FOUR REV[...]

The Sun of Saratoga, a romance of Burgoyne's surrender (1897)

In Hostile Red, a romance of the Monmouth campaign (1900)

My Captive, a tale of Tarleton's raiders (1902)

The Wilderness Road, a romance of St. Clair's defeat and Wayne's victory (1901)

JOSEPH ALTSHELER

2015 by McAllister Editions (MCALLISTEREDITIONS@GMAIL.COM). This book is a classic, and a product of its time. It does not reflect the same views on race, gender, sexuality, ethnicity, and interpersonal relations as it would if it was written today.

CONTENTS

BOOK ONE 5

THE SUN OF SARATOGA 5

A Romance of Burgoyne's Surrender 5
(A Revolutionary War Novel) 5
Chapter 1 On Watch 6
Chapter 2 A Light in the Window 12
Chapter 3 A Shot from the Window 17
Chapter 4 Out of the House 25
Chapter 5 My Superior Officer 30
Chapter 6 Belt's Ghost 36
Chapter 7 In Burgoyne's Camp 42
Chapter 8 A Night Under Fire 49
Chapter 9 My Guide 53
Chapter 10 The Sun of Saratoga 58
Chapter 11 The Night After 63
Chapter 12 We Ride Southward 68
Chapter 13 We Meet the Fleet 74
Chapter 14 The Pursuit of Chudleigh 81
Chapter 15 The Taking of Chudleigh 87
Chapter 16 The Return with Chudleigh 95
Chapter 17 My Thanks 100
Chapter 18 The Battle of the Guns 106
Chapter 19 The Man from Clinton 111
Chapter 20 Not a Drop to Drink 117
Chapter 21 The Messenger 126
Chapter 22 Capitulations 132

BOOK TWO 134

IN HOSTILE RED 134

A ROMANCE OF THE MONMOUTH CAMPAIGN 134

(A Revolutionary War Novel) 134
Chapter One—In Hostile Red 135
Chapter Two—Feeling the Way 144
Chapter Three—Sir William's Revel 152
Chapter Four—On a New Service 161
Chapter Five—The Work of Wildfoot 169
Chapter Six—A Cousin from England 174
Chapter Seven—The Quarrel 181
Chapter Eight—A File of Prisoners 185

CHAPTER NINE—*WITH THE COMMANDER-IN-CHIEF* 193
CHAPTER TEN—*THE FINE FINISH OF A PLAY* 197
CHAPTER ELEVEN—*A MAN HUNT* 203
CHAPTER TWELVE—*A DELICATE SEARCH* 207
CHAPTER THIRTEEN—*HESSIAN WRATH* 213
CHAPTER FOURTEEN—*ACCORDING TO PROMISE* 220
CHAPTER FIFTEEN—*THE PURSUIT OF WILDFOOT* 227
CHAPTER SIXTEEN—*A REBUKE FOR WATERS* 231
CHAPTER SEVENTEEN—*GREAT NEWS*... 233
CHAPTER EIGHTEEN—*THE SILENT SENTINEL* 239
CHAPTER NINETEEN—*A RIDE FOR THE CAUSE*... 248
CHAPTER TWENTY—*THE NIGHT COMBAT* 255
CHAPTER TWENTY-ONE—*KEEPING UP APPEARANCES*... 262
CHAPTER TWENTY-TWO—*A FULL CONFESSION*... 267
CHAPTER TWENTY-THREE—*GEORGE WASHINGTON'S MERCY*... 271
CHAPTER TWENTY-FOUR—*IN THE CITY AGAIN* 278
CHAPTER TWENTY-FIVE—*THE WIDOW'S MIGHT*.. 282
CHAPTER TWENTY-SIX—*AN AVERAGE NIGHT WITH WILDFOOT*.. 292
CHAPTER TWENTY-SEVEN—*PURE GOLD* 296
CHAPTER TWENTY-EIGHT—*AT THE COUNCIL FIRE*.. 299
CHAPTER TWENTY-NINE—*UNDER THE APPLE-TREES* 302
CHAPTER THIRTY—*THE DEFENCE OF THE GUN* 304
CHAPTER THIRTY-ONE—*A BATTLE AND AN ANSWERED QUESTION* 311

BOOK THREE..**315**

MY CAPTIVE **315**

A TALE OF TARLETON'S RAIDERS **315**
   (A REVOLUTIONARY WAR NOVEL).. 315
   CHAPTER 1 A TRYING SITUATION... 316
   CHAPTER 2 KEEPING A PRISONER... 321
   CHAPTER 3 THE MERIT OF A GOOD HORSE 327
   CHAPTER 4 SUPPER AND SONG 334
   CHAPTER 5 A CHANGE OF FRONT 340
   CHAPTER 6 IN A STATE OF SIEGE 349
   CHAPTER 7 THE TEMPER OF OLD PUT 355
   CHAPTER 8 JULIA'S REVENGE 363
   CHAPTER 9 AS SEEN IN A DREAM 369
   CHAPTER 10 IN MORGAN'S CAMP 375
   CHAPTER 11 THE BATTLE 379
   CHAPTER 12 LOOKING AHEAD 384

BOOK FOUR..**385**

THE WILDERNESS ROAD **385**

3

A ROMANCE OF ST. CLAIR'S DEFEAT AND WAYNE'S VICTORY 385
    CHAPTER 1 BY RULE AND COMPASS 386
    CHAPTER 2 THE CRY FOR REVENGE 390
    CHAPTER 3 THE TALE THE FOREST TOLD 397
    CHAPTER 4 THE GENERAL-WHO-NEVER-WALKS 406
    CHAPTER 5 A GENTLEMAN IN RED 414
    CHAPTER 6 A FOREST COUNCIL 417
    CHAPTER 7 THE WILDERNESS ROAD 423
    CHAPTER 8 THE PHANTOM HORDE 429
    CHAPTER 9 A DANCE BY TORCHLIGHT 437
    CHAPTER 10 A KNIGHT OF FRANCE 442
    CHAPTER 11 A MAGIC FLUTE 448
    CHAPTER 12 A BARGAIN MADE 455
    CHAPTER 13 WHITE FACE, BLACK HEART 462
    CHAPTER 14 AN UNEXPECTED OFFER 465
    CHAPTER 15 A "MADMAN'S" IDEA 473
    CHAPTER 16 AUTUMN'S LAST GLORY 477
    CHAPTER 17 A HOUSE OF GLASS 484
    CHAPTER 18 THE TERROR 492
    CHAPTER 19 A WHISPER OF INTRIGUE 498
    CHAPTER 20 A MAN OF FEAR 504
    CHAPTER 21 PLAIN TALK 511
    CHAPTER 22 A MESSENGER FROM THE NORTH 514
    CHAPTER 23 AT THE FORD 518
    CHAPTER 24 BACK TO THE SOUTH 528
    CHAPTER 25 FOR HONOUR'S SAKE 532
    CHAPTER 26 TWO YEARS LATER 538
    CHAPTER 27 OLD FACES IN NEW GUISE 543
    CHAPTER 28 THE PRIZE OF SKILL 550
    CHAPTER 29 A FEATHERED MESSAGE 557
    CHAPTER 30 HOT HEADS AND COOL 563
    CHAPTER 31 A RED ACTOR 572
    CHAPTER 32 THE DEMAND OF THE TRIBES 578
    CHAPTER 33 A GREAT TRUST 584
    CHAPTER 34 THE DEFENCE OF A FORT 591
    CHAPTER 35 A FULL CONFESSION 605
    CHAPTER 36 THE FALLEN TIMBERS 609
    CHAPTER 37 THE ONLY WAY 613
    CHAPTER 38 THE MEETING OF THE CHIEFS 616
    CHAPTER 39 THE OUTCAST'S RETURN 619
    CHAPTER 40 THE VISIT TO THE CITY 625
    CHAPTER 41 PAID IN FULL 631

BOOK ONE
THE SUN OF SARATOGA
A Romance of Burgoyne's Surrender
(A Revolutionary War Novel)

CHAPTER 1 On Watch

"You will watch this hollow and the hill yonder," said the general, "and see that not a soul passes either to the north or to the south. Don't forget that the fate of all the colonies may depend upon your vigilance."

Then he left me.

I felt much discomfort. I submit that it is not cheering to have the fate of thirteen large colonies and some two or three million people, men, women, and children, depend upon one's own humble self. I like importance, but not when it brings such an excess of care.

I looked to Sergeant Whitestone for cheer.

"We are not the only men on watch to cut off their messengers," he said. "We have our bit of ground here to guard, and others have theirs."

Then he sat down on the turf and smoked his pipe with provoking calm, as if the troubles of other people were sufficient to take our own away. I decided to stop thinking about failure and address myself to my task. Leaving the sergeant and the four men who constituted my small army, I took a look about me. The hollow was but a few hundred yards across, sparse-set with trees and bushes. It should not be difficult to guard it by day, but by night it would be a different matter. On the hill I could see the walls and roof of the Van Auken house. That, too, fell within my territory, and for reasons sufficient to me I was sorry of it.

I walked part of the way up the hillside, spying out the ground and seeing what places for concealment there might be. I did not mean to be lax in my duty in any particular. I appreciated its full import. The great idea that we might take Burgoyne and his whole army was spreading among us, and it was vital that no news of his plight should reach Clinton and the other British down below us.

I came back to Sergeant Whitestone, who was still sitting on the ground, puffing out much smoke, and looking very content.

"I don't think we need fear any attempt to get through until night," he said. "The dark is the time for messengers who don't want to be seen."

I agreed with him, and found a position of comfort upon the grass.

"There's our weak point," said the sergeant, waving his hand toward the Van Auken house.

I was sorry to hear him say so, especially as I had formed the same opinion.

"But there's nobody up there except women," I said.

"The very reason," replied the sergeant.

I occupied myself for a little while tossing pebbles at a tree. Then I disposed my men at suitable distances along our line, and concluded to go up to the house, which going, in good truth, was part of my duty.

I was near the top of the hill when I saw Kate Van Auken coming to meet me.

"Good morning, Dick," she said.

"Good morning, Mistress Catherine," I replied.

It had been my habit to call her Kate when we were children together, but I could not quite manage it now.

"You are set as a guard upon us?" she said.

"To protect you from harm," I replied with my most gallant air.

"Your manners are improving," she said in what I thought rather a disdainful tone.

"I must search the house," I continued.

"You call that protecting us?" she said with the same touch of sarcasm.

"Nevertheless it must be done," I said, speaking in my most positive manner.

She led the way without further demur. Now I had every confidence in Kate Van Auken. I considered her as good a patriot as myself, though all her family were Tory. It did not seem to me to be at all likely that any spy or messenger of the British had reached the concealment of the house, but it was my duty to be sure.

"Perhaps you would not care to talk to my mother?" she asked.

"No!" I replied in such haste that she laughed.

I knew Madame Van Auken was one of the most fanatic Tories in New York colony, and I had no mind to face her. It is curious how women are more hard-set than men in these matters. But in my search of the house I was compelled to pass through the room where she sat, most haughty and severe. Kate explained what I was about. She never spoke to me, though she had known me since I was a baby, but remained rigid in her armchair and glowered at me as if I were a most wretched villain. I confess that I felt very uncomfortable, and was glad when we passed on to another room.

As I had expected, I found nothing suspicious in the house.

"I hope you are satisfied?" said Miss Van Auken when I left.

"For the present," I replied, bowing.

I rejoined Sergeant Whitestone in the hollow. He was still puffing at his pipe, and I do not think he had changed his position by the breadth of a hair. I told him I had found nothing at the house, and asked what he thought of the case.

"We may look for work to-night, I think," he replied very gravely. "It's most likely that the British will try to send somebody through at this point. All the Van

Aukens, except the women, are with Burgoyne, and as they know the ground around here best they'll go to Burgoyne and have him send the men this way."

That was my thought too. Whitestone is a man of sound judgment. I sent two of our lads toward the house, with instructions to watch it, front and rear. It was my intent to visit them there later.

Then I joined Whitestone in a friendly pipe and found much consolation in the good tobacco. Kate's manner had nettled me the least bit, but I reflected that perhaps she was justified, as so many of her people were with Burgoyne, and, moreover, she was betrothed to Chudleigh, an Englishman. Chudleigh, an officer with Tryon in New York before the war, had come down from Canada with Burgoyne. So far as I knew he had passed safely through the last battle.

I had naught in particular against Chudleigh, but it seemed to me that he might find a wife in his own country.

The day was slow. I would rather have been with the army, where there was bustle and the hope of great things, but Whitestone, a pack of lazy bones, grunted with content. He stretched his long body on the ground and stared up at the sky through half-closed eyes. A mellow sun shone back at him.

Toward noon I sent one of the men to the house with a request for some small supply of provision, if they could spare it. We had food, a little, but we wanted more. Perhaps I ought to have gone myself, but I had my reasons. The man came back with two roast chickens.

"The old lady gave me a blessing," he said with a sour face, "and said she'd die before she'd feed rebels against the best king that ever lived; but the girl gave me these when I came out the back way."

We ate our dinner, and then I changed the sentinels at the house. Whitestone relapsed into his apparent lethargy, but I knew that the man, despite his seeming, was all vigilance and caution.

We looked for no happenings before dark, but it was yet a good four hours to set of sun when we heard a noise in the south and saw some dust rising far down the hollow.

Sergeant Whitestone rose quickly to his feet, smothered the fire in his pipe, and put his beloved companion in an inside pocket of his waistcoat.

"A party coming," I said.

"Yes, and a lot of 'em, too, I think," he replied, "or they wouldn't raise so much dust."

One of the men ran down from the hill where the view was better, and announced that a large body of soldiers was approaching. I called all the others and we stood to our arms, though we were convinced that the men marching were our own. Either the British would come with a great army or not at all.

The approaching troops, two hundred at least, appeared down the valley. The dust encased them like armor, and one can not tell what a soldier is by the dirt on his uniform. Whitestone took one long and critical look and then unbuttoned his coat and drew out his pipe.

"What are they?" I asked.

"Virginians," he replied. "I know their stride. I've served with 'em. Each step they take is exactly two inches longer than ours. They got it hunting 'possums at night."

They were in loose order like men who have marched far, but their faces were eager, and they were well armed. We halted them, as our duty bade us, and asked who they were.

"Re-enforcements for the Northern army," said the captain at their head. He showed us an order from our great commander-in-chief himself.

"Where is Burgoyne?" he asked as soon as I had finished the letter. "Is he still coming south?"

"He is but a few miles beyond you," I replied, "and he will come no farther south. There has been a great battle and we held him fast."

They gave a cheer, and some threw up their hats. To understand our feelings one must remember that we had been very near the edge of the ice, and more than once thought we would go over.

All their weariness gone, these long-legged Southerners shouldered their rifles and marched on to join the great belt of strong arms and stout hearts that was forming around the doomed Burgoyne and his army. As they passed, Sergeant Whitestone took his pipe out of his mouth and said:

"Good boys!"

Which was short, but which was much for him.

I watched their dusty backs as they tramped up the valley.

"You seem to admire them," said some one over my shoulder.

"It is they and their fellows who will take Burgoyne, Mistress Catherine," I replied.

"They can't stand before the British bayonet," she said.

"Sorry to dispute the word of so fair a lady," I replied, meaning to be gallant, "but I was at the last battle."

She laughed, as if she did not think much of my words. She said no more, but watched the marching Virginians. I thought I saw a little glow as of pride come in her face. They curved around a hill and passed out of sight.

"Good-by!" said Mistress Kate. "That's all I wanted to see here."

She went back to the house and we resumed our tedious watch. Whitestone had full warrant for his seeming apathy. After the passage of the Virginians there was naught to stir us in the slightest. Though born and bred a countryman, I have never seen anything more quiet and peaceful than that afternoon, although two large armies lay but a short distance away, resting from one bloody battle and waiting for another.

No one moved at the house. Everybody seemed to be asleep there. Some birds chattered undisturbed in the trees. The air had the crisp touch of early autumn, and faint tokens of changing hues were appearing already in the foliage. I felt a sleepy languor like that which early spring puts into the blood. In order to shake it off I began a thorough search of the country thereabouts. I pushed my way through the bushes, and tramped both to the north and to the south as far as I dared go from my post. Then I visited the guards who adjoined my little detachment on either side. They had to report only the same calm that prevailed at our part of the line. I went back to Sergeant Whitestone.

"Better take it easy," advised he. "When there's nothing to do, do it, and then be fresh to do it when there's something to do."

I took his advice, which seemed good, and again made myself comfortable on the ground, waiting for the coming of the night. It was still an hour to set of sun when we saw a mounted officer coming from the north where our army lay. We seemed to be his destination, as he rode straight toward us. I recognized Captain Martyn at once. I did not like this man. I had no particular reason for it, though I have found often that the lack of reason for doing a thing is the very strongest reason why we do it. I knew little about Captain Martyn. He had joined the Northern army before I arrived, and they said he had done good service, especially in the way of procuring information about the enemy.

Whitestone and I sat together on the grass. The other men were on guard at various points. Captain Martyn came on at a good pace until he reached us, when he pulled up his horse with a smart jerk.

"Your watch is over," he said to me without preliminary. "You are to withdraw with your men at once."

I was taken much aback, as any one else in my place would have been also. I had received instructions to keep faithful guard over that portion of the line for the long period of twenty-four hours that is, until the next morning.

"But this must be a mistake," I protested. "There is nobody to relieve us. Surely the general can not mean to leave the line broken at this point."

"If you have taken the direction of the campaign, perhaps you had best notify our generals that they are superseded," he said in a tone most ironical.

He aroused my stubbornness, of which some people say I have too much, and I refused to retire until he showed me a written order to that effect from the proper officer. Not abating his ironical manner one whit, he held it toward me in an indifferent way, as much as to say, "You can read it or not, just as you choose; it does not matter to me."

It was addressed to me, and notified me briefly to withdraw at once with my men and rejoin my company, stationed not less than ten miles away. Everything, signature included, was most proper, and naught was left for me to do but to obey. The change was no affair of mine.

"Does that put your mind at rest?" asked Martyn.

"No, it does not," I replied, "but it takes responsibility from me."

Sergeant Whitestone called the men, and as we marched over the hill Martyn turned his horse and galloped back toward the army. When he had passed out of sight behind the trees I ordered the men to stop.

"Whitestone," said I to the sergeant, who, as I have said before, was a man of most acute judgment, "do you like this?"

"Small liking have I for it," he replied. "It is the most unmilitary proceeding I ever knew. It may be that our relief is coming, but it should have arrived before we left."

I took out the order again, and after scanning it with care passed it to Whitestone.

Neither of us could see anything wrong with it. But the sergeant's manner confirmed me in a resolution I had taken before I put the question to him.

"Sergeant," I said, "every man in our army knows of what great import it is that no messenger from the British should get through our lines. We are leaving unguarded a place wide enough for a whole company to pass. I think I'll go back there and resume guard. Will you go with me?"

He assented with most cheerful alacrity, and when I put the question to the others, stating that I left them to do as they pleased, all joined me. For what they believed to be the good of the cause they were willing to take the risks of disobedience, and I was proud of them.

I looked about me from the crest of the hill, but Martyn was out of sight. We returned to the valley and I posted my men in the same positions as before, my forebodings that it would be a night of action increased by this event.

CHAPTER 2 A Light in the Window

Two of my men were stationed near the house, but I had so placed them that they could not be seen by any one inside. I had also concealed our return from possible watchers there. I had an idea, which I confided to Whitestone, and in which, with his usual sound sense, he agreed with me. He and I remained together in the valley and watched the night come.

The sun seemed to me to linger long at the edge of the far hills, but at last his red rim went out of sight, and the heavy darkness which precedes the moonlight fell upon the earth.

"If anything happens, it will happen soon," said Whitestone.

That was obvious, because if Martyn meditated treachery, it would be important for him to carry it out before the unguarded point in the line was discovered. Officially it was unguarded, because we were supposed to have gone away and stayed away.

My suspicions were confirmed by the non-arrival of our relief. Whitestone still took his ease, stretched out on the ground in the valley. I knew he missed his pipe, but to light it would serve as a warning in the dark to any one. I visited the two men near the house and cautioned them to relax their watch in no particular.

The night was now well begun and I could see no great distance. As I turned away from the last man I chanced to look up at the house, whose shape was but a darker shadow in the darkness. At a narrow window high up, where the sloping eaves converged, I saw a light. Perhaps I would not have thought much of it, but the light was moved from side to side with what seemed to me to be regular and deliberate motion. It faced the north, where our army lay.

I walked twenty steps or so, still keeping the light in view. Its regular swinging motion from side to side did not cease, and I could not persuade myself that it was not intended as a signal to some one. The discovery caused in me a certain faintness at the heart, for until this night I had thought Kate Van Auken, despite mother, brother, and all else, was a true friend to our cause through all.

I own I was in great perplexity. At first I was tempted to enter the house, smash the light, and denounce her in my most eloquent language. But I quickly saw the idea was but folly, and would stand in the way of our own plans. I leaned against an oak tree and kept my eyes fixed on the light. Though the windows in the house were many, no other light was visible, which seemed strange to me, for it was very early. Back and forth it swung, and then it was gone with a suddenness which made me rub my eyes to see if it were not still there; nothing ailed them. The building was a huge black shadow, but no light shone from it anywhere.

I went in a mighty hurry to Whitestone and told him what I had seen. He loosened the pistol in his belt and said he thought the time for us to make discoveries had come. Once more I agreed with him.

I drew my own pistol, that it might be ready to my hand, if need be, and we walked a bit up the valley. It was very dark and we trusted more to our ears than to our eyes, in which trust we were not deceived, for speedily we heard a faint but regular thump, thump, upon the earth.

"A horse coming," I said.

"And probably a horseman, too," said Whitestone.

How glad was I that we had stayed! It was not at all likely that the man coming had any honest business there. We stepped a trifle to one side and stood silent, while the tread of the horse's hoofs grew louder. In a few moments the horseman was near enough for us to see his face even in the night, and I felt no surprise, though much anger, when I recognized Captain Martyn. He was riding slowly, in order that he might not make much noise, I supposed.

I stepped forward and put my hand upon his bridle rein. He saw who it was and uttered an exclamation; but after that he recovered his self-control with a quickness most astonishing.

"How dare you stop me in such a sudden and alarming manner?" he said with an appearance of great wrath.

But, very sure now that I was right, I intended neither to be deceived nor overborne. I ordered him to dismount and surrender himself.

"You are very impertinent, sir," he said, "and need chastisement."

I told him it mattered not, and ordered him again to dismount. For reply he drew a pistol with such suddenness that I could not guard against it and fired point-blank at my face. It was the kindly darkness making his aim bad that saved me. The bullet passed me, but the smoke and flash blinded me.

The traitor lashed his horse in an attempt to gallop by us, but Whitestone also fired, his bullet striking the horse and not the man. The animal, in pain, reared and struck out with his feet. Martyn attempted to urge him forward but failed. Then he slipped from his back and ran into the bushes. My eyes were clear now, and Whitestone and I rushed after him.

I noted from the very first that the man ran toward the house, and again, even in that moment of excitement, I congratulated myself that I had expected treason and collusion and had come back to my post.

I saw the captain's head appearing just above some of the short bushes and raised my pistol to fire at him, but before I could get the proper aim he was out of sight. We increased our efforts in fear lest we should lose him, and a few steps further heard a shot which I knew came from one of my men on guard. We met the man running toward us, his empty rifle in his hand. He told us the fugitive had turned the corner of the house, and I felt that we had trapped him then, for the second man on guard there would be sure to stop him.

We pressed forward and met the man from behind the house, attracted by the sound of shots. He said nobody had appeared there. I turned to a side door, convinced that Martyn had found refuge in the house. It was no time to stand upon courtesy, or to wait for an invitation to enter. The door was locked, but Whitestone and I threw our full weight against it at the same time, and it flew open under the impact of some twenty-five stone.

We fell into a dark hall and scrambled in pressing haste to our feet. I paused a moment that I might direct the soldiers to surround the house and seize any one who came forth. Then we turned to face Madame Van Auken, who was coming toward us, a candle in her hand, a long white robe around her person, and a most icy look on her face.

She began at once a very fierce attack upon us for disturbing quiet folks abed. I have ever stood in dread of woman's tongue, to which there is but seldom answer, but I explained in great hurry that a traitor had taken refuge in her house, and search it again we must, if not with her consent, then without it. She repelled me with extreme haughtiness, saying such conduct was unworthy of men who pretended to breeding; but, after all, it was no more than she ought to expect from ungrateful rebels.

Her attack, most unwarranted, considering the fact that a traitor had just hid in her house, stirred some spleen in me, and I bade her very stiffly to stand out of the way. Another light appeared just then at the head of the stairway, and Mistress Kate came down, fully dressed, looking very fine and handsome too, with a red flame in either cheek.

She demanded the reason of our entry with a degree of haughtiness inferior in no wise to her mother's. Again I explained, angered at these delays made by women who, handsome or not, may appear sometimes when they are not wanted.

"Take the men, all except one to watch at the door, and search the house at once, sergeant," said I.

Whitestone, with an indifference to their bitter words most astonishing, led his men upstairs and left me to endure it all. I pretended not to hear, and taking the candle suddenly from Kate's hands turned into a side room and began to poke about the furniture. But they followed me there.

"I suppose you think this is very shrewd and very noble," said Kate with a fine irony.

I did not reply, but poked behind a sideboard with my pistol muzzle. Both Kate and her mother seemed to me, despite their efforts to repress it, to manifest a very great uneasiness. I did not wonder at it, for I knew they must fear to be detected in their collusion with the traitor. Kate continued to gibe at me.

"Oh, well, it's not Captain Chudleigh I'm looking for," said I at last.

"And in truth if it were, you'd be afraid to find him," replied she, a sprightly flash appearing in her eye.

I said no more, content with my hit. I found no one below stairs, and joined Whitestone on the second floor, the women still following me and upbraiding me. I looked more than once at Kate, and I could see that she was all in a tremor. I doubted not it arose from a belief that I had discovered her treachery, as well as from a fear that we would capture the chief traitor.

Whitestone had not yet found our man, though he had been in every room on the second floor and even into the low-roofed garret. At this the two women became more contumelious, crying out that we were now shamed by our own acts. But we were confident that the man was yet in the house. I pushed into a large room which seemed to serve as a spare chamber. We had entered it once before, but I thought a more thorough search might be made. In one corner, some dresses hanging against the wall reached to the floor. I prodded one of them with my fist and encountered something soft.

The dress was dashed aside and our man sprang out. There was a low window at the end of the room, and with one bound he was through it. Whitestone fired at his disappearing body, but missed. We heard a second shot from the man on guard below, and then we rushed pell-mell down the stairs to pursue him.

I bethought me at the door to bid one of the men stay and watch the house, for I knew not what further treachery the women might meditate. This stopped me only a moment, and then I ran after Whitestone, who was some steps in the lead. We overtook the man who had fired at Martyn, and he said he had hit him, so he thought.

"When he sprang from the window he rose very light from the ground," he said, "and I don't think the fall hurt him much."

We saw Martyn some twenty yards or more in advance of us, running toward the south. It was of double importance now that we should overtake him, for if we did not he would be beyond our lines, and, barring some improbable chance, would escape to Clinton with a report of Burgoyne's condition.

The fugitive curved here and there among the shadows but could not shake us off. I held my loaded pistol in my hand and twice or thrice had a chance for a fair shot at him, but I never raised the weapon. I could shoot at a man in the heat of battle or the flurry of a sudden moment of excitement, but not when he was like a fleeing hare. Moreover, I preferred to take him alive.

The moon was coming out, driving away part of the darkness, and on the bushes I noticed some spots of blood. Then the fugitive had been hit, and I was glad I had not fired upon him, for we would be certain to take him wounded.

The course led over pretty rough ground. Whitestone was panting at my elbow, and two of the men lumbered behind us. The fugitive began to waver, and presently I noticed that we were gaining. Suddenly Martyn began to cast his hands as if he were throwing something from him, and we saw little bits of white paper fluttering in the air. I divined on the instant that, seeing his certain capture, he was tearing up traitorous papers. We wanted those papers as well as their bearer.

I shouted to him to halt lest I fire. He flung a whole handful of scraps from him. Just then he came to a stump; he stopped abruptly, sat down upon it with his face to us, and drawing a pistol from his pocket, put it to his own head and fired.

I was never more shocked in my life, the thing was so sudden. He slid off the stump to the ground, and when we reached him he was quite dead. We found no letters upon him, as in the course of his flight he had succeeded in destroying them all. But I had not the slightest doubt the order he had given to me would soon prove to be a forgery. His own actions had been sufficient evidence of that.

I directed Whitestone to take the body to some safe place and we would give it quiet burial on the morrow. I did not wish the women to know of the man's terrible fate, though I owed them scant courtesy for the way they had treated me.

Leaving Whitestone and one of the soldiers to the task, I went back to the house alone.

Mistress Kate and her mother were at the door, both in a state of high excitement.

"Did he escape?" asked Madame Van Auken.

"No," I replied, telling the truth in part and a lie in part. "We captured him, and the men are now taking him back to the army."

She sighed deeply. Mistress Kate said nothing, though her face was of a great paleness.

"I will not upbraid you with what I call treachery," I said, speaking to them both, "and I will not disturb you again to-night. It is not necessary."

I said the last rather grimly, but I observed some of the paleness depart from Mistress Kate's countenance and a look strangely like that of relief come into her eyes. I was sorry, for it seemed to me to indicate more thought of her own and her mother's peace than of the fate of the man whom we had taken. But there was naught to say, and I left them without the courtesy of a good night on either side.

Whitestone and the men returned presently from their task, and I posted the guards as before, confident that no traitor could pass while I was on watch there.

CHAPTER 3 A Shot from the Window

Whitestone and I held a small conference in the dark. Though regretting that the matter had ended in such tragic way, we believed we had done a great thing, and I am not loath to confess that I expected words of approval the next day when we would take the news of it to the army. We agreed that we must not relax our vigilance in the smallest particular, for where there was one plot there might be a dozen. Whitestone went down into the valley while I remained near the house.

In my lonely watch I had great space for thought. I was grieved by my discoveries in regard to Kate Van Auken. Of a truth she was nothing to me, being betrothed, moreover, to Chudleigh the Englishman; but we had been children together, and it was not pleasing to believe her a patriot and find her a traitor. I could get no sort of satisfaction out of such thoughts, and turning them aside walked about with vigor in an attempt to keep myself from becoming very sleepy.

The moon was still showing herself, and I could see the house very well. No light had appeared in it since our last withdrawal, but looking very closely I saw what appeared to be a dark shadow at one of the windows. I knew that room to be Mistress Kate's, and I surmised that she was there seeking to watch us. I resolved in return that I would watch her. I stepped back where I would be sheltered by a tree from her sight, and presently had my reward. The window was opened gently and a head, which could be none other than that of Kate, was thrust out a bit.

I could see her quite well, even the features of her face. She was looking very earnestly into the surrounding night, and of a truth anxiety was writ plainly on her countenance. She stretched her head out farther and examined all the space before the house. I was hidden from her gaze, but down in a corner of the yard she could see the sentinel pacing back and forth. She inspected him with much earnestness for some time, and then withdrew her head, closing the window.

I was of the opinion that some further mischief was afoot or intended, but the nature of it passed me. It seemed that what had happened already was not a sufficient warning to them. I began to walk around the house that I might keep a watch upon it from every point. Sleepiness no longer oppressed me. In truth, I forgot all about it.

I passed to the rear of the building and spoke to the sentinel stationed in the yard there. He had seen nothing of suspicious nature so far. I knew he was a faithful, watchful man, and that I could trust him. I left him and pushed my way between two large flower bushes growing very close together. Standing there, I beheld the opening of another window in the house. Again the head of Mistress Kate appeared, and precisely the same act as before was repeated. She looked about with the intentness and anxiety of a military engineer studying his ground. She saw the sentinel as she had seen his fellow before the house, and her eyes rested long upon him. Her examination finished, she withdrew, closing the window.

I set myself to deciphering the meaning of this, and of a sudden it flashed upon me with such force that I believed myself stupid not to have seen it before. Kate Van Auken herself was planning to go through our lines with the news of Burgoyne's plight. She was a bold girl, not much afraid of the dark or the woods, and the venture was not beyond her. The conviction of the truth depressed me. I felt some regard for Kate Van Auken, whom I as a little boy had liked as a little girl, and I had slight relish for this task of keeping watch upon her. Even now I had caught her planning great harm to our cause.

I confess that I scarce knew what to do. Perhaps it was my duty, if the matter be considered in its utmost strictness, to arrest both the women at once as dangerous to our cause, and send them to the army. But such a course was quite beyond my resolution. I could not do it. Being unable to decide upon anything else, I continued my watch, determined that Mistress Kate should not escape from the house.

The moon withdrew herself and then there was an increase of darkness. Again I was thankful that I had been vigilant, for I saw a small door in the rear of the house open. I could not doubt that it opened to let forth Catherine Van Auken upon her traitorous errand. I made my resolution upon the instant. If she came out, I would seize her and compel her to return to the house in all quiet, in order that Whitestone and the others might not know.

My suspicions—my fears, in truth I may call them—were justified, for in a few moments her well-known figure appeared in the doorway all clothed about in a great dark cloak and hood, like one preparing for a long night's journey. I retreated a little, for it was my purpose to draw her on and then catch her, when no doubt about her errand could arise.

She stood in the doorway for perhaps two minutes repeating her actions at the window; that is, she looked around carefully to note how we were watching. I could not see her face owing to the increase of darkness and her attitude, but I had no doubt the same anxiety and eagerness were writ there.

Presently she seemed to arrange her dark draperies in a manner more satisfactory and, stooping somewhat, came out of the house. The sentinel in this part of the yard was doing his duty and was as watchful as could be, but he could scarce see this shadow gliding along in the larger shadow of the rose bushes. I deemed it good fortune that I was there to see and prevent the flight. I would face her and confound her with the proof of her guilt.

She came on quite rapidly, and I shrank a little farther back into the rose bushes. Her course was directly toward me, and suddenly I rose up in the path. I expected her to show great surprise and to cry out after the fashion of women, but she did not. In truth I fancied I saw a start, but that was all. In a moment she whirled about and fled back toward the house with as little noise as the shadow she resembled. I had scarce recovered my presence of mind when she was halfway to the house, but I pursued in the effort to overtake her and confound her.

I observed that when she came forth she had shut the door behind her, but as she fled swiftly back it seemed to open of its own accord for her entrance. She passed within, disappearing like a ghost, and the door was shut with a snap almost in my face. I put my hands upon it and found it was very real and substantial perhaps a stout two inches in thickness.

I deliberated with myself for a moment or two and concluded to do nothing further in the matter. Perhaps it had turned out as well as might be, for I had stopped her errand, and her return, doubtless, had released me from unpleasant necessities.

I made no effort to force the door or to enter the house otherwise, but visited the sentinels, telling them to be of good caution, though I gave them no hint of what had happened.

I found Whitestone in the valley sitting on a stump and sucking at his pipe, which contained neither fire nor tobacco. He told me naught unusual had happened there. I took him back to the house with me, and together we watched about it until the coming of the day, without further event of interest.

Sunrise found my men and me very tired and sleepy, as we had a right to be, having been on guard near to twenty-four hours, with some very exciting things occurring in that long space. I awaited the relief which must come soon, for we were not iron men.

The sun had scarce swung clear of the earth when a door of the house was opened and Mistress Kate coming out, a pail in hand, walked lightly toward the well. I approached her, and she greeted me with an unconcern that amazed me.

"I trust that you enjoyed your night watch, Master Shelby?" she said.

"As well as was likely under the circumstances," I replied. "I hope that you slept soundly?"

"Nothing disturbed us after your invasion of our house," she said with fine calmness. "Now, will you help me draw this water? Since the approach of the armies there is no one left in the house save my mother and myself, and we must cook and do for ourselves."

I helped draw the water, and even carried the filled pail to the house for her, though she dismissed me at the door. But she atoned partly for her scant courtesy by bringing us a little later some loaves of white bread, which she said she had baked with her own hands, and which we found to be very good.

We had but finished breakfast when the soldiers who were to relieve us came, and right glad were we to see them. They were followed a few minutes later by the colonel in charge, to whom I related the affair of Captain Martyn, and to whom I showed the order commanding us to withdraw. He instantly pronounced it a forgery and commended us for staying.

"It was a traitorous attempt to get through our line," he said, "but we are none the worse off, for it has failed."

I said nothing of Kate Van Auken's share in the conspiracy, but I told him the women in the house inclined strongly to the Tory side.

"I will see that the house is watched every moment of the day and night," he said.

Then I felt easy in mind and went off to sleep.

When I awoke it was about two by the sun, and the afternoon was fine. I heard that fresh troops had arrived from the Massachusetts and New Hampshire provinces in the morning, and the trap was closing down on Burgoyne tighter than ever. Everybody said another great battle was coming, and coming soon. Even then I heard the pop-pop of distant skirmishing and saw an occasional red flash on the horizon.

I was eager to be at the front, but such duty was not for me then. As soon as I had eaten I was sent back with Sergeant Whitestone and the same men to keep watch at precisely the same point.

"Best take it easy," said the sergeant consolingly. "If the big battle's fought while we're away we can't get killed in it."

Then he lighted the inevitable pipe, smoked, and was content.

I questioned very closely the men whom we relieved near the house, and they said there had been nothing to note. The elder woman had never come out of the house, but the younger had been seen in the yard several times, though she had naught to say, and seemed to be concerned not at all about anything.

I thought it best not to visit the house, and took my station with Whitestone in the valley, disposing the men in much the same manner as before. Whitestone puffed at his pipe with the usual regularity and precision, but some of his taciturnity was gone. He was listening to the sounds of the skirmishing which came to us fitfully.

"The bees are stinging," said he. Then he added, with a fine mixture of metaphors: "The mouse is trying to feel his way out of the trap. The big battle can't be far off, for Burgoyne must know that every day lost is a chance lost."

It seemed to me that he was right, and I regretted more than ever my assignment to sentinel duty. I do not pretend to uncommon courage, but every soldier will bear me out that such waiting as we were doing is more trying than real battle.

Of a sudden the skirmishing seemed to take on an increase of vigor and to come nearer. Flashes appeared at various points on the horizon. Whitestone became deeply interested. He stood at his full height on a stump, and I would have done likewise had there been another stump. Presently he leaped down, exclaiming:

"I fancy there is work for us!"

I saw at once what he meant. A dozen men were coming down the valley at full speed. The bright sun even at the distance brought out the scarlet of their uniforms, and there was no mistaking the side to which they belonged. Evidently a party of Burgoyne's skirmishers had slipped through our main line somehow and were bent upon escape southward, with all its momentous consequences.

That escape we would prevent. I sent Whitestone in a run to the two men near the house to bid them take refuge behind it and fight from its shelter. He was back in a breath, and he and I and the other soldiers prepared to hold the passage of the valley. Most fortunate for us, a rail fence ran across this valley, and we took refuge behind it—a wise precaution, I think, since the approaching party outnumbered us.

All of ours, except myself, had rifles, and I carried two good pistols, with which I am no bad shot. The British came on with much speed. Two of them were mounted.

I glanced toward the house. At one of the windows I saw a figure. I trusted if it was Kate Van Auken that she would withdraw speedily from such an exposed place. But I had no time to note her presence further, for just then the British seemed to perceive that we barred the way, for they stopped as if hesitating. I suppose they saw us, as we were sheltered but in part by the fence.

Wishing to spare bloodshed I shouted to them to surrender, but one of the men on horseback shook his head, said something to the others, and they dashed toward us at all speed. I recognized this man who appeared to be their leader. He was Chudleigh, the Englishman, the betrothed of Kate Van Auken, and, so far as I knew, an honest, presentable fellow.

Whitestone poised his rifle on the top rail of the fence and I surmised that it was aimed at Chudleigh. Were the matter not so desperate I could have wished for a miss. But before Whitestone pulled the trigger one of the men from the shelter of the house fired, and Chudleigh's horse, struck by the ball intended for his master, went down, tossing Chudleigh some distance upon the ground, where he lay quite still. Whitestone transferred his aim and knocked the other mounted man off his horse.

The remainder, not daunted by the warmth of our greeting and the loss of their cavalry, raised a cheer and rushed at us, firing their pistols and muskets.

I do not scorn a skirmish. It may, and often does, contain more heat to the square yard than a great battle with twenty thousand men engaged. These men bore down upon us full of resolution. Their bullets pattered upon the rails of the fence, chipping off splinters. Some went between the rails and whizzed by us in fashion most uncomfortable. One man cried out a bit as the lead took him in the fleshy part of the leg, but he did not shrink from the onset.

Meanwhile we were not letting the time pass without profit, but fired at them with as much rapidity and aim as we could. The two men at the corner of the house helped us much with fine sharpshooting.

Our fortification, though but slender, gave us a great advantage, and nearly a third of their number had fallen before they were within a dozen feet of the fence. But it was our business not only to defeat them but to keep any from passing us. I was hopeful of doing this, for the sound of the firing had reached other portions of the line, and I saw re-enforcements for us coming on the run.

Our fire had been so hot that the British when within a dozen feet of us shrank back. Of a sudden one of them, a very active fellow, swerved to one side, darted at the fence, and leaping it with a single bound ran lightly along the hillside. I called to Whitestone and we followed him at all speed. I was confident that the others would be taken by our re-enforcements, who were coming up fast, and this man who had passed our line must be caught at all hazards.

One of my men at the house fired at the fugitive, but missed. My pistols were empty, and so was Whitestone's rifle. It was a matter which fleetness would decide and we made every effort.

The fugitive curved toward a wood back of the house, and we followed. I heard a rifle shot from a new direction, and Whitestone staggered; but in a moment he recovered himself, saying it was only a flesh wound. I was amazed, not at the shot but at the point from which it came. I looked up, and it was no mistake of hearing, for there was the white puff of smoke rising from an upper window in the house. It was but the glance of a moment, as the fugitive then claimed my attention. His speed was slackening and he seemed to be growing very tired.

A little blood appeared on Whitestone's arm near the shoulder, but he gave no other sign that the wound affected him. Our man increased his speed a bit, but the effort exhausted him; he stopped of a sudden, dropped to the earth, and lay there panting, strength and breath quite gone.

We ran up to him and demanded his surrender. He was too much exhausted to speak, but he nodded as if he were glad the thing was over. We let him rest until his breath came back. Then he climbed to his feet, and, looking at us, said in the fashion of one defending himself:

"I did the best I could; you can't say I didn't."

"I guess you did," I replied. "You went farther than any of your comrades."

He was a most likely young fellow, not more than twenty, I should say, and I was very glad he had come out of the affair unhurt. We took him back to the valley, where the conflict was over. Our re-enforcements had come up so fast that the remainder of the British surrendered after a few shots. All the prisoners were delivered to one of our captains who had arrived, and he took them away. Then I turned my attention to Whitestone. Having some small knowledge of surgery, I asked him to let me see his arm. He held it out without a word.

I pushed up his sleeve and found that the bullet had cut only a little below the skin. I bound up the scratch with a piece of old white cloth, and said:

"You needn't bother about that, Whitestone; the bullet, that cut it wasn't very well aimed."

"It was aimed pretty well, I think, for a woman," he said.

"You won't say any more about that, Whitestone, will you?" I asked quietly.

"Not to anybody unless to you," he replied.

There was a faint smile on his face that I did not altogether like; but he thrust his hand into the inside pocket of his waistcoat, took out his pipe, lighted the tobacco with great deliberation, and began to smoke as if nothing had happened.

The prisoners taken away and other signs of conflict removed, we were left to our old duty, and hill and hollow resumed their quiet. I was much troubled, but at last I made up my mind what to do. Asking Whitestone to keep a good watch, I went to the house and knocked with much loudness at the front door. Kate opened the door, self-possessed and dignified.

"Miss Van Auken," I said with all my dignity, "I congratulate you upon your progress in the useful art of sharpshooting. You have wounded Sergeant Whitestone, a most excellent man, and perhaps it was chance only that saved him from death."

"Why should you blame me?" she said. "I wished the man you were pursuing to escape, and there was no other way to help him. This is war, you know."

I had scarce expected so frank an admission.

"I will have to search the house for your weapon," I said. "How do I know that you will not shoot at me as I go away?"

"Do not trouble yourself," she said easily, "I will bring it to you."

She ran up the stairway and returned in a moment with a large, unloaded pistol, which she held out to me.

"I might have tried to use it again," she said with a little laugh, "but I confess I did not know how to reload it."

She handed me the pistol with a gesture of repulsion as if she were glad to get rid of it. Her frankness changed my purpose somewhat, and I asked her how her mother fared. "Very well, but in most dreadful alarm because of the fighting," she replied.

"It would be best for both of you, for your own safety, to remain in the house and keep the windows closed," I said.

"So I think," she replied.

I turned away, for I wished to think further what disposition to make of Kate Van Auken and her mother. It seemed that they should remain no longer at such a critical point of our line, where in an unwatched moment they might do us a great evil. Moreover, I was much inflamed against Kate because of the treacherous shot which had come so near to ending Whitestone's career. But even then I sought for some mitigating circumstance, some excuse for her. Perhaps her family had so long worked upon her that her own natural and patriotic feelings had become perverted to such an extent that she looked upon the shot as a righteous deed. Cases like it were not new.

I thought it best to take Whitestone into my confidence.

"We can not do anything to-day," he said, "for none of us can leave here; but it would be well to keep a good watch upon that house again to-night."

This advice seemed good, for like as not Kate Van Auken, not at all daunted by her failure, would make another attempt to escape southward.

Therefore with much interest I waited the coming of our second night there, which was but a brief time away.

CHAPTER 4 Out of the House

The night came on and I was uneasy. Many things disturbed me. The house was a sore spot in my mind, and with the dusk the signs of battle seemed to increase. Upon this dark background the flashes from the skirmishing grew in size and intensity. From under the horizon's rim came the deep murmur of the artillery. I knew that Burgoyne was feeling his way, and more than ever it was impressed upon me that either he would break out soon or we would close in upon him and crush him. The faint pop-pop of the distant rifles was like the crackling that precedes the conflagration.

To the south there was peace, apparent peace, but I knew Burgoyne must turn his face hopefully many a time that way, for if rescue came at all it must come thence.

"Another day nearer the shutting of the trap," said Whitestone, walking up and down with his arm in a sling. I found that he could manage his pipe as well with one hand as with two.

The night was darker than usual, for which I was sorry, as it was against us and in favor of the others. Again asking Whitestone to stand sponsor for the hollow, I approached the house. I had repeated my precautions of the day before, placing one sentinel in front of it and another behind it. But in the darkness two men could be passed, and I would watch with them.

From the hill top the flashes of the skirmishing seemed to multiply, and for a few moments I forgot the house that I might watch them. Even I, who had no part in the councils of my generals and elders, knew how much all this meant to us, and the intense anxiety with which every patriot heart awaited the result. More than ever I regretted my present duty.

The house was dark, but I felt sure in my heart that Kate would make another attempt to escape us. Why should she wait?

I thought it my best plan to walk in an endless circle around the house; it would keep sleep away and give me the greater chance to see anything that might happen. It was but dull and tiresome work at the best. Around and around I walked, stopping once in a while to speak to my sentinels. Time was so slow that it seemed to me the night ought to have passed, when the size of the moon showed that it was not twelve.

I expected Kate to look from the windows again and spy out the ground before making the venture; so I kept faithful watch upon them, but found no reward for such vigilance and attention. Her face did not appear; no light sparkled from the house. Perhaps after her failures her courage had sunk. Certainly the time for her venture, if venture she would make, was passing.

As I continued my perpetual circle I approached the beat of the sentinel who was stationed behind the house. I saw him sooner than I expected; he had come farther toward the side of the house than his orders permitted him to do, and I was preparing to rebuke him when I noticed of a sudden that he seemed to be without his rifle. The next moment his figure disappeared from me like the shadow of something that had never been.

Twenty yards away I saw the sentinel, upright, stiff, rifle on shoulder, no thought but of his duty. I knew the first figure was that of Kate Van Auken, and not of the sentinel. How she had escaped from the house unseen I did not know and it was no time to stop for inquiry. I stepped among the trees, marking as closely as I could that particular blotch of blackness into which she had disappeared, and I had reward, for again I saw her figure, more like shadow than substance.

I might have shouted to the sentinels and raised hue and cry, but I had reasons—very good, it seemed to me—for not doing so. Moreover, I needed no assistance. Surely I could hold myself sufficient to capture one girl. She knew the grounds well, but I also knew them. I had played over them often enough.

The belt of woods began about fifty yards back of the house, and was perhaps the same number of yards in. breadth. But the trees seemed not to hinder her speed. She curved lightly among them with the readiness of perfect acquaintance, and I was sure that the elation coming from what she believed to be escape was quickening her flight.

She passed through the trees and into the stretch of open ground beyond. Then for the first time she looked back and saw me. At least I believe she saw me, for she seemed to start, and her cloak fluttered as she began to run with great speed.

A hundred yards farther was a rail fence, and beyond that a stretch of corn land. With half a leap and half a climb, very remarkable in woman, who is usually not expert in such matters, she scaled this fence in a breath and was among the cornstalks. I feared that she might elude me there, but I, too, was over the fence in a trice and kept her figure in view. She had shown much more endurance than I expected, though I knew she was a strong girl. But we had come a good half mile, and few women can run at speed so far.

She led me a chase through the cornfield and then over another fence into a pasture. I noted with pleasure that I was gaining all the time. In truth, I had enjoyed so much exercise of this kind in the last day that I ought to have been in a fair way of becoming an expert.

Our course lengthened to a mile and I was within fifteen yards of her. Despite my general disrelish for the position I felt a certain grim joy in being the man to stop her plans, inasmuch as she had deceived me more perhaps than any one else.

It was evident that I could overtake her, and I hailed her, demanding that she stop. For reply she whirled about and fired a pistol at me, and then, seeing that she had missed, made an effort to run faster.

I was astounded. I confess it even after all that had happened—but she had fired at Whitestone before; now she was firing at me. I would stop this fierce woman, not alone for the good of our cause, but for the revenge her disappointment would be to me. The feeling gave me strength, and in five minutes more I could almost reach out my hands and touch her.

"Stop!" I shouted in anger.

She whirled about again and struck at me, full strength, with the butt of her pistol. I might have suffered a severe, perhaps a stunning, blow, but by instinct I threw up my right hand, and her wrist gliding off it the pistol struck nothing, dashing with its own force from her hand. I warded off another swift blow aimed with the left fist, and then saw that I stood face to face not with Kate Van Auken but with her brother Albert.

There was a look upon his face of mingled shame and determination. How could he escape shame with his sister's skirts around him and her hood upon his head?

My own feelings were somewhat mixed in character. First, there was a sensation of great relief, so quick I had not time to make analysis, and then there came over me a strong desire to laugh. I submit that the sight of a man caught in woman's dress and ashamed of it is fair cause for mirth.

It was dark, but not too dark for me to see his face redden at my look.

"You'll have to fight it out with me," he said, very stiff and haughty.

"I purpose to do it," I said, "but perhaps your clothes may be in your way."

He snatched the hood off his head and hurled it into the bushes; then with another angry pull he ripped the skirt off, and, casting it to one side stood forth in proper man's attire, though that of a citizen and not of the British soldier that he was.

He confronted me, very angry. I did not think of much at that moment save how wonderfully his face was like his sister Kate's. I had never taken such thorough note of it before, though often the opportunity was mine.

Our pause had given him breath, and he stood awaiting my attack like one who fights with his fists in the ring. My loaded pistol was in my belt, but he did not seem to think that I would use it; nor did I think of it myself. His, unloaded, lay on the ground. I advanced upon him, and with his right fist he struck very swiftly at my face. I thrust my head to one side and the blow glanced off the hard part of it, leaving his own face unprotected. I could have dealt him a heavy return blow that would have made his face look less like his sister Kate's, but I preferred to close with him and seize him in my grasp.

Though lighter than I he was agile, and sought to trip me, or by some dexterous turn otherwise to gain advantage of me. But I was wary, knowing full well that I ought to be so, and presently I brought him down in a heap, falling upon him with such force that he lay a few moments as if stunned, though it was but the breath knocked out of him.

"Do you give up?" I asked, when he had returned to speaking condition.

"Yes," he replied. "You were always too strong for me, Dick."

Which was true, for there never was a time, even when we were little boys, when I could not throw him, though I do not say it as a boast, since there were others who could throw me.

"Do you make complete and unconditional surrender to me as the sole present representative of the American army, and promise to make no further effort to escape?" asked I, somewhat amazed at the length of my own words, and a little proud of them too.

"Yes, Dick, confound it! Get off my chest! How do you expect me to breathe?" he replied with a somewhat unreasonable show of temper.

I dismounted and he sat up, thumping his chest and drawing very long breaths as if he wished to be sure that everything was right inside. When he had finished his examination, which seemed to be satisfactory, he said:

"I'm your prisoner, Dick. What do you intend to do with me?"

"Blessed if I know," I replied,

In truth, I did not. He was in citizens' clothes, and he had been lurking inside our lines for at least a day or so. If I gave him up to our army, as my duty bade me to do, he might be shot, which would be unpleasant to me as well as to him for various reasons. If I let him go he might ruin us.

"Suppose you think it over while I rest," he said. "A man can't run a mile and then fight a big fellow like you without getting pretty tired."

In a few minutes I made up my mind. It was not a way out of the matter, but it was the only thing I could think of for the present.

"Get up, Albert," I said.

He rose obediently.

"You came out of that house unseen," I resumed, "and I want you to go back into it unseen. Do exactly as I say. I'm thinking of you as well as of myself."

He seemed to appreciate the consideration and followed close behind me as I took my way toward the house. I had no fear that he would attempt escape. Albert was always a fellow of honor, though I could never account for the perversion of his political opinions.

He walked back slowly. I kept as good a lookout as I could in the darkness. It was barely possible that I would meet Whitestone prowling about, and that was not what I wanted.

"Albert," I asked, "why did you shoot at Whitestone from the house? I can forgive your shooting at me, for that was in fair and open strife."

"Dick," he said so earnestly that I could not but believe him, "to tell you the truth, I feel some remorse about the shot, but the man you were pursuing was Trevannion of ours, my messmate, and such a fine fellow that I knew only one other whom I'd rather see get through with the news of our plight, and that's myself. I couldn't resist trying to help him. Suppose we say no more about it; let it pass."

"It's Whitestone's affair, not mine," I said. I was not making any plans to tell Whitestone about it.

When we came to the edge of the wood behind the house I told him to stop. Going forward, I sent the sentinel to the other side of the building, telling him to watch there with his comrade for a little, while I took his place. As soon as his figure disappeared behind the corner of the house Albert came forward and we hurried to the side door. We knocked lightly upon it and it was promptly opened by his sister. I could guess the anxiety and dread with which she was waiting lest she should hear sounds which would tell of an interrupted flight, and the distress with which she would see us again. Nor was I deceived. When she beheld us standing there in the dark, her lips moved as if she could scarce repress the cry that rose.

I spoke first.

"Take him back in the house," I said, "and keep him there until you hear from me. Hurry up, Albert!"

Albert stepped in.

"And don't forget this," I continued, for I could not wholly forgive him, "if you shoot at me or Whitestone or anybody else, I'll see you hanged as a spy, if I have to do it myself."

They quickly closed the door, and recalling the sentinel, I went in search of Whitestone.

I had some notion of confiding in Whitestone, but, after thought, I concluded I had best not, at least not fully.

I found him walking up and down in the valley.

"Whitestone," I said, "do me a favor? If anybody asks you how you got that scratch on your arm, tell him it was in the skirmish, and you don't know who fired the shot."

He considered a moment.

"I'll do it," he said, "if you'll agree to do as much for me, first chance."

I promised, and, that matter off my mind, tried to think of a plan to get Albert out of the house and back to his own army unseen by any of ours. Thinking thus, the night passed away.

CHAPTER 5 My Superior Officer

The relief came early in the morning, bringing with it the news that our army, which was stronger every day than on the yesterday, had moved still closer to Burgoyne. My blood thrilled as ever at this, but I had chosen a new course of action for myself. It would be an evil turn for me if Albert Van Auken were taken at the house and should run the risk of execution as a spy; it might be said that I was the chief cause of it.

I was very tired, and stretching myself on the turf beneath the shade of a tree in the valley, I fell into a sound sleep in two minutes. When I awoke at the usual time I found that the guard had been re-enforced, and, what was worse, instead of being first in command I was now only second. This in itself was disagreeable, but the character of the man who had supplanted me was a further annoyance. I knew Lieutenant Belt quite well, a New Englander much attached to our cause, but of a prying disposition and most suspicious. The re-enforcements had been sent because of the previous attempt to break through the line at this point, the lay of the ground being such that it was more favorable for plans of escape than elsewhere.

"You need not stay unless you wish," said Belt. "No positive instructions were given on that point. As for myself, I confess I would rather be with the army, since much is likely to happen there soon."

"I think things will drag for some time yet," I said with as careless an air as I could assume, "and I suspect that they have been more active here than they are with the army. Another attempt to break through our line may be made at this point, and I believe I'd rather remain for a day or two."

But just then, as if for the sole purpose of belying my words about dullness at the front, there was a sharp crackle of distant skirmishing and the red flare of a cannon appeared on the horizon. It called the attention of both of us for a moment or two.

"The bullets appear to be flying over there, but if you prefer to remain here, of course you can have your wish," said Belt with sarcasm.

I did not answer, as no good excuse happened to my mind, and we went up the hillside together. I looked about carefully to see what arrangements he had made, but it was merely a doubling of the guard. Otherwise he had followed my dispositions. Belt looked at the house.

"I hear that some people are there. Who are they?" he asked.

"Only two," I replied, "women both—Madame Van Auken and her daughter."

"For us, or against us?" he asked.

"Against us," I replied. "The son and brother is in the English army with Burgoyne, over there; moreover, the daughter is betrothed to an Englishman who has just been taken prisoner by us."

I thought it best to make no disguise of these matters.

"That looks suspicious," he said, his hawk face brightening at the thought of hidden things to be found.

"They might do us harm if they could," I said, "but they have not the power. Our lines surround the house; no one save ourselves can go to them, nor can they go to any one."

"Still, I would like to go through the house," he said, some doubt yet showing in his tone.

"I have searched it twice and found nothing," I said indifferently.

He let the matter drop for the time and busied himself with an examination of the ground; but I knew he was most likely to take it up again, for he could not suppress his prying nature. I would have been glad to give warning to Kate, but I could think of no way to do it.

"Who is the best man that you have here?" he asked presently.

"Whitestone—Sergeant Whitestone," I replied, glad to place the sergeant in his confidence, for it might turn out to my advantage. "There is none more vigilant, and you can depend upon all that he says."

We separated there, our work taking us in different directions. When we returned to the valley, which we had made a kind of headquarters, I heard him asking Whitestone about the Van Aukens.

"Tartars, both of 'em," said the good sergeant; "if you go in there, leftenant, they'll scold you till they take your face off."

The look on Belt's face was proof that not even Whitestone's warning would deter him. At least it so seemed to me. In a half hour I found that I had judged aright. He told me he was not in a state of satisfaction about the house, and since the responsibility for it lay with him he proposed to make a search of it in person. He requested me to go with him.

"This seems to be the main entrance," he said, leading the way to the portico, which faced the north, and looking about with very inquiring eyes. "Madame Van Auken and her daughter must be much frightened by the presence of troops, for I have not yet seen the face of either at door or window."

He knocked loudly at the door with the hilt of his sword, and Kate appeared, very calm as usual. I made the introductions as politely as I was able.

"Lieutenant Belt is my senior, Miss Van Auken," I said, "and therefore has superseded me in command of the guard at this point."

"Then I trust that Lieutenant Belt will relax some of the rigors of the watch," she said, "and not subject us to the great discomfort of repeated searches of our house."

She turned her shoulder to me as if she would treat me with the greatest coldness. I understood her procedure, and marveled much at her presence of mind. It seemed to be successful too, for Belt smiled, and looked ironically at me, like one who rejoices in the mishap of his comrade.

She took us into the house, talking with much courtesy to Belt, and ignoring me in a manner that I did not altogether like, even with the knowledge that it was but assumption. She led us into the presence of madame, her mother, who looked much worn with care, though preserving a haughty demeanor. As usual, she complained that our visits were discourtesies, and Belt apologized in his best manner. Glad that the brunt did not now fall upon me, I deemed it best to keep silence, which I did in most complete manner.

Madame invited us to search the house as we pleased, and we took her at her word, finding nothing. I was much relieved thereat. I had feared that Albert, knowing I would not make another search so long as I was in command, would not be in proper concealment. With my relief was mingled a certain perplexity that his place of hiding should evade me.

Belt was a gentleman despite his curiosity, which I believe the New England people can not help, and for which, therefore, they are not to be blamed, and when he had finished the vain quest he apologized again to Madame Van Auken and her daughter for troubling them. He was impressed by the fine looks of the daughter, and he made one or two gallant speeches to her which she received very well, as I notice women mostly do whatever may be the circumstances. I felt some anger toward Belt, though there seemed to be no cause for it. When we left the house he said:

"Miss Van Auken doesn't look so dangerous, yet you say she is a red-hot Tory."

"I merely included her in a generality," I replied. "The others of the family are strong Tories, but Miss Van Auken, I have reason to think, inclines to our cause."

"That is good," he said, though he gave no reason why it should seem good to him. After that he turned his attention to his main duty, examining here and there and displaying the most extreme vigilance. The night found him still prowling about.

Directly after nightfall the weather turned very cool in that unaccountable way it sometimes has in the late summer or early autumn, and began to rain.

It was a most cold and discouraging rain that hunted every hole, in our worn uniforms, and displayed a peculiar knack of slipping down our collars. I found myself seeking the shelter of trees, and as the cold bit into the marrow my spirits drooped until I felt like an old man. Even the distant skirmishers were depressed by the rainy night, for the shots ceased and the hills and the valleys were as silent and lonely as ever they were before the white man came.

I was thinking it was a very long and most dismal night before us, when I heard a chattering of teeth near me, and turning about saw Belt in pitiable condition. He was all drawn with the cold damp, and his face looked as shriveled as if it were seventy instead of twenty-five. Moreover, he was shaking in a chill. I had noticed before that the man did not look robust.

"This is a little hard on me, Shelby," he said, his tone asking sympathy. "I have but lately come from a sick-bed, and I fear greatly this rain will throw me into a fever."

He looked very longingly at the house.

I fear there was some malice in me then, for he had put aspersions upon my courage earlier in the day, which perhaps he had a right to do, not knowing my secret motives.

"The weather is a trifle bad, one must admit, lieutenant," I said, "but you and I will not mind it; moreover, the darkness of the night demands greater vigilance on our part."

He said nothing, merely rattled his teeth together and walked on with what I admit was a brave show for a man shaking in a bad chill. As his assistant I could go and come pretty much as I chose, and I kept him in view, bent on seeing what he would do.

He endured the chill most handsomely for quite a time, but the wet and the cold lent aggravation to it, and presently he turned to me, his teeth clicking together in most formidable fashion.

"I fear, Shelby, that I must seek shelter in the house," he said. "I would stick to the watch out here, but this confounded chill has me in its grip and will not let go. But, as you have done good work here and I would not seem selfish, you shall go in with me."

I understood his motive, which was to provide that in case he should incur censure for going into the house, I could share it and divide it with him. It was no very admirable action on Belt's part, but I minded it not; in truth I rather liked it, for since he was to be in the house, I preferred to be there too, and at the same time, and not for matters concerning my health. I decided quickly that I must seem his friend and give him sympathy; in truth I was not his enemy at all; I merely found him inconvenient.

We went again to the front door and knocked many times before any answer came to us. Then two heads—the one of Mistress Kate, the other of her mother—were thrust out of an upper window and the usual question was propounded to us.

"Lieutenant Belt is very ill," I said, taking the word from his lips, "and needs must have shelter from the cruelty of the night. We would not trouble you were not the case extreme."

I could see that Belt was grateful for the way I had put the matter. Presently they opened the door, both appearing there for the sake of company at that hour, I suppose. Belt tried to preserve an appearance in the presence of the ladies, but he was too sick. He trembled with his chill like a sapling in a high wind, and I said:

"Lieutenant Belt's condition speaks for itself; nothing else could have induced us to intrude upon you at such an untimely hour."

I fancy I said that well, and both Madame Van Auken and her daughter showed pity for Belt; yet the elder could not wholly repress a display of feeling against us.

"We can not turn any one ill, not even an enemy, away from our door," she said, "but I fear the rebel armies have left us little for the uses of hospitality."

She said this in the stiff and rather precise way that our fathers and mothers affected, but she motioned for us to come in, and we obeyed her. I confess I was rather glad to enter the dry room, for my clothes were flapping wet about me.

"Perhaps the lieutenant would like to lie down," said Madame Van Auken, pointing to a large and comfortable sofa in the corner of the room that we had entered.

But Belt was too proud to do that, though it was needful to him. He sat down merely and continued to shiver. Mistress Kate came presently with a large draught of hot whisky and water which smelled most savorous. She insisted that Belt drink it, and he swallowed it all, leaving none for me. Madame Van Auken placed a lighted candle upon a little table, and then both the ladies withdrew.

Belt said he felt better, but he had a most wretched appearance. I insisted that he let me feel his pulse, and I found he was bordering upon a high fever, and most likely, if precautions were not taken, would soon be out of his senses. The wet clothes were the chief trouble, and I said they must come off. Belt demurred for a while, but he consented at last when I told him persistent refusal might mean his death.

I roused up the ladies again, explaining the cause of this renewed interruption, and secured from them their sympathy and a large bedquilt. I made Belt take off his uniform, and then I spread the quilt over him as he lay on the sofa, telling him to go to sleep. He said he had no such intention; but a second hot draught of whisky which Kate brought to the door gave him the inclination, if not the intention. But he fought against it, and his will was aided by the sudden revival of sounds which betokened that the skirmishing had begun again. Through the window I heard the faint patter of rifles, but the shots were too distant, or the night too dark to disclose the flash. This sudden spurt of warlike activity told me once again that the great crisis was approaching fast, and I hoped most earnestly that events at the Van Auken house would culminate first.

Belt was still struggling against weakness and sleep, and he complained fretfully when he heard the rifle shots, bemoaning his fate to be seized by a wretched, miserable chill at such a time.

"Perhaps after all the battle may be fought without me," said he with unintended humor.

I assured him that he would be all right in the morning. His resistance to sleep, I told him, was his own injury, for it was needful to his health. He took me at my word and let his eyelids droop. I foresaw that he would be asleep very soon, but he roused up a bit presently and showed anxiety about the guard. He wanted to be sure that everything was done right, and asked me to go out and see Whitestone, whom we had left in charge when we entered the house.

I was averse in no particular and slipped quietly out into the darkness. I found Whitestone in the valley.

"All quiet," he reported. "I've just come from a round of the sentinels and there's nothing suspicious. I'm going back myself presently to watch in front of the house."

I knew Whitestone would ask no questions, so I told him the lieutenant was still very ill and I would return to him; I did not know how long I would stay in the house, I said. Whitestone, like the good, silent fellow he was, made no reply.

I returned to the front door. I was now learning the way into the house very well. I had traveled it often enough. I stood for a moment in the little portico, which was as clean and white as if washed by the sea. The rain had nearly ceased to fall, and the blaze of the distant skirmishing suddenly flared up on the dark horizon like a forest fire. I wondered not that the two women in the house should be moved by all this; I wondered rather at their courage. In the yard stood Whitestone, his figure rising up as stiff and straight as a post.

CHAPTER 6 Belt's Ghost

I found Belt fast asleep. The two draughts of whisky, heavy and hot, had been a blanket to his senses, and he had gone off for a while to another world to think and to struggle still, for he muttered and squirmed in his restless slumber. His hand when I touched it was yet hot with fever. He might, most likely would, be better when he awoke in the morning, but he would be flat aback the remainder of the night. He could conduct no further search in that house before the next day.

I was uncertain what to do, whether to remain there with Belt or go out and help Whitestone with the watch. Duty to our cause said the latter, but in truth other voices are sometimes as loud as that of duty. I listened to one of the other.

I drew a chair near to Belt's couch and sat down. He was still muttering in his hot, sweaty sleep like one with anger at things, and now and then threw out his long thin legs and arms. He looked like a man tied down trying to escape.

The candle still burned on the table, but its light was feeble at best. Shadows filled the corners of the room. I like sick-bed watches but little, and least of all such as that. They make me feel as if I had lost my place in a healthy world. To such purpose was I thinking when Belt sat up with a suddenness that made me start, and cried in a voice cracked with fever:

"Shelby, are you there?"

"Yes, I'm here," I replied with a cheeriness that I did not feel. "Lie down and go to sleep, lieutenant, or you'll be a week getting well."

"I can't go to sleep, and I haven't been to sleep," he said, raising his voice, which had a whistling note of illness in it.

His eyes sparkled, and I could see that the machinery of his head was working badly. I took him by the shoulders with intent to force him down upon the couch; but he threw me off with sudden energy that took me by surprise.

"Let me go," he said, "till I say what I want to say."

"Well, what is it?" I asked, thinking to pacify him.

"Shelby," said he, belief showing all over his face, "I've seen a ghost!"

A strong desire to laugh was upon me, but I did not let it best me, for I had respect for Belt, who was my superior officer. I don't believe in ghosts; they never come to see me.

"You're sick, and you've been dreaming, lieutenant," I said. "Go to sleep."

"I'll try to go to sleep," he replied, "but what I say is truth, and I've seen a ghost."

"What did it look like?" I asked, remembering that it is best to fall in with the humor of mad people.

"Like a woman," he replied, "and that's all I can say on that point, for this cursed fever has drawn a veil over my eyes. I had shut them, trying to go to sleep, but something kept pulling my eyelids apart, and open they came again; there was the ghost, the ghost of a woman; it had come through the wall, I suppose. It floated all around the room as if it were looking for something, but not making a breath of a noise, like a white cloud sailing through the air. I tell you, Shelby, I was in fear, for I had never believed in such things, and I had laughed at them."

"What became of the ghost?" I asked.

"It went away just like it came, through the wall, I guess," said Belt. "All I know is that I saw it, and then I didn't. And I want you to stay with me, Shelby; don't leave me!"

This time I laughed, and on purpose. I wanted to chirk Belt up a bit, and I thought I could do it by ridiculing such a fever dream. But I could not shake the conviction in him. Instead, his temper took heat at my lack of faith. Then I affected to believe, which soothed him, and exhaustion falling upon him I saw that either he would slumber again or weakness would steal his senses. I thought to ease his mind, and told him everything outside was going well; that Whitestone was the best sentinel in the world, and not even a lizard could creep past him though the night might be black as coal. Whereat he smiled, and presently turning over on his side began to mutter, by which I knew that a hot sleep was again laying hold of him.

After the rain it had turned very warm again, and I opened the window for unbreathed air. Belt's request that I stay with him, given in a sort of delirium though it was, made good excuse for my remaining. If ever he said anything about it I could allege his own words.

The candle burned down more on one side than on the other and its blaze leaned over like a man sick. It served but to distort.

I looked at Belt and wondered why the mind too should grow weak, as it most often does when disease lays hold of the body. In his healthy senses, Belt—who, like most New Englanders, believed only what he saw—would have jeered at the claims of a ghost. There, was little credulity in that lank, bony frame.

But I stopped short in such thoughts, for I noticed that which made my blood quicken in surprise. Belt's uniform was gone. I rose and looked behind the couch, thinking the lieutenant in his uneasy squirmings might have knocked it over there. But he had not done so; nor was it elsewhere in the room. It had gone clean away—perhaps through the wall, like Belt's ghost. I wondered what Whitestone's emotions would be if a somewhat soiled and worn Continental uniform, with no flesh and bones in it, should come walking down his beat.

I understood that it was a time for me to think my best, and I set about it. I leaned back in my chair and stared at the wall in the manner of those who do strenuous thinking. I shifted my gaze but once, and then to put it upon Belt, who I concluded would not come back to earth for a long time.

At the end of ten minutes I rose from my chair and went out into the hall, leaving the candle still burning on the table. Perhaps I, too, might find a ghost. I did not mean to lose the opportunity which might never seek me again.

The hall ran the full width of the house and was broad. There was a window at the end, but the light was so faint I could scarce see, and in the corners and near the walls so much dusk was gathered that the eye was of no use there. Yet, by much stealing about and reaching here and there with my hands, I convinced myself that no ghost lurked in that hall. But there was a stairway leading into an upper hall, and, as silent as a ghost myself, for which I take pride, I stole up the steps.

Just before I reached the top step I heard a faint shuffling noise like that which a heavy and awkward ghost with poor use of himself would most likely make. Nay, I have heard that ghosts never make noise, but I see no reason why they shouldn't, at least a little.

I crouched down in the shadow of the top step and the banisters. The faint shuffling noise came nearer, and Belt's lost uniform, upright and in its proper shape, drifted past me and down the steps. I followed lightly. I was not afraid. I have never heard, at least not with the proper authenticity, that ghosts strike one, or do other deeds of violence; so I followed, secure in my courage. The brass buttons on the uniform gleamed a little, and I kept them in clear view. Down the steps went the figure, and then it sped along the hall, with me after it. It reached the front door, opened it half a foot and stood there. That was my opportunity to hold discussion with a ghost, and I did not neglect it. Forward I slipped and tapped with my fingers an arm of the uniform, which inclosed not empty air but flesh and blood. Startled, the figure faced about and saw my features, for a little light came in at the door.

"I offer congratulations on your speedy recovery from fever, Lieutenant Belt," I said, in a subdued tone.

"It was quick, it is true," he replied, "but I need something more."

"What is that?" I asked.

"Fresh air," he replied. "I think I will go outside."

"I will go with you," I said. "Fevers are uncertain, and one can not tell what may happen."

He hesitated as if he would make demur, but I said:

"It is necessary to both of us."

He hesitated no longer, but opened the door wider and stepped out into the portico. I looked with much anxiety to see what sort of watch was kept, and no doubt my companion did the same. It was good. Three sentinels were in sight. Directly in front of us, and about thirty feet away, was Whitestone. The skirmishers and their rifles had not yet gone to sleep, for twice while we stood on the portico we saw the flash of powder on the distant hills.

"Lieutenant, I think we had best walk in the direction of the firing and make a little investigation," I said.

"The idea is good," he replied. "We will do it."

We walked down the steps and into the yard. I was slightly in advance, leading the way. We passed within a dozen feet of Whitestone, who saluted.

"Sergeant," said I, "Lieutenant Belt, who feels much better, and I, wish to inquire further into the skirmishing. There may be some significance for us in it. We will return presently."

Whitestone saluted again and said nothing. Once more I wish to commend Whitestone as a jewel. He did not turn to look at us when we passed him, but stalked up and down as if he were a wooden figure moving on hinges.

We walked northward, neither speaking. Some three or four hundred yards from the house both of us stopped. Then I put my hand upon his arm again.

"Albert," I said, "your fortune is far better than you deserve, or ever will deserve."

"I don't know about that," he replied.

"I do," I said. "Now, beyond those hills are the camp-fires of Burgoyne. You came thus far easily enough in your effort to get out, though Martyn, who came with you, failed, and you can go back the same way; but, before you start, take off Belt's uniform. I won't have you masquerading as an American officer."

Without a word he took off the Continental uniform and stood in the citizen's suit in which I had first seen him, Belt being a larger man than he. I rolled them up in a bundle and put the bundle under my arm.

"Shake hands," he said. "You've done me a good turn."

"Several of them," I said, as I shook his hand, "which is several more than you have done for me."

"I don't bear you any grudge on that account," he said with a faint laugh, as he strode off in the darkness toward Burgoyne's army.

Which, I take it, was handsome of him.

I watched him as long as I could. You may not be able sometimes to look in the darkness and find a figure, but when that figure departs from your side and you never take your eyes off it, you can follow it for a long way through the night. Thus I could watch Albert a hundred yards or more, and I saw that he veered in no wise from the course I had assigned to him, and kept his face turned to the army of Burgoyne. But I had not doubted that he would keep his word and would not seek to escape southward; nor did I doubt that he would reach his comrades in safety.

I turned away, very glad that he was gone. Friends cause much trouble sometimes, but girls' brothers cause more.

I took my thoughts away from him and turned them to the business of going back into the house with the wad of uniform under my arm, which was very simple if things turned out all right. I believed that Whitestone would be on guard at the same place, which was what I wanted. I knew Whitestone would be the most vigilant of all the sentinels, but I was accustomed to him. One prefers to do business with a man one knows.

I sauntered back slowly, now and then turning about on my heels as if I would spy out the landscape, which in truth was pretty well hid by the thickness of the night.

As I approached the yard my heart gave a thump like a hammer on the anvil; but there was Whitestone on the same beat, and my heart thumped again, but with more consideration than before.

I entered the yard, and Whitestone saluted with dignity.

"Sergeant," said I, "Lieutenant Belt is looking about on the other side of the house. He fears that his fever is coming on him again, and he will re-enter the house, but by the back door. I am to meet him there."

Sergeant Whitestone saluted again. I said naught of the bundle in the crook of my arm, which he could plainly see.

"Sergeant," said I, "what do you think of a man who tells all he knows?"

"Very little, sir," he replied.

"So do I," I said; "but be that as it may, you know that you and I are devoted to the patriot cause."

"Aye, truly, sir!" he said.

We saluted each other again with great respect, and I passed into the house.

Belt was still asleep upon the sofa and his fever was going down, though he talked now and then of the things that were on his brain when awake. The candle was dying, the tallow sputtering as the blaze reached the last of it, and without another the thickness of the night would be upon us.

I ascended the stairway into the upper hall again, but this time with no attempt to rival a ghost in smoothness of motion. Instead, I stumbled about like a man in whose head hot punch has set everything to dancing. Presently Mistress Kate, bearing a candle in her hand and dressed as if for the day—at which I was not surprised—appeared from the side door.

I begged her for another candle, if the supply in the house were not exhausted, and stepping back she returned in a moment with what I desired; then in a tone of much sympathy she inquired as to the state of Lieutenant Belt's health. I said he was sleeping peacefully, and suggested that she come and look at him, as she might have sufficient knowledge of medicine to assist me in the case. To which she consented, though ever one of the most modest of maidens.

I held the candle near Belt's face, but in such position that the light would not shine into his eyes and awaken him.

"But the lieutenant would rather be on his feet again and in these garments," I said, turning the light upon Belt's uniform, which I had carefully spread out again on the foot of the couch. Then I added:

"The wearer of that uniform has had many adventures, doubtless, but he has not come to any harm yet."

I might have talked further, but I knew that naught more was needed for Kate Van Auken.

Moreover, no words could ever be cited against me.

CHAPTER 7 In Burgoyne's Camp

Belt awoke the next morning in fairly good health, but very sour of temper. Like some other people whom I know, he seemed to hold everybody he met personally responsible for his own misfortunes, which I take it is most disagreeable for all concerned. He spoke to me in most churlish manner, though I am fair to say I replied in similar fashion, which for some reason seemed to cause him discontent. Then he went out and quarreled with Whitestone and the others, who had been doing their duty in complete fashion.

But a few minutes after he had gone out, Madame Van Auken, who was a lady in the highest degree, though a Tory one, came to me and said she and her daughter had prepared breakfast; scanty, it is true, for the rebels had passed that way too often, but it would most likely be better than army fare, and would be good for invalids; would I be so kind as to ask Lieutenant Belt to come in and share it with them, and would I do them the further kindness to present myself at the breakfast also? I would be delighted, and I said so, also hurrying forth to find Belt, to whom I gave the invitation. He accepted in tone somewhat ungracious, I thought, but improved in manner when he entered the presence of the ladies; for, after all, Belt was a gentleman, and I will admit that he had been unfortunate. As we went in to the breakfast table I said to Belt:

"You've come out of that chill and fever very well, lieutenant. You look a little weak, but all right otherwise."

"You seem to have had your own worries," he replied a bit slowly, "for something has been painting night under your eyes."

Well, it was natural; it had been an anxious time for me in truth. But I suggested it was due to long night watches.

The ladies, as they had said, had not a great deal to offer, but it was well prepared by their own hands. They had some very fine coffee, to which I am ever partial, especially in the mornings, and we made most excellent progress with the breakfast, even Belt waxing amiable. But about the middle of the breakfast he asked quite suddenly of us all:

"Do you believe in ghosts?"

I was a bit startled, I will admit, but I rejoice to think that I did not show it. Instead, I looked directly at Mistress Kate, who in truth looked very handsome and lighted-hearted that morning, and asked:

"Do you believe in ghosts?"

"Of a certainty—of a certainty," she said with emphasis.

"So do I," said I with equal emphasis.

Madame Van Auken drank her coffee.

"I don't," said Belt. "I thought I did for a while last night. I even thought I saw one while Shelby was away from me for a while."

I rallied Belt, and explained to the ladies that the fever had given him an illusion the night before. They joined me in the raillery, and trusted that the gallant lieutenant would not see double when he met his enemies. Belt took it very well, better than I had thought. But after the breakfast, when we had withdrawn again, he said to me with a sour look:

"I do not trust those ladies, Shelby."

"Well, as for that," I replied, "I told you that Madame Van Auken was a hot Tory, of which fact she seeks to make no concealment. But I don't see what harm they could do us, however much they might wish it."

"Maybe," he said; then with a sudden change:

"Why did you say this morning that you believed in ghosts, when last night you said you didn't?"

I fixed upon him the sharp stare of one amazed at such a question.

"Belt," said I, "I am a believer in ghosts. I am also a devout believer in the report that the moon is made of moldy green cheese."

He sniffed a bit, and let me alone on that point, but he returned to the attack on the ladies. I do not know what idea had found lodgment in his head; in truth it may have been due to biliousness, but he suspected them most strongly of what he called treasonable correspondence with the enemy. I asked him what course he intended to take in the matter, and he returned a vague answer; but I soon received intimation of his purpose, for in an hour, leaving me in charge for the time, he returned to the army. He made a quick trip, and when he came back he told me he had reported the case at headquarters. The general, not knowing what else to do with the ladies, had directed that they be sent to Burgoyne's army, where, he understood, they had relatives.

"He said to me," said Belt, "that at this time it would be just as well for the British to take care of their own."

Reflecting a little, I decided that the matter had fallen out very well. If they were in Burgoyne's camp it would release us all from some troubles and doubts.

"You had best go into the house and notify them," said Belt, "for they are to be taken to Burgoyne under a white flag this very afternoon."

I found Mistress Kate first and told her what Belt had done. She did not seem to be much surprised. In truth, she said she had expected it.

"I trust, Mistress Kate," I said, "that while you are in Burgoyne's army you will not let your opinions be influenced too much by your surroundings."

"My opinions are my own," she said, "and are not dependent upon time and place."

Then I said something about its being a pity that Captain Chudleigh was a prisoner in our hands at such a time and was not with his own army, but she gave me such a sharp answer that I was glad to shut my mouth.

Madame Van Auken said she was glad to go, but she would revisit her house when she came southward with Burgoyne after he had scattered the rebels, provided the rebels in the meantime had not burned the house down. Which, considering many things, I felt I could overlook. Both promised to be ready in an hour. I went outside and found that Belt was able to surprise me again.

"You are to take the ladies into Burgoyne's camp," he said. "I wished to do it myself, but I was needed for other work."

I was not at all averse to this task, though it had never occurred to me that I would enter the British lines, except possibly as a prisoner.

"I wish you luck," said Belt, somewhat enviously. "I think the trip into the British lines is worth taking."

Right here I may say—for Belt does not come into this narration again—that after the war I told him the whole story of these affairs, which he enjoyed most heartily, and is at this day one among my best friends.

The preliminaries about the transfer of the ladies to Burgoyne's camp were but few, though I was exposed on the way to much censure from Madame Van Auken because of my rebel proclivities. In truth, Mistress Catherine, I think, took after her deceased and lamented father rather than her mother, who I knew had made the signal of the light to Martyn, and to Albert, who was on foot near him. But I bore it very well, inasmuch as one can grow accustomed to almost anything.

I found that during my few days' absence our army had pushed up much closer to Burgoyne, and also that we had increased greatly in numbers. Nothing could save Burgoyne, so I heard, but the arrival of Clinton from New York with heavy re-enforcements, and even then, at the best for Burgoyne, it would be but a problem. My heart swelled with that sudden elation one feels when a great reward looks certain after long trial.

Protected by the flag of truce we approached Burgoyne's lines. There were but the three of us, the two ladies and I. Mistress Kate was very silent; Madame Van Auken, for whom I have the utmost respect, be her opinions what they may, did the talking for all three. She was in somewhat exuberant mood, as she expected to rejoin her son, thus having all her immediate family together under the flag that she loved. She had no doubt that Burgoyne would beat us. I could not make out Mistress Kate's emotions, nor in truth whether she had any; but just after we were hailed by the first British sentinel she said to me with an affectation of lightness, though she could not keep her voice from sounding sincere:

"My brother will never forget what you have done for him, Dick."

"He may or may not," I replied, "but I hope your brother's sister will not."

Which may not have been a very gallant speech, but I will leave it to every just man if I had not endured a good deal in silence. She did not take any exceptions to my reply, but smiled, which I did not know whether to consider a good or bad sign.

I showed a letter from one of our generals to the sentinel, and we were quickly passed through the lines. We were received by Captain Jervis, a British officer of much politeness, and I explained to him that the two ladies whom I was proud to escort were the mother and sister of Albert Van Auken, who should be with Burgoyne's army. He answered at once that he knew Albert, and had seen him not an hour before. Thereat the ladies rejoiced greatly, knowing that Albert was safe so far; which perhaps, to my mind, was better luck than he deserved. But in ten minutes he was brought to us, and embraced his mother and sister with great warmth; then shaking hands with me—

"I'm sorry to see you a prisoner, Dick, my lad," he said easily, "especially after you've been so obliging to me. But it's your bad luck."

"I'm not a prisoner," I replied with some heat, "though you and all the rest of Burgoyne's men are likely soon to be. I merely came here under a flag of truce to bring your mother and sister, and put them out of the way of cannon balls."

He laughed at my boast, and said Burgoyne would soon resume his promenade to New York. Then he bestirred himself for the comfort of his mother and sister. He apologized for straitened quarters, but said he could place them in some very good company, including the Baroness Riedesel and Madame the wife of General Fraser, at which Madame Van Auken, who was always fond of people of quality, especially when the quality was indicated by a title, was pleased greatly. And in truth they were welcomed most hospitably by the wives of the British and Hessian officers with Burgoyne's army, who willingly shared with them the scarcity of food and lodging they had to offer. When I left them, Mistress Catherine said to me with a saucy curve of the lip, as if she would but jest:

"Take good care of yourself, Dick, and my brother's sister will try not to forget you."

"Thank you," I said, "and if it falls in my way to do a good turn for Captain Chudleigh while he is our prisoner, I will take full advantage of it."

At this she was evidently displeased, though somehow I was not.

Albert Van Auken took charge of me, and asked me into a tent to meet some of his fellow officers and take refreshment; which invitation I promptly accepted, for in those days an American soldier, with wisdom born of trial, never neglected a chance to get something good to eat or to drink.

On my way I observed the condition of Burgoyne's camp. It was in truth a stricken army that he led—or rather did not lead, for it seemed now to be stuck fast. The tents and the wagons were filled with the sick and the wounded, and many not yet entirely well clustered upon the grass seeking such consolation as they could find in the talk of each other. The whole in body, rank and file, sought to preserve a gallant demeanor, though in spite of it a certain depression was visible on almost every face. Upon my soul I was sorry for them, enemies though they were, and the greater their misfortune the greater cause we had for joy, which, I take it, is one of the grievous things about war.

It was a large tent into which Albert took me, and I met there Captain Jervis and several other officers, two or three of whom seemed to be of higher rank than captain, though I did not exactly catch their names, for Albert spoke somewhat indistinctly when making the introductions. There seemed to be a degree of comfort in the tent—bottles, glasses, and other evidences of social warmth.

"We wish to be hospitable to a gallant enemy like yourself, Mr. Shelby," said Captain Jervis, "and are not willing that you should return to your own army without taking refreshment with us."

I thanked him for his courtesy, and said I was quite willing to be a live proof of their hospitality; whereupon they filled the glasses with a very unctuous, fine-flavored wine, and we drank to the health of the wide world. It had been long since good wine had passed my lips, and when they filled the glasses a second time I said in my heart that they were gentlemen. At the same time I wondered to myself a bit why officers of such high rank, as some of these seemed to be, should pay so much honor to me, who was but young and the rank of whom was but small. Yet I must confess that this slight wonder had no bad effect upon the flavor of the wine.

Some eatables of a light and delicate nature were handed around by an orderly, and all of us partook, after which we drank a third glass of wine. Then the officers talked most agreeably about a variety of subjects, even including the latest gossip they had brought with them from the Court of St. James. Then we took a fourth glass of wine. I am not a heavy drinker, as heavy drinkers go, and have rather a strong head, but a humming of the distant sea began in my ears and the talk moved far away. I foresaw that Richard Shelby had drunk enough, and that it was time for me to exercise my strongest will over his somewhat rebellious head.

"I suppose that you Americans are very sanguine just now, and expect to take our entire army," said the oldest and apparently the highest of the officers—colonel or general, something or other—to me.

I noted that he was overwhelmingly polite in tone. Moreover, my will was acquiring mastery over Dick Shelby's humming head. I made an ambiguous reply, and he went further into the subject of the campaign, the other officers joining him and indulging slightly in jest at our expense, as if they would lead me on to boast. To make a clean confession in the matter, I felt some inclination to a little vaunting. He said something about our hope to crush Burgoyne, and laughed as if it were quite impossible.

"English armies are never taken," said he.

"But they have never before warred with the Americans," I said.

I recalled afterward that some of the officers applauded me for that reply, which was strange considering their sympathies. The old officer showed no offense.

"Have you heard that Sir Henry Clinton is coming to our relief with five thousand men?" he asked.

"No; have you?" I replied.

I was applauded again, and the officer laughed.

"You take me up quickly. You have a keen mind, Mr. Shelby; it's a pity you're not one of us," he said.

"That would be bad for me," I said, "as I do not wish to become a prisoner."

This was a bit impertinent and ungenerous, I will admit, but I had drunk four glasses of wine and they were nagging me. They filled up the glasses again, and most of them drank, but I only sipped mine, meanwhile strengthening my rule over Dick Shelby's mutinous head. The officer laughed easily at my reply and began to talk about the chances of the next battle, which he was sure the British would win. He said Burgoyne had six thousand men, English and Hessians, and in quite a careless way he asked how many we had.

By this time I had Dick Shelby's unruly head under complete control, and his question, lightly put as it was, revealed their whole plan. Right then and there I felt a most painful regret that I had not given Albert Van Auken the worst beating of his life when I had the chance.

I replied that I could not say exactly how many men we had, but the number was somewhere between a thousand and a million, and at any rate sufficient for the purpose. He laughed gently as if he were willing to tolerate me, and continued to put questions in manner sly and most insidious. I returned answers vague or downright false, and I could see that the officer was becoming vexed at his want of success. Albert himself filled up my glass and urged me to drink again.

"You know, Dick, you don't get good wine often," he said, "and this may be your last chance."

Had not I been a guest I would have created, right then and there, a second opportunity for giving Albert the worst beating of his life. I pretended to drink, though I merely sipped the fumes. The elderly officer changed his tactics a little.

"Do you think your generals are well informed about us?" he asked.

"Oh, yes," I replied.

"How?"

"We learn from prisoners," I said, "and then, perhaps, we ask sly questions from Englishmen who come to us under flags of truce."

"What do you mean?" he asked, his face—and I was glad to see it—reddening.

"I mean," said I, "that you have brought me into this tent with purpose to intoxicate me and get valuable information from me. It was a plot unworthy of gentlemen."

He rose to his feet, his eyes flashing with much anger. But the wine I had drunk made me very belligerent. I was ready to fight a thousand come one, come all. Moreover, I leave it to all if I did not have just cause for wrath. I turned from the officer to Albert, against whom my indignation burned most.

"I have just saved you from death, perhaps a most degrading death," I said, "and I am loath to remind you of it, but I must, in order to tell your fellow officers I am sorry I did it."

I never saw a man turn redder, and he trembled all over. It was the scarlet of shame, too, and not of righteous anger.

"Dick," he said, "I beg your pardon. I let my zeal for our cause go too far. I—I—"

I think he would have broken down, but just then the elderly officer interfered.

"Be silent, Lieutenant Van Auken," he said. "It is not your fault, nor that of any other present except myself. You speak truth, Mr. Shelby, when you say it was unworthy of us. So it was. I am glad it failed, and I apologize for the effort to make it a success. Mr. Shelby, I am glad to know you."

He held out his hand with such frank manliness and evident good will that I grasped it and shook it heartily. What more he might have said or done I do not know, for just then we were interrupted by the sound of a great though distant shouting.

CHAPTER 8 A Night Under Fire

The shouting begat curiosity in us all, and we left the tent, the elderly officer leading. I perceived at once that the noise came from our lines, which were pushed up very close to those of the British and were within plain hearing distance. Among the trees and bushes, which were very dense at points, I could see in the brilliant sunshine the flash of rifle barrel and the gleam of uniform. The shouting was great in volume, swelling like a torrent rising to the flood.

I remained by the side of the old officer. He seemed anxious.

"What is it? What can that mean? It must be something important," he asked as much of himself as of me.

The reply was ready for him, as some English skirmishers came forward with an American prisoner whom they had taken but a few moments before. The man was but a common soldier, ragged, but intelligent. The officer put to him his question about the shouting, which had not yet subsided.

"That was a welcome," said the prisoner.

"A welcome! What do you mean by that?"

"Simply that more re-enforcements have come from the south."

The officer grew even graver.

"More men always coming for them and never any for us," he said, almost under his breath.

I had it in mind to suggest that I be returned at once to my own army, but the arrival of the troops or other cause created a sudden recrudescence of the skirmishing. Piff-paff chanted the rifles; zip-zip chirped the bullets. Little blades of flame spurted up among the bushes, and above them rose the white curls of smoke like baby clouds. On both sides the riflemen were at work.

The officer looked about him as if he intended to give some special orders, and then seemed to think better of it. A bullet passed through the tent we had just left. I felt that my American uniform took me out of the list of targets.

"Your sharpshooters seem to have come closer," said the officer. "Their bullets fell short this morning. I will admit they are good men with the rifle—better than ours."

"These are countrymen," I said. "They have been trained through boyhood to the use of the rifle."

I was looking at the fringe of trees and bushes which half hid our lines. Amid the boughs of a tall tree whose foliage was yet untouched by autumn I saw what I took to be a man's figure; but the leaves were so dense and so green I was not sure. Moreover, the man, if man it was, seemed to wear clothing of the hue of the leaves. I decided I was mistaken; then I knew I had been right at first guess, for I saw the green body within the green curtain of leaves move out upon a bough and raise its head a little. The sun flashed upon a rifle barrel, and the next instant the familiar curl of white smoke rose from its muzzle.

The officer had opened his mouth to speak to me, but the words remained unspoken. His face went pale as if all the blood had suddenly gone out of him, and he flopped down like an emptied bag at my feet, shot through the heart.

I was seized with a shivering horror. He was talking to me one moment and dead the next. His fall, seen by so many, created a confusion in the British lines. Several rushed forward to seize the body and carry it away. Just as the first man reached it, he too was slain by a hidden sharpshooter, and the two bodies lay side by side.

Acting from impulse rather than thought, I lifted the officer by the shoulders and began to drag him back into the camp. Whether or not my uniform protected me I can not say, but I was hit by no bullet, though the skirmishing became so sharp and so hot that it rose almost to the dignity of a battle. The officer's body was withdrawn beyond the range of the sharpshooting and placed in a tent. Though he had sought to entrap me he had made handsome apology therefor, and I mourned him as I would a friend. Why should men filled with mutual respect be compelled to shoot each other?

Albert came to me there, and said in a very cold voice:

"Dick, this sudden outburst will compel you to remain our guest some time longer—perhaps through the night."

I turned my back upon him. and when he left I do not know, but when I looked that way again he was gone, for which I was in truth very glad. Yet I would have liked to ask him about Kate and her mother. I wondered if they were safe from the stray bullets of the sharpshooters.

In the stir of this strife at long range I seemed to be forgotten by the British, as I had been forgotten by my own people. My Continental uniform was none of the brightest, and even those who noticed it apparently took me for a privileged prisoner. When I left the tent in which the officer's body lay I came back toward the American army, but the patter of the bullets grew so lively around me that I retreated. It is bad enough to be killed by an enemy, I imagine, but still worse to be killed by a friend.

The day was growing old and the night would soon be at hand. Our sharpshooters held such good positions that they swept most of the British camp. I do not claim to be a great military man, but I was convinced that if the British did not dislodge these sharpshooters their position would become untenable. The night, so far from serving them, would rather be a benefit to their enemies, for the lights in the British camp would guide the bullets of the hidden riflemen to their targets.

The bustle in the camp increased, and I observed that details of men were sent to the front. They took off their bright coats, which were fine marks for the riflemen, and it was evident that they intended to match our sharpshooters at their own business. Many of these men were Germans, who, I have heard, have always been accounted good marksmen in Europe.

Nobody caring about me, I took position on a little knoll where I could see and yet be beyond range. The sun, as if wishing to do his best before going down, was shining with marvelous brilliancy. The incessant pit-pat of the rifle fire, like the crackling of hail, drew all eyes toward the American line. It seemed to me that only the speedy coming of the night could prevent a great battle.

The crackling flared up suddenly into a volley, betokening the arrival of the fresh British skirmishers at the point of action. The little white curls of smoke were gathering together and forming a great cloud overhead. Presently some wounded were taken past.

There was a movement and gathering of men near me. Quite a body of soldiers, a company, it seemed, were drawn up. Then, with fixed bayonets, they advanced upon the American line. I guessed that the skirmishers were intended to attract the attention of our people, while this company hoped to clear the woods of the sharpshooters and release the British camp from their galling fire. The British advanced with gallantry. I give them credit for that always—that is, nearly always.

The firing had reached an exceeding degree of activity, but I did not see any man in the company fall. By this I concluded that their skirmishers were keeping our own busy, and I was in some apprehension lest this strong squad should fall suddenly and with much force upon our outposts. Forward they went at a most lively pace and preserving a very even rank, their bayonets shining brightly in the late sun. The British boast much about their ability with the bayonet. We know less about ours, because almost our only way of getting bayonets was to take them from the British, which we did more than once.

Two or three British officers gathered on the knoll to watch the movement. Among these was Captain Jervis, whom I liked well. He spoke pleasantly to me, and said, pointing at the company which was now very near to the wood:

"That charge, I think, is going to be a success, Mr. Shelby, and your sharpshooters will find it more comfortable to keep a little farther away from us."

He spoke with a certain pride, as if he would hold our people a little more cheaply than his own.

I made no reply, for another and better answer from a different source was ready. There was a very vivid blaze from the wood and the crash of a heavy volley. The head of the column was shattered, nay, crushed, and the body of it reeled like a man to whom has been dealt a stunning blow. It was apparent that our people had seen the movement and had gathered in force in the wood to repel it, striking at the proper moment.

The company rallied and advanced most bravely a second time to the charge; but the flash of the rifles was so steady and so fast that the woods seemed to be spouting fire. The British fell back quickly and then broke into a discreet run into their own encampment.

"You will perceive," said I to Captain Jervis, "that our people have not yet retired for the night."

He laughed a little, though on the wrong side of his mouth. I could see that he felt chagrin, and so I said no more on that point.

As if by concert our sharpshooters also pushed up closer, and being so much better at that business drove in those of Burgoyne. The Germans, in particular, knowing but little of forests, fared badly.

Though I was neither in it nor of it, I felt much elation at our little triumph. In truth the consequences, if not important of themselves, were significant of greater things. They showed that Burgoyne's beleaguered battalions could rest hope only on two things, the arrival of Clinton or victory in a pitched battle. But now Burgoyne could not even protect his own camp. It was reached in many parts by the fire of the sharpshooters drawn in a deadly ring around it. The night came, and as far as possible the lights in the camp were put out, but the firing went on, and no British sentinel was safe at his post.

CHAPTER 9 My Guide

I remember no night in which I saw more misery. The sharpshooters never slept, and the dark seemed to profit them as much as the day. They enveloped the British camp like a swarm of unseen bees, all the more deadly because no man knew where they hovered nor whence nor when the sting would come. Men brave in the day are less brave at night, and every British officer I saw looked worn, and fearful of the future. I confess that I began to grow anxious on my own account, for in this darkness my old Continentals could not serve as a warning that I was no proper target. I have always preserved a high regard for the health and welfare of Richard Shelby, Esq., and I withdrew him farther into the camp. There I saw many wounded and more sick, and but scant means for their treatment. Moreover, the list of both was increasing, and even as I wandered about, the fresh-wounded were taken past me, sometimes crying out in their pain.

There were many who took no part in the fighting—Tories who had come to the British camp with their wives and little children, and the wives of the English and Hessian officers who had come down from Canada with them, expecting a march of glory and triumph to New York. For these I felt most sorrow, as it is very cruel that women and children should have to look upon war. More than once I heard the lamentations of women and the frightened weeping of little children. Sometimes the flaring torches showed me their scared faces. These non-combatants, in truth, were beyond the range of the fire, but the wounded men were always before them.

It was but natural that amid so much tumult and suspense I should remain forgotten. My uniform, dingy in the brightest sun, was scarce noticeable in the half-lit dusk, and I wandered about the camp almost at will. The night was not old before I noticed the bustle of great preparations. Officers hurried about as if time of a sudden had doubled its value. Soldiers very anxiously examined their muskets and bayonets; cannon were wheeled into more compact batteries; more ammunition was gathered at convenient points. On all faces I saw expectation.

I thought at first that some night skirmish was intended, but the bustle and the hurrying extended too much for that. I set about more thorough explorations, and it was easy enough to gather that Burgoyne intended to risk all in a pitched battle on the morrow. These were the preparations for it.

Curiosity had taken away from me, for the moment, the desire to go back to my own people, but now it returned with double force. It was not likely that my warning of the coming battle could be of much value, for our forces were vigilant;

but I had the natural desire of youth to be with our own army, and not with that of the enemy, at the coming of such a great event.

But the chance for my return looked very doubtful. Both armies were too busy to pay heed to a flag of truce even if it could be seen in the night.

I wandered about looking for some means of escape to our own lines, and in seeking to reach the other side of the camp passed once more through the space in which the women and children lay. I saw a little one-roomed house, abandoned long since by its owners. The uncertain light from the window fought with the shadows outside.

I stepped to the window, which was open, and looked in. They had turned the place into a hospital. A doctor with sharp instruments in his hand was at work. A woman with strong white arms, bare almost to the shoulder, was helping him. She turned away presently, her help not needed just then, and saw my face at the window.

"Dick," she said in a tone low, but not too low to express surprise, "why haven't you returned to the army?"

"Because I can't, Kate," I said. "My flag of truce is forgotten, and the bullets are flying too fast through the dark for me to make a dash for it."

"There should be a way."

"Maybe, but I haven't found it."

"Albert ought to help you."

"There are many things Albert ought to do which he doesn't do," I said.

"Don't think too badly of him."

"I think I'll try to escape through the far side of the camp," I said, nodding my head in the way I meant to go.

"We owe you much, Dick, for what you have done for us," she said, "and we wish you safety on that account, and more so on your own account."

She put her hand out of the window and I squeezed it a little.

Perhaps that was Chudleigh's exclusive right.

But she did not complain, and Chudleigh knew nothing about it.

The British camp was surrounded, but on the side to which I was now coming the fire of the sharpshooters was more intermittent. It was the strongest part of the British lines, but I trusted that on such account the way for my escape would be more open there. At night, with so much confusion about, it would not be easy to guard every foot of ground. I walked very slowly until I came almost to the outskirts of the camp; then I stopped to consider.

In the part of the camp where I stood it was very dark. Some torches were burning in a half-hearted fashion forty or fifty feet away, but their own light only made the dusk around me the deeper. I was endeavoring to select the exact point at which I would seek to pass the lines, when some one touched me with light hand upon the shoulder.

I turned my head and saw Albert Van Auken, clad in the same cloak he wore the night he tried to counterfeit his sister. I was about to walk away, for I still felt much anger toward him, when he touched me again with light hand, and said in such a low voice that I could scarce hear:

"I am going to pay you back, at least in part, Dick. I will help you to escape. Come!"

Well, I was glad that he felt shame at last for the way in which he had acted. It had taken him a long time to learn that he owed me anything. But much of my wrath against him departed. It was too dark for me to see the expression of shame which I knew must be imprinted upon his face, but on his account I was not sorry that I could not see it.

He led the way, stepping very lightly, to-ward a row of baggage wagons which seemed to have been drawn up as a sort of fortification. It looked like a solid line, and I wondered if he would attempt to crawl under them, but when we came nearer I saw an open space of half a yard or so between two of them. Albert slipped through this crack without a word, and I followed. On the other side he stopped for a few moments in the shadow of the wagons, and I, of course, imitated him.

I could see sentinels to the right and to the left of us, walking about as if on beats. On the hills, not so very far from us, the camp-fires of the American army were burning.

I perceived that it was a time for silence, and I waited for Albert to be leader, as perhaps knowing the ground better than I. A moment came presently when all the sentinels were somewhat distant from us. He stepped forward with most marvelous lightness, and in a few breaths we were beyond the line of the sentinels. I thought there was little further danger, and I was much rejoiced, both because of my escape and because it was Albert who had done such a great service for me.

"I trust you will forgive me, Albert, for some of the hard words I spoke to you," I said. "Remember that I spoke in anger and without full knowledge of you."

He put his fingers upon his lips as a sign for me to be silent, and continued straight ahead toward the American army. I followed. Some shots were fired, but we were in a sort of depression, and I had full confidence they were not intended for us, but were drawn by the lights in the British camp. Yet I believed that Albert had gone far enough. He had shown me the way, and no more was needed. I did not wish him to expose himself to our bullets.

"Go back, Albert," I said. "I know the way now, and I do not wish you to become our prisoner."

He would not pause until we had gone a rod farther. Then he pointed toward our camp-fires ahead, and turned about as if he would go back.

"Albert," I said, "let us forget what I said when in anger, and part friends."

I seized his hand in my grasp, though he sought to evade me. The hand was small and warm, and then I knew that the deception Albert had practiced upon me a night or so before had enabled Albert's sister to do the same.

"Kate!" I exclaimed. "Why have you done this?"

"For you," said she, snatching her hand from mine and fleeing so swiftly toward the British camp that I could not stop her.

In truth I did not follow her, but mused for a moment on the great change a slouch hat, a long cloak, and a pair of cavalry boots can make in one's appearance on a dark night.

As I stood in the dark and she was going toward the light, I could watch her figure. I saw her pass between the wagons again and knew that she was safe. Then I addressed myself to my own task.

I stood in a depression of the ground, and on the hills, some hundreds of yards before me, our camp-fires glimmered. The firing on this side was so infrequent that it was often several minutes between shots. All the bullets, whether British or American, passed high over my head, for which I was truly glad.

I made very good progress toward our lines, until I heard ahead of me a slight noise as of some one moving about. I presumed that it was one of our sharpshooters, and was about to call gently, telling him who I was. I was right in my presumption, but not quick enough with my hail, for his rifle was fired so close to me that the blaze of the exploding powder seemed to leap at me. That the bullet in truth was aimed at me there was no doubt, for I felt its passage so near my face that it made me turn quite cold and shiver.

"Hold! I am a friend!" I shouted.

"Shoot the damned British spy! Don't let him get away!" cried the sharpshooter.

Two or three other sharpshooters, taking him at his word, fired at my figure faintly seen in the darkness. None hit me, but I was seized with a sudden and great feeling of discomfort. Seeing that it was not a time for explanations, I turned and ran back in the other direction. One more shot was fired at me as I ran, and I was truly thankful that I was a swift runner and a poor target.

In a few moments I was beyond the line of their fire, and, rejoicing over my escape from present dangers, was meditating how to escape from those of the future, when a shot was fired from a new point of the compass, and some one cried out:

"Shoot him, the Yankee spy! the damned rebel! Don't let him escape!"

And in good truth those to whom he spoke this violent command obeyed with most alarming promptness, for several muskets were discharged instantly and the bullets flew about me.

I turned back with surprising quickness and fled toward the American camp, more shots pursuing me, but fortune again saving me from their sting. I could hear the Englishmen repeating their cries to each other not to let the rebel spy escape. Then I bethought me it was time to stop, or in a moment or two I would hear the Americans shouting to each other not to let the infernal British spy escape. I recognized the very doubtful nature of my position. It seemed as if both the British and American armies, horse and foot, had quit their legitimate business of fighting each other and had gone to hunting me, a humble subaltern, who asked nothing of either just then but personal safety. Was I to dance back and forth between them forever?

Some lightning thoughts passed through my mind, but none offered a solution of my problem. Chance was kinder. I stumbled on a stone, and flat I fell in a little gully. There I concluded to stay for the while. I pressed very close against the earth and listened to a rapid discharge of rifles and muskets. Then I perceived that I had revenge upon them both, for in their mutual chase of me the British and American skirmishers had come much closer together, and were now engaged in their proper vocation of shooting at each other instead of at me.

I, the unhappy cause of it all, lay quite still, and showered thanks upon that kindly little gully for getting in my way and receiving my falling body at such an opportune moment. The bullets were flying very fast over my head, but unless some fool shot at the earth instead of at a man I was safe. The thought that there might be some such fool made me shiver. Had I possessed the power, I would have burrowed my way through the earth to the other side, which they say is China.

It was the battle of Blenheim, at least, that seemed to be waged at the back of my head, for my nose was pressed into the earth and my imagination lent much aid to facts. I seemed to cower there for hours, and then one side began to retreat. It was the British, the Americans, I suppose, being in stronger force and also more skillful at this kind of warfare. The diminishing fire swept back toward the British lines and then died out like a languid blaze.

I heard the tramp of feet, and a heavy man with a large foot stepped squarely upon my back.

"Hello!" said the owner. "Here's one, at least, that we've brought down!"

"English, or Hessian?" asked another.

"Can't tell," said the first. "He's lying on his face, and, besides, he's half buried in a gully. We'll let him stay here; I guess this gully will do for his grave."

"No, it won't, Whitestone!" said I, sitting up. "When the right time comes for me to be buried I want a grave deeper than this."

"Good Lord! is it you, Mr. Shelby?" exclaimed Whitestone, in surprise and genuine gladness.

"Yes, it is I," I replied, "and in pretty sound condition too, when you consider the fact that all the British and American soldiers in the province of New York have been firing point-blank at me for the last two hours."

Then I described my tribulations, and Whitestone, saying I should deem myself lucky to have fared so well, went with me to our camp.

CHAPTER 10 The Sun of Saratoga

Dangers and troubles past have never prevented me from sleeping well, and when I awoke the next morning it was with Whitestone pulling at my shoulder.

"This is the third shake," said he.

"But the last," said I, getting up and rubbing my eyes.

I have seldom seen a finer morning. The fresh crispness of early October ran through the brilliant sunshine. The earth was bathed in light. It was such a sun as I have heard rose on the morning of the great battle of Austerlitz, fought but recently. A light wind blew from the west. The blood bubbled in my veins.

"It's lucky that so many of us should have such a fine day for leaving the world," said Whitestone.

The battle, the final struggle for which we had been looking so long, was at hand. I had not mistaken the preparations in the British camp the night before.

I have had my share, more or less humble, in various campaigns and combats, but I have not seen any other battle begun with so much deliberation as on that morning. In truth all whom I could see appeared to be calm. A man is sometimes very brave and sometimes much afraid—I do not know why—but that day the braver part of me was master.

We were ready and waiting to see what the British would do, when Burgoyne, with his picked veterans, came out of his intrenchments and challenged us to battle, much as the knights of the old time used to invite one another to combat.

They were not so many as we—we have never made that claim; but they made a most gallant show, all armed in the noble style with which Britain equips her troops, particularly the bayonets, of which we have had but few in the best of times, and none, most often.

They sat down in close rank on the hillside, as if they were quite content with what we might do or try to do, whatever it might be. I have heard many say it was this vaunting over us that chiefly caused the war.

The meaning of the British was evident to us all. If this picked force could hold its own against our attack, the remainder of their army would be brought up and an attempt to inflict a crushing defeat upon us would be made; if it could not hold its own, it would retreat into the intrenchments, where the whole British army would defend itself at vantage.

Farther back in the breastworks I could see the British gazing out at their chosen force and at us. I even imagined that I could see women looking over, and that perhaps Kate Van Auken was one of them. I say again, how like it was in preparation and manner to one of the old tournaments! Perhaps it was but my fancy.

There was no movement in our lines. So far as we could judge just then, we were merely looking on, as if it were no affair of ours. In the British force some one played a tune on a fife which sounded to me like "Won't you dare?"

"Why did we take so much care to hem them in and then refuse to fight them?" asked I impatiently of Whitestone.

"What time o' day is it?" asked Whitestone.

"I don't know," I replied, "but it's early."

"I never answer such questions before sundown," said Whitestone.

Content with his impolite but wise reply, I asked no more, noticing at times the red squares of the British, and at other times the dazzling circle of the red sun.

Suddenly the British began to move. They came on in most steady manner, their fine order maintained.

"Good!" said Whitestone. "They mean to turn our left."

We were on the left, which might be good or bad. Be that as it may, I perceived that our waiting was over. I do not think we felt any apprehension. We were in strong force, and we New Yorkers were on the left, and beside us our brethren of New England, very strenuous men. We did not fear the British bayonet of which our enemies boast so much. While we watched their advance, I said to Whitestone:

"I will not ask that question again before sundown."

"I trust that you will be able to ask it then, and I to answer it," replied he.

Which was about as solemn as Whitestone ever became.

Looking steadily at the British, I saw a man in their front rank fall. Almost at the same time I heard the report of a rifle just in front of us, and I knew that one of our sharpshooters had opened the battle.

This shot was like a signal. The sharp crackling sound ran along the grass like fire in a forest, and more men fell in the British lines. Their own skirmishers replied, and while the smoke was yet but half risen a heavy jerky motion seized our lines and we seemed to lift our selves up. A thrill of varying emotions passed through me. I knew that we were going to attack the British, not await their charge.

Our drummers began to beat a reply to theirs, but I paid small attention to them. The fierce pattering from the rifles of the skirmishers and the whistling of the bullets now coming about our ears were far more important sounds. But the garrulous drums beat on.

"Here goes!" said Whitestone.

The drums leaped into a faster tune, and we, keeping pace with the redoubled rub-a-dub, charged into a cloud of smoke spangled with flaming spots. The smoke filled my eyes and I could not see, but I was borne on by my own will and the solid rush of the men beside me and behind me. Then my eyes cleared partly, and I saw a long red line in front of us. Those in the first rank were on one knee, and I remember thinking how sharp their bayonets looked. The thought was cut short by a volley and a blaze which seemed to envelop their whole line. A huge groan arose from our ranks. I missed the shoulder against my left shoulder—the man who had stood beside me was no longer there.

We paused only for a moment to fire in our turn, and our groan found an equal echo among the British. Then, officers shouting commands and men shouting curses, we rushed upon the bayonets.

I expected to be spitted through, and do not know why I was not; but in the turmoil of noise and flame and smoke I swept forward with all the rest. When we struck them I felt a mighty shock, as if I were the whole line instead of one man. Then came the joy of the savage when their line—bayonets and all—reeled back and shivered under the crash of ours.

I shouted madly, and struck through the smoke with my sword. I was conscious that I stepped on something softer than the earth, that it crunched beneath my feet; but I thought little of it. Instead I rushed on, hacking with my sword at the red blurs in the smoke.

I do not say it as a boast, for there were more of us than of them—though they used to claim that they did not care for numbers—but they could place small check upon our advance, although they had cannon as well as bayonets. Their red line, very much seamed and scarred now, was driven back, and still farther back, up the hill. Our men, long anxious for this battle and sure of triumph, poured after them like a rising torrent. The British were not strong enough, and were swept steadily toward their intrenchments.

"Do you hear that?" shouted some one in my ear.

"Hear what?" I shouted in reply, turning to Whitestone.

"The cannon and the rifles across yonder," he said, nodding his head.

Then I noticed the angry crash of artillery and small arms to our left, and I knew by the sound that not we alone but the whole battle front of both armies was engaged.

If the British, as it seemed, wanted a decisive test of strength, they would certainly get it.

For a few moments the smoke rolled over us in such volume that I could not see Whitestone, who was but three feet from me, but I perceived that we had wheeled a little, and nobody was before us. Then the smoke drifted aside, and our men uttered a most tremendous shout, for all the British who were alive or could walk had been driven into their intrenchments, and, so far as that, we were going to carry their intrenchments too, or try.

I think that all of us took a very long breath, for I still had the strange feeling that our whole line was one single living thing, and whatever happened to it I felt. The cannon from the intrenchments were fired straight into our faces, but our bloody line swept on. I leaped upon a ridge of newly thrown earth and struck at a tall cap. I heard a tremendous swearing, long volleys of deep German oaths. We were among the paid Hessians, whom we ever hated more than the British for coming to fight us in a quarrel that was none of theirs.

The Hessians, even with their intrenchments and cannon, could not stand before us nor do I think they are as good as we. Perhaps our hatred of these mercenaries swelled our zeal, but their intrenchments were no barrier to us. For a space we fought them hand to hand, knee to knee; then they gave way. I saw their slain commander fall. Some fled, some yielded; others fought on, retreating.

I rushed forward and called upon a Hessian to surrender. For answer he stabbed straight at my throat with his bayonet. He would have surely hit the mark, but a man beside him knocked the bayonet away with his sword, calling out at the same moment to me.

"That's part payment of my debt to you, Dick."

He was gone in the smoke, and as I was busy receiving the surrender of the Hessian and his bayonet I could not follow him. I looked around for more to do, but all the Hessians who had not fled had yielded, and the fight was ours. Burgoyne had not only failed in the pitched battle in the open field, but we had taken many of his cannon and a portion of his camp. His entire army, no longer able to face us in any sort of contest, lay exposed to our attack. I wondered why we did not rush on and finish it all then, but I noticed for the first time that the twilight had come and the skies were growing dark over the field of battle. I must have spoken my thoughts aloud, for Whitestone, at my elbow, said:

"No use having more men killed, Mr. Shelby; we've nothing to do now but hold fast to what we've got, and the rest will come to us."

Whitestone sometimes spoke to me in a fatherly manner, though I was his superior. But I forgave him. I owed much to him.

The battle ceased as suddenly as it had begun. The long shadows of the night seemed to cover everything and bring peace, though the cries of the wounded reminded us of what had been done. We gathered up the hurt, relieving all we could; but later in the night the sharpshooters began again.

I was exultant over our victory and the certainty of a still greater triumph to come, I rejoiced that Albert had not forgotten his debt to me and had found a way of repayment, but I felt anxiety also. In the rush of the battle, with the bullets flying one knew not whither, not even the women and children lying in that portion of the British camp yet intact were safe.

The wounded removed, I had nothing more to do but to wait. Only then did I remember to be thankful that I was unhurt. I had much smoke grime upon my face, and I dare say I was not fine to look at, but I thought little of those things. Whitestone, who also was free from active duty, joined me, and I was glad. He drew his long pipe from the interior of his waistcoat, filled it with tobacco, lighted it and became happy.

"It has been a good day's work," he said at length.

"Yes, for us," I replied. "What will be the next step, Whitestone?"

"The British will retreat soon," he said. "We will follow without pressing them too hard. No use to waste our men now. In a week the British will be ours."

Whitestone spoke with such assurance that I was convinced.

CHAPTER 11 The Night After

But a dull murmur arose from the two camps, victor and vanquished. Both seemed to sleep for the morrow. I had done so much guard duty of late that I looked for such assignment as a matter of course, and this night was no exception. With Whitestone and some soldiers I was to guard one of the little passes between the hills. We were merely an alarm corps; we could not stop a passage, but there were enough behind us whom we could arouse for the purpose. The British might retreat farther into the interior, but the river and its banks must be closed to them.

We stood in the dark, but we could see the wavering lights of either camp. The murmur as it came to us was very low. The two armies rested as if they were sunk in a lethargy after their strenuous efforts of the day. I did not regret my watch. I did not care to sleep. The fever of the fight yet lingering in my blood. I was not so old to battle that I could lie down and find slumber as soon as the fighting ended.

"Mr. Shelby," said Whitestone, "is there any rule or regulation against a pipe to-night?"

"I know of none, Whitestone," I said.

He was satisfied, and lighted his pipe, which increased his satisfaction. I strolled about a little, watching the lights and meditating upon the events of the day. The camps stood higher than I, and they looked like huge black clouds shot through here and there with bits of flame. I believed Whitestone's assurance that Burgoyne would retreat on the morrow; but I wondered what he would attempt after that. Clinton's arrival might save him, but it seemed to me that the possibility of such an event was fast lessening. In this fashion I passed an hour or two; then it occurred to me to approach the British camp a little more closely and see what movements there might be on the outskirts, if any. Telling Whitestone of my intent, I advanced some forty or fifty yards. From that point, though still beyond rifle shot, I could see figures in the British camp when they passed between me and the firelight.

There was one light larger than the others —near the center of the camp it seemed to be— and figures passed and repassed in front of it like a procession. Presently I noticed that these shapes passed in fours, and they were carrying something. It seemed a curious thing, and I watched it a little; then I understood what they were doing: they were burying the dead.

I could easily have crept nearer and fired some bullets into the British camp, but I had no such intent. That was the business of others, and even then I could hear the far-away shots of the sharpshooters.

The sights of this stricken camp interested me. The ground was favorable for concealment, and I crept nearer. Lying among some weeds I could obtain a good view. The figures before indistinct and shapeless now took form and outline. I could tell which were officers and which were soldiers.

Some men were digging in the hillside. They soon ceased, and four others lifted a body from the grass and put it in the grave. A woman came forward and read from a little book. My heart thrilled when I recognized the straight figure and earnest face of Kate Van Auken. Yet there was no need for me to be surprised at the sight of her. It was like her to give help on such a night.

I could not hear the words, but I knew they were a prayer, and I bowed my head. When she finished the prayer and they began to throw in the earth, she walked away and I lost sight of her; but I guessed that she went on to other and similar duties. I turned about to retreat, and stumbled over a body.

A feeble voice bade me be more careful, and not run over a gentleman who was not bothering me but attending to his own business. A British officer, very pale and weak—I could see that even in the obscurity—sat up and looked reproachfully at me.

"Aren't you rebels satisfied with beating us?" he asked in a faint voice scarce above a whisper. "Do you want to trample on us too?"

"I beg your pardon," I said. "I did not see you."

"If any harm was done, your apology has removed it," he replied most politely.

I looked at him with interest. His voice was not the only weak thing about him. He seemed unable to sit up, but was in a half-reclining position, with his shoulder propped against a stone. He was young.

"What's the matter?" I asked, sympathizing much.

"I'm in the most embarrassing position of my life," he replied, with a faint attempt at a laugh. "One of your confounded rebel bullets has gone through both my thighs. I don't think it has struck any bone, but I have lost so much blood that I can neither walk, nor can I cry out loud enough for my people to come and rescue me, nor for your people to come and capture me. I think the bleeding has stopped. The blood seems to have clogged itself up."

I was bound to admit that he had truly described his position as embarrassing.

"What would you do if you were in my place?" he asked.

I didn't know, and said so. Yet I had no mind to abandon him. The positions reversed, I would have a very cruel opinion of him were he to abandon me. He could not see my face, and he must have had some idea that I was going to desert him.

"You won't leave me, will you?" he asked anxiously.

His tone appealed to me, and I assured him very warmly that I would either take him a prisoner into our camp or send him into his own. Then I sat my head to the task, for either way it was a problem. I doubted whether I could carry him to our camp, which was far off comparatively, as he looked like a heavy Briton. I certainly could carry him to his own camp, which was very near, but that would make it uncommonly embarrassing for me. I explained the difficulty to him.

"That's so," he said thoughtfully. "I don't want you to get yourself into trouble in order to get me out of it."

"What's your name?" I asked.

"Hume. Ensign William Hume," he replied.

"You're too young to die, Hume," I said, "and I promise not to leave you until you are in safety."

"I'll do the same for you," he said, "if ever I find you lying on a hillside with a bullet hole through both your thighs."

I sat down on the grass beside him, and gave him something strong out of a little flask that I carried in an inside pocket. He drank it with eagerness and gratitude and grew cheerful.

I thought a few moments, and my idea came to me, as good ideas sometimes do. As he could neither walk nor shout, it behooved me to do both for him. Telling him my plan, of which he approved most heartily, as he ought to have done, I lifted him in my arms and walked toward the British camp. He was a heavy load and my breath grew hard.

We were almost within reach of the firelight, and yet we were not noticed by any of the British, who, I suppose, were absorbed in their preparations. We came to a newly cut tree, intended probably for use in the British fortifications. I put Ensign Hume upon this tree with his back supported against an upthrust bough.

"Now, don't forget, when they come," I said, "to tell them you managed to crawl to this tree and shout for help. That will prevent any pursuit of me."

He promised, and shook hands with as strong a grip as he could, for he was yet weak. Then I stepped back a few paces behind him, and shouted:

"Help, help, comrades! Help! help!"

Figures advanced from the firelight, and I glided away without noise. From my covert in the darkness I could see them lift Hume from the tree and carry him into his own camp. Then I went farther away, feeling glad.

It was my intent to rejoin Whitestone and the soldiers, and in truth I went back part of the way, but the British camp had a great attraction for me. I was curious to see, as far as I could, what might be going on in its outskirts. I also encouraged myself with the thought that I might acquire information of value.

Thus gazing about with no certain purpose, I saw a figure coming toward me. One of our sharpshooters or spies returning from explorations, was my first thought. But this thought quickly yielded to another, in which wonderment was mingled to a marked extent. That figure was familiar. I had seen that swing, that manner, before.

My wonderment increased, and I decided to observe closely. I stepped farther aside that I might not be seen, of which, however, there was but small chance, so long as I sought concealment.

The figure veered a little from me, choosing a course where the night lay thickest. I was unable to make up my mind about it. Once I had taken another figure that looked like it for Albert, and once I had taken it for Albert's sister, and each time I had been wrong. Now I had my choice, and also the results of experience, and remained perplexed.

I resolved to follow. There might be mischief afoot. Albert was quite capable of it, if Albert's sister was not. The figure proceeded toward our post, where I had left Whitestone in command for the time being. I fell in behind, preserving a convenient distance between us.

Ahead of us I saw a spark of fire, tiny but distinct. I knew very well that it was the light of Whitestone's pipe. I expected the figure that I was following to turn aside, but it did not. Instead, after a moment's pause, as if for examination, it went straight on toward the spark of light. I continued to follow. Whitestone was alone. The soldiers were not visible. I suppose they were farther back.

The gallant sergeant raised his rifle at sight of the approaching figure, but dropped it when he perceived that nothing hostile was intended.

"Good evening, Miss Van Auken," he said most politely. "Have you come to surrender?"

"No," replied Kate, "but to make inquiries, sergeant, if you would be so kind as to answer them."

"If it's not against my duty," replied Whitestone, with no abatement of his courtesy.

"I wanted to know if all my friends had escaped unhurt from the battle," she said. "I was going to ask about you first, sergeant, but I see that it is not necessary."

"What others?" said the sergeant.

"Well, there's Mr. Shelby," she said. "Albert said he saw him in that fearful charge, the tumult of which frightened us so much."

"Oh, Mr. Shelby's all right, ma'am," replied the sergeant. "The fact is, he's in command of this very post, and he's scouting about here somewhere now. Any others, ma'am, you wish to ask about?"

"I don't recall any just now," she said, "and I suppose I ought to go back, or you might be compelled to arrest me as a spy, or something of that kind."

The sergeant made another deep bow. Whitestone always thought he had fine manners. Kate began her return. She did not see me, for I had stepped aside. But I was very glad that I had seen her. I watched her until she re-entered the British camp.

When I rejoined Whitestone he assured me, that nothing whatever had happened in my absence, and, besides the men of our immediate command, he had not seen a soul of either army. I did not dispute his word, for I was satisfied.

All night long the bustle continued in Burgoyne's camp, and there was no doubt of its meaning. Burgoyne would retreat on the morrow, in a desperate attempt to gain time, hoping always that Clinton would come. The next day this certainty was fulfilled. The British army drew off, and we followed in overwhelming force, content, so our generals seemed, to wait for the prize without shedding blood in another pitched battle.

CHAPTER 12 We Ride Southward

But it is not sufficient merely to win a battle. One must do more, especially when another hostile army is approaching and one does not know how near that army is, or how much nearer it will be.

It was such a trouble as this that afflicted our generals after the morning of the great victory. That other British army down the river bothered them. They wanted exact information about Clinton, and my colonel sent for me.

"Mr. Shelby," he said, "take the best horse you can find in the regiment, ride with all haste to Albany, and farther south, if necessary, find out all you can about Clinton, and gallop back to us with the news. It is an important and perhaps a dangerous duty, but I think you are a good man for it, and if you succeed, those much higher in rank than I am will thank you."

I felt flattered, but I did not allow myself to be overwhelmed.

"Colonel," I said, "let me take Sergeant Whitestone with me; then, if one of us should fall, the other can complete the errand."

But I did not have the possible fall of either of us in mind. Whitestone and I understand each other, and he is good company. Moreover, the sergeant is a handy man to have about in an emergency.

The colonel consented promptly.

"It is a good idea," he said. "I should have thought of it myself."

But then colonels don't always think of everything.

Whitestone was very willing.

"I don't think anything will happen here before we get back," he said, looking off in the direction of Burgoyne's army.

In a half hour, good horses under us, we were galloping southward. We expected to reach Albany in four hours.

For a half hour we rode along, chiefly in silence, each occupied with his own thoughts. Then I saw Whitestone fumbling in the inside pocket of his waistcoat, and I knew that the pipe was coming. He performed the feat of lighting it and smoking it without diminishing speed, and looked at me triumphantly. I said nothing, knowing that no reply was needed.

My thoughts—and it was no trespass upon my soldierhood—were elsewhere. I hold that I am not a sentimental fellow, but in the ride to Albany I often saw the face of Kate Van Auken—Mrs. Captain Chudleigh that was to be—a girl who was nothing to me, of course. Yet I was glad that she was not a Tory and traitor, and I hoped Chudleigh would prove to be the right sort of man.

"I'll be bound you're thinking of some girl," said Whitestone suddenly, as he took his pipe from his mouth and held the stem judicially between his thumb and forefinger.

"Why?" I asked.

"You look up at the sky, and not ahead of you; you sigh, and you're young," replied Whitestone.

But I swore that I was not thinking of any girl, and with all the more emphasis because I was. Whitestone was considerate, however, and said nothing more on the subject. Within the time set for ourselves we reached Albany.

Albany, as all the world knows, is an important town of Dutchmen. It is built on top of a hill, down a steep hillside, and then into a bottom by the river, which sometimes rises without an invitation from the Dutchmen and washes out the houses in the bottom. I have heard that many of these Dutchmen are not real Dutchmen, but have more English blood in them. It is not a matter, however, that I care to argue, as it is no business of mine what hobby horse one may choose to ride hard. All I know is that these Albany Dutchmen are wide of girth and can fight well, which is sufficient for the times.

Whitestone and I rode along looking at the queer houses with their gable ends to the street. We could see that the town was in a great flurry, as it had a good right to be, with our army and Burgoyne's above it and Clinton's below it, and nobody knowing what was about to happen.

"We must gather up the gossip of the town first," I said to Whitestone. "No doubt much of it will be false and more of it exaggerated, but it will serve as an indication and tell us how to set about our work."

"Then here's the place for us to begin gathering," said Whitestone, pointing to a low frame building through the open door of which many voices and some strong odors of liquor came. Evidently it was a drinking tavern, and I knew Whitestone was right when he said it was a good place in which to collect rumors.

We dismounted, hitched our horses to posts, and entered. As plenty of American soldiers were about the town, we had no fear that our uniforms would attract special attention. In truth we saw several uniforms like ours in the room, which was well crowded with an assemblage most mixed and noisy. Whitestone and I each ordered a glass of the Albany whisky tempered with water, and found it to be not bad after a long and weary ride. I have observed that a good toddy cuts the dust out of one's throat in excellent fashion. Feeling better we stood around with the others and listened to the talk, of which there was no lack. In truth, some of it was very strange and remarkable.

The news of our great battle had reached the Albany people, but in a vague and contrary fashion, and we found that we had beaten Burgoyne; that Burgoyne had beaten us; that Burgoyne was fleeing with all speed toward Canada; that he would be in Albany before night. Those who know always feel so superior to those who don't know that Whitestone and I were in a state of great satisfaction.

But the conversation soon turned from Burgoyne to Clinton, and then Whitestone and I grew eager. Our eagerness turned to alarm, for we heard that Clinton, with a great fleet and a great army, was pressing toward Albany with all haste.

Good cause for alarm was this, and, however much it might be exaggerated, we had no doubt that the gist of it was the truth.

I made a sign to Whitestone, and we slipped quietly out of the tavern, not wishing to draw any notice to ourselves. Despite our caution, two men followed us outside. I had observed one of these men looking at me in the tavern, but he had turned his eyes away when mine met his. Outside he came up to me and said boldly, though in a low voice:

"Have you come from the south?"

"No," I said carelessly, thinking to turn him off.

"Then you have come from the north, from the battlefield," he said in a tone of conviction.

"What makes you think so?" I asked, annoyed.

"You and your companion are covered with dust and your horses with perspiration," he replied, "and you have ridden far and hard."

I could not guess the man's purpose, but I took him and the others with him to be Tories, spies of the British, who must be numerous about Albany. I do not like to confess it, but it is true that in our province of New York the Tories were about as many as, perhaps more than, the patriots. We might denounce the men, but we had no proof at all against them. Moreover, we could not afford to get into a wrangle on such a mission as ours.

"You were at the battle," said the man shrewdly, "and you have come in all haste to Albany."

"Well, what if we were?" I said in some heat. His interference and impertinence were enough to make me angry.

"But I did not say from which army you came," he said, assuming an air of great acuteness and knowledge.

I was in doubt. Did the man take us for Tory spies—I grew angrier still at the thought—or was he merely trying to draw us on to the telling of what he knew? While I hesitated, he added:

"I know that Burgoyne held his own in a severe battle fought yesterday. That is no news to you. But if you go about the town a little, you will also know what I know, that Clinton, in overwhelming force, will soon be at Albany."

I was convinced now that the man was trying to draw from me the facts about the battle, and I believed more than ever that he and his comrades were Tory spies. I regretted that Whitestone and I had not removed the dust of travel before we entered the tavern. I regretted also that so many of our countrymen should prove faithless to us. It would have been far easier for us had we only the British and the hired Hessians to fight.

Whitestone was leaning against his horse, bridle in hand, looking at the solitary cloud that the sky contained. Apparently the sergeant was off in dreams, but I knew he was listening intently. He let his eyes fall, and when they met mine, he said, very simply and carelessly:

"I think we'd better go."

As I said, the sergeant is a very handy man to have about in an emergency. His solution was the simplest in the world—merely to ride away from the men and leave them.

We mounted our horses.

"Good day, gentlemen," we said.

"Good day," they replied.

Then we left them, and when I looked back, at our first turning, they were still standing at the door of the tavern. But I gave them little further thought, for Clinton and his advancing fleet and army must now receive the whole attention of the sergeant and myself.

It was obvious that we must leave Albany, go down the river, and get exact news about the British. It was easy enough for us to pass out of the town and continue our journey. We had been provided with the proper papers in case of trouble.

We had given our horses rest and food in Albany, and rode at a good pace for an hour. Not far away we could see the Hudson, a great ribbon of silver or gray, as sunshine or cloud fell upon it. I was occupied with the beauty of the scene, when Whitestone called my attention and pointed ahead. Fifty yards away, and in the middle of the road, stood two horsemen motionless. They seemed to be planted there as guards, yet they wore no uniforms.

I felt some anxiety, but reflected that the horsemen must be countrymen waiting, through curiosity or friendship, for approaching travelers in such troublous times. But as we rode nearer I saw that I was mistaken.

"Our inquiring friends of the tavern," said Whitestone.

He spoke the truth. I recognized them readily. When we were within fifteen feet they drew their horses across the way, blocking it.

"What does this mean, gentlemen? Why do you stop us?" I asked.

"We are an American patrol," replied the foremost of the two, the one who had questioned me at the tavern, "and we can not let anybody pass here. It is against our orders."

Both wore ragged Continental coats, which I suppose they had brought out of some recess before they started on the circuit ahead of us.

I signed to Whitestone to keep silent, and rode up close to the leader.

"We ought to understand each other," I said, speaking in a confident and confidential tone.

"What do you mean?" he asked suspiciously.

I burst out laughing, as if I were enjoying the best joke in the world.

"I hate rebels," I said, leaning over and tapping him familiarly on the shoulder with my finger.

"I don't understand you," he said.

"I mean that you hate rebels too," I replied, "and that you are just as much of a rebel as I am."

"Hi should think so! Hi could tell by the look hof their countenances that they are hof the right sort," broke in Whitestone, dropping every h where it belonged and putting on every one where it did not belong.

It was Whitestone's first and last appearance on any occasion as an Englishman, but it was most successful.

A look of intelligence appeared on the faces of the two men.

"Of Bayle's regiment in Burgoyne's army, both of us," I said.

"I thought it, back yonder in Albany," said the leader, "but why did you fence us off so?"

"One doesn't always know his friends, first glance, especially in rebel towns," I said. "Like you, I thought so, but I couldn't take the risk and declare myself until I knew more about you."

"That's true," he acknowledged. "These rebels are so cursedly sly."

"Very, very sly," I said, "but we've fooled 'em this time."

I pointed to their Continental coats and to ours. Then we laughed all together.

"Tell me what really happened up there," said the man.

"It was a great battle," I said, "but we drove them off the field, and we can take care of ourselves. Six thousand British and German veterans care little for all the raw militia this country can raise."

"That's so," he said. We laughed again, all together.

"How is everything down there?" I asked, nodding my head toward the south.

"Clinton's coming with a strong fleet and five thousand men," he replied. "What they say in the town is all true."

"Small thanks he will get from Burgoyne," I said. "Our general will like it but little when Clinton comes to strip him of part of his glory."

"I suppose you are right," he answered, "but I did not think Burgoyne was finding his way so easy. I understood that the first battle at Saratoga stopped him."

"Don't you trouble yourself about Burgoyne," I said. "If he stopped, he stopped for ample reasons."

Which was no lie.

"But we must hasten," I continued. "Our messages to Clinton will bear no delay."

"Luck with you," they said.

"Luck with you," we replied, waving our hands in friendly salute as we rode away, still to the south.

Whether they ever found out the truth I do not know, for I never saw or heard of either again.

We continued our journey in silence for some time. Whitestone looked melancholy.

"What is the matter?" I asked.

"It was too easy," he replied. "I always pity fools."

He lighted his pipe and sought consolation.

CHAPTER 13 We Meet the Fleet

The night soon came and was very dark. We were compelled to stop for rest and for food, which we found at a farmer's house. But we were satisfied with our day's work. We had started, and with the appearance of fact too, the report that Burgoyne had beaten us in pitched battle. We knew the report would be carried far and wide, and Clinton would think haste was not needed. Let me repeat that to win a battle is not to win a campaign, and I hold no general's commission either.

In the morning we met a few countrymen in a state of much fright. "Clinton is coming!" was all that we could get from them. We thought it more than likely that Clinton was coming in truth, since all the reports said he and his ships ought to be very near now.

"The river is the place to look," said Whitestone.

We turned our horses that way, and in a few minutes stood upon its high banks.

"See," said Whitestone, pointing a long arm and an outstretched finger.

I saw, and I saw, moreover, that our search was ended. Far down the river was the British fleet, a line of white specks upon the silver bosom of the water. We could scarce trace hull or sail or mast, but ships they were without mistake, and British ships they must be, since we had none. It was not a pleasant sight for us, but it would have rejoiced the heart of Burgoyne had he been there to see.

We knew that Clinton must have several thousand men either on board the fleet or not far below, and we knew also that with such a strong force nothing could prevent his speedy arrival at Albany if he chose to hasten. I knew not what to do. Ought we to go back at once to our army with the news of what we had seen, or ought we to stay and find out more? On one side was time saved, and on the other better information. I put it to Whitestone, but he was as uncertain as I.

Meanwhile the fleet grew under the horizon of the river. We could trace masts and spars, and see the sails as they filled out with the wind. The little black figures on the decks were men.

A quarter of a mile or more below us we saw a rocky projection into the river. I proposed to Whitestone that we ride at least that far and decide afterward on further action.

We rode rapidly, but before we were halfway to the place we met men running frightened men at that. Their condition of mind showed plainly on their faces. They wore militia uniforms, and we knew them to be some of our citizen soldiery, who are sometimes a very speedy lot, not being trained to the military business. We tried to stop them and find out why they were running and whence they came; but all we could get out of them was, "The British are coming, with a hundred ships and forty thousand men!" At last, half by persuasion and half by force, we induced one man to halt; he explained that he had been sent with the others to man a battery of four guns on the point. When they saw the British fleet coming, some of the raw militia had taken fright and fled, carrying the others with them.

"But the ships may not be here for an hour," I protested.

"So much the better," he said, "for it gives us the more time."

We released him, and he followed his flying comrades. Whitestone and I looked ruefully after them, but I suggested that we continue our ride to the point. Even with the ships abreast us in the river, it would be easy for us to ride away and escape the British. We rode as rapidly as the ground would allow, and soon reached the point and the deserted battery.

I could have sworn with vexation at the flight of our militia. It was a pretty battery, well planted, four trim eighteen pounders, plenty of powder, shot neatly piled, and a flag still flying from a tall pole. Whoever selected the place for the battery knew his business—which does not always happen in the military life. I looked again in the direction of the fleeing militia, but the back of the last man had disappeared.

"What a pity!" I said regretfully to Whitestone. "At least they might have trimmed the rigging a little for those British ships down yonder."

"I don't understand one thing," said Whitestone.

"What is it?" I asked.

He took his pipe from his mouth and tapped the bowl of it significantly with the index finger of his left hand.

"I can smoke that pipe, can't I?" he asked.

"I should think so!"

"So could you if you had a chance, couldn't you?"

"Certainly."

"Those men who ran away could fire a cannon; so could—"

"Do you mean it, Whitestone?" I asked, the blood flying to my head at the thought.

"Mean it? I should think I did," he replied. "I used to be in the artillery, and I can handle a cannon pretty well. So can you, I think. Here are the cannon, there's ammunition a-plenty, and over us flies the brand-new flag. What more do you want?"

He replaced his pipe in his mouth, sat down on the breech of a gun, and gave himself up to content. I looked at him in admiration. I approve of so many of Whitestone's ideas, and I liked few better than this. I was young.

"Good enough, Whitestone," I said. "I, as commander, indorse the suggestion of my chief assistant."

We took our horses out of the range of the guns on the ships and fastened them securely, as we were thinking of our future needs. Then we came back to our battery. Evidently the original defenders had desired the battery to appear very formidable, for in addition to their real guns they had planted eight Quaker guns, which, seen from the center of the river, would look very threatening, I had no doubt. The four guns, genuine and true, were charged almost to the muzzle.

"I think they have seen us," said Whitestone, pointing to the ships.

It was a strong fleet—frigates and sloops. It was plain that they had seen us and had not been expecting us, for the ships were taking in sail and hovering about in an uncertain way. Officers in gilt and gold stood on their decks watching us through glasses.

"Keep down, Whitestone," I said. "We must not give them any hint as to the size of our force."

"But I think we ought to give 'em a hint that we're loaded for bear," said Whitestone. "What do you say to a shot at the nearest frigate, Mr. Shelby. I think she is within long range."

I approved, and Whitestone fired. In the stillness of a country morning the report was frightfully distinct, and the echo doubling upon and repeating itself seemed to travel both up and down the river. The shot was well aimed. It smashed right into the frigate, and there was confusion on her decks. I fired the second gun, and down came some spars and rigging on the same ship. Whitestone rubbed his hands in glee. I shouted to him to lie close, and obeyed my own command as promptly as he. The frigate was about to return our salute.

She swung around and let us have a broadside, which did great damage to the rocks and the shore. But Whitestone and I remained cozy and safe. A large sloop came up closer than the frigate and fired a volley, which sailed peacefully over our heads and made a prodigious disturbance among the trees beyond us.

"Can you get at that third gun, Whitestone?"

"Nothing easier!"

"Then give that spiteful sloop a shot. Teach her it isn't safe for a sloop to come where a frigate can't stay."

Whitestone obeyed, and his shot was most glorious. The chunk of lead struck the sloop between wind and water and must have gone right through her, for presently she began to sheer off, the signs of distress visible all over her, as if she were taking in water at the rate of a thousand gallons a minute. I clapped Whitestone on the back and shouted "Hurrah!"

But our lucky shot had stirred up the full wrath of the fleet. The ships formed in line of battle and opened their batteries on us, firing sometimes one after the other, and sometimes nearly all together. I dare say the cliffs of the Hudson, in all their long existence, have never received such another furious bombardment. Oh, it was a bad day for the trees and the bushes and the rocks, which were beaten and battered and cut and crushed by eighteen-pound shot and twelve-pound shot and six-pound shot, and the Lord knows what, until the river itself fell into a rage and began to lash its waters into a turmoil!

But Whitestone and I, with all this infernal uproar around us, lay in our brave earthworks as snug and cozy as chipmunks, and laughed to think that we were the cause of it all. I rolled over to Whitestone and shouted in his ear:

"As soon as the eruption diminishes a little we will try a fourth shot at them!"

He grinned, and both of us embraced the earth for some minutes longer. Then the fire of the enemy began to abate. We took the first chance to peep out at them, but the volume of smoke over the river was so great and so dense that we could see the ships but indistinctly.

As for ourselves, we had suffered little. One of our guns was dismounted, but it was a Quaker, and no harm was done. The fire dying, the clouds of smoke began to float away and the ships were disclosed. Whitestone and I, peeping over our earthworks, beheld a scene of great animation and excitement. The British were working hard; there was no doubt of it. The bustle on the decks was tremendous. Officers were shouting to men and to each other; men were reloading cannon and making every preparation to renew the bombardment when their officers might order it. One frigate had come too near, and was grounded slightly in shallowing water. Her crew were making gigantic efforts to get her off before our terrible battery could blow her to pieces.

The captains were using their glasses to see what was left of us, and I could guess their chagrin when they beheld us looking as formidable and as whole as ever, barring the dismounted Quaker. Our escape from injury was not so wonderful after all. We defenders were only two, and we made a very small target; while if the battery had been crowded with men the death rate would have been prodigious.

"There goes the frigate!" I cried. "They've got her off! Give her a good-by as she goes, Whitestone!"

He was lying next to the fourth gun, and he instantly sent a shot smashing into the vessel. But the shot was like a veritable torch to a powder magazine, for the fleet attacked us again with every gun it could bring to bear. The first bombardment seemed to have aroused fresh spirit and energy for the second, and

Whitestone and I, taking no chances with peeps, thrust our fingers into our ears and our heads into the ground.

But we could not keep out the heavy crash-crash of the volleys, blending now and then into a continuous roar, which the river and the horizon took up and repeated. King George must have had a pretty powder-and-shot bill to pay for that day's work.

The clouds of smoke gathered in a vast black canopy over river and ships, shore and battery. Under and through it appeared now and then the dark lines of spars and ropes, and always the blazing flash of many great guns. If the stony shores of the Hudson did not suffer most grievously, let it not be charged against the British, for they displayed a spirit and energy, if not a marksmanship, worthy of their reputation.

I rejoiced at the vigor of their fire. Its volume was so great, and they must be working so hard, that they could not know the battery was making no answer.

By and by the cannoneers waxed weary of loading and firing, and the officers of giving orders. The crash of the great guns became more infrequent. The flash of the powder bore less resemblance to continuous lightning. The smoke began to drift away. Then the defenders of the battery rose up in their courage and strength, reloaded their guns, and opened fire on the fleet.

I love to think that the British were surprised most unpleasantly. Their fire was waning, but ours was not, it seemed to them. The mischievous little battery was still there, and they had neither reduced it nor passed it. It was mirth to us to think how easily they could pass us, and yet preferred to reduce us.

"By all that's glorious," exclaimed Whitestone, "they're retreating!"

It was so. The ships were hauling off, whether to refit for another attack or to consult for future action we did not know. We gave them a few shots as they drew away, and presently they anchored out of range. Boats were launched, and men in gold-laced caps and coats were rowed to the largest frigate.

"The admiral has called a conference, I guess," I said to Whitestone.

He nodded, and we inspected our battery to see how it had stood the second bombardment. Two more Quaker guns were dismounted, but one of them we were able to put again into fairly presentable condition. That done, we took some refreshment from our knapsacks, and awaited in calmness the next movement of our enemies. As it was, we flattered ourselves that we had made a gallant fight.

We waited a half hour, and then a boat put out from the big frigate. Besides the oarsmen, it contained a richly dressed officer and a white flag. They came directly toward us.

"A flag of truce and a conference," I said. "Shall we condescend, Whitestone?"

"Oh, yes," replied Whitestone. "We ought to hear what they have to say."

"Then you remain in command of the battery," I said, "and I will meet the officer."

I scrambled down the high cliff to the water's edge and awaited the boat, which I was determined should not come too near. When it came within speaking distance, I hailed the officer and ordered him to stop.

"I am Captain Middleton," he called, "and I am commissioned by our commander to speak to your commander."

"General Arnold saw you coming," I said, "and sent me to meet you and hear what you have to say."

"General Arnold!" he exclaimed in surprise.

"Yes, General Arnold, the commander of our battery," I replied.

I mentioned General Arnold because of his great reputation then as a fighting general. And a fighting general he was, too; I will say it, traitor though he afterward proved to be.

"I thought General Arnold was with Gates," said the officer.

"Oh, they quarreled," I replied airily, which was the truth, "and General Arnold, being relieved of his command up there, has come down here to fight this battery. You have seen for yourself that he knows how to do it."

"It is true," he said, "your fire was very warm."

He looked up at the battery, but I would not let him come within fifty feet of the shore, and he could see nothing save the earthworks and some of the gun muzzles.

"It can be made warmer," I said confidently, not boastingly.

"I have come to summon you to surrender," he said. "We will offer you good terms."

"Surrender!" I laughed in scorn. "Why, my dear captain, you have made no impression upon us yet, while we have scarred your ships a bit."

"That is a fact," he said. "You have handled your eighteen-pounders well."

"Twenty-four pounders," I corrected.

"I did not know they were so heavy," he said. "That accounts for the strength of your fire."

He seemed pleased at the discovery. It made an excuse for his side.

"No doubt General Arnold can do something with a battery of twelve twenty-four pounders," he began.

"Eighteen twenty-four pounders," I corrected. "You can not see all the muzzles."

He looked very thoughtful. I knew that he was impressed by the exceeding strength of our battery.

"But about the proposition to surrender," he began.

"I will not take such an offer to General Arnold," I exclaimed indignantly. "In fact, I have my instructions from him. He'll sink every ship you have, or be blown to pieces himself."

Captain Middleton, after this emphatic declaration, which I am sure I made in a most convincing manner, seemed to think further talk would be a waste, and gave the word to his oarsmen to pull back to his ship.

"Good day," he said very courteously.

"Good day," said I with equal courtesy. Then I climbed back up the cliff and re-enforced the garrison. I watched Middleton as he approached the flagship. He mounted to the deck and the officers crowded around him. In a half hour the ships bore up again, formed line of battle, and opened upon us a third terrific bombardment, which we endured with the same calmness and success. When they grew tired we gave them a few shots, which did some execution, and then, to our infinite delight, they slipped their cables and fell back down the river.

"When they find out what we really are they'll come again to-morrow and blow us to splinters," said Whitestone.

"Yes, but we'll be far away from here then," said I, "and we may have held them back a day at least. Why, man, even an hour is worth much to our army up yonder!"

We were in a state of supreme satisfaction, also in a state of hurry. There was nothing more for us to do in the south, and it was our business to hasten northward with the news we had. I rejoiced greatly. I hoped that Clinton would continue to fiddle his time away below Albany, impressed by the risks he was taking, thanks to our brave battery.

We found our horses nearly dead from fright, but a few kicks restored life, and we rode northward in all haste. At Albany we changed horses, evaded questions, and resumed our ride. In the night we reached our own camp, and as soon as we had reported sought the rest we needed so badly, and, I think, deserved so well.

CHAPTER 14 The Pursuit of Chudleigh

Having returned, I expected to share in the pursuit of Burgoyne, and wondered to what particular duty I would be assigned. But a man never knows at seven o'clock what he will be doing at eight o'clock, and before eight o'clock had come I was called by the colonel of our regiment.

"Mr. Shelby," he said, "you have already shown yourself intelligent and vigilant on important service."

I listened, feeling sure that I was going to have something very disagreeable to do. You can depend upon it when your superior begins with formal flattery. I had just finished one important task, but the more you do the more people expect of you.

"One of our prisoners has escaped," he said; "a keen-witted man who knows the country. He has escaped to the south. As you know so well, Sir Henry Clinton is, or has been, advancing up the Hudson with a strong force to the aid of Burgoyne, whom nothing else can save from us. This man—this prisoner who has escaped—must not be permitted to reach Clinton with the news that Burgoyne is almost done for. It was important before the last battle that no messenger from Burgoyne should pass through our lines; it is still more important to-day. You understand?"

I bowed, as a sign that I understood.

"This escaped prisoner knows everything that has happened," he resumed, "and he must be overtaken. He will probably follow the direct road along the river, as he knows that haste is necessary. How many men do you want?"

I named Whitestone and a private, a strong, ready-witted fellow named Adams.

"What is the name of the man we are to capture?" I asked.

"Chudleigh—Captain Ralph Chudleigh," he replied. "A tall man, dark hair and eyes, twenty-six to twenty-eight years of age. Do you know him?"

I replied that I knew him.

"So much the better," said our colonel with much delight. "Aside from your other qualifications, Mr. Shelby, you are the man of all men for this duty. Chudleigh will undoubtedly attempt to disguise himself, but since you know him so well he can scarce hide his face from you. But remember that he must be taken, dead or alive."

I had not much relish for the mission in the first place, and, for reasons, less relish when I knew that Chudleigh was the man whom I was to take. But in such affairs as these it is permitted to the soldier to choose only the one thing, and that is, to obey.

We set out at once over the same road we had traveled twice so recently. Three good horses had been furnished us, and we were well armed. For a while we rode southward with much speed, and soon left behind us the last detachment of our beleaguering army.

One question perplexed me: Would Chudleigh be in his own British uniform, which he wore when he escaped, or did he manage to take away with him some rags of Continental attire, in which he would clothe himself first chance? I could answer it only by watching for all men of suspicious appearance, no matter the cut or color of their clothing.

We galloped along a fair road, but we met no one. Quiet travelers shun ground trodden by armies. It was past the noon hour when we came to a small house not far from the roadside. We found the farmer who owned it at home, and in answer to our questions, fairly spoken, he said three men had passed that day, two going north and one going south, all dressed as ordinary citizens. I was particularly interested in the one going south, and asked more about him.

"He was tall, dark, and young," said the farmer. "He looked like a man of small consequence, for his clothing was ragged and his face not overclean. He wanted food, and he ate with much appetite."

I asked if the man had paid for his dinner, and the farmer showed me silver fresh from the British mint. I could well believe that this was Chudleigh. However wary and circumspect he might be he was bound to have food, and he could find it only by going to the houses he saw on his southern journey.

I was confirmed in my belief an hour later, when we met a countryman on foot, who at first evinced a great desire to run away from us, but who stopped, seeing our uniforms. He explained that he knew not whom to trust, for a short while before he was riding like ourselves; now he had no horse; a ragged man meeting him in the road had presented a pistol at his head and ordered him to give up his horse, which he did with much promptness, as the man's finger lay very caressingly upon the trigger of the pistol.

"That was Chudleigh without doubt," I said to Whitestone, "and since he also is now mounted we must have a race for it."

He agreed with me, and we whipped our horses into a gallop again. In reality I had not much acquaintance with Chudleigh, but I trusted that I would know his face anywhere. Secure in this belief we pressed on.

"Unless he's left the road to hide—and that's not probable, for he can't afford delay—we ought to overhaul him soon," said Whitestone.

The road led up and down a series of lightly undulating hills. Just when we reached one crest we saw the back of a horseman on the next crest, about a quarter of a mile ahead of us. By a species of intuition I knew that it was Chudleigh. Aside from my intuition, all the probabilities indicated Chudleigh, for we had the word of the dismounted farmer that his lead of us was but short.

"That's our man!" exclaimed Whitestone, echoing our thought.

As if by the same impulse, all three of us clapped spur to horse, and forward we went at a gallop that sent the wind rushing past us. We were much too far away for the fugitive to hear the hoof-beats of our horses, but by chance, I suppose, he happened to look back and saw us coming at a pace that indicated zeal. I saw him give his mount a great kick in the side, and the horse bounded forward so promptly that in thirty seconds the curve of the hill hid both horse and rider from our view. But that was not a matter discouraging to us. The river was on one side of us not far away, and on the other cultivated fields inclosed with fences. Chudleigh could not leave the road unless he dismounted. He was bound to do one of two things, out-gallop us or yield.

We descended our hill and soon rose upon the slope of Chudleigh's. When we reached the crest, we saw him in the hollow beyond urging his horse to its best speed. He was bent far over upon the animal's neck, and occasionally he gave him lusty kicks in the side. It was evident to us that whatever speed might be in that horse Chudleigh would get it out of him. And so would I, thought I, if I were in his place. A fugitive could scarce have more inducement than Chudleigh to escape.

Measuring the distance with my eye, I concluded that we had gained a little. I drew from it the inference that we would certainly overtake him. Moreover, Chudleigh was making the mistake of pushing his horse too hard at the start.

It is better to pursue than to be pursued, and a great elation of spirits seized me. The cool air rushing into my face and past my ears put bubbles in my blood.

"This beats watching houses in the night, does it not, Whitestone?" I said.

"Aye, truly," replied the sober sergeant, "unless he has a pistol and concludes to use it."

"We will not fire until he does, or shows intent to do so," I said.

Whitestone and Adams nodded assent, and we eased our horses a bit that we might save their strength and speed. This maneuver enabled the fugitive to gain slightly upon us, but we felt no alarm; instead we were encouraged, for his horse was sure to become blown before ours put forth their best efforts.

Chudleigh raised up once to look back at us. Of course it was too far for us to see the expression of his face, but in my imagination anxiety was plainly writ there.

"How long a race will it be, do you think?" I asked Whitestone.

"About four miles," he said, "unless a stumble upsets our calculations, and I don't think we'll have the latter, for the road looks smooth all the way."

The fugitive began to kick his horse with more frequency, which indicated increased anxiety.

"It won't be four miles," I said to Whitestone.

"You're right," he replied; "maybe not three."

In truth it looked as if Whitestone's second thought were right. We began to gain without the necessity of urging our horses. Chudleigh already had driven his own animal to exhaustion. I doubted if the race would be a matter of two miles. I wondered why he did not try a shot at us with his pistols. Bullets are often great checks to the speed of pursuers, and Chudleigh must have known it.

At the end of a mile we were gaining so rapidly that we could have reached the fugitive with a pistol ball, but I was averse to such rude methods, doubly so since he showed no intent on his own part to resort to them.

A half mile ahead of us I saw a small house in a field by the roadside, but I took no thought of it until Chudleigh reached a parallel point in the road; then we were surprised to see him leap to the ground, leave his horse to go where it would, climb the fence, and rush toward the house. He pushed the door open, ran in, and closed it behind him.

I concluded that he had given up all hope of escape except through a desperate defense, and I made hasty disposition of my small command. I was to approach the house from one side, Whitestone from another, and Adams from a third.

We hitched our horses and began our siege of the house, from which no sound issued. I approached from the front, using a fence as shelter. When I was within half a pistol shot the door of the house was thrown open with much force and rudeness, and a large woman, a cocked musket in her hand and anger on her face, appeared. She saw me, and began to berate me rapidly and wrathfully, at the same time making threatening movements with the musket. She cried out that she had small use for those who were Tories now and Americans then, and robbers and murderers always. I explained that we were American soldiers in pursuit of an escaped prisoner of importance who had taken refuge in her house, and commanded her to stand aside and let us pass.

For answer she berated me more than ever, saying that it was but a pretext about a prisoner, and her husband was a better American than we. That put a most uncomfortable suspicion in my mind, and, summoning Whitestone, we held parley with her.

"You have pursued my husband until there is scarce a breath left in his body," she said.

Whereupon, having pacified her to some extent, we went into the house and found that she spoke the truth. Her husband was stretched upon a bed quite out of breath, in part from his gallop and more from fright. We could scarce persuade him that we were not those outlaws who belonged to neither army but who preyed upon whomsoever they could.

Making such brief apologies as the time allowed, we mounted our horses and resumed the search.

"It was a mistake," said Whitestone.

I admitted that he spoke the truth, and resolved I would trust no more to intuitions, which are sent but to deceive us.

Anxiety now took me in a strong grip. Our mistaken chase had caused us to come very fast, and since we saw nothing of Chudleigh, I feared lest we had passed him in some manner. It therefore cheered me much, a half hour later, when I saw a stout man, whom I took to be a farmer, jogging comfortably toward us on a stout nag as comfortable-looking as himself. He was not like the other, suspicious and afraid, and I was glad of it, for I said to myself that here was a man of steady habit and intelligence, a man who would tell us the truth and tell it clearly.

He came on in most peaceable and assuring fashion, as if not a soldier were within a thousand miles of him. I hailed him, and he replied with a pleasant salutation.

"Have you met a man riding southward?" I said.

"What kind of a man?" he asked.

"A large man in citizen's dress," I replied.

"Young, or old?"

"Young—twenty-six or twenty-eight."

"Anything else special about him?"

"Dark hair and eyes and dark complexion; his horse probably very tired."

"What do you want with this man?" he asked, stroking a red whisker with a contemplative hand.

"He is an escaped prisoner," I replied, "and it is of the greatest importance that we recapture him."

"Did you say he was rather young? Looked like he might be six and twenty or eight and twenty?" he asked.

"Yes, that is he," I said eagerly.

"Tall, rather large?"

"The very man."

"Dark hair and eyes and dark complexion?"

"Exactly! Exactly!"

"His horse very tired?"

"Our man beyond a doubt! Which way did he go?"

"Gentlemen, I never saw or heard of such a man," he replied gravely, laying switch to his horse and riding on.

We resumed our journey, vexation keeping us silent for some time.

"Our second mistake," said Whitestone at length.

As I did not answer, he added:

"But the third time means luck."

"I doubt it," I replied. My disbelief in signs and omens was confirmed by the failure of my intuition.

CHAPTER 15 The Taking of Chudleigh

We were forced to ride with some slowness owing to the blown condition of our horses, and anxiety began to gnaw me to the marrow. We had come so fast that the time to overtake Chudleigh, if in truth we had not passed him already, had arrived. In such calculations I was interrupted by the sight of a loose horse in the road, saddled and bridled, but riderless. He was in a lather, like ours, and I guessed at once that this was the horse Chudleigh had taken. In some manner—perhaps he had seen us, though unseen himself—he had learned that he was pursued hotly, and, fearing to be overtaken, had abandoned his horse and taken to the woods and fields. Such at least was my guess.

I esteemed it great good luck when I saw a man standing in the edge of a cornfield staring at us. He was a common-looking fellow with a dirty face. Stupid, I thought, but perhaps he has seen what happened here and can tell me. I hailed him, and he answered in a thick voice, though not unfriendly. I asked him about the horse, and if he knew who had abandoned him there. He answered with that degree of excitement a plowboy would most likely show on such occasions that he was just going to tell us about it. I bade him haste with his narration.

He said, with thick, excited tongue, that a man had come along the road urging his horse into a gallop. When they reached the field the horse broke down and would go no farther. The rider, after belaboring him in vain, leaped down, and, leaving the horse to care for himself, turned from the road.

This news excited Whitestone, Adams, and me. It was confirmation of our suspicions, and proof also that we were pressing Chudleigh hard.

"How long ago was that?" I asked.

"Not five minutes," replied the plowman.

"Which way did he go?" I asked, my excitement increasing.

"He took the side road yonder," replied the plowman.

"What road?" exclaimed Whitestone, breaking in.

"The road that leads off to the right—yonder, at the end of the field."

I was about to set off in a gallop, but it occurred to me as a happy thought that this fellow, knowing the country so well, would be useful as a guide. I ordered him to get on the loose horse, now somewhat rested, and lead the way. He demurred. But it was no time to be squeamish or overly polite, so I drew my pistol and warned him. Thereupon he showed himself a man of judgment and mounted, and taking the lead of us, obedient to my command, also showed himself to be a very fair horseman.

In a few seconds we entered the diverging road, which was narrow, scarce more than a path. It led between two fields, and then through some thin woods.

"You are military folks," said our guide, turning a look upon me. "Is the man you are after a deserter?"

"No," said I, "a spy."

"If you overtake him and he fights, I don't have any part in it," he said.

"You needn't risk your skin," I said. "It is enough for you to guide us."

I laughed a bit at his cowardice; but after all I had no right to laugh. It was no business of his to do our fighting for us.

"Perhaps he has turned into these woods," said Whitestone.

"No, he has gone on," said our guide, "I can see his footsteps in the dust."

Traces like those of human footsteps were in truth visible in the dust, but we had no time to stop for examination. We rode on, watching the country on either side of the road. The heat and animation of the chase seemed to affect our guide, heavy plowman though he was.

"There go his tracks still!" he cried. "See, by the edge of the road, by the grass there?"

"We'll catch him in five minutes!" cried Adams, full of enthusiasm.

Our guide was ten feet in front of me, leaning over and looking about with much eagerness. A curve in the road two or three hundred yards ahead became visible. Suddenly I noticed an increase of excitement in the expression of our guide.

"I see him! I see him!" he cried.

"Where? Where?" I shouted.

"Yonder! yonder! Don't you see, just turning the curve in the road? There! He has seen us too, and is drawing a pistol. Gentlemen, remember your agreement: I'm not to do any of the fighting. I will fall back."

"All right!" I cried. "You've done your share of the business. Drop back.— Forward, Whitestone! We've got our man now!"

In a high state of excitement we whipped our horses forward, paying no further attention to the plowman, for whom in truth we had use no longer. Our horses seemed to share our zeal, and recalled their waning strength and spirits. Forward we went at a fine pace, all three of us straining our eyes to catch the first glimpse of the fugitive when we should turn the curve around the hill.

"Two to one I beat you, Whitestone!" I said.

"Then you'll have to push your horse more," said the sergeant, whose mount was neck and neck with mine.

In truth it looked as if he would pass me, but I managed to draw a supreme effort from my horse and we went ahead a little. However, I retained the advantage but a few moments. Whitestone crept up again, and we continued to race neck and neck. Adams, upon whom we had not counted as a formidable antagonist, overhauled us, though he could not pass us.

Thus we three, side by side, swept around the curve, and the command to the fugitive to halt and surrender was ready upon our lips.

The turn of the curve brought us into a wide and bare plain, and we pulled up astonished. Nowhere was a human being visible, and upon that naked expanse concealment was impossible.

We stared at each other in amazement, and then in shame. The truth of the trick struck me like a rifle shot. Why did I wait until he was gone to remember something familiar in the voice of that plowman, something known in the expression of that face? I think the truth came to me first, but before I said anything Whitestone ejaculated:

"Chudleigh!"

"Without doubt," I replied.

"I told you the third time would not fail," he said.

"I wish it had failed," I exclaimed in wrath and fury, "for he has made fools of us!"

We wheeled our horses about as if they turned on pivots and raced back after the wily plowman. I swore to myself a mighty oath that I would cease to be certain about the identity of anybody, even of Whitestone himself. Whitestone swore out loud about a variety of things, and Adams was equal to his opportunities.

We were speedily back in the main road. I doubted not that Chudleigh had hurried on toward the south. In truth he could not afford to do otherwise, and he would profit as fast as he could by the breathing space obtained through the trick he had played upon us. I wondered at the man's courage and presence of mind, and it was a marvel that we had not gone much farther on the wrong road before detecting the stratagem.

The road lay across a level country and we saw nothing of Chudleigh. Nevertheless we did not spare our weary horses. We were sure he was not very far ahead, and it was no time for mercy to horseflesh. Yet I thought of the poor brutes. I said to Whitestone I trusted they would last.

"As long as his, perhaps," replied Whitestone.

But the truth soon became evident that he was wrong in part. We heard a great groan, louder than a man can make, and Adams's horse went down in a cloud of dust. I pulled up just enough to see that Adams was not hurt, and to shout to him:

"Follow us as best you can!"

Then on we went. Far ahead of us in the road we saw a black speck. Whether man, beast, or a stump, I could not say, but we hoped it was Chudleigh.

"See, it moves!" cried Whitestone.

Then it was not a stump, and the chance that it was Chudleigh increased. Soon it became apparent that the black object was not only moving, but moving almost as fast as we. By and by we could make out the figure of a man lashing a tired horse. That it was Chudleigh no longer admitted of doubt.

"We'll catch him yet! His trick shall not avail him!" I cried exultingly to Whitestone.

The wise sergeant kept silent and saved his breath. I looked back once and saw a man running after us, though far away. I knew it was Adams following us on foot, faithful to his duty.

I felt a great shudder running through the horse beneath me, and then the faithful animal began to reel like a man in liquor. I could have groaned in disappointment, for I knew these signs betokened exhaustion, and a promise that the pursuit would be left to Whitestone alone. But even as my mind formed the thought, Whitestone's horse fell as Adams's had fallen. My own, seeing his last comrade go down, stopped stock still, and refused to stir another inch under the sharpest goad.

"What shall we do?" I cried to Whitestone.

"Follow on foot!" he replied. "His horse must be almost as far gone as ours!"

We paused only to snatch our pistols from the holsters, and then on foot we pierced the trail of dust Chudleigh's horse had left behind him. The fine dust crept into eyes, nose, mouth, and ears. I coughed and spluttered, and just as I was rubbing sight back into my eyes I heard a joyful cry from Whitestone. I was able to see then through the dust, and I beheld Chudleigh abandoning his horse and taking to the woods on foot.

"It's a foot race now, and not a horse race!" I said to Whitestone.

"Yes, and we must still win!" he replied.

Poor Adams was lost to sight behind us.

About two hundred yards from the road the woods began. I feared that if Chudleigh reached these he might elude us, and I pushed myself as I had pushed my horse. Being long-legged and country bred, I am a fair runner; in fact, it is a muscular talent upon which I used to pride myself. The sergeant puffed much at my elbow, but managed to keep his place.

I now perceived with much joy that we could outrun Chudleigh. When he dashed into the woods we had made a very smart gain upon him, and in truth were too near for him to elude us by doubling or turning in the undergrowth. Despite the obstacle of the trees and the bushes we were yet able to keep him in view, and, better acquainted with this sort of work than he, we gained upon him even more rapidly than before. We flattered ourselves that we would soon have him. Though it was a heavy draught upon my breath, I shouted with all my might to Chudleigh to stop and yield. For answer he whirled around and fired a pistol at us. The sergeant grunted, and stopped.

"Go on and take him yourself!" he said hastily to me. "His bullet's in my leg! No bones broke, but I can't run any more! Adams will take care of me!"

Obedient to his command and my own impulse I continued the chase. Perhaps if I had been cooler in mind I might not have done so, for Chudleigh had proved himself a man; he probably had another pistol, and another bullet in that other pistol; in case that other bullet and I met, I knew which would have to yield, but I consoled myself with the reflection that I too had a pistol and some acquaintance with its use.

Chudleigh did not look back again, and perhaps did not know that he was now pursued by only one man. He continued his flight as zealously as ever. As I may have observed before, and with truth too, it incites one's courage wonderfully to have a man run from him, and seeing Chudleigh's back I began to feel quite competent to take him alone. We wound about among the trees at a great rate. I was gaining, though I was forced to pump my breath up from great depths. But I was consoled by the reflection that, however tired I might be, surely he fared no better. I shouted to him again and again, to stop, but he ran as if he were born deaf.

Presently I noticed that he was curving back toward the road, and I wondered at his purpose. A moment later he burst from the trees into the open ground. I was within fair pistol shot, and, with trees and bushes no longer obstructing, he was a good target. I doubted not that I could hit him, and since he would not stop for my voice, I must see if a bullet would make him more obedient.

I raised my pistol and took the good aim which one can do running if he has had the practice. But my heart revolted at the shot. If I could risk so much for Kate Van Auken's brother, surely I could risk something for Kate Van Auken's lover. I do not take praise to myself for not shooting Chudleigh, as I was thinking that if I did fire the shot I would have but a poor tale to tell to Mistress Catherine.

I let down the hammer of the pistol and stuffed the weapon into my pocket. Chudleigh was now running straight toward the road. My wonder what his purpose might be increased.

Of a sudden he drew a second pistol and fired it at me, but his bullet sped wide of the mark. He threw the pistol on the ground and tried to run faster.

I thought that when he reached the road he would follow it to the south, hoping to shake me off; but, very much to my surprise, he crossed it, and kept a straight course toward the river. Then I divined that he being a good swimmer, hoped I was not, and that thus he might escape me. But I can swim as well as run, and I prepared my mind for the event. When he reached the river he threw off his coat with a quick movement and sprang boldly into the stream. But I was ready. I threw my own coat aside—the only one I had—and leaped into the water after him.

If I was a good swimmer, so was Chudleigh. When I rose from my first splash he was already far from me, floating partly with the stream, and following a diagonal course toward the farther shore. I swam after him with vigorous strokes. Curiously enough, the severe exertion to which I had been subjecting myself on land did not seem to affect me in the water. I suppose a new set of muscles came into play, for I felt fresh and strong. Moreover, I resolved that I would cling to Chudleigh to the very last; that I would not let him by any chance escape me. I felt again that the entire fate of the great campaign depended upon me, and me alone. With such a feeling, one's sense of importance grows much, and I think it made my arm stronger also, which was what I needed more particularly just then.

Chudleigh dived once and remained under water a long time, with the probable intent of deceiving me in regard to his course. But the trick worked against him rather than for him; when he came up he was nearer to me than before. I thought also that his strokes were growing weaker, and I was confirmed in such belief by the amount of water he splashed about, as if his efforts were desperate rather than judicious.

I swam, my strokes long and steady, and gained upon him with much rapidity. We were approaching the shore, when he, looking back, perceived that I must overtake him before he could reach land.

With an abruptness for which I was unprepared, he swam about and faced me as much as to say: "Come on; if you take me, you must fight me first."

Chudleigh, with only his head above water, was not especially beautiful to look at. The dirt with which he had disguised himself when he played false guide to us was washed off partly, and remained partly in streaks of mud, which made him look as if a hot gridiron had been slapped of a sudden upon his face. Moreover, Chudleigh was angry, very angry; his eyes snapped as if he were wondering why I could not let him alone.

I may have looked as ugly as Chudleigh, but I could not see for myself. I swam a little closer to him, looking him straight in the eye, in order that I might see what he intended to do the moment he thought it.

"Why do you follow me?" he asked, with much anger in his tone.

"Why do you run from me?" I asked.

"What I do is no business of yours," he said.

"Oh, yes, it is," I replied. "You're Captain Chudleigh of the British army, an escaped prissoner, and I've come to recapture you."

"I don't see how you're going to do it," he said.

"I do," I replied, though, to tell the truth, I had not yet thought of a way to manage the matter, which seemed to present difficulties. In the meantime I confined myself to treading water. Chudleigh did the same.

"That was a dirty trick you played on us back there," I said, "palming yourself off on us as a guide."

"I didn't do it," he replied in an injured tone. "You're to blame yourself. You forced me at the pistol's muzzle."

He told the truth, I was forced to confess.

"We'll let that pass," I said. "Now, will you surrender?"

"Never!" he replied, in manner most determined.

"Then you will force me to a violent recapture," I said.

"I fail to see how you are going to do it," he said with much grimness. "If you seize me here in the water, I will seize you, and then we will drown together, which will be very unpleasant for both of us."

There was much truth in what he said. A blind man or a fool could see it.

"Let us swim to land and fight it out with our fists," I proposed, remembering how I had overcome Albert, and confident that I could dispose of Chudleigh in similar fashion.

"Oh, no," he said decidedly, "I am very comfortable where I am."

"Then you like water better than most British officers," I said.

"It has its uses," he replied contentedly.

There was nothing more to do just then but to tread water and think.

"Come, come, captain," I said after a while, "be reasonable. I've overtaken you. You can't get away. Surrender like a gentleman, and let's go ashore and dry ourselves. This water's getting cold."

"I see no reason why I should surrender," he replied. "Besides, the water is no colder for you than it is for me."

There was no answer to this logic. Moreover, what he said sounded like a challenge. So I set myself to thinking with more concentration than ever. There was another and longer interval of silence. I hoped that Whitestone or Adams would appear, but neither did so. After all, I had little right to expect either. We had left them far behind, and also we had changed our course. There was nothing to guide them.

I addressed myself once more to Chudleigh's reason.

"Your errand is at an end," I said. "Whether I take you now or not, you can not shake me off. You will never get through to Clinton. Besides, you are losing all your precious time here in the river."

But he preserved an obstinacy most strange and vexatious. He did not even reply to me, but kept on treading water. I perceived that I must use with him some other means than logic, however sound and unanswerable the latter might be.

Sometimes it happens to me, as doubtless it does to other people, that after being long in a puzzle, the answer comes to me so suddenly and so easily that I wonder why I did not see it first glance.

Without any preliminaries that would seem to warn Chudleigh, I dived out of sight. When I came up I was in such shallow water that I could wade. Near me was a huge bowlder protruding a good two feet above the water. I walked to it, climbed upon it, and taking a comfortable position above the water, looked at Chudleigh, who seemed to be much surprised and aggrieved at my sudden countermarch.

"What do you mean?" he asked.

"Nothing," I replied, "except that I am tired of treading water. Come and join me; it's very pleasant up here."

He declined my invitation, which I had worded most courteously. I remained silent for a while; then I said:

"Better come. You can't tread water forever. If you stay there much longer you'll catch the cramp and drown."

I lolled on the bowlder and awaited the end with calmness and satisfaction. My signal advantage was apparent.

"I'll swim to the other shore," said he presently.

"You can't," I replied. "It's too far; you haven't strength enough left for it."

I could see that he was growing tired. He looked around him at either shore and up and down the river, but we were the only human beings within the circle of that horizon.

"What terms of surrender do you propose?" he said at last, with a certain despair in his tone.

"Unconditional."

"That is too hard."

"My advantage warrants the demand."

He was silent again for a few moments, and was rapidly growing weaker. I thought I would hasten matters.

"I will not treat you badly," I said. "All I want to do is to take you back to our army."

"Well, I suppose I must accept," he said, "for I am growing devilish cold and tired."

"Pledge your honor," I said, "that you will make no attempt to escape, with the understanding that the pledge does not forbid rescue."

"I give you my word," he said.

Whereupon he swam to shore, to the great relief of us both.

CHAPTER 16 The Return with Chudleigh

We climbed up the bank, and sat for some time drying in the sun. We were wet, and, moreover, had drunk large quantities of the Hudson River. As a regular thing, I prefer dry land as a place of inhabitation.

While the sun dried our bodies and clothing I was thinking. Though I had taken my man, and that, too, single-handed, my position was not the best in the world. I was now on the wrong side of the river, and I had lost my weapons and my comrades. Also I was hungry.

"Chudleigh," I asked, "are you hungry?"

"Rather," he replied with emphasis.

"How are we to get something to eat?" I asked.

"That's your affair, not mine," he replied. "I have nothing to do but to remain captured."

I thought I saw in him an inclination to be disagreeable, which, to say the truth, was scarce the part of a gentleman after the handsome fashion in which I had treated him. In the face of such ingratitude, I resolved to use the privileges of my superior position.

"Are you about dry?" I asked.

"Yes."

"Then get up and march."

He seemed to resent my stern tone, but inasmuch as he had provoked it he had no cause for complaint. If he intended to assert all the rights of a prisoner, then I equally would assert all the rights of a captor.

"Which way?" he asked.

"Northward, along the river bank. Keep in front of me," I said.

Obedient to my orders he stalked off at a pretty gait, and I followed. We marched thus for half a mile. Chudleigh glanced back at me once or twice. I seemed not to notice it, though I could guess what was passing in his mind.

"If I hadn't given my word," he said, "I think I'd fight it out with you, fist and skull."

"I offered you the chance," I said, "when we were in the river, but you would not accept it, You've heard many wise sayings about lost opportunities, and this proves the truth of them."

"That's so," he said with a sigh of deep regret.

"Besides," I added, in the way of consolation for his lost opportunity, "you would gain nothing by it but bruises. I am larger and stronger than you."

He measured me with his eye and concluded that I spoke truth, for he heaved another sigh, but of comfort.

"Now, Chudleigh," I said, "a man can be a fool sometimes and lose nothing, but he can't be a fool all the time and gather the profits of the earth. Drop back here with me and let us talk and act sensibly."

He wrinkled his brow a moment or two, as if in thought, and accepted my invitation. Whereupon we became very good companions.

In reality I felt as much trouble about Chudleigh as myself. It was like the trouble I had felt on Albert's account. He had penetrated our lines in citizen's clothes, and if I took him back to our camp in the same attire he might be regarded as a spy, with all the unpleasant consequences such a thing entails. Having spared Chudleigh's life once from scruples, I had no mind to lead him to the gallows. I must get a British uniform for him, though how was more than I could tell. The problem troubled me much.

But the advance of hunger soon drove thoughts of Chudleigh's safety out of my mind, and, stubborn Englishman though he was, he was fain to confess that he too felt the desire for food. Along that side of the river the settlements were but scant, and nowhere did we see a house.

That we would encounter Whitestone and Adams was beyond all probability, for they would never surmise that we had crossed the river. Chudleigh and I looked ruefully and hungrily at each other.

"Chudleigh," I said, "you are more trouble a captive than a fugitive."

"The responsibility is yours," he said. "I decline to carry the burdens of my captor. Find me something to eat."

We trudged along for more than an hour, somewhat gloomy and the pains of hunger increasing. I was about to call a halt, that we might rest and that I might think about our difficulties, when I saw a column of smoke rising above a hill. I called Chudleigh's attention to it, and he agreed with me that we ought to push on and see what it was.

I was convinced that friends must be at the bottom of that column of smoke. If any British party had come so far north, which in itself was improbable, it could scarce be so careless as to give to the Americans plain warning of its presence.

It was a long walk, but we were cheered by the possibility that our reward would be dinner. Chudleigh seemed to cherish some lingering hope that it was a party of British or Tories who would rescue him, but I told him to save himself such disappointments.

In a short time we came in view of those who had built the fire, and I was delighted to find my surmise that they were Americans was correct.

They numbered some fifty or a hundred, and I guessed they were a detachment on the way to join the northern army beleaguering Burgoyne.

"Chudleigh," I said as we approached the first sentinel, "will you promise to do all that I say?"

"Of course; I am your prisoner," he replied.

I hailed the sentinel, and my uniform procured for me a friendly reception. Chudleigh I introduced vaguely as a countryman traveling northward with me. The men were eating, and I told them we were making close acquaintance with starvation. They invited us to join them, and we fell to with great promptitude.

I could tell them something about affairs at the north, and they could give me the latest news from the south. They told me that Clinton was still below Albany, hesitating and awaiting with impatience some message from Burgoyne.

I rejoiced more than ever that I had stopped Chudleigh, and felt pride in my exploit. I hope I can be pardoned for it. It was but natural that Chudleigh's emotions should be the opposite of mine, and I watched his face to see how he would take this talk. It was easy enough to see regret expressed there, though he sought to control himself.

The talk of these recruits was very bitter against the British. The Indians with Burgoyne had committed many cruel deeds before they fled back to Canada, and these countrymen were full of the passion for revenge. I often think that if the British in London knew what atrocities their red allies have committed in their wars with us they would understand more easily why so many of us are inflamed against the Englishman.

These men were rehearsing the latest murders by the Indians, and they showed very plainly their desire to arrive at the front before Burgoyne was taken. Nor did they spare the name of Englishman. I was sorry on Chudleigh's account that the talk had taken such drift. He took note of it from the first, because his red face grew redder, and he squirmed about in the manner which shows uneasiness.

"Chudleigh," I whispered at a moment when the others were not looking, "keep still. Remember you are my prisoner."

But he sat there swelling and purring like an angry cat.

While the others were denouncing them, I made some excuses, most perfunctory, it is true, for the British; but this was only an additional incitement to a bellicose man named Hicks. He damned the British for every crime known to Satan. Chudleigh was so red in the face I thought the blood would pop out through his cheeks, and, though I shoved him warningly with my boot, he blurted out his wrath.

"The English are as good as anybody, sir, and you accuse them falsely!" he said.

"What is it to you?" exclaimed Hicks, turning to him in surprise and anger.

"I am an Englishman, sir," said Chudleigh with ill-judged haughtiness, "and I will not endure such abuse."

"Oh, you are an Englishman, are you, and you won't endure abuse, won't you?" said Hicks with irony; and then to me, "We did not understand you to say he was an Englishman."

I saw that we were in a pickle, and I thought it best to tell the whole truth in a careless way, as if the thing were but a trifle.

"The man is an English officer, an escaped prisoner, whom I have retaken," I said. "I did not deem it worth while to make long explanations, especially as we must now push on after you have so kindly fed us."

But Hicks was suspicious; so were the others, and their suspicions were fed by the mutterings and growls of Chudleigh, who showed a lack of tact remarkable even in an Englishman out of his own country. Then, to appease them, I went into some of the long explanations which I had said I wanted to avoid.

"That's all very well," broke in Hicks, "but if this man is an English officer, why is he not in the English uniform? I believe he is an Englishman, as you say; he talks like it, but tell me why he is dressed like a civilian."

The others followed Hicks's lead and began to cry:

"Spy! Spy! Spy!"

In truth I felt alarm.

"This is no spy," I said. "He is Captain Chudleigh, of the English army."

"He may be Captain Chudleigh and a spy too," said Hicks coolly. "I am not sure about the Chudleigh part, but I am about the spy part."

"Hang him for good count!" cried some of the others, who seemed to be raw recruits. The talk about the Indian atrocities was fresh in their minds, and they were in a highly inflammatory state. I recognized a real and present danger.

"Men," I cried, "you are going too far! This prisoner is mine, and it is of importance that I take him back to the army."

But my protest only seemed to excite them further. In truth they took it as a threat. Some of them began to demand that I too should be hung, that I was a Tory in disguise. But the body of them did not take up this cry. The bulk of their wrath fell upon Chudleigh, who was undeniably an Englishman. Two or three of the foremost made ready to seize him. I was in no mind to have all my plans spoiled, and I snatched a musket from a stack and threatened to shoot the first man who put a hand on Chudleigh.

Chudleigh himself behaved very well, and sat, quite calm. The men hesitated at sight of the rifle, and this gave me a chance to appeal to their reason, which was more accessible now since they seemed to be impressed by my earnestness. I insisted that all I had said was the truth, and they would be doing much injury to our cause if they interfered with us. I fancy that I pleaded our case with eloquence, though I ought not to boast. At any rate they were mollified, and concluded to abandon their project of hanging Chudleigh.

"I've no doubt he deserves hanging," said Hicks, "but I guess we'll leave the job for somebody else."

Chudleigh was about to resent this, but I told him to shut up so abruptly that he forgot himself and obeyed.

I was anxious enough to be clear of these men, countrymen though they were; so we bade them adieu and tramped on, much strengthened by the rest and food.

"Captain," said I to Chudleigh, though trying to preserve a polite tone, "you do not seem to appreciate the beauty and virtue of silence."

"I will not have my country or my countrymen insulted," replied he in most belligerent tones.

"Well, at any rate," I said, "I had to save your life at the risk of my own."

"It was nothing more than your duty," he replied. "I am your prisoner, and you are responsible for my safety."

Which I call rank ingratitude on Chudleigh's part, though technically true.

It was late in the day when we met the detachment, and dark now being near at hand, it was apparent that we would have to sleep in the woods, which, however, was no hardship for soldiers, since the nights were warm and the ground dry. When the night arrived I proposed to Chudleigh that we stop and make our beds on the turf, which was rather thick and soft at that spot. He assented in the manner of one who had made up his mind to obey me in every particular.

But before lying down I had the forethought to ask from Chudleigh a guarantee that he would not walk away in the night while I was asleep. I reminded him of his pledge that he would not attempt to escape, barring a rescue.

But he took exceptions with great promptness, claiming with much plausibility, I was fain to admit, that his pledge did not apply in such a case. He argued that if I lay down and went to sleep he was no longer guarded; consequently he was not a prisoner; consequently he would go away. Since he chose to stick to his position, I had no way to drive him from it, whether reasonable or unreasonable.

"Then I will bind you hand and foot," I said.

He reminded me with an air of triumph that I had nothing with which to bind him, which unfortunately was true.

"What am I to do?" I said as much to myself as to him.

"Nothing that I can see," he replied, "but to guard me while I sleep."

Without another word he lay down upon the turf, and in less than two minutes his snore permeated the woods.

Reflecting in most unhappy fashion that if it were not for the great interests of our campaign I would much rather be his prisoner than have him mine, I sat there making fierce efforts to keep my eyelids apart.

CHAPTER 17 My Thanks

About midnight I reached the limit of endurance. I was firm in my resolution that I would not sleep, and while still firm in it I slept. When I awoke it was a fine day. For a moment I was in a cold terror, feeling sure Chudleigh had slipped away while I slept the sleep that had overpowered me. But a calm, evenly attuned snore that glided peacefully through the arches of the woods reassured me.

Chudleigh was lying on his back, sleeping. He was as heavy as a log, and I knew that he had not known a single waking moment since he lay down the night before. I dragged him about with rudeness and he opened his eyes regretfully. Presently he announced that he felt very fresh and strong, and asked me where I expected to get breakfast. He said he was sorry for me, as he knew I must be very tired and sleepy after sitting up on guard all night.

I gave him no answer, but commanded him to resume the march with me. We walked on with diligence through a breakfastless country. Chudleigh, though suffering from hunger, was frequent in his expressions of sympathy for me. He said he had the utmost pity for any man who was compelled to sit up an entire night and watch prisoners; but I replied that I throve upon it, and then Chudleigh showed chagrin.

We had the good fortune, about two hours before noon, to find the house of a farmer, who sold us some food, and cared not whether we were American or British, Tory or nothing, so long as we were good pay.

A half hour after leaving this place I decided that we ought to recross the river. Chudleigh offered no objection, knowing that he had no right to do so, being a prisoner. I had no mind to take another swim, so I made search along the bank for something that would serve as a raft, and was not long in finding it.

Having proved to Chudleigh that it was as much to his benefit as to mine to help me, we rolled a small tree that had fallen near the water's edge into the river, and, sitting astride it, began our ride toward the farther shore. I had a pole with which I could direct the course of our raft, and with these aids it seemed rather an easy matter to cross. I allowed the tree to drift partly with the current, but all the time gently urged it toward the farther shore.

We floated along quite peacefully. So far as we could see we were alone upon the broad surface of the river, and the shores too were deserted. I remarked upon the loneliness of it all to Chudleigh, and he seemed impressed.

"Chudleigh," I said, "we're having an easier time recrossing the river than we had crossing it."

"So it would seem," he replied, "but we won't unless you look out for the current and those rocks there."

I had twisted my face about while speaking to Chudleigh, and in consequence neglected the outlook ahead. We had reached a shallow place in the river where some sharp rocks stuck up, and the water eddied about them in manner most spirited. The front end of our log was caught in one of these eddies and whirled about with violence. I was thrown off, and though I grasped at the log it slipped away from me. I whirled about to recover myself, but the fierce current picked me up and dashed me against one of the projecting rocks. With a backward twist I was able to save myself a little, but my head struck the cruel stone with grievous force.

I saw many stars appear suddenly in the full day. Chudleigh and the log vanished, and I was drifting away through the atmosphere. I was not wholly unconscious, and through the instinct of an old swimmer made some motions which kept me afloat a little while with the current.

I had too little mind left to command my nerves and muscles, but enough to know that I was very near death. In a dazed and bewildered sort of way I expected the end, and was loath to meet it.

The blue sky was rapidly fading into nothing, when some voice from a point a thousand miles away called to me to hold up a little longer. The voice was so sharp and imperious that it acted like a tonic upon me, and brain resumed a little control over body. I tried to swim, but I was too weak to do more than paddle a little. The voice shouted again, and encouraged me to persevere.

In truth I tried to persevere, but things were whizzing about so much in my head and I was so weak that I could do but little. I thought I was bound to go down, with the whole river pouring into my ears.

"That's a good fellow!" shouted the voice. "Hold up just a minute longer, and I'll have you safe!"

I saw dimly a huge figure bearing down upon me. It reached out and grasped me by the collar.

"Steady, now!" continued the voice. "Here comes our tree, and we'll be safe in twenty seconds!"

The tree, looking like a mountain, floated down toward us. My rescuer reached out, seized it, and then dragged us both upon it. Reposing in safety, mind and strength returned, and things resumed their natural size and shape. Chudleigh, the Hudson River running in little cascades from his hair down his face, was sitting firmly astride the log and looking at me with an air of satisfaction,

"Chudleigh," I said, "I believe you have saved my life."

"Shelby," he replied, "I know it."

"Why didn't you escape?" I asked.

"You compel me to remind you that I am a gentleman, Mr. Shelby," he said.

That was all that ever passed between us on the subject, though I reflected that I was not in his debt, for if he had saved my life I had saved his.

We had no further difficulty in reaching the desired shore, where the sun soon dried us. We continued our journey in very amicable fashion, Chudleigh no doubt feeling relief because he was now in a measure on even terms with me. I, too, was in a state of satisfaction. Unless Burgoyne had retreated very fast, we could not now be far from the lines of the American army, and I thought that my troubles with my prisoner were almost at an end. I hoped that Burgoyne had not been taken in my absence, for I wished to be present at the taking. I also had in my mind another plan with which Chudleigh was concerned. It was a plan of great self-sacrifice, and I felt the virtuous glow which arises from such resolutions.

We paused again, by and by, for rest, the sun having become warm and the way dusty. Chudleigh sat down on a stone and wiped his damp face, while I went to a brook, which I had seen glimmering among the trees, for a drink of fresh water. I had just knelt down to drink when I heard a clattering of hoofs. Rising hastily, I saw two men riding toward Chudleigh. Though the faces of these two men were much smeared with dust, I recognized them readily and joyfully. They were Whitestone and Adams.

My two comrades evidently had seen and recognized Chudleigh. They raised a shout and galloped toward him as if they feared he would flee. I came down to the edge of the wood and stopped there to see at my leisure what might happen.

Chudleigh sat upon the stone unmoved. As a matter of course he both saw and heard Whitestone and Adams, but he was a phlegmatic sort of fellow and took no notice. Whitestone reached him first. Leaping from his horse, the gallant sergeant exclaimed:

"Do you surrender, captain?"

"Certainly," said Chudleigh.

"It's been a long chase, captain, but we've got you at last," continued the sergeant.

"So it seems," said Chudleigh, with the same phlegm.

Then I came from the wood and cut the sergeant's comb for him; but he was so glad to see me again that he was quite willing to lose the glory of the recapture. He explained that he had been overtaken by Adams. Together they had wandered around in search of Chudleigh and me. Giving up the hunt as useless, they had obtained new horses and were on the way back to the army.

We were now four men and two horses, and the men taking turns on horseback, we increased our speed greatly.

Whitestone and Adams were in fine feather, but there was one question that yet bothered me. I wanted to take Chudleigh back in his own proper British uniform, and thus save him from unpleasant possibilities. I did not see how it could be done, but luck helped me.

We met very soon a small party of Americans escorting some British prisoners. Telling my companions to wait for me, I approached the sergeant who was in charge of the troop. Making my manner as important as I could, and speaking in a low tone, as if fearful that I would be overheard—which I observe always impresses people—I told him that one of our number was about to undertake a most delicate and dangerous mission. It chanced that I had some slight acquaintance with this sergeant, and therefore he had no reason to doubt my words, even if I am forced to say it myself.

He pricked up his ears at once, all curiosity, and wanted to know the nature of the business. I pointed to Chudleigh, who was standing some distance away with Whitestone and Adams, and said he was going to enter the British lines as a spy in order to procure most important information.

"A dangerous business, you say truly. He must be a daring fellow," said my man, nodding his head in the direction of Chudleigh.

"So he is," I said, "ready at any moment to risk his life for the cause, but we need one thing."

He asked what it was.

"A disguise," I said. "If he is to play the British soldier, of course he must have a British soldier's clothes."

I made no request, but I looked suggestively at the British prisoners. The sergeant, who was all for obliging me, took the hint at once. He picked out the very best uniform in the lot, and made the man who wore it exchange it for Chudleigh's old clothes. Chudleigh, who had been learning wisdom in the last day or two, was considerate enough to keep his mouth shut, and we parted from the sergeant and his troop with many mutual expressions of good will. The uniform did not fit Chudleigh, nor was it that of an officer, but these were minor details to which no attention would be paid in the press of a great campaign.

The matter of the uniform disposed of, we pressed forward with renewed spirit, and soon reached the first, sentinels of our army, which we found surrounding that of Burgoyne. It was with great satisfaction that I delivered Chudleigh to my colonel.

The colonel was delighted at the recapture, and praised me with such freedom that I began to have a budding suspicion that I ought to be commander in chief of the army. However, I made no mention of the suspicion. Instead, I suggested to the colonel that as Chudleigh had escaped once, he might escape again, and it would be well to exchange him for some officer of ours whom the British held.

The colonel took to the idea, and said he would speak to the general about it. In the morning he told me it would be done, and I immediately asked him for the favor of taking Chudleigh into the British camp, saying that as I had been his jailer so much already, I would like to continue in that capacity until the end.

The colonel was in great good humor with me, and he granted the request forthwith. As I left to carry out the business, he said, "The exchange is well enough, but we'll probably have your man back in a few days."

In truth it did look rather odd that the British should be exchanging prisoners with us upon what we regarded as the unavoidable eve of their surrender, but they chose to persevere in the idea that we were yet equal enemies. Nevertheless, the coils of our army were steadily tightening around them. All the fords were held by our troops. Our best sharpshooters swept the British camp, and it is no abuse of metaphor to say that Burgoyne's army was rimmed around by a circle of fire.

I found Chudleigh reposing under a tree, and told him to get up and start with me at once.

"What new expedition is this?" he asked discontentedly. "Can not I be permitted to rest a little? I will not try to escape again?"

I told him he was about to be exchanged, and I had secured the privilege of escorting him back to his own people.

"That's very polite of you," he said.

I really believe he thought so.

For the second time I entered Burgoyne's camp under a white flag, and saw all the signs of distress I had seen before, only in a sharper and deeper form. The wounded and sick were more numerous and the well and strong were fewer. It was a sorely stricken army.

But I did not waste much time in such observations, which of necessity would have been but limited anyhow, as the British had no intent to let any American wander at will about their camp and take note of their situation. When we were halted at the outskirts, I asked the officer who received us for Albert Van Auken, who, I said, was a friend of mine and of whose safety I wished to be assured. He was very courteous, and in a few minutes Albert came.

Albert was glad to see me, and I to see him, and as soon as we had shaken hands I approached the matter I had in mind.

"Madame Van Auken, your mother, and your sister, are they well, Albert?" I asked.

"Very well, the circumstances considered," replied Albert, "though I must say their quarters are rather restricted. You can see the house up there; they have been living for the last three or four days and nights in its cellar, crowded up with other women, with a hospital beside them, and the cannon balls from your army often crashing over their heads. It's rather a lively life for women."

"Can't I see your sister, Mistress Catherine?" I asked. "I have something to say to her about Chudleigh."

"Why, certainly," he replied. "Kate will always be glad to see an old playmate like you, Dick."

He was so obliging as to go at once and fetch her. She looked a little thin and touched by care, but the added gravity became her. She greeted me with gratifying warmth. We had stepped a little to one side, and after the greetings, I said, indicating Chudleigh:

"I have brought him back as sound and whole as he was the day he started on this campaign."

"That must be very pleasant to Captain Chudleigh," she said with a faint smile.

"I saved him from a possible death too," I said.

"Captain Chudleigh's debt of gratitude to you is large," she replied.

"I have taken great trouble with him," I said, "but I was willing to do it all on your account. I have brought him back, and I make him a present to you."

She looked me squarely in the eyes for a moment, and said, as she turned away:

"Dick, you are a fool!"

Which I call abrupt, impolite, ungrateful, and, I hope, untrue.

CHAPTER 18 The Battle of the Guns

I returned to our camp downcast over the failure of good intentions, and convinced that there was no reward in this life for self-sacrifice. Perhaps if I were to fall in the fighting and Kate Van Auken were to see my dead body, she would be sorry she had called me a fool. There was comfort in this reflection. The idea that I was a martyr cheered me, and I recovered with a rapidity that was astonishing to myself.

An hour's rest was permitted me before my return to active duty, and I had some opportunity to observe our tactics, which I concluded must be most galling to the enemy. Some clouds of smoke hung over both encampments, and the crackling of the rifles of the sharpshooters and the occasional thud of the cannon had become so much a matter of course, that we scarce paid attention to them.

When my hour of leisure was over I was assigned to duty with an advanced party close up to Burgoyne's camp. It was much to my pleasure that I found Whitestone there too. It was but natural, however, that we should be often on duty together, since we belonged to the same company.

Whitestone, according to his habit, had made himself comfortable on the ground, and, there being no law against it, was smoking the beloved pipe, which like its master was a veteran of many campaigns. From his lounging place he could see a portion of the British camp.

"Mr. Shelby," said he, "this is like sitting by and watching a wounded bear die, and giving him a little prod now and then to hurry the death along."

So it was, and it was no wonder the soldiers grew impatient. But I was bound to confess that the policy of our generals was right, and by it they would win as much and save more life.

There was nothing for me to do, and I kept my eyes most of the time on the house Albert had pointed out to me. Crouched in its cellar I knew were scared women and weeping children, and doubtless Kate and her mother were among them. Once a cannon ball struck the house and went through it, burying itself in the ground on the other side. I held my breath for a little, but I was reassured by the thought that the women and children were out of range in the cellar.

Thus the day passed in idleness as far as I was concerned. I spent it not unpleasantly in gossip with Whitestone. The nightfall was dark, and under cover of it the British ran a twenty-four pounder forward into a good position and opened fire with it upon some of our advanced parties. My first warning of the attack was a loud report much nearer to us than usual, followed by a hissing and singing as if something were stinging the air, and then a solid chunk of iron struck the earth with a vengeful swish a few yards from us. A cloud of dirt was spattered in our faces, stinging us like bees.

When we had recovered from our surprise, and assured ourselves we were neither dead nor dying, we made remarks about chance, and the probability that no other cannon ball would strike near us during the campaign. Just as the last of such remarks were spoken we heard the roar and heavy boom, followed by the rapid swish through the air, and the cannon ball struck a full yard nearer to us than the first. We used vigorous and, I fear, bad language, which, however, is a great relief sometimes, especially to a soldier.

"They've pushed that gun up too close to us," said Whitestone. "It's among those trees across there. The darkness has helped them."

We were of opinion that the men with the gun had our range—that is, of our particular party—and we thought it wise and healthy to lie down and expose the least possible surface. I awaited the third shot with much curiosity and some apprehension.

Presently we saw a twinkle, as of a powder match, and then a great flash. The ball shrieked through the air, and with a shiver that could not be checked we waited for it to strike. True to its predecessors, it followed nearly the same course and smashed against a stone near us. One of our men was struck by the rebounding of fragments, of iron or stone, and severely wounded. It was too dark to see well, but his groans spoke for him. Whitestone and I took hold of him and carried him back for treatment. While we were gone, one man was slain and another wounded in the same way. In the darkness that British cannon had become a live thing and was stinging us. Some of our best sharpshooters were chosen to slay the cannoneers, but they could aim only by the flash of the gun, and the men loading it had the woods to protect them. The bullets were wasted, and the troublesome hornet stung again and again.

We were perplexed. Our pride as well as our safety was concerned. The idea came to me at last.

"To fight fire with fire is an old saying," I remarked to Whitestone.

"What do you mean?" he asked.

"Why, we must have a cannon too," I said.

He understood at once, for Whitestone is not a dull man. He volunteered to get the cannon and I went along with him to help. We presented our claim with such urgency and eloquence that the artillery officer to whom we went was impressed. Also he was near enough to see how damaging and dangerous the British cannon had become.

"You can have Old Ty," he said, "and be sure you make good use of him."

I did not understand, but Whitestone did. He knew Old Ty. He explained that Old Ty, which was short for "Old Ticonderoga," was a twenty-four pounder taken at Ticonderoga early in the war by Ethan Allen and his Green Mountain Boys. It had done so much service and in so many campaigns that the gunners had affectionately nicknamed the veteran Old Ty in memory of the fortress in which he had been taken.

"I've seen Old Ty," said Whitestone. "He's been battered about a good lot, but he's got a mighty bad bark and a worse bite."

In a few minutes the groaning of wheels and the shout of the driver to the horses announced the approach of Old Ty. I stood aside with respect while the gun passed, and a grim and fierce old veteran he was, full worthy the respect of a youngster such as I felt myself to be.

Old Ty was of very dark metal, and there were many scars upon him where he had received the blows of enemies of a like caliber. A wheel which had been struck by a ball in the heat of action was bent a trifle to one side, and Old Ty rolled along as if he were a little lame and didn't mind it. His big black muzzle grinned at me as if he were proud of his scars, and felt good for many more.

Just behind the gun walked a man as ugly and battered as Old Ty himself.

"That's Goss, the gunner," said Whitestone. "He's been with Old Ty all through the war, and loves him better than his wife."

On went the fierce and ugly pair like two who knew their duty and loved it.

The night, as usual after the first rush of darkness, had begun to brighten a bit. We could see the British cannon, a long, ugly piece, without waiting for its flash; yet its gunners were protected so well by fresh-felled trees and a swell of the earth that our sharpshooters could not pick them off. They were in good position, and nothing lighter than Old Ty could drive them out of it.

The British saw what we were about and sought to check us. They fired more rapidly, and a cannon ball smashed one of the horses hitched to Old Ty almost to a pulp. But Goss sprang forward, seized one wheel, and threw the veteran into place.

Old Ty had a position much like that of his antagonist, and Goss, stroking his iron comrade like one who pets an old friend, began to seek the range, and take very long and careful looks at the enemy. Lights along the line of either army flared up, and many looked on.

"Lie flat on the ground here," said Whitestone to me. "This is going to be a pitched battle between the big guns, and you want to look out."

I adopted Whitestone's advice, thinking it very good. Old Ty's big black muzzle grinned threateningly across at his antagonist, as if he longed to show his teeth, but waited the word and hand of his comrade.

"There goes the bark of the other!" cried Whitestone.

The bright blaze sprang up, the British cannon roared, and hurled his shot. The mass of iron swept over Old Ty and buried itself in the hillside.

"Much bark, but no bite," said Whitestone.

Old Ty, black and defiant, was yet silent, Goss was not a man who hurried himself or his comrade. We waited, breathless. Suddenly Goss leaned over and touched the match.

Old Ty spoke in the hoarse, roaring voice that indicates much wear. One of the felled trees in the British position was shattered, and the ball bounded to the right and was lost to sight.

"A little bite," said Whitestone, "but not deep enough."

Old Ty smoked and grew blacker, as if he were not satisfied with himself. They swabbed out his mouth and filled it with iron again.

Where I lay I could see the muzzles of both cannon threatening each other. The Briton was slower than before, as if he wished to be sure. Goss continued to pat his comrade by way of stirring up his spirit. That did not seem to me to be needed, for Old Ty was the very fellow I would have chosen for such a furious contention as this.

The two champions spoke at the same instant, and the roar of them was so great that for the moment I thought I would be struck deaf. A great cloud of smoke enveloped either cannon, but when it raised both sides cheered.

Old Ty had received a fresh blow on his lame wheel, and careened a little farther to one side, but the Briton was hit the harder of the two. His axle had been battered by Old Ty's ball, and the British were as busy as bees propping him up for the third raid.

"Rather evenly matched," grunted Whitestone, "and both full of grit. I think we shall have some very pretty sport here."

I was of Whitestone's opinion.

I could see Goss frowning. He did not like the wound Old Ty had received, and stroked the lame wheel. "Steady, old partner," I heard him say. "We'll beat 'em yet."

All at once I noticed that the lights along the line had increased, and some thousands were looking on at the battle of the two giants.

"Old Ty must win!" I said to Whitestone. "We can't let him lose."

"I don't know," said Whitestone, shaking his head. "A battle's never over till the last shot's fired."

The Briton was first, and it was well that we were sheltered. The ball glanced along Old Ty's barrel, making a long rip in the iron, and bounded over our heads and across the hill.

"Old Ty got it that time," said Whitestone. "That was a cruel blow."

He spoke truth, and a less seasoned veteran than Old Ty would have been crushed by it. There was a look of deep concern on Goss's face as he ran his hand over the huge rent in Old Ty's side. Then his face brightened a bit, and I concluded the veteran was good for more hard blows.

The blow must have had some effect upon Old Ty's voice or temper. At any rate, when he replied his roar was hoarser and angrier. A cry arose from the British ranks, and I saw them taking away a body. Old Ty had tasted blood. But the British cannon was as formidable as ever.

"The chances look a bit against Old Ty," commented Whitestone, and I had to confess to myself, although with reluctance, that it was so.

Goss was very slow in his preparations for the fourth shot. He had the men to steady Old Ty, and he made a slight change in the elevation. Again both spoke at the same time, and Old Ty groaned aloud as the mass of British iron tore along his barrel, ripping out a gap deeper and longer than any other. His own bolt tore off one of the Briton's wheels.

"The Englishman's on one leg," said Whitestone, "but Old Ty's got it next to the heart. Chances two to one in favor of the Englishman."

I sighed. Poor Old Ty! I could not bear to see the veteran beaten. Goss's hard, dark face showed grief. He examined Old Ty with care and fumbled about him.

"What is he doing?" I asked of Whitestone, who lay nearer the gun.

"I think he's trying to see if Old Ty will stand another shot," he said. "He's got some big rips in the barrel, and he may leave in all directions when the powder explodes."

Old Ty in truth was ragged and torn like a veteran in his last fight. The Briton had lost one wheel and was propped up on the side, but his black muzzle looked triumphant across the way.

The British fired again and then shouted in triumph. Old Ty, too, had lost a wheel, which the shot had pounded into old iron.

"Old Ty is near his end," said Whitestone. "One leg gone and holes in his body as big as my hat; that's too much!"

Old Ty was straightened up, and Goss giving the word, the shot was rolled into his wide mouth. Then the gunner, as grim and battered as His gun, took aim. Upon the instant all our men rushed to cover.

Goss touched the match, and a crash far outdoing all the others stunned us. With the noise in my ears and the smoke in my eyes I knew not what had happened. But Whitestone cried aloud in joy. Rubbing my eyes clear, I looked across to see the effect of the shot. I saw only a heap of rubbish. Old Ty's bolt had smote his enemy and blown up the caisson and the cannon with it.

Then I looked at Old Ty to see how he bore his triumph, but his mighty barrel was split asunder and he was a cannon no longer, just pieces of old iron.

Sitting on a log was some one with tears on his hard, brown face. It was Goss, the gunner, weeping over the end of his comrade.

CHAPTER 19 The Man from Clinton

At one o'clock in the morning I went off duty, and at five minutes past one o'clock I had begun a very pleasant and healthful slumber. At eight o'clock I awoke, and found Whitestone sitting by a little fire cooking strips of bacon, some of which he was so kind as to give me.

Whitestone's face was puffed out in the manner of one who has news to tell, and I was quite willing that he should gratify himself by telling it to me.

"What is it, Whitestone?" I asked. "Has the British army surrendered while I slept?"

"No," said Whitestone, "and it may not surrender after all."

"What!" I exclaimed.

"It's just as I say," said Whitestone, lighting the inevitable pipe. "It may not surrender after all."

"What has happened?"

Whitestone's cheeks continued to swell with a sense of importance.

"Clinton's advancing with seven thousand men," he said.

"That's nothing," I said. "Clinton's been advancing for weeks, and he never gets near us."

"But he is near us this time, sure enough," said the sergeant very seriously.

I was still unbelieving, and looked my unbelief.

"It's as I say," resumed the sergeant; "there is no doubt about it. Just after daylight this morning some skirmishers took a messenger from Clinton, who bore dispatches announcing his arrival within a very short time. It seems that Clinton is much farther up the river than we supposed, and that his army is also much larger than all our reckonings made it. I guess that with re-enforcements he got over the fright we gave him."

This in truth sounded like a matter of moment. I asked Whitestone if he was sure of what he reported, and he said the news was all over the camp. I must confess that I felt as if it were a personal blow. I had looked upon the capture of Burgoyne as a certainty, but the arrival of Clinton with seven thousand fresh men would be sure to snatch the prize from us. It looked like a very jest of fate that we should lose our spoil after all our labors and battles.

"What's to be done, Whitestone?" I asked gloomily.

"In a case of this kind," he replied, "I'm glad that I'm a humble sergeant, and not a general. Let the generals settle it. Take another piece of the bacon; it's crisp and fresh."

"Have you seen this captured messenger?" I asked.

"No," replied Whitestone. "They have him in a tent over yonder, and I think the officers have been busy with him, trying to pump him."

As soon as I finished the bacon I walked about the camp to see if I could learn anything further concerning the matter, in which attempt I failed. I saw, however, its effect upon the army, which vented its feelings largely in the way of swearing. The soldiers expected we would have to leave Burgoyne and turn southward to fight Clinton. Some said luck was always against us.

I was interrupted in my stroll by a message from my colonel to come at once. I hurried to him with some apprehension. He had expressed his high confidence in me of late, and, as I have said before, these high confidences bring hard duties.

But the matter was not so difficult as I had expected.

"Mr. Shelby," said the colonel, "we took prisoner this morning a man bearing important dispatches from Clinton to Burgoyne you have heard about it, doubtless; it seems to be known all over the camp and I am directly responsible for his safe keeping for the time being. He is in that tent which you can see on the hillside. Take three men and guard him. You need not intrude upon him, though; he seems to be a very gentlemanly fellow."

Of course I chose Whitestone as one of my three men, and we began our guard over the tent. I understood from the gossip Whitestone had picked up that the generals were debating what movement to make after the important news obtained, and probably they would examine the prisoner again later on. It was not at all likely that the prisoner, placed as he was in the center of our camp, could escape, but there might be reasons for keeping him close in the tent; so our watch was very strict.

Nevertheless, Whitestone and I chatted a bit, which was within our right, and tried to guess what would be the result of the campaign if we had to turn southward and fight Clinton, with Burgoyne on our rear. Doubtless some of these comments and queries were heard by the prisoner, whose feet I could see sticking out in front of the tent flap, but whose body was beyond our view. But I did not see that it mattered, and we talked on with freedom. Once I saw the prisoner's feet bob up a bit, as if he suffered from some kind of nervous contraction, but I made very slight note of it.

The debate of the generals lasted long, and I inferred, therefore, that their perplexity was great. Whitestone and I ceased to talk, and as I, having command of the little detachment, was under no obligation to parade, musket on shoulder,

I sat down on a stone near the flap of the tent and made myself as comfortable as I could. From my position I could still see the prisoner's boots, a substantial British pair, of a kind that we could envy, for most of the time we were nearly bare of foot, sometimes entirely so.

The camp was peaceful, on the whole. The rattle of drums, the sound of voices, rose in the regular, steady fashion which becomes a hum. The prisoner was silent—unusually silent. He seemed to have no curiosity about us, and to prefer to remain in the shadow of his tent. In his place, I would have had my head out looking at everything. I noticed presently the attitude of his boots. They were cocked up on their heels, toes high in the air. I inferred immediately that the man was lying flat on his back, which was not at all unreasonable, as he probably needed rest after traveling all night.

The hum of the camp became a murmur, and it was answered by a slighter murmur from the tent. The prisoner was snoring. He was not only flat upon his back, but asleep. I felt an admiration for the calmness of mind which could turn placidly to slumber in such an exciting situation. A curiosity about this prisoner, already born in me, began to grow. He was most likely a man worth knowing.

I concluded that I would take a look at the sleeping Englishman despite my orders. I did not mention my idea to Whitestone, because I thought he might object, and hint it was none of my business to go in. I stooped down and entered the tent, which was a small one. As I surmised, the prisoner was lying upon his back and was fast asleep. The snore, which became much more assertive now that I had entered the tent, left no doubt about his slumbers. Yet I could not see his face, which was far back under the edge of the tent.

I reached back and pulled the tent-flap still farther aside, letting in a fine flow of sunlight. It fell directly upon the face of the prisoner, bringing out every feature with the distinctness of carving.

My first emotion was surprise; my second, wrath; my third, amusement.

The prisoner was Albert Van Auken.

I do not claim that mine is the acutest mind in the world; but at a single glance I saw to the bottom of the whole affair, and the desire to laugh grew very strong upon me. It had not been twenty-four hours since I was talking to Albert Van Auken in Burgoyne's camp, and here he was a prisoner in our camp, bringing dispatches from Clinton, down the river, to Burgoyne. I believe some things—not all things.

I perceived that the bright light shining directly into Albert's eyes would soon awaken him. In truth he was yawning even then. I sat down in front of him, closing my arms around my knees in the attitude of one who waits.

Albert yawned prodigiously. I guessed that he must have been up all the previous night to have become so sleepy. He would have relapsed into slumber, but the penetrating streak of sunshine would not let him. It played all over his face, and inserting itself between his eyelids, pried them open.

Albert sat up, and, after the manner of man, rubbed his eyes. He knew that some one was in the tent with him, but he could not see who it was. I had taken care of that. I was in the dark and he was in the light.

"Well, what is it you wish?" he asked, after he had finished rubbing his eyes.

I guessed that he took me for one of the general officers who had been examining him. I have a trick of changing my voice when I wish to do so, and this was one of the times when I wished.

"I am to ask you some further questions in regard to the matters we were discussing this morning," I said.

"Well!" said Albert impatiently, as if he would like to be done with it.

"According to the dispatches which we secured when we took you," I said, "Sir Henry Clinton was very near at hand with a large army."

"Certainly," said Albert, in a tone of great emphasis.

"It is strange," I said, "that we did not hear of his near approach until we took you this morning. Our scouts and skirmishers have brought us no such news."

"It is probably due to the fact, general," said Albert politely, "that we captured your scouts and skirmishers as we advanced northward. Our celerity of movement was so great that they could not escape us."

"That was remarkable marching, in truth," I said admiringly. "You Englishmen are as rapid in movement as you are strenuous in battle."

"Thank you, general," said Albert, with complacent vanity. I felt a strong inclination to kick him. I hate Tories, and, in particular, those who would have people think they are Englishmen.

"I believe you said Sir Henry Clinton had several thousand men with him," I resumed.

"I did not say it," replied Albert, "but most unfortunately it was revealed in the dispatches which you captured upon me. I may add, however, that the number is nearer eight thousand than seven thousand."

I understood the impression he wished to create, and I was willing to further his humor.

"Eight thousand with Sir Henry Clinton," I said, as if musing, "and Burgoyne has six thousand; that makes fourteen thousand, all regular troops, thoroughly armed and equipped otherwise. We can scarce hope to capture both armies."

"Not both, nor one either," said Albert in derision. "As a matter of fact, general, I think you will have some difficulty in looking after your own safety."

"By what manner of reasoning do you arrive at that conclusion?" asked I, wishing to lead him on.

"Oh, well, you know what British troops are," said Albert superciliously; "and when fourteen thousand of them are together, I imagine that troubles have arrived for their enemies."

My inclination to kick him took on a sudden and violent increase. It was with the most extreme difficulty that I retained command over my mutinous foot.

"Perhaps it is as you assert," I said musingly. "In fact there would seem to be no doubt that it is best for us to let Burgoyne go, and retreat with what rapidity we can."

"Of course! of course!" said Albert eagerly. "That is the only thing you can do."

Now a desire to laugh instead of a desire to kick overspread me; but I mastered it as I had the other.

"I wish to tell you, however," I said, assuming my politest manner, "and in telling you I speak for the other American generals, that however little we are pleased with the news you bear, we are much pleased with the bearer. We have found you to be a young gentleman of courtesy, breeding, and discernment."

"Thank you," said Albert in a tone of much gratification.

"And," I resumed, "we have arrived at a certain conclusion; I may add also that we have arrived at that conclusion quickly and unanimously."

"What is it?" asked Albert with eager interest.

"That we have met many graceful and accomplished liars in our time, but of them all you are the most graceful and accomplished," I said with grave politeness, my tongue lingering over the long words.

Albert uttered something which sounded painfully and amazingly like an oath, and sprang to his feet, his face flushing red with anger or shame, I am uncertain which.

He raised his hand as if he would strike me, but I moved around a little, and the light in its turn fell on my face. He uttered another cry, and this time there was no doubt about its being an oath. He looked at me, his face growing redder and redder.

"Dick," he said in a tone of deep reproach, "I call this devilish unkind."

"The unkindness is all on your side, Albert," I retorted. "You have given me more trouble in this campaign than all the rest of Burgoyne's army—if that fellow Chudleigh be counted out—and here I have you on my hands again."

"Who asked you to come into my tent?" said Albert angrily. "I heard you outside a while ago, but I did not think you would come in."

"That was when your feet bobbed up," I said. "You must retain more control over them, Albert. Now that I think of it, and trace things to their remote causes, that movement first stirred in me the curiosity to see your face, and not your feet only. Have them amputated, Albert."

"What do you mean to do?" he asked with an air of resignation.

"Mean to do!" I said in a tone of surprise. "Why, I mean to retreat with all the remainder of our army as quickly as we can in order to get out of the way of those fourteen thousand invincible British veterans who will soon be united in one force."

"Now stop that, Dick." said Albert entreatingly. "Don't be too hard on a fellow."

"All right," I replied; "go to sleep again."

Without further ado I left the tent, and found Whitestone waiting outside in some anxiety.

"You stayed so long," he said, "I thought perhaps the fellow had killed you."

"Not by any means as bad as that," I replied. "I found him to be a very pleasant young man, and we had a conversation long and most interesting."

"About what?" Whitestone could not keep from asking.

"About many things," I replied, "and one thing that I learned was of special importance."

"What was that?"

"How to send Clinton and his eight thousand men back below Albany, hold Burgoyne fast, and continue the campaign as it was begun."

"That's a pretty big job," said Whitestone, "for one man, and that one, too, rather young and not overweighted with rank."

"Maybe you think so," I said with lofty indifference. "But I can do it, and, what is more, I will prove to you that I can. You can stay here while I go down to the council of generals and tell them what to do."

Not giving Whitestone time to recover, I stalked off in a state of extreme dignity.

CHAPTER 20 Not a Drop to Drink

I pressed into the council of the generals with an energy that would not be denied, also with some strength of the knee, as an officious aid-de-camp can testify even at this late day. As a matter of course, my information was of such quality that everybody was delighted with me and praise became common. Again I felt as if I ought to be commander in chief. Again I had sufficient self-sacrifice to keep the thought to myself.

As I left the room they were talking about the disposition of the prisoner who had tried to trick us into precipitate flight and the abandonment of our prey. This put an idea into my head, and I told it to a colonel near the door, who in his turn told it to their high mightinesses, the generals, who were wise enough to approve of it, and, in truth, to indorse it most heartily.

I suggested that Albert be sent back to Burgoyne with the most gracious compliments of our commander in chief, who was pleased to hear the news of the speedy arrival of Clinton, which would greatly increase the number of prisoners we were about to take. I asked, as some small reward for my great services, that I be chosen to escort Albert into the British camp and deliver the message. That, too, was granted readily.

"You can deliver the message by word of mouth," said one of the generals; "it would be too cruel a jest to put it in writing, and perhaps our dignity would suffer also."

I was not thinking so much of the jest as of another plan I had in mind.

I found Whitestone keeping faithful watch at the tent.

"Well," said he, with a croak that he meant for a laugh of sarcasm, "I suppose the generals fell on your neck and embraced you with delight when you told them what to do."

"They did not fall on my neck, but certainly they were very much delighted," I said; "and they are going to do everything I told them to do."

"That's right," said Whitestone. "Keep it up. While you're spinning a yarn, spin a good one."

"It's just as I say," I said, "and as the first proof of it, I am going to take the prisoner as a present to Burgoyne."

Turning my back on the worthy sergeant, I entered the tent, and found Albert reclining on a blanket, the expression of chagrin still on his face. To tell the truth, I did not feel at all sorry for him, for, as I have said before, Albert had been a great care to me.

"Get up," I said with a roughness intended, "and come with me."

"What are they going to do with me?" asked Albert. "They can't hang me as a spy; I was taken in full uniform."

"Nobody wants to hang you, or do you any other harm," I said. "In your present lively and healthful condition you afford us too much amusement. We do not see how either army could spare you. Put your hat on and come on."

He followed very obediently and said nothing. He knew I held the whip hand over him.

"Sergeant," I said to Whitestone, "you need not watch any longer, since the tent is empty."

Then I took Albert away without another word. I had it in mind to punish Whitestone, who was presuming a little on his age and experience and his services to me.

I really could not help laughing to myself as I went along. This would make the third time I had entered Burgoyne's camp as an escort once with Chudleigh, once with Albert's sister and mother, and now with Albert. I was fast getting to be at home in either camp. I began to feel a bit of regret at the prospect of Burgoyne's speedy surrender, which would break up all these pleasant little excursions.

Albert showed surprise when he saw us leaving our camp and going toward Burgoyne's.

"What are you going to do?" he asked.

"Nothing, except to take you back where you belong," I said. "We don't care to be bothered with you."

"You hold me rather cheaply," he said.

"Very," I replied.

The return of Albert was an easy matter. I met a colonel, to whom I delivered him and also the message from our council. The colonel did not seem to know of Albert's intended mission, for the message puzzled him. I offered no explanations, leaving him to exaggerate it or diminish it in the transmission as he pleased.

When I turned away after our brief colloquy, I saw Kate Van Auken, which was what I had hoped for when I asked the privilege of bringing Albert back. Her paleness and look of care had increased, but again I was compelled to confess to myself that her appearance did not suffer by it. There was no change in her spirit.

"Have you become envoy extraordinary and minister plenipotentiary between the two camps, Dick?" she asked in a tone that seemed to me to be touched slightly with irony.

"Perhaps," I replied; "I have merely brought your brother back to you again, Mistress Catherine."

"We are grateful."

"This makes twice I've saved him for you," I said, "and I've brought Chudleigh back to you once. I want to say that if you have any other relatives and friends who need taking care of, will you kindly send for me?"

"You have done much for us," she said. "There is no denying it."

"Perhaps I have," I said modestly. "When I presented Chudleigh to you, you called me a fool. I suppose you are willing now to take it back."

"I was most impolite, I know, and I'm sorry—"

"Oh, you take it back, then?"

"I'm sorry that I have to regret the expression, for, Dick, that is what you are."

There was the faintest suspicion of a smile on her face, and I could not become quite as angry as I did on the first occasion. But she showed no inclination to take the harsh word back, and perforce I left very much dissatisfied.

When I returned to our camp I found much activity prevailing. It seemed to be the intention of our leaders to close in and seize the prize without further delay. No attack was to be made upon Burgoyne's camp, but the circle of fire which closed him in became broader and pressed tighter. The number of sharpshooters was doubled, and there was scarce a point in the circumference of Burgoyne's camp which they could not reach with their rifle balls, while the British could not attempt repayment without exposing themselves to destruction. Yet they held out, and we did not refuse them praise for their bravery and tenacity.

The morning after my return I said to Whitestone that I gave the British only three days longer. Whitestone shook his head.

"Maybe," he said, "and maybe not so long. They've been cut off at a new point."

I asked him what he meant.

"Why, the British are dying of thirst," he said. "They are in plain sight of the Hudson—in some places they are not more than a few yards from it—but our sharpshooters have crept up till they can sweep all the space between the British camp and the river. The British can't get water unless they cross that strip of ground, and every man that's tried to cross it has been killed."

I shuddered. I could not help it. This was war—war of the kind that wins, but I did not like it. Yet, despite my dislike, I was to take part in it, and that very soon. It was known that I was expert with the rifle, and I was ordered to choose a good weapon and join a small detachment that lay on a hill commanding the narrowest bit of ground between the British camp and the river. About a dozen of us were there, and I was not at all surprised to find Whitestone among the number. It seemed that if I went anywhere and he didn't go too, it was because he was there already.

"I don't like this, Whitestone. I don't like it a bit," I said discontentedly.

"You can shoot into the air," he said, "and it won't be any harm. There are plenty of others who will shoot to kill."

I could see that Whitestone was right about the others. Most of them were from the mountains of Virginia and Pennsylvania, backwoodsmen and trained Indian fighters, who thought it right to shoot an enemy from ambush. In truth this was a sort of business they rather enjoyed, as it was directly in their line.

As I held some official rank I was in a certain sense above the others, though I was not their commander, each man knowing well what he was about and doing what he chose, which was to shoot plump at the first human being that appeared on the dead line. A thin, active Virginian had climbed a tree in order to get a better aim, and shot with deadly effect from its boughs.

I sat down behind a clump of earth and examined my rifle.

"Look across there," said Whitestone, pointing to the open space.

I did so, and for the second time that day I shuddered. Prone upon the ground were three bodies in the well-known English uniform. A pail lay beside one of them. I knew without the telling of it that those men had fallen in their attempt to reach the water which flowed by—millions and millions of gallons—just out of reach.

"It's rather dull now; nobody's tried to pass the dead line for an hour," said Bucks, a man from the mountains of western Pennsylvania, with a face of copper like an Indian's.

"Did any one succeed in passing?" I asked.

"Pass!" said Bucks, laughing. "What do you reckon we're here for? No sirree! The river is just as full as ever."

There was an unpleasant ring in the man's voice which gave me a further distaste for the work in hand. Our position was well adapted to our task. The hill was broken with low outcroppings of stone and small ridges. So long as we exercised moderate caution we could aim and shoot in comparative safety. Bucks spoke my thoughts when he said:

"It's just like shooting deer at a salt lick."

But the dullness continued. Those red-clad bodies, two of them with their faces upturned to the sun, were a terrible warning to the others not to make the trial. Two of our men, finding time heavy, produced a worn pack of cards and began to play old sledge, their rifles lying beside them.

The waters of the broad river glittered in the sun. Now and then a fish leaped up and shot back like a flash, leaving the bubbles to tell where he had gone. The spatter of musketry around the circle of the British camp had become so much a habit that one noticed it only when it ceased for the time. The white rings of smoke from the burnt powder floated away, peaceful little clouds, and, like patches of snow against the blue sky, helped out the beauty of an early autumn day.

All of us were silent except the two men playing cards. I half closed my eyes, for the sun was bright and the air was warm, and gave myself up to lazy, vague thought. I was very glad that we had nothing to do, and even should the time to act come, I resolved that I would follow Whitestone's hint.

The two men playing cards became absorbed in the game. One threw down a card and uttered a cry of triumph.

"Caught your Jack!"

"All right," said the other; "it's only two for you, your low, Jack against my high, game. I'm even with you."

I became interested. I was lying on my back with my head on a soft bunch of turf. I raised up a little that I might see these players, who could forget such a business as theirs in a game of cards. Their faces were sharp and eager, and when they picked up the cards I could tell by their expression whether they were good or bad.

"Four and four," said one, "and this hand settles the business. Five's the game."

The other began to deal the cards, but a rifle was fired so close to my ear that the sound was that of a cannon. The echo ceasing, I heard Bucks and the man in the tree swearing profusely at each other.

"He's mine, I tell you!" said Bucks.

"It was my bullet that did it!" said the man in the tree with equal emphasis.

"I guess it was both of you," put in Whitestone. "You fired so close together I heard only one shot, but I reckon both bullets counted."

This seemed to pacify them. I looked over the little ridge of earth before us, and saw a fourth red-clad body lying on the greensward near the river. It was as still as the others.

"He made a dash for the water," said Whitestone, who caught my eye, "but the lead overtook him before he was halfway."

The two men put aside their cards, business being resumed; but after this attempt we lay idle a long time. Bucks, who had an infernal zeal, never took his eyes off the greensward save to look at the priming of his gun.

"I could hit the mark at least twenty yards farther than that," he said to me confidently.

Noon came, and I hoped I would be relieved of this duty, but it was not so. It seemed that it would be an all-day task. The men took some bread and cold meat from their pouches and we ate. When the last crumb fell, a man appeared at the edge of the greensward and held up his hands. Bucks's finger was already on the trigger of his gun, but I made him stop. The man's gesture meant something, and, moreover, I saw that he was unarmed. I called also to the Virginian in the tree to hold his fire.

I thought I knew the meaning of the pantomime. I took my rifle and turned the muzzle of it to the earth so conspicuously that the Englishman, who was holding up his hands, could not fail to see. When he saw, he advanced boldly, and laying hold of one of the bodies dragged it away. He returned for a second, and a third, and then a fourth, and when he had taken the last he did not come back again.

"That's a good job well done!" I said with much relief when the last of the fallen men had been taken away. It was much pleasanter to look at the greensward now, since there was no red spot upon it. I said to Whitestone that I thought the English would not make the trial again.

"They will," he replied. "They must have water, and maybe they don't know even yet what kind of riflemen we have."

Whitestone was right. In a half hour a man appeared protecting his body with a heavy board as long as himself. He moved with slowness and awkwardness, but two or three bullets fired into the board seemed to make no impression.

"At any rate, if he reaches the river and gets back all right it's too slow a way to slake the thirst of many," said Whitestone in the tone of a philosopher.

Bucks's face puffed out with anger.

"They mustn't get a drop!" he said with the freedom of a backwoodsman. "We're to keep 'em from it; that's what we're here for."

The man looked fierce in his wrath and I did not reprove him, for after all he was right, though not very polite.

The man in the tree fired, and a tiny patch of red cloth flew into the air. The bullet had cut his clothes, but it could not reach the man, who continued to shamble behind his board toward the river.

"I'm afraid we won't be able to stop him," I said to Bucks.

Bucks had crawled to the edge of the hill and was watching with the ferocity and rancor of a savage for a chance to shoot. Often I think that these men who live out in the forests among the savages learn to share their nature.

I could not see because of the board, but I guessed that the man carried a bucket, or pail, in one hand. In truth I was right, for presently a corner of the pail appeared, and it was struck instantly by a bullet from the rifle of the man in the tree.

"At any rate, we've sprung a leak in his pail for him," said Whitestone.

I began to take much interest in the matter. Not intending it, I felt like a hunter in pursuit of a wary animal. My scruples were forgotten for the moment. I found myself sighting along the barrel of my rifle seeking a shot. The Englishman had ceased for me to be a human being like myself. I caught a glimpse of a red-coat sleeve at the edge of the board and would have fired, but as my finger touched the trigger it disappeared and I held back. Whitestone was at my shoulder, the same eagerness showing on his face. The man in the tree had squirmed like a snake far out on the bough, and was seeking for a shot over the top of the board.

The Englishman trailed himself and his protecting board along, and was within a yard of the water. Over the earthwork at the edge of the British camp the men were watching him. His friends were as eager for his success as we were to slay him. It was a rivalry that incited in us a stronger desire to reach him with the lead. In such a competition a man's life becomes a very small pawn. For us the Englishmen had become a target, and nothing more.

Bucks was the most eager of us. He showed his teeth like a wolf.

The Englishman reached the water and stooped over to fill his pail. Bending, he forgot himself and thrust his head beyond the board. With a quickness that I have never seen surpassed, Bucks threw up his rifle and fired. The Englishman fell into the water as dead as a stone, and, his board and his pail falling too, floated off down the stream.

I uttered a cry of triumph, and then clapped my hand in shame. over my mouth. The water pulling at the Englishman's body took it out into the deeper stream, and it too floated away.

The zest of the chase was gone for me in an instant, and I felt only a kind of pitying horror. Never before in my life had I been assigned to work so hateful.

Bucks crawled back all a-grin. I turned my back to him while he received the praise of the man in the tree. It was evident to me that nobody could cross the dead line in the face of such sharpshooters, and I hoped the British saw the fact as well as we.

Our enemies must have been very hard pressed, for after a while another man tried the risk of the greensward. He came out only a few feet, and when a bullet clipped right under his feet he turned and fled back, which drew some words of scorn from Bucks, but which seemed to me to be a very wise and timely act.

I thought that this would be the last trial, but Whitestone again disagreed with me.

"When men are burning up with thirst and see a river full of water running by, they'll try mighty hard to get to that river," he said.

The sergeant's logic looked good, but for a full hour it failed. I felt sleepy, again, but was aroused by the man in the tree dropping some twigs, one of which struck me in the face.

"They're going to try it again," he said.

As I have remarked, we could see a small earthwork which the British had thrown up, and whoever tried to pass the dead line would be sure to come from that point. The man in the tree had a better view than we, and I guessed that he saw heads coming over the earthwork.

Among our men was a slight bustle that told of preparation, a last look at the flints, a shoving forward for a better position. I looked at my own rifle, but I resolved that I would not allow zeal to overcome me again. I would remember Whitestone's suggestion and fire into the air, leaving the real work to Bucks and the others, who would be glad enough to do it. I saw the flutter of a garment at the earthwork and some one came over. The man on the bough above me uttered a cry, to which I gave the echo. All the blood in me seemed to rush to my head.

Kate Van Auken, carrying a large bucket in her hand, stepped upon the greensward and walked very calmly toward the river, not once turning her eyes toward the hill where she knew the sharpshooters lay. Behind her came a strapping, bare-armed Englishwoman, who looked like a corporal's wife, and then four more women, carrying buckets or pails.

Bucks raised his rifle and began to take aim.

I sprang up and dashed his rifle aside. I am afraid I swore at him too. I hope I did.

"What are you about, Bucks?" I cried. "Would you shoot a woman?"

"Mr. Shelby," he replied very coolly, "we're put here to keep the British from that water, man or woman. What's a woman's life to the fate of a whole army? You may outrank me, but you don't command me in this case, and I'm going to shoot."

I stooped down and with a sudden movement snatched the gun from his grasp.

"Don't mind it, Bucks," said the man in the tree; "I'll shoot."

"If you do," I cried, "I'll put a bullet through you the next moment."

"And if you should chance to miss," said Whitestone, coming up beside me, "I've a bullet in my gun for the same man."

The man in the tree was no martyr, nor wanting to be, and he cried out to us that he would not shoot. In proof of it he took his gunstock from his shoulder. The other men did nothing, waiting upon my movements.

"Bucks," I said, "if I give you your gun, do you promise not to shoot at those women?"

"Do you take all the responsibility?"

"Certainly."

"Give me my gun. I won't use it."

I handed him his rifle, which he took in silence. I don't think Bucks was a bad man, merely one borne along by an excess of zeal. He has thanked me since for restraining him. The women, Kate still leading them, filled their buckets and pails at the river and walked back to the camp with the same calm and even step. Again and again was this repeated, and many a fever-burnt throat in the besieged camp must have been grateful. I felt a glow when I sent a messenger to our colonel with word of what I had done and he returned with a full indorsement. How could our officers have done otherwise?

I was sorry I could not get a better view of Kate Van Auken's face. But she never turned it our way. Apparently she was ignorant of our existence, though, of course, it was but a pretense, and she knew that a dozen of the best marksmen in America lay on the hill within easy range of her comrades and herself.

"There's but one thing more for you to do, Mr. Shelby," whispered Whitestone.

"What's that?"

"Save the life of madame, her mother. She's the only one yet unsaved by you."

"I will, Whitestone," I replied, "if I get the chance."

After a while, though late, the women ceased to come for the water. Presently the sun went down and that day's work was done.

My belief that Chudleigh was a very fortunate man was deepening.

CHAPTER 21 The Messenger

I rose early the next morning, and my first wish was for duties other than keeping the enemy away from the water. I found Whitestone sitting on his camp blanket and smoking his pipe with an expression of deep-seated content.

"What are we to do to-day?" I asked him, for Whitestone usually knew everything.

"I haven't heard of anything," he replied. "Maybe we'll rest. We deserve it, you and I."

Whitestone has some egotism, though I do not undertake to criticise him for it.

It seemed that he was right, for we were like two men forgotten, which is a pleasant thing sometimes in the military life. Finding that we had nothing else to do, we walked toward the British camp, which, as a matter of course, was the great object of curiosity for all of us, and sat down just within the line of our sharpshooters. The zeal and activity of these gentlemen had relaxed in no particular, and the crackle of their rifles was a most familiar sound in our ears.

We had a good position and could note the distressed look of the British camp. The baggage wagons were drawn up with small reference to convenience and more to defense. The house, the cellar of which I knew to be inhabited by women, children, and severely wounded men, was so torn by cannon balls that the wind had a fair sweep through it in many places. Some of the soldiers walking about seemed to us at the distance to be drooping and dejected. Yet they made resistance, and their skirmishers were replying to ours, though but feebly.

While I was watching the house I saw three or four officers in very brilliant uniforms come out. After a few steps they stopped and stood talking together with what seemed to be great earnestness. These men were generals, I was sure; their uniforms indicated it, and I guessed they had been holding conference. It must be a matter of importance or they would not stop on their way from it to talk again. I directed Whitestone's attention, but he was looking already.

"Something's up," I said. "Maybe they are planning an attack upon us."

"Not likely," he replied. "It may be something altogether different."

I knew what was running through his mind, and I more than half agreed with him.

The generals passed into a large tent, which must have been that of Burgoyne himself; but in a minute or two an officer came and took his way toward our camp. He was a tall, fine fellow, rather young, and bore himself with much dignity. Of a certainty he had on his finest uniform, for he was dressed as if for the eye of woman. His epaulets and his buttons flashed back the sun's rays, and his coat was a blaze of scarlet.

The officer drew the attention of other eyes than Whitestone's and mine. In the British camp they seemed to know what he was about, or guessed it. I could see the people drawing together in groups and looking at him, and then speaking to each other, which always indicates great interest. An officer with gray hair whom he passed looked after him, and then covered his face with his hands.

The officer came on with a steady and regular step to the earthwork, where he paused for a moment.

"It may be," said Whitestone, "that you and I were the first to see the beginning of a great event."

The officer stepped upon the earthwork, raising a piece of white cloth in his hand. The fire of the sharpshooters ceased with such suddenness that my ear, accustomed to the sound, was startled at the lack of it.

"I think you've guessed right," I said to Whitestone.

He made no reply, but drew a deep breath at his pipe stem, and then let the smoke escape in a long white curl.

Some of the sharpshooters stepped from covert and looked curiously at the approaching officer.

"Whitestone," I said, "since there is no committee of reception, let us make ourselves one."

He took his pipe from his mouth and followed me. The murmur of the camps, the sound made by the voices of many men, increased. The officer came rapidly. Whitestone and I walked very slowly. He saw us, and, noting my subaltern's uniform, took me for one dispatched to meet him.

When he came very near I saw that his face was frozen into the haughty expression of a man who wishes to conceal mortification. He said at once that he wished to see our commander in chief, and without question Whitestone and I took him to our colonel, who formed his escort to the tent of our commander in chief. Then we returned to our former place near the outposts.

"How long do you think it will take to arrange it?" I asked Whitestone.

"A day or two, at least," he said. "The British will talk with as long a tongue as they can, hoping that Clinton may come yet, and, even if he don't, there will be many things to settle."

Whitestone was right, as he so often was. The generals soon met to talk, and we subalterns and soldiers relaxed. The rifles were put to rest, and I learned how little we hate our enemies sometimes. I saw one of our sentinels giving tobacco to a British sentinel, and they were swapping news over a log. Some officers sent in medicines for the wounded. No longer having fear of bullets, I walked up to the British outworks and looked over them into the camp. A Hessian sentinel shook his gun at me and growled something in his throaty tongue. I laughed at him, and he put his gun back on his shoulder. I strolled on, and some one hailed me with a familiar voice. It was Albert Van Auken.

"Hello, Dick!" said he. "Have you folks surrendered yet? How long are these preliminaries to last?"

He was looking quite fresh and gay, and, if the truth be told, I was glad to see him.

"No," I replied, "we have not surrendered yet, and we may change our minds about it."

"That would be too bad," he replied, "after all our trouble—after defeating you in battle, and then hemming you in so thoroughly as we have done."

"So it would," I said. "Sit down and talk seriously. Are your mother and sister well?"

"Well enough," he replied, "though badly frightened by your impertinent cannon balls."

He sat down on a mound of earth thrown up by British spades, and I came quite close to him. Nobody paid any attention to us.

"How goes it with Captain Chudleigh?" I asked.

"Poor Chudleigh!" said Albert. "He's lying in the cellar over there, with a ball through his shoulder sent by one of your infernal sharpshooters."

"Is it bad?" I asked.

"Yes, very," he replied. "He may live, or he may die. Kate's nursing him."

Well, at any rate, I thought, Chudleigh is fortunate in his nurse; there would have been no such luck for me. But I kept the thought to myself.

"Albert," I asked, "what did your officers say to you when I brought you back?"

"Dick," he replied, "let's take an oath of secrecy on that point even from each other."

For his part he kept the oath.

I could not withhold one more gibe.

"Albert," I asked, "what do you Tories say now to the capture of an entire British army by us ragged Continentals?"

He flushed very red.

"You haven't done it," he replied. "Clinton will come yet."

We talked a little further, and then he went back into his camp.

The talk of the generals lasted all that day and the next, and was still of spirit and endurance on the third. We soldiers and subalterns, having little to do, cultivated the acquaintance of the enemy whom we had fought so long. Some very lively conversations were carried on across the earthworks, though, of course, we never went into their camp, nor did they come into ours.

On the third day, when I turned away after exchanging some civilities with a very courteous Englishman, I met a common-looking man whose uniform was a Continental coat, distressingly ragged and faded, the remainder of his costume being of gray homespun. He nodded as he passed me, and strolled very close to the British lines. In fact, he went so close that he seemed to me to intend going in. Thinking he was an ignorant fellow who might get into trouble by such an act, I hailed him and demanded where he was going.

He came back, and laughed in a sheepish way.

"I thought it was no harm," he said.

"I have no doubt you meant none," I said, "but you must not go into their camp."

He bowed very humbly and walked away. His submission so ready and easy attracted my notice, for our soldiers were of a somewhat independent character. I watched him, and noticed that he walked in the swift, direct manner of a man who knows exactly where he is going. Being a bit curious, and having nothing else in particular to do, I followed him at a convenient distance.

He moved three or four hundred yards around the circle of our camp until he came to a place beyond sight of that at which I had stood when I hailed him. The same freedom and ease of communication between the two armies prevailed there.

My man sauntered up in the most careless way, looking about him in the inquisitive fashion of a rustic soldier; but I noted that his general course, however much it zigzagged, was toward the British. I came up much closer. He was within a yard of the British lines and our men were giving him no heed. I felt sure that in a few moments more, if no one interfered, he would be in the British camp. I stepped forward and called to him.

He started in a manner that indicated alarm, and, of course, recognized my face, which he had seen scarce two minutes before. I asked him very roughly why he was trying so hard to steal into the British camp.

"It's true," he said, "I was trying to go in there, but I have a good excuse."

I demanded his excuse.

"I have a brother in there, a Tory," he said, "and I've heard that he's wounded. Everybody says Burgoyne will surrender in a few hours, and I thought it no harm to go in and see my brother."

What he said seemed reasonable. I could readily understand his anxiety on his brother's account. He spoke with such an air of sincerity that I had no heart to scold him; so I told him not to make the attempt again, and if the tale that Burgoyne was to surrender in a few hours was true, he would not have long to wait.

Yet I had a small suspicion left, and I decided to humor it. If there was anything wrong about the man he would watch me, I knew, after two such encounters. I wandered back into our camp as if I had nothing on my mind, though I did not lose sight of him. Among crowds of soldiers there I had the advantage of him, for I could see him and he could not see me.

He idled about a while, and then began to move around the circle of our camp inclosing the British camp. I was glad that I had continued to watch him. Either this man was overwhelmingly anxious about his brother, or he had mischief in mind. I followed him, taking care that he should not see me. Thus engaged, I met Whitestone, who told me something, though I did not stop to hold converse with him about it, not wishing to lose my man.

The fellow made a much wider circle than before, and frequently looked behind him; but he stopped at last and began to approach the British line. There was nobody, at least from our army, within thirty or forty yards of him except myself, and by good luck I was able to find some inequalities of the ground which concealed me.

A British sentinel was standing in a lazy attitude, and my man approached and hailed him in a friendly manner. The Englishman replied in the same tone.

"Can I go in there?" asked the man, pointing to the British camp.

"You can go in," replied the sentinel with some humor, "but you can't come out again."

"I don't want to come out again," replied the man.

"You chose a curious time to desert," said the sentinel with a sneer, "but it's none of my business."

The man was about to enter, but I stepped forward quickly, drawing my pistol as I did so. He saw me and raised his hand, as if he too would draw a weapon, but I had him under the muzzle of my pistol and threatened to shoot him if he made resistance. Thereupon he played the part of wisdom and was quiet.

"I will take care of this deserter," I said to the English sentinel.

"I told him it was none of my business, and I tell you the same," the sentinel said, shrugging his shoulders. "We're not fighting now. Only don't shoot the poor devil."

"March!" I said to the man, still covering him with my pistol.

"Where?" he asked.

"To the little clump of woods yonder," I said. "I have something to say to you."

The fellow had hard, strong features, and his countenance did not fall.

He wheeled about and marched toward the wood. I followed close behind, the pistol in my hand. I had chosen my course with my eyes open. Our people were not near, and we reached the trees without interruption or notice. In their shelter the man turned about.

"Well, what do you want?" he asked in sullen, obstinate tones.

"Your papers," I said; "the message you were trying to carry into the British camp."

"I have no papers; I was not trying to carry anything into the British camp," he replied, edging a little closer.

"Keep off!" I said, foreseeing his intent. "If you come an inch nearer I will put a pistol ball through you. Stand farther away!"

He stepped back.

"Now give me that letter, or whatever you have," I said. "It is useless to deny that you have something. If you don't give it to me, I will take you into the camp and have you stripped and searched by the soldiers. It will be better for you to do as I say."

Evidently he believed me, for he thrust his hand inside his waistcoat and pulled out a crumpled letter, which he handed to me. Keeping one eye on him I read the letter with the other eye, and found I had not been deceived in my guess. It was from Sir Henry Clinton to Sir John Burgoyne, telling him to hold out for certain rescue. Sir Henry said he was within a short distance of Albany with a strong force, and expected to join Sir John soon and help him crush all the rebel forces.

"This is important," I said.

"Very," said the man.

"It might have changed the fate of the campaign had you reached General Burgoyne with it," I said.

"Undoubtedly it would have done so," he replied.

"Well, it wouldn't."

"That is a matter of opinion."

"Not at all."

"I don't understand you."

"The campaign is ended. Burgoyne surrendered a half hour ago."

Which was true, for Whitestone, with his skill in finding out things before other people, had told me.

"I'm very sorry," said the man in tones of sharp disappointment.

"I'm not," I said.

"What do you mean to have done with me?" he asked—"hanging, or shooting?"

I did not admire the man, but I respected his courage.

"Neither," I replied. "You can't do any harm now. Be off!"

He looked surprised, but he thanked me and walked away.

It was unmilitary, but it has always been approved by my conscience, for which I alone am responsible.

CHAPTER 22 Capitulations

I stood with Whitestone and saw the British lay down their arms, and, of all the things I saw on that great day, an English officer with the tears dropping down his face impressed me most.

We were not allowed to exult over our enemies, nor did we wish it; but I will not deny that we felt a great and exhilarating triumph. Before the war these Englishmen had denied to us the possession of courage and endurance as great as theirs. They had called us the degenerate descendants of Englishmen, and one of their own generals, who had served with us in the great French and Indian war, and who should have known better, had boasted that with five thousand men he could march from one end of the colonies to the other. Now, more than five thousand of their picked men were laying down their arms to us, and as many more had fallen, or been taken on their way from Canada to Saratoga.

I repeat that all these things—the taunts and revilings of the English, who should have been the last to cheapen us—had caused much bitterness in our hearts, and I assert again that our exultation, repressed though it was, had full warrant. Even now I feel this bitterness sometimes, though I try to restrain it, for the great English race is still the great English race, chastened and better than it was then, I hope and believe.

Remembering all these things, I say that we behaved well on that day, and our enemies, so long as they told the truth, could find no fault with us.

There was a broad meadow down by the riverside, and the British, company after company, filed into this meadow, laid down their arms, and then marched, prisoners, into our lines. Our army was not drawn up that it might look on, yet Whitestone and I stood where we could see.

Some women, weary and worn by suspense and long watches, came across the meadow, but Kate Van Auken was not among them. I guessed that she was by the side of the wounded Chudleigh. When the last company was laying down its arms, I slipped away from Whitestone and entered the British camp.

I found Chudleigh in a tent, where they had moved him from the cellar that he might get the fresher air. Kate, her mother, and an English surgeon were there. The surgeon had just fastened some fresh bandages over the wound. Chudleigh was stronger and better than I had expected to find him. He even held out his hand to me with the smile of one who has met an enemy and respects him.

"I will be all right soon, Shelby," he said, "so the doctor tells me, if you rebels know how to treat a wounded prisoner well."

"In a month Captain Chudleigh will be as well as he ever was," said the surgeon.

I was very glad on Kate's account. Presently she walked out of the tent, and I followed her.

"Kate," I asked, "when will the marriage occur?"

"What marriage?" she asked very sharply.

"Yours and Chudleigh's."

"Never!"

"What!" I exclaimed in surprise. "Are you not going to marry Chudleigh?"

"No."

"Are you not betrothed to him?"

"No. That was my mother's plan for me."

"Are you not in love with him?"

"No."

I was silent a moment.

"Kate," I asked, "what does this mean?"

"Dick," she said, "I have told you twice what you are."

Her cheeks were all roses.

"Kate," I said, "love me."

"I will not!"

"Be my betrothed?"

"I will not!"

"Marry me?"

"I will not!"

Which refusals she made with great emphasis—every one of which she took back.

She was a woman.

THE END.

BOOK TWO

IN HOSTILE RED

A ROMANCE OF THE MONMOUTH CAMPAIGN

(A Revolutionary War Novel)

(The **Battle of Monmouth** was an American Revolutionary War battle fought on June 28, 1778 in Monmouth County, New Jersey.)

CHAPTER ONE—*In Hostile Red*

"Captain the Honorable Charles Montague, eldest son and heir to Lord George Montague, of Bridgewater Hall, Yorkshire, England," said Marcel, reading the letters, "and Lieutenant Arthur Melville, son to Sir Frederick William Melville, of Newton-on-the-Hill, Staffordshire, England. Those names sound well, don't they, eh, Chester? They roll like the Delaware."

I could not restrain a smile at the prim and choppy way in which Marcel pronounced the names and titles, just as if he were calling the roll of our company. Nevertheless, I wished to hide it, feeling some sympathy for the two young Englishmen because of the grievous state into which they had fallen. As they stood a bit apart from us, they preserved the seeming of dignity, but in truth it was apparent that beneath this cloak they were sore troubled in mind; and well they had a right to be. It was a hard fate to come all the way across the ocean with letters of high recommendation to one's commander-in-chief, only to fall into the hands of the enemy, letters and all, with the place of destination almost in sight.

"They should have stood very high in the graces of Sir William Howe had they reached Philadelphia," said Marcel, "for here are letters from some of the greatest men in England, descanting upon their military merits. Perhaps, Chester, we have saved the Thirteen Colonies with this little achievement, you and I. Because, if everything in these letters be true—and it is not for me to criticise the veracity of the writers,—one of our prisoners must be an Alexander at the very least, and the other a Hannibal."

Marcel had a sprightly humor, and one could never tell how it was going to show itself. But he was not given to malice, and he spoke the latter words in a tone that the Englishmen could not hear.

"Chester," he resumed, drawing me a little farther to one side, "these young gentlemen, barring their mischance of falling into our hands, seem to be veritable pets of fortune. They are rich, of high station, and they come to join a powerful army which has all the resources of war at its command. And look at their raiment, Chester; look at their raiment, I say!"

In good truth, they were apparelled in most comfortable and seemly fashion. There is always a brave dash of color and adornment about the uniform of the British officer, and our prisoners had omitted nothing.

"Now look at our own attire," said Marcel, in tones of the utmost melancholy.

Of a verity, there was cause for his melancholy; the contrast was most piteous. Time and hard wear had played sad tricks with our regimentals, and, what was worse, we knew not when or how we were to replace them.

"I see not why we should grieve over it," I said. "The matter cannot be helped, and we must make the best of it we can."

"Perhaps," replied Marcel, fingering the letters meditatively. Then he turned and said with much politeness to Captain Montague,—

"I believe you stated that you and your friend are complete strangers to Sir William and his army?"

"Yes," replied Captain Montague; "we have no acquaintance with them at all, and we fear that the unlucky capture of us you have effected will prevent us from making any very soon."

"It was mere chance, and no fault of yours, that threw you into our hands," said Marcel, very courteously; "and it may save you from being killed on the battle-field, which fate I would take to be somewhat unpleasant."

Then he drew me aside again.

"Chester," he said, assuming his most weighty manner, "sit down on this tree-trunk. I wish to hold converse with you for a moment or two."

I occupied the designated seat and waited for him to speak, knowing that he would take his own good time about it.

"Chester," he said, the solemnity of his tone unchanged, "you know what I am."

"Yes," I replied; "by descent three parts French and one part Irish, by birth South Carolinian; therefore wholly irresponsible."

"Quite true," he replied; "and you are by descent three parts English and one part Scotch, and by birth Pennsylvanian; therefore if you were to die the world would come to an end. Now, Bob Chester, still your Quakerish soul and listen. Behold those officers! Their brave clothes and well-rounded figures, which indicate a fine and abundant diet, arouse much envy in my soul, and because of it I have taken a resolution. Now having listened, look!"

He rose and bowed low.

"Lieutenant Melville," he said, addressing himself to me, "pardon this somewhat formal and abrupt introduction, but I have heard often of your family, and I know of its ancient and honorable extraction. Perhaps my own may fairly make pretensions of a similar character. Lieutenant Melville, permit me to introduce myself. I am Captain the Honorable Charles Montague, eldest son to Lord George Montague, of Bridgewater Hall, Yorkshire. I am delighted to meet you, Lieutenant Melville, and doubly delighted to know that you also have letters to our illustrious commander-in-chief, and that we shall be comrades in arms and in glory."

"Marcel," said I, after a moment's pause, for he had taken the breath from me, "this is impossible. It would mean the halter for both of us before to-morrow night."

"Not so," he replied. "Neither of those men has a personal acquaintance in the British army. What I propose is easy enough, if we only preserve a little coolness and tact. I am tired of skulking about like a half-starved hound, and I want an adventure. It's only for a day or two. Moreover, think what valuable information we might be able to acquire in Philadelphia, and what a great service we might render to our commander-in-chief. But of course, if you are afraid to go with me, I will go alone."

So speaking, he looked at me in the most provoking manner.

Now, I hold that I am a prudent man, but the Highland fourth in my blood will get the mastery of the English three-fourths now and then, and I never would take a dare from Marcel. Besides, I had a sudden vision and I dreamed of a great service to a desperate cause, to be followed perhaps by high promotion.

"A good idea," I said. "We will go to our colonel and propose it at once."

Marcel laughed, and his manner became more provoking than ever.

"And be called a fool for your trouble," he said. "Now is your chance or not at all. Come, Bob! Our success will bring our pardon. At this moment the way of a true patriot lies there."

He pointed toward Philadelphia, and his words were most tempting.

"Very well," I said; "if you go alone you will surely be detected and hanged as a spy. Since it is necessary for me to go with you to save you, I'll have to do it."

"It is most kind of you," said Marcel; "and then if we must hang it will be pleasanter for us to hang together."

We beckoned to Sergeant Pritchard and told him our plan. He was full of astonishment and protestations. But, as he was under our command, he could do naught but obey.

The two young Englishmen were compelled to retire behind some trees and divest themselves of their fine clothes, which we donned, giving them our rags in return. All the letters and other documents that we found in their possession we put in our pockets. Then we mounted their sleek, fat horses and turned our heads towards Philadelphia.

"Sergeant Pritchard," I said, "look well to the prisoners, and see that they do not escape ere we return."

"Then they will never escape," he said. "Lieutenant Chester, you and Lieutenant Marcel could find better ways to die. I beg you to come back."

"Sergeant Pritchard," said Marcel, "we will do you the honor of dining with you, at your expense, one month from to-day. Meanwhile report to our colonel the nature of the errand upon which we are now going."

Then we bowed low to the gentlemen whose clothes we wore, and galloped off towards Philadelphia.

One can become intoxicated without drinking, and the air was so brilliant and buoyant that I think it got into our heads and created in us an unusual measure of high spirits. Moreover, we were so nobly clad and had such good horses under us that we felt like gentlemen of quality for the first time in many long and weary months. We galloped at a great rate for a half-hour, and then when we pulled our horses down to a walk Marcel turned a satisfied smile upon me.

"Lieutenant Melville, allow me to congratulate you upon the make and set of your uniform," he said with extreme politeness. "It is in truth most becoming to you, and I dare say there is no officer in the service of our gracious Majesty King George who could present a finer appearance or prove himself more worthy of his commission."

"A thousand thanks, Captain Montague," I replied. "Such a compliment from an officer of your critical discernment and vast experience is in truth most grateful. Permit me to add, without attempting to flatter you, that you yourself make a most imposing and military figure. May these perverse rebels soon give us both a chance to prove our valor and worth!"

"The warlike words of a warrior," said Marcel. "And it seemeth to me, Lieutenant Melville, that the warrior is worthy of his wage. The country about us is fair. There are hills and dales and running streams and woodland and pasture. I doubt not that when all the rebels are hanged and their goods confiscated, the king will allot brave estates to us for our most faithful services. It will be very pleasant to each of us, Lieutenant Melville, to have fair acres in this country to add to what we may have some day in England. See that tall hill afar to the right. I think I will rear my mansion upon its crest. That curtain of wood on the slope there will make a lordly pad, while my lands will roll back for miles."

"And I trust that I shall be your neighbor, Captain Montague," I replied, "for, behold, to the left is another hill, upon which a noble building shall rise, the home of the famous soldier General Melville, Duke of Pennsylvania."

Then we threw our heads back and laughed like two boys out for a frolic.

"There is one thing that both of us must bear in mind, Lieutenant Melville," said Marcel, presently.

"What is that?" I asked.

"We must not forget the tragic end of two young American officers whom we knew, Lieutenant Robert Chester, of Pennsylvania, and Lieutenant Philip Marcel, of South Carolina."

"Ah! their fate was sad, very sad," I said.

Marcel put his face in his hands and appeared to weep.

"They departed this life very suddenly," he said, "about ten o'clock of a fine morning, on the 8th of May, 1778, in his Britannic Majesty's province of Pennsylvania, about fifteen miles east of his most loyal city of Philadelphia. The witnesses of their sudden and sorrowful demise were Sergeant Pritchard, four privates in the rebel service, and two young British officers who had just been captured by the aforesaid rebels. But such, alas, are the chances of war; we must even weep their fate, for they were so young and so ingenuous! Lieutenant Melville, will you weep with me?"

We bowed our heads and wept.

"Suppose the English officers should ask us about England and our homes and kin?" I said to Marcel. "How could we answer them without at once convicting ourselves?"

"That will be easy enough," replied Marcel, gayly. "We have brains, haven't we? And if any impertinent fellow becomes too inquisitive we can do as the Connecticut man does: we can answer a question with a question of our own. Besides, there is plenty of information in these letters that we have captured, and we can study them."

We were now approaching the British lines, but were still in a region that might be called doubtful ground, since parties from either army scouted and foraged over it.

I suggested that we halt in the shade of a convenient grove and examine the letters again with minute care, rehearsing them in order that we might be perfectly familiar with their contents. This we did, and then each tested the knowledge of the other, like a pedagogue questioning his pupil.

"I think we'll do," said Marcel. "Even if we were to lose the letters, we can remember everything that is in them."

"That being granted," I replied, "I propose that we push on at once for Philadelphia. I am amazingly hungry, and I have heard that the rations of the British officers are a delight to the stomach."

We mounted our horses and rode leisurely on. As we were drawing near to the city we expected to meet scouting or skirmishing parties, and we were not subjected to disappointment.

Presently, as our road wound around a hill we heard a clanking of spurs and the jabber of voices. Through some trees we could see bits of sunshine reflected from the metal of guns.

"A British scouting or foraging party," said Marcel. "Now, Bob, remember that we are to carry it off like two young lords, and are to be as weighty of manner as if we equalled Sir William Howe himself in rank."

We shook up our horses, and they trotted forward, Marcel and I assuming an air of ease and indifference. A dozen troopers came into our view. They were rather a begrimed and soiled lot, and it was quite evident to us that they had been on a foraging expedition, for one of them carried chickens and turkeys, and another had a newly slain pig resting comfortably across his saddle-bow. The leader seemed to be a large swart man who rode in front and clutched a squawking hen in his left hand.

"They're Americans! They're of our own side, by Jupiter!" exclaimed Marcel. "We'll warn them that this is dangerous ground and that they may meet the enemy at any moment."

So we whipped up our horses and galloped forward with this benevolent purpose in view.

But, to our great amazement and to our equal indignation, the large man drew a horse-pistol of a bigness proportioned to his own, and fired point-blank at us. I heard three or four slugs whizzing in a most uncomfortable manner past my head, and, thinking it was time to stop, drew back my horse with a jerk.

"The confounded whipper-snapper dandies!" exclaimed the big man with the pistol. "Would they dare to ride us down! At them, lads, and knock them off their horses!"

"Stop! stop!" shouted Marcel. "What do you mean by attacking your own countrymen and comrades?"

But his only answer was a shout of derision and the cocking of pistols. Then I remembered that we were clad in the British uniform. The Americans might well believe that our protestations of friendship were but a sham. In truth, they could scarce be expected to believe aught else. With a quick and powerful jerk of the rein I wheeled my horse about. Marcel did likewise, and away we galloped, our countrymen hot at our heels and their bullets whistling about us.

It was lucky for us that the foragers were well loaded up with spoil and their movements and aim thus impeded. Otherwise I think we should have been slain. But, as it was, none of their bullets struck us, and the suddenness of our flight gave us a good start. We bent down upon our horses' necks, in order to present as small a target as possible.

"I think we ought to stop and explain," I said to Marcel when we had galloped a few hundred yards.

"But there is no time to explain," he replied. "If we were to check our speed we would be overtaken by bullets before we could make explanation. Our uniforms, though very fine and becoming, are much against us, and even if we should escape without wounds we would be taken back as prisoners to the American army."

"Then, Captain Montague," I said, "there is naught for us to do but continue our flight to Philadelphia and escape within the lines of his Britannic Majesty's most devoted army."

"It is even so, Lieutenant Melville," returned Marcel. "How does his Grace the Duke of Pennsylvania like to be pursued thus over his own domain by these wicked rebels?"

"He likes it not at all," I replied.

"But he must even endure it," said Marcel, grinning in spite of our predicament.

We had gained somewhat upon our pursuers, but we could hear the big man encouraging the others and urging them to greater speed. It was our good fortune that the country was not obstructed by hedges or fences, and it seemed that we might escape, for our horses evidently were the fresher.

I looked back and saw the big man fifteen or twenty feet ahead of his companions. He was making great efforts to reload his pistol, but was keeping a watchful eye upon us at the same time. It was plain to me that he was filled with the ardor of the chase and would not relinquish it as long as it seemed possible to overtake us. Presently he adjusted the charge in his pistol and raised the weapon. I saw that it was aimed at me, and just as he pulled the trigger I made my horse swerve. Nevertheless I felt a smart in my left arm and uttered a short cry.

"Are you hurt?" asked Marcel, apprehensively.

"No," I replied, "not much. I think his bullet took a piece of my skin, but no more."

For all that, a fine trickle of blood that came down my left sleeve and stained my hand made me feel uneasy.

We urged our horses to greater efforts, and the spirited animals responded. We had curved about considerably in the course of our flight, but I had a good idea of the country, and I knew that we were now galloping directly towards Philadelphia. I trusted that if our pursuers were aware of this fact they would abandon the chase, which threatened soon to take them inside the British lines. But many minutes passed, and they showed no signs of stopping.

"We have our pistols," said Marcel. "We might use them."

"We cannot fire on our own countrymen," I replied.

"No," he replied, "but we can fire over their heads, and it may reduce the infernal eagerness they show in their pursuit. A bullet properly directed discourages overmuch enthusiasm."

We twisted about in our saddles and discharged our weapons as Marcel had suggested. But, unfortunately for us, our countrymen were brave and not at all afraid of our pistols. They came on as fast as ever, while our movement had checked our flight somewhat and caused us to lose ground perceptibly. We began to grow discouraged.

But in this moment of depression we saw a smudge of red across a valley, and Marcel uttered a little shout of joy.

"A rescue! A rescue, most noble duke!" he cried. "See, the British troops are coming!"

Through the valley a body of British cavalry were galloping. There were at least fifty men in the party, and evidently they had seen us before we saw them, for many of them held their sabres in their hands, and presently they raised a great shout.

Our American pursuers, seeing that they were out-numbered, turned about and took to their heels with considerable precipitation. The next moment we galloped into the middle of the British troop, and then, a curious faintness overcoming me, I slid to the ground.

Marcel, having thrown himself from his horse, was beside me in a moment, and lifted me to my feet.

"A little water, please, as soon as you can," he said to a fine stalwart officer who had also dismounted and come to my aid. "The lieutenant was wounded in a brush we had with those confounded rebels, and I fear his strength is exhausted."

"Then here is something much better for him than water," said the officer, sympathetically.

He held a canteen to my mouth, and I took a draught of as fine whiskey as I have ever tasted. It put life back into me and I was able to stand upon my feet without assistance.

A half-dozen of the British had remained with the officer who gave me the whiskey, but the others had continued the pursuit. This man, who wore the uniform of a captain, was apparently about thirty-five, and of prepossessing appearance. He looked at us inquiringly, and Marcel, who guessed the nature of his unspoken question, said,—

"My friend here, who is so unfortunate as to be wounded, is Lieutenant Arthur Melville, and I am Captain Charles Montague. We landed but lately in New York, and we undertook to come across the country to Philadelphia, for we have letters to Sir William Howe, and we wished to see active service as soon as possible."

"You seem to have had an adventure, at any rate," said the officer.

"Why, it was nothing much, only a trifle," replied Marcel, airily. "If the fellows had not been so numerous, I think we could have given a handsome account of them. Melville here, before he got his wound, popped one of them off his horse with a bullet through his head, and I think I gave another a reminder in the shoulder which he will not forget very soon. But it was lucky you came when you did, gentlemen, for they were most persistent scoundrels, and I verily believe they would have overtaken us."

"It is a pleasure to have been in time to render you assistance," said the officer. "My name is Blake, Geoffrey Blake, and I am a captain in the Guards. I am something of a surgeon, and if Lieutenant Melville will permit me I will examine his arm and discover the nature of his wound."

The hurt proved to be very slight, but I readily saw how much the manner of our entry into the British lines was in favor of our plan. We had come up full tilt, pursued by the Americans, and an American bullet had grazed my arm. The chase, after all, was a fortunate accident, for it created a vast prepossession in favor of our assumed identity.

"It was an early and rather rude welcome that the rebels gave us," said Marcel, as we were examining the wounded arm, "but I fancy that we will yet find an opportunity for revenge."

"No doubt of it! No doubt of it!" said Captain Blake. "We have not been able to bring on a general battle for some time, but their skirmishers swarm like flies around us, and nothing is safe beyond the sight of our army. It was very bold of you, gentlemen, to undertake a journey from New York to Philadelphia across a rebel-infested country."

"We thought we might have a skirmish with the rebels," said Marcel, lightly, "and we had no great objection to such an encounter: did we, eh, Melville?"

"Oh, no, not at all, so long as Captain Blake and his gallant men were at hand to rescue us," I replied.

Captain Blake bowed and regarded us with a look of great favor. I saw that we were fast establishing our reputation with our new British friends as men of dashing courage and good nature. Presently the troopers who had pursued the Americans returned and reported that they had been unable to catch them.

"They disappeared in the woods over there," said a lieutenant, "and we can discover no further traces of them. And they carried all their spoil with them, too; not a chicken, not a turkey, could we retake."

"Let them go," replied Captain Blake. "At least we have saved our friends here from capture."

"Which the aforesaid friends consider to be not the least among your achievements," said Marcel.

Captain Blake laughed good-humoredly, and then we rode into Philadelphia, Marcel and I bearing ourselves like conquering heroes and guests of honor.

CHAPTER Two—*Feeling the Way*

We made a fine cavalcade when we rode through the streets of Philadelphia. As we had stopped at the outposts in order to comply with the usual formalities, a rumor of our adventures preceded us, and, since it is not the habit of rumor to diminish the importance of things, it made notable heroes of Marcel and me. Some part of it came to our ears as we proceeded, and we found that between us we had slain at least eight rebels and had pursued a hundred others a matter of not less than ten miles.

"I fear, captain," said Marcel to Blake, "that we have achieved such a reputation for valorous conduct that we will never be able to prove the tenth part of it."

"Trust me, gentlemen, for thinking better of you than that," replied Captain Blake, who seemed to have taken a fine fancy for us. "I doubt not that both of you will be winning honors on bloody battlefields."

"If so," said Marcel, "we trust that General Blake will be there to see it."

Captain Blake, who, like most men, was not inaccessible to flattery, seemed charmed at the high promotion Marcel had conferred so readily upon him, and certain was I that we would have a fast friend in him.

"I am going to take you immediately to Sir William himself," said the captain, "as you have letters of introduction to him, and I doubt not that he will place you on his own personal staff, where you will secure fine opportunities for conspicuous service."

"I would like to see service first at a well-loaded table," whispered Marcel to me. "I was hungry before I reached Philadelphia, and the sight of all these smug and comfortable people in the streets sharpens the pangs of famine."

And in truth the people we saw were a well-fed lot, with fat cheeks and double chins, very unlike our own lean and hungry fellows, who had to fight on empty stomachs.

We arrived in a short time at the quarters of Sir William Howe, a two-story brick house that had once been a private residence, and I was somewhat astonished at the luxury and display I witnessed there. There were as many articles for ease and adornment as ever I had seen in the mansions of our most wealthy citizens, and seeing it all I did not wonder why this general should have been called "The Sluggard." It contrasted strongly with the simplicity of our own commander-in-chief's hut, and I, who had not slept under a roof in a year, felt oppressed, as if the air were too heavy for my lungs. But it was not so with Marcel, who loved his ease and basked in rich colors.

"We have made a happy change, Chester," he said to me as we waited for Sir William. "This in truth looks to be a most comfortable place, and if we do not find much enjoyment here it will be because we are men of small resources."

I was thinking of the great risks we were incurring, and made no answer. He did not notice it. He sighed in the most contented fashion, and said it was the first moment of real enjoyment he had experienced in six months. But his lazy pleasure was soon interrupted by the entrance of Sir William Howe himself. The British commander was a swart, thick man, whose plump face and figure indicated a love of good eating. His expression was indolent, and on the whole good-natured. He received us with kindness. It was evident that some one had blown our trumpet for us already: I guessed that it was Blake.

"I am delighted to see you, gentlemen," he said. "It was in truth a daring deed to ride from New York to Philadelphia, as the rebels infest the country between. It is fortunate that Lieutenant Melville escaped with so slight a wound. I should like to hear more about your adventures, gentlemen."

Then Marcel with an air of great modesty told a most remarkable story of our encounter, how we had driven the rebels back once, and had knocked two of them off their horses, but at last under stress of numbers were compelled to retreat. I took careful note of everything he said, because if the time came for me to tell the tale alone, as most like it would, mine must not vary from Marcel's in any particular. Sir William seemed to be much pleased with the story.

"That will bear retelling," he said. "I must have you two, Captain Montague and Lieutenant Melville, at our dinner to-morrow. I am to have a company here composed of my most distinguished officers and of some of our loyal friends of Philadelphia. I shall be glad for you to come, gentlemen; and do you look your best, for there will be beauty at the banquet."

Of course we accepted the invitation with great alacrity, but a shade came over Marcel's face. The general observed it with keen eye.

"What is it that you find displeasing, Captain Montague?" he asked.

Marcel hesitated, and seemed to be in a state of perplexity.

"I fear it would anger you, general, if I were to name the cause," he replied.

"Speak out! Tell me what it is. Would you rather not come? If so, have no hesitation in declaring it," said Sir William.

But the general did not appear at all pleased at the possibility of his invitation to dinner being declined by a junior officer. At which I did not wonder, for it would have savored much of disparagement, not to say impertinence.

"It is not that, general," replied Marcel, making a most graceful genuflection. "We have already derived acute pleasure in anticipation from the banquet to which you have so graciously invited us. But, general, it is the truth that we have great need of one now. General, it pains me to have to say it in your presence, but we are starving. We have not eaten for a day. Perhaps we could have contained ourselves, if you had not spoken of a feast, but that was too much for our endurance."

The general burst into a fit of great and hearty laughter. Marcel's sly impertinence, for such it was, seemed to please him.

"Starving, eh?" he exclaimed. "Then I must see that my heroes who fought the rebels so well do not perish of hunger. Britain has not yet come to such a pass that she must deny food to her soldiers. Vivian will care for you."

He called an aide of about our own age and bade him take us to the officers' mess and give us the best that was to be found. This Vivian was a talkative and agreeable young personage. We had to tell our entire story again to him, which perhaps was not a bad thing, as it was a kind of rehearsal and served to fasten the matter in our minds. I was narrator this time, and I am confident that I followed Marcel's story so well that if the two tales had been written out a reader could have found no difference in them. It is so easy to lie sometimes.

"You are caught between luncheon and dinner," said Vivian, "but I think the cook can knock up enough for you to stay the pangs of starvation."

"I trust he may," said Marcel, devoutly, "or else he will be responsible for our deaths, and that would be too heavy a weight for a regimental cook to bear."

It was evident that the cook had faced such emergencies before, as he was nobly equal to it, and we did not restrain the expression of our gratitude when we were seated at a table in the mess-room, with an imposing meat pie, an abundance of bread and vegetables, and a flagon of wine before us.

"We can do better than this when we are warned," said Vivian.

"This is ample and most comforting," I replied; and that was about the first true thing said by either Marcel or me since we had entered Philadelphia.

There was in this mess-room the same touch of luxury and adornment, though more restrained, that we had noticed at the headquarters of the general. It was evident that his Britannic Majesty's officers lived well in the good city of Philadelphia.

"Oh, why did we not come sooner?" exclaimed Marcel, with a double meaning that I alone understood.

"The rebels seem to have hurried you along fast enough," said Vivian, with a laugh.

"We hope to reverse the case soon," replied Marcel, "and become the pursuers ourselves. Meanwhile I take great comfort in demolishing this pie."

The news of our adventure had been spread very generally about headquarters, as several officers came in while we ate. They were rather a friendly lot, and some of them I liked. Blake, our first British friend, was among them.

"I wonder the rebels had the courage to pursue you," said a very callow youth named Graves.

"Don't the rebels fight well?" asked Marcel.

"Oh, no, not at all," returned Graves, superciliously. "They take to flight at the first glimpse of a British uniform."

"Then why don't you go out and show yourself, Graves?" asked Vivian; "for they say that bands of the rebels do come alarmingly close to Philadelphia."

There was a general laugh, and Graves turned almost as red as his coat.

"There is no doubt," said an older officer, named Catron, "as to our ability to crush these rebels if we could get them into a corner. But they are most cursedly sly."

"However," said I, for I was determined to defend my countrymen despite our situation, "the rebels are the weaker, and it is the business of the weaker party to avoid being pushed into a corner. And according to all the accounts that have come to England, they seem to show much skill in this particular."

"It is true," replied Catron, "but I must persist in calling it most unhandsome behavior on their part. They don't give us a chance to win any laurels, and they won't let us go home. We are kept in a condition of waiting and uncertainty which is the most unpleasant of all things."

"Well, all that will speedily come to an end," said Marcel, "for my friend Melville has arrived, and I tell you in strict confidence, gentlemen, that Melville is the fiercest warrior since Marlborough. I doubt not that the rebels, having heard of his arrival, are even now fleeing into the wilderness across the Alleghany Mountains, that they may forever be beyond the reach of his mighty arm."

The laugh went around again, and this time at my expense.

"Perhaps, if the discourteous rebels had known that I was one of the gentlemen whom they were pursuing," I said, "it might have saved my friend Captain Montague much exasperation of spirit and the loss of a most elegant military cloak that he brought from England with him. I assure you, gentlemen, that when we were compelled to take to flight the captain's beautiful cloak trailed out behind him like a streamer, and finally, a puff of wind catching it, left his shoulders entirely. I doubt not that some ragged rebel is now wearing it as a trophy. Ah, captain, it was a most beautiful cloak to lose, was it not?"

"And it was with that very cloak upon my shoulders," said Marcel, falling into the spirit of the matter, "that I expected to make conquest of some of these provincial maidens of whom report speaks in such glowing terms. Alas, what shall I do?"

"Oh, it will be easy enough to get it back," said a young officer, whose name, as I afterwards learned, was Reginald Belfort. "These rebels are a poor lot. They cannot stand before us."

Belfort was young and handsome, but his face expressed arrogance and superciliousness. I liked him but little.

"I know not much of the rebels from personal observation," I replied, not relishing his sneer, "but General Burgoyne would hardly have said that at Saratoga."

"No," commented Vivian, "for it would be somewhat severe upon General Burgoyne to be captured with all his veterans by such a poor lot of men as Belfort says the rebels are."

"You must not forget," said Catron, good-humoredly, "that Belfort thinks the rebels are inferior in blood. Belfort, as you know, gentlemen, has a lineage that dates back to the Conquest. He claims that these rebels are the descendants of peasants and out-casts, and therefore should admit their inborn and permanent inferiority."

"And such they are," said Belfort, still sneering. "They should be ruled by the gentlemen of England, and ruled by them they will be."

"What were the Normans themselves in the beginning," I asked, "but Scandinavian pirates and peasants? The ancestors of these rebels may have been peasants, but at any rate they were not pirates."

Belfort flushed, and for a moment could not answer. He knew that I had spoken the truth, as any one who reads history knows also.

"We have come to a fine pass," he said at length, "when a man who has just escaped by the speed of his horse from the rebels sets himself up as their defender."

"That may be," I replied, for I was still somewhat angry; "but I do not think it worth our while to depreciate men who have already taken an entire army of ours, and keep all our other forces cooped up in two or three large towns."

"Melville does not want to diminish the glory of the victories that we are to achieve," said Marcel, lightly. "The more valiant and the more worthy the foe, the greater one's glory to triumph over him."

"That is a very just observation," said Vivian, who seemed anxious to avoid a quarrel, "and I propose that the quality of the rebels and the amount of resistance they will offer to our conquering armies be left to the future. Such warlike questions will keep. Milder subjects better become the present."

"Then would not the dinner that the general is to give to-morrow be a fit topic?" asked young Graves.

"Our new friends are to be there," said Vivian. "You are lucky chaps, Montague, you and Melville, to be invited, so soon after your arrival, to one of Sir William's entertainments. There is not a better diner in America, or Europe either, than the commander-in-chief."

"The banquet is to be blessed by beauty too," said Graves. "Our fair ally and her renegade father are to be there. Oh, but Sir William keeps a sharp eye on the old scoundrel, and well he deserves to be watched thus."

"I beg to avow ignorance of whom you mean," I said, my curiosity aroused. "You must remember that Montague and I have arrived but within the day and know not the great personages of Philadelphia."

"By 'old renegade' we mean John Desmond, merchant and money-lender of this city, who it is said has more wealth than any other man in all this rich colony, ay, even enough to set up a mighty estate in England, if he so chose," replied Vivian; "and by 'our fair ally' we mean his daughter Mary, as fine and fair a woman as these two eyes ever gazed upon. The old Desmond leans to the rebels, and 'tis said would help them with his money if he dared, while the daughter is all for us, as she should be, being a born subject of our liege King George, God bless him. And 'tis reported that it might go hard with the old rebel, but some of his sins are forgiven him for the sake of his loyal and lovely daughter."

I had not heard of the daughter before, but the name of the father was known to me. Secret assistance of money had reached our camp sometimes, and it was said that this John Desmond had sent it. Repute had it that he was a man of great mind and brain, who would have come in person to join us had not his rich properties in Philadelphia demanded his care and attention; and I could well believe that his situation was of a very precarious nature, despite his daughter's fidelity to the king.

"I am curious to see both the rebel and his loyal daughter," said Marcel, unconsciously speaking my own thoughts also.

"You may yield to the charms of the daughter," replied Vivian, "but I warn you that if you seek to retort her conquests upon her you will have antagonists, and our friend Belfort here would not be the least among them."

Belfort frowned as if he did not relish the allusion, but it was a jolly young company of officers, and his frowns did not prevent them from having but small mercy upon him.

"I am told," said Catron, "that the young lady looks very high, and it will not be an easy task to win her. I think, Belfort, that the uniform of a colonel would be an exceeding betterment to your chances. And even if you should achieve success with the lady, I know not how the glowering old Desmond will look upon you."

"It seems to me, gentlemen," said Belfort, a trifle warmly, "that you are over personal in your discussions."

"Then in truth it is a most serious matter with you, eh, Belfort?" exclaimed Vivian.

"Nevertheless the field is open to any of us who choose to enter, and I suspect that some of us do choose," said Catron. "Belfort must not expect to win a battle unopposed."

I saw that Belfort liked the discussion less and less, and that he did not fancy rivalry. Many of the British officers in America, with worldly wisdom, were already seeking alliances with our Colonial heiresses. I had no doubt that Belfort had such designs in his mind, and I took a dislike to him for it.

Our appetites had now been dulled, and Vivian, seeing it, suggested that perhaps we might like to seek repose, adding that we would not be assigned to any regular service for a day or two. We accepted the invitation to rest, as we were in truth tired. Evening was at hand and it had been a long day, filled with many adventures. The officers wished us a hearty good-night and slumber undisturbed by dreams of pursuing rebels, and then left us.

"I must return to Sir William," said Vivian, as he left, "but Waters will take you to your quarters.—Here, Waters, see that Captain Montague and Lieutenant Melville are made comfortable."

Waters, a large, red-headed man in the dress of a British orderly, who had just entered, stepped forward.

"Waters is American," said Vivian, "but no Englishman is more loyal to the king than he. He is a good soldier and a good fellow. In fact, he has been so useful to us in various ways that he is in some sort a privileged character, and often comes and goes pretty nearly according to his own liking. So you may know that he is esteemed by us all."

When Vivian had gone, Waters led the way to our quarters. Presently this red-headed man said to us, "The rebels are very numerous about the city, are they not, and make travelling a matter of much danger?"

"Why should you think them numerous?" haughtily asked Marcel, who was a great stickler for the formalities, and thought the man presumptuous in speaking unbidden to his superiors.

"I meant no harm, sir," replied Waters, humbly. "I heard that they pursued you and your friend there almost into the city itself."

"Well, at any rate," said Marcel, shortly, "they did not overtake us; and if you will kindly conduct us to our quarters we will undertake to get along without any further questions from you about the rebels."

"Of a certainty, sir," replied Waters. "I see that your honor pays small heed to the rebels."

This savored of fresh impertinence, but neither Marcel nor I replied. When we had reached the room and Waters was adjusting it for us, I saw him regarding Marcel with a pair of remarkably keen and intelligent eyes. It was a more comprehensive gaze than that of an ordinary attendant prompted by curiosity, and there was something in it that struck me with alarm. Presently his gaze shifted from Marcel and fell upon me, but the eyes, meeting mine, passed on. A moment or two later, Waters, having finished his task, bowed to us and left the room, walking with a light, noiseless step, although he was a large, heavy man.

Sometimes little things stir one overmuch, and it was so with this incident. The man had aroused my apprehensions to a strange degree, and I showed my alarm in my face, for Marcel, turning to me, exclaimed,—

"Why, what ails you? What are you scared about?"

Then I explained how I had noticed the suspicious and inquiring gaze of the man Waters. This made Marcel look serious also.

"Of a truth the man was over-bold in his manner," he said, "and it may be he believes I am no more Captain Montague than you are Lieutenant Melville. He is an American, I believe Vivian said?"

"Yes, one of the Tories."

"They are the worst of all."

But presently we took a more cheerful view of the matter. We reasoned that, situated as we were, the slightest sort of an incident was likely to breed suspicion in our minds.

"At any rate," said Marcel, "I shall not be unhappy just after having eaten the first substantial and plentiful meal that I have had in a year. That red-headed Tory shall not rest upon my mind."

"Nor upon mine," I said.

"That being the case," continued Marcel, "we'd better go to sleep."

Which we did.

CHAPTER THREE—*Sir William's Revel*

I had heard that Sir William Howe was of sybaritic temperament. What we had seen on the occasion of our first interview with him indicated the truth of this report, and the sight that burst upon us when we entered the apartments where his banquet of state was served was indubitable confirmation. There was such a confusion of soft carpets and silken hangings and glittering glass and other adornments of luxury that for a few moments both Marcel and I were quite dazzled and overpowered.

"I would like to turn about twenty of our starving soldiers loose here with liberty to do their will for a half-hour," Marcel whispered to me.

I smiled at the thought of the mighty wreckage and despoiling that would ensue. But Vivian and Blake were coming to greet us, and soon we were strolling about with them. We rendered our respects again to Sir William, who received us with kindly courtesy. He was in the full blaze of his most splendid and brilliant uniform, with a gold-hilted sword hanging by his side, and I have rarely seen a more bravely adorned figure.

"Suppose we get a glass of wine," said Blake, after we had performed our duty to our host and commander-in-chief.

We made assent, and he led the way to a smaller room, where there was spread a fine array of bottles and glasses. An attendant hastened to fill the glasses for us, and when he handed mine to me I recognized the face of the man Waters. Perhaps it was my imagination again, but his eyes seemed to dwell upon me for a moment with a look of suspicion or knowledge. But it was only for a moment, and then his face became as blank and stupid as that of a well-trained attendant ought to be. But the feeling of alarm was aroused in me as it had been aroused the night before, and I drank off the wine at a draught to steady my nerves and to still my fears. It had the effect desired: my blood grew warm in my veins again. Then I saw how foolish I had been. The imagination loves to trick us, and if ever we give it any vantage it will treat us in precisely the same way again.

Waters was asking me in the most respectful tone for the privilege of refilling my glass, but I declined, and passed on with my friends. I determined to say nothing to Marcel about this second alarm that Waters had given me, for I knew that his volatile Southern temperament had long since thrown off the effects of what he might have felt the previous night, and he would only laugh at me.

Marcel and the two Englishmen said by and by that they wanted another glass of wine, and decided to return to the room in search of it. I wished to keep my head cool, and declined to go with them.

"Very well," said Vivian. "Take care of yourself, and we will rejoin you presently."

So they left me; and I was not ill content to be alone,—that is, in so far as one can be alone in the midst of a crowd,—as I wished to look on and to note well, since I apprehended that in the course of our adventure we would need a great store of knowledge as well as tact. I was thinking such thoughts, and meanwhile failing to look about me with the acuteness that I had intended, when I turned an angle of the hall and barely saved myself from a collision with the most beautiful young woman I had ever seen. Startled by my absence of mind and awkwardness, she stepped back with a little cry, while I stammered out some sort of an apology, though all the while I kept my eyes upon her face, which was of that clear, fine, and expressive type that I so much admire. The slight look of annoyance appearing at first in her eyes passed away. I suppose it was my look of admiration that placated her, for I have heard old men who know much of women say that no one of them is so good or so indifferent as not to be pleased by evident admiration. A half-dozen brilliantly uniformed officers were around her, and one of them— Catron it was—stepped forward.

"Miss Desmond," he said with easy grace, "permit me to introduce to you the valiant Lieutenant Melville, who is one of the heroes of yesterday's encounter with the rebel band, of which you perhaps have heard.—Lieutenant Melville, make obeisance to Miss Desmond, our fairest and most faithful ally."

So this was the woman. As traitorous as she was fair! The apostate daughter of a patriot father! Not all her beauty—and I was fain to confess to myself that it was great—could prevent the anger from rising within me.

But I concealed my feelings and made a most lowly obeisance.

"You are just from England, I hear, Lieutenant Melville," she said. "Ah, that is a happy land! There the king's subjects are loyal and devoted to his welfare, while this wretched country is rent by treason and war."

Her words increased my anger.

"Miss Desmond," I said, "I am a soldier of his Majesty King George, and hope to serve him well, but I can condemn the rebels as rebels only and not as men also. I hear that Mr. Washington and many of his officers are, aside from their lack of loyalty, most worthy persons."

These words had a bold sound, but I had determined to adopt such a course, as I believed it would come nearer to allaying suspicion than any over-warm espousal of Britain's cause. This in truth seemed to be the case, for two or three of the officers murmured approval of my words.

"You seem to be as frank as you are bold," said Miss Desmond, coldly. "But perhaps it would be wise for you to keep these opinions from Sir William Howe."

"He has not yet asked me for my opinions," I replied; then adding as an apology for the rudeness, "but if any one could convert me by argument to the belief that the morals of the rebels are as bad as their politics, it would be Miss Desmond."

"Then," she said, somewhat irrelevantly, "you do not believe that all these men should be hanged when the rebellion is crushed?"

"Miss Desmond," I replied, "you cannot hang an entire nation."

"Fie! fie!" broke in Catron, "to talk of such a gruesome subject at such a time! Melville, acknowledge yourself one of Miss Desmond's subjects, and come with us."

"I yield willingly to such overwhelming odds," I said.

"You are just in time," said Catron, "for here comes Belfort, who is even more fierce against the rebels than Miss Desmond."

Belfort saluted Miss Desmond in his most courtly manner, but was chary of politeness to the remainder of us. It was evident that he wished to assume a certain proprietorship over Miss Desmond, but the gay crowd around her was not willing to submit to that, and Miss Desmond herself would not have allowed such cool appropriation. So among us we made Belfort fight for his ground, and, though it is wrong, perhaps, to confess it, I extracted much enjoyment from his scarce-concealed spleen. In this pleasant exercise we were presently aided by Marcel, who saw how matters stood as soon as he joined us, and turned all the shafts of his sharp wit upon Belfort.

But these passages at arms were soon broken up, as the time for the banquet arrived. The largest room in the house was set apart for the feasting, and the great table which ran almost its full length supported an array of gold and silver plate of a splendor and quality that I had never seen before. In the adjoining chambers were stationed two of the regimental bands, the one to play while the other rested. Scores of wax candles in magnificent candelabra shed a brilliant light over gold and silver plate and the gorgeous uniforms of the gathering guests. Of a truth the British army lived well. How could we blame our ragged and starving men for leaving us sometimes?

Sir William, as a matter of course, presided, with the general officers on either side of him. But a seat or two away from him was a large man in civilian's dress. This man was of a noble but worn countenance, and I guessed at once that he was John Desmond. I soon found that I was right, and I wondered why Sir

William had brought him to the banquet, but supposed it was for his daughter's sake.

Miss Desmond was near the upper end of the table, with Belfort by her side. Nor was she the only beauty at the banquet, as the wives and daughters of our rich Philadelphians were very partial to the British, whose triumph in America they considered certain. This fact was not a matter of pleasure and encouragement to good patriots.

I would have liked to be near Miss Desmond, as I wished to draw her out further in regard to her political principles. I did not understand why an American woman could be so bitter against the best of her countrymen, and moreover there is a certain pleasure in opposition. We soon grow tired of people who always agree with us. But it was not my fortune to be near enough to converse with her. Nevertheless I could watch the changing expression of her brilliant countenance.

The viands and the liquors were of surpassing quality, and under their satisfying influence the dinner proceeded smoothly. There was much talk, mostly of the war and its progress, and everybody was in fine feather. Despite the late successes of the Americans in the North, there seemed to be no one present who did not anticipate the speedy and complete triumph of the British arms.

"Sir William expects to be made a marquis at least," said Blake, who was one of my neighbors, to me, "and if he should take Mr. Washington he would deserve it."

"Of a certainty he would deserve it if he should do that," I said.

Miss Desmond was talking with great animation to some officers of high rank, but my attention presently wandered from her to her father, and was held there by his square, strong, Quakerish face and moody look. This man wore the appearance of a prisoner rather than that of a guest, and replied but curtly to the questions addressed to him, even when Sir William himself was the questioner. I was near enough to hear some of these questions and replies.

"It is a gay and festal scene, is it not, Mr. Desmond?" said Sir William. "It seems to me that the pinched condition of the rebels, of which we hear so much, would contrast greatly with this."

"You speak truly, Sir William," said Mr. Desmond, "but you do not say in whose favor the contrast would be."

I inwardly rejoiced at the bold and blunt reply, but Sir William only smiled. In truth I soon saw that he and some of the high officers around him had set out to badger the old Philadelphian, which I deemed to be a most ungallant thing, as he was wholly in their power.

"Mr. Desmond still feels some lingering sympathy for his misguided countrymen," said a general. "But perhaps it is as well that he does, is it not, Sir William? they will need it."

"It is a characteristic of my countrymen to show patience and endurance in adversity," said Mr. Desmond, proudly.

"Let us attribute that to their British blood," said Sir William.

"And the bad qualities that they show," added a colonel, "we will attribute to their American birth."

"If you will pardon me for making the observation, gentlemen," said Mr. Desmond, with great dignity, "it was such attempts at discrimination, such reflections upon the American birth of British subjects, that were among the many causes of this present unfortunate war."

I would have applauded the stanch old merchant had I dared, and I listened without any reproach of my conscience for more, but Sir William's reply was lost amid a jangle of talk and the clinking of glasses. Moreover, at that precise moment an insinuating voice at my elbow asked me if I would have my wineglass filled again. There was a familiar tone in the voice, and, turning my head slightly, I beheld the leering visage of Waters. At least there seemed to me to be a leer upon his face, though I am willing to admit that imagination may have played a trick upon me.

Either this man was dogging me, or it was a curious chance that put him so often at my elbow. But I preserved my equanimity and curtly ordered him to fill my glass again. This he did, and then passed on about his business, leaving me much vexed, and all the more so because I had lost the thread of the most interesting dialogue between Mr. Desmond and the British officers. Mr. Desmond's face was flushed, and there was a sparkle in his eye that told of much anger.

"They're worrying the old rebel," said Blake to me, "but he has a stern spirit, and, as he is aware that his opinions are known, it is not likely that he will try to curry favor."

"It seems to me to be scarce fair to treat him thus," I said.

"Perhaps not," he replied, "but it is not so bad as it would appear, for by my faith the old man has a sharp tongue and the spirit to use it."

"Do you have many such events as this in Philadelphia?" I asked, meaning the banquet.

"We do not suffer from a lack of food and drink," replied Blake, with a laugh, "and on the whole we manage to while away the hours in a pleasurable manner. But we have a bit of the real military life now and then also. For instance, the day we rescued you and Montague from the rebels, we were out looking for that troublesome fellow Wildfoot and his band. A loyal farmer brought us word that he was lying in the woods within a few miles of the city."

"Did you find him?" I asked.

"No," said Blake, with an expression of disappointment, "but we found where he had been, for every horse and cow of the aforesaid loyal farmer had been carried off in his absence."

"It was not very far from serving him right," I said.

"From the standpoint of an American it was extremely even-handed justice," said Blake.

Now, this Wildfoot was a most noted partisan or ranger who had come up from Virginia, and, though I had not seen him yet, our army—and the British army also, I doubt not—was filled with the tale of his deeds, such as the cutting off of British scouting and skirmishing parties and the taking of wagons loaded with provisions, which last were worth much more to us than the taking of prisoners; for we could not eat the prisoners, though I have seen the time when I was sorely tempted to do so.

In consequence of these things, all patriotic Americans regarded Wildfoot with pride and gratitude. But, as the tale went, I had been so short a time in America it was not meet that I should know much about him; so I requested Blake to enlighten my understanding on the point, which he proceeded to do, and to my great delight, gave a most marvellous account of the pestiferous fellow's misdeeds.

"He is here, there, and everywhere, chiefly everywhere," said Blake; "and I must admit that so far his ways are past finding out. He is doing more harm to us than a big battle lost. What is most annoying is the fellow's impertinence. One afternoon he and his band rode up to the river within full sight of the city and stopped a barge loaded with soldiers. They could not carry off the men, but they took their muskets and bayonets and all their ammunition, and, what is more, they got away without a scratch."

I had heard of the deed. In truth, some of the muskets taken on that occasion by Wildfoot and his men found their way to our regiment, where they proved a most welcome and serviceable addition, for, as I have said before, the British always arm and equip their soldiers well.

Blake was going into some further account of Wildfoot's exploits, when he was interrupted by the toast. Very heavy inroads had been made upon the wine supplied by his Majesty to his officers in America, and though the guests were not so far advanced into a state of hilarity as to render the absence of the ladies necessary, yet it was manifest that their spirits were rising. It was in truth fit that the toast-making should not be put off much longer, for, though the capacity of the British stomach is one of the wonders of the world, there is a limit to all things.

Sir William rose in a very stately manner, considering his deep potations, and called for a toast to his Britannic Majesty.

"And may he soon triumph over his rebellious subjects here and wherever else they choose to raise their heads!" said Sir William.

My glass had been filled before this toast by the ready Waters, as those of all the others had been filled for them, and I was even compelled to drink it. I looked across at Marcel and caught his eye. It twinkled with humor. It was easy to see that he did not look at the matter in the same serious light as I, and that reconciled me to it somewhat. But as I swallowed the wine I changed the toast and said to myself,—

"Here is to the long life and success of General Washington and his patriot army!"

This eased my conscience still further. Then there was another toast to the "speedy destruction of Mr. Washington and his rebels."

I drank to this also, as drink I must, but again I said to myself,—

"I drink to the speedy destruction of the army of Sir William Howe and of all the other armies of the oppressor in America, even as the army of Burgoyne was destroyed."

These and other toasts were accompanied by great applause; and when there was some subsidence of the noise, Sir William, whose face, through overmuch drinking, was now a fine mottle of red and purple, turned towards Mr. Desmond and exclaimed,—

"We have had loyal and heartfelt expressions for our king and country, but they have all come from Britain. His Majesty has other subjects who owe him allegiance. I call upon my guest, the loyal Mr. Desmond of the good city of Philadelphia, to propound a toast for us. Fill up your glasses, gentlemen. We await your sentiments, Mr. Desmond."

The noise of the talk ceased at once, for I think all were surprised at this request from Sir William, knowing as they did that Mr. Desmond thought not much of their cause. I wondered how the old merchant would evade the matter, and looked at his daughter, who was watching his face with evident anxiety. But Mr. Desmond, though the traces of anger were still visible on his countenance, seemed to be in no state of perplexity. He rose promptly to his feet with a full glass in his hand, and said, in a voice that was very firm and clear,—

"Yes, gentlemen, you shall have a toast from a loyal American, loyal to what is right. I drink to the health of General Washington, the best and the greatest of men, and likewise to the health of his gallant and devoted soldiers."

So saying, and before a hand could be lifted to stop him, he raised the glass to his lips and emptied it at a draught, I and many others doing likewise, I because it was a toast that I liked, and the others because it was the wine that they liked, and they seized the opportunity to drink it before their dazed brains comprehended the nature of the toast. Replacing the glass upon the table, Mr. Desmond looked defiantly about him. For a moment there was the heavy hush which so often succeeds impressive events, and then the company burst into a confused and angry clamor. One officer, who had been performing most notably at the wine-cup, leaned over, his face quite gray with passion, and would have struck at the daring speaker, but another less heated seized him and threw him not lightly back into his seat. Sir William turned furiously upon the old man and exclaimed,—

"How dare you, sir, how dare you speak thus in my presence and in the presence of all these gentlemen, loyal subjects of the king?"

"Sir William," said a clear voice, "you must not forget that you asked him for a toast. I say it with all due respect; but you knew his principles, and perhaps you could not have expected anything else. Let his daughter plead for his forgiveness, Sir William."

Miss Desmond was standing. One hand rested upon the table in front of her, the other was slightly raised. Her eyes were aflame, her attitude was that of fearlessness. Above her white brow shone the black masses of her hair like a coronet, and a ruby placed there gathered the light and flashed it back in a thousand rays. Tory and traitor though she was, she seemed to me then as noble as she was beautiful.

"I need no defence," said Mr. Desmond, rising; "at least not from my own daughter."

She flushed deeply at the rebuke, but she went on nevertheless.

"Sir William," she said, "remember that this was said at a banquet where much wine has been drunk, and under provocation."

"Sir William must yield to her," said Blake to me.

"Why?" I asked.

"Because it is as she says," he replied. "Bear in mind the place and the incitement. Sir William brought the retort upon himself. If he punishes the old rebel, the report of this is sure to get back to England, and see what a reflection it would be upon the dignity and duty of the commander-in-chief. High though his favor be, the king and the ministers are but ill pleased with Sir William's conduct of the war, and the tale of such an incident as this would do him much hurt in their esteem."

It was even as Blake said. Sir William hesitated. Moreover, I am not loath to relate that many of the British officers were ruled by a spirit of gallantry and fair play. They crowded around Sir William and told him to let the matter pass as a jest. I suspect he was glad of their interference, because he soon yielded.

"Since the daughter pleads for the father's forgiveness, it shall even be awarded to her," he said. "To beauty and loyalty we could forgive greater sins."

Miss Desmond bowed, but the frown gathered more deeply on the old patriot's face.

"I admire his spirit," said Blake, "but I would that it were displayed on the right side. It is such stubborn men as he that make this country so hard to conquer."

"There are many such," I said, and I spoke with more knowledge than Blake suspected.

"I doubt it not," he replied.

The banquet proceeded, but all the spirit and zest had gone out of it, and very soon it ended, as in truth it was time it should. When we withdrew from the apartment, I came near to Miss Desmond. She had thrown a rich cloak over her shoulders in preparation for her departure, and some traces of excitement or other emotion were still visible on her face. Belfort was standing near. The man was always hovering about her.

"Lieutenant Melville," said Miss Desmond, "you are only a short time in this country, but you find that strange things happen here."

"Not so strange, perhaps, as interesting," I replied. "However much I may condemn your father's sentiments, Miss Desmond, I would be a churl in truth to refuse admiration for the boldness and spirit with which they have been expressed to-night."

I spoke my opinion thus, knowing that she had the events of the evening in mind. But she turned upon me sharply.

"If it is unwise in my father to speak such sentiments so openly, it is still more unwise in you to commend him for them, as he is an American and may have some excuse, while you are an Englishman and can have none," she said.

Then she turned away with Belfort, who took her triumphantly to her father.

"Chester," said Marcel, when we were back in our quarters and were sleepily going to bed, "the old Desmond hath a temper of which I approve, and his daughter is fair, very fair."

"But she has the tongue of a shrew," I said.

"I am not sorry for that," he replied, "for she may exercise it on that fellow Belfort when she is Madame Belfort."

"Marcel," said I, after a silence of some minutes, "do you not think our position is growing more dangerous every hour? Suppose Sir William detects us."

"Sir William," said Marcel, half asleep, "is not a great general, but his wine is good, very good, and there was a noble supply of it."

CHAPTER FOUR—*On a New Service*

When we awoke the next morning we found that the man who had put our uniforms in order and attended to the other duties about the quarters was Waters. There he was, grinning at us in the familiar way that made my anger rise. Again I became suspicious of the fellow, although there was nothing particular upon which I could rest my apprehensions, unless it was the air of secret knowledge and importance I fancied I saw so often on his face. But I reflected that such looks were as much the characteristic of fools as of sages, and with this reflection I turned very cheerfully to receive the morning draught which Waters handed to me. The taste of it left no doubt that he was a noble compounder of beverages, and when I had drunk it all I readily forgave him his wise looks, for, as everybody knows, a cool draught in the morning is a necessity after a revel of the night before. Moreover, in a talkative way he volunteered us much information concerning the army and its prospects. Suspecting that this would be useful to us, we had no hesitancy in listening to him.

I knew that the attendants about the quarters of the officers often came into possession of valuable information, so I asked him, though I pretended a very careless and indifferent manner, if anything weighty were afoot.

"A company of mounted dragoons are looking for Wildfoot, the American ranger," he said, "and a wagon-train loaded with provisions gathered from the farmers is expected in the afternoon. The general thinks the train may draw Wildfoot and his robbers, and then the dragoons will come down on him and put an end to him and his band."

That Waters spoke the truth we soon had good proof, for somewhat later both Marcel and I were ordered to join a troop commanded by Blake, which was intended to co-operate with the body of dragoons already in search of Wildfoot. Good horses had been secured for us, and we had no choice but to go and serve against our own countrymen.

"Let us trust to the luck which has never deserted us yet," said Marcel. "We may be of service to this Wildfoot without betraying ourselves."

That was a very reasonable and consoling way of putting the matter, and I mounted my horse with a feeling of relief at the prospect of being out in the country again. At least the hangman's noose was not drawn so tightly around our necks there. We attracted attention from the populace as we rode through the city, and in truth a fine body of men were we, well mounted, well clothed, and well armed. Some of the people cheered us, but I could see other faces glowering, and

I liked them the better. Though this Philadelphia, our finest city, lay under the heel of the enemy, I knew it yet contained many faithful friends of the good cause.

A light rain had fallen in the morning, and the beads of water still lay on bush and blade of grass. Forest and field glowed in living green, and the south wind, which had the odor of flowers in its breath, was fresh as the dew upon our faces.

"It makes one think of the mountains and lakes, and of sleep under the trees," said Vivian, who was of our company.

"I warn you that you will not have a chance, Vivian, to go to sleep under a tree or anywhere else," said Blake. "We have more important business than day-dreaming in hand. This fellow Wildfoot, who is worse than a plague, must be trapped to-day."

"I trust that we shall have him hanging from a strong oak bough before nightfall," said Belfort, who also had been sent on the service.

"I can scarce say that," continued Blake, who was a gallant fellow. "I would rather fight these people with the sword than with the cord."

The country seemed to be the abiding-place of peace. The district through which we rode had not been harried, and we saw some farmers going about their business.

They noticed us but little; doubtless soldiers had ceased long since to be an unaccustomed sight to them. The fresh air and the beauty of the country acted like a tonic upon us. We broke into a gallop, our sabres clanking at our sides. I forgot for the moment that I was with enemies,—official enemies.

"We should meet Barton somewhere near here," said Blake.

Barton was the commander of the first troop that had been sent out to trap Wildfoot. Blake had been sent along later, for fear Barton's squad would not be strong enough for its task. Blake was to command both detachments when they united.

"Barton may not like to be superseded thus," said Blake, "but it is the general's orders. He did not wish to take unnecessary risks."

"Anyway, we will make sure of the rebels," said Belfort, "and a bit of service like this does not come amiss, after so many weeks of feasting and dancing in Philadelphia."

"Those must be our friends on that distant hill-side yonder," broke in Marcel, "for against the green of the grass there is a blur of red, which I take to be British coats."

Marcel was right, and the two parties soon formed a junction. Barton, a middle-aged officer, did not seem so displeased as Blake thought he would be at the coming of the reinforcements and his own supersession in the command.

"What news?" asked Blake eagerly of him. "Have you seen anything of the rebels yet?"

"No," replied Barton; "but if you will ride with me to the crest of this hill, I will show you the wagon-train."

Blake beckoned to several of us to accompany him, and we ascended the hill, which was crowned with oak-trees.

"See, there they are," said Barton, pointing into the valley beyond, "and I think those wagons carry enough food to tempt the starving rebels to almost any desperate deed."

About thirty large Conestoga wagons, each drawn by four stout bullocks, were moving along slowly and in single file. From where we stood we could hear the creaking of the wagon wheels and the cracking whips of the drivers.

"You are right about the temptation," said Blake, "and if Wildfoot and his men mean to make the dash upon them according to our advices, this is the place for it. It would be a matter of great ease for them to surround the wagons in that valley. You have been careful to leave no evidence of your presence, Barton?"

"Yes; this is the nearest that we have been to the wagons," replied Barton. "If the rebels are about, they cannot suspect that the train has other guard than the soldiers you see riding with it."

"I think it would be wise to keep watch as long as we can from this summit," said Blake. "It is well wooded, and will serve to conceal us from the rebels."

"Captain," said a soldier who had ridden up hastily, "Lieutenant Vivian wishes your presence immediately."

Vivian had been left in charge for the moment of the soldiers down the hill-side; and Blake, saying to us, "Come on, gentlemen," galloped back to him. We found the entire troop drawn up as we had left them, but all were gazing towards the north. We looked that way too, and at once saw the cause of this concentrated vision. Just out of musket-range and under the boughs of a large oak-tree were three or four horsemen. Their reins hung loose, and their attitudes were negligent and easy, but all wore the uniforms of Continental soldiers. Their coats were ragged and faded, as in truth were all the uniforms in our army, but enough of the color was left to allow no room for doubt.

"By heavens, this savors much of impertinence!" said Blake. "How came they there?"

"We do not know," responded Vivian. "One of the men called my attention, and we saw them sitting there just as they are now."

I had been examining the men with great attention. The one who was nearest to us was large, dark, and apparently very powerful. His figure did not appear altogether strange to me. I was vexing my brain in an endeavor to account for the recollection, when Marcel leaned over and whispered to me,—

"Behold him, Chester. It is the lively gentleman who chased us so hotly when we fled into the arms of our friends the British."

"What is that you say?" asked Blake, who saw Marcel whispering to me.

"I was reminding Lieutenant Melville," replied Marcel, "that we had unexpectedly renewed an acquaintance. The large man who sits nearest to us is the leader of the band who chased us into the midst of your troop the other day."

"We failed to take him then," responded Blake, quickly, "but I do not think he can escape us now."

"It would be a pity to use arms on such skulkers," said Belfort. "They should be lashed into submission with whips."

A hot reply was rising to my lips, but Blake said lightly: "Then we will even delegate the task of lashing them to you, Belfort. We will look on while you ride forward and perform your duty. But wait! what does that fellow mean?"

The large man had taken notice of us apparently for the first time. With deliberate action he hoisted a piece of white cloth on the muzzle of his gun-barrel, and then began to ride slowly towards us.

"Does he mean that they surrender?" asked Blake.

"I think not," said Marcel. "That is a flag of truce. He wishes to confer with you."

"I would hold no conference with him," said Belfort. "He is a rebel and not worthy of it. Let us ride forward and shoot them down."

"Not so," said Blake; "we must recognize a certain degree of belligerency in them, rebels though they be, and we will hear what he may have to say. Let no one raise a weapon against him while he bears that white flag. The honor of England forbids it."

Belfort was silent under the rebuke, but I could see that it stung him. The American continued to approach, but when he was midway between us and his companions he stopped.

"Come," said Blake, "we will meet him." Accompanied by a party of officers—Marcel, Belfort, Vivian, and myself among the number—he rode forward. We stopped within speaking-distance of the man, who waited very composedly. Then Blake hailed him and demanded his name and his errand.

"I am Captain William Wildfoot, of the American army," said the man, "and I have somewhat to say to you that may be to your profit, if you take heed of it."

There were some murmurs in our group when the famous ranger so boldly announced himself, and Blake said, in an undertone, "It would in truth be a great mischance if the fellow escaped us now."

Then he said to Wildfoot: "We have heard of you, and I may say have been looking for you, but did not expect that you would come to meet us. What is your message?"

"I demand the surrender of your command," replied the ranger. "I would spare bloodshed, which is distasteful to me, and I pledge you my word that I will treat you well, all of you, officers and men."

At this marvellous effrontery Blake swore a deep oath, and a murmur arose from the soldiers behind us, who heard the demand, as the ranger probably intended they should.

"You may be witty, but you are not wise, Sir Rebel," returned Blake. "Yield yourself at once, and perhaps you may secure the pardon of Sir William, our commander-in-chief, though your misdeeds are many."

"Not so fast, my friend," returned Wildfoot. "What you call my misdeeds are deeds of which I am proud. At least they have been of some service to our cause and of some disservice to yours, and that, I take it, is the purpose of war. My demand for your surrender you may receive in jocular vein, but I make it again."

The man spoke with dignity, but it made no impression upon the English officers, some of whom angrily exclaimed, "Ride the insolent rebel down!" But Blake again restrained them, calling their attention to the flag of truce.

"Rejoin your companions," he said to Wildfoot "To that much grace you are entitled, but no more, since you choose to boast of your treason and other misdeeds."

"It shall be as you wish," rejoined Wildfoot, "but I will find means to let Sir William Howe know that I gave you fair warning. He cannot say that I took advantage of you."

He turned his horse and rode placidly back to his companions, while Blake sat all a-tremble with rage. The moment Wildfoot reached his comrades, who had been waiting for him in apparent listlessness, he pulled off his wide-brimmed hat, which had shaded his face during the interview, waved it to us, and galloped away through the forest, while we, with a wild shout, galloped after him.

"He will soon bitterly rue his theatrical display," said Blake, "for I doubt not that Sir William will show little mercy to such a marauder as he. So ho, my lads! Yonder goes the chase! Lose not sight of them!"

The little American band had disappeared from our view for a moment, but as we came into an opening we saw them again galloping ahead of us just out of range.

"Give them a hunting call!" said Blake to a trumpeter who galloped by his side. "We will show these fellows what we think of them."

The man raised the trumpet to his lips, and the clear and inspiring strains of a hunting catch rang through the forest. It was a note of derision, a summons for the hunter to pursue the game, and in recognition of its meaning the troopers burst into a cheer.

"It will be a fine hunt,—ay, finer than to pursue the fox or the deer," said Belfort.

The fugitives were well horsed, for the distance between them and the pursuers did not diminish. Some scattering shots were fired at them, but all fell short, and Blake commanded the firing to cease until the opportunities for execution grew better.

The flight of the Americans led us gradually towards the foot of the slope, and we came to a broad sweep of country which was free from trees or undergrowth. Here the British pushed their horses to the utmost, and Blake commanded his men to spread out fan-like, in the hope of enclosing the fugitives if they sought to turn or double like foxes. There seemed to be wisdom in this plan, for beyond the open the stretch of ground practicable for horsemen narrowed rapidly. The country farther on was broken by hillocks and curtained with scrubby woods.

"We have them now," exclaimed Blake, joyously. "So ho! So ho! my lads!"

The trumpeter again merrily blew his hunting catch, and the men cheered its inspiring notes. I could easily understand why Blake was so eager to overtake Wildfoot, who in himself would be a very important capture, while his conduct on this occasion had been most irritating. It was his wish to get within firing range of the fugitives before they crossed the open stretch, but it was soon evident that such effort would be in vain. The long easy stride of the horses that Wildfoot and his men rode showed that they had strength in reserve.

"There is a ravine in front of that wood," exclaimed Belfort, who rode at my left hand. "Mr. Fox and his friends have trapped themselves."

So it seemed. But, though Wildfoot must have seen the ravine, he and his men galloped towards it without hesitation.

"Forward, my men," cried Blake; "we'll take them now."

Wildfoot and his men were at the edge of the gully, which we could now see was wide and lined with bushes. They checked their horses, spoke to them soothingly, and the next moment the gallant animals, gathering themselves up, leaped over the bushes into the ravine, horses and men alike disappearing from our view.

"'Tis but a last desperate trick to delude us," cried Blake. "On, my lads!"

In a wide but converging line we swept down upon the gully. We were scarce fifty feet from it when I heard a sharp, brief cry like a command, and from the dense wood that lined its farther bank there burst forth a flash of flame like the gleaming edge of a sword, only many times longer and brighter, and the next moment we went down as if smitten by a thunderbolt.

In war there is nothing that strikes fear to the heart like a surprise. While the front ranks of the British force crumbled away like a wrecked ship before the beat of the sea, cries of terror burst from those behind, and, mingling with the groans and the terrified neighing of the horses, produced a din that bewildered me. From this stupor I was aroused by the plunging of my horse, which had been wounded in the neck. I seized the reins, dropped from my hands in the first shock, and was endeavoring to draw back the frightened animal, so that he might not trample upon the fallen, when Marcel's face appeared through the dense smoke, and he shouted to me,—

"Shelter yourself behind your horse as much as you can. It is time for them to give us another volley!"

I took his advice not a whit too soon, for almost as he spoke, the withering flame flashed from the wood a second time, and once again our command cried out under the force of it.

But the British—I will give them credit for bravery and all soldierly qualities—began to recover from their surprise. Blake shouted and cursed, and the officers, with a fine display of gallantry, helped him to restore order in the command. Thus was the column beaten at length into some sort of shape and the fire of the ambushers returned, though no one could see whether the counter-fire did any execution.

After a few moments of this fusillade the British began to retreat, which was the wisest thing to do, for one who falls into a trap must needs try to get out of it the best he can. But we heard a loud shout on the slope above us, and a party of horsemen led by Wildfoot himself burst from the covert and charged down upon us.

"Here are enemies whom we can see!" shouted Blake. "At them, my lads!"

The whole troop turned to meet the charge, but they were ill fitted to endure it, for their flanks were still quivering beneath the fire from beyond the gully. The two bodies of horsemen met with a crash, and the British line staggered back. The next moment Wildfoot and his men were among us.

"By all the saints, I will do for him!" exclaimed Belfort, who had a ready pistol in his hand. Wildfoot and Blake were crossing swords in so fierce a combat that the ring of their blades was like the beat of the hammer upon the anvil.

Belfort levelled his pistol point-blank at the partisan, and would have slain him then and there, but at that moment, why I need not say, my horse stumbled and fell almost with his full weight against Belfort's. His pistol was knocked from his hand, and he barely kept his seat in his saddle.

"Damnation!" he roared. "What are—" and the rest of his words were lost in the din.

Just then the duel between the two leaders ended. Blake was unable to cope with his larger and more powerful antagonist, and his blade was dashed from his hand. Wildfoot might have shorn his head from his shoulders with one blow of his great sabre. Instead, he thrust the weapon into his belt, seized Blake by both shoulders, and hurled him to the earth, where the stricken man lay, prone and still.

Daunted by the fall of their leader, the British line bent and broke, and the men fled towards the cover of the forest. My heart sickened at the plight of Blake, enemy though he was.

The Americans, much to the surprise of the British, did not pursue, but drew off towards cover. Blake lay between the two detachments, his face almost concealed in the grass. I could not leave him there while life might still be in his body, to be trampled to pieces in the next charge of the horsemen, and driven by a sudden impulse, I sprang from my saddle, ran forward, and seized him by the shoulders, just as the great ranger whirled his horse and galloped by me. He had his sabre in his hand again, and I thought he was going to cut me down, as he might easily have done, but, to my unutterable surprise and relief, he made no motion to strike. Instead he said to me, as he galloped by,—

"You are a brave man, but you are a fool, a most wondrous fool!"

I stayed not to reflect wherein I was a most wondrous fool, but, with a strength which was a creation of the emergency and the excitement, I ran back towards the British lines, dragging poor Blake after me. Every moment I expected to feel an American bullet in my back, but none came, nor did I hear the sound of shots.

Then, after a space of time which it seemed to me would never come to an end, I reached the trees, and strong hands seized both Blake and me, dragging us under cover.

CHAPTER FIVE—*The Work of Wildfoot*

I remained for a minute or two in a stupor, superinduced by the excitement of the fight and my great physical exertions. From this I was aroused by Barton, who was now in command, Blake being disabled.

"It was gallantly done, Lieutenant Melville," he said. "You have saved our captain's life."

"Are you sure he is still living?" I asked.

"He is stunned by the shock he received when that great rebel hurled him to the ground," said Barton, "but he will be well enough in time."

"You have saved more lives than Blake's," whispered Marcel, as Barton turned. "You have saved yours and mine, for that villain Belfort suspected that you threw your horse purposely against his. In face of this he dare not declare his suspicions."

"By the way," resumed Marcel, a moment later, "you might ask our haughty Norman noble over there if the rebel dogs can fight."

I did not ask the question, though, had time and place been otherwise, it would have pleased me much to do so.

All the troopers had dismounted and were putting themselves in posture of defence behind the rocks, hillocks, and trees. Barton expected another attack upon the instant, but it was not made. In fact, when he examined with his field-glass the wood into which Wildfoot and his men had withdrawn, he announced that he could see naught of them.

"I see nothing among those trees over there," he said; "not a horse, not a man. Verily the fellows have learned to perfection the art of hiding themselves. By St. George, they need it in their dealings with us!"

It was sometimes the temper of the British in our country to boast and to show arrogance even when sore outwitted and outfought by us, and then to wonder why we did not love them. Perhaps this fault was not theirs, exclusively.

"Likely enough this silence is some new trick," said Belfort, "some scheme to draw us into another ambush."

"I suspect that you speak the truth," replied Barton. "Stand close, men. We have suffered too much already to risk another trap."

The men were quite willing to obey his order and stand close. Thus we waited. Blake revived by and by, and a careful examination showed that he had no bones broken, though he was sore in every muscle and still somewhat dazed in mind. But he was urgent in entreating his officers not to take excessive risks.

"I fancy that we have nothing to do but to wait here," said Barton to him, "for the rebels will of a surety attack us again very soon."

But in this Barton was mistaken, for the Americans seemed to have gone away. We waited a full hour, and then, as they gave no evidence of being anywhere near us, a small scouting-party was sent out, which presently returned with word that they were in truth gone, and that the woods were empty.

"They feared to attack us when we were on our guard," said Barton, triumphantly. "There is naught for us to do now but to go and escort the wagon-train back to the city."

We gathered up the wounded and rode over the ridge in search of the wagon-train. We found with ease the tracks of the wheels and followed them towards the city, expecting to overtake the wagons. Presently, as we turned around a hill, we rode almost full tilt into three or four of them lying upon the ground, too much shattered and broken ever to be of use again.

In his surprise Barton reined back his horse against mine, for I rode just behind him.

"What is this?" he exclaimed.

"It seems that we have the wagon-train, or what is left of it," said Marcel. "There is a placard; it may inform us."

A pine board was stuck in a conspicuous place upon one of the wagons, and some words had been written upon it with a piece of charcoal. We rode forward and read,—

"To Sir William Howe or His Representative.

For the Wagons and their Contents

We Are Much Indebted

As we were Hungry

And You Have Fed Us.

We Give You Leave to Take Repayment

At Such Time and Place

As You May Choose.

"WILLIAM WILDFOOT."

Barton swore in his rage. It was easy enough to see now why the patriots had withdrawn after the first attack. The provision-train was more valuable than arms or prisoners to the American army, and, barring the broken wagons, Wildfoot and his men had carried off everything. Nor were the British in any trim to pursue, a business at which, most like, they would have had their faces slapped.

Barton swore with a force and fluency that I have seldom heard surpassed, and Blake said with a melancholy smile,—

"It is well that I have this broken head to offer as some sort of an excuse, or I think it would go hard with me."

He spoke truly, for, though his expedition had been a most dire failure, his own condition was proof that he had done valiant duty.

The British gathered up their wounded again and began their march to the city. The country glowed in the brilliant sunshine of a summer afternoon, but I was in no mood to enjoy its beauty now. Our column marched mournfully along, as sad as a funeral procession. Even though the victory had gone where I wished it to go, yet there were others before my eyes, and I felt sorrow for them in their wounds and defeat.

When we approached Philadelphia, some people on horseback turned and galloped towards us. As they came nearer, I saw that two of them were women, one of whom I recognized as Miss Desmond. They were accompanied by two British officers whom I had seen at the banquet, Colonel Ingram and Major Parsons. The other young woman I learned afterwards was the daughter of a rich Tory of Philadelphia.

Belfort rode forward to meet them, and Marcel and I followed, though at a somewhat slacker pace. We could take this privilege, as we were now within the lines. I judged that the officers and the ladies had been taking a ride for the sake of the air and the exercise, and such proved to be the case.

"Here comes Blake's expedition," exclaimed Ingram, as they rode up, "and I see wounded men. Verily I believe we have taken the rebel Wildfoot at last."

"Is it true, Lieutenant Belfort?" asked Miss Desmond. "Has the robber Wildfoot been taken?"

Belfort was thrown into a state of embarrassment by this question, to which he knew he must return an unwelcome answer; and he hesitated, pulling uneasily at his bridle-rein. But Marcel, the readiness of whose wit was equalled only by his lack of a sense of responsibility, spoke up.

"I fear, Miss Desmond," he said, "that we have but sad news. The wounded men you see are not rebels, but our own. As for Mr. Wildfoot the robber, we suspect that he has had fine entertainment at our expense. Of a certainty he gave us all the sport we wanted."

"It was a trick, a dastard American trick!" exclaimed Belfort. "They gave us no chance."

"Then you have not captured this Wildfoot?" asked Miss Desmond.

"No," replied Marcel. "He came much nearer to capturing us, and in addition he has taken off our wagon-train, provisions, bullocks, drivers, and all, which I dare say will be welcome food to the Americans, drivers included, for we hear that they are starving."

"They did not stay to fight us to the end," broke in Belfort, "but ran away with the spoil."

"No doubt they had obtained all they wanted," said Miss Desmond, dryly. "Do not forget, Lieutenant Belfort, that, however misguided my countrymen may be, they are able to meet anybody in battle, Englishmen not excepted."

"For you to say anything makes it true," said Belfort.

"You should also take note," said Marcel, "that Miss Desmond is more chivalrous than some other opponents of the Americans."

"I do not take your full meaning," said Belfort.

"It is easy enough to understand it," said Marcel. "Miss Desmond gives to our enemies the credit for the bravery and skill which they have shown so plainly that they possess."

"I think you have taken a very long journey for strange purposes," said Belfort, "if you have come all the way from England to defend the rebels and to insult the officers of the king."

A fierce quarrel between them might have occurred then, for it was breeding fast, but Miss Desmond interfered.

"If you say any more upon this subject, gentlemen," she said, "I shall not speak to either of you again."

"Where no other penalty might prevent us, Miss Desmond," said Marcel, with a low bow, "that of a surety will."

Marcel was a graceless scamp, but I always envied his skill at saying things which fitted the matter in hand.

Our shot-riddled party had now come up, and while the colonel and the major were receiving the full story from Barton, I found myself for a few moments the only attendant upon Miss Desmond.

"Since I can now do it without risk of sudden death, our friend Lieutenant Belfort being absent, I assure you again that your countrymen showed great bravery and military skill in our action with them," I said.

"The appearance of your column," she replied, looking pityingly at the wounded soldiers, "is proof that you came off none too well."

"It would be better," I said, "to avow the full truth, that we were sadly beaten."

"Lieutenant Melville," she said, "why are you so quick in the defence and even the praise of the rebels? Such is not the custom of most of the British officers. It seems strange to me."

"Does it seem more strange," I asked, "than the fact that you, an American, espouse the cause of the British?"

The question appeared to cause her some embarrassment. Her lip quivered, and an unusual though very becoming redness came into her face. But in a moment she recovered her self-possession.

"If you had been born an American, Lieutenant Melville," she asked, "would you have fought with the Americans?"

"The question is unfair," I answered hastily.

"Then let the subject be changed," she said; and changed it was. In a few more minutes we entered the city, where the news we brought, and the abundant evidence of its truth that we likewise brought with us, carried much disturbance, and I may also add joy too, for there were many good and loyal patriots among the civilians of Philadelphia, and some who feared not to show their feelings in the face of the whole British army.

My rescue of Blake, more the result of impulse than of resolution, came in for much praise, which I would rather not have had, and of which I was in secret not a little ashamed. But there was naught for me to do but to receive it with a good grace, in which effort I was much aided by the knowledge that the incident formed a coat of armor against any suspicions that Belfort might have formed.

"Well, Lieutenant Melville," said Marcel, as we were returning to our quarters, "you have distinguished yourself to-day and established yourself in the esteem of your fellow-Britons."

"And you," I said, "have almost quarrelled with one of these same Britons, who hates us both already and would be glad to see us hanged."

"My chief regret," replied Marcel, "is that it was not a quarrel in fact. It would be the pleasantest task of my life to teach our haughty Norman nobleman a lesson in manners."

"Such lessons might prove to be very dangerous to us just now," I remarked.

"This one would be worth all the risk," replied he.

I saw that he was obstinate upon the point, and so I said no more about it.

CHAPTER SIX—*A Cousin from England*

By the time we regained our quarters that afternoon I was feeling decidedly serious. In adopting the wild suggestion of Marcel and riding into Philadelphia in British red, I had never expected such a complication as this. We were to do our work quickly, ride away and be with our own again, in true colors. But the inch had become a yard, and here we were, involved already in a perfect network of circumstances. Some one who knew the real Melville and Montague might arrive at any moment, and then what would become of us? Walking on bayonet points may be well enough as a novelty, for a moment or two, but as a regular thing I prefer solid ground.

I know that I looked exceedingly glum, but Marcel's face was careless and gay. In truth the situation seemed to delight him.

"Marcel!" I exclaimed, "why did the Lord create such a rattle-brained, South-Carolina, Irish-French American as you?"

"Probably he did it to ease his mind after creating you," he replied, and continued humming a dance air. His carelessness and apparent disregard of consequences annoyed me, but I remained silent.

"If I were you, Bob," he said presently, "I'd leave to old man Atlas the task of carrying the earth on his back. He's been doing it a long time and knows his business. A beginner like you might miscalculate the weight, and think what a terrible smash up we'd have then! Moreover, I don't see what we have to worry about!"

"I don't see what we don't have to worry about!" I replied.

"I'm sure that I have nothing," he continued calmly. "I know of no young man who is better placed than my own humble self. Behold me, the Honorable Charles Montague, heir to the noble estate of Bridgewater Hall in England, a captain in the finest army on the planet, comfortably quartered in the good city of Philadelphia, which is full of gallant men and handsome women. I already have friends here in abundance, and a reputation, too, that is not so bad. I am satisfied, and I recommend you, Lieutenant Melville, who are equally well situated, to accept your blessings and cease these untimely laments.

'The lovely Thais sits beside thee.

Take the goods the Gods provide thee!'"

He looked at me with such an air of satisfaction and conceit that I was compelled to laugh. Of course that was an end of all attempts to argue with Phil Marcel, and nothing was left to me but resignation.

"You don't complain of your company, do you?" he asked.

"I do not," I replied; "the English officers are a jolly lot,—a fine set, I will say,—if they are our enemies; and it's a pity we have to fight them,—all except Belfort, who I know does not like us and who I believe suspects us."

Marcel looked grave for a moment.

"Yes, Belfort's the possible thorn in our side," he said; "but your saving Blake as I have told you once before has been a great advertisement for us. You did that well, Bob, very well for you, though not as gracefully as I would have done it if the chance had been mine. Can you tell why it is, Bob, that I always have the merit and you always have the luck?"

"Perhaps it's because, if you had both, your conceit would set the Delaware on fire."

Catron and Vivian came in, a half-hour later, and urged us to spend the evening at the former's quarters, where we would meet all the men whom we knew, for a good time. They would accept no excuse. Marcel's spontaneous wit and gayety made him a favorite wherever he went, and I was a temporary hero through that happy chance of the Blake affair, and so we were in demand. Secretly I was not unwilling, and Marcel certainly was not. This lively, luxurious, and careless life, this companionship of young men who knew all the ways and gossip and pleasant manners of the great world, took instant hold of me, and I felt its charm powerfully. Having gone so far, it seemed to me the best thing we could now do was to do as those around us did, until our own opportunity came.

I do not speak of the luxurious and unmilitary life of the British in Philadelphia that season in any spirit of criticism, or with a desire to call special attention to it as something extraordinary. If the case had been reversed, the American army probably would have done the same thing. Nearly all the English generals regarded the rebellion as dead or dying, and many Americans were of the same opinion. Then why not let it die without being helped on by slaughter? Moreover, many of the British officers had no feeling of personal hostility whatever towards us, and all of us know, or ought to know, and remember with gratitude, that a powerful party in England defended us to the end.

Marcel looked at me with his suggestive smile and drooping of the eyelid when Catron and Vivian had gone.

"It seems to me that we have found favor at court," he said, "and must do as the king and courtiers do. Come, Bob, let's float with the stream."

Vivian, a young officer named Conant, and Vincent Moore, an Irish lieutenant, came for us about eight o'clock in the evening, and on the way to Catron's quarters we stopped a few moments to enjoy the fresh air. The day had been hot, and all of us had felt it.

"I don't think the Lord treated this country fairly in the matter of climate," said Vivian. "He gave it too much cold in winter and too much heat in summer."

"Oh, that's nothing," said Marcel; "you'll soon grow used to these hot summers."

"Why, what do you know about them?" asked Moore, quick as lightning, "when you've been here less than a week."

I almost groaned at my comrade's thoughtless remark, and my heart paused for a long time over its next beat. But Marcel was as calm as the sphinx.

"Why shouldn't I know a great deal about the heat here?" he replied. "Did I not make my entry into Philadelphia at the rifle muzzles of a lot of American rascals? Did they not make it warm enough for me then to become an expert on the subject of heat? Don't you think that I can endure any temperature after that?"

"You certainly came in a hurry," said Moore, "but you have redeemed yourselves as quickly as if you were Irishmen, and, after all, what a pity you were not born Irishmen!"

"Ireland is always unfortunate; she misses everything good," said Marcel, briefly.

The next instant we met Belfort, and I was devoutly thankful that he had not been present when Marcel made his remark about our hot summers. Its suggestive nature would not have been swept so quickly from his mind as it had been swept from the minds of the others.

But Belfort was in a good humor and was courteous, even cordial, to us. He complimented us on our share in the skirmish, and to me especially he hoped that further honors would soon come. Just as we reached Catron's door he turned to Marcel and said,—

"I've a pleasant bit of news for you, Captain Montague. Your cousin Harding—Sir John Harding's son, you know—arrived to-day on a frigate that came up the Delaware, and no doubt he will be as glad to see you as you will be to see him."

I was thankful for the darkness, as I know I turned pale. Already I felt piercing me those bayonet points on which we had been dancing so recklessly. Of course, this cousin arriving in such untimely fashion would expose us. Confound him! Why had not a merciful Providence wrecked his ship?

"I hope that I shall meet him soon, to-morrow or perhaps the next day, when he has fully recovered from the long journey," said Marcel.

"There will be no such wait as that," replied Belfort, cheerfully. "He will be here to-night, to meet all of us. Catron invited him, and he was glad to come. I saw him this afternoon, and as he is a good sailor, he needed no rest."

"So much the better," said Marcel, with unbroken calm. "We can initiate him to-night into the mysteries of Philadelphia. But all of our family take readily to new countries."

We were in the anteroom now, and I thought it best to imitate Marcel's seeming unconcern. It was impossible to withdraw, and it was more dignified to preserve a bold manner to the last.

A servant opened the door for us, and we passed into the rooms where the others were gathered. I was blinded for a moment by the lights, but when my eyes cleared I looked eagerly about me. I knew every man present, and curiously enough the knowledge gave me a sense of relief.

"I do not see my cousin," said Marcel, as we returned our greetings. "Belfort told us that he would be here."

"He will come in half an hour," replied Catron. "Remember that he landed from the ship only this afternoon, and we are not usually in a break-neck hurry to see cousins, unless they be of the other sex, and very fair."

We drank wine, and then began to play cards,—whist, picquet, and vingt et un. Belfort was at our table, and apparently he sought to make himself most agreeable. As it was unusual in one of his haughty and arrogant temper, it deceived completely all except Marcel and myself. But we understood him. We knew that he was expecting some great blow to fall upon us, and that his good humor arose wholly from the hope and expectation. What he suspected of us— whether he believed us to be in false attire, or merely considered us enemies because I had been so bold as to admire Miss Desmond, the lady of his choice—I could not say. Yet he undoubtedly expected us to be knocked over by the arrival of this unexpected and unknown cousin of Marcel's, and it was equally sure that he hated us both.

He began to talk presently of Harding,—Rupert Harding he called him; and though he pretended to have eyes only for his cards, I believed that he was covertly watching our faces. Marcel thought to lead him to a pleasanter subject, but he would not follow, and the life, career, and ambitions of Rupert Harding seemed to have become a weight upon his mind, of which he must talk. Chills, each colder than its predecessor, raced up and down my backbone, but my face looked calm, and I was proud that I could keep it so.

Marcel, unable to draw Belfort away from Rupert Harding, began by and by to show an interest in the subject and to talk of it as volubly as Belfort himself. But I noticed that nearly everything he said was an indirect question, and I noticed, too, that he was steadily drawing from Belfort a full history of this troublesome young man, for the arrival of whom we were now looking every moment.

Marcel dropped a card presently, and when he leaned over to pick it up, he whispered,—

"You are keeping a splendid face, old comrade. Let it never be said that we flinched."

A certain spirit of recklessness now took possession of me. We were past all helping, we had suffered the torments of anticipated detection, and having paid the penalty, we might endure the short shrift that was left to us. I laughed with the loudest and grew reckless with the cards. Luck having deserted me at all other points, now, as an atonement, made me a favorite at the gaming-table, and I won rapidly. The arrival of Harding was long delayed, and I hoped it would be further postponed, at least long enough for me to win ten more pounds. Then my ambition would be satisfied.

"It has been a long time since you have seen Harding, has it not?" asked Belfort of Marcel.

By pure chance all the players happened to be quiet then, but it seemed as if they were silent merely to hear his answer.

"It has been such a while since I have held a good hand of cards," replied Marcel, with a comic gesture of despair, "that my mind can hold no other measurements of time."

"Don't be downcast, Montague," said Catron, laughing; "your luck will change if you only play long enough."

"Unless the bottom of my pocket is reached first," said Marcel, with another rueful face.

Only he and I knew how little was in that pocket.

"Why is that cousin of mine such a laggard?" asked Marcel, presently. "We have been at the cards nearly an hour and he has not come."

"He will be here," said Belfort. "Does he play a good game?"

"If he doesn't play better than I do," replied Marcel, "he ought to be banished forever from such good company as this."

"Come, come, Montague!" said Catron, "a soldier like you, who can look into the angry face of an enemy, should show more courage before the painted face of a card."

I saw that no suspicion had entered the mind of any save Belfort, and he pressed his lips together a little in his anger at the way in which his questions were turned aside. But he was too wise to make a direct accusation, for all the others would have taken it as absurd, and would have credited his feelings immediately to the jealousy which he had shown of me.

The door opened, and a tall young man of our own age in the uniform of a British officer entered, and stood for a moment looking at us. His face was unknown to me, and this I felt sure must be Marcel's cursed cousin Rupert. I saw

Marcel's lip moving as if he would greet the stranger but he remained silent, and I, resolving to keep a bold face throughout, played the card that I held in my hand.

"You are late, Richmond," said Catron, "but your welcome is the greater. There are some present whom you do not know. Come, let me introduce you. This is Lieutenant Moore, and this is Captain Montague, and this, Lieutenant Melville; the last two just arrived from England, and of whose adventures you perhaps have heard. Gentlemen, Lieutenant Henry Richmond of Pennsylvania, one of his Majesty's most loyal and gallant officers."

So it was not the cousin after all, but a Tory, and my heart sprang up with a strange sense of relief. A place was made for him at one of the tables, and the game, or rather games, went on.

"It is warm to-night," said Belfort to me. He called one of the servants, who opened another window. With Marcel's blunder fresh before me, I was not likely to repeat it, and I continued to play the cards in silence.

"Do you not regard the insurrection as dead?" he asked.

"I have been too short a time in America," I replied in a judicial tone, "to be an authority, but I should say no."

"What do they think at home?" he asked.

"Some one way and some another," I replied. "Fox and Burke and their followers think, or pretend to think, that the rebels will yet win, and the loyal servants of the king, who are in the great majority, God bless him! think that if the insurrection is not dead it soon will be. But why speak of politics to-night, Lieutenant Belfort, when we are here for pleasure?"

I was afraid that he would lead me into treacherous fields. He listened, and then turned back to the subject of Harding.

"He is unusually late," he said, "but I suppose that Captain Montague can stand it."

"Undoubtedly," I replied. "Cousins are usually superfluous, any way."

I had made up my mind that we would maintain the illusion until the actual exposure and my nerves had become steady.

The door opened once more, and another young man entered. His features were unmistakably English. He looked around with the air of a stranger, and Marcel and I again were silent, just waiting.

"Harding!" exclaimed Catron. "You have found us at last. I was afraid that you had lost your way."

"So I did," said Harding, "but some one was kind enough to set me on the right road."

His eyes went from one to another of us, lingered for a moment on Marcel, and passed on without the slightest sign of recognition. Then I noticed that the card I held was wet with the sweat of my hand. Catron began to introduce us, beginning with Vivian. I believed that Belfort was watching Marcel and me, but I did not dare to look at him and see.

"I have a cousin here, have I not?" broke in Harding,—"Charlie Montague of Yorkshire? At least I was told that I would find him here, and as we have never seen each other, I am curious to meet him. Strange, isn't it, that one should have to come to America to meet one's English kin who live in the next county."

He laughed a hearty resonant laugh, and a painful weight rolled off my brain. He had never seen his cousin Montague before! Then he might look upon his cousin Marcel with safety,—safety to us. My own face remained impassive, but I saw Belfort's fall a little, and as for Marcel, the volatile and daring Marcel, he was already metaphorically falling into his cousin's arms and weeping with joy at the sight of him. Moreover I knew Marcel well enough to be sure that he could take care of the conversation and guide it into far-away channels, if Cousin Rupert wished to lead it upon the subject of their mutual interests and ties in England.

CHAPTER SEVEN—*The Quarrel*

Harding was the last arrival, and in his honor the card games were discontinued for a little, while we talked about home. Marcel justified my confidence in him; he discoursed so brilliantly upon England that one would have fancied he knew more about the old country than all the remainder of us combined. But Marcel has at times a large, generous way, and he talked wholly of extensive generalities, never condescending to particulars. This period of conversation was brought to a successful end by glasses of wine all around, and then we settled again to the more serious business of cards. Belfort had been very quiet after his failure with Harding, and he looked both mortified and thoughtful. I was inclined to the belief that his suspicions about our identity had been dissipated, and that he would seek a quarrel with at least one of us on other grounds.

The game proceeded, and I won steadily. My luck was remarkable. If I ever succeeded in escaping from Philadelphia with a sound neck, my stay there was likely to prove of profit.

The night advanced, but we played on, although it was far past twelve o'clock, and probably we would have played with equal zest had the daylight been coming in at the windows. The room was hot and close; but we paid no attention to such trifles, having eyes only for the cards and the money, and the shifting chances of the game. My luck held, and the little heap of shining gold coins gathered at my elbow was growing fast.

"Evidently the Goddess, fickle to others, favors you," said Belfort, at last. He regarded me with no pleasant eye. Much of his money had gone to swell my yellow hoard. Doubtless it seemed to the man that I was destined always to come in his way, to be to him a sort of evil genius. I was in an exultant mood, my winnings and my release from the great fear that had fallen upon me lifting me up, and I had no wish to soothe him.

"If the Goddess favors me, it is not for me to criticise her taste," I replied.

"No; that can safely be left to others," said Belfort.

He had been drinking much wine, and while all of us were hot and flushed, he seemed to have felt the effects of the night, the gaming, and the liquors more than anybody else. But despite our condition, his remark created surprise.

"Pshaw, Belfort, you jest badly!" said Vivian.

Belfort flushed a deeper red, but did not reply. Neither did I say anything. I have heard that the card-table is more prolific in quarrels than any other place in the world, and I saw the need of prudence. I had concluded that it would be very unwise to quarrel with Belfort, and my reckless mood abating, I determined not to lead him on. But a chance remark of Moore's set flame to the fuel again.

"I would pursue my luck, if I were you, Melville," he said. "Any Irishman would, and an Englishman ought not to be slack."

"How?" I asked.

"In the two accompaniments of cards, war and love. You have shown what you can do in cards and in a measure in war. Now, to be the complete gentleman, you must be successful in love."

"Melville has proved already that he has a correct eye for beauty," said Vivian.

"You mean Miss Desmond," said Catron, "but his eye has been neither quicker nor surer than those of others. There are enough officers at her feet to make a regiment."

I was sorry that they had brought up Miss Desmond's name, yet these young officers meant no disrespect to her. In our time all beautiful women were discussed by the men over cards and wine, and it was considered no familiarity, but a compliment.

"I wish you would not speak so often and with such little excuse of Miss Desmond," exclaimed Belfort, angrily.

"Why not?" I asked, replying for Vivian. His manner of appropriating Miss Desmond, a manner that I had noticed before, was excessively haughty and presumptuous, and it irritated every nerve in me.

"If you speak for yourself," he replied, turning a hot face upon me, "it is because you have known her only a few days and you have assumed an air which impresses me particularly as being impertinent."

It seemed as if there could be no end to his arrogance. He even made himself the sole judge of my manners, dismissing all the others as incompetent. Yet I was able to control my temper in face of such an insult in a way that surprised me.

"Your opinion of impertinence, Mr. Belfort, appears to differ from that of other people, and I fear you are not an authority on the subject," I replied, and I think there was no break in my voice, "yet I am willing to discuss the subject in any fashion you wish until we shall have reached some sort of a conclusion."

I knew he was bent upon forcing a quarrel upon me, and I did not see how I could honorably make further attempts to avoid it.

"Nonsense!" exclaimed Catron. "You shall not quarrel. I am your host, and I forbid it. You have both taken too much wine, and the code does not demand that hot words spoken at three o'clock in the morning shall breed sparks the next day."

Now, I had drank very little wine, and Catron knew it, but he included me in his indictment in order to ease Belfort, and I did not object. I waited, willing, even after what had been said, that peace should be made between us, but Belfort shook his head.

"Lieutenant Melville's words amounted to a challenge," he said, "and I would deem myself but the small part of a man if I refused it."

"I have nothing to withdraw," I interrupted. It seemed best to me to have it out with Belfort. I had been willing to smooth over all differences with him until he made Mary Desmond the issue between us. Somehow I could not pass that by, although she might never be anything to either him or me. Even in that moment when the quarrel was hot upon me, I wondered at the hold this Tory girl had taken upon my mind,—a girl whom I had seen but two or three times, and from whom I had received nothing but haughtiness.

"So be it, then," said Catron, impatiently, "but I trust that both of you will permit me to say what I think of you."

"Certainly! Tell us!" I said.

"Then I think you are both confounded fools to push a quarrel and cut each other up with pistol bullets or sword blades when you might dwell together in peace and friendship. Moreover, you have disturbed the game."

"We can go on with the cards," I suggested, "and Lieutenant Belfort and I will settle our affairs later."

"Of course," replied Catron. "You cannot fight at night, and we will meet here to-morrow in the afternoon to arrange for this business that you and Belfort seem bent on transacting. Meanwhile we will make the most of the night's remainder."

A few moments later we were absorbed in the cards, and the subject of the duel seemed to be banished from the minds of all, save those most concerned.

"What do you think of it?" I asked Marcel, when I was first able to speak to him, unheard by others.

"It is unfortunate, on the whole, though you are not to blame," he replied, pursing up his lips. "If you were to run him through with your sword, his inquisitive tongue would be silenced and his suspicious eyes shut forever. And yet I would not wish you to do that."

"Nor I," I said with deep conviction.

The gray in the east soon grew, and the world slid into the daylight. I looked at my comrades, and they were all haggard, their features drawn and great black streaks showing under their eyes. I shoved my gold into my pockets and said that we must go.

"And all the rest of us, too," said Moore. "Heavens! suppose that Sir William should have some active duty for us to-day! What would he think that we had been doing?"

His query was certainly pertinent, and the little gathering hastily dissolved, Marcel bidding his new-found cousin an affectionate good-night or rather good-morning.

As Marcel and I were about to pass out of the room, Waters appeared before us with a hot glass of mixed spirits in either hand.

"Better drink these before you go," he said. "They will freshen you."

The presence of this man with his evil eyes and significant glance coming upon us like an apparition was startling and decidedly unpleasant. I disliked him almost as much as I did Belfort, and in my soul I feared him more. I saw that self-same look of smirking satisfaction on his face, and I trembled not only with anger, but because I feared that the man possessed our secret and was playing with us for his own malicious sport. However we accepted his invitation and drank.

"When do you fight Lieutenant Belfort?" he asked, looking me straight in the eye as I handed back to him the empty glass.

"Is it any business of yours?" I said, flushing with anger.

"No, but I wondered why you and Lieutenant Belfort were so eager to quarrel," he replied, his eyes showing no fear of me.

"What damned impertinence is this!" broke out Marcel. "How dare you, a servant, speak in such a manner?"

"I beg your pardon, sir, I spoke hastily, I meant no harm," said the man, suddenly becoming humble, as if frightened by Marcel's heat.

"Then see that hereafter your actions conform better with your intentions," continued Marcel, as we passed out.

"That man is more to be feared than Belfort," I said a little later, speaking the thought that was in my mind.

"Yes, I think so, too," replied Marcel. "Confound him! Those eyes of his look me through, and I have the fancy that he is all the time laughing at us."

But Marcel's ill humor and suspicion lasted less than half a hour, and he was cheerfully humming a love song when he finally jumped into bed.

CHAPTER EIGHT—*A File of Prisoners*

We rose at noon the next day, and after the fashion of those times strolled toward the centre of the city to meet our friends and hear whatever news might chance to be going. Twenty-four hours earlier I would have escaped from Philadelphia if possible, but now I felt that my engagement with Belfort held me there. It was singular how circumstances combined to prevent our flight. "*Our* flight," I said, and yet I did not know that Marcel would go with me even if I fled. "*My* flight," I should say, and that, too, was impossible until I met Belfort. Then? Suppose I should slay him!

We met Vivian and Moore looking as fresh as if they had slept all the preceding night instead of playing cards, which, though perhaps not surprising in an Irishman, is somewhat beyond the power of most other people. A few moments later we met Belfort also, and he and I saluted gravely as became men who were to meet in another fashion soon.

"Come and see the American prisoners," said Moore. "The light cavalry took more than twenty yesterday, and they are just passing down the street to the prison, where I suspect that they will get better fare, bad as it is, than they have had for a long time."

The prisoners filed past, a lean and ragged band, and my heart was filled with sympathy.

"What a deuced shame that we should have to fight them!" said Moore. "Why couldn't they go back to their farms like peaceable men and obey King George like the loyal subjects they ought to be? That would end the trouble at once, and how simple! What a logician I am!"

"But the Irish don't obey King George," I said, "and they are his subjects too."

"That's different," rejoined Moore, quickly. "The Irish don't obey anybody, and never will."

Marcel suddenly pulled my arm, and when I looked around at him his face was pale. The fourth man in the line of prisoners was gazing intently at us, and his eyes expressed two emotions,—first recognition and then deep, bitter hatred. All soldiers detest traitors, and this man was one of the four whom Sergeant Pritchard had commanded. He knew us well, as we stood there in the gay uniforms of the enemy, and while he could not divine what we intended when we rode away in our borrowed plumage, he could believe but one thing now. His lips moved as if he were about to speak and denounce us; but I shook my head, gave him the most

185

significant look I could, and then putting my hand on Marcel's shoulder to indicate clearly that I was speaking to him, said in a loud voice,—

"Captain Montague, look at the fourth man in the line; does he not look wonderfully like one of the villains who chased us into the city?"

Thank heaven the man—Alloway was his name—was as quick as a flash. He heard me call Marcel Montague, and everything else may have been obscure to him, but he knew that we were not there under our right names, and that that probably meant something else other than treason. He dropped his head, looked no more at us, and walked on as impassive as the rest.

Two others had seen and taken notice, the two whom we dreaded most. They were Belfort and the scoundrel Waters, whom I now for the first time saw standing behind us, his red head towering above those around him. He seemed to have made it his special business to follow Marcel and me and to spy upon our doings. That hateful look of cunning was in his eyes, while Belfort's blazed with triumph. But both quickly dismissed all unusual expression, and Belfort was silent until the last man in the file had passed. Then he said,—

"I propose that we go to the prison and talk to those men. They are broken down and starving, and would gladly tell their woes to those who bring them food. We may acquire wonderful information concerning Mr. Washington and his army."

"It would be but a useless annoyance of prisoners," I said, seeing the drift of his mind.

"Not so," he replied. "It is a worthy object and is in the service of the king. I can easily get the necessary permission from the commandant of the prison."

Unluckily enough, Moore was greatly taken with the idea, and Vivian too liked it. They were all for talking with the prisoners, and Marcel and I were compelled to yield. We could have refused to go, but that, I felt sure, would be our undoing. I preferred that the questions Belfort wished to ask should be asked in our presence.

Belfort called Waters and sent him to the commandant with a request for the necessary permission, and we proceeded with our stroll until his return.

"This man Belfort is bound to catch us, if not by one method then by another," whispered Marcel to me. "You should not have looked with such admiring eyes upon the lady whom he has chosen for his own."

"But she has not chosen him, so far as you know," I replied, "and Mr. Belfort is not to be the master of my inclinations."

"Oh, well, don't pick a quarrel with me about it," he replied, with a wry face and then a smile. He did not seem to feel any apprehension, and I wondered if fear for the future was ever a quality that entered into his mental constitution. I had begun to believe that it did not, and that he was not to be held accountable for it.

Belfort burst suddenly into smiles and began to bow with great energy. Miss Desmond was approaching, and with her was Miss Rankin, a Tory's daughter. Miss Desmond was very simply dressed in light gray, and wore a single pink rose in her corsage. Her bearing was full of dignity, and she looked very beautiful, but, as always, cold and distant. We began to speak of the usual topics, for in our little pent-up city news soon became common; but at that moment Waters arrived with the necessary permission.

"The prisoners are sulky, sir," said Waters, with a respectful bow to Belfort, "and are not disposed to talk to anybody, but the commandant says that you may try."

I wondered if he had some sort of an understanding with Belfort. It did not seem wholly unlikely.

"At any rate it will be a novelty to talk to them," said Belfort, "and to see the inside of a prison, knowing that you can leave it whenever you wish. But I think that at least one of them will talk."

It was impossible for Marcel or me to mistake the significance of his last sentence or his intentions. Nothing else could account for this sudden desire to visit the prisoners, which looked to an ordinary observer like the freak of some one who had more time than occupation. Yet I could see purpose, determined purpose, in it.

"We are going to ask some American prisoners, just taken, why they are so foolish and wicked as to fight against the king," said Belfort, looking at Miss Desmond. "Will you not, Miss Desmond, and you, Miss Rankin, go with us and hear what they have to say? I assure you that it will be both interesting and instructive."

The man's effrontery amazed me, but I fathomed the depth of his malice and his proposed method. His defeat the night before had lulled his suspicions, but the look and manner of the prisoners had caused them to flame afresh. Now he hoped to expose us in the presence of our friends, and above all in the presence of Miss Desmond. Fortune seemed at last to have put all the chances in his favor.

"Oh, do let's go!" spoke up Miss Rankin, a young woman whose mind was not too important. "I have never been in a prison, and I should like to see how they live there."

"Believe me it is not a joyous sight, Miss Rankin," I said, hoping to keep the ladies away.

"Are you fully acquainted with it?" asked Belfort, in a low voice.

"Not as well, perhaps, as some others ought to be," I said in the same tone.

"Come, Miss Desmond, will you not go?" repeated Belfort. "It will be a valuable experience, one worth remembering."

Her eyes wandered over us, but I could not read the expression in them. They dwelt for a moment on Waters, as if wondering why a man of his condition was with us; and then she said that she would go, a flush of interest showing in her face. So we walked together toward the city prison, Belfort and Vivian escorting Miss Desmond, while the others devoted themselves to Miss Rankin. Marcel and I dropped a little behind.

"Phil," I said, "the gauntlet is nicely prepared for us."

"But we may run it," he replied cheerfully. "There's always a chance."

We were soon at the prison, and the commandant made no difficulties. In truth, Belfort seemed to have much influence with him, and five minutes later we were in the presence of the new prisoners, all of whom sat in one room where the dirt and cobwebs had gathered against the low ceiling, and where the light came dimly in at the narrow and iron-barred window. It was a gloomy place and its influence was visible at once upon us all. Even Miss Rankin ceased her chatter. The prisoners had just taken their food, and were making themselves as comfortable as they could, some upon two old wooden benches against the stone wall and some upon the floor. It suddenly occurred to me that they would send us here before they hung us, and the idea was not cheerful.

I wondered what the prisoners thought of us and our presence there, but they showed no curiosity. The man Alloway was sitting on the floor in a slouching attitude and took no notice.

"Here sit up, you!" exclaimed Waters, taking him roughly by the shoulders and jerking him up. "Do you not see that there are ladies present?"

"I can't imagine that they have come to this place for bright company," said Alloway, grimly.

Then Belfort began to talk to one of the men, purposely delaying his examination of Alloway as if he would linger over a choice morsel. I paid little attention to his questions, which seemed to elicit no satisfactory answer, but kept my eyes on Miss Desmond. Could a woman, young and beautiful, a Tory even, be without sympathy in the presence of her unfortunate countrymen, locked thus in a prison for no crime save fighting in defence of their own land, if that can be called a crime? Could she have so little heart? I did not believe it. In spite of her coldness and pride there was some charm about her which had drawn me to her, and I would not believe that a woman without heart could influence me so. Therefore I watched her closely, and at last I saw the light appear in the impassive eyes. When the others were not looking, she bent over the youngest of the prisoners and slipped something in his hand. I saw the flash of the golden guinea and the look of deep human feeling, and I knew that my lady had a heart. But she said nothing either to the prisoners or to us, and I believed that in her Tory soul she still condemned while for the moment she pitied.

I wished to speak to the man Alloway, to give him some hint, while Belfort was examining the others but I could find no opportunity. Always Belfort was watching me out of the corner of his eye, and Waters had the gaze of both eyes, full and square, upon me and Marcel. It was impossible for either of us to speak to Alloway without being seen or heard.

"Suppose we try this hulking fellow here, colonel," said Belfort to the commandant, pointing to Alloway.

"Would you like to ask him some questions, Captain Montague?" said Belfort, politely, to Marcel.

"No," replied Marcel, "it is no part of a British officer's duty."

Belfort flushed at the reply, and so did the commandant, who was an accessory to this proceeding. I saw that Marcel had made a new enemy.

"Come, my man, won't you give us some information?" said Belfort to Alloway.

Alloway's face settled into a defiant frown, but his eyes met mine once, and the swift look he gave me was full of curiosity. Nor did I read any threat there.

"We are all friends of yours; that is, all of us want to be your friends," said Belfort.

"Is that so? Then do your people have a habit of locking up in prison those of whom you think most?" returned Alloway, ironically.

"While we are all friends," resumed Belfort, "some of us are perhaps better friends than others, or better acquaintances. Are you sure there are not several of us whom you knew before to-day?"

"Why, what a strange examination, Lieutenant Belfort!" exclaimed Miss Desmond. Others, too, were looking at him in surprise. Belfort reddened, but it was not in him to be daunted.

"I asked for an excellent reason," he said politely to the commandant. "When these prisoners were passing through the street, this man seemed to recognize one of us and I wished to know which it was."

"What of that?" asked the commandant.

"It may lead to something else that I have in mind," replied Belfort, with tenacity.

"Proceed then," said the commandant, wonderingly.

"Do you not know some one of us?" asked Belfort of Alloway. His face showed the eagerness with which he put the question.

"Yes," replied Alloway.

Perhaps I had no right to expect anything else, but the answer came like a thunderbolt, and my heart fell. Alloway would betray us, and after all there was no reason why he should not.

Belfort's eyes flashed with triumph, and his hopes overran his caution.

"Who is it? who is it?" he cried. "Is it not he?" and he pointed his finger straight at me.

Alloway examined me critically, and then said, "No, I never saw him before in my life. There's the man I meant!" He pointed at Moore and continued: "He was a prisoner with us for a while after White Plains, and I was one of the escort that took him to the British lines when we exchanged him and others."

"It's true! It's true!" said Moore. "I remember you very well since you have spoken of it; and polite you were to me, for which I thank you. Right sorry am I to see you here."

It was another release from the hangman's rope, and Belfort was defeated for the second time. He recognized the fact and fell back, looking at me in a puzzled and mortified way. I believe he was convinced then that his suspicions were wrong. Why Alloway denied me I could not guess, for surely the look from me in the street was not sufficient to disclose such a complicated situation as ours. But it had happened so, and it was not for Marcel or me to complain.

"Have you finished, Lieutenant Belfort?" asked the commandant. "I understood that something important was to follow these questions or I would not have consented to such an irregularity."

"It is a mistake! I was upon the wrong path! I will explain another time!" said Belfort, hurriedly.

Marcel tapped his forehead suggestively, and all looked curiously at Belfort. They seemed to think that there was something in Marcel's idea. Of course, Belfort might have accused us openly, but he had no proof whatever, and the chances seemed at least a hundred to one that he would make himself ridiculous by such a declaration. No, I was not afraid of that, unless something else to arouse his smouldering suspicions should occur.

As we left the prison, Miss Desmond said to me, "I wish to ask Lieutenant Melville about Staffordshire."

"Ah, Miss Desmond," spoke up Moore, "if you want to know the truth about any part of England, you should ask an Irishman."

So saying, he placed his hand upon his heart and bowed.

"An Irishman always talks best about the thing of which he knows least," said Vivian.

But all walked on, and Miss Desmond and I were the last of the company. I wondered why she had chosen me thus. There was very little that I could tell her about Staffordshire, and in truth, it seemed a poor subject for conversation just then.

"Lieutenant Melville," she said, "why are you and Lieutenant Belfort to fight a duel?"

Her question was so sudden and direct that it startled me. I had not suspected that she knew of our quarrel.

"It is because we could not agree upon a point of honor," I said.

"Do you think that it is a proper business for two of the king's officers?" she asked.

"Since you wish me to be frank, I do not," I replied, "but it was impossible for me to avoid it, and perhaps my antagonist will say the same concerning himself."

"Why do you fight?" she asked. Then I knew that she had not heard the full tale, the cause of our quarrel, and I reflected for a moment while she looked at me with bright eyes. I felt like a little boy called up for punishment and seeking excuse.

"It was over the cards," I said. "There was some talk about the measures that should be taken against the rebels. Lieutenant Belfort advocated more severity, I more mildness. I do not think the opinion of either would have had any influence on the policy of the Government, but that did not restrain our heat. We quarrelled like cabinet ministers at odds. There was a blow, I think, a demand for an apology, which was refused; and what followed is to be left to the seconds, who have not yet been named."

"I do not believe you," she said, still holding me with her calm, bright eyes.

I felt the hot blood flushing my face, but neither in her tone nor manner did she condemn me or speak as one who despised a man caught in a falsehood. Rather she was reproachful.

"There is some other reason," she said, "and you will not tell it to me, but I shall not ask you again."

I was silent, and she resumed,—

"Promise me that you will not fight this duel, Lieutenant Melville."

I was as much surprised at the request as I had been when she asked me why Belfort and I were to meet. It was my first thought that she was in fear for him, and I asked with a little malice,—

"Do you make the same request of Lieutenant Belfort?"

When I saw the faint flush of color rising in her face, I was sorry that I had asked the question.

"No," she replied, "I would not make such a request of him, although I have known him longer than I have you."

I was pleased, greatly pleased; but she reminded me that I had not answered her question.

"The challenge has been issued," I said, "and if I withdraw at so late a moment I should be called a coward. Would you have me bear such a name in Philadelphia?"

"No; but is there no other way?"

"None that I know of."

A look of sadness replaced the flush on her face.

"It is a barbarous custom, I think," she said, "and belongs to a barbarous age. It is merely the better swordsman or marksman who wins, and not of necessity the better man. It decides no more than the hot ploughshare of the Middle Ages, and of the two customs I think the trial by hot iron was the saner."

I was silent, again not knowing what to answer, and she too said no more. I believe that at the last, and after weighing my evasions, she began to guess why Belfort and I had quarrelled. In a few moments we joined the others, and we bore the ladies company to their houses. Belfort was silent and moody over his failure, and bade us a brief adieu. It was ten o'clock then, and soon we were due at Catron's rooms to arrange for the duel. But before the time had elapsed the man Waters came to our quarters, his evil eyes peering under his shock of red hair.

"Confound it," I cried, "your company is an honor that I can well do without!"

"I would not intrude," he said, "but I am sent by the commander-in-chief, Sir William Howe, himself, who wishes you to come at once to his headquarters."

I was startled. The detection of our identity, or punishment for preparing to fight a duel were the ideas that sprang up in my head. But the first disappeared quickly. If Sir William had discovered who we were, he would have sent a file of soldiers for both of us, and not an order to me alone to come to his headquarters.

"You have no choice but to go," said Marcel, "and if you do not return in time I will report to Catron what has happened. I will see that Belfort does not make any charges against you."

CHAPTER NINE—*With the Commander-in-Chief*

I knew that my honor was safe in Marcel's hands, and I followed Waters to Sir William Howe, whom I found dictating to his secretary. He gave me a little nod and said,—

"I have sent my aide, Vivian, away on other duty and I wish you to take his place. You will find a chair there and you can wait."

I sat down, and he paid no further attention to me for a long time. Then he relieved the secretary, who looked worn out, and put me in his place. I write a fair round hand with a goose quill, and Sir William seemed pleased with my work. The letters were on official business, mostly to cabinet ministers in London, and to this day I often wonder if the British archives still contain documents written by that most disloyal rebel Robert Chester.

Evidently it was a busy day with Sir William Howe, as we wrote on hour after hour, long past four o'clock, the time for arranging the duel, though my work did not keep me from noticing more than once the luxury of Sir William's quarters, and the abundant proof that this man was made for a life of easy good-nature and not for stern war. How well the British served us with most of their generals! I inferred that busy days such as this were rare with Sir William Howe.

Orderlies came in with reports and went directly out again. The night darkened through the windows at last, and supper was brought to us, which I had the honor of sharing with Sir William.

It was full ten o'clock when he sat down in a chair and ceased to dictate, while I opened and shut my cramped fingers to be sure that I still had over them the power of motion.

"You are tired, Melville," said Sir William, "and you have honestly earned your weariness."

"I hope that I have served you well, Sir William," I replied. I was thoroughly sincere when I said this. God knows that I had cause only to like Sir William Howe, and in truth I did like him. I thought of him as a good man in the wrong place.

"Yes, you have done well," he said, "but I did not send for you merely to help me in this work. I wished to break up the plans for that silly duel that you and Lieutenant Belfort are trying to arrange. Do not flush; none of your friends have betrayed you. I heard of it through a proper channel. I could have arrested and punished you both, but I preferred a milder method. I liked you from the first, Lieutenant Melville, and I do not wish my young officers to kill one another. You cannot serve either the king, me, or one another by sharpening your swords on the bones of your comrades. No protestations, but understand that I forbid this! Do I wish either you or Lieutenant Belfort to come to me with British blood on his hands? Is it not bad enough when the Englishmen of the Old World and the New are cutting one another's throats?"

It was a time when silence became me, and in truth no answer was needed. Sir William seemed to be excited. He walked hurriedly back and forth, and apparently forgot the lowness of my rank when he continued,—

"I have been blamed by a numerous and powerful party in England because I have not pushed the campaign more vigorously, because I have not used more severity. I say this to you, a young man, because every one knows it. A wasted country, burning towns, and slaughtered people do not look so bad when they are thousands of miles away. But put yourself in my place, in the place of the general-in-chief. Did I wish to kill the sons and grandsons of Englishmen? Did I wish to waste this English domain, greater than England herself? I hoped, when leaving England, that the quarrel would be made up, that all Englishmen would remain brethren. My brother and I made offers, and I still hoped, even after the battle of Long Island and our capture of New York, that the rebels would come back to us. But they have not, and those who remain loyal, like the rich of this city and New York, do not seem to know the temper and resources of their own countrymen who oppose us. How could I fight well with the torch of peace in one hand and the torch of war in the other? There must be either peace or war. A country cannot have both at the same time."

"It is certain," I said, "that if any other country possessed these colonies it would not have treated them as well as England has done."

In making that assertion I was thoroughly sincere. While convinced that we had ample cause for rebellion, I had always felt that the cause would have been much greater had our mother nation been any other than England. She ruled us mildly or rather let us rule ourselves until we grew strong and proud, and then suddenly and against the wishes of many of her best, sought to give us a master when we had never known one.

"It is true, or at least I hope so," said Sir William, "but that does not end the war. How are we to achieve the conquest of a country six or seven times as large as England, and inhabited by a people of our own race and spirit? If we beat an army in one place, another appears elsewhere; if we hold a city, it is merely an island in a sea of rebels, and we cannot convert the whole thirteen colonies into one huge camp!"

As I have said before, Sir William seemed much agitated. I noticed a letter with the royal seal lying upon the table, to which his eyes frequently turned and which he took in his hand several times, though he did not reopen it in my presence. I judged that its contents were unpleasant to him, though I could not guess their nature. That and his agitation would account for the extraordinary freedom with which he spoke to me, a comparative stranger. And I was sincerely sorry for him, knowing his unfitness for the task in which he had failed, and believing too that he bore my countrymen no ill will. He continued his uneasy walk for a few minutes, and then sitting down endeavoured to compose himself.

"Do not repeat any of the things that I have said to you, Melville; see that you do not," he said to me; but he added in a lower tone, as if to himself, "But I know of no good reason why my opinions should not be heard."

I assured him that nothing he had said would be repeated by me, and in truth I had no thought of doing so, even before he gave his caution.

"Melville," he said, "you are tired and sleepy, and so am I. I shall not send you to your quarters, but there is a lounge in the anteroom upon which Vivian sleeps. You may take his place there to-night, and consider yourself the commander of my guard. Merely see that the sentinels are on duty at the door and have received proper instructions. Then you may go to sleep."

I bade him good-night, found that all was right with the sentinels, and lay down in my clothes on the lounge. I was worn out with the long work, but I did not go to sleep. I was compelled to reflect upon the extreme singularity of my position. I, Robert Chester, a lieutenant in the rebel army and most loyal to the Congress, was on watch at the door of Sir William Howe, the British commander-in-chief, as commander of his guard. And moreover I meant to be faithful to my trust. Upon these points my conscience gave me no twinge, but it urged with increasing force the necessity of our speedy flight from Philadelphia. Our errand had been a fruitless one. Honor called us away and danger hurried us on. Only the duel with Belfort stood in the way of an attempt to escape. It is true that Sir William Howe had forbidden the meeting, but I did not feel that I could withdraw from it despite his command. I was too deeply involved.

Shortly after I lay down I heard loud voices, and two men who gave the countersign passed the sentinel and entered the room where I lay. I had not put out the light, and I saw their faces distinctly. They were Hessians, and colonels, as I judged by their uniform. Now I always hated the sight of a Hessian, and when they told me that they wished to see Sir William Howe on important business, I examined them long and critically, from their flushed faces down to their great jackboots, before I condescended to answer.

"Don't you hear us?" exclaimed the younger with an oath and in bad English. "We wish to see Sir William Howe!"

"Yes, I hear you," I said, "but I do not know that Sir William wishes to see you."

"He himself is to be the judge of that," replied the elder, "and do you tell him that we are here."

Their faces were sure proof that both men had been drinking, but evidently the potations of the younger had been the deeper. Otherwise even a Hessian would scarcely have dared to be so violent in manner. I told them that Sir William probably had retired, and on no account could they disturb him. They insisted in angry tones, but I would have stood by my refusal had not Sir William himself, who had heard the altercation, appeared, fully dressed, at the door, and bade them enter. I was about to retire, but Sir William signed to me to stay, and I sat down in a chair near the window.

It was merely a matter concerning the Hessian troops,—a claim of the colonels that they had received an over-share of danger and an under-share of rations, while the British had been petted; and I would not put down the narration of it here had it not produced an event that advanced me still further in the good graces of Sir William.

Hessian soldiers in those days even ordinarily had but few manners, but when in liquor none at all. They seemed to presume, too, upon the widely reported fact that Sir William Howe was fast losing credit with his government and might be supplanted at any time. They were accusing, even violent in their claims; and the red flush appeared more than once upon the swarthy skin of Sir William's face. I wondered how he could restrain his anger, but he was essentially self-restrained, and though he was their commander he did not reply to them in kind. At last the younger man, Schwarzfelder was his name, denied outright and in an insulting manner some statement made by Sir William, and I rose at once. Sir William's eye met mine, and his look was in the affirmative. I took the Hessian colonel, who in truth was staggering with drink, dragged him through the anteroom, and threw him into the street. This brought his comrade to his senses, and he apologized hastily both for himself and Colonel Schwarzfelder.

"Deem yourself fortunate," said Sir William, sternly and with much dignity, "that you and Colonel Schwarzfelder do not hear more of this. I am yet the commander-in-chief of his Majesty's forces in America, and I am not to be insulted by any of my subordinates, either here or elsewhere. Go back, sir, to your quarters at once and take your drunken comrade with you. Lieutenant Melville, I thank you again for your services."

The officer retired in great confusion, and Sir William sent me back to the anteroom. I left him sitting at his table, looking thoughtful and gloomy.

CHAPTER Ten—*The Fine Finish of a Play*

When I reached our room the next morning, I found Marcel just rising, though there were black lines under his eyes, from which I judged that his sleep had not been adequate to the demands of nature. Yet he seemed happy and contented. There was upon his face no shadow, either of troubles past, present, or to come.

"Ah, Philadelphia is a pleasant place, Robert my bold knight!" he said. "I would that I could stay here long enough to exhaust its pleasures. It is seldom that I have met fellows of such wit, fancy and resource as Moore, Vivian, and the others. They have an abundance to eat here, cards without limit, beautiful women to look upon and admire and dance with; a theatre where they say the plays are not bad, and upon the stage of which the beautiful Mary Desmond herself is to appear with honor and distinction, for she could not appear otherwise. Now tell me, out of the truth that is in your soul, Robert Chester, can life at Valley Forge compare with life in Philadelphia?"

The mention of Mary Desmond's name in such a connection of course caught my attention, but I deferred all question about it until I could draw from Marcel the narration of what had occurred at Catron's room when I did not come to arrange the duel.

"We had a game, a most beautiful game," said Marcel, in reply. "Vincent Moore and I were partners, and we won everything that the others could transfer from their pockets to the table. Upon my soul, Bob, I love that Irishman almost as much as I do you!"

"But the duel?" I said; "what explanation did you make for me?"

"By my faith," he cried, "Vivian and Belfort and Catron wanted us to explain how we could win so handsomely and so continuously. They said that Old Nick was surely at our elbow, and if you consider the invisible character of the gentleman aforesaid, I cannot deny that he was or wasn't."

"But the duel, the duel?" I said. "Marcel, be serious for two consecutive minutes!"

"Oh, that little affair of yours and Belfort's! I had forgotten about it in the midst of more important subjects. Why do you bother so much over trifles, Chester? It's that confounded Quakerish sense of responsibility you have. Get rid of it. It will never do you any good in this world or the next, and will spoil many otherwise pleasant moments. But your little affair? I see that you are growing red in the face with impatience or annoyance, and are not to be satisfied without a narration. Well, I arrived at Catron's room on time, and explained that you had been summoned by Sir William Howe, and would communicate with us as soon as you could escape from the honor conferred upon you by the commander-in-chief. All of which I spoke in most stately and proper fashion, and the result seemed extremely satisfactory to every gentleman present, saving his High Mightiness, Lieutenant Reginald Belfort, who was disposed to impugn your courage or at least your zeal for a trial at arms, whereupon I offered to fight him myself, without delay, in that very room and at that very minute. Moore was eager for it, saying that the proposition was most becoming to a gentleman like myself (I gave him my best bow) and was in the highest interest of true sport, but the others lacked his fine perceptions and just appreciation of a situation and would not allow it. Then Moore proposed cards, and we sat down to the game at exactly ten minutes past four o'clock by my watch, and we did not rise until ten minutes past four o'clock this morning by the same watch, rounding out the twelve hours most handsomely. At some point in those twelve hours,—I do not remember just when, for I held a most beautiful hand at that moment,—Sir William's secretary came in with a report that you had been installed for the night in his place, which, of course, checked any further aspersion on your honor that Belfort might have had in store for you."

Then I told him that Sir William Howe knew of the projected duel and had forbidden it.

"What do you say now, Marcel?" I asked.

"Why, it was a pretty affair before," he exclaimed, and his face expressed supreme satisfaction, "but it is famous now. A duel is a duel at any time, but a forbidden duel is best of all. You and Belfort are bound to fight since the commander-in-chief has forbidden it. I can conceive of no possible set of circumstances able to drive us away from Philadelphia until the edges of your swords shall have met."

"But how?" I asked helplessly.

"Don't worry," he said with confidence. "Moore and I will arrange it. With that man to help me, I would agree to arrange anything. Now, Bob, you just be calm and trust me. Don't bother yourself at all about this duel until you get your sword in your hand and Belfort before you; then do your best."

It is the truth that I had no wish to fight a duel, but I did not intend that I alone should appear unwilling; so I left the affair in Marcel's hands, meanwhile seeming to look forward to the meeting as a man does to his wedding. Then I asked Marcel what he meant by the appearance of Miss Desmond in the play.

"I was going to tell you of that," he said. "You know the little theatre in South Street. It has been the scene of some famous plays during the past winter. They have officers here who write them and act them too. There's 'The Mock Doctor,' and 'The Devil is in it,' and 'The Wonder,'—the wonder of which last is a woman who kept a secret,—and maybe a dozen more. Well, they are going to give one to-night that has in it many parts for gallant knights and beautiful ladies. The British officers are, of course, the gallant knights, and our Tory maidens are the beautiful ladies. They asked Miss Desmond to take a leading part. She objected to appearing on the stage, and her father, the crusty old merchant, sustained her in the refusal. But they tacked about and poured in a broadside from another quarter,—it was a naval officer who told me about it. They said that she was the most conspicuous of the Tory young ladies in Philadelphia, and she would seem lacking in zeal if she refused to share in an affair devised, given, and patronized by the most loyal. Whereupon she withdrew her refusal, and I suppose has prevailed upon her father to withdraw his also,—at least he has made no further objection. You will go, of course, Robert, and see her act."

Yes, I would go, but I was conscious in my heart of a secret dislike to the appearance of Mary Desmond upon the stage. It was an affair for ladies and gentlemen, and but few of the general public would be present; still it was not a time when play acting was regarded with very favorable eyes, especially in America. Yet I was conscious that my objection was not founded upon that feeling. I did not wish to see Mary Desmond, to whom I was naught, seeking the applause of a crowd, and above all, I was not willing to hear these men from England discussing her as they would discuss some stage queen of their own London.

Belfort, who was a fine actor, so Marcel told me, was to have the hero's part, and he was to make love to Miss Desmond.

"But I promise you it's all in the play, Bob," said Phil, looking at me from under his eyebrows.

I was not so sure of that, but this additional news increased my distaste for the play, and I would have changed my mind and stayed away if Marcel had not assured me that it could not be done.

"You are to go with us behind the scenes, Bob," he said. "We have already arranged for that. Moore is one of the managers, and he has made me his assistant. Behold, how invaluable I have become to the British army in the few days that we have been in Philadelphia! We may need your help, too. You are to be held in reserve, and Moore will never forgive you if you do not come."

I was a little surprised at his eagerness on the point, but at the appointed time I went with him to the theatre. It had never lacked for attendance when the plays were given in the course of the winter, and to-night, as usual, it was crowded with British and Hessian officers, and Philadelphia Tories with their wives and daughters. I peeped at the audience from my place behind the curtain, and it had been a longtime since I had seen so much white powder and rose-pink and silk ribbon and golden epaulet.

I do not remember much about the play or even its name, only that it had in it a large proportion of love-making, and fighting with swords, all after the approved fashion. I might have taken more careful note, had not Reginald Belfort and Mary Desmond filled the principal parts, and my eyes and ears were for them in particular rather than for the play in general. There was a great chorus of "Bravos," and a mighty clapping of hands when she appeared upon the stage as the oppressed and distressed daughter of a mediæval English Lord whom the brave knight, Lieutenant Reginald Belfort, was to win, sword in hand, and to whom he was to make the most ardent love. Belfort did his part well. I give him full credit for that. He did not miss a sigh or vow of passion, and his voice, his looks, his gestures were so true, so earnest, that the audience thundered its applause.

"Doesn't he play it splendidly?" said Marcel, in an ecstasy to me.

"Yes, damn him!" I growled.

And she! she merely walked through the part for a long time, but she gradually caught the spirit of the lines—perhaps in spite of herself, I hoped—and became the persecuted and distressed maiden that the play would have her. Then her acting was real and sincere, and, with her wondrous beauty to aid her, the audience gave her an applause even exceeding that they had yielded to Belfort.

"It's a dazzling success!" said Marcel to me, with continued enthusiasm at the end of the second act.

I was bound to own that it was.

"But the best scene is to come yet," said Marcel, as he hurried away. "It will close the play."

The curtain soon fell on the last act and the distressed maiden and the gallant knight who had rescued her, drawn sword yet in hand, had been united forever amid the applause of all. This I supposed was the best scene, though I could not see why Marcel should say so, and I was about to leave, when he reappeared again and seemed to be in great haste.

"Come this way, Bob!" he said, putting his hand on my shoulder. "If you go in that direction, you will lose yourself among the scenes and stage trappings."

I let him lead me as he wished, and in a few moments we came out, not into the street as I had expected, but in an open space at the rear of the theatre, where the moonlight was shining upon five men who were standing there. They were Vivian, Catron, Moore, Harding, and two others in plain dress who looked like surgeons. Marcel put a sword in my hand.

"This is to be that last, the best scene, of which I told you," he said gleefully.

At that moment Belfort appeared escorted by Moore. Belfort still held in his hand the sword that he had carried on the stage.

There was no time for either of us to take thought; perhaps we would not have taken it if there had been. The love-making scenes of the play were fresh in my memory, and as for Belfort he hated me with sincerity and persistency. We faced each other, sword in hand.

"Isn't it glorious?" I heard Marcel say behind me. "Moore and I arranged it. Could we have conceived of a prettier situation? And as the finishing act, the last perfect touch to the play!"

Belfort's eye was upon mine, and it was full of malice. He seemed glad that this opportunity had come. I was only a fair swordsman, but I was cool and felt confident. We raised our swords and the blades clashed together.

But the duel was not destined to be. The fine erection of circumstance which Marcel and Moore—fit spirits well matched—had raised with so much care and of which they were so proud, crumbled at a stroke to the ground.

Mary Desmond, still in her costume of the play, but changed from the distressed maiden to an indignant goddess, rushed amongst us.

"For shame!" she cried. "How dare you fight when Sir William Howe has forbidden this duel! Are you so eager to kill each other that you must slip from a stage at midnight to do it?"

I have always remembered the look of comic dismay on the faces of Marcel and Moore at this unhappy interference with their plans, but Marcel spoke up promptly.

"So far as time and place are concerned, Miss Desmond," he said, "Lieutenant Melville and Lieutenant Belfort are not to blame. Moore and I arranged it." (Moore bowed in assent.)

She paid no attention to them, but reminded Belfort and me of our obligations to obey the orders of the commander-in-chief. She looked very beautiful in her indignation, the high color rising in her cheeks, and, even with a fear of the charge that I dreaded the combat, I was inclined to promise her that I would not fight Lieutenant Belfort.

"Lieutenant Melville, will you not escort me back to the dressing-room in the theatre?" she asked suddenly of me.

I bowed, handed my sword to Marcel, and went with her, happy that she had chosen me, though hardly knowing why.

"I have no wish to hurt Lieutenant Belfort, and certainly none to be hurt by him," I said, as we passed between stage scenery. "If it grieves you to think that perchance he should be wounded by me, I will not fight him at all."

Perhaps I was not wholly sincere in that, but I said it.

"I saw him to-night in the play," I continued, "and he was most earnest and successful."

"But it was a play, and a play only. Do not forget that," she said, and was gone.

When I returned to the court, I found no one there, save Waters, who had helped that night in moving the scenery.

"You are disappointed, Lieutenant Melville," he said, leering at me with his cunning eyes. "You cannot have your duel. I came up just as you left with Miss Desmond; there was an alarm that the provost guard was at hand, and they all ran away, carrying Lieutenant Belfort with them. It may have been part of Miss Desmond's plan."

I did not even thank the man for his information, so much did I resent his familiarity, and I resented, too, the fear which I felt of him and which I could not dismiss despite myself. I went to my room, and found Marcel waiting for me.

"We have concluded to abandon the duel, Bob," he said. "Fate is apparently against it. But 'tis a great pity that 'tis so. The finest situation that I ever knew spoiled when it seemed to be most successful. But don't think, Bob, that I wanted the life of you, my best friend, put in risk merely for sport. Since I could not get the chance, I hoped that you would give the insolent fellow some punishment, and I can tell you in confidence, too, that Moore and the others had the same wish."

I needed no apology from Marcel, as I knew that if necessary he would go through fire for me; and I told him so.

CHAPTER Eleven—*A Man Hunt*

The next day was dull, and the night began the same way, but it was not destined to remain so. Great results accrue from small causes, and it seemed that the arrival of Marcel and myself had given a fillip to the quiet city and the lazy army reposing there. At least it flattered our vanity to think so.

Having nothing to do in the evening, our footsteps inevitably took us toward Catron's quarters. I had not intended to go there, but the way of amusement and luxury is easy, and I went. Moreover it was policy, I persuaded myself, for us in our situation to live this rapid life, as it would divert suspicion, and I found my conscience somewhat eased by the thought.

Catron had most comfortable quarters, and he was rarely troubled with useless messages about military duty. So it had become a habit with the others to gather there, and when we arrived we found Moore, Blake, who was now quite well, and several others already present. Vivian was on duty at Sir William's headquarters and could not come. They received us warmly. Moore and Marcel indulged in some laments over their upset plans of the night before, told each other how much better the affair would have terminated had they been the principals instead of the seconds, and then forgot it. Belfort came in promptly, and nodded to us in a manner that indicated neither friendship nor hostility. I believed that he had given up, unwilling to risk more failures, or perhaps convinced that we were really what we claimed to be, but I decided to remain wary and watch him.

The night was dark, the clouds making threats of rain, and we felt it was a good time to be indoors. Taking advantage of this feeling, Catron and Moore began to urge cards. I feared the fascination of gaming, and would have avoided the challenge, but I knew that I should have thought of that before coming. Being there, it was not permitted me to escape, and I sat down to picquet with the others. About the beginning of the second hour of the play we heard a musket-shot, and in a moment or so, several others, fired in a scattering volley.

We threw down the cards and ran to the door. The night had darkened further, and rain had begun to fall in a fine drizzle. Just as we reached the door, we saw the flash of another musket-shot and the dim forms of men running.

"What is it?" we cried, stirred by the flash and the report and the beat of flying feet.

"The American prisoners have broken from the jail and the guards are pursuing them!" some one replied.

"A chase! a chase!" cried Moore and Catron, at once. "Come, lads, and help the guards!"

Hastily buckling on our swords, we rushed into the street and joined in the pursuit. It was far from the thoughts of either Marcel or me to aid in the seizure of any countrymen of ours who might be in the way of escape, but in truth we were compelled to take up the chase with the others. It was our duty as British officers, and I reflected with some degree of pleasure that it was easy to pretend zeal and have it not.

Brief as was my stay in Philadelphia, I had often looked at the gloomy building on Washington Square, the Walnut Street jail, where so many of my countrymen were confined and where so many of them suffered so grievously. Once, in truth, I had been inside of it, at the harrying of Alloway, and that visit did not increase my love for the place. It was of such strength, and guarded with such care, that the report of all the prisoners breaking from it seemed past belief. In truth, we soon found that only a score had escaped, the score the next minute became a dozen, then three or four, and, at last, only one.

We rushed through the square brandishing our swords, firing two or three shots from our pistols, and showing great enthusiasm. Belfort suddenly caught sight of a fugitive form, fired a shot at it, and gave chase, shouting that it was the escaped prisoner. He was right, for as we followed, the man turned suddenly, discharged a pistol at his pursuers, the bullet breaking a private's leg, and then ran toward the encampment of the Hessian grenadiers between Fifth and Seventh Streets.

On we sped through the dim light after him, and I began to revolve in my mind some plan for helping the desperate fugitive. The very numbers of the pursuers were an advantage, as we got in one another's way, and moreover, a pursuer was sometimes mistaken for the prisoners, the mistake not being discerned until he was overtaken with great violence. Some of the people joined in the hunt, and I was heartily ashamed of them. Presently a spacious citizen and myself collided with excessive force. He sank to the ground, gasping, but I, who had some expectation of the event, ran on, sure that I had done a good deed. Yet, in spite of myself, I felt the enthusiasm of the chase rising in me. I suppose that it does not matter what a man hunts so long as he hunts. But the fugitive winding among streets and alleys led us a long chase and proved himself to be noble game. Presently I heard Moore panting at my elbow.

"The fellow runs well!" he exclaimed to me. "I'd like to capture him, but I hope he'll escape!"

Moore, it is to be remembered, was an Irishman.

We lost sight of the fugitive a little later, but in a few moments saw him again, his figure wavering as if he were approaching exhaustion. I felt deep pity for him, and anger for myself because I had found no way to help him in his desperate plight. He had succeeded in shaking off, for the time being, all except our own party, which I now noticed had been reinforced by Waters. Where he came from, I do not know, but he seemed to be watching Marcel and me more than the fugitive.

It was now hare and hounds, and the hare suddenly dashed into an alley, which cut the middle of a city square. The others followed at once, but, unnoticed, I left them and took a different direction, intending to curve about the square and meet the fugitive on the other side, as I thought it likely that he would turn when we came out of the alley and run toward the north, which presented the best side for escape. It was a chance, but I was determined to take it and it served me well.

The rain was whipped into my face by the wind, and it half blinded me at times, but I ran on, and presently the sounds of the pursuit up the alley died. I was much bent upon helping the fugitive, and great was my pleasure when I reached the parallel street to see a dim figure running towards me. Even at a distance the figure showed great signs of weariness, and I was sure that it was our man.

I do not think that he saw me until he was very near, and then he threw up his hands as if in despair. But he recovered himself in a moment, and coming on quite fiercely struck at me with his unloaded pistol. Then I saw, to my infinite surprise, that it was Alloway. I held my sword in my hand, but I did not raise it against him or make any hostile movement, and the fact made him look at me more closely. Then he saw my face and knew me.

"What are you going to do?" he asked.

"Don't you hear the shouts of men before you?" I said. "The way is closed there, and you know that others are hot behind you! You must hide, and escape when the pursuit dies! See that house, the one with the lawn in front and the gardens behind! Run! hide yourself there! It's the house of John Desmond, a friend!"

Without my noticing it until then, the windings of the chase had brought us before John Desmond's home, and I saw no chance for Alloway unless he could hide for the time in the house or gardens.

"Quick," I cried, "over the fence! See, there is a light appearing in the house now! It may be John Desmond himself! If it is an old man of noble appearance, trust him, but put yourself in the hands of no woman, and say nothing of me!"

He obeyed, leaped the fence, and disappeared instantly in the shrubbery just as the hue and cry emerged from the alley and swept up the street towards me.

I was in the shadow of the buildings, and I ran forward with great energy, plunging violently into the arms of somebody who went down under the shock of the collision. But he held tightly to me and shouted,—

"I have him! I have him! It's my capture!"

I displayed a similar fierce zeal, and clung to him, exclaiming,—

"I thought that I would cut you off, and I have done it! Yield yourself!"

I reinforced my victory by sundry sound blows on the side of my antagonist's head, but in a few moments the crowd surrounded and then separated us, disclosing the bedraggled features of Moore, my captive.

"Thunder and lightning!" exclaimed the Irishman, a broad smile overspreading his face. "I thought you were a fool as you came straight towards me, and you must have thought I was a fool coming straight towards you; and sure both of us were right!"

"Didn't you see him?" I cried, affecting the greatest impatience. "He turned and ran back this way! He must have passed, as one of the crowd!"

"Aye, yonder he goes, that must be he!" cried Moore, pointing in a direction that led far away from Mr. Desmond's house. I think that Moore saw double through the violence of his meeting with me, or perhaps he mistook the dim figure of some one else for the fugitive. But as it was, we followed the wrong trail at good speed. Belfort in the lead and I last, wondering at the escape of Alloway and its singular timeliness, for however well disposed he might be toward us, he might let slip at any time, and without intending it, a word or two that would betray us.

I knew that Belfort had no suspicions of my intervention in this case, but the man Waters was there, and I believed that he was watching me always. He dropped back presently to my side and said,—

"Do you think that the man will escape, lieutenant?"

"I have no thoughts upon the subject," I said roughly, "and if I had I certainly would not confide them to you."

"I meant no harm, sir," he replied, "but one sometimes feels a little sympathy for such poor hunted fellows."

But I was not to be betrayed by such dangerous admissions. I would not allow a man of his humble rank to question me, and I did not answer him.

The chase died presently. You cannot keep a fire going without fuel, and since there was no longer a fugitive, we were no longer able to maintain a pursuit. At last we gave up entirely and returned slowly and wearily to Catron's quarters. I was sure that Alloway had been concealed by John Desmond, and later on would slip out of the city. On the whole I felt extreme satisfaction with the evening's work. My old wonder about the timeliness of Alloway's escape returned, but there was no solution. What Belfort thought of it he did not care to say, being silent like myself.

CHAPTER TWELVE—A Delicate Search

I was aroused early the next morning by Marcel, who stood at my bedside shaking me vigorously.

"Get up, Bob," he said, "there is work for you to do."

He was dressed already, and regarding me curiously, his gaze containing a faint suggestion of humor.

"What is it?" I asked, sitting up and rubbing my eyes sleepily.

"Your particular friend, Mr. Waters, is here with orders," he replied, stepping to the door and giving a signal.

The big, red-headed orderly entered and handed me a letter, gazing the while respectfully at the wall, although I was sure that in his inmost heart he suspected us and enjoyed our danger. I took the paper and held it a moment between thumb and finger, fearing to read its contents, but in a moment I dismissed my alarm as unworthy of a man and broke the seal.

Lieutenant Melville is ordered to take a file of men at once and search the house of John Desmond for one Alloway, an American soldier who escaped from the prison last night and is believed to have hidden himself there. The search is to be conducted with all the courtesy consistent with thoroughness.

HOWE, Commander-in-chief.

I felt a rush of blood from the heart to the head when I read this order. Who had betrayed Alloway? Marcel's fate and mine were in a way bound up with his, and whoever had seen him entering the Desmond house might too have seen me advising him to hide there. I looked fixedly at Waters, but he was still gazing at the same spot on the wall and his face was without expression. I studied his profile, the heavy cheek-bones, the massive projecting jaw, and the steady black eyes, the whole forming a countenance of unusual strength and boldness, and I felt that he would dare anything. This was a man who could use his power over Marcel and me merely for his own sport, torturing us until he chose to crush us.

And then another thought, even more unpleasant, came into my mind. Perhaps it was Mary Desmond herself who had betrayed Alloway! It was altogether likely that she would discover him in her father's house. But I rejected the thought the next instant, since, Tory though she was, she could not have stooped to such an act.

"You can go," I said to Waters; and he left, first saluting both Marcel and me, his face remaining a complete mask.

Then I showed the order to Marcel.

"I trust that you will find nothing," he said significantly, "but you know, Lieutenant Arthur Melville of Newton-on-the-hill, Staffordshire, England, that there is naught for you to do but go and do it."

"I know it," I replied, "and I shall not hesitate."

"Take care that you search properly," said Marcel, looking me straight in the eye. I believed that he understood, but he said no more now, and I went forth to do my distasteful duty. I took ten men and proceeded towards the Desmond house. We attracted no attention in the street, as soldiers had long since grown to be a common sight in Philadelphia, but on the way we met Belfort and the Hessian Colonel Schwarzfelder, whom I had thrown out of General Howe's room. They seemed to be acquainted and on good terms, and I did not like this alliance of two men whom I knew to be my enemies. I liked still less the question that Belfort asked me.

"On duty, eh, Melville?" he said jauntily, as if he knew what I was about, but preferred that I should tell it.

I glanced at Schwarzfelder too, and noticed a sneering look on his face as if he were prepared to enjoy a triumph over me. Perhaps it was Belfort, after all, who was the cause of the proposed search. But I did not hesitate to tell them the truth.

"I am going to search John Desmond's house for the man who escaped from the prison last night," I replied calmly. "It is the order of General Howe."

"And the beautiful Miss Desmond such a good Royalist!" said Belfort. "I do not envy you."

"I do not envy myself," I replied frankly, and walked on with my men, arriving presently at Mr. Desmond's house, which looked as if all its occupants were yet asleep. And in truth they might well be, since the sun was just showing his red rim above the eastern hills, and in the west the mists of early dawn yet lingered.

I ordered my men to stand ready, and then I struck the door a resounding blow with the great brass knocker. I listened a minute or two, but no one answered, nor could I hear anything within the house to indicate life and movement. I knocked a second and a third time, and presently there was a sound on the inside as of some one moving a bar from the door, which was opened the next moment by John Desmond himself. He was fully dressed in sober Quaker gray, and regarded us with the greatest sternness. I own that I was much embarrassed and felt extremely uncomfortable. John Desmond was a man of imposing appearance and severe countenance, and when he was angry, such being his present state of mind, as any one could easily see, not even the most brazen subaltern could be flippant in his presence.

"What is it?" he asked; "why am I summoned at such an hour by an armed guard? May I ask if his Majesty's officers have begun a systematic persecution of all those who are friendly to the Congress?"

"I am ordered to search your house, Mr. Desmond, for an American soldier who escaped from the prison last night," I replied, "and who may have hidden here. It is the order of General Howe."

The old man's eyes flashed with anger.

"I know nothing of this soldier," he said, "and there is nobody concealed in my house, nor has there been."

I said to myself that he was a good actor, but I also saw Belfort and Schwarzfelder standing on the other side of the street and I knew they were watching me. Every consideration demanded that I do my duty promptly.

"My orders are to search your house, Mr. Desmond," I said respectfully, but in decided tones, "and surely you have seen enough of armies recently to know what orders are. I shall have to enter and perform my task."

"He speaks the truth, father, and we should not resist," said a voice that I knew behind him, and Miss Desmond appeared in the hall, composed and as beautiful as ever. My suspicion returned. Could it be possible that this girl in her zeal for Britain would give up Alloway, and thereby destroy both Marcel and me? But she could know nothing of our false attire, and I quickly absolved her of that intention.

"Conduct your search," said Mr. Desmond; and placing six of my men about the house as guards, I took the remaining four and entered. One, Sergeant Blathwayt, an especially zealous man in the British cause, I kept beside me in order that he might see how well I performed my trust, as I knew not what consequences might arise from the incident.

Mr. Desmond, haughtily indignant, withdrew to his own room, saying that the search was an outrage upon the rights of a peaceable citizen, and if the British could find no better way of making war, they should not make it at all. I took his rebuke in silence, feeling the truth of his words and my own inability to resent them. Miss Desmond, too, was silent until her father disappeared, and I watched her, wondering at the strength, calmness, and courage that this young girl always showed. Did she ever feel fear? In truth she must feel it, but never before had I seen a woman who could so well conceal all emotion.

"Kindly continue the search, Lieutenant Melville," she said, in even cold tones, "but I assure you in advance that my father tells you the exact truth."

She added the last sentence proudly and with another uplift of her high head.

"I trust, Miss Desmond, that for your father's sake the search will prove fruitless," I said; "no one could wish a vain result of my task more than I."

She did not acknowledge my courtesy, and I proceeded with the work. Blathwayt, in his eagerness, was already poking among the rooms, looking behind curtains, opening the clothes-closets, and seeking in all manner of possible and impossible places for the hidden man. I did not rebuke his zeal, but began to pretend also to a similar enthusiasm, although I remained in constant fear lest we should discover Alloway. I was sure that he was in the house somewhere, and I did not see how we could avoid finding him, to the consequent ruin of Marcel and myself. Mine was a most peculiar position, and the chills coursed down my spine. Yet Mary Desmond's cold eye was upon me, and I would rather have died than shown apprehension while she looked so at me. The strange mingling of motives in her character and conduct, her loyalty to the Royal cause and her equal loyalty to her father, impressed me even then in that moment of danger.

We continued the search with vigor, going through all the rooms on the lower floors, and then into the cellars. It was a large and fine house, with spacious rooms, well stocked with furniture of mahogany and brass, and we saw in the cellars so many bottles of Madeira and port and old Spanish wines that the eyes of my English comrades began to glitter. "'Ow I would like to 'elp loot this 'ouse," said a good-natured private to me. I did not doubt the sincerity of his statement, but I saw no chance for him.

Miss Desmond accompanied us into the cellars, and as far as she showed any feeling at all, apparently wished to facilitate my task. The cellars were so extensive, and contained so many dark recesses, that the search there lasted a full half-hour. We were about to return to the upper floors, when I noticed a small door painted the color of the stone wall, and fitting into it so neatly that we might well have passed over it at a first look. Blathwayt himself had not seen it, but my eyes lingered there, and when I looked up Miss Desmond was gazing at me. My heart began to beat more rapidly. Alloway was behind that little gray door. I divined it at once. But what were Miss Desmond's feelings? What would she wish me to do? Was her loyalty to her father overcoming her loyalty to the king? And then another question intervened. I alone had passed it by; would she call attention to it?

I hesitated a little, and then walked unnoticing past the door, but I could not refrain from giving her a look of understanding, to tell her that I had seen it but would save her father. Her eye glittered, whether with scorn I could not say.

"You are overlooking the alcove, Lieutenant Melville," she said.

I paused, astounded, and I looked reproachfully at her, but her expression did not change. Then I walked a little farther, as if I had not heard, and she repeated,—

"You are overlooking the alcove, Lieutenant Melville."

The others were at the far end of the cellar and could not hear her.

"Miss Desmond," I said, "I have more regard than you for your father's safety."

Her eyes flashed.

"Lieutenant Melville," she said, "I demand that you search the alcove."

I hesitated, murmuring that I did not think it worth while; no one could lie concealed in such a small, close place.

"I shall report you to the commander-in-chief himself unless you search it," she said, looking at me steadily.

There could be no mistake; her manner and her tone alike indicated decision, and that I must obey. Yet I did not withhold these words,—

"I know that you are a Tory, Miss Desmond, but I did not think that you would go to such extremes."

She made no reply, and surrendering all hope for Marcel and myself, I turned the bolt and threw open the little door of the alcove.

It was empty!

I stood still, too much surprised to speak; relief, at that moment, not having any part in my emotions, although it came later.

"You know now, Lieutenant Melville, that your belief is as false as it was unjust," said Miss Desmond, proudly. "You have wronged my father."

"It is true," I confessed; and I confessed too, though not aloud, that perhaps I had wronged some one else yet more. Then I called to Blathwayt and censured him for overlooking the alcove.

"The fugitive might have lain there safely hidden from all of us," I said, "but I saw the place, and perhaps we may find others like it."

He admitted his error humbly, and we passed to the other floors. Here the feeling of relief disappeared from my mind, as we would surely find Alloway near the roof since he was not in the cellar. We searched three rooms, and then I put my hand upon the bolt fastening the door of the third.

"It is my bedroom," said Miss Desmond.

"I regret to say that I am compelled to search it too," I replied.

She bowed, making no further opposition, and, turning the key, I entered. It was a large, light apartment. In a corner the high bed stood within its white curtains, there were heavy rugs on the floor, a little round table of ebony, and at the far end of the room, tongs and shovel of brass hung beside the grate, in which two brazen fire dogs upheld haughty heads. It was a handsome room, worthy of its mistress, and yet I could not spare it. I looked everywhere,—behind the curtains, under the bed, and in the clothes-closets,—but I did not find Alloway.

When I finished Miss Desmond said to me,—

"I hope you believe that no man is concealed in my room."

The color had risen in her cheeks, and I replied in great haste,—

"I have not believed it any time, Miss Desmond, and only my duty compelled me to look here."

What a consoling word those four little letters, "d-u-t-y," sometimes spell! Blathwayt came to me the next moment, and reported that he had searched the upper rooms and the garret without finding the lost soldier. "But what a house it would be to loot!" he added in a whisper to me, showing, like his comrade, those predatory instincts which the British soldier often loves to indulge.

I pretended to a belief that he had not searched well the top of the house, and to show my zeal insisted upon conducting a hunt in those regions myself. But I thought, as I ascended the last stairway, that it would be rather a grim joke on me, if I found Alloway there after Blathwayt had failed to do so. But no such bad luck happened, and ten minutes later I announced with great but secret joy that his Britannic Majesty's army in Philadelphia had done Mr. Desmond an injustice; no soldier was concealed in his house, and I was sure that none ever had been. But while I said this I was wondering what had become of Alloway; he had entered the Desmond house, I knew beyond a doubt, and he must be in it yet, hidden in some secret recess. Well, at any rate, the luck which Marcel claimed was watching over us was still on guard.

"I shall be pleased to tell your father how vain our search has been," I said to Miss Desmond. But Mr. Desmond was yet in his own room and would not come forth. The haughty old Quaker, as was evident to us all, considered this search of his house a piece of gross insolence.

"I trust that I shall never again be sent on such an errand," I said to Miss Desmond as we prepared to go.

She made the formal reply that she hoped so too, and I could read nothing in her eyes. I was sure now that she had never known of Alloway's presence in the house. Then I took my soldiers and went into the street.

CHAPTER THIRTEEN—
Hessian Wrath

There was a narrow lawn in front of Mr. Desmond's house, and between that and the street an ornate iron fence. As I opened the gate that permitted egress, I saw Belfort and Schwarzfelder leaning upon the fence, while Waters hovered near. The two officers were twirling their mustaches after the most approved style of Old World dandies, and were looking at me in a manner that I could interpret only as insolent. I inferred at once that they and the Frenchman Waters were responsible for the search, and had gone there to enjoy a triumph containing the sweetest of flavor, my exposure and disgrace compelled by my own act. I became sure of it when I saw the look of triumph on the faces of Belfort and Schwarzfelder give way to one of surprise and disappointment.

"Where is your prisoner, Lieutenant Melville?" exclaimed Belfort, unable to control himself.

I gave him a stare as haughty as I knew how to make it.

"Did I understand you to ask where my prisoner was, Lieutenant Belfort?" I asked.

Both he and Schwarzfelder nodded.

"Permit me to remark that this is very extraordinary," I said, continuing my haughty manner, which suited my state of mind. "I am sent on a secret errand of great importance by Sir William Howe, and before I can report to him I am called to account concerning it in the streets of Philadelphia by one of his Majesty's sublieutenants. Or perhaps I have made a mistake, and General Howe has resigned in your favor. Do I have the pleasure of addressing General Belfort, and not Lieutenant Belfort?"

I gave him an extremely polite bow as I added the last sentence, and my tone grew most humble. But he did not seem to appreciate my homage. His face turned red.

"Lieutenant Melville," he said, "I shall have satisfaction for this insolence."

"Don't make a fuss about it," I said lightly. "I was merely speaking for your good, because if I had reported to you earlier than to Sir William he might have resented it. Still, I don't mind telling you, lieutenant, that we did not find the man, although we searched the house most thoroughly."

I was now happy, feeling my triumph somewhat, which may account for my levity; but the mention of the prisoner again set Belfort on fire.

"Did you look everywhere?" he asked eagerly. "It is certain that he took refuge there."

"Oh yes, sir!" interrupted Blathwayt, touching his cap, "we searched every square inch of the house, and it was impossible for a man to be hid there, and us not find him."

It was disrespectful of Blathwayt to interrupt when his superiors were talking, but for obvious reasons I did not correct him.

"He must have been there! he must have been there!" repeated Belfort, in disappointed tones. "Schwarzfelder says that he saw him dart among the shrubbery around the house, and he did not come out of it again last night."

So it was Schwarzfelder who had played the spy! But even so, he had not seen me give Alloway the warning or he would have betrayed me at once. I began to bear towards Schwarzfelder a feeling akin to that I felt for Belfort.

"I think that Colonel Schwarzfelder must have been mistaken," I said. "It is well known that our valiant Hessian officers often see double, especially when it is so late at night. Forward, march, men!"

I gave the order in a loud, peremptory tone, and my soldiers marched at once in their stiffest and most precise manner. Schwarzfelder was standing in the middle of the pavement, and they would have walked into him had he not skipped to one side in the most undignified way. I think that they would have been glad to do it, as generally the English soldiers hated the Hessians.

Schwarzfelder glowered at me, first because I had taunted him with his German drunkenness and the memory of his ejection from Sir William's headquarters, and secondly because in a metaphorical sense I had thrown him off the sidewalk. But he said nothing. He was choking too badly over his German wrath to enunciate words. I marched on with my men, leaving him and Belfort to concoct whatever mischief they would.

The man Waters, whom in truth I dreaded more than either Belfort or Schwarzfelder, had drawn somewhat nearer and was gazing steadily at me.

"Are you too looking for this American soldier, Waters?" I asked. "It seems that the commander-in-chief is receiving a great deal of voluntary assistance."

"Your pardon, sir," said Waters, with respect, or the assumption of it, "but I could not help hearing what the search was about, and I was merely wondering if that old rebel John Desmond was caught at last."

"Mr. Desmond may be a rebel," I replied angrily, "but it is not for you to speak of him in such a manner."

"I beg your pardon, sir, if I was presumptuous," he said meekly, dropping his eyes. Yet I was sure that he was deriding me, and I walked off, feeling an unpleasant chill again. I reported duly to Sir William that the search had brought forth nothing, and he expressed disappointment.

"I cannot understand how the man escaped," he said thoughtfully. "It was told to me that he was in the Desmond house, and I should have been glad to find him there, because it would give me a power over this rebellious old Quaker which I should be glad to use. I chose you for the task because I felt sure of your loyalty and devotion to the king, and also I know that you are a good friend of mine. There might have been promotion in it for you."

I thanked him humbly for his consideration, and I began to feel that the well-meant friendship of Sir William Howe would prove troublesome. Yet I was able to preserve a thankful countenance. Then he excused me, saying, as I departed, that I might look for further rewards at his hands, even in the short time left to him. Again I gave him thanks, and went out into the street, where I knew that I should find some of my new comrades ogling the pretty Philadelphia maids. The first that I beheld were Marcel and Vincent Moore, walking arm in arm. Marcel was in a splendid new uniform that fairly glittered with gold lace,—where he got it he has never told me, although I suppose that promptly after its arrival from England he won it at cards from some brother officer, perhaps from Harding, the new cousin, as they were about of a size and the uniform fitted Marcel beautifully. Moore also had achieved his utmost splendor, looking almost as fine as Marcel, and I saw clearly that the two were out to "kill" whatever beauty came their way.

"And you did not find the man, Melville?" exclaimed Marcel, seizing me by the arm; I was sure that he had heard the vain result of the search.

"If the bird was ever there, it had flown before our arrival," I replied, putting as much regret into my tones as I could.

"Then let war go! Come with us and look for the smiles of beauty," said Marcel, in his high flown manner. In truth, after inviting me, they gave me no choice, for Marcel took me by one arm and Moore by the other, and I could not escape swaggering on with them. I felt such relief from the situation of the morning, and the sunshine was so brilliant and inspiring, that I began to share their exultant views of life. We presently met Miss Rankin and another girl whom we knew, and, turning in our course, we walked beside them, exchanging the courtesies of the day, pouring out extravagant compliments, and otherwise behaving in a manner not unusual to masculine youth on such occasions.

Marcel, with incredible effrontery, began to tell some of the latest news about people of fashion in London, speaking as if he knew them intimately. I supposed that he had picked up the gossip, like the uniform, from Harding. This lasted a full ten minutes, and then we met Miss Desmond and her father, also walking in the sunshine. We gave them most ornate salutations, but their reply was not in kind. Miss Desmond's slight bow was accompanied by a look of surprise and disdain directed towards me. I know that I reddened under the glance, for, in truth, I became suddenly ashamed of myself, being fully aware that I had been behaving like a Jack o' dandy with more youth than brains. But there was no escape for me, and I walked on with my chattering companions, suddenly become silent, although they did not notice it, since they were making so much noise themselves. The ladies left us in another ten minutes, and then I would have excused myself from Marcel and Moore, but they would not hear of it.

"If we don't keep you, you will get into mischief," said Marcel, with a significance that Moore did not see, and they retained hold of my arms. Shortly after, our party was increased by Vivian and Catron, and we filled the sidewalk from edge to edge, all talking in lively fashion except myself, Marcel being in his element. In truth, there was no need that I should talk, since Marcel and Moore were doing enough and to spare for us all. They continued to twirl their mustaches and look for the pretty maids, but our next acquaintances who approached us were men not maids, being, in truth, Belfort, Schwarzfelder, and Graves, arm in arm, with the German in the centre. They walked straight towards us, and I saw that unless either they or we turned aside, a most unpleasant collision would occur, as the sidewalk was narrow. I observed no evidence of an intent on the part of either my comrades or Belfort and his friends to change their course, and I was annoyed excessively at the prospect of a collision and a quarrel. In fact, I have never felt any desire to be a swaggerer, and I began to wonder how I could get out of the difficulty. If the others insisted upon trouble for themselves, they might have it.

I saw no solution of the difficulty; but, to my great amazement, my friends suddenly stepped to one side when we were within a half-dozen paces of our antagonists, forming a line at the edge of the sidewalk, as if we were a guard of honor stationed there to give distinction to the passage of Belfort and his companions; furthermore, they strengthened the idea by taking off their caps and giving the others a bow of astonishing sweep and depth, which Graves returned in kind, Belfort slightly, and Schwarzfelder not at all. Not a word was said, the three stalking solemnly past us, and then disappearing down the street, while we returned to our natural place on the sidewalk, and walked on in the way that we had been going.

"Gentlemen," I said gravely, when we had gone about twenty yards, "I did not think this of you."

"And why not?" replied Marcel. "Could we have done otherwise after the delicate attentions that you have received from Colonel Schwarzfelder. We were the larger party, and therefore it was our duty, under the circumstances, to give way to the smaller. Is that not so, Moore?"

"Certainly," replied Moore. "We did our duty."

I looked at them questioningly, and Marcel's eye began to twinkle.

"Oh, you have not heard of the billet-doux that Schwarzfelder has written you?" he asked.

"What are you talking about?" I replied.

"It was done in the most perfect manner," said Moore; "I wish that it had come for me."

"I refuse to go a step farther unless you tell me what you are talking about," I said, and I stopped short. They could have carried me on only by dragging me, and that would have looked undignified.

"Suppose we let him have the letter,—Schwarzfelder's masterly production," said Marcel.

"Yes, let him see it," said Vivian.

Marcel accordingly took from his waistcoat pocket, an envelope with a broken seal, superscribed in a large heavy hand, "To Captain, the Honorable Charles Montague." I put it to my nose, and it smelled of both tobacco and wine.

"But think of its contents," said Marcel.

I opened it, and stared at the writing, of which I could not read a word. It was in German. The others burst into laughter.

"That billet-doux," said Marcel, "is a challenge from your dear friend, Schwarzfelder. It seems that you did him a wrong this morning, or at least he thinks so, and off he rushed to his headquarters so blindingly angry that he must challenge you at once. He thinks of me as your best friend, and, still mad with anger, he forgets himself so far as to write the body of the letter in German, and also to ignore the use of a second for himself. But Belfort has set all of that right. Now it seems that fate won't let you fight Belfort; but I don't see how you can keep from meeting Schwarzfelder. Lieutenant Melville, if I had your quarrelsome disposition, I certainly should expect to die on the field of honor before I was turned twenty-five."

Then they laughed again, enjoying my plight and vexation.

"Belfort is at any rate a gentleman," I said; "but Schwarzfelder is at least three-fourths ruffian, and I think that it would be a disgrace to meet him."

"But you cannot refuse on that account," said Catron, gravely, "these men seem bent upon persecuting you, Melville, and you will have to put a stop to it with either sword or pistol. Suppose that we go to your quarters and discuss it."

I was willing, and ten minutes later we were around a table in our room, talking over the situation. Marcel had ordered wine from the commissariat, and the glasses were filled by the orderly, Waters, who was silent, and, as usual, apparently respectful.

"It is obvious that our friend Melville must meet Schwarzfelder," said Marcel, at length. "This Hessian is a drunkard and a bravo; but he is an officer of rank, even of much higher rank than Melville. Our man, therefore, must teach him a lesson. Do you say so, gentlemen?"

"We do say so," replied Catron, Moore, and Vivian together.

I saw that they were right, according to the code of the day, and I began, in spite of myself, to feel a willingness for the combat. Catron said that they were persecuting me, and that word "Persecute" began to inflame my anger. I would show them that persecuting had its risks.

"I am not much of a swordsman," I said; "but I am a good shot, and so I choose pistols at twenty paces."

"Then pistols it is," said Catron; "and now for a letter to Belfort, who is to be Schwarzfelder's second, which will show that we know how to manage such an affair as this in the most courteous manner."

Then we set ourselves to the task of writing the letter,—a labor that was by no means small,—and while we were hard-set at it, Waters came into the room again and saluted.

"Well?" said Catron, impatiently.

"Your honor," said Waters, apologetically, "there is some news of interest in the city, and I thought that you would pardon me for telling it to you."

"Wait! Do you not see that we are busy? You should not interrupt!" replied Marcel.

"But this is a most extraordinary affair, and the whole town is ringing with it," rejoined the man.

I saw now that his eyes were sparkling after the manner of one who has a budget of good gossip to tell and is anxious to tell it. The others noticed it too, and our own curiosity began to rise.

"What is it, Waters?" I asked.

He opened his hands, showing a piece of white paper about a foot long and perhaps half as wide.

"There is writing upon it; I ask your honor to read it," he said.

I took it and read:

To SIR WILLIAM HOWE, *Commander-in-chief of His Britannic Majesty's forces in Philadelphia:—*

I beg to present to you my compliments, and to notify you that I shall pay a visit to the City of Philadelphia one night this week, in order that you may prepare a reception worthy of yourself and me.

Yours faithfully,

WILLIAM WILDFOOT,
Captain in the Continental Army.

"It is said that over twenty of these have been found in the city to-day," said Waters, "all exactly alike, and written in the same hand."

The penmanship was large, rough, and angular, evidently that of a man more accustomed to grasping the sword than the goose quill.

Catron swore a tremendous oath.

"Well, of all unmitigated impertinences this is the greatest!" he exclaimed.

"It's mere bravado," said Vivian. "Of course the man will not think of venturing into Philadelphia."

"They say that he surely will come," said Waters; "it is the gossip of the city."

"If he does," added Vivian, scornfully, "he will come only to be hanged."

I was not so sure, but I said nothing. I remembered our former encounter with Wildfoot, and the singular words that he shouted to me as he dashed past. The others discussed the insolent placards with some degree of heat.

"Have you heard what Sir William says about this piece of presumption?" asked Vivian of Waters, letting his curiosity overcome his dignity.

"I have heard only, sir, that he was extremely angry," replied Waters.

"An entirely natural emotion under the circumstances," added Marcel.

Then we returned to the discussion of my own affair, and shortly after the important letter was finished, notifying Belfort that I accepted Schwarzfelder's challenge, naming pistols as the weapons, and stating that Captain Montague would call upon him as soon as possible to make arrangements as to time and place.

"There," said Marcel, his face flushing with satisfaction, as he looked at the completed letter, "I think that's as pretty a piece of work as any one of us has done in many a day. I don't want you to kill that Hessian fellow, Melville; but if you could let a lot of blood from him with a bullet, say in his shoulder, it would improve both his appearance and his manners."

Waters was deputed to bear the letter to Belfort, and then we went out to enjoy the small portion of the day and the sunshine that was left to us. This was Tuesday, and Marcel and Moore began to calculate when they could have the duel, the two undertaking to manage it, just as they had managed my abortive affair with Belfort. Marcel was of the opinion that the meeting could be held within two or three days, the time to be just at dawn, and the place to be a spot in the Northern suburbs, barely within the line of the British pickets, but where they could not see us.

We were not permitted to think long of the proposed duel. Wildfoot's placard was making a great buzz in the city, and many of the British officers who believed that he would keep his promise thought that the time to catch him had come.

CHAPTER FOURTEEN—
According to Promise

I was at mess when an orderly arrived from Sir William, bidding my immediate presence at his quarters, a command that I could not think of disobeying, however reluctant I might be to go. It was in truth somewhat unpleasant to leave the brilliantly lighted room with its glittering china and silver, its abundant wines, and the talk and laughter of the good comrades who were there, for the loneliness and work of the commander-in-chief's house. I like to be popular with my superior officers, but now and then popularity is burdensome, and I leave it to anybody if Sir William's favor was not extremely embarrassing to one in my position. So I rose and apologized with reluctance for my departure, which I said I must take at once, and at the same time naming the cause.

"Farewell, Melville," they shouted with mock solemnity. "He goes to sure promotion, and this is another good man lost to those who love him."

I found Sir William at the table in his workroom, and the heap of papers that lay before him was larger than the one which had been there the first night that I had helped him. These were the closing days of his command, and much remained to be done. He was, as I have said before, and as all the world knows, an easy, sluggish, good-natured man, fond of pleasure, and his work always came last. Vivian was there helping him, and not looking over-happy. I was sure that he, like myself, was thinking longingly of the mess and its lights and the good company. But his face brightened a bit when he saw me, knowing now that he would have a companion in misery.

Sir William turned to me a face upon which annoyance was plainly written, and I saw in his hand a placard like that which Waters had shown to us.

"Melville, have you heard of this?" he asked, holding up the placard.

"Yes, sir, I have heard of it."

"This placard, or paper, or whatever it may be, is the most unexampled impertinence," he said, the red flushing into his swarthy face. "I think that it is intended as a personal insult to me. This outlaw Wildfoot must know of my forthcoming departure for England, and he is seeking to taunt me. But he shall not do it! I tell you, he shall not do it!"

He struck his fist upon the table to give emphasis to his statement that he would not allow a rebel partisan to upset his dignity, but it was entirely obvious that it *was* very much upset.

"If the man is so foolish and reckless as to enter Philadelphia," continued Sir William, "he will never get out again. I shall at least have the satisfaction of disposing of this troublesome fellow before I go to England."

The thought gave him consolation, and he began to dictate to us orders about the watch for Wildfoot, doubling the sentries, cautioning them to increase their vigilance, and making new dispositions of the pickets which he thought would guard the city better. Many of these movements could not be executed before the next morning; but Sir William did not look for Wildfoot for two or three nights, provided he came at all, and his countenance and voice began, by and by, to express satisfaction.

"We shall have our trap set," he said, "and the outlaw will walk into it just as we wish."

The time passed slowly, and we were reinforced presently by another secretary, who proved to be young Graves, a man who was the friend of Belfort and Schwarzfelder, and more or less hostile to me. But he was in a good humor, thinking of the prospective duel, in which he was to have a part as one of the managers,—a circumstance which flattered his pride, and he was very courteous to me. He exchanged a word occasionally with me about it in a whisper, and informed me, by and by, that he was not sure Schwarzfelder would win.

In a short while, Graves was sent to the anteroom to copy some documents there. He sat at a table near the wall, and once, when I went to take him some papers, I saw the sentinel, loaded gun on shoulder, walking back and forth in front of the door. I heard the sound of footsteps outside and, looking through the window, beheld a company of troops marching past. It was evident that Sir William's anger over Wildfoot's impertinence was producing activity. Then I went back to the commander-in-chief's table and resumed my work there.

I think it was about 10 o'clock when Sir William told me to go and help Graves, who seemed to be falling behind in his task. I drew up a chair and sat down at the table facing Graves, and with my back to the door. He, feeling his importance, wanted to exchange with me more whispered comments on the duel; but I wished to avoid the subject, and worked so industriously that he gave up the attempt.

We heard nothing during the next quarter of an hour but the scratching of our goose quills and the occasional words of Sir William in the next room as he gave an order. Then, chancing to look up, I beheld a most extraordinary expression on the face of Graves. His eyes were distended to a great width, and the white in them was shot with little specks of red, the muscles of his face were drawn, and his whole look was that of a man suffering from the most alarmed surprise.

"Why, what under the sun is the matter, Graves?" I exclaimed.

He did not say a word, but pointed behind me. I wheeled around to see; but powerful hands grasped me by the throat, while other hands thrust the muzzle of a pistol into my face. It was not necessary for anybody to say to me: "Move a foot, or say a word, and you shall be a dead man!" I knew it perfectly well without the telling, and I neither moved nor spoke. Graves, who at the same instant had been served as I was, showed a similar wisdom. Something soft, but very filling, was thrust into my mouth, and, with an expedition as unpleasant as it was astonishing, I was bound tightly to the table. Then the strong hands slipped off me, and I was at liberty to gaze as much as I wished into the eyes of Graves, who sat opposite me just as he had sat when we were at work, and who was as securely bound and gagged as I. I always fancy that we made a pretty pair, trussed up there like two turkeys ready for the spit. I would have given much for a few words to express my feelings, but my mouth was too full. I merely read the various looks in the eyes of Graves, all of which expressed anger.

The men, four in number, who had performed this impolite deed, brushed past me, and I saw only their backs, which were large and powerful. The door between our room and Sir William's was shut; but they opened it, leaving it so, and entered. I faced the apartment, and I saw distinctly all that passed. Thus it was my fortune, while listening to the most amazing conversation that I ever heard, to see also those who talked, though only the back of one of the most important.

Sir William and Vivian were writing busily at the large table in the centre of the room, when the intruders entered. Sir William sat at the side of the table facing us, and Vivian was at the end. I saw the faces of both clearly by the light of wax candles. Sir William had begun to wear his usual placid look. I inferred that he was pleased at what he was writing just then, and I think that it was instructions which he felt soon would cause the capture of Wildfoot. The largest man of the four put his hand on a chair, and drawing it up to the table sat down opposite to Sir William and with his back to me. Neither Sir William nor Vivian noticed their entrance until then, as they had walked with extreme lightness. But when Sir William looked up and beheld the stranger sitting uninvited and so calmly before him, his face flamed into anger. I could see the rush of blood to his head.

"Who are you, and how dare you come here?" he cried, springing to his feet.

"Be seated, Sir William, be seated," replied the man, in a strong, clear, and soothing voice. "There is no occasion for surprise or wrath. I am not an intruder. I sent you word in writing that I would call."

I saw Sir William's face turn quite black, and he began to choke.

"You are—you are—" he gasped.

"You have divined it, Sir William," replied the man. "I am Captain William Wildfoot, captain of rangers in the Continental service. Your guest, if you please, and I must warn you and your assistant not to shout for help, or my men will shoot you instantly. The young lieutenants in the front room, as you can see for yourself, will keep very quiet."

What I wished most of all at that moment was to see the man's face. His effrontery, his astonishing recklessness, inspired me with the deepest curiosity. I thought that Marcel and I had shown considerable presumption, but we were children, raw beginners, compared with this man.

"What do you want?" asked Sir William, at last.

"First, that you and your assistant put your hands upon the table, or else I shall have to bind you," replied Wildfoot.

Sir William frowned and choked again; but there was no recourse, and he and Vivian both laid their empty hands upon the table.

"That is better," said Wildfoot, in a pleased tone; "I know that it is undignified in you, but the good of our service demands it. And now for serious talk. I came to show you, Sir William, the insecurity of your position, and the great resources of the patriots."

"I must say," replied Sir William, "that I never before saw a man so anxious to give his side of the argument."

"Yes," replied Wildfoot, "I have been at some trouble and risk to do so."

I saw a faint gleam of humor appear in the eyes of Sir William, and I inferred that the quality of geniality or good fellowship in him, which perhaps made him such a poor soldier, was rising to the surface. He seemed to appreciate, to a slight degree at least, the humor of the situation. His eye suddenly sought mine, and then I distinctly saw a trace of amusement mingling with his perplexed and annoyed expression.

"You seem to have made sure of the attention of Lieutenant Melville and Lieutenant Graves," he said.

"I have no doubt that they can maintain their interest," replied Wildfoot, "and their present position is only temporary."

"You say that you came to show me the strength and resources of the colonists. Will you tell me how this is so?" asked Sir William.

"That I am here is the proof of it."

"It is true that you are here, but I have an idea, Captain Wildfoot, that you will not go away again."

"Why not?"

"I am hospitable. We need you. Philadelphia needs you."

"I know it, and so I shall come back again."

"No, we wish you to stay with us now."

I should have laughed at this point had not the gag been in my mouth, not at the conversation of Sir William and Wildfoot, but at the funny look on the face of Graves. He had a great sense of dignity and aristocratic importance, and it was hurt by the sudden intrusion of Wildfoot. I said: "Never mind, Graves, it will soon be over," but the words stopped short against that gag, and he did not hear them. I did not even hear them myself. Vivian, on the contrary, was bearing himself like a gentleman. He sat perfectly still, with his eyes either on Sir William or Wildfoot, and so far as I could see, his face was without expression. The three men who accompanied Wildfoot remained standing, but motionless, each with a cocked pistol in his hand. One stood with his face turned towards me, but every feature was hidden by a thick, bushy, black beard.

"So I take it, that you have done this thing merely in a spirit of bravado," said Sir William, "and I wish you to understand, Captain Wildfoot, that I thoroughly appreciate your daring. I could wish that you were one of us; in the king's service you would be a colonel at least, and not a mere rebel captain; moreover, your neck would be in no danger."

"But I would be colonel in a losing cause," replied Wildfoot, "and to tell the truth, Sir William, I enjoy my captaincy among the rebels, as you call them, much more than any man enjoys his colonelcy among the king's men. No, Sir William, I am happy where I am; then why seek unhappiness elsewhere?"

"Are you quite sure that you are happy where you are?"

"Quite sure."

"Then it is not worth while to attempt persuasion; but to return to another point, Captain Wildfoot, we value men of your spirit and daring too much to give them up when they come once among us. We must even detain you by other means than persuasion."

"I thank you for the honor, Sir William," said Wildfoot, with a grateful inflection, "but I had formed another plan, somewhat different in manner but similar in the result that you mention."

"May I ask just what you mean?"

"It is not necessary for us to be separated under my plan."

"I do not understand yet."

"I had thought, Sir William, of taking you with me when I left Philadelphia."

The deep red flushed Sir William's swarthy face again. My amazement at Wildfoot's presumption increased, but I remembered the case of the English general Prescott, who had been kidnapped in Rhode Island by the daring American captain, Barton.

"Do you mean that you would carry me off as a prisoner?" asked Sir William.

"Such was my intention, if you will pardon the rudeness," replied Wildfoot, humbly. "And if you will excuse me again, Sir William, we must hurry."

I saw Vivian suddenly lean over in his chair, throw out his arms, and sweep from the table the candles, extinguishing them instantly, while Graves, with a single strong puff of his breath, blew out the one in front of us. The rooms were plunged into darkness, and what had seemed comedy before, became tragedy, especially for Graves and me, bound as we were to the table and powerless to cry out. I heard the quick, heavy tread of feet, and the crack of a pistol shot, the flash of the powder casting for a moment a fantastic light by which I saw rapidly moving figures, and then the sound of shattering glass and another shot.

I do not think that I breathed for a minute or two. The next room, with the darkness, the pistol shots, the occasional flashes of light and the trampling feet, furnished every evidence of a deadly struggle, and at any moment a pistol ball might take me in the breast, while I sat there bound to the table, powerless to help myself, and unable even to make myself heard.

A man brushed suddenly past me, threw open the outer door, and shouted to the guards, who were already crowding into the room. But the sounds in the inner chamber ceased with great suddenness, and in a moment, a flame flared up. It was Vivian relighting a candle. He was very pale, and the blood was dripping from his left arm, which was limp by his side. Save for himself, the room was empty. Broken glass from both windows lay on the floor. Near the table was a large spot of blood.

"They escaped through the windows, Sir William," said Vivian, "but I think that one has carried with him the mark of my bullet."

"And you have the mark of his," replied Sir William, who was at the outer door. "One of you men run for a surgeon at once. I owe too much to you, Vivian, to forget this."

Then he began to give hasty orders for the pursuit of Wildfoot and his men. All the anger and chagrin which he had concealed so well in their presence surged up.

"They shall be caught! They shall be caught!" he cried. "I will give a hundred guineas myself to the man who first lays hands on this Wildfoot. Send the alarm to all the pickets, and permit nobody to leave Philadelphia on any pretext whatever!"

He continued his orders, and messengers rushed with them to the outposts, impressed by the anger and emphasis of the commander-in-chief which would permit no delay. Two or three minutes passed thus, and the fierce mental exertion seemed to calm Sir William. More candles had been lighted, and looking about the room, he saw Graves and me still motionless and confronting each other across the table, as silent as sphinxes.

"What, are you bound?" he exclaimed. "Why didn't you call for help?"

And we were yet silent.

He stared at us in surprise, and then he burst into laughter. I think it was partly relief from the nervous strain that made him laugh.

"I have heard often," he said, "that silence is a virtue, but this seems to me to be carrying it to an extreme point."

He promptly gave orders to have the gags and thongs removed, and I stretched my muscles with a feeling of deep relief. Wildfoot might be a great partisan commander, but there was such a thing as pernicious activity. I was a good American, and it was a grievous insult to be bound and gagged by another good American.

"How did this happen?" asked Sir William.

"I do not know," I replied, glad to be able to speak again. "We were bent over the table, busy with our writing, when we were seized from behind. I cannot understand how they passed the sentinel unnoticed."

Sir William swore a frightful oath.

"The sentinel has disappeared," he said. "Undoubtedly he was in league with them, perhaps an American whom we took to be a faithful Tory. We will capture this Wildfoot before morning, and you shall help."

I exchanged a word or two with Vivian, and found that he was not badly hurt. A small bone in his left arm was broken by the bullet, but it would heal perfectly in a week or two. Then I hurried out with Sir William and Graves.

CHAPTER FIFTEEN—*The Pursuit of Wildfoot*

The general was so eager that Graves and I were several yards behind him when we emerged from the house into the midst of a great tumult, orderlies galloping from the door with despatches, and others returning for more, while lights were increasing rapidly in the city, and soldiers were gathering for duty. It was evident that Sir William was thoroughly aroused, and intended to capture Wildfoot if it were possible to do such a thing. My first feeling of anger against the ranger because of his treatment of me passed, as I reflected that he naturally took me for a British officer, and could not have done otherwise, even had he known the difference. Now I began to fear for him. I did not wish this bold man, so valuable to our cause, to be captured, possibly to be hanged upon some pretext or other. But Sir William did not give me much time to think.

"Be sure you follow me, Melville," he said.

He was already on horseback, and, mounting a horse that an orderly held for me, I galloped after him. He had gathered several other aides in his rapid pursuit, and we made quite a cavalcade, the hoofs of our horses thundering upon the hard street. The whole city was awake now; night-capped heads were thrust from windows, and trembling voices asked what was the matter. But we paid no heed, galloping on.

Catron was among the officers who had joined us, and pointing towards Germantown, he said:—

"They ran this way; I saw four men with pistols in their hands dash down the street. One was very large."

"That was Wildfoot! It was he! Sound the call!" Sir William shouted joyfully to a trumpeter.

The man put the instrument to his lips and blew the hunting call. Merrily rose the notes, and Sir William's spirits rose with them. He felt sure that already he held Wildfoot in the hollow of his hand.

Our rapid ride was bringing us near the outskirts of the city, where the British intrenchments and fortifications lay, and I imagined that it was Sir William's plan to establish first a thorough picket line, and then to search every house in Philadelphia for Wildfoot and his comrades. But, turning my eyes to the southward, I saw a sudden rosy glow under the dark horizon which deepened in a moment into pink and then into red, rising in a lofty pyramid. Sparks shot from it. I pointed it out to Sir William at once. He paused, perplexed.

"It is a fire, clearly enough," he said; "but I wonder what it can be!"

His doubt lasted only a moment. An aide, much excited, galloped up and informed us that the cantonments of the troops to the southward had been set on fire, and were now burning fiercely.

"An accident?" asked Sir William, deeply annoyed.

"The men are sure that it was caused by the rebels," replied the aide.

"There is nothing to be done but to put it out as best you can," replied Sir William, and he began to give instructions; but even as he spoke the report of rifle-shots came from a point a little farther to the north, distant yet distinct, sounding so far away like the popping of a hickory log under the flames. There were red sparks too, no bigger than fire-flies, and both the cracking noises and the sparks increased. Sir William stopped his horse and gazed anxiously at the little red flashes.

"An attack by the rebels, and at this of all times," he said in tones of great annoyance, but to himself rather than to us. It was not likely that our ragged little army could storm fortified Philadelphia and defeat the powerful and far more numerous force that defended it; but Sir William was so much engrossed with the pursuit of Wildfoot that he resented any interference demanding his attention. He swore again in his wrath.

"Catron," he said, "you must go at once to that point. If the force there is not sufficient, hurry forward these."

He began to name regiments that would be available.

Catron galloped away, and before the sound of his horse's hoofs had died, more rifle-shots were heard still farther to the northward, coming from a point entirely new. The fire quickly blazed up there like a flame in a tinder dry forest, indicating another attack, heavier perhaps than the first. We paused, uncertain which way to go; and while we hesitated, the attack developed at a fourth point far to the southward, some of the ships in the river replying, the deep boom of the cannon rising like the notes of a funeral bell above the crackle of the musketry. A hum sprang up too from Philadelphia, the alarm of the people deepening as the firing seemed to spread and ring them around. They feared another battle fought almost at their doors, like that of Germantown. The cantonments, mostly light wooden structures, burned brightly, adding to the alarm, and casting a glow over the hurrying regiments. I confess, American as I was, and much as I should have enjoyed the doubts of the British, that I, too, was in a daze. My own peculiar position was assuming most perplexing phases.

"If I only knew what this meant!" exclaimed Sir William. "Perhaps, after all, I can leave my men to brush off those rebels while I continue my search for Wildfoot."

His eagerness to capture the partisan seemed to increase, and I did not wonder at it. I should have felt the same way in his place. We were joined at this moment by more officers, among whom I saw Belfort and Schwarzfelder. The German's face was inflamed by drink, and his talk was full of warlike fury. It died, however, when Sir William looked towards him, although it was Belfort's hand on his arm that warned him to make less noise.

Another light flamed up at the central point of attack, and one of the officers stated that it was a farmhouse occupied as quarters by the troops, evidently set on fire, like the other cantonments, by the rebels. The rapid br-r-r of the rifle-shots there indicated that it was the heaviest point of attack.

This seemed to decide Sir William, and he rode towards the farmhouse, ordering us to follow. I looked back and saw the lights of the city twinkling behind us, and I felt sure that Wildfoot and his comrades lay hidden there, perhaps in the houses of trusty patriots. The attack at this particular time was either a lucky chance, or part of a clever scheme, and my admiration of the man, always great, increased. We approached the scene of the combat, and the volume of the firing swelled rapidly, the shouts of the combatants coming to our ears; yet we could see but little of the battle. The night was dark, and the assailing force which had driven back the pickets was sheltered by a rail fence standing within the original British lines. The little jets of flame ran along the fence for some hundreds of yards, but the Americans remained invisible. None could even make a guess at their numbers.

"Stop, Sir William!" exclaimed Belfort, suddenly. "Let us dispose of these skirmishers before you advance."

Belfort never lacked courage, and his remark was well-timed. I heard the br-r-r of a bullet over our heads, and then another, and then many others. Two men were struck the next instant, and a horse was killed. It was obviously not the place of the commander-in-chief to ride into such a hornet's nest, and he drew off a bit. An unusually heavy volley burst from the fence, and the British pickets were driven back. The officers with us gathered up the fugitives, and led them in a charge.

"Stay with me, Melville," said Sir William to me. "I shall want you for despatches."

I was devoutly thankful for his order, not being willing to join in a charge against my own countrymen, and I sat willingly on my horse beside him. I was of the opinion that the attack of the British would fail, as they were in too small force, and should have waited for the regiments which were coming up rapidly.

All the officers were on horseback save the one whose mount had been shot from beneath him, and a bulky figure which I recognized even in the dark as Schwarzfelder's led the van. The German, for all I knew, was a brave man; but the wine that he had been drinking was now more potent in bringing him on and putting him in the foremost place.

The attacking force of English numbered about a hundred, and, despite their scanty numbers, they rushed forward with the greatest gallantry, shouting to each other and uttering a hearty cheer. The top of the fence burst into a long streak of flame, and the crack of many rifles together made a heavy crash, followed by an irregular crackle, as more rifles were fired. All but a few in the front ranks of the attacking column were cut down, and those in the rear still pushing on, dropped fast before the deliberate fire of the concealed sharpshooters.

"It's a trap," I said to Sir William; "the English are sure to be beaten."

We heard a rapid drum behind us, and the footsteps of an advancing regiment; but they would be too late to save the forlorn hope charging the fence. The crackling fire swelled again into a volley, and the red blur made by the uniforms of the advancing English became dimmer. I heard a groan beside me. It was Vivian, pale and weak, with a limply hanging arm, who had ridden up.

"They will all be killed," he said.

The charging force was now approaching the fence, and always in the van was the bulky figure of Schwarzfelder, bestriding his horse, man and beast apparently alike untouched, the German brandishing a huge sword, and shouting as if he were possessed by a demon.

"Certainly Schwarzfelder is brave," muttered Sir William, who perhaps remembered the night that I had cast the German out of his quarters. The forlorn hope was almost at the fence, and then the fire of the riflemen increased rapidly. Many of the English fell, and the few who were left, unable to stand such a leaden sleet, turned and ran, as they should have done long before, all except Schwarzfelder, who rode straight at the fence.

Then I saw an unusual thing. Two men, evidently large and powerful, and at the distance the first looked to me remarkably like Wildfoot, sprang over the fence and seized Schwarzfelder from either side. Then, while one tore the sword from his hand, the other, the one who looked like Wildfoot, sprang up behind him, and, holding him around the waist, jumped the horse over the low fence. Then we heard the distant thud of hoofs as they disappeared in the darkness.

"What an insult to Hessian dignity!" said Vivian beside me. Then he added in a low voice, that Sir William might not hear: "There's an end to your duel, Melville. The gods are surely unwilling for you to fight."

When the regiment advancing to the relief reached the fence, the Americans were gone and no one could discover where. The attack at the other points ceased almost simultaneously, and the fires burned out slowly. The search for Wildfoot in the city was continued, but no trace of him could be found, and, eating his heart out in his anger, Sir William returned to his quarters.

CHAPTER SIXTEEN—*A Rebuke for Waters*

The next day was a gloomy one in Philadelphia, which was then largely a British town, not only because of the army of occupation, but because most of the patriot population had gone away, leaving the Tories in possession. The feelings of all were hurt by Wildfoot's extraordinary daring, his easy disappearance with his men, and the utter lack of respect he had shown for the commander-in-chief. Men said: "What if he had really carried off Sir William! What an irregular mode of warfare!" They repeated that they did not fear the American armies, but that they did object to an antagonist who appeared at such unexpected moments and in such an unexpected manner; the irregularity of the thing was what they especially disliked.

A number of us visited Vivian at his quarters as soon as we could obtain leave, and condoled with him over his wound. But he was suffering little pain, and reckoned the bandage upon his arm a badge of distinction. So we gave him our congratulations instead of our condolences.

"I should have been glad to have had the other arm broken, if thereby we could have captured Wildfoot," he said. The words were spoken without affectation, and we knew that he meant them.

Belfort was there too, and he was gloomy, despite the fact that he had been commended by Sir William for gallantry in action. Vivian rallied him on his looks.

"It is because our luck is bad," replied Belfort. "That prisoner who might have told things of importance has disappeared completely, and Wildfoot seems to be able to enter the city, do what he pleases, and then disappear with impunity. I am of the opinion that there are traitors in Philadelphia."

"If you mean rebels, of course there are," said Vivian; "all of us know that, but they are in a great minority."

"I don't mean rebels precisely, at least not self-confessed rebels," replied Belfort.

"Then whom do you mean?" said the sprightly Marcel; "if you mean Sir William, or Vivian there, who has a rebel bullet through his arm, or my chum Melville and myself, who arrived in Philadelphia amidst a leaden shower, or our lamented friend Schwarzfelder, who rode his own horse among the rebels, and a truly gallant sight he was—why speak out in the name of justice and the king."

Belfort flushed with vexation. There was no adequate reply that he could make, whatever his thoughts might be. But after some hesitation he said,—

"I am glad that you mentioned Schwarzfelder. Why should he disappear at such a time, literally kidnapped, as that bandit wished to kidnap Sir William?"

"It seems to me that Schwarzfelder is irrelevant," interrupted Vivian. "At least he has no connection with these rebel disappearances. He was to fight a duel with

Melville, and scarcely can you charge that Melville bribed Wildfoot to come here and carry him off, in order to escape the duel, especially when Wildfoot treated Melville with excessive discourtesy, binding him to a table and thrusting an unfeeling gag into his mouth."

"I don't mean to impeach Melville's courage," said Belfort, hastily. "I spoke merely of the singularity of these events."

Our little party was broken up presently by orders from Sir William which gave us all work to do. It seemed that he was seized with another spasm of energy, and he resumed the search of the city for both Wildfoot and Alloway. He was not at all sure that Wildfoot had succeeded in joining the rebels who made the attack the night before, and fancied he might still be hidden in the city. So there was a great hunt for him, and my part of it was of an exceedingly unpleasant nature. I was to go to the Desmond house, search it again, and address various penetrating interrogations to the owner thereof.

I acquitted myself in the best style of which I was capable. I found both John Desmond and his daughter in the house, and, much to my surprise, he answered all my questions quite readily and politely. I thought that his courtesy was due, perhaps, to the presence of his daughter at his elbow, but both search and examination, as before, revealed nothing.

As I was returning to Sir William's quarters to report the fruitless task, I met Waters. I would have passed him without notice, but he said,—

"I take it that it was again a fruitless search at Mr. Desmond's house, was it not, sir?"

This savored most strongly of impertinence in one of his rank, and I felt anger. I disliked his incessant watch of Marcel and me, and in spite of my belief that he either knew or suspected us, caution was swallowed up in wrath.

"Waters," I said, "your question was impertinent and your tone insolent."

He did not apologize as he had done before, but held up his head and his bold eyes looked steadily into mine.

"All the city, sir, is talking of this Wildfoot, and every loyal man wants him captured. The wish is as strong among us of a lower rank as it is among those of a higher."

I thought that I saw a peculiar significance in his words, and I would have given much to keep down the flush that reddened my face.

"What do you mean to intimate, Waters?" I asked.

"Nothing," he replied. "You are pleased, sir, to dislike me, although I do not know why, and to become angry because I ask you about the search of Mr. Desmond's house, a task which I felt sure was most unwelcome to you."

His eyes did not flinch as he said these bold words, and manner and words alike confirmed my long felt fear that he knew me to be an impostor. I hesitated a little, uncertain what course to take, and then, turning scornfully from him, marched on with my men.

CHAPTER SEVENTEEN—
Great News

As neither Marcel nor I was assigned to any duty for the remainder of the day, we thought to while away a portion of the time by strolling about Philadelphia.

"We need not make spies of ourselves," said Marcel; "but I know no military law against the gratification of our own personal curiosity."

Guided by such worthy motives, we spent some time that was to our amusement and perhaps to our profit also. Barring the presence of the soldiery, Philadelphia showed few evidences that war was encamped upon its threshold. I have seldom witnessed a scene of such bustle and animation, and even of gayety too, as the good Quaker City presented. A stranger would have thought there was no war, and that this was merely a great garrison town.

The presence of fifteen or twenty thousand soldiers was good for trade, and gold clinked with much freedom and merriment. Though wagon-trains of provisions were taken sometimes by the Americans, yet many others came safely into Philadelphia, and the profits were so large that the worthy Pennsylvania farmers could not resist the temptation to take the risks, though most of them would have preferred to sell to the patriots, had the latter possessed something better than Continental paper to offer them.

"The British boast much of their bayonets," said Marcel; "but they fight better with their gold."

"And we have neither," said I.

"Which merely means," said Marcel, "not that we shall not win, but that we will be longer in the winning."

Our conversation was diverted from this topic by my observance of a peculiar circumstance. Often I would see four or five men, gathered at a street corner or in front of a doorway, talking with an appearance of great earnestness. Whenever Marcel and I, who were in full uniform, and thus were known to be British officers as far as we could be seen, approached, they would lower their tone or cease to talk. This had not happened on any day before, and was not what we would have expected from citizens who had grown used to the presence of the British army. I asked Marcel to take note of it.

"Something unusual that they do not wish to tell us of has happened," he said. "I propose that we find out what it is."

"How?" I said.

"I know no better way than to ask," he replied. "Suppose we seize the very next opportunity, and interrogate our Quaker friends concerning the cause of their strange and mysterious behavior."

Presently we saw four men engaged in one of these discussions. Three appeared to be citizens of Philadelphia, or at least we so judged from the smartness of their dress; the fourth had the heavy, unkempt look of a countryman. We approached; on the instant they became silent, and there was a look of embarrassment upon their faces.

"Friends," said Marcel, in his courtly manner, "we wish not to interrupt your most pleasant discourse, but we would ask what news of importance you have, if there be no harm in the telling of it."

"It rained last night," said the countryman, "and it is good for the spring planting."

"Yet one might have news more interesting, though not perhaps more important, than that," replied Marcel; "for it has rained before, and the crops have been planted and reaped likewise before."

"Even so," said the countryman, "but its importance increases when there are twenty thousand red-coats in Philadelphia to be fed."

"But is that the whole burden of your news?" asked Marcel. "We have seen others talk together as you four talk together, and we do not think it accords with nature for all Philadelphia to be agog because it rained the night before."

"Some heads hold strange opinions," said the countryman, curtly; "but why should I be held to account for them?"

So saying, he walked off with his companions.

"You can't draw blood from a turnip," said Marcel, "nor the truth from a man who has decided not to tell it."

"Not since the torture-chamber was abolished," I said, "and I would even guess that this countryman is no very warm friend to the British, from the insolent tone that he adopted towards us."

"And I would guess also that his news, whatever it may be, is something that will not be to the taste of the British, or he would tell it to us," said Marcel.

But we were not daunted by one repulse, and we decided to try elsewhere. From another little group to which we addressed ourselves we received treatment perhaps not quite so discourteous, but as unproductive of the desired result. All this we took as further proof that there was in reality something of importance afoot. At last we went into a little eating-house where strong liquors also were sold.

"Perhaps if we moisten their throats for them," said Marcel, "they may become less secretive. It is a cure I have rarely known to fail."

There were eight or ten men in this place, some citizens of the town and some countrymen.

"What news?" I asked of one who leaned against the counter. "There seems to be a stir about the town, and we ask its cause."

"You are British officers," he replied. "The British hold this town. You should know more than we."

"But this town has a population of such high intelligence," I said, thinking to flatter him, "that it learns many things before we do."

"If you admit that," he said, "then I can tell you something."

"Ah! what is it?" I asked, showing eagerness.

"Perhaps you may not like to hear it," he said, "but Sir William Howe was nearly carried off last night by Wildfoot."

Then all of them laughed in sneering fashion.

"I was afraid you would not like my news," said the man, pretending of a sudden to be very humble; "but you would not be satisfied until I told it, and so I had to tell it."

"We must even try elsewhere," said Marcel.

Marcel was a jester, but, like most other jesters, he did not like a jest put upon himself. So we left the eating-house, and as we went out we saw the man Waters coming towards us. As I have often said, I did not like this fellow, and moreover I feared we had reason to dread him, but I thought he could tell us what we wished to know, as he had such a prying temper.

He saluted us with much politeness, and stopped when I beckoned to him. The men in the eating-house had all come to the door.

"Good-morning, Waters," I said. "Can you tell us what interests the people of this city so much, the news that we have been seeking in vain to learn? Here are gentlemen who have something that they would cherish and keep to themselves like a lady's favor."

"It would scarce be proper for me, who am but an orderly, to announce weighty matters to your honors," said the man, with a most aggravating look of humility. The loungers who had come to the door laughed.

"We will overlook that," said Marcel, who kept his temper marvellously well. "But tell us, is not the town really in a stir as it seems to be?"

"It is, your honors," said Waters, "and it has cause for it."

The loungers laughed again; but I did not mind it now, as I was eager to hear what Waters had to say.

"Let us have this mighty secret," I said.

"I fear your honors will not like it," replied Waters.

"Never mind about that," I said, impatiently. "I do not believe that it amounts to anything at all."

"It is only that the King of France has joined the Americans and declared war on the English," said Waters.

For a moment I could scarce restrain a shout of joy. There had been talk for some time about a French alliance, but we had been disappointed so often that we had given up hope of it. Now the news had come with the suddenness of a thunderclap. I believe that Marcel felt as I did, but it was of high importance that we should keep our countenances.

"Whence did you get such a report as that?" I asked, affecting to treat it with contempt and unbelief.

"From the people of the city," replied Waters.

"Where did they get it?" asked Marcel.

"I think it was brought in from the American army," replied the man, "and if your honor will pardon me for saying it, there is no doubt whatever about its truth."

"King George will now have two enemies to fight instead of one, and he has not whipped the first," said one of the loungers.

"Fear not that his armies will not be equal to the emergency," said I, thinking it needful to preserve my character as a British officer.

"Then they will have to do something more than feast and dance in this city," said the bold fellow. The others murmured their approval and applause, and Marcel and I, bidding them to beware how they talked treason, strolled on.

"I'm sorry to be the bearer of such bad news," said Waters, humbly.

"King Louis and the Americans are responsible for the news, not you," said Marcel. "Still, we thank you for narrating it to us."

His tone was that of curt dismissal, and Waters, accepting it, left us. Marcel and I looked at each other, and Marcel said:—

"If we were able, half-armed, untrained, and unaided, to take one British army at Saratoga, what ought we not to do now with King Louis's regulars to help us, and King Louis's arsenals to arm us?"

"The alliance suggests many things," I said, "and one in particular to you and me."

"What is that?" asked Marcel.

"That we leave Philadelphia at once, or at least as soon as we can find an opportunity," I replied, "and rejoin our army. This should portend great events, perhaps a decisive campaign, and if that be true we ought to share it with our comrades."

"Without denying the truth of what you say," replied Marcel, "we nevertheless cannot leave the city to-day, so we might as well enjoy the leisure the gods have allotted to us. The counting-house of our rich patriot, old John Desmond, is on this street. Perhaps he has not heard the news, and if we were the first to tell it to him he might forgive our apparent British character, though I fear it would be but small recommendation to his handsome Tory daughter."

We entered the counting-house, where Mr. Desmond still contrived to earn fair profits despite the British occupation. Our British uniforms procured for us a certain amount of respect and deference from the clerks and attendants, but the stern old man, who would not bend to Sir William Howe himself, only glowered at us when we came into his presence.

"I fear I can give you but little time to-day, gentlemen," he said, with asperity, "though I acknowledge the honor of your visit."

"We are not in search of a loan," said Marcel, lightly, "but came merely to ask you if you had any further particulars of the great news which must be so pleasing to you, though I admit that it is less welcome to us."

"The news? the great news? I have no news, either great or small," said Mr. Desmond, not departing from his curt and stiff manner.

"Haven't you heard it?" said Marcel, with affected surprise. "All the people in the city are talking about it, and we poor Britons expect to begin hard service again immediately."

"Your meaning is still strange to me," said Mr. Desmond.

"It's the French alliance that I mean," said Marcel. "We have received positive news this morning that King Louis of France and Mr. Washington of America, in virtue of a formal treaty to that effect, propose to chastise our master, poor King George."

I had watched Mr. Desmond's face closely, that I might see how he took the news. But not a feature changed. Perhaps he was sorry that he had yielded to his feelings at the recent banquet, and was now undergoing penance. But, whatever the cause, he asked merely, in a quiet voice,—

"Then you know that the King of France has espoused the American cause and will help General Washington with his armies and fleets?"

"Undoubtedly," replied Marcel.

"Then this will be interesting news for my daughter, though she will not like it," he said. He opened the door of an inner room, called, and Miss Desmond came forth.

She looked inquiringly at us, and then spoke with much courtesy. We returned the compliments of the day in a manner that we thought befitting highborn Britons and conquerors in the presence of sympathetic beauty. I took pride to myself too, because my affair with Belfort had ended as she wished. It seemed to give me a claim upon her. But I observed with some chagrin that neither our manners nor our appearance seemed to make much impression upon Miss Desmond.

"Daughter," said Mr. Desmond, in the same expressionless tone that he had used throughout the interview, "these young gentlemen have been kind enough to bring us the news that France and the colonies have signed a formal treaty of alliance for offensive and defensive purposes. The information reached Philadelphia but this morning. I thought it would interest you."

I watched her face closely, as I had watched that of her father, expecting to see joy on the father's, sorrow on the daughter's. But they could not have been freer from the appearance of emotion if they had planned it all before.

"This will complicate the struggle, I should think," she said, dryly, "and it will increase your chances, Captain Montague and Lieutenant Melville, to win the epaulets of a colonel."

"We had expected," I said, "that Miss Desmond, a sincere friend of our cause, would express sorrow at this coalition which is like to prove so dangerous to us."

"My respect to my father, who does not believe as I do, forbids it," she said. "But I think the king's troops and his officers, all of them, will be equal to every emergency."

We bowed to the compliment, and, there being no further excuse for lingering, departed, patriot father and Tory daughter alike thanking us for our consideration in bringing them the news.

"The lady is very beautiful," said Marcel, when we had left the counting-house, "but she sits in the shadow of the North Pole."

"Self-restraint," I said, "is a good quality in woman as well as in man."

"I see," said Marcel. "It is not very hard to forgive treason when the traitor is a woman and beautiful."

"I do not know what you mean," I said, with frigidity.

"It does not matter," he replied. "I know."

CHAPTER EIGHTEEN—*The Silent Sentinel*

I doubted not that the news of the French alliance would incite Sir William Howe to activity, for any fool could see that, with his splendid army, splendidly equipped, he had allowed his chances to go to ruin. There was increasing talk, and of a very definite nature too, about his removal from the chief command. So far as the subalterns knew, his successor might have been appointed already, and this would be an additional inducement to Sir William to attempt some sudden blow which would shed glory over the close of his career in America, and leave about him the odor of success and not of failure.

My surmise was correct in all particulars, for both Marcel and I were ordered to report for immediate duty, and though this cut off all chance of escape for that day, we had no choice but to obey. We found an unusually large detachment gathered under the command of a general officer. Belfort, Barton, Moore, and others whom we knew were there; but, inquire as we would, we could not ascertain the nature of the service for which we were designed. In truth, no one seemed to know except the general himself, and he was in no communicative mood. But there was a great overhauling of arms and a very careful examination of the ammunition supply. So I foresaw that the expedition was to be of much importance.

"Perhaps it will be another such as the attempt to capture our brother-in-arms Mr. Wildfoot," said Marcel.

"If we come out of this as well as we did out of that," I replied, "we will have a right to think that Fortune has us in her especial keeping."

"Dame Fortune is kindest to those who woo her with assiduity," said Marcel, "and she cannot complain of us on that point."

But I knew how fickle the lady is, even towards those who woo her without ceasing, and I was uneasy.

The detachment had gathered in the suburbs, and we were subjected to a long period of waiting there. I also learned that no one was to be allowed to pass from the city during the day, and from this circumstance I inferred that Sir William was building great hopes upon the matter which he had in hand, and which he had placed under the direction of one of his ablest generals. I would have given much to know what it was, but I was as ignorant as the drummer-boy who stood near me. It was not until dusk that we marched, and then we started forth, a fine body, four thousand strong,—a thousand horse and three thousand foot.

"If there is a time for it to-night," I said to Marcel, when the opportunity came for us to speak together in secrecy, "I shall leave these people with whom we have no business, and return to those to whom we belong."

"And I," said Marcel, with one of his provoking grins, "shall watch over you with paternal care, come what may."

The night was half day. A full silver moon turned the earth—forests, fields, and houses—into that peculiar shimmering gray color which makes one feel as if one were dwelling in a ghost-world that may dissolve into mist at any moment. Our long column was colored the same ghostly gray by the moon. There were no sounds, save the steady tramp of the men and the horses, and the occasional clank of the bayonets together.

I did not like this preternatural silence, this evidence of supreme caution. It warned me of danger to my countrymen, and again I wished in my soul that I knew what business we were about. But there was naught to do save to keep my mouth shut and my eyes open.

We followed one of the main roads out of Philadelphia for some distance, and then turned into a narrower path, along which the detachment had much difficulty in preserving its formation. This part of the country was strange to me, and I did not believe that we were proceeding in the direction of the American encampment. Still, it was obvious that a heavy blow against the Americans was intended.

As the hours passed, clouds came before the moon, and the light waned. The long line of men ahead of me sank into the night so gradually that I could not tell where life ended and darkness began, and still there was no sound but the regular tread of man and beast and the clanking of arms. My sense of foreboding increased. How heartily I wished that I had never come into Philadelphia! I silently cursed Marcel for leading me into the adventure. Then I cursed myself for attempting to throw all the blame on Marcel.

The night was advancing, when we came to a long, narrow valley, thickly wooded at one end. We halted there, and the general selected about three hundred men and posted them in the woods at the head of the valley. I was among the number, but I observed with regret that Marcel was not. A colonel was placed in command. Then the main army followed a curving road up the hill-side and went out of sight over the heights. I watched them for some time before they disappeared, horse and foot, steadily tramping on, blended into a long, continuous, swaying mass by the gray moonlight; sometimes a moonbeam would tip the end of a bayonet with silver and gleam for a moment like a falling star. At last the column wound over the slope and left the night to us.

About one-third of our little force were cavalrymen; but, under the instructions of our colonel, we dismounted and gave our horses into the care of a few troopers; then all of us moved into the thick woods at the head of the pass, and sat down there, with orders to keep as quiet as possible.

I soon saw that the rising ground and the woods which crowned it merely formed a break between the valley which we had entered at first and another valley beyond it. The latter we were now facing. I had not been a soldier for two years and more for nothing, and I guessed readily that we were to keep this pass clear, while the main force was to perform the more important operation, which I now doubted not was to be the entrapping of some large body of Americans. Perhaps in this number was to be included the general-in-chief himself, the heart and soul of our cause. I shuddered at the thought, and again cursed the reckless spirit that had placed me in such a position.

At first we had the second valley in view; but our colonel, fearing that we might expose ourselves, drew us farther back into the woods, and then we could see nothing but the trees and the dim forms of each other.

I looked up at the moon, and hoped to see the clouds gathering more thickly before her face. I had confirmed my resolution. If the chance came to me, I would steal away from the English and enter the valley beyond. I doubted not that I would find my own people there. I would warn them of the danger, and remain with them in the future, unless fate should decree that I become a prisoner.

But Dame Fortune was in no such willing humor. The clouds did not gather in quantities, and, besides, the English were numerous around me. Belfort himself sat on the grass only a few feet from me, and, with more friendliness than he had shown hitherto, undertook to talk to me in whispers.

"Do you know what we are going to do to-night, Melville?" he asked.

"It seems," I said, "that we are to sit here in the woods until morning, and then to be too hoarse with cold to talk."

Then I added, having the after-thought that I might secure some information from him,—

"I suppose we are after important game to-night. The size of our force and the care and secrecy of our movements indicate it, do they not?"

"There is no doubt of it," he replied, "and I hope we shall secure a royal revenge upon the rebels for that Wildfoot affair."

Our conversation was interrupted here by an order from the colonel for me to move farther towards the front, from which point I was to report to him at once anything unusual that I might see or hear. The men near me were common soldiers. They squatted against the trees with their muskets between their knees, and waited in what seemed to me to be a fair degree of content.

An hour, a very long hour, of such waiting passed, and the colonel approached me, asking if all was quiet. I supplemented my affirmative reply with some apparently innocent questions which I thought would draw from him the nature of his expectations. But he said nothing that satisfied me. As he was about to turn away, I thought I heard a movement in the woods in front of us. It was faint, but it resembled a footfall.

"Colonel," I said, in a hurried whisper, "there is some movement out there."

At the same moment one of the soldiers sprang to his feet and exclaimed,—

"There is somebody coming down on us!"

"Be quiet, men," said the colonel. "Whoever it is, he stops here."

Scarce had he spoken the words when we heard the rush of many feet. The woods leaped into flame; the bullets whistled like hailstones around our ears. By the flash I saw the head of one of the soldiers who was still sitting down fall over against a tree, and a red streak appear upon his forehead. He uttered no cry, and I knew that he was dead.

For a few moments I stood quite still, as cold and stiff as if I had turned to ice. There is nothing, as I have said before, that chills the heart and stops its flow like a sudden surprise. That is why veterans when fired upon in the dark will turn and run sometimes as if pursued by ghosts.

Then my faculties returned, and I shouted,—

"Back on the main body! Fall back for help!"

The colonel and the men, who like me had been seized by surprise, sprang back. Almost in a breath I had formed my resolution, and I ran, neither forward nor back, but to one side. When I had taken a dozen quick steps, I flung myself upon my face. As I did so, the second volley crashed over my head, and was succeeded by yells of wrath and pain.

"At them, boys! At them!" shouted a loud voice that was not the English colonel's. "Drive the bloody scoundrels off the earth!"

I doubted not that the voice belonged to the leader of the attacking party. I arose and continued my flight. Behind me I heard the British replying to the fire of the assailants, and the other noises of the struggle. The shots and the shouts rose high. I knew that I was following no noble course just then, that I was flying alike from the force to which I pretended to belong, and from the force to which I belonged in reality; but I saw nothing else to do, and I ran, while the combat raged behind. I was in constant fear lest some sharpshooter of either party should pick me off, but my luck was better than my hopes, and no bullet pursued me in my flight.

When I thought myself well beyond the vortex of the combat, I dropped among the bushes for breath and to see what was going on behind me. I could not hear the cries so well now, but the rapid flashing of the guns was proof enough that the attack was fierce and the resistance the same.

As I watched, my sense of shame increased. I ought to be there with the Americans who were fighting so bravely. For a moment I was tempted to steal around and endeavor to join them. But how could I fire upon the men with whom I had been so friendly and who had looked upon me as one of their own but ten minutes ago? I was no crawling spy. Then, again, I was in full British uniform, and of course the patriots would shoot me the moment they caught sight of me. Richly, too, would I deserve the bullet. Again there was naught for me to do but to resort to that patient waiting which I sometimes think is more effective in this world than the hardest kind of work. And well it may be, too, for it is a more trying task.

I could not tell how the battle was going. So far as the firing was concerned, neither side seemed to advance or retreat. The flashes and the shots increased in rapidity, and then both seemed to converge rapidly towards a common centre. Of a sudden, at the very core of the combat there was a tremendous burst of sound, a great stream of light leaped up and then sank. The firing died away in a feeble crackle, and then I knew that the battle was over. But which side had won was a question made all the more perplexing to me by my inability to decide upon a course of conduct until I could learn just what had happened.

As I listened, I heard a single shot off in the direction from which the Americans had come. Then they had been beaten, after all. But at the very moment my mind formed the conclusion, I heard another shot in the neck of the valley up which the British had marched. Then the British had been beaten. But my mind again corrected itself. The two shots offset each other, and I returned to my original state of ignorance and uncertainty.

My covert seemed secure, and, resorting again to patience, I determined to lie there for a while and await the course of events. Perhaps I would hear more shots, which would serve as a guide to me. But another half-hour passed away, and I heard nothing. All the clouds had fled from the face of the moon, and the night grew brighter. The world turned from gray to silver, and the light slanted through the leaves. A lizard rattled over a fallen trunk near me, and, saving his light motion, the big earth seemed to be asleep. Readily could I have imagined that I was some lone hunter in the peaceful woods, and that no sound of anger or strife had ever been heard there. The silence and the silver light of the moon falling over the forest, and even throwing streaks across my own hands overpowered me. Though knowing full well that it was the truth, I had to make an effort of the will to convince myself that the attack, my flight, and the battle were facts. Then the rustling of the lizard, though I could not see him, was company to me, and I hoped he would not go away and leave me alone in that vast and heavy silence.

At last I fell to reasoning with myself. I called myself a coward, a child, to be frightened thus of the dark, when I had faced guns; and by and by this logic brought courage back. I knew I must take action of some kind, and not die there until the day found me cowering like a fox in the shelter of the woods. I had my sword at my side, and a loaded pistol was thrust in my belt. In the hands of a brave man they should be potent for defence.

Without further ado, I began my cautious journey. It was my purpose to proceed through the pass into the second valley and find the Americans, if still they were there. Then, if not too late, I would warn them of the plan against them, that this was not merely the raid of a few skirmishers, but a final attempt. Success looked doubtful. It depended upon the fulfilment of two conditions: first, that the Americans had not been entrapped already, and, second, that I should find them. Still, I would try. I stopped and listened intently for the booming of guns and other noises of conflict in the valley below, but no sound assailed my ears. I renewed my advance, and practised a precaution which was of the utmost necessity. For the present I scarce knew whether to consider myself English or American, and in the event of falling in with either I felt that I would like to make explanations before any action was taken concerning me. I stood up under the shadow of the big trees and looked around me. But there was naught that I could see. Englishmen and Americans alike seemed to have vanished like a wisp of smoke before the wind. Then with my hand on my pistol, I passed on from tree to tree, stopping ofttimes to listen and to search the wood with my eyes for sight of a skulking sharpshooter. Thus I proceeded towards the highest point of the gorge. The crest once reached, I expected that I would obtain a good view of the valley beyond, and thus be able to gather knowledge for my journey.

As I advanced, my opinion that the wood was now wholly deserted was confirmed. Victor and vanquished alike had vanished, I felt sure, carrying with them the wounded and the dead too. After a bit, and when almost at the crest, I came to an open space. I walked boldly across it, although the moon's light fell in a flood upon it, and as I entered the belt of trees on the farther side I saw the peak of a fur cap peeping over a log not forty feet before me. It was a most unpleasant surprise, this glimpse of the hidden sharpshooter; and, with the fear of his bullet hot upon me, I sprang for the nearest tree and threw myself behind it.

I was too quick for him, for the report of no rifle lent speed to my flying heels, and I sank, empty of breath, but full of thanks, behind the sheltering tree. Brief as had been my glimpse of that fur cap, I knew it, or rather its kind. It was the distinguishing mark of Morgan's Virginia Rangers, the deadliest sharpshooters in the world. I had seen their fell work at Saratoga when we beleaguered the doomed British army, where not a red-coat dared put his foot over the lines, for he knew it would be the signal for the Virginia rifle to speak from tree or bush. I do not like such work myself, but I acknowledge its great use.

Again I gave thanks for my presence of mind and agility of foot, for I had no wish to be killed, and least of all by one of our own men.

I lay quite still until my pulses went down and my breath became longer. I was fearful that the sentinel would attempt some movement, but a cautious look reassured me. He could not leave his covert behind the log for other shelter without my seeing him. It was true that I could not leave the tree, but I did not feel much trouble because of that. I had no desire to shoot him, while he, without doubt, would fire at me, if the chance came to him, thinking me to be a British officer.

The tree grew on ground that was lower than the spot from which I had seen the sentinel. In my present crouching position he was invisible to me, and I raised myself carefully to my full height in order that I might see him again. But even by standing on my toes I could see only the fur tip of his cap. I could assure myself that he was still there, but what he was preparing I knew not, nor could I ascertain. Yet I doubted not that his muscles were ready strung to throw his rifle to the shoulder and send a bullet into me the moment I stepped from behind the tree. The unhappy part of my situation lay in the fact that he would fire before I could make explanations, which would be a most uncomfortable thing for me, and in all likelihood would make explanations unnecessary, considering the deadly precision of these Virginia sharpshooters. Confound them! why should they be so vigilant concerning me, when there was a British army near by that stood in much greater need of their watching? But it was not worth while to work myself into a stew because I had got into a fix. The thing to do was to get out of it.

After some deliberation, I concluded that I would hail my friend who was yet an enemy, or at least in the position of one. I was afraid to shout to him, for most likely, with his forest cunning, he would think it a mere device to entrap him into an unwary action that would cost his life. These wilderness men are not to be deluded in that manner. However, there might be others lurking near, perhaps British and Americans both, and either one or the other would take me for an enemy and shoot me.

But at last I called in a loud whisper to the sentinel. I said that I was a friend, though I came in the guise of an enemy. The whisper was shrill and penetrating, and I was confident that it reached him, for the distance was not great. But he made no sign. If he heard me he trusted me not. I think there are times when we can become too cunning, too suspicious. This I felt with a great conviction to be one of such times.

As a second experiment, I decided that I would expose my hat or a portion of my uniform, in the hope that it would draw his fire. Then I could rush upon him and shout my explanations at him before he could reload his gun and shoot a second bullet at me. But this attempt was as dire a failure as the whispering. He was too wary to be caught by such a trick, with which he had doubtless been familiar for years.

I almost swore in my vexation at being stopped in such a manner. But vexation soon gave way to deepening alarm. I could not retreat from the tree without exposing myself to his fire, and there I was, a prisoner. As I lay against the tree-trunk, sheltering myself from the sharpshooter, a bullet fired by some one else might cut my life short at any moment. I waited some minutes, and again I raised myself up and took a peep. There he was, crouched behind his log, and still waiting for me. He seemed scarce to have moved. I knew the illimitable patience of these forest-bred men, the hours that they could spend waiting for their prey, immovable like wooden images. I repeat that I had seen them at work at Saratoga, and I knew their capabilities. I liked not the prospect, and I had good reason for it.

The old chill, the old depression, which was born part of the night and part of my situation, came upon me. I could do naught while my grim sentinel lay in the path. I knew of no device that would tempt him to action, to movement. I wearied my brain in the endeavor to think of some way to form a treaty with him or to tell him who and what I was. At last another plan suggested itself, I tore off a piece of the white facing of my uniform, and, putting it on the end of my gun-barrel, thrust it out as a sign of amity. I waved it about for full five minutes, but the watcher heeded not; perchance he thought this too was a trick to draw him from cover, and he would have none of it. Again I cursed excessive caution and suspicion, but that did me no good, save to serve as some slight relief to my feelings.

A strong wind sprang up, and the woods moved with it. The clouds came again before the moon, and the color of trees and earth faded to an ashen gray. The light became dimmer, and I felt cold, to the bones. Fear resumed sway over me, and dry-lipped, I cursed my folly with bitter curses.

But the shadows before the moon suggested one last plan to me, a plan full of danger in the presence of the watchful sentinel, but like to bring matters to a head. I unbuckled my sword and laid it upon the ground behind the tree. I also removed everything else of my equipment or uniform that might make a noise as I moved, and then crept from behind the tree. I had heard how Indians could steal through the grass with less noise than a lizard would make, and I had a belief that I could imitate them, at least to some extent.

I felt in front of me with my hands, lest I should place the weight of my body upon some stick that would snap with a sharp report. But there was only the soft grass, and the faint rustle it made could not reach the ears of the sentinel, no matter how keen of hearing or attentive he might be. All the time I kept my eyes upon the log behind which he lay. Each moment I trembled lest I should see a gun-barrel thrust over the log and pointed at me. Then it was my purpose to spring quickly aside, rush upon him, and cry out who I was.

But the threatening muzzle did not appear. I grew proud of my skill in being able thus to steal upon one of these rangers, who know the forest and all its tricks as the merchant knows his wares. Perchance I could learn to equal them or to surpass them at their own chosen pursuits. I even stopped to laugh inwardly at the surprise and chagrin this man would show when I sprang over the log and dropped down beside him, and he never suspecting, until then, that I was near. Of a truth, I thought, and this time with a better grace, there could be an excess of caution and suspicion.

When I had traversed about half the intervening space, I lay flat upon my face and listened, but without taking my eyes off the particular portion of the log over which I feared the gun-muzzle would appear. But the watcher made no movement, nor could I hear a sound, save that of the rising wind playing its dirge through the woods. Clearly I was doing my work well. Bringing my muscles and nerves back to the acutest tension, I crept on.

I must have been aided by luck as much as by skill, perhaps more, and I made acknowledgment of it to myself, for never once did I make a false movement with hand or foot. No twigs, no dry sticks, the breaking of which would serve as an alarm, came in my way. All was as smooth and easy as a silk-covered couch. Fortune seemed to look kindly upon me.

In two more minutes I had reached the log, and only its foot or two of diameter lay between me and the sentinel. Complete success had attended my efforts so far. It only remained for me to do one thing now, but that was the most dangerous of all. I lay quite still for a moment or two, drawing easy breaths. Then I drew in a long one, inhaling all the air my lungs would hold. Stretching every muscle to its utmost tension, and crying out, "I'm a friend! I'm a friend!" I sprang in one quick bound over the log.

I alighted almost upon the ranger as he crouched against the fallen trunk, the green of his hunting-shirt blending with the grass, and the gray of his fur cap showing but faintly against the bark of the tree. As I alighted by his side he moved not. His rifle, which was clutched in both his hands, remained unraised. His head still rested against the tree-trunk, though his eyes were wide open.

I put my hand upon him, and sprang back with a cry of affright that I could not check.

The sentinel was dead and cold.

CHAPTER NINETEEN—A
Ride for the Cause

When I discovered that I had stalked a dead man as the hunter stalks the living deer, I was seized with a cold chill, and an icy sweat formed upon my brow. My muscles, after so much tension, relaxed as if I had received some sudden and mortal blow, and I fell into a great tremble.

But this did not last long. I trust that I am not a coward, and I quickly regained possession of my limbs and my faculties. Then I turned to the examination of the dead man. He had been shot through the head, and I judged that he had been dead a good two hours. A stray ball must have found him as he lay there watching for the enemy and with his rifle ready. I thought I could still trace the look of the watcher, the eager attention upon his features.

I left him as he was, on duty in death as well as in life, and hurried through the grass, still hoping to reach the Americans in the valley beyond, in time.

A second thought caused me to stop. I knew that in the rush and hurry of the fight our horses must have broken from the men, and perchance might yet be wandering about the woods. If I could secure one, it would save much strength and time. I began to look through the woods, for I had little fear of interruptions now, as I believed that everybody except the dead and myself had left the pass. My forethought and perseverance were not without reward, for presently I found one of the horses, saddled and bridled, and grazing peacefully among the trees. He must have been lonely, for he whinnied when he saw me, and made no effort to escape.

I sprang into the saddle, and was soon riding rapidly into the farther valley. The slope was not so steep as that up which I had come with the British, and the woods and the underbrush grew more scantily. There was sufficient light for me to see that I would soon be on cleared ground, where I could make good speed and perchance find the object of my search quickly.

There was increase to my joy when my horse's foot rang loud and clear, and, looking down, I saw that I had blundered into a good road. It led straight away down the valley, and, with a quickening gait, we followed it, my good horse and I.

The night brightened somewhat, as if to keep pace with the improvement of my fortune. I could see fields around me, and sometimes caught glimpses of houses surrounded by their shade-trees. From one of these houses a dog came forth and howled at me in most melancholy tune, but I heeded him not. I rode gayly on, and was even in high enough mood to break forth into a jovial song, had I thought it wise. Such was my glee at the thought that I had left the British, had cast off my false character, and was now about to reassume my old self, the only self that was natural to me, and take my place among the men with whom I belonged.

It was shortly after this that my horse neighed and halted, and, had not my hand been firm on the reins, he would have turned and looked behind him. I urged him forward again, but in a few moments he repeated the same suspicious movement. This caused me to reflect, and I came to the conclusion that some one was behind us, or my horse would not have acted in such fashion. I pulled him to a stand-still, and, bending back, heard with much distinctness the sound of hoof-beats. Nor was it that only; the hoof-beats were rapid, and could be made only by a horse approaching with great speed. Even in the brief space that I listened, the hoof-beats of the galloping horse became much more distinct, and it was evident to me that if I did not put my horse to his own best speed, or turn aside into the fields, I would be overtaken. But I had no mind either to follow the difficult route through the fields or to flee from a single horseman. My loaded pistol and my sword were in my belt; and, while I did not wish to slay or wound any one, it did not seem becoming in me to take to flight.

I eased my grasp on the bridle-rein and took my pistol in my hand. Then, twisting myself round in my saddle, and watching for the appearance of my pursuer, if pursuer it were, I allowed my horse to fall into a walk.

I knew I would not have long to wait, for in the still night the hoof-beats were now ringing on the road. Whoever it was, he rode fast and upon a matter of moment. Presently the figure of the flying horse and rider appeared dimly. Then they grew more distinct. The rider was leaning upon his horse's neck, and as they rushed down upon us I saw that it was a woman. Great was my surprise at the sight.

My first impulse was to rein aside, but when the woman came within twenty feet of me she raised her face a little, and then I saw that it was Mary Desmond, the Tory. Even in that faint light I could see that her face was strained and anxious, and I was struck with a great wonderment.

I turned my horse into the middle of the road, and she was compelled to rein her own back so suddenly that he nearly fell upon his haunches.

"Out of my way!" she cried. "Why do you stop me?"

"I think you will admit, Miss Desmond," I said, "that the meeting is rather unusual, and that surprise, if nothing else, might justify my stopping you."

"Why is it strange that I am here?" she demanded, in a high tone. "Why is it more strange than your presence here at this time?"

"I am riding forward to join a detachment of the American army which I believe is encamped not much farther on," I said.

In reassuming my proper American character I had forgotten that I still wore the British garb.

"Why are you doing that?" she asked, quickly and keenly.

"I wish to take them a message," I replied.

"Who are you, and what are you?" she asked, abruptly, turning upon me a look before which my eyes fell,—"you whose garb is English and speech American."

"Whatever I am at other times," I replied, "to-night I am your servant only."

"Then," she replied, in a voice that thrilled me, "come with me. I ride to warn the Americans that they are threatened with destruction."

"*You!*" I exclaimed, my surprise growing. "*You* warn them! *You*, the most bitter of Tories, as bitter as only a woman can be!"

She laughed a laugh that was half of triumph, half of scorn.

"I have deceived you too, as I have deceived all the others," she said. "But I should not boast. The part was not difficult, and I despised it. Come! we will waste no more time. Ride with me to the American army, if you are what you have just boasted yourself to be."

Her voice was that of command, and I had no mind to disobey it.

"Come," I cried, "I will prove my words."

"I know the way," she replied. "I will be the guide."

We galloped away side by side. Many thoughts were flying through my head. I understood the whole story at once, or thought I did, which yielded not less of satisfaction to me. She was not the Tory she had seemed to be, any more than I was the Briton whose uniform I had taken. Why she had assumed such a *rôle* it was not hard to guess. Well, I was glad of it. My spirits mounted to a wonderful degree, past my ability to account for such a flight. But I bothered myself little about it. Another time would serve better for such matters.

The hoof-beats rang on the flinty road, and our horses stretched out their necks as our pace grew swifter and we fled on through the night.

"How far do we ride?" I asked.

"The American encampment is four miles beyond," she said. "The British force is coming down on the right. Pray God we may get there in time!"

"Amen!" said I. "But, if we do not, it will not be for lack of haste."

We passed a cottage close by the roadside. The clatter of our horses' hoofs aroused its owner, for in those troublous times men slept lightly. A night-capped head was thrust out of a window, and I even noted the look of wonderment on the man's face; but we swept by, and the man and his cottage were soon lost in the darkness behind us.

"It will take something more than that to stop us to-night," I cried, in the exuberance of my spirits.

Miss Desmond's face was bent low over her horses neck, and she answered me not; but she raised her head and gave me a look that showed the courage a true woman sometimes has.

We were upon level ground now, and I thought it wise to check our speed, for Miss Desmond had ridden far and fast, and her horse was panting.

"We will not spare the horse," she said. "The lives of the patriots are more precious."

"But by sparing the former we have more chance of saving the latter," I said; and to that argument only would she yield. The advantage of it was soon seen, for when we increased our speed again the horses lengthened their stride and their breath came easier.

"Have you heard the sound of arms?" she asked. "Surely if any attack had been made we could hear it, even as far as this, in the night."

"I have heard nothing," I replied, "save the noise made by the galloping of our own horses. We are not yet too late."

"No, and we will not be too late at any time," she said, with sudden energy. "We cannot—we must not be too late!"

"How strong is the American force?" I asked.

"Strong enough to save itself, if only warned in time," she replied.

We came to a shallow brook which trickled peacefully across the road. Our horses dashed into it, and their flying hoofs sent the water up in showers. But almost before the drops could fall back into their native element we were gone, and our horses' hoofs were again ringing over the stony road.

Before us stretched a strip of forest, through the centre of which the road ran. In a few moments we were among the trees. The boughs overhung the way and shut out half of the moon's light. Beyond, we could see the open country again, but before we reached it a horseman spurred from the wood and cried to us to halt, flourishing his naked sword before him.

We were almost upon him, but on the instant I knew Belfort, and he knew me.

"Out of the way!" I cried. "On your life, out of the way!"

"You traitor! You damned traitor!" he shouted, and rode directly at me.

He made a furious sweep at my head with his sabre, but I bent low, and the blade circled over me, whistling as it passed. The next moment, with full weight and at full speed, my horse struck his, and Belfort's went down, the shriek from the man and the terrified neigh from the horse, mingling as they fell.

With a snort of triumph, my horse leaped clear of the fallen and struggling mass, and then we were out of the forest, Mary Desmond still riding by my side, her head bent over her horse's neck as if she were straining her eyes for a sight of the patriots who were still two miles and more away.

"You do not ask me who it was," I said.

"I know," she replied; "and I heard also what he called you."

"'Tis true, he called me that," I replied. "But he is in the dust now, and I still ride!"

We heard musket-shots behind us, and a bullet whizzed uncomfortably near. So Belfort had not been alone. In the shock of our rapid collision I had not had the time to see; but these shots admitted of no doubt.

"We will be pursued," I said.

"Then the greater the need of haste," she replied. "We cannot spare our horses now. There is a straight road before us."

No more shots were fired at us just then. Our pursuers must have emptied their muskets; but the clatter of the horses' hoofs told us that they were hot on the chase. Our own horses were not fresh, but they were of high mettle, and responded nobly to our renewed calls upon them. Once I took an anxious look behind me, and saw that our pursuers numbered a dozen or so. They were riding hard, belaboring their mounts, with hands and feet, and I rejoiced at the sight, for I knew the great rush at the start would tell quickly upon them.

"Will they overtake us?" asked Mary Desmond.

"It is a matter of luck and speed," I replied, "and I will answer your question in a quarter of an hour. But remember that, come what may, I keep my word to you. I am your servant to-night."

"Even if your self-sought slavery takes you into the American lines?" she asked.

"Even so," I replied. "I told you my mission, though you seemed to believe it not."

With this the time for conversation passed, and I put my whole attention upon our flight. My loaded pistol was still in my belt, and if our pursuers came too near, a bullet whistling among them might retard their speed. But I held that for the last resort.

So far as I could see, the men were making no attempt to reload their muskets, evidently expecting to overtake us without the aid of bullets. I inferred from this circumstance that Belfort, whom I had disabled, had been the only officer among them. Otherwise they would have taken better measures to stop us. Nevertheless they pursued with patience and seemingly without fear. By and by they fell to shouting. They called upon us to stop and yield ourselves prisoners. Then I heard one of them say very distinctly that he did not want to shoot a woman. Mary Desmond heard it too, for she said,—

"I ask no favor because I am a woman. If they should shoot me, ride on with my message."

I did not think it wise to reply to this, but spoke encouragingly to her horse. He was panting again, and his stride was shortening, but his courage was still high. He was a good horse and true, and deserved to bear so noble a burden.

Presently the girl's head fell lower upon the horse's neck, and I called hastily to her, for I feared that she was fainting.

"'Twas only a passing weakness," she said, raising her head again. "I have ridden far to-night; but I can ride farther."

The road again led through woods, and for a moment I thought of turning aside into the forest; but reflection showed me that in all likelihood we would become entangled among the trees, and then our capture would be easy. So we galloped straight ahead, and soon passed the strip of wood, which was but narrow. Then I looked back again, and saw that our pursuers had gained. They were within easy musket-range now, and one of the men, who had shown more forethought than the others and reloaded his piece, fired at us. But the bullet touched neither horse nor rider, and I laughed at the wildness of his aim. A little farther on a second shot was fired at us, but, like the other, it failed of its mission.

Now I noted that the road was beginning to ascend slightly and that farther on rose greater heights. This was matter of discouragement; but Miss Desmond said briefly that beyond the hill-top the American encampment lay. If we could keep our distance but a little while now, her message would be delivered. Even in the hurry of our flight I rejoiced that the sound of no fire-arms save those of our pursuers had yet been heard, which was proof that the attack upon the Americans had not yet been made.

The road curved a little now and became much steeper. Our pursuers set up a cry of triumph. They were near enough now for us to hear them encouraging each other, I could measure the distance very well, and I saw that they were gaining faster than before. The crest of the hill was still far ahead. These men must be reminded not to come too near, and I drew my pistol from my belt.

As the men came into better view around the curve, I fired at the leader. It chanced that my bullet missed him, but, what was a better thing for us, struck his horse full in the head and killed him. The stricken animal plunged forward, throwing his rider over his head. Two or three other horsemen stumbled against him, and the entire troop was thrown into confusion. I struck Miss Desmond's horse across the flank with my empty pistol, and then treated my own in like fashion. If we were wise, we would profit by the momentary check of our enemies, and I wished to neglect no opportunity. Our good steeds answered to the call as well as their failing strength would permit. The crest of the hill lay not far before us now, and I felt sure that if we could but reach it, the British would pursue us no farther.

But when I thought that triumph was almost achieved, Miss Desmond's horse began to reel from side to side. He seemed about to fall from weakness, for, of a truth, he had galloped far that night, and had done his duty as well as the best horse that ever lived, be it Alexander's Bucephalus or any other. Even now he strove painfully, and looked up the hill with distended eyes, as if he knew where the goal lay. His rider seemed smitten with an equal weakness, but she summoned up a little remaining strength against it, and raised herself up for the final struggle.

"Remember," she said again to me, "if I fail, as most like I will, you are to ride on with my message."

"I have been called a traitor to-night," I said, "but I will not be called the name I would deserve if I were to do that."

"It is for the cause," she said. "Ride and leave me."

"I will not leave you," I cried, thrilling with enthusiasm. "We will yet deliver the message together."

She said no more, but sought to encourage her horse. The troopers had recovered from their confusion, and, with their fresher mounts, were gaining upon us in the most alarming manner. I turned and threatened them with my empty pistol, and they drew back a little; but second thought must have assured them that the weapon was not loaded, for they laughed derisively and again pressed their horses to the utmost.

"Do as I say," cried Miss Desmond, her eyes flashing upon me. "Leave me and ride on. There is naught else to do."

But my thought was to turn my horse in the path and lay about me with the sword. I could hold the troopers while she made her escape with the message that she had borne so far already. I drew the blade from the scabbard and put a restraining hand upon my horse's rein.

"What would you do?" cried Miss Desmond.

"The only thing that is left for me to do," I replied.

"Not that!" she cried; "not that!" and made as if she would stop me. But, even while her voice was yet ringing in my ears, a dozen rifles flashed from the hill-top, a loud voice was heard encouraging men to speedy action, and a troop came galloping forward to meet us. In an instant the Englishmen who were not down had turned and were fleeing in a panic of terror down the hill and over the plain.

"You are just in time, captain," cried Miss Desmond, as the leader of the rescuing band, a large, dark man, came up. Then she reeled, and would have fallen from her horse to the ground had not I sprung down and caught her.

CHAPTER TWENTY—*The Night Combat*

But Miss Desmond was the victim only of a passing weakness, and I was permitted to hold her in my arms but for a moment. Then she demanded to be placed upon the ground, saying that her strength had returned. I complied of necessity; and turning to the American captain, who was looking curiously at us, she inquired,—

"Captain, the American force, is it safe?" "Yes, Miss Desmond," he replied; and I wondered how he knew her. "It is just over the hill there. The night had been quiet until you came galloping up the hill with the Englishmen after you."

"Then we are in time!" she cried, in a voice of exultation. "Lose not a moment, captain. A British force much exceeding our own in strength is even now stealing upon you."

The message caused much perturbation, as well it might, and a half-dozen messengers were sent galloping over the hill. Then the captain said,—

"Miss Desmond, you have done much for the cause, but more to-night than ever before."

But she did not hear him, for she fell over in a faint.

"Water!" I cried. "Some water! She may be dying!"

"Never mind about water," said the captain, dryly. "Here is something that is much better for woman, as well as for man, in such cases."

He produced a flask, and, raising Miss Desmond's head, poured some fiery liquid in her mouth. It made her cough, and presently she revived and sat up. She was very pale, but there was much animation in her eye.

"You have sent the warning, captain, have you not?" she asked, her mind still dwelling upon the object for which she had come.

"Do not fear, Miss Desmond," said the leader, gravely. "Our people know now, and they will be ready for the enemy when they come, thanks to your courage and endurance."

Then he beckoned to me, and we walked a bit up the hill-side, leaving Miss Desmond sitting on the turf and leaning against a tree.

"A noble woman," said the captain, looking back at her.

"Yes," said I, fervently.

"It was a lucky fortune that gave you such companionship to-night," he continued.

"Yes," replied I, still with fervor.

"Lieutenant Chester," he said, "that is not the only particular in which fortune has been kind to you to-night."

"No," I replied, with much astonishment at the patness with which he spoke my true name.

"I have said," he continued, with the utmost gravity, "that fortune has been very kind to-night to Lieutenant Robert Chester, of the American army. I may add that it has been of equal kindness to Lieutenant Melville, of the British army."

"Who are you, and what are you?" I cried, facing about, "and why do you speak in such strange fashion?"

"I do not think it is strange at all," he said, a light smile breaking over his face. "So far as I am concerned, it is a matter of indifference, Lieutenant Chester or Lieutenant Melville: which shall it be?"

I saw that it was useless for me to pretend more. He knew me, and was not to be persuaded that he did not. So I said,—

"Let it be Lieutenant Robert Chester, of the American army. The name and the title belong to me, and I feel easier with them than with the others. I have not denied myself. Now, who are you, and why do you know so much about me?"

"Nor will I deny myself, either," he said, a quiet smile dwelling upon his face. "I am William Wildfoot, captain of rangers in the American army."

"What! are you the man who has been incessantly buzzing like a wasp around the British?" I cried.

"I have done my humble best," he said, modestly; "I even chased you and your friend Lieutenant Marcel into Philadelphia. For which I must crave your forgiveness. Your uniforms deceived me; but since then we have become better acquainted with each other."

"How? I do not understand," I said, still in a maze.

"Perhaps you would know me better if I were to put on a red wig," he said. "Do not think, Lieutenant Chester, that you and Lieutenant Marcel are the only personages endowed with a double identity."

I looked at him closely, and I began to have some glimmering of the truth.

"Yes," he said, when he saw the light of recognition beginning to appear upon my face, "I am Waters. Strange what a difference a red wig makes in one's appearance. But I have tried to serve you and your friend well, and I hope I have atoned for my rudeness in putting you and Lieutenant Marcel to such hurry when I first saw you. It is true that I have had a little sport with you. I thought that you deserved it for your rashness, but I have not neglected your interests. I warned Alloway in the jail not to know you, and I helped him to escape. I learned about you from Pritchard, but no one else knows. I bound you, too, in Sir William Howe's room, but I leave it to you yourself that it was necessary."

His quiet laugh was full of good nature, though there was in it a slight tinge of pardonable vanity. Evidently this was a man much superior to the ordinary partisan chieftain.

"Then you too have placed your neck in the noose?" I said.

"Often," he replied. "And I have never yet failed to withdraw it with ease."

"I have withdrawn mine," I said, "and it shall remain withdrawn."

"Not so," he replied. "Miss Desmond must return to her father and Philadelphia. It is not fit that she should go alone, and no one but you can accompany her."

I had believed that nothing could induce me to take up the character of Lieutenant Melville of the British army again, but I had not thought of this. I could *not* leave Miss Desmond to return alone through such dangers to the city.

"Very well," I said, "I will go back."

"I thought so," returned Wildfoot, with a quick glance at me that brought the red blood to my face. "But I would advise you to bring Miss Desmond to the crest of the hill and wait for a while. I must hurry away, for my presence is needed elsewhere."

The partisan was like a war-horse sniffing the battle; and, leaving Miss Desmond, myself, and two good, fresh horses on the hill-top, he hastened away. I was not averse to waiting, for I expected that a sharp skirmish would occur. I had little fear for the Americans now, for in a night battle, where the assaulted are on their guard, an assailing force is seldom successful, even though its superiority in arms and numbers be great.

From the hill-top we saw a landscape of alternate wood and field, amid which many lights twinkled. A hum and murmur came up to us and told me that the Americans were profiting by their warning and would be ready for the enemy.

"You can now behold the result of your ride," I said to Miss Desmond, who stood by my side, gazing with intent eyes upon the scene below, which was but half hidden by the night. She was completely recovered, or at least seemed to be so, for she stood up, straight, tall, and self-reliant.

"We were just in time," she said.

"But in good time," I added.

"I suppose we shall see a battle," she said. "I confess it has a strange attraction for me. Perhaps it is because I am not near enough to mark its repellent phases."

She made no comment upon my British uniform and my apparent British character. She did not appear to remark anything incongruous in my appearance there, and it was not a subject that I cared to raise.

"See, the fighting must have begun," she said, pointing to a strip of wood barely visible in the night.

Some streaks of flame had leaped up, and we heard a distant rattle which I knew must be the small arms at work. Then there was a lull for a moment, followed by a louder and a longer crackle, and a line of fire, flaming up and then sinking in part, ran along the edge of the woods and across the fields. Through this crackle came a steady rub-a-dub, rub-a-dub.

"That is the beat of the drums," I said to Miss Desmond, who turned an inquiring face to me. "The drum is the soldier's conscience, I suppose, for it is always calling upon him to go forward and fight."

I spoke my thoughts truly, for the drum has always seemed to me to be a more remorseless war-god than the cannon. With its steady and tireless thump, thump, it calls upon you, with a voice that will not be hushed, to devote yourself to death. "Come on! Come on! Up to the cannon! Up to the cannon!" it says. It taunts you and reviles you. Give this drum to a ragamuffin of a little boy, and he catches its spirit, and he goes straight forward with it and commands you to follow him. It was so at Long Island when the Maryland brigade sacrificed itself and held back the immense numbers of the enemy until our own army could escape. A scrap of a boy stood on a hillock and beat a drum as tall as himself, calling upon the Maryland men to stand firm and die, until a British cannon-ball smashed his drum, and a British grenadier hoisted him over his shoulder with one hand and carried him away. There is a league between the drum and the cannon. The drum lures the men up to the cannon, and then the monster devours them.

Above the crackle rose the louder notes of the field-pieces, and then I thought I heard the sound of cheering, but I was not sure. We could see naught of this dim and distant battle but the flame of its gunpowder. The night was too heavy for any human figure to appear in its just outline; and I saw that I would have to judge of its progress by the shifting of the line of fire. The British attack was delivered from the left, and the blaze of the musketry extended along a line about a half-mile in length. Though while the light was leaping high at one place it might be sinking low at another, yet this line was always clearly defined, and we could follow its movements well enough.

The line was stationary for full fifteen minutes, and from that circumstance we could tell that the Americans had profited well by the warning and were ready to receive the attack. Still, the action was sharper and contested with more vigor than I had expected. Having made the attack, the British seemed disposed to persist in it for a while at least. But presently the line of fire began to bend back towards the west at the far end.

"The British are retreating!" exclaimed Miss Desmond.

"At one point, so it would seem," I said.

"Yes, and at other points too," she cried. "See, the centre of the fiery line bends back also."

This was true, for the centre soon bent back so far that the whole line was curved like a bow. Then the eastern end yielded also, and soon was almost hidden in some woods, where it made but a faint quivering among the trees. In truth, along the whole line the fire was dying. The sputter of the musketry was but feeble and scarce heard, and even the drum seemed to lose spirit and call but languidly for slaughter.

"The battle is nearly over, is it not?" asked Miss Desmond.

"Yes," I replied, "though we could scarce call it a battle. Skirmish is a better name. I think that line of fire across there will soon fade out altogether."

I chanced to be a good prophet in this instance, for in five minutes the last flash had gone out and there was naught left but a few echoes. It was clear that the British had suffered repulse and had withdrawn, and it was not likely that the Americans would follow far, for such an undertaking would expose them to destruction.

I now suggested to Miss Desmond that it would be the part of wisdom for us to begin our return to Philadelphia, and we were preparing for departure, when we heard the approach of horsemen, and in a moment or two Wildfoot and three of his men approached. "It was not a long affair," said the leader, "though there was some smart skirmishing for a while. When they found that we were ready, and rather more than willing, they soon drew off, and they are now on the march for Philadelphia. I tell you again, Miss Desmond, that you have ridden bravely to-night, and this portion of the American army owes its salvation to you."

"My ride was nothing more than every American woman owes to her country," replied Miss Desmond.

"True," replied Wildfoot, "though few would have had the courage to pay the debt. But I have come back mainly to say that some of my scouts have brought in Lieutenant Belfort, sorely bruised, but not grievously hurt, and that he will have no opportunity to tell the English of your ride to-night, Miss Desmond, at least not until he is exchanged."

I had forgotten all about Belfort, and his capture was a lucky chance for both of us. As for the other Englishmen who had pursued us, I had no fear that they would recognize me, even if they saw me in the daylight, and they had seen me but dimly in a hot and flurried pursuit.

Captain Wildfoot raised his hat to us with all the courtesy of a European nobleman and rode away with his men, while we turned our horses towards Philadelphia, and were soon far from the hill on which we had stood and witnessed the battle's flare. Miss Desmond knew the way much better than I did, and I followed her guidance, though we rode side by side.

"You do not ask me to keep this matter a secret," I said, at length, when we had ridden a mile or more in silence.

"Is not your own safety as much concerned as mine?" she asked, looking with much meaning at my gay British uniform.

"Is that the only reason you do not ask me to speak of it?" I said, still bent upon going deeper into the matter.

"Will you speak of it when I ask you not to do so?" she said.

I did not expect such a question, but I replied in the negative with much haste. But presently I said, thinking to compliment her, that, however my own sympathies might be placed, I must admit that she had done a very brave deed, and that I could not withhold my admiration. But she replied with some curtness that Captain Wildfoot had said that first,—which was true enough, though I had thought it as early as he. Had it been any other woman, I would have inferred from her reply that her vanity was offended. But it was not possible to think such a thing of Mary Desmond on that night.

"Have you any heart for this task?" she asked me, with much suddenness, a few minutes later.

"What task?" I replied, surprised.

"The task that the king has set for his army,—the attempt to crush the Colonies," she replied.

There was much embarrassment in the question for me, and I sought to take refuge in compliment.

"That you are enlisted upon the other side, Miss Desmond," I replied, "is enough to weaken the attachment of any one to the king's service."

"This is not a drawing-room," she replied, looking at me with clear eyes, "nor has the business which we have been about to-night any savor of the drawing-room. Let us then drop such manner of speech."

She was holding me at arm's length, but I made some rambling, ambiguous reply, to the effect that a soldier should have no opinions, but should do what he is told to do,—which, though a very good argument, does not always appease one's conscience. But she did not press the question further,—which was a relief to me.

When we became silent again, my thoughts turned back to our successful ride. On the whole, I had cause for lightness of feeling. Aided by chance or luck, I had come out of difficulties wondrous well. Within a very short space I had seen our people twice triumph over the British, and I exulted much because of it.

I think I had good reason for my exultation aside from the gain to our cause from these two encounters. While accusing us of being boasters, the British had quite equalled us at anything of that kind. I think it was their constant assumption of superiority, rather more than the tea at the bottom of Boston Harbor, that caused the war. Then they came over and said we could not fight. They are much better informed on that point now, though I will admit that they showed their own courage and endurance too.

Our return journey was not prolific of events. The night seemed to have exhausted its fruitfulness before that time. When we were within a short distance of the British lines, Miss Desmond pointed to a low farmhouse almost hidden by some trees.

"That is my retreat for the present," she said. "It was from that house I started, and I will return to it. For many reasons, I cannot be seen riding into Philadelphia with you at this hour."

"But are the inhabitants of that house friends of yours?" I asked, in some protest.

"They can be trusted to the uttermost," she replied briefly. "They have proved it. You must not come any farther with me. I have a pass and I can come into the city when I wish without troublesome explanations."

"Then I will leave you," I replied, "since I leave you in safety; but I hope you will not forget that we have been friends and allies on this expedition."

"I will not forget it," she said. Then she thanked me and rode away, as strong and upright and brave as ever. I watched her until she entered the trees around the house and disappeared. Then, although I might have fled to the American camp, I turned towards Philadelphia, a much wiser man than I was earlier in the night.

Some of the stragglers were coming into the city already, and it was not difficult for me, with my recent practice in lying, to make satisfactory explanation concerning myself. I told a brave tale about being captured by the rebels in the rush, my escape afterwards, and my futile attempts to rejoin the army. Then I passed on to my quarters.

In the course of the day the entire detachment, save those who had been killed or wounded in the skirmish, returned, and I learned that Sir William was much mortified at the complete failure of the expedition. He could not understand why the rebels were in such a state of readiness. I was very uneasy about Marcel, but he rejoined me unharmed, although he admitted that he had been in much trepidation several times in the course of the night.

CHAPTER TWENTY-ONE—
Keeping up Appearances

I wished to hold further conversation with Marcel that morning on a matter of high interest to both of us, but I did not find the opportunity, for we were sent on immediate duty into different parts of the suburbs. Mine was soon finished, and I returned to the heart of the city. I noticed at once that the invading army had suffered a further relaxation of discipline. Evidently, after his failure of the preceding night, Sir William took no further interest in the war, and but little in the army, for that matter, except where his personal friends were concerned. But most afflicting was the condition of mind into which the Tories had fallen. Philadelphia, like New York, abounded in these gentry, and a right royal time they had been having, basking in the sunshine of British favor, and tickling themselves with visions of honors and titles, and even expecting shares in the confiscated estates of their patriot brethren.

Now they were in sore distress, and but little of my pity had they. Among the rumors was one, and most persistent it was too, that a consequence of the French alliance would be the speedy evacuation of Philadelphia by the British, who would in all probability seek to concentrate their strength at New York. This was a misfortune that the wretched Tories had never foreseen. What! the British ever give up anything they had once laid their hands upon! The descendants of the conquerors of Crecy, Poitiers, and Agincourt, the grandsons of the men who had humbled Louis the Great at Blenheim and Malplaquet, to be beaten by untrained, half-armed, and starving farmers! The thing was impossible. And Tory and Briton vied with each other in crying to all the winds of heaven that it could not be. The British were most arrogant towards us in those days, for which reason we always took much satisfaction in beating them, admitting at the same time that they were brave men, and we never cared much about our victories over the Hessians, who, to tell the truth, were very fierce in the pursuit of a beaten enemy, but not quite so enduring in the main contention as the British.

But I had ever had more animosity against the Tories than the British, and I felt much secret delight at their manifest and troublous state of mind. Some, who had their affairs well in hand, were preparing to depart with their beloved British, who little wanted such burdens. Others were mourning for their houses and goods which they had expected to see wrenched from them as they would have wrenched theirs from the patriots. All seemed to expect that the American army would be upon them immediately, such were their agitation and terror. Curses, too, were now heard against King George for deserting his faithful servants after making so many great promises to them. Well, it is not for those who shake the dice and lose, to complain. We, too, had had our sufferings.

Nevertheless, the British, as is their wont, put a good face upon the matter. That very night, many of the officers were at a reception given with great splendor at the house of a rich Tory, and they talked of past triumphs and of others soon to be won. I also was there, for I had contrived to secure an invitation, having special reasons for going.

As I had expected, Miss Desmond was present. She seemed to neglect none of the fashionable gayeties of the city, and to me she looked handsomer and statelier than ever. I wished for some look, some suggestion that we had been companions in danger, and that we were rather better friends than the others present; but she was cold and proud, and there was nothing in her manner to show that we had ever met, save in the formal atmosphere of the drawing-room.

"I hear, Lieutenant Melville," she said, "that you were in the unfortunate attack last night and fell into the hands of the rebels."

"Yes, Miss Desmond," I replied, "but good fortune succeeded bad fortune. I escaped from them in the darkness and the confusion, and am back in Philadelphia to lay my sword at your feet."

Such was the polite language of the time; but she received it with small relish, for she replied, with asperity,—

"You have barely escaped laying your sword at the feet of the rebels. Is not that enough of such exercise?"

Then some British officers, who heard her, laughed as if the gibe had no point for them.

I had no further opportunity for conversation with her until much later in the evening. The rooms were buzzing with the gossip of great events soon to occur; and though I sought not the part of a spy, and had no intent to put myself in such a position, I listened eagerly to the fragments of news that were sent about. This was not a matter of difficulty, for all were willing, even eager, to talk, and one could not but listen, without drawing comment and giving offence.

"'Tis reported," said Symington, a colonel, to me, "that the French king will despatch an army in great haste to America. But we shall not care for that—shall we, Melville? I, for one, am tired of playing hide-and-seek with the old fox, Mr. Washington, and should like to meet our ancient foes the French regulars in the open field. Then the fighting would be according to the rules as practised by the experts in Europe for many generations."

I thought to throw cold water upon him, and said I feared the Americans and the French allied might prove too strong for us; and as for the ancient rules of war, campaigns must be adapted to their circumstances and the nature of the country in which they are conducted. If the Americans alone, and that too when at least one-third of them were loyal to our cause, had been able to confine us to two or three cities practically in a state of besiegement, what were we to expect when the full might of the King of France arrived to help them?

But he would have naught of my argument. He was full of the idea that glory was to be found fighting the French regulars in the open field according to the rules of Luxembourg and Marlborough. But I have no right to complain, for it was such folly as his that was of great help to us throughout the war, and contributed to the final victory over the greatest power and the best soldiers of Europe.

Although much interested in such talk as it was continued by one or another through the evening, I watched Miss Desmond. Now, since I knew her so well, or at least thought I did, she had for me a most marvellous attraction. At no time did she betray any weakness in the part she played, and though more than once she found my eyes resting upon her, there was no answering gleam. But I was patient, and a time when I could speak to her alone again came at last. She had gone for air into the small flower-garden which adjoined the house after the fashion of the English places, and I, noting that no one else had observed her, followed. She sat in a rustic chair, and, seeing me coming, waited for me calmly, and in such manner that I could not tell whether I came as one welcome or repugnant. But I stood by her side nevertheless.

"You have heard all the talk to-night, Lieutenant Melville, have you not?" she asked.

"I suppose that you have in mind the new alliance with the French that the rebels have made?" I said.

"Yes," she said. "That has been the burden of our talk."

"I could not escape it," I replied. "It is a very promising matter for the rebels, and for that reason a very unpromising one for us."

"The French," she said, "would consider it a glorious revenge upon us for our many victories at their expense, if they could help the rebels to certain triumph over us. It would shear off the right arm of England."

I looked with wonder at this woman who could thus preserve her false part with me when she knew I knew so well that it was false. I thought she might never again refer to our night ride, our companionship in danger. It was not anything that I wished to forget. In truth, I did not wish to forget any part of it. Yet if I had reflected, I should have seen that she had reason to forget that night's ride, since she must distrust me. Evidently Wildfoot had not told her who I was, and while I must be a friend in some way or the ranger would not have let me go, she could not guess the whole truth.

"Do you think, Lieutenant Melville," she asked, turning a very thoughtful face towards me, "that this alliance will crush the English, or will the French intervention incite them to more strenuous efforts?"

"I think, Miss Desmond," I replied, piqued and suddenly determining to play my part as well as she, "that we will defeat Americans and French combined. You know we are accustomed to victory over the French."

"It is as you say," she said; "but when one reads French histories one finds French victories over the English also."

Which is very true, for it is a great gain to the glory of any country to have expert historians.

"We will underrate the French," I said, "for that would depreciate such triumphs as we have achieved in conflict with them."

"You make very little of Americans," she said. "Do you not think that you will also have to reckon with my misguided countrymen?"

"Mere louts," I said, thinking that at last I had found away to provoke her into an expression of her real opinions. "Perchance they might do something if they were trained and properly armed. But, as they are, they cannot withstand the British bayonet."

She looked at me with some curiosity, at which I was gratified, but, in imitation of her own previous example, I had discharged expression from my face.

"I had thought sometimes, Lieutenant Melville," she said, "that you had been moved to sympathy for these people, these rebels."

"Then you are much mistaken, Miss Desmond," I said, "although I hope I am not hard of heart. I am most loyal to the king, and hope for his complete triumph. How could I be otherwise, when you, who are American-born, set me such a noble example?"

"That is but the language of compliment, Lieutenant Melville," she said, "the courtly speech that you have learned in London drawing-rooms, and—pardon me for saying it—means nothing."

"It might mean nothing with other men," I said, losing somewhat of my self-possession, "but it does mean something with me."

"I do not understand you, Lieutenant Melville," she said, turning upon me an inquiring look. "You seem to speak in metaphors to-night."

"If so," I replied, "I may again plead your noble example. I do not understand you at all to-night, Miss Desmond."

"Our conversation has been of a military character," she replied, smiling for the first time. "So gallant an officer as you, Lieutenant Melville, should understand that, while all of it may well be a puzzle to me, a woman, whom the sound of a trumpet frightens, it is easy enough for you to comprehend it."

"It is this time I who ask the pardon, Miss Desmond," I replied, "if I say that is the language of compliment, of the drawing-room."

She made no reply, but bent forward to inhale the odor of a flower that blossomed near her. I too was silent, for I knew not whether she wished me to go or stay, or cared naught for either. From the drawing-room came the sound of music, but she made no movement to go.

"I have had thoughts about you, too, Miss Desmond," I said, at length, after some minutes of embarrassment, for me at least.

"I trust that such thoughts have been of a pleasant nature, Lieutenant Melville," she said, turning her deep eyes upon me again.

"I have thought," I continued, "that you too felt a certain sympathy for the rebels, your misguided countrymen."

"What reasons have I furnished for such a supposition?" she replied, coldly. "Are you in the habit, Lieutenant Melville, of attributing treasonable thoughts to the best friends of the king's cause."

This I thought was carrying the matter to a very extreme point, but it was not for me, who called myself a gentleman, to say so aloud.

"I would not speak of it as treason," I said; "it seems to me to be in accord with nature that you, who are an American, should feel sympathy for the Americans."

"Then," she replied, "it is you who have treasonable thoughts, and not I."

"I trust I may never falter in doing my duty," I said.

"I trust I may not do so either," she said.

"Then," I exclaimed, flinging away reserve and caution, "why play this part any longer?"

"What part?" she asked, her eyes still unfathomable.

"This pretence of Toryism," I cried. "This pretence which we both know to be so unreal. Do I not know that you are a patriot, the noblest of patriots? Do I not honor you for it? Do I not remember every second of our desperate ride together, and glory in the remembrance?"

I paused, for I am not accustomed to making high speeches, even when under the influence of strong emotion.

Her eyes wavered, for the first time, and the red flush swept over her face. But she recovered herself quickly.

"Then say nothing about it, if you would serve me," she said, and rising abruptly she went into the house.

CHAPTER TWENTY-TWO—*A Full Confession*

Marcel and I had some leisure the next morning at our quarters.

"Marcel," said I, "I wish to talk to you on a matter of serious import."

"It must be of very high import, in truth," said Marcel, "if I may judge of its nature from the solemn look that clothes your face like a shroud."

"It is no matter of jest," I replied, "and it is of close concern to us both."

"Very well," replied Marcel, carelessly, flinging himself into a chair. "Then let it be kept a secret no longer."

"It is this, Marcel," I replied, and I was in deep earnest. "I am tired of the false characters we have taken upon ourselves. The parts are awkward. We do not fit in them. We have been required to serve against our own people. Only luck, undeserved luck, has saved us from the rope. I want to reassume my own character and my own name, to be myself again."

I spoke with some heat and volubility. I was about to add that I was sorry ever to have gone into such a foolish enterprise, but the thought of a fair woman's face recalled the words. And this brought me another thought—that I was unwilling to continue this false *rôle* with Mary Desmond's eyes upon me.

"Is that all?" asked Marcel, beginning to whistle a gay dancing-tune which some newly arrived officers had brought over from London.

"No, it is not," I replied. "I said I wished to be myself again, and that I mean to be."

"I think I shall do likewise," said Marcel, cutting off his tune in the beginning. "I am tired of this piece of stage-play myself, but I wanted you to say so first."

"It is time to leave it off," I added, "and go back to our duty."

"You speak truly," said Marcel. "It would not be pleasant to be killed by American bullets, or be forced to fire upon our old comrades. And yet the adventure has not been without interest. Moreover, let it not be forgotten that we have had plenty to eat, a good luck which we knew not for two years before."

He said the last in such a whimsical tone of regret that I laughed despite myself.

"There is no need to laugh," said Marcel. "A good dinner is a great item to a starving man, and, as you know, I am not without experience in the matter of starvation."

Wherein Marcel spoke the truth, for during our long campaigns hunger often vexed us more sorely than the battle.

"I shall be glad to see our comrades and to serve with them again. When will we have a chance to leave?" he asked.

"I do not know," I said; "and I do not see that it matters. I am not going."

"Then will his lordship condescend to explain himself?" said Marcel. "You speak in riddles."

"We have come into this town, Marcel," I said, "in the guise of Englishmen and as the friends of the English. We have eaten and drank with them, and they have treated us as comrades. If I were to steal away, I would think that I had played the part of a mere spy."

"What then?" asked Marcel.

"I mean to take what I consider to be the honorable course," I said. "I mean to go to Sir William Howe, tell him what I am and what I have done, and yield myself his prisoner."

"You need not look so confoundedly virtuous about it," said Marcel. "I shall go with you and tell what I am and what I have done, and yield myself his prisoner in precisely the same manner that you will. Again I wanted you to say the thing first."

I never doubted that Marcel would do what was right, despite his habitual levity of manner, and his companionship strengthened me in my resolution.

"When shall we go to Sir William?" asked Marcel.

"To-day,—within the hour," I said.

"Do you think he will hang us as spies?" asked Marcel, gruesomely.

"I do not know," I said. "I think there is some chance that he will."

In truth, this was a matter that weighed much upon me. Do not think that I was willing to be a martyr, or wanted to die under any circumstances. Nothing was further from my desires.

"He is like enough to be in a very bad humor," said Marcel, "over his failures and his removal from the chief command. I wish for our sakes he felt better."

By representing to an aide that our business was of the most pressing importance, we secured admission to Sir William Howe. I think we came into the room before he expected us, for when we entered the doorway he was standing at the window with the grayest look of melancholy I ever saw on any man's face. In that moment I felt both sorrow and pity for him, for we had received naught but kindness at his hands. I stumbled purposely, that I might warn him of our coming, and he turned to meet us, his face assuming a calm aspect.

"You sent word that your business is pressing," he said. "But I hope that Lieutenant Melville and Captain Montague are in good health."

"We know not the bodily condition of Lieutenant Melville and Captain Montague," I said, "but we trust that both are well."

"What sort of jesting is this?" he said, frowning. "Remember that, though my successor has been appointed, I am yet commander-in-chief."

"It is no jest," I replied. "We speak in the utmost respect to you. I am not Lieutenant Melville of the British army, nor is my friend Captain Montague. Those officers are prisoners in the hands of the Americans."

"Then who are you?" he asked.

"We are American officers," I replied, "who, in a moment of rashness and folly, took the places of Captain Montague and Lieutenant Melville."

"Is this truth or insanity?" he asked, sharply.

"I think it is both," I replied, soberly.

He smiled somewhat, and then asked more questions, whereupon I told the whole story from first to last, furnishing such proofs that he could not doubt what I said. For a while he sat in a kind of maze. Then he said,—

"Are you aware, gentlemen, that the most natural thing for me to do is to hang you both as spies?"

We admitted with the greatest reluctance that the laws of war would permit it.

"Still, it was but a mad prank," said Sir William, "and you have given yourselves up when you might have gone away. I cannot see of what avail it would be to the British cause, to me, or to any one to hang you. I like you both, and you, Lieutenant Chester, as you call yourself, and as I suppose you are, threw that Hessian colonel into the street for me so handsomely that I must ever be in your debt, and I don't suppose that you had anything to do with the attempt of that villian, Wildfoot; moreover, it seems that you are quite capable of hanging yourselves in due time. I will spare the gallows. But I wish you were Englishmen, and not Americans."

I felt as if the rope were slipping off our necks when Sir William spoke these words, and my spirits rose with most astonishing swiftness. I must say that Sir William Howe, though a slothful man and a poor general, was kind of heart sometimes, and I have never liked to hear people speak ill of him.

"Your case," he said, "is likely to be a source of mighty gossip in this town; but I shall not leave you here long to enjoy your honors. We exchange for Lieutenant Belfort and some prisoners who are in the hands of the rebels. You will be included in the exchange, and you will leave Philadelphia soon. You need not thank me. In truth, I ought to hang you as spies; but I am curious to know what act of folly you will commit next."

I am confident that Sir William in reality liked us greatly, for he was fond of adventure. Perhaps that was the reason he was not a better general.

"I shall have to place you under guard," said Sir William, calling an aide, "and if ever this war ends and we are alive then, I should like to see you both in England, and show you off as the finest pair of rascals that ever deserved to be hanged and were not."

"It appears to me that we came out of that matter easily," said Marcel, as we left the room.

We remained for a while in Philadelphia as prisoners of the British, and, to our great amazement and equal pleasure, found ourselves heroes with the men who had been our comrades there for a brief space. They considered it the finest and boldest adventure of which they had heard, and Marcel's new cousin, Rupert Harding, was not last in his appreciation.

"I think that I shall prefer you to the real cousin, when I see him," said Harding to Marcel, "and I shall always claim the kinship."

We parted from them with sincere regret when Sir Henry Clinton, who, succeeding Sir William Howe in the chief command, saw no reason to change the latter's plan in this matter, sent us to the American army in exchange for Belfort and others.

CHAPTER TWENTY-THREE—
George Washington's Mercy

"Bob," said Marcel, as we rode under escort towards the American army, "the British have dealt handsomely with us,—we have no right to complain of Sir William Howe,—but how about the Americans?"

"The Americans are our countrymen."

"Which proves nothing. When I am at fault, I would rather receive the sentence of my official enemy than that of my official friend."

"Don't talk of it," I replied. "We have fared so well in the first four acts of this play that our luck cannot change consistently in the fifth and last."

"Yet I would there were no fifth," he grumbled. I said nothing more, wishing to dismiss the subject from my mind. But I had been thinking of it before Marcel spoke, and his words chimed so well with my own thoughts that my apprehensions grew. The subject would not depart merely because I ordered it to do so. We had left our army without leave. Practically, we were deserters, and General Washington, as all the world knows, was a severe man where a question of military discipline was concerned.

"But I am not sorry I went," I said aloud. I was thinking of Mary Desmond and that thrilling night ride of ours when the hoof-beats of my horse rang side by side with the hoof-beats of hers. I remembered the flush on her face and the light in her eye.

"I am not sorry either," said Marcel, aloud. Of what he was thinking I do not know. Perhaps that same wild strain in his blood which had led us into the adventure was speaking. Yet I should, and shall be, the last man in the world to blame him for it.

It was a glorious day. The wind blew, the grass waved, and the sun shone. A young man could not remain unhappy long over misfortunes yet unfelt. My memories were pleasant and so were my comrades. A half dozen other American officers, to be exchanged for an equal number of the enemy, accompanied us, and the two British officers in charge of the escort, of whom Catron was one, were men of wit, manners, and friendly temper. We made a lively party and found one another agreeable. We had always possessed the liking of Catron, but in truth we now seemed to have his unbounded admiration as well.

"Ta-ra-ra, ta-ra-ra," rang the British bugle through the forest, announcing our approach to the American army. The journey had been all too fast. I never thought that I would part from an enemy with so much reluctance, and I became grave again when the first American sentinel stopped us.

Our mission was explained, and an officer came and attended to the exchange. We bade our friends the British, good-bye, and then, according to orders, walked towards headquarters for instructions. As we passed down one of the camp streets we heard a cry of surprise, and looking about saw Sergeant Pritchard to whom we had once bade a good-bye that he thought would be eternal.

We dropped back a little behind the others.

"Sergeant Pritchard," said Marcel, "you owe me a dinner, but as provisions are scarce in the American camp I will not collect it."

This was generous of Marcel, but I suspect that the true cause was his unwillingness to dine in state with a sergeant.

"I reported that you had taken the places of the Englishmen and gone to Philadelphia," replied the good sergeant. "He made no comment in my presence, and I know not what he said to the general about it. Nor do I know what will come of the matter."

Then he shook his head gloomily.

"General Washington should behave as handsomely as Sir William Howe," said Marcel, and I was quite sure that it was General Washington's duty to do so.

I acted as spokesman, and laid the case before our colonel, concealing nothing save my ride with Mary Desmond. He was a middle-aged man, amiable, and he liked us. In truth, both us had been fortunate enough to receive his praise for good service in action, but he could see no mitigating circumstances.

"There is nothing to do but report the case to the commander-in-chief," he said. "I am sorry, for I esteem you two boys, and you have been of value."

His solemn, even despondent tone depressed us. We began to feel afraid of the future and to wonder what General Washington would say to us. Our period of suspense was not long, as within two hours we were summoned to appear before the commander-in-chief.

An aide led us to his headquarters, a small square log-house such as frontiersmen build for themselves. A sentinel was watching at the door, but we passed in and stood before the general, who was alone writing at a table.

The aide withdrew to the further end of the room and left us standing there, watching the goose quill, held in the large muscular hand, as it travelled over the paper, writing perhaps the instructions for our own execution as deserters. I shall never forget the few minutes that we stood in that room hearing only the scratch of the quill on the paper. I have dreamed of them often, and have awakened to hear the rustle of the quill in my ears.

No one could feel frivolous or flippant in the presence of General Washington. The air was never very warm about him, and I have noticed that it is usually so with men of great mental powers and great responsibilities.

On went the goose quill. Scratch! Scratch! I hate the sound of a goose quill to this day. I looked at the silent aide, but his face gave no encouragement. I looked at Marcel, but he was looking at me for the same purpose, and neither was able to be a help to the other.

The general wiped the goose quill and put it away. Then he turned to us, and his face was as stern as any into which I ever looked. I saw no ray of mercy in those severe, blue eyes.

"Lieutenant Robert Chester?" he said to me. I bowed, and then Marcel bowed when his name, too, was called.

"You deserted, according to your own confession, to the enemy, and Sir William Howe, not thinking you of sufficient value, has sent you back to me."

I flushed at both the charge and the irony, and protested that we were not deserters, and had never meant to be. Moreover, we had sent word by Sergeant Pritchard of our intention. Then I begged him to let me repeat the whole story. He bowed slightly, and told me to proceed. I fear that I was disturbed somewhat by the steady gaze of those cold, blue eyes, which never left me, and I limped more than once in my narrative. Whenever I did so, he made me go back and take up the loose thread. It was his way to be exact in all things.

"A likely tale! A likely tale!" he said, when I finished, "and does credit to your powers of narration. I shall not enter into a discussion of its truth or falsity; but even if true, you left without permission, the army to which you belonged and masqueraded as officers of the enemy. It seems to me that you have succeeded in being false to both Americans and British, and I do not see how anything could be more serious, though you young gentlemen may choose to call it an adventure or a jest or a whim. Sirs, a great war is a deadly matter, and it is not to be won with jests!"

The blue eyes grew colder and sterner than ever. I wished to say something, but I could think of nothing that would avail, and I was silent. I fear that my lips trembled, not from fright, but at the rebuke. I know my comrade's did, and Philip Marcel, the gay and irrepressible cavalier, was wordless for once in his life.

"Take them to the guard-house, Mordaunt," said the commander-in-chief to the aide, "and we will have them disposed of to-morrow. See that they have no chance to escape. Nor shall they be permitted to send messages to any one."

Then he turned his cold face away, and began to write again. I think that the shock of this sudden and terrible sentence was taken from me by the flame of indignation that leaped up in my heart. We were no deserters, however foolish we had been, and however great the liberty we had taken! I felt that we did not deserve such a punishment. Both Marcel and I had served our country well, and to put us to death for this adventure, although it might come within the military law, was harsh, beyond all measure. I considered ourselves martyrs.

"Do not be afraid that we will try to escape," I burst out, "and if this is to be the reward of men who serve their country, no wonder that our cause is in such straits!"

He did not appear to notice us, but wrote calmly on, and the deadly scratching of the goose quill was unbroken. The aide beckoned to us, and we followed him from the room.

"I am sorry, very sorry," said Mordaunt, when we were outside, "and, in truth, I think that your sentence is far too severe."

His face showed deep concern.

"Don't be afraid that we will repeat your opinion to your hurt in the general's good graces," said Marcel, with a laugh that was pathetic. "We won't have many opportunities in the next twenty-four hours, and after that—well, the best story in the world will not interest us."

We were put in a one-room house of logs, and we sat there in silence for many hours watching the day fade. I was still hot with indignation. We deserved punishment, it was true, I repeated, but not death, an ignominious death such as that decreed for us. What good end could be served by such a deed?

But with the fading of the day my anger faded also. Then I thought of Mary Desmond, the curve of her check, the blue of her eye, and the sunshine in her hair. She did not hate me I knew. "O Mary," I said under my breath, "I shall never see you again!" and I covered my face with my hands.

"Bob," said Marcel, presently, holding out his hand, "forgive me."

"Forgive you, for what?"

"For leading you into that wild adventure. It was I who dared you to do it, who provoked you into joining me."

I could not accept any such assertion, and I told him so, adding that I did not wholly regret our excursion into Philadelphia.

"Miss Desmond!" said Marcel, understandingly, "she is worth any man's winning, and you might have won her if—if—"

Then he stopped abruptly and stared blankly at me, unwilling to finish the sentence. The night came presently, and they brought us food, which we scarcely touched. There was no light in our prison, but through the single iron window we could see flickering camp-fires outside. The low murmur of the army came to us.

We sat on our stools for a long time in silence. I was trying to prepare myself for the future, and I suppose that Marcel was occupied with a similar task. It must have been past 10 o'clock when the door of the prison was opened and our colonel came in. Sincere sorrow was written plainly on the good man's face.

"I have heard about you," he said, "and I went to him at once, and pleaded with him. I urged your previous good service and your youth, but I could not shake him a particle. There have been too many desertions lately, and the army is at a low ebb. You are officers, and your fate will be an example for all."

"Our case is past mending," said Marcel. "We thank you for your good wishes and your efforts, but I don't think that anything can be done."

"That is so," said the colonel. "The next life is what you must now consider."

Our colonel was a good man and a good soldier, but he was never noted for tact. Somehow he could not get off the subject of our execution, and when he left with tears in his eyes, and an expressed hope that he might deliver our last messages for us, he took with him our few remaining grains of courage, and we felt that death was very, very near.

Bye and bye, two more officers whom we knew well came to bid us good-bye. They had obtained permission from the general, they said, and they too had interceded for us, but fruitlessly; they could offer us no hope whatever. They were frank in condemning the severity of General Washington, and this knowledge that our friends regarded our punishment as far out of proportion to our crime, made it all the more bitter to us.

"General Washington may be a great man and a fine commander," said Marcel, after they had gone; "but he will never get forgiveness for this."

I pressed my dry lips together and said nothing. In an hour three more officers came, and one by one bidding us farewell went out again. Their gloomy manner depressed us still further.

"Curse it!" exclaimed Marcel. "I wish they wouldn't come here with their solemn faces, and their parting sermons! They make me afraid of death!"

He expressed my state of mind exactly, but there were more farewells. It was about midnight when the last of them came, a major who had been a minister once, and was never known to laugh. He talked to us so dolefully about the future, and the duty of all men to be prepared for the worst, that my nerves were jumping, and I could scarce restrain myself from insulting him. We were glad to see him go, and if ever I was thoroughly unprepared for death it was when the major left us.

The long night dragged wearily on, every minute an hour. Once I laughed aloud in my bitterness, when I thought of Mary Desmond hearing the news of my death.

We slept by snatches, a few minutes at a time; but we were wide-eyed when the day came. I saw black lines under Marcel's eyes, and I knew that my own face was haggard too. The sentinel brought us breakfast; but did not retire as we ate, and when I looked at him inquiringly, he said,—

"Your escort is waiting outside."

The food choked me, and I could eat no more. "Come," I said to Marcel, "let's get it over."

We arose, and, walking out at the door, met soldiers who fell in before and behind us. The camp, or at least nearly all of it, was yet slumbering. Only a few fires were burning. Over the forests and fields the new-risen sun shone with a clear light.

They marched us to a little grove, and there General Washington and a half-dozen officers, our colonel among them, met us.

"I think that he might have stayed away," said Marcel, when he saw the commander-in-chief.

But General Washington, looking closely at us, said: "You do not appear to have slept well."

"Our time was so short that I thought we could not afford to waste any of it in sleep," I replied, with a sad attempt at a jest.

"General, kindly shoot us at once and have done with it!" exclaimed Marcel, who was ever an impatient man and now, expecting death, felt awe of nobody.

"Who said that I was going to have you shot?" asked General Washington, regarding us intently.

"Did you not tell us so yesterday?" I exclaimed.

"Not at all," he replied, his grim face relaxing. "I merely said that I would dispose of you to-day. I said nothing about shooting. That is an assumption of your own, although it is what you had a right to expect, and perhaps my words indicated such action. At any rate you seem to have had a fore-taste of what you expected."

The officers, all high in rank, our colonel among them, laughed aloud. At another time I would have been deeply mortified, but not now. I began to see. I understood that our punishment was not to be death; but we had already paid the price, the night's expectation of it.

"Fortune loves us," whispered Marcel to me.

"What did you say?" asked the commander-in-chief, seeing the motion of his lips.

"I was telling Lieutenant Chester how thankful we should be that our understanding of your words was a misunderstanding," replied Marcel, promptly, and with that smile of his which few people could resist.

"Call it a jest. Do you imagine that you are the only jesters in this camp?" said the general, laughing a little. "I thought that you needed punishment, and you were too brave and useful to be shot. So I decided upon another plan, and I think it has been successful."

This, they say, was the only jest of General Washington's life, but I thank God that he made the exception. Marcel joins me.

"Moreover, some pleas have been made in your favor," continued the general. "Sir William Howe himself, before leaving, took the trouble to write to me and ask that you be treated gently. You are lads whom he loves, he said. Certainly I could afford to do so small a favor for the man who has made it necessary for his successor to give up to me the city of Philadelphia. And there is a young lady, too, who speaks well of you."

"A young lady!" I cried, suspecting.

"Yes, a young lady, Miss Mary Desmond, to whom we owe much, and who has just added to our debt, because last night when you were preparing so well for your future life, she was riding to us with the news that the British were about to depart from Philadelphia. She has told too, Mr. Chester, how she met you that night you were on the way to warn us of the British attack, and how you rode on together. The circumstance was much in your favor. Yonder she is. You might speak to her, and then make ready for duty, like the valiant and loyal officers that you have been always—that is nearly always."

He smiled in kindly fashion, and patted us both on the shoulder. We thanked him with deep and fervent sincerity, and then I hurried away to Mary Desmond.

She stood under the boughs of one of the trees, holding her horse by the bridle.

"I am glad to see you, Lieutenant Chester, in your own proper guise," she said.

I took her warm little hand in mine, as I replied: "And I to see you again in yours." Then I added: "You have brought the news that the British are leaving Philadelphia?"

"Yes," she replied.

"Then may I come to see you there, still in my own proper guise?"

"If General Washington gives you time," she replied. "But to tell you the truth, I don't think you will stay long in Philadelphia. Now, good-bye."

I helped her upon her horse, and she gave me her hand again. Perhaps I held it a second or two longer than custom demands, but of that I shall say nothing more.

I watched her as she rode away, the morning sunshine rippling on her hair, a slender figure, yet so strong and brave. There, I knew, beat a dauntless heart. Her spirit and courage led me on to love her from the first, and then the mystery about her, the strange, magnetic charm had drawn me too. She might take my love and tread upon it if she would, but it was hers, and no woman could ever dispossess her.

CHAPTER TWENTY-FOUR—
In the City Again

A detachment of our army entered Philadelphia the next day, hot upon the heels of the retreating British, and Marcel and I were among the first dozen Americans who rode into the city, Wildfoot, the ranger, commanding the little band which had the honor of taking the lead. Seldom have happier horsemen galloped to the music of triumph.

"See, Lieutenant Chester!" said Wildfoot to me, pointing across the fields.

I followed his long forefinger with my eyes, and saw the tips of Philadelphia's spires, a most stimulating sight. Philadelphia was then our largest, richest, and most important city. The great Declaration had been made there, and in a way we considered it our capital. It had been a heavy blow to us, when we were forced to yield it to Howe, and now when his successor, Clinton, felt himself obliged to give it back to us, our spirits, so long depressed, sprang up with a bound.

"Aye, it's Philadelphia," said Wildfoot, "and we've worked and waited long to get it back again."

I thought I saw a mist appear in the eyes of the strong backwoodsman, and I knew that he was deeply moved. Certainly no one had worked more than he, and perhaps none other had taken such great risks. He was entitled to the honor of leading the vanguard.

We expected to find skirmishers and bands of the British prepared to make our way troublesome; but we met no foe and galloped, unopposed, into the city, from which the British had gone but a few hours, and from which more than three thousand Tories, too, had fled. The departure of the enemy had been so abrupt, and we were so close behind, that several British officers, either laggards or late risers, were captured by our men, and our little troop, scattering, galloped about the streets, hoping to take more such trophies.

Marcel and I turned into one of the cross streets, and saw a hundred yards ahead of us two officers in red-coats, riding at a great rate.

"British!" cried Marcel.

"So they are!" I replied, "and they must be ours!" We were wild with enthusiasm, and even with General Washington's lesson fresh in our memories, we thought little of consequences while in that state of mind.

We shouted to our horses, and followed the Englishmen at full speed, eager to make the capture. They heard the clattering of hoofs, and, seeing us, fled at a greater speed. We were but two, and no doubt they would have turned and fought us; but they knew the American army to be at our back, and there was nothing for them to do but gallop.

On they sped, lashing their horses, and after them came Marcel and I, also lashing our horses. The dust flew from the street, and pedestrians scuttled to safety.

"It will be something for us to talk of if we take them!" said Marcel.

"It must be done!" I replied, as I sought to draw more speed from my panting horse. The distance between us was decreasing, slowly it is true, but yet at a rate that could be noticed. I called Marcel's attention to our gain, and his face flushed with the hope of triumph.

"We shall take them to the general himself," he said, "and it will help us in his eyes."

The horses of the fugitives began to stagger, and I noticed it with exultation. Obviously, they could not escape us now. We soon gained rapidly, and I shouted to them to halt. One of the men whirled about quickly and fired a pistol. The bullet whizzed between Marcel and me, and its only result was to add anger to the motives that drew us on. We gained yet more rapidly, and cried anew to them to halt. A second pistol bullet was the reply, but, like its predecessor, it went wide of the target. We galloped on, and each of them fired at us again, and missed.

"We have them now!" cried Marcel. "Their pistols are empty, and they cannot reload them while going at this pace!"

In truth they were doomed apparently to be our prisoners and that, too, speedily. Our horses were the swifter and stronger, and our loaded pistols were in our belts. The fugitives seemed helpless.

"Stop or we fire!" we shouted.

They looked back as if studying their chances, and I saw their faces clearly. When they had fired their pistols, the glimpse had been too fleeting, but I knew them now. They were Vivian and Belfort.

My heart thrilled with various emotions. Vivian was our good friend, a man of whom we had the most pleasant memories. We could not fire upon him. Belfort was my enemy, yet I believed that I had triumphed over him, and surely one can afford to forgive the enemy from whom he has taken the victory. I could not fire upon him, in such a situation, any more than I could fire upon Vivian.

"Lower your pistol!" I cried to Marcel. "Do you not see who they are?"

"I do see, and you are right," said Marcel, as he replaced his weapon in its holster. We gradually checked the speed of our horses, and in a few moments the fugitives began to draw away from us. Five minutes later they galloped across the fields and to the safety of their own army. Whether they recognized us or not, I do not know.

As we turned and rode back through the suburbs, a woman on horseback met us. It was Mary Desmond.

"Why did you let them go?" she asked, speaking to me, rather than to Marcel.

"They were Vivian and Belfort," I replied. "Surely you would not have had us to fire upon either?"

"I should not have forgiven you, if you had," she replied.

She said that she had come out to meet the American force, and she had seen part of our pursuit. She, too, bore the flush of triumph upon her face, and in truth it was a great day for her as well as for us. She had done a man's work, and more than a man's work in the cause of her country.

"Yes, I am glad you let them go," she repeated as we rode back together. "It is not likely that we shall ever see either again."

We rode with her to her father's house, and then went to quarters. Just about sunset a colored man came to us with a note from John Desmond, asking us to dinner at his house that night. No excuse would be accepted, he said, and as for leave, that had been granted already by our colonel. There was no probability that either Marcel or I would seek an excuse to stay away from John Desmond's house, and as soon as we could put our toilets in proper trim we went to his residence, a great square brick building, lighted with many lights. Some carriages stood in the street in front, yet we were badly prepared for a company of the extent and rank that we found assembled there, with General Washington himself at its head. In truth, we were somewhat abashed, thinking ourselves out of place with generals and colonels; but the commander-in-chief shook our hands, and seemed to be in a gay humor, uncommon for him.

"Mr. Desmond and his daughter were bound to have you," he said. "They told me that they met you first at a banquet under embarrassing circumstances, and it is only fair to have you now at a dinner where everybody appears as what he is."

Mary Desmond came in presently, and never before had I seen a woman so shine as she did that night. She had dressed herself as for a triumph, and jewels glittered on her neck and in her hair. Her face was illumed by a great joy, all her reserve was gone, but the charm which had first drawn me to her cast a more potent spell than ever. If I had not already been deep in love with her, I should have become so then. I wondered why every man present was not eager to lay his heart at her feet. Perhaps I was not the only one present who was!

Our dinner was brief, for the generals could linger only a little when an enemy must be pursued. In truth, the main army was already in pursuit, and it was known to only a few that General Washington was at John Desmond's house. His was but a flying visit. Yet the dinner was joyous. All believed that this return to

Philadelphia marked the swift rise of our fortunes. Presently wine-glasses were filled, and General Washington stood up.

"I have heard of a toast that some drank in the presence of Sir William Howe," he said, "and I wish to return it. Let us drink to the health of John Desmond, one of our truest and most useful patriots."

We drank, and the old man flushed deep with gratified pride.

"And now," resumed the general, "let us drink to the best patriot of all, the daring messenger and horsewoman, Miss Mary Desmond. Happy the country that can claim her, and happy the man! To Miss Mary Desmond!"

No toast was ever drunk with a better will.

The commander-in-chief and the generals went away in a few minutes, but Marcel and I stayed a little longer.

"We pursue the enemy to-morrow," I said to Mary Desmond as I bade her good-night, "and there will soon be a battle."

She looked steadily into my eyes, but in a moment a light flush swept over her beautiful face.

"May you come back safely, Lieutenant Chester," she said.

"Will you care?" I asked.

"I do care," she replied. I thought I felt her fingers quiver as she gave me her hand, but she withdrew it in an instant, and I came away.

Our vanguard under Wildfoot, with Marcel and me by his side, began the pursuit of the British the next day.

CHAPTER TWENTY-FIVE—
The Widow's Might

The troop, led by Wildfoot, numbered not more than fifty horsemen, but all were strong and wiry, and bore themselves in the easy alert manner that betokens experience, and much of it. Moreover, they were well mounted, a point of extreme importance. Marcel and I deemed ourselves fortunate to be included in such a band, and that we were high in the partisan chief's favor, we had good evidence, because before we started he brought us two exceptionally fine horses and bade us exchange our mounts for them, temporarily.

"You must do it, as you are likely to need their speed and strength," he said, when we showed reluctance, for good cavalry horses were worth their weight in silver, at least in those days, and we did not like to take the responsibility of their possible loss.

"Then you mean to give us some work, I take it," said Marcel.

"Not much to-day," replied the partisan, "as I operate best in the dark; so shall I wait until sun-down, but I hope that we shall then get through with a fair night's work."

Wildfoot's men seem to trust him absolutely. They never asked him where they were going or what they were expected to do, but followed cheerfully wherever he led. The partisan himself continued in the great good humor that had marked him when we entered Philadelphia. He sang a bit under his breath and smiled frequently. Whether he was happy over deeds achieved or others to come, I could not tell. But I saw that our duties were to be of a scouting nature, as was indicated clearly by the character of the force under his command.

We rode for a while in the track of the British army, a huge trail made by the passage of sixteen thousand troops, and a camp train twelve miles long. Many Tories, too, not fortunate enough to secure passage on the ships down the river, had followed the army, filled with panic and dreading retaliation from the triumphant patriots whom some of their kind had persecuted cruelly in the days when our fortunes were lower.

It was easy enough for us to overtake the British army, which was dragging itself painfully over the hills and across the fields. A body of fifteen or twenty thousand men can move but slowly in the best of times, and in the terrible heat which had suddenly settled down, the British forces merely crept towards New York. Soon we saw their red coats and shining arms through the trees, and heard the murmur of the thousands. However we bore off to one side, passing out of sight, and made a wide curve, apparently for the purpose of examining the country, and to see whether the British had sent out skirmishing or foraging parties. But we saw neither, and shortly after sunset our curve brought us back to the enemy's army, which had gone into camp for the night, their fires flaring redly against the background of the darkness. We stopped upon the crest of a little hill, from which we could see the camp very well and sat there for a few minutes, watching. Being in the darkness we were invisible, but many blazing heaps of wood shed their light over the hostile army.

"They seem to be taking their ease," said Wildfoot. "It ought not to be allowed, but we will not disturb them for the present."

Then he withdrew our men about a mile, and, halting them in a thick wood, ordered them to eat of the food in their knapsacks. But Marcel and me he summoned to go with him on a little journey that he purposed to take.

"We shall not be gone more than an hour or two," he said, "and we will find the men waiting for us here when we come back."

We curved again as we rode away. In truth, we had been making so many curves that it was hard for me to retain any idea of direction. In a half hour we saw a light, and then the house from which it came, a low but rather large building of heavy logs, standing in a small clearing in the forest.

Wildfoot had not spoken since we left the other men, and as he seemed to be in deep thought we did not interrupt him with vain questions, merely following him as he rode quietly into the thickest part of the woods behind the house. When he slipped from his horse there, we did likewise, and waited to see what he would do next.

"We will tie our horses here," he said. "No one will see them, and as they are old campaigners, they are too well trained to make a noise."

Again we imitated his example, and tethered our horses to the boughs of trees.

"Now," said Wildfoot, when that was done, "we will call on a lady."

The moon was shining a little, and I thought I saw a faint smile on his face. I was full of curiosity, and Marcel beside me uttered a little exclamation. The name of woman was always potent with this South Carolina Frenchman; but we said nothing, content, perforce, to be silent and wait.

"She is not so handsome as Miss Mary Desmond," continued Wildfoot, smiling again a little, and this time at me. "Few are; but as she finds no fault with it herself, none other should."

But Marcel had begun to brush his uniform with his hands, and settle the handsome sword, which was his proudest adornment, a little more rakishly by his side.

We walked to the door and knocked, and when some one within wished to know in a strong voice who was there, Wildfoot responded with a question.

"Are you alone?" he asked.

"Yes," said the voice. "Who is it?"

"Wildfoot and two friends."

The door was opened at once, and we entered, beholding a woman who seemed to be the sole occupant of the house. At least none other was visible.

"I hope you are well, mother," said Wildfoot, and the woman nodded.

But I saw at once that she was no mother of his, although old enough. She, too, was large and powerful, almost masculine in build, but there was no similarity whatever in the features.

"Lieutenant Chester and Lieutenant Marcel of the American army, good friends of mine and trusted comrades," said Wildfoot, "and this, gentlemen," he continued to us, "is Mother Melrose, as loyal a patriot as you can find in the Thirteen Colonies, and one who has passed many a good bit of information from the British army in Philadelphia on to those who needed it most. Mother, can't you find us something to eat while we talk?"

The woman looked pleased with his praise, and speedily put upon a table substantial food, which we attacked with the zest that comes of hard riding. Yet from the first I studied the room and the woman with curiosity and interest.

The note of Mother Melrose's manner and air was self-reliance. She walked like a grenadier, and her look said very plainly that she feared few things. She must have been at least sixty, and perhaps was never beautiful. I surmised, from the complete understanding so evidently existing between her and Wildfoot, that she helped him in his forays, warning him of hostile expeditions, sending him news of wagon trains that could be cut off, and otherwise serving the cause. There were many such bravewomen who gave us great aid in this war. But I wondered at a fortitude that could endure such a lonely and dangerous life.

"Do you know that the British army is encamped near you, mother?" asked Wildfoot, as we drank a little wine that she brought from a recess, probably captured by Wildfoot himself from some wagon train.

"I know it," she replied, her old eyes lifting up, "and glory be to God, they have been forced to run away from Philadelphia at last!"

She passed presently into a rear room which seemed to be a kitchen, and Marcel said:—

"A fine patriot, but has she no sons, nobody to help her here and to protect her, maybe?"

"She can protect herself well enough," replied Wildfoot, "and there is nobody else in this house except a serving lad, who, I suspect, is in the kitchen helping himself to a little extra supper. But she has sons, three of them. They're in our business, and far away from here."

"Three for the cause," I commented. "That is doing well."

"Two fight for the Congress and one for the king," said Wildfoot. "The one who serves the king is her youngest and best beloved. Nothing can change that, although, as far as her power goes, the king has no greater opponent than she."

"Strange!" said Marcel.

But it did not seem so very strange to me.

The woman was coming back, and I looked at her with deeper respect than ever. We talked a little more, and Wildfoot's questions disclosed that his object in coming to the house was to see if she had any better information than he had been able to pick up. But she could tell him of no hostile party that he might cut off.

Our conversation was ended suddenly by a shock of red hair thrust in at the door, and a voice, coming from somewhere behind the red hair, announcing that some one was coming. It was the serving boy who gave us the timely warning.

"It must be the enemy," said Wildfoot. "No Americans except ours are near here, and they would not come contrary to my express order. How many are they, Timothy?"

"Three men on horseback, and they are British," replied Timothy.

"You can go out the back way and escape into the forest without any trouble," said the woman.

"I don't know that we want to escape," replied Wildfoot, "especially as we are three to three. Neither are we looking for a skirmish just now; so, by your permission, mother, we will step into the next room, and wait for your new guests to disclose themselves."

Mother Melrose offered no objection, and we entered a room adjoining the one in which we had been eating. It was unlighted, but the house seemed to have been a sort of country inn in more peaceful times, and this apartment into which we had just come, was the parlor.

"Leave the door ajar an inch or two, that we may see," said Wildfoot, and the woman obeyed. A minute later there was a heavy knock, as if whoever came, came with confidence. Mother Melrose opened the door in an unconcerned manner, as if such knocks were a common occurrence at her house, and three British officers entered, that is, two were Englishmen, and the third was a Hessian. The faces of the Englishmen were young, open, and attractive, but that of the Hessian I did not like. We did not dislike the English officers in this war, who were mostly honest men serving the cause of their country; but we did hate the Hessians, who were mere mercenaries, besides being more cruel than the British, and when I say "hate," I use the word with emphasis.

They, too, seemed to have taken the place for a sort of country inn, and sat down at the table from which Mother Melrose had hastily cleared the dishes of our own supper.

"Can't you give us something to eat, mistress?" asked one of the Englishmen. "We are tired of camp fare, and we pay gold."

"Provisions are scarce," replied Mother Melrose; "but I am willing to do my best, because you travel in such haste that I may never have another chance to serve you."

"She has pricked you very neatly, Osborne," laughed the other Englishman, "but I am free to confess that we would travel faster if the weather were not so deucedly hot. We don't have such a Tophet of a summer in England, and I'm glad of it. Any rebels about, mistress?"

It was the merest chance shot, as we were ahead of the British army rather than behind it, and we were not expected in this quarter; but Mother Melrose never flinched. "No, you are safe," she replied.

"That's for you, Hunston," said Osborne, laughing in his turn, "but I would have you to know, good mistress, that we are giving up Philadelphia to your great Mr. Washington out of kindness, pure kindness. He starved and froze, out there at Valley Forge, so long that we thought he needed a change and city comforts, and as there is plenty of room for all of ours in New York, we concluded,—and again I say it was out of the kindness of our souls,—to give him Philadelphia."

"Well, the Lord loveth a cheerful giver," said Mother Melrose, with unction.

Both Englishmen laughed again, and with great heartiness. Evidently they were men who knew that life was worth living, and were not prone to grieve over evils unbefallen. I was sorry that I could not laugh with them. There was no smile on the face of the ill-favored Hessian. His eyes wandered about the room, but he seemed to have no suspicion. I took it that his sour temper was the result of chronic discontent.

"What ails you, Steinfeldt?" asked Osborne. "Why don't you look happy? Isn't the hospitality of the house all that you wish?"

"Haven't you any wine?" asked Steinfeldt. "I can't drink the cursed drinks of this country, cider and such stuff! faugh!"

Mother Melrose produced the same bottle from which she had poured wine for us, and filled the glasses.

"That's better," said Steinfeldt. "Fill them again, can't you?" His eyes began to sparkle, and his face to flush. It was easy to tell his master passion. But Mother Melrose filled the glasses again, and then a third time, producing a second bottle. The house was better stocked than I had thought it could possibly be. Steinfeldt's temper began to improve under the influence of the liquor, and he grew talkative. Evidently Mother Melrose's taunt about the British evacuation of Philadelphia rankled in his mind, though the two Englishmen themselves had passed it off easily enough.

"We will come back," he said. "You don't imagine that we will let Mr. Washington keep Philadelphia long?"

"I don't think he will ask you about it," replied Mother Melrose.

"It's too good a country to give up," continued Steinfeldt, "and we must keep it. It is rich land, and the women are fair. The men may not want us; but the women do."

One of the Englishmen angrily bade him be silent; but the wine was in his blood.

"But the women do want us, don't they?" he repeated to Mother Melrose.

She lifted her hand, which was both large and muscular, and slapped him in the face. It was no light blow, the crack of it was like that of a pistol-shot, and Steinfeldt reeled in his chair, the blood leaping to his cheeks.

"Damnation!" he cried, springing to his feet, and snatching his sword from its scabbard.

"Steinfeldt, stop!" cried Osborne, "you cannot cut down a woman."

"I wish you were a man," said the Hessian to Mother Melrose, "then you'd have to fight for that."

"Don't trouble yourself about my not being a man," said she, coolly. "I'll fight you any way."

One of the Englishmen had hung his sword and belt on the back of his chair while he ate, and, to my unbounded surprise, Mother Melrose stepped forward, took the sword, and putting herself in the attitude of a genuine fencing-master, faced the German. I was about to make a movement, but Wildfoot put a restraining hand on my shoulder. His other hand was on Marcel's shoulder.

"Madame, what do you mean?" asked Osborne.

"The gentleman seems to be angry, and I am the cause of his anger, so I offer him satisfaction," she replied. "He need not hesitate. I am probably a much better swordsman than he."

Steinfeldt's face flushed. He raised his weapon, and the two swords clashed together. But we did not intend that the matter should go farther, and we stepped into the room just as the Englishmen also moved forward to interfere.

Their surprise was intense, but they drew weapons promptly. Marcel, whose blood was hotter than mine or Wildfoot's, raised his hand as a signal to be quiet.

"Since the German gentleman wants to have satisfaction, he ought to have it," he said, "and since he has insulted the women of our country, we also want the satisfaction which we ought to have. If the quarrel is not handsomely made up, I never heard of one that was. I'll take Mother Melrose's place."

The woman put the sword on the table, and stepped aside, content with the way affairs were going. The Englishmen looked dubiously at us.

"Why not?" asked Wildfoot.

His query seemed pertinent to me. According to the military law, all of us ought to fight; but since we would make a most unpleasant muss in the house it was best that a champion of each side should meet. It was proper, too, that Marcel should be our man, since he was a better swordsman than I. Wildfoot was our leader, and it was not fitting for him to take the risk.

"Why not?" continued Wildfoot. "I may tell you, gentlemen, that I have a large party near, and perhaps I could get help in time to make you prisoners, but I assure you that the affair would interfere with other and more important plans of mine. You would much better let them fight."

The Englishmen whispered together a moment or two.

"Let it be as you propose," said Osborne.

Their eyes began to sparkle, and I saw that the love of sport, inherent in all Englishmen, was aroused. Marcel and Steinfeldt faced each other and raised their swords. I was astonished at the animosity showing in the eyes of these two men who had never seen each other until a few minutes ago and who had no real cause of quarrel. Yet they seemed to me at that moment to typify their two races which, since then, and in these Napoleonic times, have come into such antagonism. Still it would not be right to say that I care more for the French than for the Germans, although Marcel, who was of French descent, was my fast friend. I have no great admiration for the faults of either race.

Steinfeldt was the larger and apparently the stronger of the two; but Marcel was more compact and agile, and I felt confident of his success. They crossed swords, testing each other's attack and defence, and then began to fight in earnest, their eyes gleaming, their faces hot, and their breath coming short and hard. A candle on a table cast a dim light, and shadows flickered on the floor.

The German was no bad swordsman, and the influence of the wine had passed. At first he pressed Marcel back with fierce and rapid thrusts, and for a moment I was alarmed for my friend. Then I saw that Marcel's face was calm, and his figure seemed to gather strength. My eyes passed on to Mother Melrose; but she stood, impassive, against the wall, silently watching the swordsmen. A red head appeared at the kitchen door, and there was the serving lad following the contest with staring eyes. As for myself, I was uneasy. I did not like the situation; it seemed to me irregular, and we might be interrupted at any time by a force of the enemy. Yet I reasoned with myself that I should not be disturbed when Wildfoot, who was a veteran, seemed not to be, and I soon forgot my scruples in the ring of steel and the joy of combat that rose in my blood, as it had risen in that of the Englishmen.

The Hessian paused a little, seeming to feel that he had been too violent in the beginning, and I noticed that his breath had shortened. Marcel, whose back was against the wall, feinted, and followed up the feint with a thrust, quick as lightning. But the Hessian had no mean skill, and he turned aside the blade which flashed by his arm with a soft sound like scissors snipping through cloth. His coat-sleeve was laid open and the flesh grazed.

"He guards well," said one of the Englishmen, nodding towards Steinfeldt.

The Hessian heard the remark, and it seemed to give him new strength. His sword became a beam of light, and he thrust so straight at Marcel's breast that I held my breath in fear; but my comrade was quick, and the blade, caught on his own, flashed harmlessly by.

"Well fought; well fought, by Pollux!" exclaimed the Englishman Osborne. "This is worth seeing."

The duellists were now almost in the centre of the room, and they paused a moment for breath. I knew, by the compression of their lips, that each was preparing for his greatest effort, and we were silent, awaiting the issue.

The sword play began again, and the weapons rang across each other. The heavy breathing of the combatants sounded distinctly, and the soft beat of their footsteps, as they shifted about the room, made a light, sliding noise, like the restless tread of wild animals in a cage.

The Hessian's sword passed close to Marcel's side, cutting his coat; but when Marcel's blade flashed in return, it came back with blood upon it. The keen edge had passed along the Hessian's wrist, leaving a red thread.

The cut was not deep, but it had a sting to it, and Steinfeldt shut his teeth hard. Marcel's sword was now making lines of light about him, and the Hessian's part in the combat soon became a defence only. He was pressed back, an inch or two at a time, but without cessation. Then I saw the great skill of my comrade. His lips were shut tight, but his eyes remained calm and confident, and the sword seemed to have become a part of himself, so truly did it obey his will.

The Hessian's face slowly darkened, and the light in his eyes, that had been the light of anger and defiance, became the light of fear. And it was the fear of death. He read nothing else in the gleaming blade and calm look of the man before him. Two or three drops of perspiration stood out on his forehead.

"Bad, bad! Steinfeldt has lost!" I heard the Englishman Osborne say under his breath.

I studied Marcel's face, but I could not discover his intentions there. That he carried the Hessian's life on the point of his sword, everyone in the room now knew, and the Hessian himself knew it best of all. But Steinfeldt had courage, I give him all credit for that, whatever else he may have been. A man must be brave to fight on, in the face of what he knows is certain death.

Back went the Hessian, closer and closer to the wall, and always before him was the calm, unsmiling face and gleaming sword that whistled so near and threatened every moment to strike a mortal blow. The suspense became unbearable. I felt like crying out: "Have done and end such a game," and I bit my lip to enforce my own silence.

The Hessian's back suddenly touched the wall, and the sword of Marcel flashed a second time along his wrist, leaving another red thread beside the first. Then it flashed back again, and the weapon of the Hessian, drawn from his hand, fell clattering on the floor.

The defenceless man stood as if he expected a stroke; but I knew that Marcel would never give it. He thrust his own sword into its scabbard, bowed to his opponent with the easy and graceful politeness that he loved, and turned to us as if awaiting our will. I have often wondered where Marcel got that manner of his, and I have concluded that it came from his French blood.

"Take your friend and go," said Wildfoot to the Englishmen. "He is not hurt much, and it is time for all of us to rejoin our commands."

The Englishmen hesitated, as if it were not right for official enemies, in the height of a hot campaign, to part in such a manner. In truth, it was not, but Wildfoot had a set of military rules peculiarly his own, and was not called to account for anything that he might do.

Their hesitation ceased quickly, and each taking an arm of Steinfeldt, they hurried with him out of the room, not neglecting, however, to give us a farewell salute. But they forgot to take Steinfeldt's sword, and Marcel, picking it up, said that he would keep it as a remembrance.

"You must admit that Lieutenant Marcel made a good substitute for you," said Wildfoot, turning to Mother Melrose.

"None could have been better, but I might have beaten the Hessian myself," she replied sturdily. "My husband was a great swordsman and he taught me."

It was now our turn to go, and we bade this remarkable old woman good-night. She showed no signs of fear and was already wiping from the floor the drops of blood that had fallen from Steinfeldt's wrist.

We secured our horses again, and sprang upon their backs. I heard a faint sound like a laugh, and saw a broad smile on the face of Wildfoot.

"I did not expect to see such fine sport when we went to the house," he said.

The ranger obviously was enjoying himself. Events like this pleased his wild and energetic nature. I saw that he was in truth a man of the forests and the night and war, and loved danger.

"Aside from the risk of a fight with them, I did not wish to hold those Englishmen," he continued. "Although they are not likely to report the full and exact facts of our meeting, they will say, when they rejoin their army, that the

American forces are in the vicinity, and that is what I wish the British to know. Unless you are planning a secret attack, it is important to keep the enemy worried, to let him think that you are everywhere, and it will exhaust his strength and patience. Growing tired, he will do something rash and costly."

I understood Wildfoot's logic; but I wondered what would be his next movement, waiting, however, as usual, to let the deed disclose itself. We rejoined our men, who were resting in the wood undisturbed, and all rode on another circuit.

CHAPTER TWENTY-SIX—*An Average Night with Wildfoot*

The night was bright with the moonlight, and we soon saw the blaze of the British camp-fires again. We rode slowly towards them, and at last stopped at a distance of several hundred yards.

"They should have a picket near here," said Wildfoot, "and I fancy it is over yonder in the shadow."

He pointed towards a clump of trees on our right, and Marcel, whose eyes were wonderfully keen, announced that he saw there the color of uniforms.

"Six men are in the group," said Wildfoot, a moment later, "and they appear to be resting, which is wrong. No British picket should be taking its ease in a campaign like this. We will furnish them some excuses for being on watch."

He gave word to two of his men, who lifted their rifles and fired towards the group under the trees. I heard the bullets cutting through the leaves in the few minutes of intense silence that followed. Then a great clamor arose, the noise of many voices, a drum beating, and scattered shots returning our fire. We saw soldiers leap up in the camp and run to arms.

We were far enough away to be hidden from the sight of our enemies, and we rode swiftly on, leaving the clamor behind us. It was a huge camp, spreading out for miles, and partly surrounded by woods, which always make easy the approach of a concealed foe. Yet there was not enough open space in the vicinity for the whole British army, and their commanders were not to blame.

Wildfoot still led the way, appearing to know the country thoroughly. He divided our little force, presently, into three troops, naming a place at which we were to reunite some hours later. He placed trusted leaders over the first two troops, and took the third himself, Marcel and I being included in it. We rode through the deep woods, the twigs whipping our faces, but always ahead of us was the large dark figure of Wildfoot, horse and man passing on silently, like a ghostly centaur.

In a half-hour we stirred up another picket, which saw us in the moonlight and fired their bullets so close to our heads that I felt anxious. But they were only four men, and we soon sent them running back to their army. Then an entire company came out to beat up the woods for us, but we were gone again, flitting on to new mischief. Wildfoot was an expert at this business. Anybody could see it at a glance. He knew when to do a thing, and when not to do it, which comes very near to being supreme wisdom. He knew whether to attack or to wait, whether to ride on or to stay, and the entire British right flank was soon in an uproar, their musketeers returning the fire of an enemy whom they could not see, and cavalry galloping through the forests after the foe whom they could not overtake. While Wildfoot led us often into danger, he always led us out again, and we continued our circle of the British camp, all our horsemen unharmed.

"Isn't this glorious?" said Wildfoot to me presently. "Such nights as these a man remembers long."

I gazed at him in wonder, but there was no sign of affectation in his voice or eye. I knew that there was none in his heart either. But I looked at my torn clothing, felt my bruised face, where the twigs had struck like switches, stretched my muscles, sore from so much riding, and replied,—

"If I were the British commander, Captain Wildfoot, and I could catch you, I would hang you to the top of the tallest tree in this forest."

"I admit that it is somewhat annoying," he replied, smiling broadly at what impressed him as a great compliment; "but, as I told you, we must not let the enemy dwell in peace. If we can disturb his sleep, impair his digestion, and upset his nerves, he won't be enthusiastic when he goes into real battle."

A half-hour later we were dashing through the woods pursued by a formidable company, entirely too large for us to oppose, but again we were unharmed. In truth, the darkness—for the moon had faded somewhat—was our protector. The enemy could not see to hit us with the musket-bullets, and presently we gathered together again in the friendly shadows, with the hostile troop left far behind.

"I wish I knew where General Clinton himself lies," said Wildfoot, who was ambitious. "I should like to send a bullet through his tent, not to hurt him, but merely to let him know that we are here."

His face was full of longing, but there was no way for us to discover or approach General Clinton's tent, and I feared that his desire must go unfulfilled. Nevertheless, his zest and energy did not decrease, and he seemed bent upon completing the circuit of the British army with his irritating methods. I was worn to the bone, but in spite of it I caught some of Wildfoot's militant enthusiasm, and aided him to the utmost.

Clouds obscured the moon again, and the added darkness helped us. After midnight we found a company camped on a hill-side on the fringe of the army, but a little farther from the main body than usual. The tethered horses grazed on the grass near by, and I was willing to swear that I knew several of them.

"Yes," said Wildfoot, at whom I looked questioningly, "that's the company with which you rode the night you and Miss Desmond brought us the warning. I have no doubt that your friend Belfort, who was exchanged for you, and other friends of yours, too, are there. We will rouse them up a bit."

He signalled to his men, and a half-dozen bullets clipped the grass among the tents. The return fire came in an instant, and it was much fiercer than we had expected. The musket-balls whistled around us, and two men and a horse were grazed. We sent back a second volley, and the British, rushing to their horses, galloped after us, at least a hundred strong. Away we crashed through the woods, expecting to shake them off in a few minutes, as we had rid ourselves of the others, but they managed to keep us in sight and hung on to the chase.

"We must discourage such enthusiasm," said Wildfoot, and he gave orders to our men, who had reloaded their rifles, to fire again, cautioning them to take good aim. Two troopers fell to our volley, and others seemed to be hurt. The pursuit slackened for a few minutes, but was resumed to the accompaniment of scattering rifle-shots that urged us to renewed speed. Three of our men were wounded, though slightly, and the affair was growing decidedly warm.

But the darkness of night and our knowledge of the country gave us a vast advantage, which we used to good purpose. Wildfoot ordered us to curve farther away from the British camp, and in five minutes we entered the deeper forest. Marcel and I were thankful now that Wildfoot had made us take the horses. All the men were specially well mounted, in truth, on horses trained for such work, and our pursuers began to diminish in number, the slower ones dropping off. They decreased rapidly from a hundred to fifty, and then to twenty-five, and then to less. But a small group clung persistently to us until at last Wildfoot laid a restraining hand on the rein of his horse, and said: "Not more than seven or eight men are following us now. We must show them that they are rash."

We stopped and raised our rifles, all except Marcel and I, who had none, pistols taking their place. Our pursuers were too eager and too hot with the chase to notice instantly that we were no longer fleeing, and dashed at us like knights riding down an antagonist at a tournament. The man at their head was Belfort,—I saw him plainly,—who never lacked bravery and zeal, however unlikable he may have been otherwise. I had spared his life once, and I would not fire at him now, but of course I was not responsible for what the others might do.

Our weapons flashed, and two of the pursuing horsemen fell. One horse also went down. The unhurt, warned by this terrible volley that they had come too far, whirled about and fled—all except two.

The two who did not flee were a wounded man who had fallen from his saddle and the one whose horse had been killed. Both wore the uniform of officers.

The dismounted man might have darted among the trees and eluded us easily, but he did not run. Instead he raised up his wounded companion, who began to limp away. I saw that the latter was Belfort, but I judged that he was not badly hurt, the blood on his coat indicating that the bullet had struck him in the shoulder. The moonlight fell on the face of the man who led him, and we saw that it was not a man at all, merely a fair-haired English boy of seventeen or eighteen years. He put his arm under Belfort's shoulder, and the two walked towards one of the horses that stood near with empty saddle.

"Surrender!" shouted Wildfoot.

The boy turned towards us, and his face showed defiance. Then he shook his fist, and walked on with his comrade towards his horse.

We held the lives of both at our mercy, and the boy probably knew it, but he never flinched. We might fire or we might not; but he did not intend to desert a comrade or surrender. One of our men raised his rifle, but Wildfoot struck it down.

"There is some English mother whom we can spare!" he said.

So we sat there on our horses until the boy helped Belfort into the saddle, and climbed up behind him. Then he looked at us intently for a moment, and raised his hand. I thought he was going to shake his fist in our faces again; but the hand went to his head, and he gave us a military salute. Then, with his wounded comrade, he rode away towards the British army.

"A fine spirit and fine manners," said Wildfoot.

We, too, rode off in the forest, and I was very glad that the ranger had spared the boy. He had given me my life once, but then he knew that I was not an Englishman.

There was no cessation of the work for hours, and we continued our circuit, stirring up alarm after alarm, Wildfoot, sleepless and untiring, at our head. At last when day was bright, and our three bands had reunited, he looked at the rising sun and said, with a deep sigh of regret:—

"I'm afraid we'll have to quit and go back to General Washington's camp."

"Don't you think that we've had rather an active night?" I asked.

"It's been a fair average night," he replied.

Such was the man.

When the sun was well risen, we were riding into camp.

CHAPTER TWENTY-SEVEN—
Pure Gold

I was so sleepy and tired that I practically fell from my horse when we reached quarters; but I had slept only three or four hours when a messenger from General Washington himself came to me, bearing instructions for me to go to John Desmond's house in Philadelphia with ten armed men and bring what he would give. I was to show Mr. Desmond a sealed order which the messenger brought.

The armed men were waiting, and I rode at their head to John Desmond's house, wondering what the nature of my errand could be. Yet my ill-humor at being awakened so early had vanished when I found where I was to go. It was Mr. Desmond's residence, not his counting-house, and I found him in the parlor, where I gave him a note. He was not alone. He sat at one side of a wide table and on the other side was a man whom I knew to be a trusted aide of General Washington. Between them lay a heap of shining gold of English and French coinage, and they were counting it. It was a fine yellow heap, one of the most luscious sights that I had beheld in a long time, and my eyes lingered over it.

"It is this that you are to take," said Mr. Desmond, with a smile, and indicating the gold, when he had read my sealed order.

"For what is it?" I could not restrain myself from asking.

"For the cause," he replied. "It is the contribution of some of Philadelphia's merchants and bankers to the Continental army. They have awaited this opportunity a long time."

I suspected that his own contribution was the largest of all, and such I afterwards found to be the truth.

"It is well to be exact," continued Mr. Desmond, "and so we are counting it in order that Captain Reade here may give us a receipt for the exact amount. It will take us more than a half hour yet to finish the task, and you might walk into the garden while you are waiting."

He indicated the way, and going into the garden I found Mary Desmond there. She wore June roses on her shoulder, their pink and red gleaming against her white dress, and her face was bright. The charm of her eyes did not depart in the daylight.

"So you have come back unharmed," she said. "But you have returned early."

"We have not fought the battle yet," I replied.

"But you look worn," she said. "Have you not seen service?"

"Yes," I replied, "I have spent a night on duty with Wildfoot."

"I might have known," she replied, as she laughed. "That man never sleeps—at least not in the night. He is always seeking to do something for our cause, which may have friends more powerful, but never better."

"I know it," I replied earnestly.

We walked on between the flower beds. It was just such another garden as that at the Tory's house, in which we had talked at cross-purposes after our night's ride, but somehow we seemed to understand each other much better here. The atmosphere was different.

I began to tell her of our night with Wildfoot, and first of our visit to the lonely house where Mother Melrose challenged the Hessian. Her eyes filled and grew tender.

"I know her well," she said, "and she is as loyal and true as Wildfoot himself. She has been one of the links in our chain of communication with the American army, as perhaps Wildfoot told you. I have left messages there myself more than once, and sometimes I have urged her to go away to a safer place. But she seems never to be afraid in that lonely house!"

I looked with admiration at this young girl who spoke with such praise of another's bravery, but was unconscious of her own.

"But if Mrs. Melrose should be afraid there," I said, "should not you be afraid to ride alone, at night, in our service through the dangerous forests?"

"I never thought of that," she replied simply. "I had ridden all about Philadelphia before the war, and I knew the country. It seemed easy for me to go, and I was sure that none would ever suspect me, I claimed to be such an ardent Tory, and I seemed to be all that I claimed. Then we needed friends in Philadelphia."

"In truth we found the best," I replied with earnestness.

She blushed, but did not look wholly displeased.

"You flatter like a courtier, Lieutenant Chester," she said, "and this is too grave a time for flattery."

"But were you never afraid?" I persisted.

"Once I was," she said, "when some horsemen, I know not whether they were soldiers or robbers, pursued me. They followed me five miles; but my horse was too swift, and when they saw the lights of the picket they turned back. I had a pass from Sir William Howe, but I know that my hand trembled when I showed it to the sentinels. I was too ill to leave our house the next day, but I went again a week afterward."

I looked with increasing wonder and admiration at the slender figure that could dare so much. If our women even were so brave, surely our cause could not fail!

"Why did you talk so strangely to me when we met for the first time after that night's ride together?" I asked. "Why did you seem to have forgotten it or to pretend that it had never been?"

"I did not know who and what you were as well then as I do now; Captain Wildfoot did not tell me," she replied. "One, perforce, had to be cautious then, Lieutenant Chester."

"But were you not afraid that I would betray you after that ride we took together."

"I was sure you would not do so."

"Why?"

She looked me directly in the eyes for a moment, and then turned her face away. But she was not so quick that I did not see the red coming into her cheeks.

We walked on among the roses in the golden sunshine, and the time was all too short for me.

"Will you not wish me success in the coming battle?" I asked, when they called me to take the gold.

"Yes, and you may wear my colors, if they will last long enough," she said. She took one of the roses from her shoulder, and pinned it on my coat. As she bent her head over the rose, silken strands of her hair blew in my face.

I forgot myself then, but I have no excuse for it now. I bent down suddenly and kissed her. She sprang away from me, uttering a little cry, and her cheeks were flaming red.

"Mary," I said, "I don't ask any forgiveness. I kissed you because I could not help myself. You were not afraid that I would betray you after that ride to the American army, and it was because you knew that I loved you. No, I would not have betrayed you even had I been Lieutenant Melville, the British officer that I seemed to be. But much as I loved you then, I love you more now. Mary, will you marry me?"

An elusive smile came into her eyes, as she made me a pretty bow, and replied: "Lieutenant Melville of Newton-on-the-Hill, Staffordshire, England, I thank you for your offer, but I have resolved never to marry an Englishman."

Then, before I could stay her, she ran into the house. But she had left her rose with me, and I did not despair.

I carried the gold to General Washington, and our main force pressed forward a little later in pursuit of the British army.

CHAPTER TWENTY-EIGHT—
At the Council Fire

The British, going from Philadelphia to New York, marched on a slightly curving route, while we, almost parallel with them, were advancing in a straight line; that is, they were the bent bow and we were its cord. Therefore we held the advantage, and it was obvious that we would overtake them. Great hopes began to rise among us. The British army was the larger, composed of regular troops, and far better armed than ours; but it had just given up the chief city of the colonies, and was in retreat. It was suffering from depression, while we were elated over the French alliance and the sudden and favorable turn of our fortunes. Many of us believed that a heavy blow, well directed, might now end the war. We heard, too, that it was General Washington's own hope, and it was my fortune to discover, through personal observation, that this was so.

It was several nights after my return with the gold. Our scouts had been engaged in some skirmishing with British outposts, and just as the evening fell, Marcel and I returned with a report of it. The weather was still intensely hot, and the men, terribly tired by forced marches in such a temperature, were lying on the ground with their faces to the sky that they might feel the first coolness of the evening. The cooks were preparing supper, and fires blazed here and there; but we were too languid to show much energy, and the camp was unusually quiet.

We made our report to the colonel; but he considered it of sufficient importance to be heard by the general-in-chief himself, and he directed me to take it to him.

"You will find him among the trees," he said, pointing to a small wood. Under the boughs of the largest tree, a fire was burning and over it swung a camp-kettle. Several men, sitting on logs in front of the fire, were talking earnestly, and now and then looking at a map. The one who held the map was large and straight-shouldered, and I knew the figure to be that of the general-in-chief. As I approached, I recognized, too, the swarthy face of Charles Lee, the foreigner who came to us with such an air of superior wisdom, and whom we put in high place, but whom the real soldiers already hated. Then I recognized Wayne, with his trim figure and fine frank eyes, Greene, the silent Rhode-Islander who afterward became so great, and others.

The council—if council it was—seemed to have developed some heat. General Washington's blue eyes plainly showed anger, and Lee was whipping his own high cavalry boots with a small switch. I approached with much embarrassment and hesitation. My Philadelphia exploits in company with Marcel were yet fresh in the memory of men, and to appear presumptuous was, of all things, the one that I wished least. I was sorry that Marcel had not been chosen to deliver the report. It was a situation that would have pleased him.

But General Washington saw me as I came near, and delivered me from further embarrassment by calling to me in very kind tones,—

"A report for me, is it not, Lieutenant Chester?" he asked.

I said yes, and stated it briefly, while the others listened with attention. Then I stood awaiting the general's further orders.

"It is just as I told you," he said emphatically to Charles Lee, and seeming to forget my presence. "Our army will overtake theirs in three days at furthest, and we must strike with all our strength. We may be able to destroy Clinton's army, and then our cause will be won."

"But Clinton has more men than we," replied Charles Lee, in protesting tones, "and his equipment is much superior."

"He retreats, and we pursue," said the general-in-chief.

"That is true," rejoined Lee; "but I think we should be very cautious."

His words and tone did not indicate zeal. How heartily I have since cursed the traitor, and how many others have done the same.

"And why so cautious?" burst in the impetuous Wayne. "One cannot win a battle unless he fights!"

"You might have found caution a good thing, General Wayne," replied Lee, in smooth, soft tones. "Remember how they cut you up at Paoli."

Wayne flushed with anger, but he was too manly to deny his only disaster.

"It is true," he said, "but the fault was mine. My troops did not get a chance to fight. Here they will have it."

"We shall invite our own rout," said Lee. "The Americans cannot stand the British grenadiers."

It was the feeling of an old race towards a new one that spoke in him, and this man, who proved himself a traitor to two countries, the old and new, was unwise enough to say it.

"You are mistaken," said the commander-in-chief, promptly and emphatically. "That is a delusion which the British may cherish, but not we. This war has furnished too many instances to the contrary. The attack shall be made, General Lee, and you shall lead it. We must end this war as soon as possible, and benefit two nations; for I take it that Englishmen do not love to kill Americans, any more than Americans love to kill Englishmen."

Throughout the talk Greene said nothing, sitting there upon the log, looking calm and decided. I like this quality of stanchness in the New Englanders. They stick fast, whatever else you may say about them, and that I think wins more than anything else.

I received my instructions a moment later and retired. As I walked away, I met Marcel.

"Was it a council of war?" he asked.

"I think so."

"I hope that you gave them the proper instructions."

"I did my best," I replied in the same spirit.

"They had no right to expect more," rejoined Marcel; "but it's a great pity I was not in your place."

Perhaps he would have given them advice. Marcel had great confidence in his judgment.

CHAPTER TWENTY-NINE—
Under the Apple-Trees

We lay gasping under the apple-trees. The hottest sun that ever I felt or saw, was dissolving our muscles and pinning us to the earth, mere flaccid lumps. The heat quivered in the air, and the grass turned dry blades to the brown soil. I ran my finger along the bare edge of my sword, and the skin was scorched. My throat burned.

"What a day to fight!" said Marcel. "The red coats that the British over yonder wear blaze like fire, and I dare say are as hot. I wish I were a private and not an officer. Then I could strip myself."

He looked longingly at a huge soldier who had taken off coat and shirt, and was lying on the grass, naked to the waist, his rifle ready in his hands.

"Leave old Father Sun alone," I said: "I believe he will settle the business for both armies. At least he seems to be bent upon doing it."

I tried to look up at the sun, but His Majesty met me with so fierce a stare that I was glad to turn my eyes again, blinking, to the earth. When they recovered from the dimness, I looked along the line of panting soldiers, and saw one who had dropped his rifle on the grass and flung his arms out at ease.

"Stir up that man, there," I said; "he must keep his rifle in hand and ready."

"If you please, sir," said the bare-waisted soldier, "he won't be stirred up."

"Won't be stirred up?" I said, with natural impatience; "why won't he?"

"Because he can't be," said the soldier.

"Can't be?" I said, not understanding such obstinacy. "What do you mean?"

"He can't be stirred up," replied the soldier; "because he's dead, sir."

I examined the man, and found that it was true. We had marched long and hard in the stifling heat before we lay down in the orchard, and the man, overpowered by it, had died so gently that his death was not known to us. We let him lie there, the dead man in the ranks with the quick.

"Doesn't the concussion of cannon and muskets cause rain sometimes?" asked Marcel.

"I have heard so," I replied. "Why?"

"Because, if it does," said Marcel, "I hope the battle will be brought on at once, and that it will be a most ferocious contention. Then it may cause a shower heavy enough to cool us off."

"Whether it brings rain or not," I said, "I think the battle will soon be upon us."

Up went the sun, redder and fiercer than ever. The heavens blazed with his light. The men panted like dogs, and their tongues hung out. The red coats of the British opposite us looked so bright that they dazzled my eyes. The leaves of the apple-trees cracked and twisted up.

"It would be funny," said Marcel, "if the British were to charge upon us and find us all lying here in a placid row, dead, killed by the sun."

"Yes," said I, "it would be very funny."

"But not impossible," said the persistent Marcel.

We lay near the little town of Freehold in the Jersey fields, where we had overtaken the retreating British, and intended to force a battle, although we were much inferior in numbers and equipment.

I can say with truth that the men were eager for the fight. They had starved long at Valley Forge, and now with full stomachs they had come upon the heels of a flying enemy. Moreover, we had been raised up mightily by the French alliance. We did not know then how much the French were to disappoint us, and how little aid they were to give us until the final glorious campaign.

"Listen!" exclaimed a soldier near me.

"What is it, Alloway?" I asked.

"The battle! It's begun!" he replied.

The sound of a rifle-shot came through the hot air across the fields, and then many more sang together. A half mile away, under the low lines of trees, a cloud of smoke was rising, and the base of it was red with flashes. Presently a cannon boomed its deeper note, and the echo of shouts came faintly. At last the battle had begun, and our men, panting already in the heat, grew hotter with impatience. It was hard to lie there under the burning sun while the battle swelled, without us. But we had no choice, and we pulled at the dry grass, while we watched the growing combat.

CHAPTER THIRTY—*The Defence of the Gun*

Marcel and I, with some others, were moved presently to the outskirts with the skirmishers. We lay among some trees by the roadside, and in the road one of our cannon with its complement of men was stationed to drive back a large body of the British troops which threatened us on that wing. We did not have to wait long for the attack. The heavy red squares of the English appeared, pressing down the road. Then the gun, a beautiful bronze twelve-pounder, became active, and the men who fought it were full of zeal.

They fired for a time, working rapidly, skilfully, and without friction, like a perfect machine, only the sergeant in command speaking, his short, sharp orders snapping out like the crackling of a whip. The faces of all were impassive, save for the occasional flash of an eye when a shot beat its fellows. The gun was alive now, pouring a stream of missiles from its bronze throat, the British replying with both cannon and muskets.

Presently the men fell back a little with the gun, until they came to a hillock, and then unlimbered again just beyond the crest, where they were somewhat sheltered. They seemed to think that the new position was good, and they would fight where they were. Ross, the sergeant in command, a tall, thin Jerseyman with an impassive face, gave the order to unlimber the cannon, and the six horses dragged the limber to the proper distance in the rear. At an almost equal distance in the rear of the limber stood the caisson, also with its six horses. The chief of caisson, a short, stout man, was behind the limber ready to supply ammunition when needed, his face calm, his nerves unmoved by the roar and blaze of the combat, which rolled towards him in a flaming curve, tipped with steel.

There were thirteen men with the gun and caisson, and the eyes of all were on Sergeant Ross, who commanded it, a man worthy of his post and fit for battle. The twelve horses stood in the rear. We were still near them among the trees by the roadside, firing our rifles, and could hear the few words that they said.

"We must stay here," resumed Sergeant Ross to the corporal, his gunner, a tall, thin Jerseyman like himself and as calm and impassive. The corporal looked at the heavy squares pressing forward as if to crush them, listened a moment to the swell of the battle, but said nothing. The men were at work already, serving in silence.

There had been no lull in the combat, and the advancing British line looked like a red wave of fire. A shell burst over the men around the gun, and a fragment struck the lead horse of the limber chest in the neck. The animal uttered a single neigh of pain, and then let his head drop, while the blood poured from his wound.

His eye expressed melancholy and resignation precisely like that of a stricken veteran. He fell softly in a few moments, and died.

The battle was coming very near, and made many threats. The reserve men cut the gear of the dead horse, dragged his body aside, and replaced him with one of the six from the caisson. They did this without comment, and the sergeant and the gunner took no notice.

"To your posts!" called Sergeant Ross.

His men sprang instantly to position. No. 7 took a charge of shot and powder from the limber chest and passed it to No. 5, who handed it to No. 2. No. 2 inserted it in the gun, while No. 1 rammed it home. The gunner took aim at the black mass of the British army, red at the crest with flame. Sergeant Ross gave the command to fire, and No. 4 obeyed. The twelve-pound shot rushed through the air, but though watching and eager to see, the men could not tell what damage it had done. The advancing line was hidden at that moment by the floating smoke and the flash of the firing. Those at the gun bent to their work. No. 1 ran his sponge into the black muzzle, swabbed out the barrel, and No. 2 inserted a fresh charge. These impassive men seemed to show no fear; they loaded and fired as if unconscious of the showers of balls and bullets.

The British army pushed on, and its line of battle converged nearer, but the men at the gun were still without emotion. This machine, whose parts were human beings, worked in a beautiful way, and we admired them. Again the cannon was alive, pouring forth its rapid stream of shot.

"We must drive 'em back!" said Sergeant Ross.

"We'll blow 'em to hell with this twelve-pounder," said the corporal.

He patted the gun, a polished piece kept in perfect order. They fired again, and the shattered British line crumpled up before the rage of the twelve-pounder, which was pouring its fire into it, faster and faster; the rows had already become thinner at that point, the bulk of the force turning aside against the heavier Continental battalions. The hopes of the men with the gun rose.

"We'll mow 'em down," said No. 1, the sponger and rammer, a boy of twenty.

They showed feeling at last, and their faces brightened up. They were young, in fact, boys rather than men; the oldest of them was under twenty-five, and the youngest was not more than seventeen.

The battle veered a little, and thundered to right and left; but the thinner line in front of the gun was still advancing, and its muskets threatened. A battery, a little distance in its rear, threw shot over its head; but the regular and precise work of the men was not disturbed.

"Depress that gun a bit!" said Ross to the corporal, in his sharp, snapping voice. It was done. The discharge that followed swept down a row of advancing men in red. The gunner smiled, and the captain of the gun nodded approvingly. The cannoneers said nothing, but No. 7 passed another cartridge.

A shell screamed through the air, took off Sergeant Ross's head and passed on. The corporal made no comment, but joined the duties of captain of the gun to his own duties as gunner. The regularity and precision of the work was not disturbed for a moment. The gun had aroused more attention in the British lines, and it became necessary to silence it and destroy the men who served it. It was merely a small incident in the course of a great battle, but the gun had become an obstacle.

"They know we are here," said the corporal to the new gunner, a faint smile appearing on his brown face.

"Yes, and they are throwing us bouquets," replied the gunner, as a shower of bullets flew over their heads.

There was a crash in their ears, a blaze of light like that struck by steel, and the cannon toppled over. The four men nearest it fell to the ground, three sprang up quickly; but the fourth, who was No. 5, a cannoneer, lay still and dead. A reserve man instantly took his place. The others ran anxiously to the cannon. They paid no attention to the dead man. The wounded gun was of far more importance than many men.

"The wheel's smashed! No harm beyond that!" said the corporal. Then he shouted,—

"Change wheels!"

The rubbish was dragged away, the extra wheel, provided for such cases, was brought as by another turn of the perfect machine from its place on the caisson, and fitted on the axle. No. 4, a cannoneer, was killed by a bullet while they were doing it; but the second reserve man took his place, and the battery went on with its work as well as ever.

The gun was fired rapidly again, and the men saw that the effect was good; the red line of their enemy had been shattered once more. The corporal glanced a little to the left, and said, in an unchanged voice:

"A cavalry charge is coming; stand steady!"

The red line of infantry was suddenly blotted out, and in its place a line of horsemen rose out of the smoke. They were riding at a gallop, firing from their pistols, their sabres ready for the swinging blow when the charge was driven home, a swelling wave, edged with fire and steel. It was a glittering and magnificent sight.

The boys about the gun looked anxious at the sight of the cavalry, but the corporal was calm.

"Load with grape, triple charges!" he said, and his voice cracked louder and sharper than ever.

The grape, triple charges, was rammed into the twelve-pounder, and the wonderful machine that handled the gun increased its speed. The British cavalry galloped into a stream of fire. The gun was hidden from them by the incessant blaze and smoke of its discharges, and the triple loads of grape whizzed among them, killing horses and horsemen, destroying the precision of their ordered lines, crumpling up those in front, and heaping the dead in the way of those behind. But the unslain horsemen galloped on, and always before them roared the engine of death, the gun, and always about them whistled the showers of grape. Presently they were into the flame and the smoke, and before them rose the gun and its detachment.

"Stretch prolonge ropes!" shouted the corporal to his men.

The drivers cracked their whips over the horses, and whirled the caisson and the limber chest about, bringing them, horses and all, into line with the piece, and in a moment, heavy ropes were stretched from the cannon to the limber chest, and from the limber chest to the caisson, and the fighting men were crouching in their appointed positions between the wheels, and around the gun, holding in hand their pistols and artillery swords, short, heavy weapons with which they could slash as with axes. The cavalry company was charging upon a breastwork held by an armed force.

"Let 'em have it with the pistols!" cried the corporal to his men.

The pistols began to crack, and more holes appeared in the charging lines of horsemen. When a trooper was hit hard in the breast or shoulder, up went his hands, and he fell back from his horse; if struck in the limbs, he fell forward and rolled off. Some horses that had lost their riders kept place in the charge and galloped on. Two or three others turned to one side, and ran about, neighing with fear and alarm, but would not leave the field. All sprang aside when they came to a wounded or dead man lying on the ground.

The cavalry company was not large, and many saddles were empty before it smashed into the gun and its defenders. Then a terrible tumult arose. There was a confused mêlée of rearing horses, men leaning in the saddle, firing with pistols and slashing with sabres. Other men, brown and wiry, reaching over and bending forward among the wheels, striking upward with short heavy swords, killing horses and riders, and darting about like Indians, evading alike the hoofs of the horses and the slashes of the horsemen. There was a sickening whit of steel cutting through flesh, the gasp of last and hard-drawn breaths, and the sound of falls. The horses became entangled among the ropes, and stumbled over the gun and caisson, throwing their riders to the earth. The sinewy forms of their enemies slipped in and out like snakes, escaping the blows aimed from above, but steadily deepening the stains on their own red swords. Shouts, cries, and the stamp of horses' feet came from the whirling ball of fire and smoke, which began presently to throw forth men and horses. The cavalrymen who still rode, galloped away, and those who were on foot now, followed. Many of the horses were riderless, and they joined others that ran up and down the field, always keeping the battle in view. Then the ball split asunder entirely, and each half began to shred off in fragments; the dying combat, and the men, the living and the dead, rose out of it. The ground over which they had fought was a soaking red mire, and the wheels of cannon, caisson, and limber were sunk deep in it. But the cavalry had been beaten; entangled in the breastwork of the gun and its equipment and the prolonge ropes, they had been unable to withstand the slashing and the thrusting of the short artillery swords, and those who lived fled to the main line of their army, knowing their defeat and not seeking to hide it. A trumpet sounded the recall, and the riderless horses, ceasing their restless race to and fro on the field, fell into line like the veterans they were, and followed the bugler back to the army which owned them.

The men about the gun may have enjoyed their victory; but they gave no sign, and the seven who were left, four having fallen, were reloading as if nothing had happened to interrupt the regular firing of their one gun battery. No. 1, the sponger and rammer, had been killed by a pistol-shot. No. 2 had taken his place, his own place being taken in turn by No. 3, and so on, each moving up a step in the promotion of death. There was no reserve men now, and the force at the caisson was reduced. The corporal was bleeding from a sabre-cut on the head; but he took no notice of it, nor did the men comment on the appearance of his face, which was dyed red. Such things had grown common.

"We gave 'em hell that time," said the corporal.

"And we can do it again," said he who had been No. 2, but now was No. 1.

The men, though saying nothing, began to feel their victory. They were making a great fight and they knew it. Their beloved cannon was excelling itself. They patted the barrel and the wheels, and ran their hands along the shining bronze, saying, "Good old boy!" and "Well done!" The prolonge ropes were taken down, the limber chest and caisson were sent back to the rear, and the great one gun battery again went into action.

"Aim at that mass of infantry across the hill there," said the corporal, and the shot was placed in the appointed spot.

The fires of many British guns was turned upon this cannon which had become most annoying, stinging like a wasp. The defeat of the cavalry furnished mortification too, and the necessity to silence the gun and annihilate its detachment grew more imperative. A sleet of lead and iron beat about it. A hot shot struck the limber chest, and a volcano of fire and smoke, accompanied by a terrific explosion, gushed up. Pieces of iron and steel and oaken wood whizzed through the air, and for a few moments both men and horses were blinded by the dazzling burst of flame.

The limber chest was no longer there; but a deep hole appeared in the earth where it had been, and the space about it was strewed with old iron. It had been blown up by the hot shot, and the corporal, who was taking charges from the chest, and three horses were blown up with it. The other horses, torn loose from their gear and chest, had run away, bleeding. The new driver of the caisson cracked his whip over the heads of his horses, and whirled the limber into the place of the limber destroyed. The chief of caisson proceeded to supply ammunition to the gun, which did not slacken its industry.

The main battle rolled a little further away, and the horses and the gun formed a projection of the American line extending into the British. But the nature of the ground on either side, and the occupation furnished by our army to the bulk of the British troops, protected their flanks. The danger lay directly in front of them.

The gun was getting hot, and they were forced to let it cool a little.

The corporal watched the enemy, while his gun rested. He never turned his eyes towards his comrades, knowing they would do their duty.

"They advance slowly," he said to the new No. 1.

"They do not like the kisses of old Hammer and Tongs here," replied No. 1, patting the gun.

"Is that sponge burnt out?" asked the corporal.

No. 1 did not reply.

"Why don't you answer?" asked the corporal, a little impatiently.

"He's quit talking," said Acting No. 2.

The corporal did not ask, as he knew there could be only one reason for No. 1's inability. A bullet had passed through the man's heart, and he had died gracefully and without noise. All the men moved up another step, but both the gun and the caisson were shorthanded. They were too few now to have repulsed a second cavalry charge; but, luckily for them, the second charge was not forthcoming. Infantry and guns alone were before them.

"Begin firing!" said the corporal.

The silent Jerseyman who was chief of caisson passed the charges, and in a moment the deep note of the gun blended with the surge and roar of the battle. Shot followed shot. The machine was reduced, but no change was apparent in the quantity or quality of its work.

"The old gun can still talk good English," said the corporal, with intense satisfaction.

A fragment of grape cut him in half. The chief of caisson was promoted to the command of the gun, and took his new office without friction or delay. Six men with such a willing and experienced cannon could yet hold eloquent converse with their enemy. Still there were disadvantages. The force at the limber was so small that the charges were handled with difficulty, and the firing speed was reduced. The hostile line of battle was pressing alarmingly near, and, moreover, it had begun at last to converge on the flanks of the gun. Although we with our rifles were protecting them as much as we could, one of the reserve men looked behind him and spoke of retreat.

"This gun is tired of retreating," said the new captain. "It stays right here, and we stay with it."

Fierce and defiant, the rapid note of the twelve-pounder boomed out.

A minute later the new wheel that had been supplied to it from the caisson was smashed like its predecessor by a round shot; to fill its place, they took off the hinder part of the caisson, leaving it a cripple, and put it on the gun, which became again as good as new.

The fire of the twelve-pounder was undiminished.

"We still hold 'em back; we've won our day's pay and perhaps a little more," remarked the new captain, rather in a tone of soliloquy than address.

The balance of pay was never collected. A whiff of grape exterminated him and the man who stood nearest him, and the gun had only four assistants in its work. Two of these four men were wounded, and they might have thought of retreat; but a shot struck the caisson, blew it up, and killed the drivers, and all the horses except two. It was no longer possible to carry away the gun, and the three men who were left would not abandon it to the enemy.

The surviving horses hovered near, turning about in a small circle.

The man who had been No. 5, a cannoneer, was the senior, and took command. He was wounded, but he lost little blood and concealed the hurt.

"Shall we run?" asked one of his comrades.

"One more shot for good count!" he replied.

They aimed with deliberation, though the balls and bullets rained around them. The cannoneer chose the densest red of the advancing mass, and sent the shot straight to the mark. Before the smoke from the discharge sank, three British shells burst, almost simultaneously, among the last defenders, and when the smoke cleared no one was standing there. The gun, blown from its wheels and torn open at the breech, was useless forever.

CHAPTER THIRTY-ONE—*A Battle and An Answered Question*

The gun and its defenders were gone, but the heavy British force had been held off our flank long enough to suit our purpose. Our line, during the interval, had extended itself in such a manner that now it could not be surrounded, and we resumed our original place in the centre, where the battle was increasing.

The columns of smoke before us rose and broadened, the flashes of fire that shot through it, increased and twinkled in thousands. The shouting came more distinctly to our ears, and the drifting smoke made the dense tremulous heat more oppressive. I knew that Charles Lee commanded our engaged division, and, having in mind the talk at the council fire, I was uneasy. If only Wayne or Greene were there!

The cloud of fire and smoke suddenly began to move towards us, and the shouting grew louder. The battle was shifting its face, and approaching us. It had but one meaning, and that was the retreat of the Americans. A universal groan arose from our ranks.

"It can't be! It can't be!" shouted Marcel, and he swore.

But it was. Across the fields came our men in full flight, with Charles Lee himself, thrice-accursed traitor, at their head. All the world knows how he ordered his own men to flee, when they were winning the victory, and it need be told to no one what such a movement would mean to an army in the height of a battle. I could have wept for despair at this lost opportunity, at this useless flight which might mean our own destruction. On streamed the fugitives, and suddenly a great man on a great horse galloped forward to meet them. Everybody in our company knew that the rider was Washington, and we uttered a mighty shout. Then we were silent, while Washington rode directly in front of Charles Lee, and stopped his horse across his path.

We could not hear the words that were said, the words that must have burned into the man's soul; but we saw the red, wrathful face of Washington, and the white, scared face of Lee. Never was Washington so fiercely angry, and never with better cause. Branding the traitor with hot words, he sent him away under arrest, and then, among the stinging bullets, he reformed the men, who cheered their great commander, turned their faces to the enemy, and began anew the battle that had been all but lost.

"Leftenant," said the bare-waisted man, who had been so thirsty, and who had accompanied us with the skirmishers, "ain't it about time to let us have another drink? The inside of my throat's so dry it's scalin' off."

We had filled our canteens with water before this last march; but I had allowed my men to drink but sparingly, knowing how much they would need it later. Now I pitied them as well as myself, and I gave the word to turn up the canteens; but I ordered that the drink should be a very short one.

Up went the canteens as if they had been so many muskets raised to command. There was a deep grateful gurgle and cluck along the whole line as the water poured into the half-charred throats of the men. But Marcel and I had to draw our swords and threaten violence before they would take the canteens away from their lips.

"Leftenant," said the bare-waisted man, reproachfully, "I was right in heaven then, and you pulled me out by the legs."

"Then you may be sent back to heaven or the other place soon enough," I said, "for here come the British. Ready, men!"

"Confound the British!" growled the big man. "I don't mind them, but I hate to be baked afore my time."

The British opposite the orchard, who, like ourselves, had been waiting, were forming in line for an attack. The trumpets were blowing gayly, and the throbbing of the drums betokened the coming conflict. Presently across the fields they came, a long line of flashing bayonets and red coats, with the cavalry on either wing galloping down upon us. General Wayne himself passed along our line, and, like Putnam at Bunker Hill, told our men to be steady and hold their fire until the enemy were so close that they could not miss.

The British fired a volley at us as they rushed across the fields, and then, with many an old score to settle, we rose and poured into them, at short range, a fire that swept away their front ranks and staggered the column. But they recovered, and charged us with the bayonets, and we met them with clubbed rifles, for few of us had bayonets.

In a moment we were in a fierce turmoil of cracking guns, flashing swords, and streaming blood and sweat. The grass was trampled into the earth; the dust arose and clogged our throats and blinded our eyes. Over us the sun, as if rejoicing in the strife and seeking to add to it, poured his fiercest rays upon us, and men fell dead without a wound upon them. A British sergeant rushed at me with drawn sword when I was engaged with another man, and I thought the road to another world was opening before me; but when the Englishman raised his sword to strike, the weapon dropped from his limp fingers to the ground, and he fell over, slain by the sun.

Had the cavalry been lucky enough to get in among us with their sabres, they might have broken our lines and thrust us out of the orchard; but we had emptied many a saddle before they could come up, and the horses that galloped about without riders did as much harm to the enemy as to us. The British showed most obstinate courage, and their leader, a fine man, Colonel Monckton, I afterwards learned his name to be, encouraged them with shouts and the waving of his sword, until a bullet killed him, and he fell between the struggling lines.

"Come on!" I shouted, under the impulse of the moment, to the men near me. "We will take off his body!"

Then we rushed upon the British column. Some of our men seized the body of their fallen leader, and they made a fierce effort to regain it. But the British did not have raw militia to deal with this time, and, however stern they were in the charge, equally stern were we in resisting it. The colonel's body became the prize for which both of us fought; and we retained our hold upon it.

The clamor increased, and the reek of blood and sweat thickened. The pitiless sun beat upon us, and rejoiced as we slew each other. But, however they strove against us, we held fast to the colonel's body; nay, more, we gained ground. Twice the British charged us with all their strength, and each time we hurled them back. Then they gave up the struggle, as well they might, and with honor too, and fell back, leaving us our apple orchard and their colonel's body. We had no intent but to give suitable burial to the fallen chief, and a guard was formed to escort his remains to the rear.

As the broken red line gave ground, some of their men turned and fired a few farewell shots at us. I felt a smart blow on my skull, as if some one had suddenly tapped me there with a hammer. As I threw up my hands with involuntary motion to see what ailed me, black clouds passed of a sudden before my eyes, and the earth began to reel beneath me. Marcel, who was standing near, turned towards me with a look of alarm upon his face. Then the earth slid away from me, and I fell. Ere I touched the ground my senses were gone.

When I opened my eyes again, I thought that only a few minutes had passed since I fell; for above me waved the boughs of one of the very apple-trees beneath which we had fought. Moreover, there were soldiers about, and the signs of fierce contention with arms were still visible. But when I put one of my hands to my head, which felt heavy and dull, I found that it was swathed in many bandages.

"Lie still," said a friendly voice, and the next moment the face of Marcel was bending over me. "You should thank your stars that your skull is so thick and hard, for that British bullet glanced off it and inflicted but a scalp-wound. As it is, you have nothing but good luck. The commander-in-chief himself has been to see you, and has called you a most gallant youth. Also, you have the best nurse in America, who, moreover, takes a special interest in your case."

"But the army! The battle!" I said.

"Disturb not your mighty mind about them," said Marcel. "We failed to destroy the enemy, having to leave that for a later day; but we won the battle, and the British army is retreating towards New York. I imitate it, and now retreat before your nurse."

He went away, and then Mary Desmond stood beside me. But her face was no longer haughty and cold.

"You here!" I cried. "How did this happen?"

"When the American army followed the retreating British, we knew there would be a battle," she said. "So I came with other women to nurse the wounded, and one of them I have watched over a whole night."

She smiled most divinely.

"Then, Mary," I cried, with an energy that no wound could lessen, "will you not marry an American?"

Her answer?

It was not in words, but I saw in her eyes the light that shines for only one, and I asked no more.

THE END

BOOK THREE

MY CAPTIVE

A TALE OF TARLETON'S RAIDERS

(A Revolutionary War Novel)

CHAPTER 1 A Trying Situation

I looked at the prisoner, and I was vexed by doubt. With a battle on one side of him and a woman on the other, what is a man to do? She returned my gaze with great, pure eyes, which seemed to say I was a villain, a monster; yet I had been doing my exact duty, that of a faithful soldier in the cause of the Continental Congress and freedom, while she—a woman, a girl—had presumed to turn from the things for which God had intended her and to meddle with war. I was more than vexed—I was angry: angry at her for attempting such a task, and angry at myself for being forced into a situation so full of troubles.

On the right, in the fringe of woods a quarter of a mile away, the last rifle-shot had been fired, and its echo was speeding across the far hills. The powder flashed no more, and the smoke rose in lazy coils over the ground on which men had fought and some had died. The victors, the captured detail with them, were riding away. I almost fancied I could hear the beat of their horses' hoofs, and the dead, I knew, lay with their faces upturned to the sun, waiting there until the last trump called them to rise again. And here was I, an atom, left in the drift of the armies, cut off from my comrades, and alone with this girl.

The horses shifted about uneasily, stamped their feet, and once mine raised his head and neighed, as if in truth he heard the beating hoofs of the galloping detachment. He knew that his comrades too were leaving him, though I cannot say that it was a desertion intended by either horse or man.

The girl's look of reproach turned to one of inquiry. She sat on a log, her little riding-whip hanging idly in her hand. For the first time I took note of her face—the delicate but firm moulding of each feature; the clear depths of her dark-blue eyes; the bronze gold of her hair, clustering in tiny curls around her forehead; the rose red of her cheeks, like a flush; her lithe, strong young figure. Why is it that when God wishes to make women especially wicked and troublesome He makes them beautiful?

"Well, you rebel," she said, "when do you propose to set me free?"

"When you give your word of honor that you will tell Cornwallis nothing about the strength of Morgan's forces and our present movements."

"That I will not do."

"Then you remain my prisoner."

Yet I would have been a fool even to have taken her word of honor. What woman has any regard for the truth in military matters? If she could find a chance, she would certainly give information that would bring Cornwallis, as well as Tarleton, on Morgan.

"I think that it is enough for Englishmen themselves to fight us without sending their daughters also against us," I said.

"My father did not send me," she said quickly; "I came of my own accord."

"So much the worse," I replied.

But nothing was to be gained by standing there and talking. Besides, it is never well for a soldier to dispute with his prisoner. A captor should bear himself with dignity and reserve. I would show my quality.

I untied the horses and led them to the log on which she was sitting.

"Get up!" I said curtly and in a tone of command.

The natural rose-flush of her cheeks deepened a little.

"You speak as if you were my master," she said.

"That is just what I am—for the present," I replied. "Mount your horse at once."

She gave me a sidewise look from eyes that flashed, but she stood upon the log.

"This log is too low, and the saddle is too high," she said.

I stepped forward and held out my hand to assist her.

"Don't touch me, you rebel!" she cried, and leaped lightly into the saddle.

I felt hurt.

"I wish you wouldn't call me a rebel," I said.

"Why?"

"It's impolite."

"But it's true."

"Well, perhaps it is in a way, and in a way too I am proud of it. Are you proud of your King?"

"Yes."

"It doesn't take much to arouse English pride."

"You will think more of him when the war is over. It will pay you to do so."

"Meanwhile we will wait until then."

"What do you purpose to do with me—keep me a prisoner?"

"It is my misfortune."

"The courtesy of a rebel."

"I shall take you to General Morgan."

"Then Tarleton will rescue me. Your Morgan cannot stand before him."

I was afraid that she spoke the truth. We were outnumbered, and, besides, more than half our force was raw militia. The odds were great against us, and knowing it, I did not reply to her taunt.

While we were talking she sat in the saddle with the easy seat of a good horsewoman. I held my horse loosely by the bridle. She was twiddling the whip in her hands. Suddenly she leaned over and lashed my horse across the eyes with her whip. The blow was given with all her might, and the startled animal reared, jerked the bridle out of my hand, and ran away.

"Good-by, Mr. Rebel!" she shouted, and drawing her whip across her own horse galloped off in the opposite direction.

I believe I swore. I was angry and alarmed too, for this girl, with her messages and accurate news about us, was a formidable enemy, escaped, who might cause the destruction of the entire army of the south and the loss of all the southern colonies. I drew a pistol, it being my idea to kill the horse, but it was a shot that I could not risk. I thrust the weapon back in my pocket and ran after my horse. He was thirty or forty yards away, half-mad with rage and pain, his bridle swinging beside him.

I am a very good runner, but I do not claim to be as swift as a horse. Nevertheless, I made speed as I ran after him, and I whistled and shouted with a vigor that must have convinced him of my intentions. I looked back once, and the girl and the horse she rode were growing smaller as they sped over the desolate and unfenced fields. My need of a horse too was growing more pressing. Mounted, there was hope; afoot, there was none.

I whistled all the calls that a friendly and well-treated horse should know, and meantime did not neglect to run after him with the best speed that I could command. Presently he seemed to understand and to remember that I was not responsible for the blow. He slackened his pace, looked back over his shoulder at me, and whinnied. I whistled encouragingly, he whinnied again, and, remembering who I was, his best friend, came to a full stop, for he was a most intelligent animal. In half a minute I overtook him, leaped into the saddle, and turned his head the other way.

"Now, old horse," I cried, "you can gallop, but you gallop my way."

I wore my spurs, and I gave him a touch of the steel. That was enough, for he was always ambitious and proud of his speed, and away we flew over the fields after the disappearing girl. She was a full quarter of a mile away, and her figure was growing dim on the horizon. Another quarter of a mile and she would be in the woods, where the concealment of the trees would enable her to elude my pursuit. Moreover, these English girls are often daring horsewomen, and even at the distance I could see that she rode like a trooper. But I knew the country and she did not, and I hoped to secure from it some chance that would enable me to overtake her.

I encouraged my horse. I did more than encourage—I appealed to his pride and his sense of gratitude. I reminded him how I had ridden him all the way from the Hudson when I came south with Greene; how I had tended him and cared for him and fed him, often when I was compelled to go hungry myself. I appealed to him now not to let that girl escape when so much depended on her capture, when I would be eternally disgraced, and he with me, if we permitted ourselves to be tricked and outwitted at such a time by one red-cheeked English girl.

He was a sensible animal, and he understood. He said nothing, not even a little snort, but his stride lengthened, and the swift and regular beat of his hoofs on the turf was music.

"Good horse, Old Put, good lad!" I said. I had named him Put, after Old Put, the famous Connecticut General, because he was so reliable and steady. He shook his ears slightly as a sign that he would do his best for me, having no time to say more, and ran a little faster. I kept a sharp watch for stones and holes in the ground, having no mind to risk a fall, which might ruin all, and nursed my comrade's strength, for on land as well as sea a stern chase is a long one.

The figure of the girl and the horse she rode was growing larger; good proof that I was gaining, which was not enough, however, for I might continue to do so, and yet she could elude me in the woods unless I was close upon her when she reached them. Her long hair had fallen down and was streaming behind her like a ribbon of spray with the sunshine on it, but I felt like giving that yellow hair a jerk just then could I have put my hands upon it.

"Steady, Put!" I said to my faithful comrade. "Do you see that girl with the yellow hair? Yes? Well, note the horse that she is riding, a common troop-horse, clumsy, ill-bred, no pedigree. Are you going to let yourself be beaten by him?"

His ears wagged violently, and he ran a foot to the second faster. We struck a piece of beautiful turf, evidently an old field left to itself until it could recover its fertility, and with the soft grass deadening and easing his footfalls Old Put raced for life. I could almost count the yards that we gained, and still she was not in the forest. She had not looked back until then, and it was a hasty glance, followed by a quick lashing of her mount. I judged that she too had noticed the gain and would now be unmerciful to her horse. I was exultant, willing to boast of it, and I shared my feelings with Old Put.

"Notice that yellow-haired girl again, Put," I said. "When we catch her this time we will take care that she does not serve us such a trick again. If we cannot trust an Englishman, Put, how on earth can we put any faith in an English woman?"

Put had received a slight slash once from the sabre of an Englishman who, offering to surrender to me, had tried to back out of it, and he knew what I meant.

For the first time he uttered a slight snort, called one new muscle into play, and we steadily shortened the distance between us and the girl.

She would have got into the wood a few moments later, but she abruptly reined in her horse, turned him half about, and galloped off to the left. I guessed the trouble at once. The heavy rains often wash great gullies in our South Carolina soil, and a kind Providence, wishing to oblige me, had placed one of these in her way. It was equal to a gain of two hundred feet without an effort, and I turned Old Put at once into the course she was taking.

"Don't you see, Put," I said, "that the Lord is on our side, and she and that burnt-brown cob of hers, who has passed most of his life hitched to a sutler's wagon, will be delivered into our hands?"

Old Put fairly neighed, his first real expression of triumph. He was as sure of the victory now as I, and I had confidence in the judgment of my old comrade.

"Stop! stop!" I shouted to the girl. "If you don't stop, I'll shoot!"

I had a long-barrelled horse-pistol, which I drew and flourished magnificently. I was within hearing though not shooting range, and I trusted that I would be able to frighten her into yielding.

But she did not stop. She had worn her whip into shreds, and thin red streams of blood zigzagged across the horse's sides, but she pounded on with the stump. I felt a genuine pity for her horse, hack though he was, but none for her.

CHAPTER 2 Keeping a Prisoner

No more gullies thrust themselves across the way, and the girl was within twenty feet of the wood. She took another hurried look at me, and seeing my rapid gain, alarm appeared on her face. She drew a little toy pistol from the cloak she wore and levelled it at me, or at least that seemed to be her intention. I call it a toy pistol, because I, a full-grown soldier, would have felt deep shame had I been caught with such a weapon in my possession. She pulled the trigger, and the bullet cut the uncomplaining air somewhere, but not in my neighborhood. This bombardment cost her at least twenty feet of the distance between us, but she thrust the terrible weapon back in her cloak and galloped on, with Old Put thundering at her heels. Then she was into the wood, and I was not far behind, shouting to her to stop, telling her that I would surely overtake her and she was merely wasting the breath of both our horses and our own. Still she paid no heed, guiding her horse between the trees and through the bushes with considerable skill.

But, seeing the wood thicken presently, I was tempted to laugh. It was obvious now that the end of the race had come and I was the winner. The forest became so dense, the bushes clustering in thickets and the vines interlacing from tree to tree, that it formed an impenetrable wall. What I had feared would help her had been my best ally.

She stopped short and sat stiffly on her horse, her back turned to me. I wondered if she would draw out that amazing pistol again and threaten me with it, but she made no such attempt, evidently having arrived at wisdom at last. She dropped the stump of her switch on the ground and kept the back of her head towards me. Some beams of sunshine came through the tall trees and gleamed across the long curls of tawny gold, tinging them for the moment as if with fire.

I rode up by her side, and then, as she seemed to ignore me, I asked Old Put to take me around in front of her. There I could see her face. It was pale, sad, and reproachful, and a tear ran down either cheek. For the moment I felt a little pity for her despite her perverse nature and all the trouble she had given me. .

"I am sorry I have to do this," I said.

"Sorry for what?" she asked.

I saw that I had made a mistake. One should always be polite to a woman, but never apologetic.

"That I had to overtake you," I replied.

"Yours is the better horse," she said, wiping away the tears with an angry little brush of the hand. "I like to ride, and I always enjoy a good race. That was the reason I challenged you to it, though I did not know you had such a good horse."

This was a new view of the case, but I had a thought, or, rather, a reflection.

"It was a good race," I said, "but wasn't that a false start?"

"How so?"

"Didn't you take an advantage?"

"I was entitled to it. I am a woman."

"So women expect to carry that rule even into warfare?"

"Certainly."

I was glad that I had never been forced to wage war with one of the feminine sex before, and hoped never to meet the necessity again. One likes to stick to the rules in military matters, and then he has some idea what to expect.

"The horses are very tired," I said.

"They look like it," she replied.

The poor animals were panting, and their coats were damp. I took the reins of her horse from her hand and held them firmly in mine.

"What are you going to do?" she asked.

"I think I'd better hold the reins of both," I said. "Will you please dismount?"

I set her a good example by jumping down myself. She could not say that the prisoner was compelled to walk while the captor rode. I stepped forward to assist her, but again she refused my help, and sprang to the ground unassisted.

Old Put gazed angrily at the girl who had struck him. Then he snorted with triumph and looked contemptuously at the horse beside him. The latter seemed to be ashamed of himself, and his attitude was apologetic, but he had done his best, and therefore should not have been blamed.

"Come," I said, "we will get out of this wood and walk back across the fields. Keep by my side. I will watch you; I do not want any more treachery."

I spoke with great sternness, as the mite of pity I felt when I saw the tears had gone. She obeyed with surprising meekness and walked beside me, while I led the horses, holding both bridles in one hand. I was glad that I had been so sharp with her, and I saw now it was the proper way with rebellious women. A man has only to show towards them a stern, unyielding temper, and they submit at once. She was crushed, and again that mite of pity rose up in my breast, for nearly always we feel a trace of sympathy for those whom we have vanquished.

Her head drooped, there was a faint appeal in her eyes, and her walk showed weariness. She seemed to have forgotten that her hair was loose down her back, as she let it hang in long curls of gold, burnished where the sunshine fell upon it, dark in the shadow.

The yellow of the sun was deepening into red, a sign that the afternoon was waning, and I was anxious about the future, for which, like a good soldier, I felt it my duty to provide. She must have seen the care in my face, for she asked,—

"Are you thinking how we shall reach General Morgan?"

"General Morgan or someone else."

"Is it far to his camp?"

"I cannot say. I do not know where he is. The American camp just now is of a shifting character."

"To keep out of Tarleton's way, I suppose?"

"Either that or to find him."

Then she seemed to repent of her gibe at our running away from the British.

"But General Morgan is a brave man, I have heard," she said.

That warmed my heart.

"He is a brave man," I replied, "and, what is more, he is a fine soldier and general."

"What a pity he is not on the right side!"

"Let's not quarrel about that again."

I thought I could afford to be generous, my situation was so superior to hers.

After that we walked along in silence for several minutes. The red tint of the sun deepened; faint shadows appeared in the blue velvet of the sky.

"I want to ask you one question," she said presently.

"There is nothing to prevent your asking it."

"But I want an answer, direct and correct."

"If it does not interfere with the progress of the campaign."

"I don't think it will do that."

"What is it?"

"What is your name?"

I laughed. It had never occurred to me before to tell her.

"It is true," I said, "that we have not had an introduction, though we are seeing a good deal of each other's society, but it is not too late. My name is Philip Marcel."

"Why, that sounds like French, and I thought you were an American."

"Both are true. I am an American, and the name Marcel used to be French. I am of French descent partly, and I may have British blood too, though I shall not boast of it. There are many of us in South Carolina."

"But I thought you were Northern. You said you had been serving in the Northern army of the rebels——"

"The patriots!"

"Well, the patriots, then, under Mr. Washington."

"General Washington!"

"Well, General Washington."

"Yes, I have been serving in the Northern army of the patriots under General Washington, but he has sent me south with General Greene and the others, mostly Southerners themselves, to redeem this part of the country from the British raiders. But I am a South Carolinian."

She relapsed into silence again, and I imitated her example. I had enough of importance anyhow to think about without talking to a girl, an enemy, but presently I recollected.

"Pardon me," I said, "but you have forgotten something too."

"What is it?"

"You have not told me your name."

"That is true, and the introduction cannot be complete until I do."

"Certainly not."

"My name is Howard."

"Howard! What Howard?"

"Julia Howard. My father is John Sinclair Howard, major in Tarleton's legion. I was born in Devonshire, England, and I am here with my father, having nobody else to look after me, until such time as these rebellious colonies are put down and restored in their allegiance to their lawful sovereign, George III., King of England, Scotland, Wales, and Ireland, God bless him!"

I thought that God could find something better to do than to waste His time blessing King George, a fat German blockhead, but I kept the thought to myself just then.

"Then, mark my words, Miss Julia Howard, of Devonshire, England," I said, "you have come here to stay."

"I don't believe it."

"It is a prediction; it will come true."

Her look was full of unbelief, and we relapsed into silence again. The shadows grew in the sky. The sun blazed like fire, and my old trouble about the future came back.

The horses ceased to pant and walked now with springy steps, their weariness gone. Old Put thrust his nose under my arm and whinnied gently. He was talking in the language that we two understood. I rubbed his soft nose.

"Yes, old fellow," I said to him, "you have done your duty well, as you always do. We'll stop soon, and then I'll find you something to eat."

He whinnied again and rubbed his nose on my sleeve, for he understood.

"He looks like a good horse," said the girl.

"Never better," I replied, and with emphasis.

"I like a good horse," she said.

"So do I. That's the reason I'm so fond of Old Put."

"I wonder if he would be as friendly with me?"

"I don't know. He usually likes old friends best, but still he is a horse of fine taste."

Her evident admiration of Old Put appealed to me, and I thought I would give her the little compliment. Women like such things, and, again, I felt as if I could afford to be generous.

She put her hand upon his nose and stroked it gently. It was a white, well-shaped hand, with pretty, tapering fingers. Old Put must have admired it. He assisted in the rubbing task, swaying his nose gently to and fro, and he whinnied once softly, after his custom when he was talking to me. He seemed to have forgotten the blow she had given him.

"See," she said triumphantly, "he has found a new friend, a good friend, and he knows it. He is almost as fond of me as he is of you."

I was surprised, greatly surprised. Heretofore Old Put had always proved himself to be an excellent judge of character, and now he was putting his trust in this English girl, who had shown herself to be unworthy of any confidence whatever. Poor Old Put! Another masculine dupe! He was growing old; he was falling into his dotage. I felt a certain sadness at these signs of mental decay in my faithful horse. But they marched on, his silky nose pressed closely against her arm, and meanwhile the sun was sinking and the shadows were deepening and lengthening.

"I do not think it is necessary for us to walk any more," I said. "The horses are now thoroughly rested from their race and are willing to do their part, which is to carry us."

She looked at her ugly brown hack in some dismay.

"He's such a rough traveller, I believe I'd rather continue walking," she said.

He certainly had a most irregular, jumping kind of gait, which would make him an unpleasant mount for anybody, but there seemed to be no resource. Horses were not running loose around us for me to catch.

"But we can't help it," I said. "We can ride slowly. If he misbehaves, use that switch you have picked up."

She walked steadily on.

"Now, if he were like this one," she said, stroking Old Put's nose, "I would be glad to ride again."

"Suppose I change the saddles, then," I said, "and let you ride Old Put?"

It was a great concession for me to make, but her appreciation of my horse had touched me for the moment.

"Do you think he would let me?" she said, looking at Old Put doubtfully and timidly.

Now I was indignant. It was a slur upon the character of Old Put, one of the gentlest and best bred of horses, to insinuate that he would behave badly with a lady on his back.

"No man except myself has ridden him in years," I replied. "Perhaps no woman has ever ridden him at all, but that is no reason why one should not ride him now."

"But I am afraid," she protested again in timid fashion. All her courage seemed to have gone. Again I say you have only to be stern with a woman to keep her at your feet.

"Nonsense!" I said a little roughly. "We'll stop talking about this and do it at once."

I halted the horses and changed the saddles, while she looked doubtfully on. Old Put submitted like an angel, and I drew the girth tight. Then I continued,—

"Now, if you would know what a real saddle-horse is, Miss Howard, just jump up there."

"Will you help me?"

Another proof of her subdued condition!

I held out my hand in most gallant fashion. She leaned on it a moment for support, and sprang into the saddle. Then, giving Old Put a cut with the switch which she had picked up, she galloped away.

"Good-by, Mr. Marcel!" she shouted. "I ride the better horse now."

She turned Old Put's nose to the southwest, and away she went at the very best speed of which my good horse was capable, and that was much. Her yellow hair flew in the wind, as before, like the streamers of a defiant battle-flag, and either with or without intent the red cap she wore was set rakishly and saucily on one side of her head.

CHAPTER 3 The Merit of a Good Horse

I paused, not to swear this time, but for a momentary reflection on the vanity of man and the deceitfulness of woman in taking advantage of it, and then I sprang upon the back of that old brown hack—confound him for an army mule without the ears!—and gave chase. I had no switch or whip, but I rowelled him and kicked him in the sides until I frightened him into a greater speed than he or anyone else believed to dwell within his long frame. He gave a wild snort, and we plunged after the fleet girl, rocking and swaying like a boat in a stormy sea, but even with such exertion he could not compare with Old Put. Despite the anxiety of the moment, I noted his inferiority with some pride, but then I remembered how much depended upon the success of the pursuit, and continued to urge on my own mount.

Strive and strain as we could and ride and thump as I would with all my arms and legs, we lost ground rapidly. The girl turned her head once to look at me, and I thought I saw a look of triumph on her face, but I suppose it was my imagination, which was industriously tormenting me just then. I groaned at the certainty of her escape, and then hope seized me, for I remembered suddenly that I too had a trick to play. Old Put and I possessed a common language in which we often talked with perfect understanding. I put two fingers to my lips and blew between them a long, shrill whistle, which cut the air and travelled like the scream of a fife. It was a request, a command even, to him to stop and wait for me. He twisted his long neck in the manner of one listening, looking back at me to see what I meant, but he went on, though with slightly diminished speed, his manner indicating that he was uncertain what I had said.

The girl was belaboring him with the switch, for she must have noticed his decreasing gait. I whistled again, and as Old Put's pace sank to a trot she beat him fiercely. A third whistle, and Old Put, now in perfect accord with me, stopped stock still; not only that, but he faced about and neighed joyously. The girl threw the remains of her switch upon the ground and began to cry, not pitifully, but angrily, fiercely. I rode up slowly and held out my hand to Old Put, who rubbed his nose against it. He knew his master and best friend. Never had I beaten him, and now there were stripes and welts on his side where she had pounded him.

"Why did you not tell me what sort of a horse he was," she cried, "and then I would not have made myself look so ridiculous, sitting here as if I had been tied and waiting for you to come up?"

"Miss Howard," I replied in some astonishment, "do you expect me to show you the way to escape?"

"I do not expect anything from you, a rebel," she said, "Do not speak to me again."

All right; that suited me. I did not wish to talk to her. She used words only to inveigle me into some incautious mood. But it was necessary for me to tell her to dismount in order that I might change saddles again, as I did not intend to give her another such opportunity. I did not offer to assist her, having had enough of that, but stood beside the brown hack, watching her with a look that was now strictly military.

"Why don't you help me down?" she said angrily. "Have you no courtesy for a lady?"

"You have declined such assistance from a rebel before," I replied to her unexpected question.

"And I decline again. You needn't offer it," she said abruptly, springing to the ground, when I had no thought of offering it.

As soon as she was off his back Old Put showed the greatest distrust of her and aversion. He shied as far away from her as my hold on his bridle would let him, and his big, dark eyes shone with wrath. I was glad that he had come back to his senses, and he, like I, should have known her thoroughly from the first and always.

"We don't intend to be deceived by her again, do we, old comrade?" said I to him.

He nodded his head in emphatic fashion, and his big eye winked intelligently. Her face flushed a little, but she took no other notice.

"Look well at this lady, Put," I said. "Do you note her?"

He nodded.

"She's English, we're Americans, and therefore she's an enemy and not to be trusted. Watch her well," I continued.

He nodded violently.

"Now, Miss Howard," I said severely, "I've changed those saddles, and they are ready for our use when we need them, but meanwhile we'll walk again, as we've tired our horses out for the second time, and all your fault too."

She said nothing, but walked on in the way which I had indicated, keeping eight or ten feet from me. She had ceased to cry and had given her features a fixed and angry set.

I was troubled greatly. We had wasted so much time over her futile efforts to escape that the problem of a night's shelter had grown more difficult and pressing, and I intended that my attention should not be diverted from it again. Therefore

I would take precautions. I drew from my pocket a long silk handkerchief, a trophy of the Monmouth campaign, which I had preserved with great care.

"Hold out your hands," I said.

"What would you do?" she asked, turning upon me a look of fire.

But I was firm. My experience had been too great.

"Hold out your hands," I repeated. "I intend to bind them together. You play too many tricks."

"You are not a gentleman."

"You have told me that three or four times already. It won't bear further repetition."

"I will not submit to such a thing."

"Then I will have to use force, which will make it much more unpleasant for you."

I hated to do what I had planned. It was rude and severe, but then there are few who have had women prisoners like mine, and consequently there are few who are in a position to judge me. I prefer greatly to deal with the regular forces, but in this case I had no choice, and so I strengthened my will and proceeded.

"Hold out your wrists," I repeated. "I shall not hurt you. I merely wish to keep you out of further mischief."

"I shall never forgive you," she said.

I could afford to laugh at such a threat.

"I trust that nobody will forgive me until I ask it," I replied.

She looked at me, her eyes full of rebellion. I thought she was going to raise her hand to strike me, but women are so changeable and uncertain. Instead she held out her hands meekly.

I bound her wrists together and noticed that they were white and well moulded. The handkerchief was soft and could not pain her at all, and, besides, her hands were bound in front of her and not behind her. She need feel no inconvenience, but she must realize that her opportunities for mischief were diminished vastly. Old Put looked at her with an air of triumph, as much as to say, "Now, miss, you are being punished, and punished deservedly, for beating me so much." That seemed to be her own understanding of herself.

We resumed our march, the horses walking behind us. The rim of the sun was now meeting the rim of the earth, and the western skies were tinged with ruddy fire. In the east the misty gray of twilight was descending on field and forest, and the chill of night was creeping over everything. Even in our South Carolina latitudes the nights are cold in midwinter, and I shivered as a twilight wind, with a raw edge to it, swept over the plain.

There was a heavy cloak hanging at her saddle-horn, for she had not ventured upon her journey unprepared. I took it off and threw it over her shoulders. It fell below her waist like a greatcoat, and I buttoned it securely around her neck.

"You are a barbarian," she said.

"I know it," I replied, "but I do not intend to let you suffer more than is necessary for your own good. That is the kind of barbarians we are in this country."

The land was lone and desolate, for we were on the sterile slopes of the hills. It was thinly peopled at the best of times, but now, raided incessantly by Tarleton's Legion, which knew no mercy to anything, whether animate or inanimate, and plundered too by wild bands which claimed to belong to either army, as the occasion served, and perhaps belonged to neither, the people had fled to securer regions, where one side or the other was master. Only those who have seen it know the sufferings of a country harried by opposing armies and predatory bands. I had hoped to find some friendly farmer bolder than the rest with whom my prisoner and I could obtain shelter, or if not that, at least an abandoned house which would give us a roof, but I saw no sign of a human face except our own, and no roof appeared either in the fields or among the trees. It was a solitude bleak and cold, and the declining sun, now half-way behind the earth, warned me that it would soon be time to stop. The darkness would be upon us, and in a land of hills, gullies, and no roads we could not travel well without light.

Despairing of such shelter as I had expected, I turned our course towards a thick grove of trees rising like a great castle on the left. When we entered it, the shadows already made darkness there, and the night-wind moaned among the dry branches of the trees. I saw the girl shiver, and again I felt pity for her in spite of all that she had tried to do, though I lost none of my distrust and caution.

Almost in the centre of the grove was a small open space, sheltered from the rush of cold air by the great trees which grew so thickly around it. It seemed to me the likeliest spot we could find for a camp. I hitched the horses to boughs of the trees and took from my pocket a small flask of that cheer which a good soldier seldom neglects. I drew the stopper and handed it to the girl.

"Take a little of this," I said. "You must if you do not expect to catch your death of cold."

"I would if I could," she replied, "but I cannot while my hands are tied."

"I had forgotten the handkerchief," I continued, "but I don't think we'll need it any longer. You have been warned sufficiently."

I unbound her wrists and replaced the handkerchief in my pocket.

"But don't forget," I said, "that this handkerchief is an evidence that I have put my mark upon you and that you belong to me—that is, you are my prisoner until such time as I choose to give you up."

Her face flushed.

"I will not endure such talk," she replied, "from a rebel who within six months may be hanged by his outraged King for treason."

"You can't escape it," I said, "and the King can't hang me before he catches me. It's a long way from London to South Carolina, and I hear the King is fat and lazy and suffers from seasickness."

But she drank the whiskey, just a little of it, though enough to put more sparkle in her eye, and handed the flask to me without a word of thanks. Then she sat down on a fallen tree and looked idly in front of her, as if she had no interest whatever in anything.

I gathered up armfuls of the dry brushwood and tossed them into a heap, which I ignited with the flint and steel I always carried. The fire blazed up rapidly and snapped as it bit through the wood. Its merry crackling drowned the desolate moan of the wind, and the long red ribbons of flame and the fast-forming bed of live coals threw out a kindly heat that fended off the chill of the night. Even the girl, angry and humiliated as she seemed to be, felt the influence of the light and warmth, and edged along the log until she was much closer and the fire could shine directly upon her face. Old Put was frank in his appreciation, coming to the full length of his tether and wagging his head in a manner which said to me as plain as day, "You have done well." Even the stupid brown hack understood and imitated Old Put's example.

Higher rose the fire and drove back the shadows, but the darkness was now rolling up to the circle of light, and beyond the sparkle of the flames began to rise like a wall. The sun was gone, and a faint, fading pink tint in the west marked the way his flight had taken him. Over all the world the twilight drooped, and the winter wind mourned the dead day.

"Are there ghosts in the forest?" suddenly asked the girl.

"None that I ever heard of," I said.

"It is so unlike England."

"How?"

"So much wilder."

I had heard of their forests there, or rather what they call forests, —some acres of trees, with the undergrowth cut away and the lawns shaven, every rod patrolled by keepers or workmen, a mere plaything of a forest,—but here in America are the real forests, just as nature made them, the desolate wilderness through which the wild animals howl, while the lone wind plays its song on the branches or leaves of the trees. This is the real forest, a place in which man becomes about as big as a cork on the sea. Never the lone hunter, though fifty years his home, fails to feel its immensity and desolation. The girl drew the edges of her cloak a little more tightly and moved as close to the fire as the end of the log would allow her.

"If you will permit me," I said, "I will give you a better seat by the fire than that."

She rose without a word, and I rolled the log well within the warmth of the blaze. She resumed her seat, and the firelight flickered and played over her face, tinting her cheeks with deep red and spangling her bronze-gold hair with patches of scarlet and crimson. The little red cap had been pulled securely down on her head, and, sitting there in the alternate light and darkness, her figure lithe and strong, she looked like some Saxon wood-nymph.

But I did not cease my good deeds. I call myself a forethoughtful trooper, and from the saddle-bags I carried across my saddle-bow I took a cold chicken, a piece of cold boiled ham, and some hard biscuits, a dinner fit for a prince, or rather an honest American citizen, which was better, in these hard times of war. To this royal collation I added a canteen well filled with water, remembered the stout little flask in my breast-pocket, and the repast was complete, all but the serving.

Her eyes sparkled at the sight of the good things. Wood-nymphs, Saxon or other, must eat.

"Let me carve the chicken," she said.

"You have neither a table, plates, nor a knife," I said.

"This log will serve as a table, some of those clean dry leaves as plates, and you can lend me a knife."

"How could I lend you a knife, a weapon, after all the tricks you have tried to play upon me? You don't forget this, do you?"

I took the little toy pistol with which she had tried to shoot me out of my pocket and held it up before her, but she laughed. Women don't seem to have any conscience, or at least they forget their crimes, which is convenient for their peace of mind.

"Give me the knife," she said, "and don't waste time. I'm hungry."

I distrusted her as much as ever, even more, but I opened the blade of my clasp-knife and handed it to her.

"A very good knife," she said, "but I have no doubt it was stolen from an Englishman. Ah, here it is—the name of an English maker on the blade!"

"It was not stolen!" I exclaimed indignantly. "I took it from him fairly at the battle of Monmouth, where he fell into my hands."

"That, I suppose, is a good enough title for a rebel," she said, and began to carve the chicken.

It was a fine, fat chicken, beautifully roasted, and she showed that she knew how to carve, for she deftly clipped off a leg, which she held up before me.

"That looks fat and good to eat," she said, "and it's a fine chicken, but I've no doubt it was stolen from a loyal subject of King George."

"It's not true!" I exclaimed in some wrath. "He was a Tory farmer, I admit, but I did not steal the chicken. I took it before his eyes, and he never said a word."

"Afraid, I suppose; but it doesn't make any difference to you. It will taste just as good to a rebel. Here, take your piece on this big, clean leaf, and eat."

I obeyed. She carved off a portion for herself too, and ate with a good appetite. Then I handed her the canteen of water and told her to drink.

"Don't be afraid," I said. "I took that water out of a clear brook in the wilderness, and the land through which it flowed belonged to God, not to any Englishman or Tory."

"But how about the canteen?" she asked. "Did you steal that from any English soldier or take it by violence, which is worse?"

I showed her the name of the maker, a Boston man, upon it.

"A vile rebel town, the worst of them all," she said.

But she took a good drink out of it, and when she handed it back to me I imitated her example. Then, while the fire crackled and blazed higher and the circle of light widened and the darkness beyond it thickened, we ate and drank, and I grew cheerful. I had defeated all her attempts, and to-morrow I would find Morgan and give her into other hands and be rid of all my troubles; yet I was compelled to admit once again that she was very beautiful with the firelight flickering and playing over her face and hair, but all the world knows, as I have said, that the handsome women are most dangerous, the most cunning, and I was on my guard against any new attempt of hers to escape. Still, when I looked around at the blackness of the night and heard the sigh of the cold wind above the crackling of the fire, I did not think that she would dare to attempt it. I knew no woman would venture alone on a winter night into that uncanny wilderness, and, knowing it, I felt easy.

CHAPTER 4 Supper and Song

The horses looked jealously at our supper. I was sorry for them, especially Old Put, whose great, intelligent eyes said in the purest English, "I too am hungry, master." But I could do nothing. I had no provender for horses, and so I told him to wait as best he could until morning and I would find something for him, if I had to rob a patriot farmer to do it. He bowed his head in resignation like the wise horse he was, while the brown hack, not so well bred, tugged at his bridle-rein and thrashed about until I threatened him with a big stick.

After the chicken the girl served the cold ham and drank from the canteen again. I did likewise. Moreover, I urged her to wet her lips at the flask a second time as a further precaution against cold, which she did literally and no more. I was liberal rather than literal, for I was a soldier and knew its value. I took my blanket from my saddlebow and urged her to wrap it around herself, but she said "No;" that her heavy cloak was sufficient, and she would not deprive me, even if I was a misguided rebel. I saw that she spoke truly, as her cloak was of the most ample character, and so, having no further compunction, I wrapped the blanket around me, Indian style, and, sitting down on the dry leaves in front of the fire, leaned my head against the log. She sat on the log at the other end, leaning her head against a dead bough which was thrust straight up in the air. I had put the remains of the provisions back in my saddle-bags.

Triumphant, warm, well fed, my cheerfulness, my satisfaction with myself, increased. I stared into the bed of red coals and saw figures, pictures, there. Near the centre of the bed the coals had fallen into such shape that I could trace distinctly the epaulets of a general, and I knew that those epaulets were for me. The coals crumbled into new shapes and built the house which was to be mine when the war was victoriously over and I was ready to retire to it with my honors. She too seemed to be engaged in the same business, for she was staring with half-closed eyes into the dreamy coals.

"Why are you a rebel?" she asked. "Is it from pure perverseness? They say all you Americans are so."

"They tell many things about us in England that are not true," I replied, "and this is one of them. The English themselves have often been rebels, and their present royal family, one of the worst they have ever had,—and they have had the Stuarts,—was placed on the throne by a just rebellion."

"You must know," she replied, "that in England the character of the sovereign is nothing. It is the sovereign principle. The worse the sovereign, the better the court likes him."

We relapsed into silence and our study of the red coals. Old Put whinnied gently, raised his head, and looked beyond the fire, as if he saw something in the darkness impenetrable to all but horse eyes.

"I'd better look to that," I said. "Old Put is not going to give a warning for nothing. He has a character to lose."

"A wild-cat, maybe," she suggested.

"Perhaps, but I'll see."

I rose, still keeping my blanket wrapped around me, and ordered her to stay where she was under pain of being bound again. She promised, and I believed that she would not stir from her position on the log. The darkness and the desolation were not inviting.

I walked out into the black bank of the night, but could neither see nor find anything. I made a complete circuit around the oasis of light from the fire, and all was peaceful and quiet. I returned to the log, ready to scold Old Put for giving a false alarm, but refrained, reflecting that he might be nervous and irritable, owing to his lack of food.

"What did you find?" asked the girl, looking at me with bright eyes.

"Nothing."

"I thought you wouldn't find anything. It was a wild-cat, or maybe a harmless little squirrel."

"Aren't you afraid of the wild animals?"

"Not with such a brave rebel as you near me."

I opened my eyes a little wider and looked at her. It was the first time that she had complimented me, even in that half-handed way, and I was surprised.

"I thought you did not allow me the possession of any desirable quality whatsoever," I said.

"You are improving," she replied. "Perhaps it is due to my society. I may yet make you a loyal follower of King George and save you from the hangman."

I had my doubts about the "loyalty," which is a term devised for the protection of sovereigns in their crimes, but I said nothing just then. She too relapsed into silence. The heap of coals grew and glowed in the depths with deep crimsons and scarlets, throwing out a generous heat and wooing me to sleep. Despite my sense of caution and the efforts of my will, my eyelids drooped. The castles in the coals became more indistinct and wavered as if they were made of red mist.

Old Put whinnied again and raised his head high in the air, like one who listens. I was wide awake in an instant and on my feet again.

"Put," I said, "if I find that you have given a false alarm a second time you shall have nothing to eat in the morning."

"I wouldn't bother about it," said the girl. "It's only a squirrel or a rabbit. Any horse would notice the passing of such an animal. Their senses are keener than ours."

She was growing very considerate of me!

But I searched the wood again, and finding nothing returned to my comfortable place. Old Put was restless and shuffled about; but, angry at his idle alarms, I commanded him roughly to keep quiet, and he obeyed.

The girl was humming softly to herself, as if she were thinking of her far-away English home. I supposed she was lonely and homesick, and again some pity for her crept into my heart.

"Are you singing of your sweetheart?" I asked, meaning to cheer her up.

"I have none," she replied.

"Not now, perhaps, but you will have some day."

"That is a different matter."

"What kind of a sweetheart would you choose?"

"A soldier, a gallant English soldier, one loyal to his King through all."

She continued to hum her little song, whatever it was. Something stirred in the wood, and Old Put, despite my previous command, whinnied and stamped his feet.

"Confound that beast, whatever it may be!" I said. "It must be a wild-cat attracted by the light of our fire."

"Let the wild-cat go," she said. "Listen and I will sing you a song that will tell you what my future betrothed and husband shall be. It's an old Scotch song of devotion and loyalty, but we English sing it too, and like it as well as the Scotch. 'Dumbarton's Drums' we call it."

"Sing," I said.

Then she sang:

Dumbarton's drums beat bonnie O,

When they mind me of my dear Johnnie O!

How happy am I

When my soldier is by,

While he kisses and blesses his Annie O!

Tis a soldier alone can delight me O,
For his graceful looks do invite me O!
While guarded in his arms
I'll fear no war's alarms,
Neither danger nor death shall e'er fright me O!

My love is a handsome laddie O,
Genteel, but ne'er foppish or gaudy O!
Though commissions are dear,
Yet I'll buy him one this year,
For he'll serve no longer a cadie O!
A soldier has honor and bravery O,
Unacquainted with rogues and their knavery O!
He minds no other thing
But the ladies or the king,
For every other care is but slavery O!

Then I'll be the captain's lady O!
Farewell, all my friends and my daddy O!
I'll wait no more at home,
But I'll follow with the drum,
And whene'er that beats I'll be ready O!
Dumbarton's drums sound bonnie O!
They are sprightly like my dear Johnnie O!
How happy I shall be
When on my soldier's knee,
And he kisses and blesses his Annie O!

Her voice was deep and true, and the old war ballad was music in my ears. As the melody rose and fell in the lonely night my eyes drooped again and my brain became dim with advancing slumbers, like a child soothed to sleep by the song of his mother. I was tired as a dog, I had ridden long and far and had worked much, and every nerve and muscle in me cried aloud for rest. But I roused myself as she finished and the last note of her song died in the darkness.

"That is a proper military song," I said, "and nobly sung, but I object to the sentiments of your hero. He minds no other thing but the ladies or the King. The ladies are all right, but no King. Leave the King out!"

Old Put was stamping his feet again.

"That's right, Put," I said. "Applaud the song, for it was well sung, though you and I, who are good Americans, don't altogether like the sentiments. That, I take it, is an old song of loyalty to the Stuarts. It is a singular thing to me how wholesome-minded English people can invest the Stuarts, whom they kicked out of their country, with so much romance and charm when all history shows they were an utterly debased lot, and nobody knows it better than the English themselves."

"The sentiments of the song, King and all, are perfectly correct, and I'll sing that verse to you again."

She looked at me with a look half of defiance, half a smile, and sang:

My love is a handsome laddie O,

Genteel, but ne'er foppish or gaudy O!

Though commissions are dear,

Yet I'll buy him one this year,

For he'll serve no longer a cadie O!

A soldier has honor and bravery O,

Unacquainted with rogues and their knavery O!

He minds no other thing

But the ladies or the king,

For every other care is but slavery O!

She sang it still more softly and gently than before, and, though my eyelids drooped again, I turned my gaze from the bed of coals to her face. The firelight played ruddily over her eyes and cheeks, and the expression there seemed tender and far-away, as if her thoughts had gone from this dark night and the war-torn fields of South Carolina to the green English meadows and peaceful sunshine.

When she finished, I raised my hands and clapped them together.

"Well done!" I said. "Well done!"

"Done well enough for us," said someone, and strong hands reached over the log and grasped me by the wrists. My languor and my sleepiness were gone in an instant, and I made a powerful effort to wrench myself loose, but I had been taken too suddenly. Three or four men flung themselves upon me, and I was crushed under a great weight, while the firm grip was still on my wrists. I managed to deal somebody a heavy kick and heard a grunt of pain, but in a few seconds I was overpowered, and, like a wise man, ceased to struggle further.

Singularly enough, one of my early thoughts in that moment was of relief that Old Put should prove to be a true prophet, having enjoyed such a good character in that respect so long. I had been a fool not to take his warning more seriously. Then I wondered why the girl did not cry out at the sight of struggling men and the sound of oaths and blows, a violent medley usually very terrifying to women. I caught one glimpse of her, and she was sitting on the log, her back against the upthrust bough, leaning upon it as lazily as if she were in a rocking-chair in a parlor. The firelight still played over her face and eyes, but the soft and tender expression which had pleased me was gone. Instead the look that she turned upon me was a mixture of dislike, malice, and triumph.

After meeting such a glance it was a relief to me to look another way and see who had captured me.

CHAPTER 5 A Change of Front

"Truss him up good," said one. "These rebels are not to he trusted, even when they are tied."

I gave careful notice to the man who spoke, evidently the leader of the party. He was of middle size, middle age, and truculent features. His most noticeable characteristic was his drooping eyelids, which would induce the casual observer to think he was fast asleep, though in reality he was wide awake. He was dressed in the uniform of a captain in the British army. I set him down as a partisan chief on a small scale. He had five comrades, cast in the same mould as himself, all dressed in British soldiers' uniforms and rather wild of look.

They bound me securely and set me with my back to the log and my face to the fire, much in the position that I had occupied while the girl was singing. Confound her for lulling away my caution and suspicions in such a manner! I had no doubt now that she had seen the red uniforms of the British when first I went into the wood to search for the cause of the noise. I was a fool to let my distrust of her decrease for a moment.

"That was a complete job, Miss Howard," said the leader, "well done by everybody, and your part is the best done of all."

"You have rescued me from the hands of a rebel, Captain Crowder," she replied, "and I am back with my own people, for both of which I thank you."

I thought it was time for me to say something.

"It is true you have trapped me between you, Captain Crowder, for so I hear the lady call you," I said, "but I wouldn't exult, because the next chance might be mine, and it would hurt your feelings for me to pay you back."

"I don't know about any next chance for you," he replied, "because here in the South we generally hang rebels."

I did not reply to his threat, thinking that I had said enough, and turned my head away. My glance fell now upon Old Put. His eyes were full of reproach to me. The I-told-you-so expression was there, and the I-am-sorry-for-you-and-myself expression was mingled with it. "I will never lose faith in you again, best of all comrades!" I signalled back.

Captain Crowder, having seized me, also seized my camp, evidently with the intention of spending the night there. He posted one sentinel, while the others sat around the fire, making themselves comfortable. The girl occupied her old seat on the tree-trunk, leaning against the projecting bough.

"Do you know where my father is, Captain Crowder?" she asked.

"With Tarleton," he replied.

"And where is Tarleton?"

"Hot on the chase of the rebel, Morgan, and his men."

"Can we overtake Tarleton by noon to-morrow?"

"Undoubtedly, for he has to go rather slowly, not knowing just where Morgan is. He doesn't want to run past the game. Morgan's hard to catch, but when Tarleton once comes up to him there'll be an end to one rebel army."

I listened to this conversation with the closest attention and continued to listen while he described Tarleton's movements, force, and equipment. If I could escape him and the hangman's rope with which he had threatened me, this information would be of great value to our cause. I was glad that, for the sake of precaution, I had torn up the girl's letters and other written facts about us when I captured her, for now she could rely only upon speech. I waited for her to tell Crowder about me, but she said nothing upon that point, and I reflected that her reticence was natural, as she would want to give her information herself to Tarleton, and thus secure all the credit, instead of letting the guerilla, Crowder, claim at least half of it.

Two of the men disappeared in the wood and returned in a few moments, leading the horses of the band, which they tethered to the trees near by. I guessed that they had seen the light of our fire at a distance and, leaving their mounts there, had crept upon me.

"You will excuse us, Miss Howard, while we eat and drink a little," said Crowder. "We've ridden far to-day, and we're tired and hungry."

Their appearance was sufficient indication that they needed food and rest, as the grime of travel was thick upon them. They rummaged their haversacks and saddle-bags and produced bread and meat, which they began to eat greedily. They were absorbed like wild animals in their repast and paid no attention to anything else.

The girl rose and walked over to me. Reaching down, she seized the end of my silk handkerchief, which was projecting from my pocket, and jerked it forth. She threw it into the fire and watched it burn, the red heat gripping the delicate silk and converting it in a moment to ashes. Then she turned upon me a face of flame.

"You dared to bind me," she said—"you a rebel, and I an English woman, the daughter of a loyal English officer! You dared to insult me so!"

"And I presume that is the reason you burn the handkerchief with which I bound you," I said.

"Yes."

"Now that you have begun the job of burning, I suppose you would like to burn me too, as I am the man who tied the handkerchief, and I did so because you deserved it."

She was silent, but her cheeks were as red as ever.

"I congratulate you upon your rescue, your rescuers, your company," I said.

"They are loyal British soldiers."

"They wear the British uniform. Any ruffian and robber may do that."

"I have seen Captain Crowder himself in the army of Cornwallis. My father knows him, and I do too."

"You know his face, and that is all. He may be a good enough British soldier when he is with Cornwallis, but elsewhere he is anything that suits his purpose. Look at him and his comrades now."

Every man had produced a bottle and was drinking deeply from it. The odor rose and was too strong to be swept away by the wind.

"Look at them," I repeated. "I congratulate you on your company."

They drank deeply and replaced their bottles in their pockets, where I was sure they were not destined to remain long. The red fled from the girl's face, but she said nothing, and giving me the same curious look of mingled triumph and defiance, went back to her old place on the log. There she sat, staring straight into the fire, as if she were wholly oblivious of me and the other men around her.

The partisans were in great glee. They laughed and cracked rough jokes, and presently, as I had expected, pulled out the bottles again and took long, deep draughts, once, twice, thrice. Their faces flushed from the effect of the strong spirits, and the loudness and roughness of their talk increased. Crowder, the leader, was the loudest and roughest of them all.

"That was a fine song you sang to that fellow there when you set him a-napping for us to catch, Miss Howard," he said presently, "and we like music too, don't we, boys?"

"Yes, yes!" they roared, all together.

"And won't you kindly sing that song or another as good for us, Miss Howard?" he continued.

She made no answer, staring straight at the red embers, her cheeks pale.

"I say, Miss Howard, don't you hear?" exclaimed Crowder roughly.

"Yes, I hear," she replied, "but I'm sorry I can't oblige you. I can't sing any more."

"If you can sing for that d—d rebel there," continued Crowder, "I should think you could sing for us, who are good and loyal English like yourself."

342

She was silent again.

"Didn't we rescue you?" he continued. "Aren't we your saviors? Don't you owe us gratitude?"

Still unanswered, he swore an oath and said to his comrades:

"Here's gratitude for you, lads. Well, if she won't sing for us, we can sing for her. How do you like this, my lady? It's called 'I'll Owre the Muir to Maggy,' and it goes very well with the song you gave us just now."

Then he sang the old song, which like the girl's was Scotch:

And I'll owre the muir to Maggy—
Her wit and sweetness call me—
There to my fair I'll show my mind,
Whatever may befall me.
If she loves mirth, I'll learn to sing,
Or likes the Nine to follow,
I'll lay my lugs in Pindar's spring
And invocate Apollo.

If she admire a martial mind,
I'll sheath my limbs in armor;
If to the softer dance inclined,
With gayest airs I'll charm her;
If she love grandeur, day and night
I'll plot my nation's glory,
Find favor in my prince's sight,
And shine in future story.

Beauty can work wonders with ease
Where wit is corresponding,
And bravest men know best to please
With complaisance abounding.
My bonnie Maggy love can turn
Me to what shape she pleases,
If in her breast that flame shall burn

Which in my bosom blazes.

His voice was not unmusical, and he had some idea of rhythm and measure. His comrades joined him, and they roared out a chorus which must have penetrated to the farthest edge of the wood.

"I'll not only sing for you, Miss Howard," said Crowder, "but I'll dance for you too."

It was plain enough that the man was drunk, and was relapsing into his natural condition of savagery. I hoped that he would fall into the fire, but he did not. His drunken head swayed from side to side, but he kept step to the measure of the song.

One of the men drew his empty bottle and beat upon its side with his knife-blade. It made a lively tinkle that sounded like music, and the others, seeing his success, imitated him. Crowder had not only a vocal but an instrumental chorus as well. His zeal increased, and he danced like an Indian at a scalp-dance, while the men roared out the song and beat their bottles with enthusiasm.

"Again I congratulate you on your company, your glorious band of rescuers, Miss Howard," I called out to her.

I know she heard me, but she did not reply. Her lips were set firmly, although her cheeks were growing paler and paler, and she seemed to be white to the hair. I tugged at my bonds, but I could not move them.

The song stopped for a moment, and Crowder, looking around for further amusement, spied me.

"A good song, boys, and good fun," he cried, "but here's better fun. Let's hang the prisoner and see him squirm."

The others, as drunk as their leader, shouted their approval, but the girl sprang up.

"You shall not do that!" she cried.

"And why not, miss?" asked Crowder. "He is our prisoner."

"Because I will not permit it!" she cried.

They roared with laughter.

"If you do," she said, "I will report your act to Colonel Tarleton. This man is an important prisoner. He can guide Tarleton to Morgan, and he will do it to save his life. He must be taken safely to the British camp. Tarleton will reward you well."

"All right, if you say so, Miss Howard," he said. "Anything to oblige, especially one as handsome as you are. And we won't hang him to-night. Maybe we will do it in the morning anyhow, but that's no reason why we should stop the fun now. A soldier's life is hard, and he ought to make merry while he can."

He took a large flask from his haversack and shared it with his men. Then they began to sing and dance again, all of them wild with drink.

It was an orgy of savages. The fire died down and ceased to blaze; only the red embers glowed in the darkness. I could feel the blackness of the night as it rolled up and encircled us more closely. The girl was immovable. Her tawny hair shone in the dim light, and I saw that her face was still white, but that was all.

One of the men fell down presently from sheer exhaustion.

"Let him lie," said Crowder. "He'll sleep as well there as anywhere."

The man never moved, but began to snore, and a second one yielded to exertion and whiskey and, stretching himself out on the ground, went to instant sleep. Crowder himself was the third, and was followed speedily by the others, including the sentinel, who had joined without objection in the orgy. The six men were sound asleep in a slumber heavy with weariness and liquor.

A last brand fell over in the coals and blazed up. The girl rose from the log, and by its light I saw that her face had turned from white to red. She walked quickly over to me and said in a voice shaking with excitement and alarm:

"Take me away from here, Mr. Marcel! Take me away at once! I would rather be with you than these men, these savages, these brutes! Nor is your life safe here!"

"They wear the British uniform; they must be loyal British soldiers," I could not keep from saying.

"I do not know what they are," she replied, with alarmed insistence, "but let's go. Pray take me at once."

She pulled at my shoulders as if she would have me rise and go on the instant.

"Untie my wrists," I said.

She tugged at the cords, but could do nothing. They were tied too tightly.

"Take a knife from that drunken fool's belt," I said, indicating one of the men. "Don't be afraid. He won't wake."

She secured the knife and cut my bonds. I rubbed my wrists together for a few minutes to take out the stiffness and restore the circulation. Again she urged me to start without delay.

"Wait a minute," I said. "We must provide ourselves."

They had taken my arms from me when they bound me, and I recovered them, adding to my supply Crowder's pistol and some ammunition. Then I turned to the horses.

Old Put's great dark eyes flamed with approval and gladness. He had stood at his halter's length, watching the orgy and my rescue with attention and understanding.

"We'll bid farewell to these beasts now, old comrade," I said in a whisper, patting his nose.

He was too cautious to whinny a reply. The brown hack was near him, but I saw another among those belonging to the guerillas which I fancied much more than him. I hastily changed Miss Howard's saddle to his back, assisted her to mount, and sprang upon Old Put.

I turned the heads of our horses towards the northwest, but as the woods before us were dense and interlaced with wiry bushes and creeping vines, we dared not attempt more than a walk. The horses stamped and neighed as we left them. The girl's mount stepped on a large, dry branch, which broke with a crack like a pistol-shot. Nor did ill luck stop at that. The abandoned horses, frightened by the report, neighed and stamped again, creating a great uproar.

The sentinel, who was the least drunk of the party, sprang to his feet. He was yet half-dazed with sleep and liquor, but he saw the dim figures of a man and a woman riding away from the little encampment, and he knew that, according to the plans of Captain Crowder, it was not what should be. He fired a hasty pistol-shot in our direction, the bullet clipping the dry twigs above our heads, and then shouted to his comrades to awake, giving emphasis to his cries with many sturdy kicks.

"Look out for your head!" I shouted to Miss Howard. "An untoward bough might prove fatal. And be sure you stay with me."

"I'll not leave you," she said.

"Now, Old Put," I continued, "lead us out of this."

He curved his long neck in the darkness and looked ahead with sharp brown eyes. I let the reins fall loose, and he wound about among the trees with a judgment that was never at fault. The other horse kept close at his side. Behind us we heard the cries of the awakened men as they leaped upon their horses and rode after us, shouting to us to stop. Two or three more pistol-shots were fired, but the air received them.

If the men could see at all, it was but dimly, though they could follow us by the hoof-beats of our horses and the tearing of the vines and slapping of the bushes as we passed. They made such a prodigious cursing and swearing that we were never in any doubt as to where they were. I had a mind for a moment to send towards them a pistol-ball which would stop their noise, but I concluded that the greater uproar they made the better it would be for us, as it gave us exact warning of their approach. They did not seem to be gaining upon us, which was a satisfaction for the present. Out on the plain they would see us more distinctly, but I believed that our horses could leave them there.

I saw a beam of light shining through the lattice-work of the boughs, and then another and another, and knew that we would soon be in the open. The girl's horse stumbled, and she uttered a little cry of dismay, but in a moment the animal was steady on his feet again, and we went on. The beams grew more numerous and fused into a broad shield of moonlight. Two minutes more and we would be out of the wood and into the cleared ground, with the fields racing behind us.

But the light had its evil for us. Against it broad silver disk we were silhouetted like the man in the moon, and the popping of pistols told us that we had become good targets. One bullet passed so close to my head that I thought it must have cut a lock of hair in its passage, and I took it as a warning to hurry.

"Haste, Miss Howard!" I said. "We want to be beyond pistol-shot in the cleared ground, for the light will help them there."

She was riding well, and her expression was firm and courageous. We shook the reins against the necks of our horses, and, taking the chances of bush and vine, sped into the open as a volley of pistol-shots whistled after us.

I uttered a shout, half of pleasure, half of defiance, to our pursuers, and bade Old Put show them what it was for a real racer to run his best. I had confidence too in the horse that the girl rode, for he was long-limbed. He looked like a strong animal, and he certainly had a clean, fast gait that kept him alongside of Old Put.

I regarded our escape as assured, and the girl seemed to take a like view of the case. Belief showed in her eyes.

"Miss Howard," I said cheerfully and egotistically, "I congratulate you on the improvement in your company."

"At any rate, you are still a rebel, with a rope around your neck."

"I seem to have been preferred to the British behind us, who do not have ropes around their necks, but deserve them. Remember that I ride with you at your own invitation."

"Then you consider me still your prisoner?"

"Oh, I am yours; but, whether one or the other, I am to be guide."

The men behind us were silent, and we were sure of gaining upon them. I could see their figures rising out of the plain in the misty gray light, gigantic and distorted in shape, and the thud, thud of their horses' hoofs, as regular as the ticking of a clock, came to our ears.

"Which way do we go?" asked the girl.

"To Morgan, of course."

"Then I shall soon be with my father and friends again."

"Why do you think so?"

"Because Tarleton will certainly take Morgan, and, of course, I shall be recaptured."

She looked at me with much of the old sparkle and defiance and the absolute faith in British valor that British defeats seemed unable to shake. I was annoyed, and my patriotic pride was hurt.

"You take it for granted that Tarleton will win if he should overtake Morgan?"

"I do."

"Yet you have heard the news from King's Mountain?"

"A chance, an accident."

"The same chance, the same accident, may happen again."

"Never."

I could not say her nay, for were we not retreating steadily before the advance of Tarleton, a retreat that seemed to all to be the part of wisdom, for again let it be said that we were fewer in numbers, far inferior in equipment, and more than half of our little army were raw troops, farmers! The exhilaration of the flight and escape disappeared for the time, and a heavy depression took its place.

CHAPTER 6 In a State of Siege

Old Put stretched his neck, and the regular, steady beat of his flying hoofs was music to a man who loves a good horse. But the new horse too lengthened his stride and kept by my side. I judged that he was a good comrade for Old Put. The plain, grassy and undulating, rolled away before us, and I could not see its end.

Our pursuers hung on, and I distrusted their silence. It betokened resolution, a determination to follow us mile after mile, to cling to the chase like hounds after a deer. I judged that among Crowder's motives chagrin at having made such a fool of himself and a desire to repair the error were the strongest. The men did not spread out fan-shape, but followed us in a close group. I was still sure that we were gaining, though very slowly, and they seemed to think so too, for presently they fired two or three shots, as if they hoped to frighten us with spent balls. The girl's horse swayed a bit to one side, and I thought he had stumbled again, but she said he was merely startled by the pistol-shots, and pulling him back into the true course we galloped on.

We crossed a swell of the earth, and far out on the plain I saw the dim outlines of a small house, or rather log cabin, rising from the earth. The girl's horse threw up his head and uttered a neigh, or rather a cry or a great sigh, for it was almost like that of a human being, and staggered from side to side, his pace sinking quickly from a sure gallop to a shaky trot. His great eyes were distended with pain and fear, and blood and foam were on his lips. A dark-red clot of blood appeared upon his side, and I knew then that one of the bullets which I thought would fall short had struck him and the wound was mortal.

Without my hand pulling upon his rein Old Put stopped and looked at the other horse with eyes of pity and sorrow, for he knew what was going to happen—he knew he was going to lose one who had been proving himself a worthy running mate and comrade.

I leaped from Old Put's back and snatched the girl from the saddle just as her horse reeled and fell, giving up his honest life with one great groan.

I half-lifted, half-pushed the girl upon Old Put's back, where she sat securely despite the man's saddle. Once she protested, but I roughly bade her be silent and obey me and we would escape yet. Then she said no more.

"See the house yonder?" I said. "We will reach that and beat them off. Maybe we will find allies there. This should be a patriot region."

I rested one arm on Old Put's shoulder. The girl was on the horse's back, and I, partly supported by him, ran by his side. It is a trick that the borderers will tell you is common and useful enough. Old Put gave me great assistance, for he understood, and as we flew along my feet at times seemed not to touch the ground.

Our pursuers reached the crest of the swell and raised a shout of triumph as they saw the dead horse in the path, and the single horse running on, carrying one of the fugitives and half-carrying the other.

I took a quick look backward and calculated that we would reach the hut in time. Our pursuers evidently did not think so, for they fired no more shots. The girl was silent, her hands folded upon the pommel of my saddle and her face all white again. She left the direction of everything to me.

The cabin continued to rise from the plain, the corners, the eaves, and the roof appearing until it stood before us distinct and near at hand.

"Now, Put, old comrade, greatest of horses," I cried, "we are nearing the goal! Show them how much strength and speed you have kept in reserve for this last effort! Show them what you can do when you try your best!"

He replied by deed, and I fairly swung through the air as we raced straight to the cabin. I expected some tousled head to appear, roused by the thunder of so many hoofs, but none came. The place remained silent and lone. There was a small garden, but no fence around either it or the house.

Old Put dashed straight for the door, as if he knew what was wanted of him, which, in fact, he did, and stopped five feet in front of it so abruptly that the girl would have shot over his head had I not held her.

She sprang to the ground. I slipped the bridle off Old Put, gave him a slap, and cried,—

"Go!"

He galloped around the house and disappeared, his hoof-beats dying away in the darkness. Then I pushed open the door and rushed in, dragging the girl after me. I slammed it back and looked for the bar that is commonly used as a fastening in such frontier houses. There is was, and I shoved it into its place. Nothing but a battering-ram could break in that door now!

"Safe for the time!" I cried. "I defy them to take us in this fort!"

Then I looked around me. The girl, half-fainting, had staggered against the wall and was leaning there. It was a house of but a single room. On a wide brick hearth a fire was still burning, or rather smouldering, yet it threw out enough light to disclose the contents of the place. No human being was there. Everything of value except the heavy furniture, which was of the rudest description and worth not much more than raw lumber, had been removed, and the whole appearance of the room indicated that its occupants had taken a hasty departure. It was easy enough to guess the cause. Some poor family, frightened by the converging of the armies upon this region, and with good reason too,—for no other State was harried in this war as was ours of South Carolina,—had gathered up their portable goods and fled to safer quarters, and perhaps not an hour before our arrival, as the fire still burning proved.

"They might have made things a little more comfortable for us," I said cheerfully, for my spirits had gone up with a leap; "but it's good as it is, and we haven't any right to complain. Mr. South Carolina Farmer, whoever you are and wherever you are, we thank you."

The girl smiled faintly and walked mechanically to the fire, where she sat down on a rude stool and spread out her fingers before the coals as if she were in her home.

"Take a little of this," I said, for I saw that she was half-dazed. There was yet some whiskey in my flask, and I handed it to her. She obeyed me like a child and drank.

Then I turned my attention to the single window, which was closed with a heavy but ill-fitting shutter, a few wandering moonbeams finding a way through the cracks. Peeping out, I could see the guerillas dismounted beyond pistol-shot and holding a conference.

"They are talking, but let 'em talk, my dear," I said to the girl. "They can't get us in this cabin. What a neat, stout little place it is!"

I really began to have a friendly feeling towards her. We had been through so many dangers together, and, besides, she was my prisoner. It is much easier for the conqueror to be generous to the conquered than for the conquered to be generous to the conqueror.

She did not reply either to my words or my manner. Her cheeks, which had been so white before, were faintly flushed with pink, but I could not tell whether it was the fire or not. She seemed to me to be in a state of collapse, natural to a girl, even the strongest and bravest, after so much.

"Now set the table for us," I said. "We must eat a little after our long, hard ride, for we will need our strength. See if you can't find a candle in that cupboard. And here, take my bundle and get out the food."

I handed her the wallet of bread and meat which I had snatched from Old Put's back almost with the same motion with which I had swept off his bridle. She took it, drew the rough pine table to the centre of the room, and spread the food upon it. Then, sure enough, she found in the cupboard a piece of old tallow candle, which she lighted and stuck in the middle of the table. These simple household duties seemed to revive her. Her eyes brightened, her color came back, and her first thought was half to defend, half to apologize, for her previous collapse.

"I was tired merely," she said. "I did not lose courage. Don't think that. I'm an English girl."

"I never said you lost courage," I replied. "I think that you have borne yourself bravely, almost as well as an American girl would have done in the same situation."

"Show me the one who would have done better," she said, with a snap of the eye.

But that was manifestly impossible at the time, and I made no such attempt.

"The table is ready, and we wait only for the army to take a seat and enjoy itself," she said in a light tone.

"Come and have a look at our enemies first," I said, noticing how her strength and courage had come back and how well they became her.

She put her eyes to one of the cracks and looked out. Crowder and his men, unconsciously imitating us, had begun to make themselves comfortable, first by building a great bonfire, and then by sitting around it and keeping warm. They had tethered their horses near, and from their position they could watch the house very well and detect us if we came forth.

"Why do they follow us so persistently?" the girl asked.

"For a variety of reasons," I replied. "I might mention as one that they are anxious to take me. You know you informed them that I was the bearer of very important news which I would tell, under proper pressure, to Tarleton."

"But that was not true."

"They do not know that it was not."

"I wish they were real British soldiers," she said. "I do not believe that any of them ever saw England. I believe they are American Tories, maybe American rebels in British uniforms."

I did not care to argue with her, such is the strength of prejudice founded on teaching and training, especially British prejudice, and most especially the prejudice of British women.

"Why did you take off his bridle?" she asked as she turned away from the window.

I had hung up Old Put's bridle on a nail in the wall.

"In order that I may have it when I want to put it on him again, which won't be long, I hope," I replied.

"Why, the horse is gone!" she said.

I laughed, laughed in her face, which turned red, and then, seeing that it was red, deliberately laughed again. Here was a woman who prided herself on her intelligence and quickness of mind, and with good cause too, so I had begun to believe, and yet after passing a day and part of a night in Old Put's presence she knew so little about him!

"Why do you laugh?" she asked redly and angrily.

"I laugh at your ignorance," I replied, "the fact that you know so little of our comrade, in many respects the shrewdest and ablest of us three, as he is certainly the swiftest and the strongest. That horse has not left us. I merely took his bridle off in order that he might not be troubled with it, that he might eat better, for no doubt he will find, somewhere around here, even in winter, a bit of grazing on some sheltered and sunny southern slope. He will take care of himself and come back to us when we need him."

"But suppose the guerillas take him?"

"I wish I was as sure that they would not take us," I said.

Then I led the way to the table. I drew up the stool for the lady and an old pine box that I found in a corner for myself. A little water was left in the canteen. She drank part of it and said,—

"Here's to the health of King George!"

"Yes," I said as I drank the remainder of the water, "this is to the health of King George—George Washington! I'm glad to see that your conversion has begun."

She frowned at me, but we had an amicable dinner over the scraps nevertheless. I stopped at intervals to watch the progress of the partisans outside. They had not yet made any movement against us, and all sat or lay around the fire. I counted them—six—and I knew that all were there, as choice a lot of scoundrels as one could find on the soil of the thirteen colonies.

I turned my eyes away from the crevice to look at the girl. The rest and the bite of food had made a wonderful improvement. She was a true English rose, I could see that—a rose of Devon or Warwick or Kent, or whatever is fairest among their roses—a girl with yellow hair that shone like fresh gold in the sun, tinted with red in the firelight, and a brow of white and cheeks of the warm pink that is the heart of the pink rose. Oh, well, as I said twice before, everybody knows that the most beautiful women are the most dangerous, and I wondered if these Saxon maidens of England were ever an exception. For a moment I felt a feeling of warmth and kinship to old England, but then this England, which is so kind to herself and so appreciative of her own merits, has never been anything but an enemy to us.

"What are you thinking of, Mr. Marcel?" she said suddenly, as she looked up. "Why are you so serious?"

"I am astonished that you should address me as Mr. Marcel and not as a rebel with a rope around his neck."

She patted the floor meditatively with her foot and looked away from me and at the fire.

"It was a mistake due to forgetfulness," she replied with an air of resentment. "I will not do it again."

"I would not forget epithets when you speak of us," I said. "You will get out of practice, and then you will be unlike the remainder of your countrymen and countrywomen."

"Do you want another quarrel?" she asked pointedly. "I should think that we had enough to do to carry on our quarrel with those men outside."

She went to the window and took a long look.

"They are still by the fire," she said, "and I see your horse too. He is dining, like the rest of us."

"Where?" I cried, for I was somewhat surprised at the early reappearance of Old Put.

"There's another crack here. Use it," she said. "Don't you see him grazing over there to the left in that field surrounded by a tumbledown fence, or rather the rails of what used to be a fence?"

In truth it was Old Put, about fifty yards to the left of the cavalrymen and grazing with supreme horse content, as if no enemy were within fifty miles of him. It was a southern slope on which he stood, and I suppose some blades of grass had retained their freshness and tenderness despite the wintry winds. It was these that Old Put sought, with the assiduous attention to detail and keen eye for grist characteristic of him.

There was a fine, full moon, shedding a silver-gray light over the earth. Old Put was clothed in its radiance, and we could see him as distinctly as if he stood at the window—the tapering head; the velvety nose, which slid here and there over the grass in search of the tender stems; the sinewy neck, and the long, powerful body, marked often, it is true, by wear and war, but in the prime and zenith of its strength. My saddle was still upon his back, but that was a trifle to which he had long since grown accustomed in his life with a cavalryman.

How rash of him, I thought, to come so near the British! The doubt which I had of Old Put when he allowed himself to be deceived by the girl came back to me. Perhaps he was really growing old, falling into his dotage. Surely nothing else could account for his taking such a risk! I would have shouted to him to go away had I thought he could hear me, but I knew my voice could not reach him, and in suspense and anxiety I merely watched that old horse as he continued to graze almost within the light of his enemy's camp-fire.

CHAPTER 7 The Temper of Old Put

My fears found ample justification, for the men soon turned their attention to the horse, and two rose and approached him. I looked upon him as one impounded, and he alone was to blame, for he should have known better. One of the men made a wide circuit and came up carefully behind, while the other approached with equal caution from the front, whistling in a soft and coaxing way and holding out his hand. Evidently they appreciated the value of a good horse, and no doubt they had stolen enough from patriot farmers to have experience. Old Put never raised his head to look at them, but continued his hunt for blades of grass. He certainly heard their approaching footsteps, and I was convinced now that his dotage was really at hand.

"I thought you said he was the most intelligent of us three," said the girl ironically, "and here he is, gone to sleep and letting himself be taken, to be used perhaps as a common cart-horse."

Her words were an insult to us both, Old Put and me, but I knew no timely reply, and I endured them in silence.

The man in front, emboldened by Old Put's gentleness, approached more rapidly and was soon within fifteen feet of the horse. Old Put raised his head, and looking at the intruder a moment lowered it and went on nipping the grass.

The fellow, holding out his hand, stepped forward and seized Old Put by the neck. The horse, with a neigh that was human in its anger, turned and bit deep into his shoulder. A scream, wilder, more fearful than any I have ever heard before or since, rose from the man's throat as the horse reared high in the air and smote him to the earth with his forefeet. The girl turned her eyes away in horror as he was crushed to pulp beneath the fierce beat of the steel-shod hoofs, time for but one cry being given to him, but I kept mine at the crevice, though I will confess that the blood was rather a chilly torrent in my veins.

The other man, the one behind, faced about and fled when he saw the death of his comrade, and the single look that I had of him showed fright to the marrow. The horse, raising his head, trotted away over the hill. The moonlight fell upon him there in distorted rays and enlarged him into a gigantic figure. In the gray light he looked like some phantom horse, a wild creature that brought death.

The band, recovering from the momentary paralysis caused by the sudden acquaintance of their comrade with death, snatched out their pistols and fired at the horse as they would have fired at a man in his place, but their aim was wild, for Old Put gave no sign of a hit, trotting steadily on, his figure growing larger and more threatening in the exaggerating rays of the moonlight, until he disappeared beyond the swell of the earth. The thing that had been living lay in the dead grass, and I was glad that it was hidden almost by some rocks and the roll of the earth.

"He is gone, Julia," I said, "and I don't think those men will try to take my horse again."

I laughed a little, with a rather forced gayety, for the influence of the sudden tragedy was still upon me. Yet I was glad that Old Put had redeemed himself so conclusively from the charge of incaution and dotage, which I would never again bring against him, even should they come to be true in the course of the years.

The girl came back to the crevice, and we watched the British for some minutes. After the hasty discharge of the pistols they returned to the fire, making no movement either to pursue Old Put or to remove the body of their dead comrade. They would have liked well enough to obtain a good horse, but they were not going to bother about such a trifle as a dead man.

"Do you think they will attack us?" asked the girl.

"Well, no; not yet, at least," I replied. "The advantages of the defence are too great, and these men are mere raiders and robbers. They are not going into a dangerous venture unless the chances are on their side. Perhaps they think we will become frightened and surrender to-morrow."

"You surely will not do that?"

"I had no such intention, worthless rebel as I am, but if you say surrender I will go out and notify them this minute."

"You know I meant nothing of the kind."

She spoke rather sharply, and leaving the window went back to the table, which she began to clear away. She gathered up the scraps and put them back neatly. Then she brushed the crumbs off in her hand, for lack of anything else, and threw them in the fire, and having done that pushed the table to one side against the wall. I made no offer to help her, as she did everything with such skill and despatch, and I was content to watch her. Nor did she say anything to me, but, her work done, took her stool again and sat down at the corner of the hearthstone, leaning her head against the wall of the chimney and gazing into the dying fire.

The last log was smouldering on the hearth and threw but a feeble light. I blew out the candle, thinking we might need it in case our enemies made any hostile movement, and the darkness gathered at once in half the room, only a dim light showing as a fringe to the fire.

"I think you'd better go to sleep," I said to the girl. "It is always well to save one's strength, and now is a chance for rest."

"And you?"

"I don't want any sleep. I'll stay at the window and watch."

"But you need rest as well as I."

"Why do you bother yourself about a villanous rebel who is going to be hanged anyway by his justly angry King?"

"I wish you would stop talking that way."

Her tone was rather plaintive. Undoubtedly she was tired and worn by anxieties, and I obeyed her request. I made her wrap her cloak around her, and though she declared stoutly that she would not go to sleep, merely wishing to lean her head against the wall and rest, her eyelids drooped and fell, and in two minutes she slumbered.

The fire sank lower, eating its way along the log until only a few inches of wood were left. The girl slept soundly. The curve of the chimney into the wall formed a kind of nook, and her head and shoulders rested easily there like a picture framed against the rough logs, which were unplastered and not even smoothly hewn. I trusted that she would sleep the night through, and as the fire sank lower and lower and the darkness crept up to the hearthstone, almost hiding her figure, the stillness of midnight came, and I could hear her regular breathing in the dead silence.

I went back to the window. The fire of the British faced it, and I could see that three of the men had lain down and gone to sleep. The other two were sitting up, weapons at hand, and I inferred that, they had been detailed as sentinels, though their lazy attitudes showed well enough that it was a job they did not like. For all I could tell at the distance, these men too might be asleep sitting.

I watched them for a half hour or more, and grew very tired of the business. The brightness of the moonlight culminated, and the earth lost its silver tint, shading into a dark, dull gray. The figures of our besiegers became shadowy and shapeless. It was a time for sleep, and I felt it in all my bones. A trooper doesn't ask much. If I could have taken my blanket and put myself down on a reasonably smooth piece of turf under the shade of a tree, with the certainty that no enemy would waken me, it would have been sufficient. I would have slept the sleep of the just, or the tired unjust, which is often as good.

I drew the old pine box up to the window and sat on it, resolved to listen, now that I was weary of looking. I wondered what had become of Old Put, the manslayer, and tried to discover why I had been such a fool as to distrust him even for a moment.

Thus musing, I discovered that the fire had gone out; that I could see nothing—in fact, that the room was pitchy dark. I opened my eyes, remembering that all things must be dark to a man with his eyes shut, and saw again the flickering fire and the figure of the girl half-reclining in the chimney-corner.

This would not do. I was the whole army—horse, foot, artillery, and baggage-wagons, commander-in-chief, colonel, captains, and privates—and we could never go to sleep all at once. I undertook to walk briskly around the room in order to stir my sluggish blood into watchfulness, but that would wake the girl, and I did not want to do such a cruel thing. I stopped in front of her and looked at her face attentively. Asleep she did not look at all the spitfire she was awake. Mingled with her beauty now was a certain wanness, a something that was pathetic, a look that appealed to a man for protection and strength. After all, she was but a girl, and why should I care for the bitter things she said when probably half the time she said them she was sorry?

I went back to the window and looked out once more. The besieging army was taking its comfort. The part which had stretched itself on the ground remained stretched, and the part which watched sagged more than ever towards the horizontal. It was a lazy army, that was evident, and I resolved that I would set it an example of superiority.

Having made these brave resolutions, I sat down on the stool and leaned my head once more against the wall, not because I was tired and sleepy, but merely that I might reserve my strength for a crisis, the most necessary thing in the world to a soldier, every man of experience knowing that an army fights better if it goes into battle well fed, well clothed, and well rested. It was a good argument, that bore extension, and I closed my eyes that they too might have rest, as they felt weary and clogged. Then, do what I would or could, weariness and sleep took charge of me. Tired muscles rose in open and defiant rebellion against mind and will. The combat was short and fierce, but matter triumphed over mind, and in five minutes I was in the midst of a sleep that was heavenly with rest, unpeopled by bad dreams, with my head back against the wall and my breathing long and regular. Meanwhile the bed of coals on the hearth became smaller and paler. The rim of fire narrowed. Coals turned from red to black and then to gray and crumbled into ashes. The darkness crept up to the very edge of the hearthstone and then invaded it. The girl was completely in the shadows, and the pale glimmer of the fire was but a faint light left in the room.

The sleeping man and the sleeping girl were tired, very tired, and they slept soundly. If they had dreams, they were pleasant ones, and no thought of danger entered into them. The men around the camp-fire had moved away to the other side of the world, and the little cabin was peaceful for them, inside and outside. Sleeping thus, they did not see the men rise from the camp-fire and approach the hut, now veiled in a darkness which made such a movement safe. They reached the cabin without alarm or a sign from the watcher who was not watching, and at last the leader tried the shutter of the window. He pried at it with his knife and moved it a little. Then he put his ear to the crack and could hear nothing within. Replacing his ear with his eye, he saw the feeble glimmer of the fire and no more. He was sure that those whom he wished to take were asleep, and he exulted, for a fierce anger mingled with his other desires to recapture both. He pried again at the window, and with greater leverage it yielded further, and wood scraped against wood. He stopped and listened once more, but the inmates of the cabin never stirred.

Putting his ear to the wide crack that now intervened between the shutter and the wall, he listened again and heard the steady, regular breathing of someone inside and below. He knew it was the breathing of a sleeping man, too loud and strong for a woman, too even for one awake, and he reached up and pulled the shutter wide open on its rude leather hinges. Then he grasped the edge of the window with both hands and raised himself up.

My sleep grew troubled at last and then turned into a nightmare. Some huge wild beast, after the fashion of beasts in nightmares, was sitting on my chest and blowing his breath in my face, while I had no power to move a muscle. I was cold to the marrow and waited for him to devour me, but instead he dwindled away and became misty. With one great effort I threw him off my chest and sprang to my feet. My head struck against somebody else's head as I sprang up, and that somebody else swore an oath that had the savor neither of a nightmare nor a dream, but of reality.

Cold air and moonlight rushed in at the window, but most of the passage was filled up by the shoulders and head of a large man whose face I could not see owing to the imperfect light. He held in his hand a pistol which he fired at me, but now the imperfect light was to my advantage and not his, for his bullet, avoiding me, buried itself with a chuck in the log walls, and the report confined in the small room roared like a cannon-shot.

Moved more by impulse and instinct than by thought, I snatched out my own pistol and fired at the head in the window. The man uttered a deep sigh; the body dropped forward and swayed there; I heard the light drip, drip of something on the floor, and then the body fell inside the room.

The girl, suddenly awakened by the terrible sounds and half in a maze, cried out in fright and then began to ask in a high, trembling voice what had happened.

"The British have attacked us," I said. "One of them was in the shadow, and I threw him back. Stand out of the range of the window."

I did not want her to see the thing lying on the floor under the window, and I shoved the table in front of it.

She obeyed, for I spoke the last sentence very sharply. The window was wide open, and, expecting to see another face there, I held my second pistol ready; but none appeared, and I had no doubt that they feared Crowder was dead.

Taking the risk, I reached out an arm, seized the shutter, and slammed it shut, securing it as best I could with the leather strap and nail used as a fastening. Then, with my ear near the crevice, I listened, but could not hear our enemies. I feared at first to look out lest I should receive a bullet, but still hearing nothing I applied my eye and saw that the men had gone back to their fire. They were all there—four. I counted them and knew that none was missing. They were deliberating evidently over the fall of their leader and what next to do, and I took an immediate resolution.

"Light the candle," I said to the girl. "Hold it to the fire. There's enough heat left to start the wick to burning."

She did so, and saw that something lay behind the table.

"What is that?" she cried.

"The dancer and singer of last night," I replied, seeing that I would have to tell. "The leader of those desperadoes outside came into our fort, but he came into his grave."

She retreated, shuddering, to the farthest corner of the room.

"Now, you do exactly as I say," I continued. "Remember that you are the rank and file of this army, and I am its commander."

"I will obey you," she said.

I quickly reloaded my pistol.

Then I shoved the table away again and, overcoming my repulsion, dragged the dead body to a sitting position. A chill struck into my marrow, but I pulled off the red British coat and, having thrown off my own, put it on. Then I gathered up the wallet of food and Old Put's bridle and took down the bar from the door.

"Come," I said; "we are going to leave this place while they are planning by the fire and their backs are turned to us."

It was a bold measure, involving many risks, but I believed that it would succeed if we kept our courage and presence of mind. For at least two or three minutes they would think I was Crowder, victorious, and that would be worth much. When I had taken down the bar, I stopped a moment.

"Keep by my side," I said. "Remember that we must become separated by no chance. Here, take this pistol! You can shoot, can't you?"

She said "Yes," and took the pistol. Then I opened the door and we dashed out, running with quick and noiseless steps across the clearing towards the wood, which rose in a dim line ahead of us.

While the window opened towards the camp-fire of the besiegers the door did not, and we had gone perhaps fifty yards before they saw us. This I knew by the surprised shout that came to our ears, and looking back I saw them hesitating, as if in doubt about my identity, and at last running towards their horses. I was glad that they would pursue on horseback, and I had taken that probability into consideration when we made a dash from the house, for even at the distance I could see that the dim forest looked dense and a poor place for the use of horses.

"Courage, Julia!" I said, taking her hand. "In a minute or two we will be into the woods, and they mean safety."

I looked back a second time. The guerillas had reached their horses, mounted them, and turned their heads our way, but in doing it their time lost was our gain. Unless lamed by some unlucky pistol-shot, we would surely gain the wood. They fired once or twice, and I heard the thunder of their horses' hoofs, but I had little fear. I still held the girl's hand in mine, and she made no effort to draw it away. She was running with a firm, sure step, and, though her face was white and her eye excited, she seemed to retain both her courage and presence of mind.

The wood was not as far as I had calculated, and when our pursuers were many yards away we dashed into it at such headlong haste that I tripped over a vine and fell upon my nose, burying it in a pile of soft leaves, which saved it from harm. But I was up again, rejoicing at the accident, for in a wood interlaced with vines horses could make no progress.

"I hope you are not hurt?" asked Julia anxiously.

"Hurt? Not a bit of it!" I replied. "What a blessing these woods are! How dark it is in here, and what a blessing that is too!"

In fact, the wood was our good luck and our best luck at that, for even we on foot found it difficult to make our way through it. Afar we could hear the British cursing in profusion and variety as they strove to force their horses through the dense bush.

"Hold my hand," I said to Julia, "for otherwise I might lose you in all this darkness and density."

But instead of waiting for her to take my hand, which she might not have done, I took hers, and, bidding her again to step lightly, I led the way, curving among the trees and bushes like a brook winding around the hills in search of a level channel. My object was to leave our pursuers at a loss concerning our course, and we soon ceased to hear their swearing or the struggles of their horses. I dropped into a walk, and, of course, the girl did likewise.

"I think we are safe now," I said. "There is not one chance in a hundred to bring them across our path again. What a fine wood! What a glorious wood! There is no such wood as this in England. It grew here especially for our safety, Julia."

"It did grow up in time," she replied, "but now that you think us safe again you can call me Miss Howard, and not Julia."

"That's true, and now that we are safe again I must ask you, Miss Howard, as an especial favor to me, to please quit holding my hand."

"I am not holding your hand, Mr. Marcel!" she replied indignantly. "It is you who are holding mine, but you shall not do so a moment longer."

She tried to jerk her hand away. I let her jerk three or four times, and then I added as an afterthought:

"It is very dark here, and there is still danger that we might become separated. I think I will let you hold it a little longer, but I shall endure it merely because it is a military necessity."

She gave her hand a most violent jerk, and it nearly slipped from me, but I renewed my grip in time.

"Simply a military necessity," I repeated, and, seeing that it was useless, she made no further effort to withdraw the hand. I could not see her face, the darkness being too great, and therefore had little opportunity to judge of her state of mind. We walked on in silence, winding here and there through the wood, with an occasional stop to listen, though we heard nothing but the common noises of a forest—the crackling rustle of dry leaves and twigs, the gentle swaying of some old tree as the wind rocked it, and the soft swish of the bushes as they swung back into place after we had passed between.

CHAPTER 8 Julia's Revenge

We walked for nearly an hour, and during the last three-quarters of it kept straight to the northwest, in which direction I thought Morgan, with his little army, lay, or rather marched. At last the bush became thinner and the trees stood farther apart. I inferred that we were approaching the end of the forest, and I was not sorry, as the travelling was hard, and I believed that we had lost our pursuers. Presently we came into the open, and I let the girl's hand drop.

"Which way are we going now?" she asked.

"Wait a moment," I said.

I put two fingers to my lips and blew between them a whistle, soft and long and penetrating.

"Why do you do that?" asked the girl in a fright, coming towards me. "You will bring them upon us again."

"Wait," I repeated, and I blew the whistle a second time. We stood motionless for two minutes, and then I heard a faint crush, crush, as of approaching footsteps.

"They are coming!" cried the girl, seizing my arm. "Let us run into the wood again."

"Wait," I said for the third time.

The footsteps approached rapidly, and a figure, gigantic and formidable in the gray light, appeared through the trees. The girl cried aloud in a panic of terror and gripped my arm.

"Don't be alarmed, Julia dear," I said. "See who it is!"

Old Put walked up to me, gave his glad, familiar whinny, and rubbed his nose on my disengaged arm. Then he started back, and his eyes flamed with wrath.

"Don't be angry, old comrade," I said. "It is true I wear a red coat, but it is only a disguise, a ruse, and I will get rid of it as soon as I can."

He wagged his head as a sign that my apology was sufficient, and made no further protest. I slipped the bridle on him, and the girl broke into a nervous laugh of relief.

"Did you think Old Put would desert a comrade?" I asked.

"Wait here just a moment," I continued. I led Old Put a little distance and, gathering up some dry leaves, wiped the stains off his hoofs. Then I returned with him to her and told her to jump upon his back, but the horse shied away from her, showing aversion and anger.

"Never mind, Old Put," I said. "It is all right. She won't beat you again. She likes us both."

"It seems to me that you are rather inclusive in your statements," she said.

"Get up," I ordered, and, giving her a hand, I assisted her to jump upon the back of Old Put, who had received my explanation with perfect confidence and assumed a protecting air towards her.

"And now once more for Morgan," I said.

"Which, of course, means Tarleton in the end," she said. "And I want to say, Mr. Marcel, that when the rebel army is taken I shall not forget the service that you have done me at a great risk to yourself. My father has influence with Colonel Tarleton, and I shall ask him to secure your good treatment while in captivity."

She spoke with quite an English—that is to say, quite a patronizing —air.

"You are very kind," I replied, "but Morgan has not been caught yet, has he, Old Put?"

Women think it their right to abuse a man and receive nothing but chivalry in return.

The old horse shook his head defiantly, and I felt encouraged. We had entered a good country for travelling and at last came into something that was meant evidently for a road, but it very much more resembled a gully washed out by the rains. It led in the right direction, and I followed it, despite my persuasion that we were now in territory practically occupied by the British, and were much more likely to meet them in the road than in the fields or forest. But I was tired of such difficult travelling, and, being extremely anxious to rejoin Morgan, I chose the course which promised the best speed.

Old Put carried the girl, and I walked on before, holding his bridle in my hand. I sank into a kind of walking doze—that is, I slept on my feet and with my feet moving. I was but dimly conscious, but I knew that I could put my trust in Old Put and that he would warn me if she made any attempt to escape. Whether the girl was asleep or wide awake I knew not, for my brain was too tired and dull then to tell me, but, looking back once, she seemed to be awake. She had slept well in the hut, while only a short nap had fallen to me.

We were in the darkest hours, those that stretch out their length between midnight and dawn, and I walked on over a dim and shadowy world. Sometimes I was not conscious that my feet touched anything but air. This queer feeling that I was walking on nothing lasted for nearly an hour, and then my half-sleep took another phase. I came back to earth, and the red clay of the road took on for a while the color of blood. The trees by the roadside raced past, rows of phantoms, holding out withered arms and making gestures that I did not understand. Once the dead face of Crowder rose up out of the road and confronted me, but when I said, "You were a murderer and worse, and compelled me to kill you," and walked boldly at him he melted away like so much smoke, and I laughed aloud at such a poor kind of ghost that would run at the first fire.

"What on earth are you laughing at?" demanded the girl from the horse's back.

I awoke with a jerk and replied,—

"At your gratitude."

But I was on the verge of sleep again in five minutes, and the trees and the hills and the bushes were playing new tricks with me. The bushes were especially impudent, nodding to me and then to each other and then saying aloud:

"Here he goes! Look at him—making a fool of himself and wasting his time over an English girl who hates him and all his countrymen!"

I picked up a stone, threw it at one excessively impudent bush, and shouted at the top of my voice,—

"It's a lie!"

"For Heaven's sake, Mr. Marcel," cried the girl, "what's the matter? Have you a fever?"

"I was dreaming," I said confusedly, and I made no further explanation, for she asked no more, merely saying that she hoped it was not worse than that.

The trees and bushes did not cease to nod at me and waggle their heads at each other and make jeering remarks about me, but I paid no further attention to them, treating them with the lofty scorn of silence, which is supposed to be the most effective of all replies. The road led into hilly country, but I tramped on in my dream, becoming dimly conscious that it was growing light. Afar off there in the east, just where the sky touched the earth, was a bar of light. As I looked it broadened and began to roll up like a great wave of molten silver. On the horizon the hills and trees rose out of the darkness.

Old Put turned his face to the daylight and whinnied approval. An answering whinny came as twenty cavalrymen galloped around a hill, opening in two lines and closing up again, with us in the centre.

"Wake up! Wake up, man! Why, you'll walk into a river or over a cliff if you sleep on in this way," said one of the cavalrymen, leaning over and slapping me vigorously on the shoulder.

I awoke and looked up at his bewhiskered English face and his be-striped English coat, and was filled with confusion and dismay.

"Why, he isn't awake even yet!" said the officer, with a laugh. "Are you from Cornwallis?"

His tone, though eager, was friendly, and the reason for his question flashed upon me. It was the red coat that I wore, Crowder's coat, which had served me one good turn already.

"Yes," I said, "my name's Hinkle, and I'm from Cornwallis with an important message for Tarleton. I was pursued last night by a gang of rebels, who shot my horse, but I escaped them in the wood. An hour ago I overtook Miss Howard here, who also has an important despatch for Tarleton, and I am trying to pilot myself and her to him at the same time."

The officer raised his hat to Miss Howard and regarded her with open admiration.

"Your bravery and loyalty equal your beauty, Miss Howard," he said. "England can never suffer when we have such as you. Don't you remember me? I'm Lieutenant George Cuthbert, and I had the honor of an introduction to you at Lord Cornwallis's ball in Charleston some months ago."

"Indeed I do," she said in a tone of recognition, "and I hope that we shall meet again soon under such peaceful circumstances, but now I must hasten on, for my message will not wait, and so must this kind soldier, who has been such an assistance and protection to me. Can you direct us by the best road to Tarleton?"

"Keep straight in the way you are going," replied the officer, "and if you hurry you ought to overtake Tarleton before noon. Have no fear of the rebels. Tarleton is driving them all ahead of him, except one small party to the south of here, for which we are looking. I'd give you an escort into Tarleton's camp, but I need all my troopers for the task I have in hand."

"I thank you for your courtesy and information, Lieutenant Cuthbert," she replied, "and I hope that we shall meet again soon in Charleston when all these rebels are taken."

"And that will not be long, Miss Howard," he said with a gallant bow.

He gave the word to his troopers, and they galloped on.

During this ordeal the behavior of Old Put was something wonderful to see. Though he hated a redcoat as a cat hates a snake, he seemed to understand that he had a part to act and that he must act it well. All his true character disappeared. He was a shambling, drooping horse, with his head down and ready to submit to anything, just an ordinary, oppressed British horse of the lower classes, not a proudspirited American horse, conscious of the Declaration of Independence and the truth that all men and horses are born free and equal.

But when the last of the British troops had disappeared around the hill and the gallop of their horses had sunk into a mere echo, Old Put resumed his former and true character—his figure expanded, he held up his head once more. He was the true patriot, equal to all. I was glad to see the change, for that was the character in which I liked him best.

We went on for a long time in silence, barring a request from the girl that I ride and let her walk in my place. I declined abruptly, saying I was a cavalryman, with such few opportunities for walking that I intended to enjoy one when I had it.

The sun, following the new light in the east, had appeared above the hills. The far crests and forests flamed with red gold, and we trod silently on in the shining light of the morning. "Why did you not take your opportunity," I asked at length, "and return to your own people? Why did you not tell them back there who and what I was?"

She remained silent, and I looked back at her.

"Julia," I said, and she did not seem to notice that I had called her by her first name again despite her command, "why did you not tell them who I was and let them take me a prisoner?"

"I have called you a rebel with a noose around your neck, and it is true. The noose is always there, and it was pressing very close at that moment. For you to have been taken a prisoner then meant your death. I could have taken the chance of returning to my own people then only by hanging you."

"How? I do not understand you."

"Look at the red coat you wear. 'A spy,' says Tarleton, who knows no mercy. 'Hang him at once!' and you are hanged."

I had forgotten the coat, which, having served me well twice, might serve me very ill the third time.

"I must get rid of this coat soon," I said. Then I added as an afterthought: "But what is it to you were I hanged? It would be only one more wicked rebel meeting the fate that he deserves. Why should you put yourself to trouble for me?"

I looked back over my shoulder, though I may not have had the appearance of looking. I saw a flush as of the morning that was around us overspread her face, and she gazed afar over my head, her eyes shining with something I had not seen there before. I asked her no more, but the morning continued to grow into a splendor and radiance passing all previous knowledge of mine.

The sun crept up, and the light reached all the earth, west as well as the east. We were still in the red-clay road, winding among lone hills and deserted fields and patches of primitive forests. We came to a brook of cool, clear water, babbling over the stones.

"Here we rest," I said, "and eat breakfast. Jump down, Julia."

She sprang down, and all three drank at the brook—Julia, Old Put, and I. Then we ate the remains of our provisions, while the horse found some tender stems of grass by the brookside.

"I think we had better leave the road now," I said, "for this is the enemy's country, and I do not want to meet any more of Tarleton's men."

It was my purpose to make a circuit around Tarleton and join Morgan, and she made no objection, but suggested that she walk with me.

"I am tired of riding," she said, "and it will be good for the horse too."

I threw the bridle-reins over Old Put's head, told him to follow us, and we started on our great curve around Tarleton. Being a Charleston man, I knew very little of that part of the country, but in my campaigning with Greene and Morgan I had obtained some idea of the lay of the land, and I knew the general course I ought to follow. Besides, I felt very good, and I was full of enthusiasm. But little of the country had been cultivated, and as the forest was not dense there was nothing to stay our progress. We marched steadily on, and what impressed us most was the desolation of the land. But thinly peopled in the first place, everybody here, as in the country through which we had travelled the day previous, had fled before the advance of the armies. We passed two abandoned cabins in the scanty fields, but saw no other sign of human habitation. Yet it did not sadden me. The sunshine was beautiful, and the old world was fresh and young.

"In a few years, Julia," I said, "when the last of Tarleton's raiders is sent across the sea or to his final home, and we win our freedom, all this will be peaceful and populated."

She said nothing—nothing about the valor of the English and the speedy destruction of the rebels—but looked abroad over the country with kindling eyes. It was fair to see, even in winter, with its rolling hills and sloping valleys and streams of sparkling water, a fit place for the growth of a noble race of freemen. But just then it was the most unhappy part of all our continent. Neither man nor woman could expect mercy where Tarleton's raiders came, and all the books will tell you—and tell you rightly—that the war was more ferocious in the South than in the North, and most ferocious of all on the soil of South Carolina. Where partisan bands ravage and fight, and the people of the soil themselves are set and embittered against each other, then war is seen at its worst.

CHAPTER 9 As Seen in a Dream

We were young and vigorous. The girl was tall, straight, almost as strong as I, and mile after mile dropped behind us. The air had the crisp, fresh coolness of a South Carolina winter, like a Northern day in autumn. The sun, climbing steadily towards the heavens, shone in full splendor and in an atmosphere as pure as that over the sea. We could see far to right and left and before us, but we saw neither men nor horses, just the rolling hills and valleys and the straggling forests.

"So much the better," I said to Julia, "for the lonelier the country the less obstacle there will be to our flight. Morgan is retreating towards the Broad River, and as we have surely passed around Tarleton by this time, we ought to overtake him by night. I hope he will have plenty to eat, for I think that you and I will miss our dinner."

"Do you know," said she, "I begin to hope that Tarleton will not catch Morgan? It would be an awful scene, and perhaps some of the rebels are good men after all."

"Perhaps."

"Couldn't the war be ended in some way without more years of fighting — by some sort of compromise? Suppose each side should give up a little?"

"We might make the proposition, you and I, to Congress and the King."

"Don't jest. I'm in earnest."

"Then I'm afraid there's no chance for a compromise, and there hasn't been for four or five years. Either we go free or we do not. You English like to boast of your courage and tenacity, and we make the same boast of ourselves. It has to be fought out to the end, win or lose."

"I am sorry."

She spoke truthfully, as she looked her sadness, but the wind soon blew it away, bringing back the sparkle to her eyes and the rose-flush to her cheeks. We stopped about noontime to rest, and Old Put made use of the opportunity to hunt for green grass, stopping at times to look benevolently at us and to indicate that his state of mind was content. We were both hungry, but we had nothing better to do than to watch Old Put nibble for his dinner, which he did very industriously until I called to him and told him it was time to start.

Julia again refused to mount the horse, and we strolled on together. I felt safe now, and, coming to a cabin whose owner had been bold enough to remain and guard his own, I offered to trade him the fine British coat I wore for any coat of his own, however old, provided it would hold together on my shoulders. He produced the garment and made the trade, by which he was a great gainer, and asked me no questions, differing therein from the country-people of the Northern regions through which I had campaigned so long. Moreover, he looked very curiously at the tall girl with me.

"You are American," he said to me just before we started.

"Yes."

"The lady looks English."

"She is English."

"It is very strange."

"You are right. It is strange."

Such were my thoughts as we walked away. The man, who seemed to live there alone, half hunter, half farmer, stood in his cabin-door and watched us until we passed out of sight.

I prevailed upon the girl to ride awhile, but after an hour on horseback she dismounted again, saying that she preferred to walk. About the middle of the afternoon we met a farmer who confirmed my belief that Morgan had passed on towards the Broad River, though he knew nothing of Tarleton. An hour later, as we were passing through thick woods, someone cried out to us to halt. I almost sprang up in my astonishment, and the girl uttered a little cry of fright, for neither of us supposed anyone to be near, having seen and heard nothing, and Old Put, I suppose, was tired or dreaming.

"Stop," I said to Julia; "it may be friends."

Two men on horseback came from a position among the dense trees. They were dressed in rough homespun gray, and looked like Americans, the two facts together inducing the belief that they were militia scouts of Morgan's.

"An American and his lady," said the foremost to me. "You are a soldier, are you not?"

"Yes," I replied.

"And on the way to Morgan too, I take it. Keep straight to the northwest, and you will overtake him. We are good patriots too."

"Thank you," I said. "Morgan seems to keep a sharp watch. I hope that we shall overtake him before nightfall."

He had ridden very close to me.

"I don't think it, my fine fellow," he said. "We will take good care of both you and the lady, for we are Tarleton's scouts, not Morgan's."

I saw then that the appearance and manner of the men had deceived me, but no thought of surrender to them entered my mind. I snatched at my pistol. The fellow, who was as wary as a panther, saw the movement and drew his own weapon. We fired almost at the same time. I saw him reel in his saddle, but not fall, and I was conscious of a thrill of pain in my head, followed by a heavy, crushing sensation, as if I had been struck by a hammer. I staggered, falling to the ground upon my hands and knees. Consciousness left me entirely for a few minutes and then came back dimly, just enough for me to dream and to create events for myself.

In this dream I saw a girl with tawny gold hair and blue eyes raise a pistol and fire at the second rider, who had drawn a cavalry sabre. The man, shouting with pain, dropped his sabre, clapped his other hand to his shoulder, and galloped after his comrade, whose horse, frightened by the shots, was running away with him. Both disappeared in the wood, and the girl, who stood for a minute or two watching, the empty pistol in her hand, seemed to feel sure that they would not come back, for she rushed to the wounded man on the ground and raised his head in her arms.

I watched her with a curious interest, this blond girl who had been so bitter of speech and yet so much the master of herself. The man had risen to his knees once, but had fallen back from weakness. His eyes closed almost, his face became very white, and there was blood on his hair. She raised his head and kissed his face, once, twice, and more, and begged him not to die. "Live! Live for yourself and for me, Philip, for I love you, my hero!" she said, and a great bay horse stood looking and listening. She flew to a little brook she saw flowing through the wood, and bringing water in her cap poured it upon the man's face, while the horse nodded approval. Then she washed the blood out of his hair and bound up the wound with something white. "No, Put, I will never leave him," she said, "I will never leave him, for he has saved me from death and worse, and I love him—I tell you I love him!" whereupon the great horse nodded his approval with extreme vigor.

I came to myself, and I was sorry that the dream was over. It had been pleasant, very pleasant, and I was willing to dream on. I had a headache, but when I put my hand to the spot which ached I knew that the wound was not serious,— that it was nothing but a trifle. A bullet, clipping under the skin, had glanced along my skull and passed on, inflicting a slight concussion, like a heavy blow from a man's fist, but that was all. I had seen many men who had suffered similar wounds in battle and were as good as ever the next day.

"You are not going to die, are you, Mr. Marcel?" tearfully asked the most modest and demure of blond English maidens, standing before me.

"My intentions are the precise opposite," I replied. "I have so much to live for."

It is curious how rapidly the feelings develop under the stress of great hardships and danger. The day and a half that I had been with her were equal to a year and a half of ordinary time.

"Would you bring me a little of that cool water to drink in your cap?" I asked. "I see that the cap is wet already, and it won't hurt it."

She brought the water, and I drank. It was as cold as ice and as refreshing as nectar as it ran down my throat. I have seen men lying on the battlefield begging for water as if it were the one great gift of heaven to our kind.

I felt twice the man that I was a minute before. The girl was strangely quiet, even shy, and more than ever I believed it my chief duty to protect her.

"No, Julia," I said; "this rebel against the King means to live. So far from dying, I haven't had anything more than a knockdown which has left a sore spot on my head and a little ache inside it, but I can travel as well as ever. Here, Old Put is waiting for you. Get up and ride."

But she declined with indignation.

"I will not do that," she said. "You may be a rebel—in fact, I know you are—but you shall not walk while you are wounded. You must ride."

As I was still a little dizzy I yielded at last, though I did not like to do it, and rode for a couple of hours. Then, feeling as strong as ever, I dismounted and made Julia take her turn on horseback. But at the end of an hour she too dismounted, and we walked on together as before, not talking much, but happy. The sun was again retreating before the night, and the western skies were aflame. The light fell full upon the girl's face, and her beauty, splendid and glowing before, was tender and spiritual now.

"We shall be in Morgan's camp soon, Julia," I said, "and I will have to resign my prisoner."

"I shall consider myself your prisoner until I am retaken by the English," she said.

I did not reply, but I was willing to accept my responsibilities.

Old Put, who was walking slowly behind us, after his custom, raised his head and neighed. It was not a whinny, but a loud, sonorous neigh that could be heard afar. It was full of meaning too. And a quarter of a mile ahead of us on one of the open ridges I saw the cause—a troop of a dozen horsemen riding towards us at a half-gallop. Old Put neighed again, long and loud.

"Ought we not to escape into the wood?" exclaimed Julia in alarm. "There is time yet. Those troopers may be English."

She did not seem to notice the strangeness of a suggestion from her that she hide from the English, but I was confident.

"They are not English," I said. "They are Americans. Old Put knows his friends. Trust him."

In truth, the horse uttered his loud and joyous neigh a third time, and I had not the slightest apprehension, for it was impossible to deceive Old Put when he was wide awake.

The horsemen saw us and quickened their pace to a gallop. As they approached I could recognize the Continental buff and blue, and, telling Julia that it was all right, we walked gravely on to meet them. Old Put, his demonstrations of joy made, followed after with equal sobriety.

They were dashing riders, those men, and their curiosity must have been aroused by the sight of the girl, for they came on at the long, swinging gallop of the good cavalryman, and quickly enclosed us.

"Good-evening, Colonel," I said to the leader, saluting. "I am happy to see you again and to join your command."

It was Colonel William Washington, the distant cousin of our great Commander-in-Chief, one of the finest cavalry commanders of our time, a fine, open-faced man of about thirty.

"Why, Marcel—Phil Marcel!" he cried in surprise, "is it you?"

"Yes, it is I, Colonel."

"And the lady?"

"The lady is my prisoner, Colonel, an English spy!"

"Did she give you that wound on your head?"

"I said a lady, Colonel."

Every hat came off, and there was admiration as well as respect in the bow that each trooper made.

"The lady carried the news of our most important movements," I said, "and I was compelled to hold her a prisoner."

"You have done well, Mr. Marcel," said my Colonel.

I thought so too. Perhaps I had done better than I thought.

"Now that I have brought the prisoner in," I said, "I will have to resign her into your hands, Colonel."

"It will be but for a brief space, as the camp of Morgan is only three miles back. There are some American women there who will take care of her."

"But I wish to remind you of one thing, Colonel."

"What is that?"

"A lady cannot be shot or hanged as a spy, even though she be a spy."

He laughed the hearty laugh that I like to hear from a man. "Have no fear," he said. "We are Americans." Then he laughed again that deep, resonant laugh which I like. "I will send two men back with you and the prisoner, but I am on a scout to find Tarleton and ascertain when he is likely to attack us." "Do we mean to make a stand?" I asked. For the third time he laughed. "Why, boy," he said, "you don't expect Morgan, who, with Arnold, was the hero of Saratoga, to run away, do you? He only wanted a little time to drill his men and get his grip on them, and now he's ready to welcome Tarleton to the fray."

"Then you will have Tarleton by morning," I said, and I explained all that I had heard or learned otherwise in my flight with the prisoner, to which he listened with an interest that indicated its importance and made me feel mine.

"Good! Good, Marcel!" he exclaimed more than once. "This is precisely what we wanted to know. And so Mr. Tarleton is hot on our heels and will attack in the morning? Well, Philip Marcel, I think you will see to-morrow as pretty a little battle as was ever fought on this continent, and neither Colonel Tarleton nor I nor any other can tell yet what the result will be."

Julia was standing by me, and her old spirit suddenly flamed up.

"I can," she said, "and I only hope that instead of falling in the battle you will be taken a prisoner, for to-morrow night your army will not exist."

"Miss Howard," said Colonel Washington, bowing—I had given her name—"we have more admiration for the ladies than confidence in their military predictions."

CHAPTER 10 In Morgan's Camp

Then we proceeded to the encampment, and Colonel Washington himself went with us, his plans being changed by my news. My head was buzzing with excitement. We were going to fight Tarleton at last, though with all the odds against us, numbers, discipline, and arms, while Tarleton himself had won his reputation as the ablest and most successful cavalry commander in the British service. We might again experience the disgrace and disaster of Camden, but Morgan was no Gates, and perhaps, on the other hand, we might equal the exploit of the wild borderers at King's Mountain, though it was a little too much to hope for that. But still we would fight, and to a young man it always seems better to fight than to run.

"Old comrade," I said to my horse, "we meet the enemy to-morrow!"

He nodded joyously and then looked gravely at the bandage around my head.

"It is nothing," I said. "I will take it off to-night. My head is well."

He nodded again, as if all his troubles were over.

The wife of Captain Dunn, of the South Carolina militia, was in the camp, a lady whom I knew, my distant kinswoman, and Julia was given into her charge.

"Take good care of her, Cousin Anna," I said. "Remember that she is my prisoner."

"Your prisoner, is she?" she replied enigmatically. "But remember, Philip, that the captor often becomes the captive."

"Cousin Anna," I said indignantly, "I hope you are not going to preach our defeat by Tarleton on the very eve of battle. It will have a discouraging effect."

"I said nothing about the battle. Go and attend to your work, Philip. I will take care of the girl."

To Julia I said:

"We fight to-morrow, and I may not see you again."

Then I bent down and kissed her lips.

She replied very simply and earnestly:

"May you live through it, Philip!"

Cousin Anna's back was to us, and she did not see or hear.

I turned away and began to examine the camp and this field, destined to be the scene of a memorable battle which was itself the opening of one of the greatest, most skilful, and successful campaigns ever conducted on the soil of our continent.

We were on a long slope, consisting of several hills rising above each other like the seats of an amphitheatre, though at a much greater elevation, as the slope was so slight that it offered no impediment to the gallop of a horse. The men were gathering up fence-rails, which they were using for the camp-fires, and I noticed many old tracks of the feet of animals. To my question one of the men said:

"We are going to fight where the cows pastured. Don't you know that this army is camped on the cow-pens of a very worthy man named Hannah? And these rails are the last that are left of his pens."

Behind us flowed the wide, deep, and unfordable Broad River, retreat thus being cut off in case of defeat. I asked the meaning of this strange military maneuver, which meant either victory or destruction, and again the explanation was ready:

"More than half of our men are militia, and you can never tell whether militia will run like rabbits or fight like devils. All early signs fail, and General Morgan says it's cheaper to have the river behind us and make 'em fight than to station regulars in the rear to shoot down the cowards."

Presently I saw General Morgan himself passing among the men and preparing for the expected attack in the morning.. This was one of our real heroes, a fighter and leader and no politician, a man whom the great Washington esteemed and loved to reward. I had seen him at Saratoga and elsewhere, and his figure as well as his name always drew attention. Over six feet high and built in proportion, with a weight of two hundred pounds, and a large, fine, open face, he was a type of the true American, the best of all men in mind and body.

There was plenty of provender in the camp, and I gave Old Put the first solid meal that had come to him in several days. I wanted him to be in good trim for the morrow, for he and I were to take our proper place with Washington's cavalry, to which we belonged, only a handful of men, but able and true and capable of doing great things in the nick of time. There had been some question about the bandage on my head, which I wore as a precaution against taking cold in the scalp-wound, but I showed that it was only a trifle, and Colonel Washington rightfully remarked that such a slight wound would only increase a man's efficiency on the battle-field. Then he presented me with a fine sabre, which I needed badly, and told me to lie down on the ground and go to sleep; but I could not sleep just then, and with the freedom of our colonial armies I roamed about the encampment.

The camp-fires flared up in the cold January darkness. The men sat around them, talking and playing with old greasy cards or singing the songs of the hills and the woods. Some of the soldiers were asleep on their blankets or the bare ground, for we were always a ragged and unhoused army at the best, and only a few of the officers had tents.

A sharp breeze came across the river, and the flames bent to it, their light flickering over wild, brown faces that knew only the open air, wind, rain, hail, or whatever came. Most of them still carried curved and carved powder-horns and bullet-pouches, inseparable companions, over their shoulders, and long, slender-barrelled rifles, so unlike the British muskets, lay at their sides.

Smoke rose from the fires and blew in the faces of the men, deepening the brown and giving them another shade of the Indian. A curse mingled now and then with the singing and the talk of the card-players, and from the borders of the camp came the stamp of the horses and an occasional neigh. In the darkness, half-lighted by the reeling fires, the camp became a camp of wild men, whose faces the wavering light moulded into whatever grotesque images it chose.

We were but a little army, only nine hundred strong, but many of us had come great distances and from places wide apart. An arc of a thousand miles would scarce cover all our homes. There were the militia, South Carolinians and Georgians, raw troops, whom one can never trust; then the little remnant of the brigade that De Kalb had led on the fatal day of Camden, splendid soldiers whose line the whole British army could not break, the survivors now eager to avenge the disgrace their brethren suffered on that day; then the stanch Virginia troops, that we knew would never fail, and near them our two or three score of cavalrymen under Washington—a little army, I say again, but led by such leaders as Morgan, Washington, Howard, and Pickens! Down the slopes the sentinels were on watch, but there was no fear of a surprise, for the scouts were just bringing in word that Tarleton could not come before daylight, and then, owing to the slope and the open ground, his approach would be seen for a great distance.

The new men talked the most, some about the coming battle, eagerly, volubly, others about things the farthest from it, but in the same eager, voluble, unreal tone. The veterans were silent mostly, and already with the calm and hardihood of long usage were seeking the rest and sleep which they knew they would need. A tall, thin man, with a wild face, whom I took to be one of the preachers at the great revival meetings so common on the border, rose in the midst of the camp and began to speak. Some listened, and some went on with the talking and card-playing. I could hear the rustle of the pasteboard as the cards were shuffled. He was a fighting preacher, for he exhorted them to strike with all their strength in the coming battle, and if they must die, to die like Christian heroes. He prayed to God for the success of our arms, then stepped from the stump on which he stood and disappeared from my sight. He fought in the front line of the South Carolina militia the next day.

I sought my own place in our troop and lay down upon one half of my blanket, with the other half above me. Old Put gnawed at some fodder by my side.

"Wake me up in the morning when you see the first red gleam of the British coats, old comrade," I said, and, knowing that he would do it, I closed my eyes.

But sleep would not come just yet, and I opened my eyes again to see that the fires were sinking and the darkness was coming down nearer to the earth. Half the men were asleep already; the others were quiet, seeking slumber, and the steady breathing of nearly a thousand men in a close space made a strange, whistling noise like that of the wind. A flaring blaze would throw a streak of light across a sleeping soldier, showing only a head or a leg or an arm, as if the man had been disjointed. I would hear the faint rattle of a sentry's fire-lock and the heavy hoof of a horse as he crowded his comrades for room. An officer in dingy uniform would stalk across the field to see that everything was right, and over us all the wind moaned and the darkness gathered close up to the edge of the dying fires. Weakness overpowered my excited brain and nerves, and I slept.

CHAPTER 11 The Battle

I was awakened in the morning by the shoving of Old Put's cold nose, which said as plain as speech, "Rise, my master, and prepare for the enemy." Most of the other men were up, and the camp cooks had breakfast ready, bread, meat, and coffee. I threw off my blanket and began to eat with the others.

It was the misty region between night and day. The scouts told us that the British would soon be at hand, and by the time the breakfast had been despatched the rim of the sun appeared in the east, and the day was coming. Then the General formed the line of battle, and each of us took his appointed place.

On the first rise of the slope stood the South Carolina and Georgia militia, the raw troops, in a line about a sixth of a mile long, under the command of the iron-nerved Pickens. They were expected to give way before the charge of the enemy, but Pickens was ordered to hold them in line until they could deliver at least two volleys with the precision in firing which all these farmer boys possessed. Then they were to retire behind the veteran regulars under Howard, who were on the second slope, one hundred and fifty yards in their rear. An equal distance behind the second rise sat we cavalrymen on our horses, commanded to pull on our reins and wait the moment upon which the fate of the combat should turn.

Thus stood our little army, expecting the rush of the battle which, as I have said, was to be one of the most important and decisive of our war. I stroked Old Put's neck and bade him be cool, but he was as calm as I and needed no such encouragement. The man on my left, Bob Chester, a Pennsylvanian, suddenly whispered:

"Don't you hear that faint rumbling noise, Phil? That's the hoof-beats of cavalry."

"Silence there!" called the Colonel.

No one spoke again; but, bending my ear forward, I could hear the far drum of the horses' hoofs, and I knew that the English army was coming. Old Put raised his head and snuffed the air. A red gleam appeared upon the horizon and broadened rapidly. A thrill and a deep murmur ran the length and breadth of our army.

"Oh, if those militiamen will only stand until the General bids them retire!" groaned the Colonel.

That he believed they would not I knew, since it is a hard thing for new men to stand the rush of a seasoned army superior in numbers and equipment.

The sun was just swinging clear of the earth, and betokened a brilliant morning, yet it was cold with the raw damp that often creeps into a South Carolina winter, and I for one wished that the men could see a little more of the day and loosen their muscles a little better before they fought.

The whole British army now appeared in the plain, cavalry, infantry, and field-pieces, in a great red square. I could plainly see the officers giving their orders, and I knew that the attack would come in a few minutes.

"Eleven hundred of them and no raw troops," said Colonel Washington. "We know that exactly from our scouts. I think our cavalry will have something to do to-day."

One officer, in the gayest of uniforms, I took to be the barbarian Tarleton, the British leader whom we hated most of all, for, with all his soldierly qualities, he was a barbarian, as most of his brother British officers themselves say.

I wanted to see the faces of those farmer boys down there on the slope who were to receive the first and fiercest rush of the enemy and to check it. I knew that many of them were white to the eyes, but their backs were towards me, and I could not see.

"They don't appear to move," whispered Chester. "Their line looks as firm as if it were made of iron."

"Like untempered iron, I guess," I replied—"break like glass at the first shot."

A bugle sounded in the front of the British squares, and its notes, loud and mellow, came to us, but from our ranks rose only the heavy breathing and the shuffling of men and horses.

The trumpet-call was followed by a cheer from more than a thousand throats, and then the British rushed upon us. The brass field-pieces on their flanks opened with the thunder that betokens the artillery, and mingled with their roar were the rattle of the small arms, the throb of the drums, and the clamorous hoof-beats of their numerous cavalry.

The face of their red line blazed with fire, their red uniforms glowing through it like a bloody gleam, while the polished bayonets shone in front.

"They are firing too soon and coming too fast," said Colonel Washington. "By God! look at those militiamen! They are standing like the Massachusetts farmers at Bunker Hill!"

It was so. The raw line of plough-boys never wavered. It bent nowhere, and was still as straight and strong as an iron bar. The plough-boys knelt down, and, as the British cheer rose and the red line flaming in front swept nearer, up went the long-barrelled border rifles. I fancied that I could hear Pickens's command to fire, but I did not, and then all the rifles in a line a sixth of a mile long were fired so close together that the discharge was like the explosion of the greatest cannon in all the world.

The smoke rose in a thick black cloud, which a moment later floated a dozen feet above the earth and revealed the British squares shattered and stopped, the ground in front of them red with the fallen, the officers shouting and reforming their lines, while our own plough-lads, still as firm as the bills, were reloading their rifles with swift and steady hands.

We cavalrymen raised a great shout of approval, which the regulars on the rise in front of us took up and repeated. A second volley was all that we had asked from the militiamen, and it was sure now. Even as our cheer was echoing it was delivered with all the coolness and deadly precision of the first. Again the British squares reeled and stopped, but they were veterans, led by the fiery Tarleton, and they came on a third time, only to meet the third of those deadly volleys, which swept down their front lines and blocked the way with their own dead and dying.

"The battle is won already," shouted Colonel Washington, "and it's the farmer boys of South Carolina and Georgia who have won it!"

Never did veteran troops show more gallantry and tenacity than those same farmer boys on that day. Two volleys were all that were asked of them, yet not merely once or twice, but many times, they poured in their deadly fire at close range, again and again hurling back the British veterans, who doubled them in number and were supported by artillery and many cavalry, while we old soldiers in the two lines behind stood silent, not a gun or a sabre raised, and watched their valor.

They retired at last, not broken, but in perfect order, and at the command of Pickens, that we who stood behind them might have the chance to do our part of the day's work.

The smoke hung low in clouds and half hid both armies, British and American. A brilliant sun above pierced through it in places and gleamed on clumps of men, some fallen, some still fighting. Shrieks and groans strove for a place with the curses and shouts.

Again rose the British cheer from the throats of all those who stood, for, the militiamen retiring before them, they thought it was a battle won, and they charged with fresh courage and vigor, pouring forward in a red avalanche. But the regulars, the steady old Continentals, who now confronted them, received them with another volley, and more infantrymen fell down in the withered grass, more riderless horses galloped away.

The battle rolled a step nearer to us, but we cavalrymen, who formed the third line, were still silent and sat with tight reins, while directly in our front rose a huge bank of flame and smoke in which friend and enemy struggled and fought. Even Old Put, with his iron nerves, fretted and pulled on the reins.

The long line of the British overlapped the Continentals, whom they outnumbered three to one, and the General, whose gigantic figure I could see through the haze of smoke, ordered them to retreat lest they should be flanked.

Again the British cheer boomed out when they saw the regulars giving ground, for now they were sure that victory was theirs, though more hardly won than they had thought. But the retreat of the regulars was only a feint, and to give time for the militiamen behind them to come again into action. General Morgan galloped towards us, waving his sword to Washington, and every one of us knew that our moment had come.

"Forward!" was the single command of our leader, and the reins and the sabres swung free as we swept in a semicircle around the line of our friends and then at the enemy. At the same moment the regulars, ceasing to yield, charged the astonished foe and poured in a volley at close range, while the militiamen threw themselves in a solid mass upon the British flank.

We of the cavalry were but eighty strong, with fifty more mounted volunteers behind us under Major McCall, but we were a compact body of strong horses and strong horsemen, with shortened rifles and flashing sabres, and we were driven straight at the heart of the enemy like the cold edge of a chisel.

We slashed into the British, already reeling from the shock of the Continentals and the militiamen, and they crumpled up before us like dry paper before a fire. Our rifles were emptied, and the sabres were doing the silent but more deadly work. Amid all the wild din of the shouting and the musketry and the blur of the smoke and the flame I knew little that I was doing except hack, hack, and I was glad of it. I could hear steel gritting on bone, and the smell of leather and smoke and blood arose, but the smoke was still in my eyes, and I could only see enough to strike and keep on striking. We horsemen, one hundred and thirty strong, were still a solid, compact body, a long gleaming line like a sword-blade thrust through the marrow of the enemy. We cut our way directly to the heart of the English army, and their broken squares were falling asunder as our line of steel lashed and tore. The red army reeled about over the slope like a man who has lost power over his limbs. I struck at a trooper on my left, but he disappeared, and a second trooper on my right raised his sabre to cut me down. I had no time to fend off the blow, and in one swift instant I expected to take my place with the fallen, but a long, muscular brown neck shot out, two rows of powerful white teeth inclosed the man's sword-arm, and he screamed aloud in pain and fright.

"Do you surrender?" I cried.

"Yes, yes, for God's sake, take him off!" he shouted. "I can fight a man, but not a man and a wild devil of a horse at the same time!"

"Let him go," I said to Old Put, and, the horse unclasping his teeth, the man gave up his sword.

The smoke was lifting and clearing away somewhat, and the fire of the rifles declined from a steady crackle to jets and spurts. A dozen of the militiamen seized one of the brass field-pieces of the British, and Howard's Continentals already held the other. Everywhere cries of "I surrender! I surrender! Quarter! quarter!"

arose from the British horse and foot, who were throwing down their arms to receive from us that quarter which we willingly gave, but which the bloody Tarleton had so often denied to our men.

I could scarce believe what I saw. The whole British army seemed to be killed, wounded, or taken. The muskets and bayonets, the swords and pistols, rattled as they threw them upon the ground. Whole companies surrendered bodily. An officer, his gay uniform splashed with mud and blood, dashed past me, lashing his horse at every jump. It was Tarleton himself, and behind him came Washington, pursuing with all his vigor and lunging at the fleeing English leader with a bayonet fastened at a rifle's end. He returned after awhile without Tarleton, but there was blood on his bayonet. Tarleton, though wounded in the shoulder, escaped through the superior speed of his horse, to be taken with Cornwallis and the others at Yorktown.

The General raised his sword and cried to us to stop firing and striking, for the field was won and the battle over, and he spoke truly. Far away showed the red backs of some of the English fleeing at the full speed of their horses, but they were only a few, and almost their entire army lay upon the field, dead and wounded, or stood there our prisoners. The defeat that so many of us feared had proved to be the most brilliant little victory in our history, a masterpiece of tactics and valor, the decisive beginning of the great campaign which won us back the Southern colonies, one of the costliest of all her battles to England. I have told you how it was, just as the histories, both English and American, tell it to you. All honor and glory to the gallant plough-boys of South Carolina and Georgia, who received the first shock of the British army and broke it so bravely! Of the eleven hundred British veterans who attacked us only two hundred escaped from the field, and we took all their cannon, baggage, ammunition, and small arms, even of those who escaped, for they threw them away in their flight. The killed, wounded, and taken just equalled the numbers of our entire army, and we had only twelve men dead.

CHAPTER 12 Looking Ahead

I returned towards the Broad River, where, under the lee of a little hill, a tent had held six or seven friendly women. Julia came out, her face still pale, for she had heard all the crash and tumult of the battle.

"It is over, Julia," I said,—I had hid my bloody sword,—"and the British army no longer exists."

"And the victory is yours! Yesterday I thought it impossible."

"Your countrymen make the same mistake over and over again, but they pay the price."

We walked towards the field, and we met some men bringing in a gray-haired prisoner, a tall, fine-looking officer. Julia, crying aloud in her joy, ran forward and embraced him. He returned the embrace again and again with the greatest tenderness.

"Father," said Julia, "we are now prisoners together."

I watched them for a few minutes, and then I stepped forward and said:

"Good-morning, Major Howard."

He stared at me in the icy way of the Englishman who has been addressed by a stranger.

"I do not know you, sir," he said.

"My name is Philip Marcel, and I am your future son-in-law."

He was now unable to speak.

"It is true, sir," I said. "Ask your daughter."

He looked at her. She smiled and reddened.

Old Put was standing by, and he nodded his head in approval. He had liked her from the first.

"Your daughter is to be my wife," I continued with emphasis, "and you are to live with us and like us."

These were resounding boasts for a young soldier to make, but they all came true after Yorktown.

THE END.

BOOK FOUR

THE WILDERNESS ROAD

A ROMANCE OF ST. CLAIR'S DEFEAT AND WAYNE'S VICTORY

(During the Northwest Indian War immediately after the Revolutionary War)

CHAPTER 1 By Rule and Compass

They were dividing lands—enough for a nation—with a rule and compass, and their faces showed their feelings as they bent over the map and cut off a principality for each. Jasper's lips were quite white—it was a curious trick that he had when he was deeply moved—and Mr. Carew watched the lines on the paper with an intent gaze. I knew that avarice and ambition were working somewhere back of his eyes, and, for the moment, I wondered that a man who had so much should crave so much more.

"Our grant covers all the region here along the Miami and the Little Wabash," said Mr. Carew, turning to me, "and I am told that the soil is most fertile, is it not?"

"There is none better," I replied.

"We shall take it at once and have it surveyed. It is well to attend to these matters promptly," said Jasper.

"But you forget that the land is occupied already," I said. It was the first time I had spoken, unless asked a question.

Mr. Carew looked up from the map, and there was inquiry in the gaze that he turned upon me.

"The tribes," I added. "It is their home and hunting ground. They are numerous and warlike. You remember Harmar?"

Mr. Carew made a gesture of contempt.

"The affair of Harmar was nothing, and these tribes are nothing," he said. "St. Clair will brush them out of the way. He is coming with an army, you know, and we shall concern ourselves no further about savages."

I shook my head, but I did not speak, knowing how vain my words would be; and they, turning back to the map, began to divide anew the lands which another race held. I saw the same look upon the faces of them all—Jasper, Mr. Carew, the large man Curry, and the slim-faced lawyer Knowlton. It was a fine map, in beautiful blues and reds and yellows, but it seems to me that any map of the West should be all red. We had to colour it thus to buy it.

I watched them a little as they parcelled so easily among themselves the country that others would have to water with their blood, and then I felt the eyes of Rose Carew upon me.

"You think they are making the division too soon," she said, knowing that the others, their souls gripped by earth-hunger, would not hear.

"They have bought, from those who can not sell, something which they can not take," I replied.

"You know this wilderness?"

"As well as any man, I suppose. Their rule and compass go through it without a halt, but they in person can not do as much."

She had regarded me before with curiosity, and the same question was in her look now. I saw that my manner and speech, contrasting with my garb—half wild, half civilized—puzzled her, but I did not seek to change either gesture or accent.

"And your name is Lee, too," she said, "the same as Captain Lee's?"

"Lee is a common name in both East and West, and its ownership means nothing."

Jasper looked covertly at me, with his sly and hateful smile, but I ignored him.

"Will you come to the door, Miss Carew?" I asked.

She glanced at her father and his friends.

"They will not miss you at this moment," I said.

Nor would they. There was nothing in the world just then so beautiful to them as the vivid blues and reds and yellows of their map. Miss Carew sighed a little as she read the emotions of her father, and then came with me.

"Do you see that woman passing?" I said. "She had a husband and children once; the tomahawk took them. And the boy there; he is the only one left of his name; the tribes slew all the others, but spared him for ransom. And yonder is another woman waiting for her husband to come back from the forest; he will never come. I know where his bones lie, but I dare not tell her."

"Why do you speak to me of these dreadful things?" she asked, the colour leaving her face.

I was silent then, because I was thinking of her father as he apportioned to himself the soil on which our powerful foe lived; but when I looked into this girl's pure eyes I knew that I could not cite such a contrast to her. Instead I said:

"It is well to know what a new land costs us. And no one can say that we shall keep it even at such a price."

"You are a prophet of evil," she said.

"Some one should be so, when others think to wish a thing is to have it. The arm of the nation is weak, and it is a long way across the mountains."

Perhaps I should not have spoken in such a manner to a young girl, but I knew how the land about me had been harried and torn. Moreover, I felt a certain sense of anger in the presence of these people from the East, who would not understand us, and dismissed all our troubles and triumphs alike as trifles. This was to them but the back door of the nation, and yet ruin may come in as readily by the back as the front door.

"I do not like to hear of these slaughters and captures," she said. "They were so strange and far away when I was at home in Philadelphia that one never thought much of them. They have scarcely seemed real."

"That is just the trouble," I replied.

As she stood there, in rich attire, her face unburned by the sun, she typified this difference. What the West suffered was in truth far away and unreal to her.

Mr. Carew, raising his head from the map, called his daughter, and she turned back, but before going asked me:

"Shall we see you once more while we are in Danville, Mr. Lee?"

"I do not know," I replied.

"Come again," she said, "and tell me of this wilderness. It has its romance."

"A romance when seen from afar," I replied. But I promised to come.

I was followed from the house by Jasper, though not knowing it until he stood beside me, with his hand lightly touching my arm.

"You create difficulties for us, John," he said.

"One can not create that which exists already," I replied.

"But St. Clair will brush them out of the way, as Mr. Carew told you. Remember that these tribes have not yet had to face our best."

"The best are always ourselves."

He laughed lightly.

"It is true. I too shall go with St. Clair, and so certain am I of the result that I have been, as you saw, selecting my share of that wilderness through which you roam. Yet I avow that I did not expect to meet you here when I came across the mountains. May I ask what you are doing in Kentucky, Cousin John?"

"There were cities of refuge in the olden times," I said, "and there are countries of refuge now. It is to one such that I have come."

He looked thoughtful, puckering his thin lips, and not speaking for another minute or two, although he kept by my side. I wondered why he had not denounced me, especially when he found me in the company set aside for himself.

"It behooves you to walk in a straight path, John," he said at length, "and I shall keep silent about you if you do as you should."

His tone was patronizing, and therefore most insulting, but I did not reply. Yet I resolved that my actions should not wait upon his pleasure, whatsoever the result.

"I have chosen a course," I said, "and I shall follow it."

"Are you averse to telling it?"

"Not at all. I have decided to serve with St. Clair."

He puckered his lips again.

"It is dangerous," he said. "I advise you not to do so."

"I thank you for your advice," I replied, "but my mind is quite made up."

He changed the subject, though I was sure that it was still in his mind, and began to talk to me of his prosperity, no sense of delicacy keeping him back. He and Mr. Carew were fast friends, he said, and they had obtained great land grants in the West, where climate and soil alike were of the best. He was to become the richest man in America, and soon he should want a wife. Then he spoke of Rose Carew, and I could have wished her a better fate.

I own that I felt much bitterness at this moment. The contrast between Jasper's career and mine seemed so great that the spirit in me was not improved when he went back to Mr. Carew and his daughter.

CHAPTER 2 The Cry for Revenge

We had in Danville the next day one of those public meetings which we call a convention. Kentucky was to become a State in the following year, and her leaders would take measures for that important event. Moreover, they were to send men to St. Clair, for, as I have said, it was a heroic vanguard which bled and suffered much and never gave back; but that terrible cloud of Indian war in the North had long hung upon it, and the air was growing too heavy to breathe. They must have relief, and it was St. Clair who should bring it. Therefore they, the men of the border, in their absolute freedom, hating military leaders and military discipline, would give to St. Clair all the help that they could, hoping to find relief through him. So they came, and, whether it was for peace or war, every one brought a rifle. The time was not yet, when a man in the West could afford to ride without a weapon in his hand.

It was a serious and solemn race that gathered there, bearing already upon its face the stamp of its trials, and the prevailing note that day in the voice of all these men was the cry for revenge. When you study their case you will not blame them. I do not find in history a record of any people who endured more cruel sufferings than they. It is an honour to be the vanguard of a mighty movement, but you pay a price. In all that crowd there was scarcely one who knew what it was to have an untroubled night's sleep. At any moment he might hear the blow of his cruel enemy at the door. When he came from his work in the field he would hasten his footsteps to see if his house had been burned and his wife and children slain in his absence. As he passed through the forest he looked about him with wary eyes, for behind any tree his ambushed foe might be lurking; and in winter, when the work was over and he sat before the red coals, he always listened amid the chatter of the children for something else. His intent ear dreaded to hear outside the soft crunch of moccasined feet on the snow, and his eye often turned to the rifle lying on its hooks on the wall. It was no wonder that he prized this weapon next to wife and children, insisted that it always be of the finest make, and that it should be, too, his chosen comrade, cleaving to him even closer than a wife; there was safety, what safety was to be had, in its long barrel—not for himself alone, but for the others who clung to him and looked to him for protection.

Even a stranger would have noted the effect of such a life upon these men. In the town itself they were wary and suspicious, keeping their rifles in their hands, examining everybody with care, looking about for enemies, eyes keen and shifting like those of a tiger, since danger might come from any point of the compass. The faces were thin and seamed. Long years of watching had left deep lines there. They had been forced to adopt the tactics of their elusive foe, to acquire the skill of the wild animal, in sight, scent, and sound, and in following his customs they had borrowed some of the nature of that foe. They, too, were fierce and relentless toward their enemies, but very generous to their friends.

To-day they called for revenge. There was nothing said about the right cheek. Had one among them preached such a doctrine, the others would have turned upon him in amazement and equal anger. There was no man who had not suffered from the red enemy. From nearly every house a wife or son or daughter had been taken, never to come back again. So those who were left remembered only their griefs, and did not pause to consider the claims of their enemies. That was to them sheer nonsense, a waste of time. What they wanted was blood for blood. I repeat that a wild life among wild foes does not teach softness, and their cry was natural. Moreover, they wished their revenge to be sweeping and final. They were sorry that St. Clair's army was not to be three or four times larger. They wanted nothing to be left of the tribes. They would exterminate them, because there is no peace with poisonous snakes; they would destroy the villages to the last lodge, and make the dark woods across the Ohio, which looked so threatening, and kept their threats, as safe as the open fields in the East. They were impatient, too, with that East which seemed so far away and so indifferent. Men there, who knew nothing about the savages, shilly-shallied with them, they said, and talked about treaties and mutual rights, while they of the West lay under the tomahawk and saw their wives and children scalped and slain. So their anger against the East increased, and many thought that they should not join St. Clair and submit to the noxious military rule of those whom they considered so much less skilful than themselves; an independent force would be better, and then they might do what seemed most fit. But the advice of others prevailed; the soldiers and the Westerners should be united, and when the blow was struck it could be struck with all the greater force.

These men met, amid surroundings of absolute democracy, in the open air under the shade of mighty oaks and beeches, and each said the thing that was in his mind. One was as good as another. There were to be no officers until they were chosen by the crowd, and then the others would obey them—if they saw fit.

The setting of this scene appealed to me, even with all my experience of the West, because I knew that from this little centre the men of my race, so long held to the seashore by the ridge of mountains behind us, would spread over a continent.

It was early autumn. The leaves bore the first delicate tints of red and yellow, and afar the forest glowed. The air, pure and clear, was a joy to breathe, and the glorious foliage hid the newness of the little town beside us. Danville was an island of civilization in a wilderness, but here were the men who would make good their kingdom.

Miss Carew was among those who looked on, and I soon found myself near her. The scene impressed her imagination too; she saw its poetry, and her deepest feelings were stirred. But she paled a little as she listened to the fiery speeches.

"How dark and fierce they look!" she said.

"You can understand what they feel only when you become one of their kind," I replied.

"I am beginning to understand," she continued. "But I wish, Mr. Lee, that they would not regard themselves as separate from the rest of us. The East is not hard and insensible; it simply does not know, or rather it does not know all."

"They are a valiant race," said Mr. Carew.

"They have need to be," I added.

Mr. Carew presently left us, taking with him Jasper, who had made himself one of our company, and began to talk with the Kentuckians. I saw readily his design, a plan in which he wished Jasper to help. He had a great stake in the West, and meant to become one of its people; he would please them and grow popular among them, thus opening the road to high advancement. So thinking, he exercised all his arts, which were not a few. He also offered much material help; he would equip a company out of his own pocket, and the success of his efforts showed in his exultant face. In addition to the help of Jasper he had that of Knowlton, a man of persuasive voice and insidious ways, and I began to wonder just what particular object Mr. Carew had in view. I saw his daughter presently watching him too, and there was a cloud upon her face, as if she would check his ambition did she but know the way.

The meeting broke up, all things being agreed to, and Mr. Carew rejoined us, followed soon by Jasper.

"Walk with us a little, will you, Mr. Lee?" he said.

"I have somewhat to say to you."

I complied willingly, and he spoke of his pleasure in meeting so many people and the friendships he was making. He trusted that their impression of him would be as good as his of them. Evidently he was all for personal glory and gain, and I judged that I had a part in his calculations. What he would say to me concerned my probable use to him. But he did not announce it then, merely asking me to come to his house again in the evening, when we should discuss the affairs that he had in mind. I agreed to his request, curious to know of what he would talk, and yet willing to wait for knowledge until the event should disclose itself. In a way he attracted me strongly with his ambition and his great schemes. I do not blame ambition when it travels the right path, and there had been a time when I had much of it myself. I knew, too, that if the past were changed it could blossom anew in my mind, and it was therefore with a certain sadness that I turned away from his house. But I walked only a few yards, stopping there and watching the lights in the building. Then I saw Rose Carew pass before the window, and I was sufficient judge of myself to know that it was not Mr. Carew alone who drew me.

"You were ever a fool, John Lee," I said to myself, "and time can not cure you."

I turned away again and met Knowlton. I disliked the man. We are open and free in our dealings with each other in the wilderness, with but little taste for the law and its chicane. Moreover, Knowlton was an unpleasing specimen of his class. I would have passed him, but he clung to me.

"A great man!" he said, nodding toward Mr. Carew's house.

"By which I take it that you mean Mr. Carew."

"Even so," he replied.

"I do not know," I said; "but if he does not possess greatness he craves it."

But Knowlton would have it that Mr. Carew was already the most promising figure in the West; he was rich—richer than any other this side of the mountains—his influence was bound to extend in the Western country wherever white men lived, and there was no honour which might not be his for the winning. Nor would his friends be forgotten. This last clause I suspected was of the utmost importance to Mr. Knowlton. But he skimmed lightly over it, and talked of the opportunities sure to come when St. Clair should have crushed the Northwestern Confederation. Then all would recognise the importance of Mr. Carew in furthering this expedition.

"Perhaps the first governorship of the State will not be too great a reward for him," said Knowlton.

"I think he is not to have it," I replied. "The people are more likely to choose a man who has shared their dangers. Like likes like. The bravest fighter is yet the most valuable citizen here, and some one of those whom you saw in that group under the trees is almost sure to be the first ruler of this new State."

He received my words with a discontented air, but did not return directly to the subject of Mr. Carew's promotion. I would have left him then perforce, but I stopped to listen to many hoof-beats. It was those who had gathered that day riding home, either to prepare for the war or to stand guard while the others fought. These I knew were the makers of the West, and not such as Knowlton or Mr. Carew; a race of men in the depths of the wilderness who had forgotten how to laugh. They came in the morning in silence, and now they were going back at night in the same silence, sombre but resolute.

I suppose that thoughts of this kind were passing through Knowlton's mind, too, as he stopped with me and listened without a word until the sound of the last hoof-beat died. Then he left me, saying, "You shall see me again very soon, Mr. Lee."

I returned at the appointed time, and when I knocked upon the Carew door it was Rose Carew who received me, holding a candle high above her head, and peering into the darkness to see who came. I noticed then how tall and straight she was, the deep blue of her eyes, and the yellow gold of her hair. With her easy grace and frank ways she was a new type in the West, where woman, like man, under the shadow of countless dangers, was yet shy and difficult. She had shown me friendship from the first—blended, so I thought, with a certain restrained curiosity as to what I was. Her uncertainty about me, I was reader enough of women's hearts to know, was not my loss.

"You come with so light a step that I heard only your knock," she said. "Do you know that this is what has impressed me most in the West—the footfalls of men and women make no sound."

"The first children in Kentucky learned early to be soundless as they passed," I replied. "It was always better—at least far safer—to hear than to be heard."

"What a life!"

"And yet many have lived it."

"They are waiting for you in the next room," she continued. "I suppose that you are to plan some great campaign, while I stay here and read a book. But I am not sure that I shall not be the better employed."

I went into the apartment she designated and found Mr. Carew, Knowlton, and Jasper there—Mr. Carew expansive and smiling, Knowlton furtive and watchful, and Jasper silent. Mr. Carew welcomed me with great warmth. But his cordiality always seemed to me too inclusive; it was elastic enough to embrace all who might be of use. He gave me a glass of wine, the first that had passed my lips in ten years, but I drank it and put the glass back upon the table without comment.

"Are you an expert in wines?" asked Jasper, with his usual covert sneer.

"Why do you ask?" I replied.

"I thought that you might be," he said.

Mr. Carew did not notice, but Knowlton gave me a quick, inquiring look. However, he remained silent, and Jasper, too, said nothing more just then.

"I want to talk to you again about the Northwest," began Mr. Carew, in smooth, persuasive tones. "You rove at random through the wilderness, and, as you have told me, you know this country well. It is fertile, and its value must be great when these pestilent tribes shall have been cleared away."

"Undoubtedly," I said.

"The grants of myself and my associates cover a large part of this wilderness," he continued, "and as soon as St. Clair finishes his task we shall want to turn it to account. We shall need some one who knows the country well to guide us in our surveys, and we think that we have found such a man."

His intent was now clear to me, and I quickly ran the matter over in my mind.

"In brief," he said, with the air of one who does an important favour, "it is you of whom we are thinking. I am the head of this affair, Captain Lee is my lieutenant, Mr. Knowlton keeps us informed about the law which goes into the very marrow of the case, and you are to be our guide through the woods."

Had any one told me a week earlier that I was to accept such an offer, I should have laughed at him. Even Jasper saw the oddity of the situation, for when I caught his eyes there was in them a flicker of amusement. His look decided any lingering doubts that I may have felt. I did not wish Jasper to be amused at my expense.

"You make no movement until after St. Clair wins his victory?" I asked Mr. Carew. "Because I go with him, as I told you, and my service there precludes my work with you until the former shall have been finished."

"Certainly not," he replied. "'Twould indeed be premature for us to go into the Northwest now. Moreover, Captain Lee also marches with St. Clair. As you see, all our movements wait upon those of the general."

"Then, with this proviso—not until after St. Clair's victory—I shall enlist in your employ," I said.

Mr. Carew seemed pleased, though Jasper looked black; but at that moment my thoughts were in the next room.

I shall admit that I felt compunctions when I entered into this agreement, though I was drawn on by something foreign to the matter in hand, and thinking, too, perhaps, that it was a vague affair which could never come to a head. But Mr. Carew did not consider it such. He talked very freely now of great opportunities. The white wave was soon to roll on and submerge all that opposed it, and those who came close behind should reap great profits. I listened to him awhile, and then I told him that I must go, as I was to depart in a day or so for the Northwest.

"Do not forget your promise," he said, giving me his hand.

"I shall not," I replied, and I left them. Jasper rose to follow me, but Mr. Carew called him, and again I found Rose Carew alone. I stopped a moment, though feeling that I should not do so.

"Is the great campaign launched?" she asked, looking up from her book.

"It is," I replied, "and I am to enter your father's service after St. Clair shall have defeated the Indians."

"And he will defeat them, will he not?" she asked. "I have heard so much of those cruel tribes, Mr. Lee, that I begin now to share your Western feelings. St. Clair is sure to crush them, is he not?"

"No one knows," I replied, "but I am certain that the hopes of all the West go with St. Clair."

I lingered yet a little longer, and she showed me a mind that could grasp the affairs of a statesman—perhaps not so uncommon a quality in woman as we think. She was the most zealous of patriots, and all the country back to the Pacific she wished to be ours.

"We must not let the powers of Europe forestall us," she said.

"The Romans won the world by shortening their swords," I replied, "and what we have here under our hands no nation across the sea can prevent us from holding."

She spoke again of her father's plan. She seemed to know somewhat of its nature, and not wholly to favour it. She, like myself, believed, apparently, that the country should belong to those who were shedding their blood for it.

When I took my leave she came again to the door with her candle.

"May I light you on your way, Mr. Lee?" she said, holding it above her head as before.

And this to me, a man who had travelled night after night through the wilderness, with no light at all! But I accepted it with alacrity, and when I looked back she was still holding the candle at arm's length, and after the young face under it faded in the darkness it beamed, until it too went out.

CHAPTER 3 The Tale the Forest Told

I met, the next morning, Winchester, the English trader with whom I had come, an honest man of open countenance, and we walked together. Yet we said little, each finding his thoughts sufficient for the moment.

I was of the forest now, and the sight of this little town rising from the recent wilderness was unreal to me. I shut my eyes, and that wilderness, sombre and unconquerable, came back again. The veneer of civilization seemed so thin and weak that a hostile touch must sweep it away. But I knew better. Where the man of my race had come to make his home there he would stay. Yet it would be a bitter struggle, and I sighed for those around me, though I saw then nothing but peace hovering over a beautiful open country of grassy hills and slopes, with the little city set in the centre like a jewel.

While we walked a procession came into the town, and it was of a kind not strange to the West. Two half-grown girls, rescued from the savages, were just returning to their own people, and, even as we looked, those who loved them most ran to meet the saved as if they had risen from the dead, and others crowded about, with an involuntary wish to share in the joy. Soon I saw Miss Carew standing near, and her eyes were wet.

"What you told no longer seems unreal and far away," she said.

"There is scarcely a family in Kentucky that has not lost some one," I replied.

"But these have come back."

"Most of them never come back."

Jasper approached at that moment, and began to talk to her, ignoring my presence. He would have her to think that he took a philosophical view of all such incidents. The vanguard of every nation must suffer; it shed its blood that those who came later might reap a harvest from the soil thus so richly watered. But his fine theories had no effect upon her then, and being ill-timed, were of little profit to his own cause. Yet he went with her back to her father's house, and Winchester and I remained in the open air, talking with those whom we knew upon the one topic—the advance of St. Clair and the expected destruction of the Northwestern Confederacy.

Kentucky, I repeat, had been making a lone fight, begun when our Union was in the desperate throes of the Revolutionary War, and could send no help. The resolute vanguard was surrounded by a mighty wilderness in which dwelt a wary, numerous, and cruel foe, who continually struck at it, emerging from those shades when no one knew that they came, and hiding in them again when the blow had fallen. Men bled and suffered, but never gave back an inch. I knew the dangers clustering so thickly around these people, and I knew, too, the joy that they felt as the army of St. Clair prepared for its advance into the great Northwestern forests to meet their bitter and treacherous enemy. The East, so populous and wealthy by comparison with the West, had not forgotten them, and was coming to their defence; they would be released from the long scourge, and could now develop the land as they pleased. Theirs was a rich and fine country, well worth the toil of any race to win, and they had my sympathy both in their sufferings and the hope of release.

I went again, despite Jasper's warning eyes, to the house of Mr. Carew, and in the presence of many spoke boldly with his daughter. I saw that I had stirred her imagination. I was a rover of the great wilderness; I seemed to her wild in aspect, and yet I spoke a cultivated tongue; it was the contrast that appealed to her, though she did not know it. I too was drawn, but it was by the sight of a beautiful face and the sound of a familiar accent after so many years.

As I talked to her I was smitten suddenly and so keenly with the longing for home that I was willing to risk everything, and Jasper's warning seemed to me a little thing. After all, I had nothing to lose.

Mr. Carew received me with smooth words; it was not his part to be either cold or warm until he knew his man better. I had read him from the first—a fencer by nature, one always seeking to test the guard of another and measure his skill and value to himself, John Carew. He was, in truth, to use another comparison, his own yardstick.

"You go soon to join St. Clair?" said Miss Carew to me.

"Such is my intention," I replied. "All in the West should serve now when there is so much need of it."

"And St. Clair will get a valuable soldier in Mr. Lee," said Jasper, who was near.

"I do not doubt it," said Miss Carew, coming warmly to my defence as she saw Jasper's purpose to gibe.

"An efficient and valuable officer," continued Jasper. He had given me his warning, which I had defied, and now it was evident to my mind that he wished to torture me in the presence of Miss Carew.

"I infer, from what Captain Lee said, that you have been a soldier?" she asked, turning bright and inquiring eyes upon me.

"Captain Lee sees fit to jest," I replied calmly. "I shall not be an officer with St. Clair; merely a common soldier, or rather a scout. A life spent in the wilderness fits me for nothing else."

She did not accept my statement wholly, an air of doubt hanging over her, increased speedily by Jasper's words. The man had in him something of the cat, liking to inflict cruelty for cruelty's sake. He called the past to my mind by a hundred suggestions and in a hundred ways, and yet at no time did he say anything that would give Miss Carew a clew. No, that was not his purpose. He would save his knowledge of me to use when there was a profit in it. It was not Jasper's way to waste any resource. But he let me alone by-and-bye, and I resolved to have a plain talk with him as soon as I might.

Miss Carew, with an insistence which I knew was steadily swelling Jasper's anger—and I was glad then to have his anger—kept me beside her. She wanted to hear more of the great wilderness, of the woods so dense and dark that the sunlight never entered them, of rivers unmarked and unnamed, of the vast plains beyond, and of adventures by flood and forest. The fascination and mystery of the mighty West were upon her, and though I was loath to tell at first, I soon found myself launched upon the full stream of narrative, current and wind together carrying me on. She listened like a new Desdemona, and when I stopped suddenly, recalling to myself that I was about to lose my caution, she exclaimed:

"It is, indeed, to have been a man to have seen and to have done all these things!"

"But not many can get the chance," said Jasper, over her shoulder. "There are few of us who have cause to turn wilderness rovers."

She wheeled upon him with a questioning look, but he said nothing more, and I, waiting until he left for the evening, followed close behind him.

"You wished to talk with me two nights ago, Cousin Jasper," I said, "and now I wish to talk with you."

"Well?"

"I told you then that I should serve with St. Clair."

"And I warned you against it."

"So you did, but I chose to let the warning pass; instead, I wish now to give you one. If you undertake to deride or torture me I shall reply with the sword. I do not fear you, Jasper Lee."

He gave me a look which he intended to be one of scorn, but it fell before mine.

"You grow bold in the light of a lady's smile," he said.

I felt my face flush despite myself.

"Oh, I have seen how Rose Carew hung upon your words," he continued. "You spin a fine tale, and any girl might well listen, but think who and what you are to dare so much."

"I have not dared anything yet," I said, "and your threat upon that point is not needed."

He changed suddenly from a hostile to a friendly air, asking me of my life in the woods, St. Clair's probable line of advance and the chance that the allied forces of the tribes would await his coming. He was to be on the general's staff, he added, and he anticipated honours sufficient to warm the heart of any man. I said him nay in no case, and, even as we talked, runners arrived calling for volunteers to serve with St. Clair. A great and crushing blow was to be struck, and the Kentucky militia must help.

There was a willing response, the way being prepared already. One company left Danville on the following day, and another, I heard, had gone from Lexington. The border was on fire with ardour, and people spoke of the time soon to come when the Indian tomahawk should have no more terrors for them.

I felt that I too ought to hasten, and yet I lingered a little longer, receiving a day or two later a message from Mr. Carew that he wished to see me again.

"You are going with St. Clair," he said, when I came, "and so is Captain Jasper Lee. He is a young man who is dear to me, and with your knowledge of the forest you may help him in this arduous campaign. I think I can rely upon you to be his good friend, can I not?"

This was a strange request to make of me, that I should be the ally of Jasper, of all men in the world, in a measure watching over him and contributing to his future, and it seemed such a jest of Fate that I was tempted to smile. Yet I refrained, nor could I see anything in Mr. Carew's look to indicate a sense of the true situation.

"Captain Lee shall have all the aid that I can give him," I replied, and I spoke with truthful intent. "Perhaps he will need it. Our Eastern officers do not appreciate the immensity and dangers of the wilderness."

I was full of the subject, and I began to tell him of the vast distances, the wily character of the foe, and the ignorance inherent in such an army as St. Clair led, but he scoffed at me.

"Think you," he said, "that a nation which fought, and fought with success, all the power of Great Britain, has need to fear a few prowling savages?"

And with that I was forced to be content. He would not hear more of such talk, his mind being set upon his great land enterprises, already counting with eager anticipation the profits of the soil on which the tribes still dwelt. Then he told me that he was going on the following day to the Falls of the Ohio, and his daughter with an escort would follow later. His wife, an invalid who had come down the Ohio by boat, and who was not yet prepared to take the land journey to Danville, was there now, waiting for them.

"I shall be at the Falls myself shortly," I said, "as my duties will take me that way."

He invited me with much courtesy, in such event, to visit him and his family, and again he gave me that shrewd look by which he seemed to estimate my worth. It was increasingly evident that he thought me useful to him, and did not intend that I should wander again into the forest without returning a dividend upon my value.

I bade Miss Carew good-bye the next day, and Jasper, who was present, did not like my appearance there; nor did I fancy his calm air of ownership.

"You go into the great wilderness," she said. "I wish sometimes that I were a man, that I might penetrate its mysteries."

"It is well enough for men," I said, "but not for women."

"An excellent place for some men," said Jasper, with cunning intimation. She glanced quickly at him and then at me, but our eyes showed nothing, and presently I left her, glad that my face was turned again toward the forest. She recalled too much. I liked to be in her presence, but it made me think, nevertheless, of all that I had lost, and the thought was not pleasant. I had not spent so many years in putting down memory to have it rise afresh at the mere sound of a woman's voice, and my mind turned now toward the forest and my chosen comrade, Osseo, who would meet me beyond the Ohio.

Winchester and I travelled together, he intending to follow St. Clair at once, and I to join the general a little later, a letter which reached me at Lexington from Colonel Darke, of the Kentucky militia, asking me first to obtain news of the tribes and their intentions. I saw, as we advanced, more fully than ever before, the work that was going on west of the mountains. On every side hung the cloud of Indian war—a kind of war so terrible and ghastly that the whole tale of it can never be told—but the people still came, down the rivers, through the forest, and over the hills, stopping at nothing, daunted by no report of suffering from those who had gone before. The armies, the red and the white, gathered, but, careless of either, the men, the women, and the children advanced, lured by tales of rich soil and good climate, and anxious for new wonders. They knew that the tomahawk was there threatening them, but they dared it. If one fell beneath its edge, another was left, and the human stream flowed on.

"The earth-hunger is the keenest hunger of all, and our Anglo-Saxon race suffers most from it," said Winchester to me.

And when I judge from what I have seen and heard, I think that he was right.

I knew that the tribes would not yield this land without a struggle, and with the advantage they had in their forests I was unable to say which would succeed. They were gathering now for an effort mightier than the red man had ever made before on our soil. The great chief, Little Turtle, had called them to war, and all the valiant and numerous tribes of the Northwest were coming, the Miamis, the

Shawnees, and the Wyandots leading them. Already the daring settlers beyond the Ohio beheld bloody warnings.

Winchester left me at the river, and I passed into the Northwest, following for days upon Indian traces, and finding everywhere new proofs that St. Clair would have to face the might of the allied tribes. Then I turned back toward the south, and at a place appointed by us a month before I met my friend Osseo, whose name means in the Iroquois tongue Son of the Evening Star.

He was a strange Indian in many ways. I never knew his tribe. He would paint himself, but he did not follow any method by which he could be classified. He wore his hair sometimes in the scalp lock, and then would let it fall down his back in long, coarse strings like a horse's mane. He had some relics of a missionary education, the better parts of which he seemed to like, and he was disposed to be friendly to the whites, being well hated by the Northwestern Indians. I have always thought that he was the last survivor of some old Eastern tribe, a man without a nation. I should add to this that he was the finest master of woodcraft I ever knew, and my good friend. He was painted now as a warrior of the nation of the Iroquois, of the tribe of the Mohawks, of the totem Cahenhisnhonen.[1] He smiled when we met, and the corner of his eye drooped in a most suggestive manner. Osseo had a sense of humour.

"It was as such that I went among them five days ago," he said. "I was Nokalis, the Mohawk who had come from the far East to help them fight the white men, and lo! I bring news that the warriors continue to gather; they come from all the forest, and even from the grass plains beyond. It is not an idle wind that will blow into the face of the white general."

I knew that Osseo spoke the truth. What his eyes beheld was but cumulative testimony to the proof of mine, and I lingered no longer, hastening on with him toward the Falls of the Ohio.

It was only a little town by the Falls that they had built—Louisville they called it, after the French king, to whom we owed much—and my business there was of scant weight, but I did not turn back from the journey. Perhaps I should now be with St. Clair, I reflected as I went on, but it would be easy for Osseo and myself, travelling so light, to overtake the general, and I was resolute to keep my promise to Rose Carew.

I did not seek to conceal to myself the chief reason that took me to the Falls. The face of woman is beautiful to all men, and one who has lived long in the woods hungers most for the sight of it. She had spoken to me with sympathy and listened in suspense to my tales of the wilderness. Nor could Jasper's sly words, with their hint at something unknown, poison her against me.

---

[1] The totem or insignia of the Mohawk tribe

We travelled toward the southwest into the eye of the setting sun, and drew near our destination, crossing the Ohio at last, and pursuing our journey along the southern shore, within the line of travel now from the older towns like Danville and Lexington to the Falls. It was the same beautiful country, a little wilder perhaps, with higher hills and deeper forests, but, like the region which we call the Bluegrass, a noble territory for the white man to win.

And it was not yet won. The axe had just begun to level the oaks, and here was where the red warriors passed but yesterday; yonder across the broad stream they still lay in the unbroken forests. Truly it was a black wilderness on the other shore, and good cause had the white women of this new land to look toward it in dread and fear.

"The warriors are there," said Osseo, following my eyes, "and the river will not hold them back."

He spoke the truth. While St. Clair prepared to crush them the tribes were striking. Daring bands more than once had crossed the Ohio into the land which they still claimed, and the tomahawk was falling on defenceless heads. Hoyoquim, the chief of the Wyandots, the boldest of all the Northwestern warriors, led the strongest party, it was said, and we found the terror of his advance spreading before us. Armed men were gathering, but none could tell where such an elusive foe would pass or when he would strike. It was like pursuing a shadow.

"They reach out a hand for Hoyoquim," said Osseo, "and he is not there. While they wonder, he strikes from behind; and then he is gone, and no one can follow."

He described the case truly, and I hastened our journey, being told, at a house within one day's travel of the Falls, that a lady riding with three men, the latter evidently of inferior degree, had passed but a few hours before. "Tall, with blue eyes, yellow hair like corn silk, and very young," they said, and I knew that it was Rose Carew. The men most likely were in her father's employ, and were the escort of which he had spoken.

I had grown daring in these days, and I might go with her, so I thought, to the little town by the Falls. Surely there would be none to dispute my right save Miss Carew herself, and it was yet for her to say.

I suggested to Osseo that we travel faster, and he obeyed without question. It was a part of this man's nature to fulfil the wishes of a friend and never ask the reason why.

The way led now through the woods, and then through little stretches of open. Man, even on the south side of the river, had yet made but little mark upon the forest, and for the present we saw none at all. It was the wilderness as God had left it. I swept the circle of my vision, but saw the smoke of no chimney—only the black rim of the forest; heard nothing but the chattering of the squirrels in the oaks and the fall of the acorns.

Osseo stopped suddenly, gazed intently at the earth, and when he looked up again his face was full of gravity.

"Lee," he said, "the warriors have passed."

I followed his pointing finger and beheld the footsteps. I doubted not that they were those of Hoyoquim, a man whom I knew well, and whose valour and skill I respected. A sudden great dread seized me, and when Osseo said, "It is well to hasten," I felt the full truth of his words. This was yet no man's land, and there was safety only within a circle of armed hands.

"A white lady and three men have passed on ahead," I said to Osseo. "Think you that their journey will be untroubled?"

"Manito alone knows," he said, and even as he spoke a horse, saddled and bridled, but riderless, galloped ahead of us through the woods, his eyes wild with terror, and foam on his flanks.

"Manito knows, and he has spoken his will," said Osseo.

The fear in my heart leaped up again, and I rushed forward at utmost speed. I did not think until days later that Osseo made no effort to restrain me after his cautious fashion when he feared an ambush—he knew even then that such danger had passed for us.

We reached the darkest shadow of the forest, and there we beheld the sight of which my fears had warned me, and which even before my eyes looked upon it I felt doomed to see. The three men lay dead under the trees, smitten down by an unseen foe, but the girl was gone, vanished, no more trace of her left than if made of thin air she had melted away before a wind.

Overpowered, I put my face in my hands and groaned, and yet it was but such a tragedy as this land had seen a thousand times before. Abrupt it might be, but not more so than many others.

"Hoyoquim and the Wyandots passed here," said Osseo.

"Which way do their footsteps lead?" I asked.

"To the river, They have crossed it now, and taking the white girl as their prisoner, go back with the other warriors to meet the white general."

I confess that this event was like a sudden blow. I had long since become hardened in a measure to the news of women captured and men slain. It was the wilderness road that we were compelled to tread, and many in the West had ceased to count the price, knowing that it must be paid. But she was not of the West; hers were another land and atmosphere; she had spoken of such things as far away and unreal; even when she witnessed the return of the captives in Danville the full truth was but the impression of the moment, and must soon grow distant and unreal again. Now she was proving in her own person what it was to tread this wilderness road. I felt a great pity for her, and it was in my mind to follow at once and bring her back if I could. Surely forest skill might be of some avail. But later thought showed that such a purpose was folly. We must go on to the Falls and spread the news there, and then my duty would call me. St. Clair was advancing, and the blow that he struck might save not Rose Carew alone, but many. Her best chance lay in his victory, and I was cool enough now to see it. One could not speak to the savages of ransom while they were preparing to meet St. Clair. It was my part, too, to contribute all I could to the weight of the arm that was to strike this blow, and we hastened to the Falls, I faintly hoping for her, Osseo saying nothing.

We found the little town in deep alarm over the forays, and our tale did not help. Mr. Carew had not yet come, Jasper was with St. Clair, and the mother was there alone. But she sent for me, and I came at once to her call. When I saw the grief in that worn, pale face, I felt that it was such as she who had most to suffer as we built up the nation in the West. She said that Rose Carew had written of me, telling about the famous woodsman whom she had met in Danville; I had saved others from the savages, and now I must save her daughter, the girl who had believed in me; surely I would do it—I could not deny her.

When she had spoken thus, she lay back and gazed at me with great eyes, to whose demand I dared not say nay. I could not refuse such an infinite grief, and yet when I came away from her presence I cursed myself and my fate because my hands were tied for the time.

"Will Lee go for the girl now?" asked Osseo, his inscrutable eyes upon me.

"How can I, Osseo, how can I?" I asked.

I was to march the next day with the detachment to join St. Clair. I had made a boast to Jasper that I would join the army. I was not my own man now, and it behooved me more than any other whom I knew to walk in the straight path, as Jasper had said. The liberty of choice was not left me.

"I shall seek her, Osseo," I replied, "but I shall seek the army first."

"Lee is right," said Osseo. "He has promised that he will fight beside the Long Knives, and he can not break his word. Moreover, the white army goes where Lee would go."

We left an hour later, hurrying away, because I was not willing to look again into the face of that poor invalid, or to have her know while I was there that I was not hastening at once for her daughter. I received permission from our captain to go on before as a scout, and with Osseo by my side I plunged into the Northwestern forest, speeding through the deep woods, now burning in the full glory of autumn colours, and thinking of Rose Carew and her fate. What a blow it must be to the ambition of her father!

CHAPTER 4 The General-Who-Never-Walks

Five days and nights we travelled through the forest, and while I still thought of Rose Carew I also thought of what awaited me in the camp of St. Clair. Jasper's threats had scarcely been veiled, and I knew, too, that I had aroused in him a feeling of jealousy—I laughed to myself, though it was a bitter laugh, to think how little was the cause. I was the last man in the world of whom he should feel jealous. But Osseo spoke words of comfort. The maid, beyond a doubt, had been taken to the Miami town on the Wabash, and there the army was marching. I reflected upon what he said, and saw new reasons why I should stay with St. Clair. Perhaps we were advancing to certain rescue.

Osseo, as we neared our destination, led the way. Once I turned to him and asked:

"Are you sure that you are taking the right path?"

"Yes," he answered. "I lead you straight toward the General-who-never-walks."

"To the General-who-never-walks?" I said, mystified.

"Yes," repeated Osseo, "the old, sick, white chief, who comes on the shoulders of his men; the one who builds his fires in the forest that all his enemies may see where he goes."

Such was his term for General St. Clair, who led our army against the great confederation of the Northwestern tribes. Now that he was so near, I thrilled with strong emotion. Yet I refused to turn back. I felt a strange, stubborn pride, and it would not permit me.

Early on the morning of the sixth day Osseo pointed toward the sunrise. A thin dark line dividing the heavens showed there distinctly against the red and gold.

"The smoke from a camp fire; it must be the army of General St. Clair," I said.

He nodded.

We hastened on now, and soon reached the outposts, finding that, in truth, it was St. Clair's army which lay before us.

A soldier levelled his gun at Osseo and was about to pull the trigger, but I knocked his hand away in time.

"Don't you see that it's a friend?" I cried. "'Tis Osseo, the smartest Indian in all the Northwestern Territory."

Then I introduced myself to the captain of the pickets, a self-contained man of middle age.

"Lee! John Lee?" he said; "I have heard the name. You volunteered to serve us as a scout?"

"So I did," I said, "and I have information."

He asked us to sit by one of the camp fires, where breakfast would be given to us, and he would report meanwhile our arrival to St. Clair. We obeyed, and while we were there Winchester came to us, giving my hand the warm grip of friendship, and telling us that his business as a trader had kept him with the army. But the captain—Hardy was his name—returned in an hour, saying that General St. Clair wished to see me.

Then he led the way. I liked his manner and his trim appearance, and I knew at once that he was an old Continental Officer. He had the military walk and rigidity of figure never cultivated by our Western people. I could not speak so well of his men. The scouts, in truth, were fitted for their work, being alert fellows without pretence. Some of them I knew, such as Ben Strong, Dick Bates, and old Joe Grimes, the guide, a short, thick, bandy-legged man of immense strength and endurance, who considered all soldiers fools, and despised all governments as a useless tyranny.

I shook hands with my friends and looked again at the soldiers. It was certain that these were not men who knew the wilderness road; the ways of the forest were strange to them. I remembered the type. Their faces showed a lack of healthy colour; they were white in the cheeks and black under the eyes, and their muscles were loose and flabby, being, in fact, but sodden lumps, drawn from the vilest drinking taverns and brothels of our great Eastern towns and sent into this far wilderness to fight the wariest and most enduring of all foes, the Northwestern Indians. In truth, our President could then find no other, as we were rebuilding a country exhausted by the long years of the Revolutionary struggle. I felt both pity and contempt for these men as I looked upon them, some even trembling for the want of that rum with which they used to soak themselves in the cities.

Captain Hardy saw my attentive look and smiled in a deprecatory way.

"They will be fit in time," he said. "We are training them."

Osseo, whose watchful eyes followed mine, said in a low voice, "Rotten like a tree that has lost its roots." The savage's look expressed contempt only, and with this contrast before me, I could not deny a favourite contention of his, that the red was the superior race. Beside me stood the Indian, a perfect specimen of manhood, the bronze of his skin without a splotch, his eyes as clear as the waters of a brook, his muscles as elastic and hard as hickory, all the strength and all the virtues of the primitive man in his brain and heart; and before me this rum-sodden lot, whose rotting flesh was ready to fall from their bones, and whose dim eyes gazed only in a vague wonder and distrust at the mighty forest in which they were lost. Most truly the breath of the wilderness is sometimes the breath of God.

"The camp is near to good water, I hope," I replied, speaking on the impulse of the moment, "and suitable for defence too. The general has thrown out scouts, has he not?"

Captain Hardy turned a keen look upon me.

"General St. Clair might resent such questions," he responded, "and so might I, one of his officers; but I do not, knowing that they are suggested by a good motive. The precautions of which you speak have been taken—at least part of them."

A look of depression appeared upon his face, and he was silent as we approached the main camp. I did not see, despite his assertion, the evidence of a vigilant watch, needed in such a country. Some sentinels were about, and the borderers, more of their own volition than by order, maintained a constant search through the woods for a foe, but that was all; otherwise the army felt itself secure in its numbers and strength. But the camp, it should be admitted, was selected with good judgment, lying on both sides of a clear creek, in an open space, where the forest was at least a quarter of a mile from any of the tents.

"That is General St. Clair's marquee," said Captain Hardy, pointing to the largest of them all. "He is not an altogether well man, and I ask you to be patient."

I made no promise, reserving to myself my birthright of independence. We approached the general's tent slowly, Osseo and I meanwhile still examining the army to the best of our opportunity. I judged that it numbered seventeen or eighteen hundred men, wholly from the East, except some companies of sunburned Kentuckians—the border contribution—who in their deerskins or home-made jeans formed a contrast to the pallid Easterners in faded uniforms. Numbers of the soldiers were playing cards on fallen logs, and others slouched about without aim or purpose, which I take to be the mark of an idle mind. I saw also at least a dozen buxom women, strapping wenches, evidently the wives of corporals or sergeants, and probably better men than their husbands.

A sentinel, musket on shoulder, watched at the entrance to the general's marquee, but he stepped aside when Captain Hardy told who we were, and we entered.

It was a large tent, and on a litter in the corner lay a man of near sixty, with high-coloured, smooth-shaven face. He wore a fine American uniform, with a great puff of orange ribbon at the throat. His hair was drawn in a knot behind and tied with ribbon. An attendant was replacing the bandages upon a much-swollen foot.

It was the face of a brave, choleric, and headstrong man, with both the virtues and the vices of the race from which he sprang. General St. Clair was not an

American, either by birth or breeding—only by adoption—although it must be said that he was an honourable soldier who had done us good service in the Revolutionary War, though always the cocksureness of his race clung to him, inherited like the gout from which he was now suffering.

I gave him the proper military salute, and he looked me slowly over, as if he would estimate my temper and worth.

"Are you the scout Lee?" he asked.

"I am a hunter primarily, and a scout secondarily," I replied.

"Your salute and your attitude are both military; these things are the result of training."

"It may be that I have served, sir."

"Where and when, pray?"

"That, General St. Clair, you must permit me to keep as my secret."

Additional colour flushed into his red face, but he retained control of himself and said:

"You are not a member of my immediate command, sir; if you were, I might compel another tone; but the matter may pass, and we will to the business in hand. Your name is not unknown to me, Mr. Lee, but I have no acquaintance with the savage who accompanies you."

"This, General St. Clair," I said, "is Osseo, an Indian, the loyal friend of the whites, and the best woodsman on the face of the earth."

The general nodded slightly. Osseo's salute was full of pride and haughtiness. His bearing was that of a man who acknowledged no superior and few equals, but he spoke no word, waiting in silence for me to say all that was needed.

"What do you know of the Indians whom we are sent against, Mr. Lee?" asked the general.

"They are gathering in great force on the Wabash and Miami Rivers," I replied. "All the Northwestern tribes are coming—Wyandots, Miamis, Shawnees, Ottawas, Sacs, Foxes, Pottawatomies, and some even from the shores of Superior, armed with bows and arrows. Little Turtle, Blue Jacket, Black Eagle, and the renegades Girty and Blackstaffe lead them."

"Be it so," said the general. "Let them gather and form one band. It will be easier to strike off one head than many."

"But, general," I could not refrain from saying, "these savages are bold and most dangerous. Caution is needed."

"Yes, caution is needed," he replied with satirical emphasis, "more perhaps than advice. Let it suffice you, Mr. Lee, that I am already taking all the necessary measures."

I bowed, and he added in a kindlier tone:

"I am glad that you stay with us, Mr. Lee, and glad to have the Indian too. This is a difficult business, I will admit, and we need men who know this accursed wilderness. I prefer war in the more open country of the East; but that is neither here nor there. How far over yonder does this forest extend?"

He waved his hand toward the Northwest.

"To my knowledge no man has ever reached the end of it yet," I replied.

He uttered an oath, but it was not due to impatience at my answer; merely to an extra twinge in his gouty foot.

"I suppose you think, Mr. Lee," he said, and he smiled as he said it, "that gout is the last thing a true forester ought to have."

"I never heard of one who had it," I replied.

"Which is only another way of saying that I am no forester."

I was silent, but he did not seem to be offended, and, if I may be pardoned for saying it, I did not care greatly about his state of mind. There was in truth something most startlingly incongruous in the spectacle of a gouty old general, carried on a litter through an unbroken forest, to fight Indians. But on the whole, though testy when the gout was lively, he was a gentleman, and I gave him willingly all the information at my command, describing the various tribes in the league against us, their characteristics, their probable numbers, and the quality, of their leaders. Osseo supplemented my story with other details, but never for a moment relaxed his dignity. Then the general thanked us both with much courtesy, and bidding him good-day, we went from his tent into the camp. The first man whom we met was Captain Hardy.

"Mr. Lee," he said, "there is an officer of your name in our army who has heard of your arrival and wishes to see you. I inferred from what he said that he was some kind of a relation of yours."

These words, so lightly uttered by this unsuspecting and good-hearted captain, sent all the blood in a rush to my head. I did not doubt that Jasper, since he had spoken openly of our kinship, meant to betray me. The strange feeling of jealousy that he seemed to harbour—and again I said with so slight a cause—was urging him on. Well, let him do it, if he chose. It was an emergency that I must face sooner or later, and I hardened my heart. Behold, he was here now with his lank figure, thin face, and saturnine smile, ready to keep the threat made in Danville. Some people thought that the ways of my cousin, Jasper Lee, were of the best mode and fashion, but others did not like them, and among such was I.

"We meet again, Cousin John," he said, "and I warned you not to come."

"The nature of a warning depends upon the one who warns," I replied.

"You will find that I keep my promises."

I said nothing.

"And perhaps they ought to hear about you," he added, with his malicious smile.

Whether he felt deep grief for Rose Carew, and surely he must have felt it, and when or how he had heard of her capture I knew not, but he did not speak of it then nor until long afterward.

I turned my back upon him. Captain Hardy was regarding us with a look of surprise. This most certainly was not an affectionate greeting by cousins, but he was too well bred to say anything. I told him that Osseo and I would sit again by one of the fires and rest, and he made no opposition.

As we sat there and refreshed ourselves I noticed again the situation of the camp, the flabby and sullen soldiers, and the forest. It seemed to me that the autumn had advanced greatly in the last few days. The foliage blazed with intense colours in the sunshine. Afar a fine haze hung in the air, which was so pure that the lightest wind was instinct with strength and life. But the soldiers lounging near me found no beauty in it. I heard many words of discontent. Perhaps they were lamenting the gin and rum in the taverns of New York and Philadelphia. Farther on a dozen Kentuckians in fringed hunting shirts were declaiming against the military discipline of General St. Clair, a rule irksome and offensive to all borderers. The conditions in this camp, as I well knew from my brief inspection, were like the meeting of fire and tow, but perhaps the gouty general in his litter saw only through military glasses, which most seldom reveal all the phases of an affair. My mind reverted from these matters to my cousin, and I was sure now, as I had supposed, that he had much influence in St. Clair's army.

Osseo seemed to divine that trouble rested upon my mind, and, with the instinctive delicacy always shown by him, asked no questions, remaining in complete silence. We sat there by the fire a long time enjoying the luxury of rest after an arduous journey.

I was aroused from my thoughts by loud laughter, followed by loud talking, both proceeding from a group of officers gathered at the centre of the camp. The words were made indistinct by the distance, but I saw the men looking toward me as they laughed, and my cousin was among them. It was my fancy, perhaps, but I detected the sneer in both laugh and speech, and I was sure the old tale was being told again. They walked near me presently, led by Jasper, and still laughing—that is, part of them; some were silent and grave, and most evidently their glances rested upon me as if they were examining a rare animal just brought into captivity. I gave them no notice save once to meet the look of my cousin with a gaze into which I tried to put all the dislike and contempt that I felt, in which I may have succeeded, as he dropped his eyes, though laughing louder than before.

These things could not escape the notice of Osseo, and with his acute perceptions he must have made some guess at their meaning, but his manner did not change, and he spoke only once.

"Lee will stay with the soldiers, will he not?" he asked.

"Such is my intent," I answered.

"Then I too will stay," he said. "Where Lee goes Osseo goes too."

Deep in my soul I thanked him for his confidence, but I said nothing. We arose after awhile and strolled through the camp, noting the signs of discontent and confusion. Nearly all the troops were sullen—the Eastern soldiers, who constituted the great bulk of the army, because they were underpaid and engaged in a service of which they knew nothing; and the Kentuckians because they revolted at the methods of the old Continental general, believing that encroachments were made upon their independence. As far as they were concerned a mutiny seemed perilously near, and my sympathies were divided, knowing so well the strength that was in the contention of both borderer and Continental; it was merely a difference in the point of view, but that difference was very wide.

Some one tapped me on the shoulder. It was Captain Hardy.

"General St. Clair would like to see you in his tent again," he said. The captain's manner had changed; it was no longer genial, but cold and reserved, yet not actively hostile. He had beyond a doubt heard Jasper Lee's tale, but I was equally sure that he reserved his opinion.

"I am willing to go to the general at once," I said, "but I should like to take Osseo with me."

"I know of no objection," he replied.

He led the way, and once more we were in the commander in chief's tent. General St. Clair, merely irritable before, was now distinctly suspicious. The look that he gave me was even longer and more critical than the one that he had bestowed upon me when I was first in his presence. There was something, too, in his gaze that made my face flush and every combative instinct in me rise.

"I have had news of you since morning, Mr. Lee," he said dryly, "which makes me change somewhat my opinion of you—that is, if it be true."

"I presume that your news comes from my cousin, Mr. Lee."

"You are correct in your surmise; it comes from Captain Jasper Lee. I can not on the whole call him a very cousinly cousin, but perhaps he was right in telling me this; at least I should know it, since I intended to proceed to some extent upon the strength of the information that you gave me this morning. Captain Lee said to me that you were drummed out of the Continental army for treason, and that you fled shortly afterward to this Western wilderness to hide your face from those who knew you. Is it true, Mr. Lee, that you were drummed out of the Continental army for treason?"

His gaze as he asked me this question was keen and curious, and in spite of myself I felt the blood rise to my face. But the emotion lasted only a moment.

"Such was the charge," I replied steadily.

"You of course deny the truth of that charge."

"Do not all men declared guilty of a crime, General St. Clair, claim their innocence?"

"Then you admit that you were guilty?"

"I have not said so."

He looked at me in doubt and perplexity.

"But surely there were extenuating circumstances." he continued. "You were only a boy then; perhaps it was some rash act, done under hot impulse?"

"It is true that I was a boy then," I replied, "but I knew perfectly well what was and what was not treason."

He swore an impatient oath—an oath that did not have its origin in his gouty foot.

"Mr. Lee," he continued, "you are a strange man. When this charge is brought against you, you neither affirm nor deny. How can I trust you in the face of such a thing? If you were a traitor then, it is quite likely that you are a traitor now. There are white renegades among the Indians—Girty and Blackstaffe and others; how do I know that you are not such yourself, and that you are not seeking to lead us into a trap?"

"You do not know it, General St. Clair," I replied, and I said it with pride—the opening of old wounds is not pleasant, and it incites one to anger.

"And yet, so I hear, you have served the border well," he said. "That is in your favour, and a man may commit a wrong act and be sorry for it. Probably poor Arnold—I say poor Arnold purposely—has repented ten thousand times of his own treason. Mr. Lee, I am absolutely sure that you were a rash and foolish boy carried away by angry impulses. You thought that a wrong had been done you, and you rushed into folly."

"It is not so," I replied stubbornly.

"I repeat that it is so," he said in a loud and choleric tone. "Do not dare to contradict me, sir; I am the commander in chief of this army. I insist that you were a thoughtless boy, who, smarting under some rank injustice, did a thoughtless deed. Now, listen, sir. You and your Indian friend can have the liberty of this camp, but you will be watched, closely watched—I can do nothing else under such circumstances—and perhaps you will have a chance to redeem yourself upon the battlefield. By God, sir, if I were in your place I should jump at the opportunity!"

"I shall stay, general," I replied quite calmly—to stay seemed best to me—"and I thank you for your consideration."

Then we left the tent and walked through the camp, intending to sit by one of the fires on the outskirts. The officers whom we passed turned their backs on me. Captain Hardy, who had been with us in the tent, went away silently. I had not understood until then, even after so many years, how bitter it would be, and I sank down by the fire in a fit of deep depression.

CHAPTER 5 A Gentleman in Red

The skies took the gray hue of my own mind. The brilliant foliage of Indian summer was dropping from the trees, and the dying leaves rustled as they fell. I repeated to myself that all the years since then had not softened the bitterness of exposure. And yet I had not really sought to hide. I had stayed in the forest because I loved it, and I had borne my own name because I was proud of it—the name John Lee. No one could truthfully say that I had sought a disguise.

I felt a light hand upon my shoulder. It was Osseo. He had been sitting beside me in silence for more than an hour. When I looked around he rose to his feet, and never had I seen him look taller and more impressive. He pointed to the northwest, where the forest stretched away a thousand miles.

"Come, my brother," he said. "Our home is there."

The Indian's eyes were flashing. I think it was the first time that I had seen him show emotion.

"Come," he continued. "Lee is accused of a crime by those of his own race, and he does not deny it. Osseo will never believe that he did it, but even if he was a traitor to his race, as the Long Knives have said, it does not change my heart. Come! all the wilderness is ours; we know it and we do not fear it. We may go where we choose."

He swept with his arm the whole semicircle of the west as he stood before me, his mighty chest heaving and his eyes still glittering. The spirit in me again leaped into life as I looked at him and listened to his words. In truth, Osseo was a gentleman, a gentleman in red, the finest gentleman I ever met. His invitation was most tempting, too. He spoke the truth when he said that we knew the forest and did not fear its shadows; it had many joys for those who were able to tread the wilderness road. But I shook my head at last. I could not go when I was on trial.

"No, Osseo," I said; "God knows that I thank you for many things, but I can not leave this army now. I must stay with it until it meets the tribes."

This, too, despite the danger of Rose Carew and the wan face of that woman in Kentucky who had put her faith in me.

"If Lee does not go I do not go either," he said quietly, and sat down again by my side, resuming his silence, his face once more impassive, the man motionless, as if he were a block of reddish-brown marble. I did not thank him, feeling the uselessness of words in such a case, and knowing, too, that he would not wish them, but he had lifted me from the depths of depression. Nor was he my only friend. It happens sometimes that we do not learn in what esteem we are held by those who know us best until we fall into ill repute with the majority. The old scouts and borderers in this camp whose opinion I respected, and with most of whom I had shared dangers, were not backward in showing their faith.

Old Joe Grimes was the first to seek me. Old Joe was not handsome to look upon; in truth, he was so ugly that his appearance was humorous, being as broad as he was long, with features devoid of system or arrangement. But he was nearly as skilful in the woods as Osseo, and a more honest man in intent wind and hail never beat upon. Now he came to me and extended his huge hand as a sign of friendship, saying:

"I don't believe a word of the durned yarn, John. You might as well whistle jigs to a milestone as tell me it's true. I can't forgit how you helped beat off the Shawnees that time they come against my cabin, and helped save the old woman and the gals from the red rascals. Put 'er thar, John."

And I put my hand inside his, receiving a grip that would have made a bear wince. "It's some lie of these durned soldiers," he said. "Guv'mints are always doin' such things. I don't believe in guv'mints nohow. They're slower'n molasses anyway, and so far as we of the West are concerned, we are just children in the house of a stepmother."

And the others came, too, with word or act of friendship—Dick Bates, Ben Strong, Sam Peabody, Swiftfoot Tom Houck, the fastest runner in the West, and all the others who knew me. Their manner strengthened my resolve to remain with General St. Clair's army while the expedition lasted. This, I gathered from the conversation about me, could not be much longer. The general intended to march immediately against the Miami towns on the Wabash, sweeping out of his way such bands as sought to impede him, and the necessity of speedy action was apparent, as winter, which in our Northwestern woods is often a bitter winter indeed, would soon be at hand. I saw about me all the signs of early cold weather. The north wind which was blowing that morning had an unusually keen edge. The leaves were beginning to lose some of their vivid tints and curl up at the edges. They were falling in showers, too, before the blast.

Many of the raw Eastern soldiers shivered and hovered more closely around the camp fires, casting anxious glances at the unbroken forest, which curved about them. I fancy that this seemed a strange campaign to them, so far from cultivated land and the homes of men. Even the two little companies of regular troops, disciplined, steady fellows, were not free from the sombre influence. It was unknown ground to them; they had learned none of the secrets of the wilderness, and everywhere they found it strange and gloomy.

"There will be snow soon," said Osseo, speaking at last, "and the march will be hard for the Long Knives."

"Yes, Osseo," I replied, "and this is not the place for the drilled and stiff soldier of the old country. If we could only trade them all for half their number of good foresters!"

"The General-who-rides-on-the-shoulders-of-his-men does not think so," he replied.

I could not discern whether there was the intent of irony in his speech, but such was its effect upon me.

Twenty Indians were gathered around a fire near by, talking in low tones in their own language. They were friendly Chickasaws, warriors from the far South, whom General St. Clair had brought with him as scouts and skirmishers. Osseo watched them for awhile with a contemplative eye, but did not speak. He rose presently, and without explanation entered the woods.

CHAPTER 6 A Forest Council

It was about noon when Osseo went into the forest, and I ate dinner with the scouts, still uncertain what to do next, though resolved to stay with the army and await the issue, hoping too that a successful battle would lead to a speedy rescue of Rose Carew.

I had seen my true kind again after many years, and though I had come in repellent guise to a harsh welcome, it was only to verify what the presence of Rose Carew in Kentucky had told me already. I could not change my nature, nor the character formed in all the years preceding manhood, and the honest and rough men with whom I now sat, though good friends, were of another breed. I had long prided myself on my forest skill, but all at once it seemed a little thing to the great world with which this army had again brought me in touch. Then I was ashamed of such thoughts, when I looked around at the brown hunters who refused to believe any ill of me.

I inquired what course the army would take. It seemed to me that we should have been on the march since dawn, but I learned that no movement would be made until the next day, because of trouble with some of the militia or raw troops. General St. Clair was now unable to leave his tent, owing to a violent attack of gout aggravated by worry; and General Butler and Colonel Sargent, his chief assistants, were seeking to overcome the difficulties, though the wilderness was a blank to them, and they sought none who could tell them its ways.

The gray and chilly day did not improve, nor did the troubled camp. Extremes met here—the stiff military discipline of the East and the absolute independence of the Western forester; while the honest but incompetent old general, whose duty it was to reconcile them, writhed with a swollen foot on his couch.

Osseo returned to the camp about dusk and sat down beside me in front of one of the fires, which were now a necessity, owing to the increasing cold. I handed him a piece of venison, and he ate it in silence. I, too, held my peace, knowing that he would speak in his own good time, and that when he did so speak it would be to much purpose.

"Indian sign," he said at last. "Plenty of it."

"Where, Osseo?" I asked.

"All around," he replied. "Before, behind, on both sides. Wyandots and Miamis on right, Ottawas and Shawnees on left. General-who-never-walks should be General-who-never-sleeps. Forest full of danger—dangers as thick as those."

He pointed toward the dying leaves, which were falling to the earth in showers before the keen north wind.

"I see, Osseo," I replied, and I felt a deep sadness as I spoke, "but I am in no position to give advice to General St. Clair. God knows that no man ever needed it more than he!"

I was thinking then of the great hopes that rested upon St. Clair's army: a whole people expected now an end to the cruelties that had so long ravaged the border; and there too was the rescue of Rose Carew which this force ought to further.

Osseo remained, after his brief report, in silence, pondering upon I knew not what. Winchester joined us presently. He, too, had heard my cousin's tale about me, and his manner of handling it was according to his nature. "It's an infernal lie, Lee!" he said. "I would not believe it if you yourself were to swear to me that it is true, and I do not want to hear a word about the matter." Then he took his seat beside us in front of the coals and talked of other things. His mind moved slowly as a rule, but it moved in right channels.

Osseo and I bade Winchester good-night shortly after dusk, and taking our rifles, prepared to leave the camp. We could do as we chose in this particular, ours being the loose duty of scouts, which means freedom in the West. In truth, the scouts made their movements according to their own judgment. All their reconnoitring seemed voluntary. General St. Clair apparently was stupefied by the forest, which lay upon him like a wet cloth, and did not fill the woods with his spies.

Most of the men were asleep. Osseo looked at them a moment or two and then said:

"Only a fool sleeps without fear in the forest."

We reached the fringe of the camp, and were about to pass the sentinel there, but he stopped us.

"You can not pass," he said.

"We are scouts; we intend to examine the woods for Indian signs," I said in some surprise.

"The Indian may go, but not you, Mr. Lee," replied the man.

"Why?" I asked. His tone seemed to me to smack of insolence.

"Orders of Captain Lee, the officer of the guard."

Captain Lee himself appeared a moment later, and explained in his usual suave manner.

"We are forced to distrust you, my gentle cousin," he said. "Remembering what you were once, we fear that you are the same to-day. Now, I am quite sure that if you go into the forest there you go merely to confer with the Indians our enemies."

"Jasper Lee," I replied, "you know that you lie!"

He flushed and raised his hand as if he would strike me, but in a moment recovered himself—he knew better than to deal me a blow—and then said, quite coldly:

"Have it as you please; I can afford to take any sort of abuse from you. You are too far below me for me to answer you."

"Perhaps," I said, stung somewhat by his taunt, "when you were dispensing news about me to the camp to-day, you did not tell how much you had profited by my condemnation. My outlawry and disappearance have enabled you to enjoy what were mine.'"

"And rightly so," he replied with some heat. "You were the traitor, not I."

"Be it as you say," I continued; "I warn you not to interfere with me. As you see, I have friends here, and if a contest should come between us I might not be the one to suffer the more. Still I do not seek it."

He looked at me wonderingly, as if fearing that I possessed some hidden weapon, and then he turned carelessly to the sentinel.

"Let him pass," he said.

Osseo and I left the camp behind us and entered the forest. We stood a few moments in the shade of a great oak tree, and looked back at the smouldering fires. Then we proceeded a little farther, and turning again, saw no light behind us. The wilderness had received the army and hidden it as it could have hidden one a hundred times larger. Around us stretched the loneliness of desolation, and a silence broken only by the rustle of the dying leaves as they fell. We renewed our journey and passed a herd of deer feeding quietly in a little open space.

"The Indian has not been here, or the deer would not be so quiet," said Osseo.

We turned toward the left, and after ten minutes' walking heard the faint hoot of an owl to the southward. It was answered from another point perhaps a mile distant. Clearly the savages were alert if General St. Clair was not.

"Wyandots," said Osseo. "They have passed this way."

He pointed to faint traces on the earth, visible in the moonlight.

I suggested to him that we pursue the band and perhaps we could steal near enough to hear their talk, his assent being given at once. So we followed the trail in the moonlight through the forest, over hills and across little brooks and through thickets, but never losing it for a moment. Engaged upon this intent and delicate business, all my old sanguine feelings returned I was again in the woods, free to go where I chose; the world was mine, and the most trusty of all comrades was by my side.

Soon we beheld a subdued light in the forest, as if those who kindled it did not wish to be seen afar. Lying down among the bushes and creeping with hand and knee, we drew near enough to discern about twenty warriors sitting in a glen and talking with great earnestness. Among them were two of our Chickasaw scouts—not prisoners, but most evidently on good terms with our inveterate enemies.

The little circle of Indians, sitting there in the forest and holding such grave converse, gave the impression of dignity. They were mostly men of importance, as I could tell by their dress, which in every instance was elaborate and rich according to the Indian ideas. Their moccasins were of the finest and neatest-fitting deerskin, and as they sat the seamless soles were turned up to the fire. Their leggings were of blue or red cloth, purchased at the British forts, decorated around the bottom and up one side with a border of beads, and trimmed in two or three cases with tiny bells. Their hunting shirts also were made of blue or red broadcloth or fine, tanned deerskin, the bottom and front covered with an embroidery of many-coloured beads, the fringe of the shirt falling to the knee.

Each carried around him, with all the gravity and grace of a Roman senator wearing the toga, a blanket of blue or red or yellow, made of the finest broadcloth, and about two yards square. Two or three wore headdresses after the fashion of the Iroquois, which consisted of a close-fitting splint band with a cross band curving over the top, from which hung a cluster of feathers, while another and larger feather was set in the centre of the head-dress and waved defiantly aloft. This was the war plume. The weapons in every case were a rifle, tomahawk, and knife.

"War chiefs in council," whispered Osseo. "When they talk thus together there will soon be wailing in the settler's cabin."

I knew full well the truth of his words, but I did not withhold admiration from the circle that made the brilliant and impressive picture before me. Theirs was truly a life in all its wildness and freedom that many a man might covet. We crept a little nearer, but still we could not understand what they were saying, and we dared not attempt a further approach, as Indian ears are so cunning that, near by, no skill may deceive them. The Wyandot chief Hoyoquim, whom I recognised, had been talking, but at this moment the warrior next to him, a man of great age, but still strong and erect, arose and began to make a formal address after the Indian custom, speaking with much eloquence, a quality not at all rare among the tribes. As he raised his voice we could hear his words.

He was an Iroquois named Haqua, and he told of the fate that befell the Six Nations because they did not unite against the white invaders. He urged the Western tribes to avoid a similar mistake, speaking with a forest eloquence that soon drew murmurs of approval.

"The warriors of the West are brave," said Haqua in conclusion, "and they are many. They have come even from the far shores of the greatest lake, and their most famous chiefs lead them. Let none go home until we strike and destroy the army that the General-who-never-walks leads through the forest. Then the white man will be sent beyond the Ohio, and he will not dare to come again into the land which you have said with your rifle and tomahawk is yours and shall remain yours. *Hero koué*."

When he uttered his guttural cry "*Hero koué*," which means, in the Iroquois, "This is the end," the murmur of approval became a subdued cry, it being evident that there was but one mind among them all. Hoyoquim next sprang to his feet, and made a fiery speech, in which he seconded all that the old Iroquois had said, and two others also spoke.

The council was now over and the chiefs rose. We, too, turned away, and our self-chosen expedition lasted throughout the night, taking us in a wide circuit around the camp. Everywhere we found Indian signs. The army of General St. Clair advanced through many dangers. We met Joe Grimes and Dick Bates near morning, and they made the same report. Old Joe shook his head ominously.

"I don't like it, Lee—I don't like it," he said, "We could tell General St. Clair that the warriors are gathering, but you might as well sing psalms to a dead horse. He'll think we're just stuffing mush in his ears."

I feared that he was right, but, right or wrong, we took our way back to the army at rise of sun, intending to report what we had seen.

The camp presented a cheerful aspect in the early morning light, the blaze of many fires rising in the crisp, frosty air. The men were preparing to make an early start, and for once they showed zeal.

The officer in charge of the guard was Captain Hardy, and he did not object when I told him that I wished to see General St. Clair, being the bearer of important information. The general, he said, was up betimes from his bed, and was in a fairly good humour, his swollen foot having been relatively kind to him the night before. Captain Hardy's bearing toward me was neither hostile nor friendly, its general note being that of one who reserved his decision for a future which should be determined by my conduct. I cared much for the good opinion of this officer, as his frank, honest manner was so evidently the index of a fine nature, and silently I thanked him for withholding his verdict.

General St. Clair was in his tent, eating his breakfast, which was served by an orderly, and with him were his second in command, Major-General Richard Butler, whose yellow face and pinched features told of illness; his adjutant general, Colonel Winthrop Sargent; and my loving cousin, Captain Jasper Lee. Jasper, by one of those curious turns of his nature, welcomed me with seeming great frankness.

"General, it is my cousin, Mr. Lee," he said. "No doubt he has a busy night's work to relate."

My tale was quickly told. General St. Clair listened with surprise, which soon turned, as I saw by the expression of his face, into incredulity. He was more than half suspecting that I sought to deceive him. Jasper's sharp eyes too caught the fact, and his look soon became an imitation of the general's; but when I met my cousin's gaze I stared so steadily at him, prompted as I was by indignation and the sense of right, that his eyes fell. Nevertheless I continued my tale to the end, keeping to the straight of it, and determined that he should hear all I knew.

"Do you mean to tell me, Mr. Lee," said General St. Clair when I finished, "that the forces of the savages are on all sides of us, and that you have listened to one of their war councils?"

It was certainly so, I replied, and I cited the absence of all the Chickasaws from the camp, a fact that I had noted immediately upon my return. The general sent his orderly for confirmation of my report, and the soldier soon returned with the news. General St. Clair's face clouded and his look became depressed.

"The Chickasaws no doubt have deserted us," he said, "and it is a grave defection at such a time."

"But perhaps they will return before nightfall," said Jasper insinuatingly. "They may be on only a scouting expedition. No doubt many besides my cousin have noted their absence from the camp."

"That is true," said the general more cheerfully.

Then I saw his face harden and all his stubbornness concentrate in his brow. It was idle to proffer advice to General St. Clair at that moment, however humbly, but I did it nevertheless, calling attention to the numbers and warlike ardour of the Northwestern warriors and our own isolated position in the huge forest. And all the time Cousin Jasper stood by, with his ironic face, but not saying a word. General Butler and Colonel Sargent occasionally made a comment, though they took no active part.

"I don't wish to wrong you, Mr. Lee," General St. Clair finally said, "and so I again give you the benefit of the doubt. I thank you for your report if it should be correct. I appreciate also your anxiety for the success of the army, but be assured that I shall take all the measures necessary to win victory."

And with that I felt myself dismissed, quite sure that I had made a mistake when I came to General St. Clair with ominous news.

CHAPTER 7 The Wilderness Road

The army took up its march, advancing slowly and with pain. General St. Clair was borne upon a litter carried by four men, who were changed at intervals. He swore profusely, and so did his army. The scouts went ahead, and after them came the axemen, as it was necessary to cut a way through the forest for the wagons and the artillery. Behind trod the soldiers, grumbling; the volunteers as usual complaining of their food and pay, and the militia discontented with the military yoke.

Yet the forest was a noble sight. The grayness had left the air, and the ground was dry in the sunshine. The woods on this last day of October still glowed with much of Indian summer's beauty. Beneath our feet the soil was deep, rich, and black. Game sprang up in front of us, deer rushed by, while squirrels chattered overhead on every bough. Any fool could see that it was a magnificent country worth fighting to gain or to keep. One's spirits were bound to rise with such a prospect, and mine were no exception. Osseo and I remained with the column. Although we had received such small thanks when I went to the general's tent that morning, my mind did not incline me to regret the experiment, at least for the present.

Captain Jasper Lee came up presently, riding a very fine horse. He asked me why I was not out with my rifle searching the woods for hostile Indians.

"General St. Clair did not choose to believe my narrative," I answered, "and I suppose that the others take the same view of it. All of you are alike, and I do not care to make reports that nobody will listen to."

He gave me a fierce look, but I repeat that we of the West are a very free people. Moreover, I had no mind to take impertinence from him.

"Mr. Lee," he said, "you should remember that you are with us on tolerance."

"General St. Clair needs all the men whom he can get," I replied.

He did not reply, but, giving his horse a cut with the whip, rode to the head of the column.

We halted a little later for the noon rest, and when we started again General St. Clair swore with a point and vigour that I have seldom known surpassed. Sixty of the militia, taking advantage of the confusion at the dinner hour, had deserted, and were now well on their way southward and toward home. Redder than ever in the face with wrath, he instantly despatched one of our two little regular regiments in search of the deserters, against the protests of some of our officers; and, thus weakened, we continued our march toward the Indian towns on the Wabash through woods apparently as wide and pathless as the sea itself.

We heard shots late that afternoon, but it was only some of the scouts skirmishing with wandering Indians. One of our men lost his life, but an Indian was slain, and the officers seemed to think it a fair exchange. These officers, I will say, were a gallant set, brave and disciplined, but out of their element in the woods, and inclined to hold the foe too lightly. Some of the younger told me their hope of finding the savages this side of their towns, and I could only reply that our foes were evasive creatures, and quote our Western proverb, "All signs fail in dry weather," which means that in midsummer the sight of clouds does not betoken rain, and if one saw an Indian now it did not indicate an Indian battle on the morrow; nor would it be wise to say that it did not—in truth, one could never know what the savages intended, their methods of warfare being most irregular.

Winchester was still with us, and, his turn of mind being philosophic, appeared not overmuch disturbed by his situation. He had a fine way of taking matters as they came, and concerned himself a great deal with the present, very little with the future.

"I scarce know what I ought to do, Lee," he said to me. "My nation is at peace with these savages, and it is my business to trade for their furs. Luckily, I have done so well that I intended in any event to return to England in the spring. I expected to leave your army and go to Detroit, but I think that I shall postpone that trip until after the battle."

While the army crept through the dark woods, Osseo said to me one day: "I go upon an errand for Lee, and perhaps I shall bring him news that he will wish to hear." I divined his meaning at once, and I replied, "Osseo, no man ever had a better friend than I have in you."

Then he slid away, his brown form blending with the brown of leaf and bush. In our ill-ordered camp he was not missed save by some of the old frontiersmen such as Joe Grimes, to whose questions I replied that he had gone to spy out the country, the excuse sufficing. I was sitting by the camp fire at dawn a few days later, when the figure of Osseo suddenly stood beside me as if he had risen like a mist from the earth. There was a light in his eyes, and I waited with patience, though with eagerness, until he should speak.

"I have seen the white maid," he said, "and she is well though not happy. I was again Nokalis of the totem Cahenhisnhonen, of the tribe of the Mohawks, of the nation of the Iroquois, and I have been to the village of the Miamis, where Hoyoquim the Wyandot took the maid when he captured her, and where she is to be kept a close prisoner until after the fighting with the General-who-never-walks, when the Wyandot chieftain means to take her to his own village."

"How does she bear it?" I asked.

"She is brave," he replied. "What tears she had to shed she has shed, for she does not weep now, but she sits in the prison lodge, and her face is ever turned toward Kaintuckee. Hope is still in her heart, because she believes that some one will yet come to save her."

"And who is that some one, Osseo?" I asked.

"I did not get a chance to talk with the maid and tell her that I was not Nokalis the Mohawk at all, but Osseo, a friend, and so I can not say," he replied. "But I saw her and I know that she does not despair. I saw too that she was beautiful, and I know also that if Lee should risk his life for her she is worth the risk."

"You spoke truth there, Osseo!" I said to myself, and again I was tempted to leave the army, take the Indian, and seek a rescue at once. But upon cold consideration it seemed so vain a plan! With every warrior alert and watching for St. Clair, it would be impossible to enter their village. No, I must wait until St. Clair struck, hoping that the blow would serve Rose Carew as well as the nation. My mind reverted also to her father. I knew that many of his plans depended upon the success of this expedition, and while he loved his daughter—of that there was no doubt—he could not wholly forget them, even when she was in captivity. I wondered too what direction his ambition would take if we were to fail, and I was sure that it would carry him into some new channel.

Late in the afternoon following Osseo's return I heard the forest calling; in truth, it had been calling all the day, but I would not heed its voice until then; I could not now resist the feeling that my place was out there among the trees and undergrowth, looking for our enemies, and not here in the close ranks, where I was of no more use than the merest lump of a soldier pining for his New York tavern and dose of gin. So I gave the signal to Osseo, who, while he was with the army usually waited upon my initiative, and shouldering our rifles we trickled quietly away from the column and into the dense woods. There we were quickly invisible, although we could yet hear the sound of the axes as the men cleared the road for the army and the crack of the whips as the drivers brought up the wagons.

Osseo's eyes twinkled faintly as he looked at me.

"My friend Lee would not like to be a soldier and carry only a gun," he said. "He would be a Long Knife. He wishes to be a general and swear at the men like the General-who-never-walks, and not be a soldier and have the general swear at him. My friend Lee is wise."

"You speak truth, Osseo," I replied, unable to restrain a smile at his discernment and dry comment. "I would rather be an officer any day than a private, but just now I would rather be here in the woods with you, neither master nor man, than be either."

"The General-who-never-walks," continued Osseo, "swears more every day, and also Manito has stricken him blind. Osquesont[2] flashes before his eyes, but he sees it not. Manito has stricken him deaf too. Annemeekee[3] is in his ears, but he hears it not. The tribes sharpen Dayanoaqua,[4] but the General-who-never-walks knows it not.

"It is true, Osseo," I said.

"Wabun[5]" is whispering secrets in my ears, he replied, "and I tell them to my friend Lee."

His tone now was not only earnest but warning. Osseo himself was fit to pronounce impressive words—a warrior over six feet high, as straight as the hickory tree, and as strong; a man of broad brow with the great width between the eyes that one often sees in the Northern Indians. He was always most scrupulous about his attire. Among the whites on the border, who are rather slovenly in dress, the same care would have been called dandyism, but with him it was merely pride and self-respect.

His blanket, partially folded across his back, and made of as fine a piece of broadcloth as I ever saw, was in colour a dark reddish brown. He wore one of the Iroquois frames over his head, and from the centre of it rose the eagle feathers, the special emblem of the Iroquois. I do not think he was an Iroquois, although he spoke their dialects perfectly, and he probably wore eagle feathers as a defiance. His deerskin hunting suit was also coloured a reddish brown, and was heavy with bead ornamentation. His rifle was silver-mounted and cost a pretty penny—I ought to know, as it was a present from me—his tomahawk had a highly polished horn handle, and the hilt of his knife was silver. In short, his dress was worthy of his figure and mien, and Osseo would have compared favourably in appearance with any of the world's great men.

"What Wabun whispers to me," he continued, "Kabibonokka[6]" also whispers, and it roars in my ears like Baimwana,[7] yet the General-who-never-walks will not hear.

---

[2] The tomahawk

[3] The thunder.

[4]. The scalping knife.

[5] The east wind

[6] The north wind

[7] The sound of thunder.

"Come, Osseo," I said, "let us not lament. But you and I will do the best we can."

It required no close search now to find the Indian trails. We crossed and recrossed them at every turn, mostly those of small parties, of a half-dozen warriors or so, but in two or three instances larger bands of twenty or thirty. I saw the truth of Osseo's metaphorical assertion that every wind brought the sound of the savages sharpening the scalping knife. But another simile also occurred to my mind: our army was like a huge and unsuspecting dragon-fly, around which many fierce little spiders were cautiously weaving a web.

"How far is it to the Miami villages, Osseo?" I asked. The Miami villages were our immediate destination.

"Lee and I could reach them in the space between two morning suns," he replied, "but the General-who-never-walks will need ten."

I made a calculation based upon this report, and found that the distance was about sixty miles. Ten days was a long period for our army, which, bad now, was declining in quality, and, moreover, winter was coming apace. Men with such soft bones as our city troops could not stand the fierce cold of these Northwestern forests.

We continued our circuit around the camp, meaning to return to it about halfway between midnight and sunset, but just as we were preparing for the homeward journey we crossed a new and decidedly fresh trail. We turned aside and followed it a few hundred yards, when both Osseo and I sank to the earth as if we had done so in response to some preconcerted signal.

A little more than rifle shot in front of us was a glade with a hillock in the centre. A half-dozen warriors watched at the edges of the glade, but it was not they who drew our eyes; instead, they were fastened upon a group of men standing upon the hillock.

"The war chiefs!" said Osseo. "Even now they look at the camp of the General-who-never-walks."

A great tower of smoke rose above the trees in front of us a half mile away, marking where the army lay, and upon this smoke the eyes of the eight men who stood on the hillock were intent. It was the second time in the last few days that Osseo and I had come upon an Indian council, but the second assembly was evidently more important than the first, and we could not now creep within hearing distance.

The chiefs were of different tribes. I recognised even at the distance Hoyoquim the Wyandot, often called Black Eagle, the captor of Rose Carew, and there too was Mechecunnaqua, or, as the whites knew him, Little Turtle, the famous war chief of the Miamis, now the head chief of the whole Northwestern Confederacy, and chiefs of the Ottawas, Pottawatomiea, Delawares, Shawnees, and others, not excepting a leader of the Chippewas from the far country beyond

Lake Superior. Little Turtle pointed occasionally toward the smoke of our camp fire, and so far as I could judge he was the principal speaker, as became his position at the head of the confederacy. He raised his tomahawk presently, and with it threatened the distant smoke, making the motion of a blow. All in turn did likewise. Then they stepped from the hillock and they and their guards faded away in the forest. I said to myself that the battle could not be far off, but Osseo and I returned to camp without comment to each other upon what we had seen. I did not offer a report, as I knew I was a discredited witness, but the other scouts were bringing in news of the same character, and I felt that what we had seen was not lost.

I lay down to sleep a little later, not having closed my eyes in forty-eight hours, and was soon in slumber-land. The next day was gray and wintry, a slight snow falling and the cold increasing so much before night that ice formed on the little pools of water, standing here and there in the forest, and the dead leaves fell in showers. But the rotting army still dragged its slow and painful length through the dismal forest, and the second evening thereafter encamped on the eastern bank of the Wabash River, now but a baby stream fifteen or twenty yards wide, where most of the soldiers—horse, foot, and artillery—were jammed together on a little plateau, although the militia went in camp some distance beyond the stream.

The night was wintry cold, fingers were chilled when they touched the metal of rifle or cannon, and the men shivered as they hung over the smoking fires. There had been no skirmishing between the scouts and Indian parties since morning, and the silence of desolation hung over the forest, where the leaves were still falling in showers. Never before had the army felt so lonely and so far from the haunts of men. The cold crept into the marrow of the soldiers, and the dwellers in cities looked fearfully at the solemn woods.

I had been all day, and most of the night before, in the woods seeking Indian sign—and finding plenty of it—and night being at hand, I was worn to the bone. Despite the coldness with which I was received, I made one or two additional reports to General St. Clair, which were received with but little comment, and if I needed further proof it became fully evident that he reposed much faith in his own foresight and judgment. Saying no more, I crossed the shallow river, and joined Osseo with the militia, who were in advance.

I was too tired to do scouting work that night, and, lying down near Osseo before one of the fires, I soon fell into a deep sleep.

CHAPTER 8 The Phantom Horde

"Awake, my friend; the enemy comes!"

Osseo stood beside me in the chill of early dawn, his dark eyes glowing, and every nerve and muscle taut.

I sprang to my feet and saw naught but the sentinels, heard naught but their footsteps. The great forest rimmed us round, as silent and lonely as when we lay down to sleep. The ice glittered on the river and the pools.

"The enemy coming, Osseo? I see nothing."

"There is a warrior in every bush. The ring of the tribes has closed around us. The General-who-never-walks does not believe, but Osseo knows. The end is in Manito's keeping. *Hero koué.*"

It was a solemn speech, and I no longer doubted. I grasped my rifle more tightly and saw that my powder-horn and bullet pouch were full. A thin, cold mist was rising from the snow-covered earth.

The awakening trumpet sounded, and the army rose from its slumbers. The sentinels reported that all was well. The wintry sun crept above the rim of the earth, and the same silence still reigned in the great woods. Yet the forest now spoke to me in many tongues. I longed to shout its news into the ears of the stubborn general, but I knew that he would order me in scorn from his tent. The militia began to form in ranks, and smoke rose from the growing fires.

"The enemy comes!" said Osseo again in low and thrilling tones.

A bead of fire appeared in a bush straight ahead of us. expanded and went out, just as the sharp crack of a rifle sped, echoing, through the desolate forest. A soldier, one of our Kentucky militiamen, standing nearest the trees, pitched forward upon his face, stone dead. The bullet had passed through his head. A yell—long, quavering, but full of sound, like the howling of thousands of hungry wolves—rose and then died in a whine, more ferocious than its highest note. It was the war-cry of the savages, and it came from every point of the compass and all the points between. Osseo had spoken from the fulness of knowledge. The attack had begun.

The single bead of fire was followed by many others sparkling among the bushes or in the shadows of the forest, singularly vivid in the cold, still morning. The sound of the rifle shots was like the rapid cracking of a huge whip, and the echoes repeated themselves. No wind was stirring. The dead and dying leaves did not move, and the spurts of smoke rose straight upward.

Our men fell rapidly, the bullets flying fast. Some died without noise, and some cried out in surprise rather than pain when they were struck. Their comrades stood in disordered groups, bewildered by the attack, despite the warnings of the last few days, staring stupidly at the officers, who shouted opposing orders and who sought to form their ranks.

The fire of the savages increased; once again rose their war-whoop, fierce and triumphant, but the harried soldiers saw nothing. The forest was full of foes who shot with deadly aim. The beads of flame appeared and reappeared among bushes and trees, and the soldiers began to fire now at the flashes and the smoke, but still they saw no human beings save themselves. The sound of battle was in their ears, but it was only the crack of the weapons, their own cries, or the occasional war-whoop. Dusky forms were flitting from tree to tree, but they made no sound as they passed. Our men knew not whether any of their bullets slew. They could only fire into the forest, which was wide and sent back no tales; but they saw their own dead heaping up at their feet, and the hail of bullets that cut them down was thickening fast.

Our vanguard was quickly driven over the little river and into the main army, but it did not find rest and peace there. The fire of the invisible foe swept in a ring around the entire force, and the swift bullets cut through every rank. The army was driven into a huddled mass, and its bewilderment grew as the companies were struck down by the unseen death. When the survivors were pressed together they made a better target for the savages, who crept closer and closer, firing from behind every tree and bush and log at the great yellow and blue mass of white men who stood in the open. The crackle of the rifle shots was accompanied by cries, groans, and falls.

It is a terrible thing for the soft dweller in cities to be surprised in the desolate forest by an unseen but none the less deadly foe; to see the fire and smoke of his rifle shots, but never that foe; to hear the hiss of the bullets, and to see them cutting down the disordered ranks; then the chill of fear creeps into the marrow and paralyzes the brain. Panic ran through our raw Eastern levies. It was not such fighting as this that they had come to do; they expected at least an enemy whom they could see, and whenever the war-whoop rose it was to them a true death chant.

The officers sought to restore order and organize the defence. There were men among them who might have known more, but none are braver than those officers proved themselves to be. The Indian bullets struck them down as they gave orders and threatened with the flats of their swords, but the survivors shirked no duty. Pride and discipline kept them erect, although the storm of bullets came thicker and thicker.

I saw General St. Clair rush from his tent, believing at first that it was but a skirmish; but when he knew at last that the danger which he had despised was upon us he showed himself a brave man, walking calmly among the soldiers, upbraiding them for panic terror, and giving them an example of coolness, while the bullets of the savages pierced his own clothing. But to lead troops in battle one needs more than courage, and though the general stood in the midst of the army and encouraged it to fight, the fire of the Indians increased in volume and accuracy, and lashed our ranks through and through.

Now the soldiers began to see figures through the haze, mere glimpses of coppery faces leaping from bush to bush and gone when they fired. The clouds of smoke rising from so many rifle shots made the forest around them dimmer, and all that it contained vague and unreal.

Our cannon were firing, and the heavy roll of the discharges made a thunderous echo. The black smoke of the great guns rose and added to the dimness, but the gunners, like the riflemen, saw no target. The cannon-balls crashed in the forest, and from some other point the warriors yelled defiance. The cavalrymen sprang upon their horses and galloped into the woods, but the fire of the savages emptied the saddles and no one saw whence the bullets came. Regular troops, cannon in the centre and on their flanks, reckless of death, charged among the trees; the warriors melted away before them, and lo! no foe was there; when they were forced to fall back upon the mass of the army the Indians swarmed again on every side, their bullets striking on human bodies like the pattering of rain drops on water.

"o God," groaned a regular beside me, "if I could only see a single enemy—something to shoot at!"

The next instant a bullet from a hidden foe cut short his hopes and his life. I loaded and fired my rifle as fast as I could, and Osseo, bent in a stooping position, sending his bullets into the woods, was by my side.

The camp was now swept by the rifle fire from every side, with the ring of the savages pressing closer and ever closer. I saw General St. Clair again, and as I looked a bullet clipped a lock of the gray hair which hung in such profusion beneath his three-cornered hat, and another pierced his coat. He continued his steady walk up and down the lines; and General Butler, our second in command, just risen from a sick-bed, did the same, each trying to preserve order on his wing and passing and repassing in grave silence. There was something tragic and pathetic in the bearing of these two old generals, both so brave and both so unfit for the work they had to do.

"A hot morning, General Butler!" said General St. Clair once as he passed.

"An exceedingly hot morning, General St. Clair." replied General Butler with the same coolness; "but I fancy that it will not last."

General St. Clair bowed courteously to indicate agreement, and walked on. This was a fine dignity on the part of two old soldiers, and I admired it duly; but not all the merits of manner removed the facts of the surprise, nor abated for one moment the fury and baffling nature of the savage attack. We were being cut down precisely as a British army under Braddock had been cut down more than thirty years before; and the great President, then in his youth, who witnessed all the horrors of Fort Duquesne, had warned St. Clair of just such another ambush. "Beware of Indian stratagem," he said. "Fill the woods with your scouts, and heed what they tell you!" But all in vain; the headstrong general would have his way, and behold the issue!

Our gallant officers still led the charges into the woods, and the cannon boomed above the crash of the rifles, balls and grape-shot doing much damage to trees and bushes, and always the wary foe sank away like the mist; but when the charge spent itself and the soldiers returned to the main force, back the savages came again, fiercer and more deadly than ever, pouring their bullets into the huddled mass of white men who yet stood like a shining mark in the open. Our charges became fewer. The artillery horses were shot down and the screams of the wounded animals were the most fearful sounds on all that battlefield. The officers fell fast, their bravery and their epaulets marking them as special targets, the army was driven more and more toward the common centre, and the ring of smoke in which so many beads of fire sparkled grew thicker all around it. The two generals were still walking up and down the lines, calling out orders and bidding the men to fight.

General St. Clair's uniform was torn in a half dozen places by the rifle bullets, but so far as I could see he was unharmed. General Butler's arm suddenly dropped to his side, broken by a ball; but the general threw oft his coat, and when one of the men put the arm in a sling he continued his calm walk, the blood from his wound falling drop by drop upon his uniform. Another bullet struck him in the side, and he fell at last, but struggled to his feet again. He could not stand, and two men, lifting him up, carried him to the middle of the camp, where he sat propped against a great heap of knapsacks, which would never be put to use again by our soldiers. General St. Clair walked on, but alone.

The disorder of the battle grew as the Indian bullets cut us down like grass; the ranks could not be kept, the cannon could not be moved, the horses being killed, the confused shouts told nothing, the increasing clouds of smoke hid every movement; all became a horrible tumult and jumble.

Now panic and terror ran through the veins of our men. They knew not the number of the savages, but they felt their sting. The foe was a phantom host who escaped their blows, but struck back with deadly interest. There was safety in neither attack nor defence, and whichever way they faced, the bullets swept every corner of the battlefield. Our dead lay throughout our camp, dozens at first, then scores, now hundreds, and above the shouts of our men, the whoop of the savages, and the rattle of the rifle shots, rose the scream of the wounded horses. I have seen battles between civilized foes; I was at Princeton when the British came with the bayonet, and I was at Monmouth on that burning day when "Mad" Anthony led the charge, but there it was mercy for the conquered, and the cry for quarter once uttered, foes became friends. Those were the mere polish of war to this savage encounter in the wilderness, where a man once down prayed a speedy death, for otherwise the fagot and the stake were his.

The terror of the phantom host multiplied in the minds of the raw soldiers. They seemed to be fighting invisible demons, as in truth they were. They began to give way, and with shouts of horror turned to flee. The savages now ran in, and bounding here and there, struck down with war axe and tomahawk.

General Butler was still lying against the knapsacks, and as I looked he sent his last aide with an order to another part of the field. A gigantic figure, naked to the waist, sprang up before the reclining officer. It was Hoyoquim, his face streaked horribly with the warpaint and his tomahawk uplifted. I raised my rifle with involuntary motion, but I had just fired at a savage, and there was not time to reload. The next instant the tomahawk descended and clove the head of the brave general to the neck. Uttering a piercing cry of triumph, Hoyoquim sprang back into the bushes, and the confusion and slaughter around us increased. The crackle of the rifle firing grew louder, but the note of the cannon sank, and for the best of reasons; nearly all the gunners and cannoneers were killed. Some of the men, unused to the forest, and appalled by this battle, in which the blows of the enemy seemed as mysterious and deadly as strokes of lightning, ceased to use their weapons, and, shivering, cowered over the fires, though, had they known it, the shivering was from terror and not from cold. Others burst into the tents and drank what liquor they could find, wishing to stupefy themselves or find an artificial joy in the face of death. The officers struck them with the flats of their swords, but these men took the blows in silence or laughed stupidly. Our regular troops in this strange and terrible position showed undaunted courage, charging often with the bayonet, driving back the savages and raising them out of the bushes and grass like partridges, but when the charge spent its force in the woods the savages, as before, swarmed back, shooting down from many coverts. Every one of the regular officers was killed or wounded, but their men fought on, and once General St. Clair himself led their charge, only to get more bullets through his clothes, but to escape the death which perhaps he then coveted.

We were being forced slowly toward the forest, and when we charged back at times to scatter the cloud of Indians who hung on our rear we noticed that our dead, who lay so thickly upon the ground, were now scalped, while the yelling savages as they leaped from bush to bush brandished in triumph the horrid trophies.

A dozen Indians suddenly sprang from the thickets, and rushing forward, seized one of the cannon; all the artillerymen had been killed beside it. They began to drag it away, but the regulars recovered it with a charge which sent the warriors flying into the bushes, from the cover of which they decimated our ranks with rifle balls. In a few moments another cannon was lost, and then retaken, but at the same expense, and now all the old scouts began to see that the courage of the regular troops and officers—boys, many of the latter were, though never did men die more bravely—was of no avail; the battle was lost beyond the hope of saving, and with it half the army, slain in that vast forest; all knew there would be no wounded, save those whom we could take away with us, and these would be but few.

Now a lone trumpet sounded the retreat. The cannon were spiked and abandoned. The way was plain; behind us lay the broad trail that our advancing army had made, and into it pressed the wild pell-mell of the fugitives, driven on by the fear of death in its most terrible form, bullets pelting the huddled and fleeing mass. Osseo and I had managed to keep together in all the turmoil, and when we turned to retreat with the others we ran toward the head of the column, where the savages had closed across the path of flight, wild with triumph and the greatest scalp-taking that their generation had known, and wishing to destroy the whole of the army as they had already destroyed half of it. The Indian coil now encircled us; but our army, some still animated by courage and some by the fear of death, drove straight along the road and at the savage line. General St. Clair, mounted on a horse that an aide had caught for him, rode in the centre, and on we went, leaving behind us our cannon and our hurt, the wildest rout that troops of our nation have ever known, and by far the most terrible.

Colonel Darke, one of our brave border officers, led the charge, and around him gathered all the frontiersmen and the stanchest of the soldiers. So fierce was our rush that the Indians were thrown from the road, and through the opening the remains of the army dashed, the savages at once closing in behind and hanging upon the rear of our flying force, busy with tomahawks and scalping knives.

Such a defeat as ours is bad, but such a flight is far worse. Only the oldest and wariest Indian fighters retained their presence of mind. The raw army, hacked continually by Indian bullets, the savage war-whoop sounding always behind it, was mad with terror. Many of the men threw away their guns, knowing that any weight would impede their flight, while the bravest turned to defend the rear as best they could and hold back the merciless pursuit. Many deeds of courage, too, did I witness on that day. I saw a provision packer, who had already given his horse to a wounded soldier, enabling the latter to escape, pick up a boy fallen from exhaustion, and carry him on his back in the press and whirl of the flying army. I learned long afterward that both escaped, although the brave packer stopped again on the way to bind up the hurt of a wounded man. Such things as these offset acts of cowardice, and I have noticed often that in moments of panic and despair the greatness and baseness of the human race alike are shown.

The old frontiersmen and the few regulars left were now the last bulwark of the fleeing army, its sole defence against the horde of savages, who followed it through the woods and strove to complete with bullet and tomahawk the ruin that they had begun. Nor should I forget Osseo, that valiant Indian who on this day achieved deeds worthy of the best knight who ever rode through the pages of a French romance. I think that a song of battle was singing in his ears; all the impulses passed down by many generations of savage life were sweeping him on; his black eyes were alight, his muscles drawn like whipcord; his brown body would flash past me, and some warrior, too daring, would fall beneath his tomahawk; now and then he uttered his own long, thrilling war-whoop as a defiance to our enemies, and though the savages sought zealously for his life, no bullet or blade touched him. He fought like one who had a grievance against the Northwestern tribes, and I, although not knowing what it was, remembered to be thankful that we profited by it.

Just in front of us a sergeant's wife fell to the ground in terror, and another woman carrying a little child in her arms sank down exhausted. Osseo seized the child, the woman shrinking from him in fright, and then rushing at him with her hands to rescue her little one, thinking that he belonged to the savage army. But Osseo took her by the arm, and still carrying the child, helped them on in their flight. I raised the sergeant's wife to her feet, and having found a place for her in a wagon, the horses of which still survived the Indian bullets, rejoined Osseo.

The retreat now demanded the whole attention of all who knew the ways of the woods. If one flees in a panic and the object that causes the panic pursues, it is but natural for the panic to increase. The danger that hangs on behind grows manifold, and when that danger was so real and terrible as ours there was naught that could restrain the more timorous among our troops. Such men as these no longer felt any sense of disgrace, and they had no thought but to reach Fort Jefferson, the last post built by the army in its advance into the Northwest, and shelter themselves behind its stockades.

But another thought was in the minds of the old frontiersmen who sought to keep back the pressing swarms of Indians, and it was of the border people whom this routed and fleeing army had come to protect and avenge. The tale of the Indian atrocities already filled with horror the minds of those who heard; but, flushed by such a victory, the tribes would become far bolder and more enterprising than ever. There would not be in all the circuit of the West a cabin that was safe. The tomahawk and the scalping knife would find victims from Pennsylvania to the Mississippi. The woods would he filled with warriors seeking to emulate the great killing when St. Clair was beaten, and the rage for white scalps, whether of man, woman, or child, would burn in the veins of every tribe, even to those beyond the farthest end of Lake Superior, and such was what came to pass. White men have done wrongs on the border, but surely nothing that ever justified such cruelties as our vanguard of settlers have suffered.

The Indian pursuit began to slacken after a distance of four or five miles and then ceased altogether. It may be that they wished to return to the field and make their ghastly collection of scalps. Surely there was enough for them, as upon that fatal day between six and seven hundred of our men—about half the army—were killed outright and scalped, and half the remainder were wounded. Nearly all the officers were slain, and among them Colonel Oldham, the leader of the Kentucky militia, who fell gallantly at the head of his men early in the action, and Major Clark, who was shot down while seeking to cover the retreat. Colonel Darke, who commanded one wing, saw his youngest son killed upon the field, and he himself was badly wounded, though escaping with his life. But why should I continue the tale and tell of so many good men losing their lives through the stubborn folly of General St. Clair, who despised his enemy and neglected the commonest precautions? I say with deliberation that his was the chief fault.

We met later in the day the little regiment of regular troops that had been sent back after the deserting militia, so missing the battle, but serving very well now to cover our retreat. Thus the ghastly procession continued until about nightfall it reached Fort Jefferson, thirty miles from the battlefield, and took refuge behind its palisades. Never did the sun set upon a more miserable band.

I saw my cousin, Jasper Lee, once in this flight—I heard that he fought cautiously in the battle—and he said to me in a patronizing tone that was more insolent than abuse:

"You have borne yourself very well to-day, John."

"Have I?" I replied. "I hope that I shall be able to speak as well of you."

I wasted no more words upon him, having made a resolution which I awaited only our arrival at the fort to carry out.

CHAPTER 9 A Dance by Torchlight

The sun went down on the forest, which now hid the black tragedy of St. Clair's defeat, but those who lay behind the walls of Fort Jefferson still beheld the tomahawk in every bush. They looked fearfully over their scanty numbers, and saw that half were gone. They quivered at the lightest sound, and told each other that they had not come from New York and Philadelphia to fight invisible demons for two dollars a month, thus mingling unconscious comedy with such real tragedy. I felt true pity for men who had been led blindly into a situation with which they were so little fitted to cope, and one could not afford to despise even the fraction that had shown cowardice. Better troops both of our own nation and others, taken in surprise by the savages, had fled more than once, and mingled with these, the only thought of whom had been flight, were the many who had risked their lives over and over again to save the army from destruction. But my duty there was done, and it was not for me to linger at Fort Jefferson.

I refilled my bullet pouch and powder-horn, and sought Osseo, finding him by the palisade, leaning against it, with his eyes almost closed, yet watching the forest. He was resting, permitting himself to float upon the border-land of sleep, and yet not dulling his senses so far that he could not watch for enemies. Winchester was near him; he had seen the defeat, and as he stood there with closed eyes I knew that he was thinking of the great tragedy.

"Osseo," I said, "it is time to go, and I need your help."

"I am ready," he replied I knew from the first that he would be waiting.

"And so am I," said Winchester quietly.

"You!" I exclaimed. "Why, Winchester, this is no work of yours!"

"It is," he said in the same quiet but stubborn tone. "I know that you are going for Miss Carew, and I want to help. Besides, I've been thinking, Lee, how I'd feel if the girl at home in England—there's one, you know—were in her place. I don't understand as much about this forest business as you and the Indian, but I might be handy in case of a fight. I'm going."

This was a long speech for Winchester, but there was no bluster about him, the firm temper of the man speaking in his voice.

"The Englishman is brave," said Osseo, "and he is ready to give his life for his friend. He shall go with us."

When our gratitude is strongest we like but little to speak of it, and so I merely said to Winchester:

"I owe you for much, Winchester, and the debt is growing."

He made a slight gesture as if he would wave the matter aside, and with that it was settled.

Although the work for which I had volunteered was done, and we of the West, as I repeat, were a very free people, I thought it right, inasmuch as I had served with St. Clair through a most arduous affair, to secure a formal leave of absence, and with such intention I sought an officer empowered to give the necessary authority. I was passed from one to another until I reached my cousin, Jasper Lee.

"And so," he said with peculiar insolence, "you wish to leave us upon some vague adventure, which for all we know may be a traitorous expedition to the savages."

"I doubt whether the savages would look upon me as a friend, Jasper, after the history of to-day," I replied, "and, moreover, I seek the rescue of Miss Carew. I also wish to inform you that if I do not obtain your permission I shall go without it."

But he kept his countenance fairly well.

"I shall seek Miss Carew myself," he said. "I have always had it in mind. Only my duty here has delayed me. It is fitting that I should do so, and with an armed force. You can not accomplish anything."

"The more numerous the rescuing parties the better it will be for Miss Carew," I said, "and I wish to tell you again, Jasper, that I shall depart within the half hour on my errand."

"Go talk to General St. Clair," he replied in an ill humour. "He is within there. The affair is not mine in any particular, and I will have naught to do with it."

He jerked his finger over his shoulder, as he spoke, toward the door of an inner room, which I pushed open and entered when I received the reply "Come," in response to my knock. It was merely a rude log chamber, such as one would expect to find even as the commandant's office in a frontier fort, and General St. Clair sat in a chair near the window which looked out upon the courtyard. I say "sat" through courtesy, as his appearance was more like that of a dead man placed in a sitting position, and though his eyes were turned upon the courtyard he saw nothing. His heavy features had fallen, the usually ruddy face was pallid, and the lids drooped over his eyes. The same blanket coat that he had worn throughout the battle, pierced now by eight bullets, still hung from his shoulders. This man, the grandson of an earl, full of preconceived opinions, despising his enemy, having all the faults of the class to which he had been born in the Old World— faults which he transplanted with himself to the New—was now, despite his courage, crushed by his great disaster. Perhaps he was thinking then, in turn, of the massacre that he had just beheld, and the warning given to him by the great President back there in the East who repeated over and over again: "Beware of an ambush! Beware of an ambush!" I felt a certain pity and sympathy for him, and it was mingled with anger, too, because he had brought such a terrible misfortune upon the border.

He did not see me, or, if seeing me, it made no impression upon his mind, and I stood there a few moments, determined to uphold my own dignity as a free ranger of the Western woods and my own master in all things. But his manner and speech were contrary to my expectations.

"What is it, Mr. Lee?" he asked at last in a most gentle tone. "Is it possible that I can now do anything for anybody?"

I related to him briefly the story of Miss Carew's capture, and my wish to rescue her if possible.

"I thank you for your courtesy, Mr. Lee," he said with the greatest and most sincere politeness. "I know well that you need not ask me for such permission, and I know still better that if I had heeded your words I would, not now be here behind these logs, mourning my men, lying scalped and mutilated there in that hideous forest. Oh, my poor lads!"

He put his face in his hands, as if he would hide from his eyes the sight upon which they had looked that morning, and I, feeling an increase of sympathy, and knowing there was nothing more to be said, slipped from the room, leaving General St. Clair to his remorse.

It was a cold moonlit night when we three—Osseo, Winchester, and I—left Fort Jefferson and entered the, forest, going back upon the trail of the stricken army. A few hundred yards from the fort the lights disappeared, and with them all sound. Again the wilderness, lone and bare, stretched around us. The white skim of snow was yet on the earth and the trees, and the air was so still that the dry leaves gave forth no rustle.

"The warriors rejoice over their triumph," said Osseo, "and it is easy for us to pass through the woods."

We followed for many miles the broad road over which the army had fled, passing now and then horses dead of their wounds, and came after awhile to the point where the pursuit had ended.

I was sure that the Indians would gather at the battlefield, rejoicing there over their victory, and we advanced cautiously in that direction, searching the forest for the lightest noise or other sign that would indicate the presence of our foes or danger of an ambush. But we saw nothing, and no sound save the ordinary voices of the night came to our ears. We veered more than once from the woods and approached the road over which the army had advanced and fled alike, beholding now the ghastly traces of the rout, the dead and scalped bodies of our soldiers, and bands of wolves gathering already for the feast. But we saw no

Indians. Nor was it needful to them to throw out scouts lest our army should return and seek with some sudden blow vengeance upon the victors. A force cut up as ours had been could not strike back for many a month.

We drew near to the fatal field, still following a slow course, by choice, through the densest undergrowth, pressing as close as we could, and lying down at last in a thick clump of bushes, whence we could see the lights of torches dancing in the open, where our camp had been, and hear the chant of the Indian song of triumph. I judged that it was the old squaws hanging upon the rear of the savage army who sang, while the warriors occupied themselves with collecting the spoil—the weapons, provisions, clothing, and scalps—a rich booty, the finest that they had taken since Braddock's defeat, so like St. Clair's.

The number of torches increased by and by, and the light grew better. We saw hundreds of warriors passing and repassing while the chant of the Indian women went on.

"The warriors make merry," whispered Osseo. "It is not often that a leader like the General-who-never-walks comes against them."

Not often, fortunately!

"Let us creep a little closer," I said.—"Be careful, Winchester! A sound no lighter than that made by the squirrel as he trips over the bark might betray us."

"Don't be afraid that I'll be rash," he replied. "I don't want to fall into the hands of those yelling devils, at least not until I have a chance to prove that I'm an Englishman."

We crept a rod or two farther, lying almost flat upon our faces, and unmindful of the light veil of snow that covered the earth, stopping at last at the crest of a tiny hill crowned with bushes, where we could see the battlefield, and ourselves lie hidden.

"What a sight!" said Winchester.

"Yes," I replied. "'Tis a bad thing enough to war with Christians, but 'tis the ghastliest of all to war with savages, always bearing in mind that such gentlemen as Osseo here are not savages."

More than a hundred torches illuminated the stretch of open that had been our camp, and was the scene, too, of our greatest slaughter, but it was a fantastic light that they made as they were moved about by the warriors and the old squaws, who were now dancing the scalp dance. Well had they the right, their ways considered, to dance it. The chant of the women was monotonous, hardly ever varying in tone, but the warriors often broke into a shout like unto the war-whoop as they waved aloft the horrid trophies which I shall not name nor describe.

Three or four fires were burning, but the dancing warriors, despite the coldness of the weather, wore only the breech clout, and their brown bodies appeared and reappeared in the fantastic and fitful light like shadows; truly they had fought us that day like a phantom, but none the less terrible, host. Others stood about, laden with their spoil—rifles, muskets, pistols, swords, blankets, and all the other supplies of an army. The cannon which we had spiked and abandoned stood near; and everywhere—between the feet of the dancers, among those who looked on, and in the edge of the wood—lay our dead, hundreds of them.

"I thank God," whispered Winchester, "that I shall never again see such a sight, and yet it is well to have seen it."

I saw presently the man for whom I was looking. Hoyoquim, the Wyandot—in the full panoply of his rank, the battle stains gone from him, his blanket thrown over his shoulder, an officer's splendid sword, taken from its fallen owner, swinging at his side—walked among the warriors, grave, dignified, and most evidently a king of his kind. I knew that the breast of the savage throbbed with a mighty exultation; and this, too, was the captor of Rose Carew.

Hoyoquim presently joined Little Turtle, the head chief of the confederation, and to them soon came other chiefs. They drew apart, and after talking earnestly for a little while gave some orders to the warriors. The dancing then ceased abruptly, most of the torches were extinguished, and each man taking his spoil began to put it in most convenient shape.

"The warriors are about to depart for their villages," said Osseo.

It was even so. The Indian army was scattering with the same facility with which it had gathered, each band going to its own wigwams, and already some were departing. We lay very close, but we were in rough ground where the savages were not likely to pass, and we had little fear. In a few moments all the noises ceased, and the last warrior vanished in the forest.

CHAPTER 10 A Knight of France

We did not follow directly upon the Indian trail, knowing that such would be a vain proceeding, and bristling with danger. Impatience must yield to prudence—a necessity nearly always present in the life of the frontiersman—and so we turned in a great curve with a general northwesterly direction, and sped on our path as fast as the breath of Winchester, the slowest of the party, would permit us.

The village of the Wyandots was far away on the shores of Lake Huron, and I was convinced that Hoyoquim, her captor, knowing of St. Clair's advance, had not found time to take Rose Carew there; it was probable, therefore, that he had left her at the village of the Miamis, and I wished to learn as soon as possible the truth or falsity of my surmise.

Both Osseo and I knew the country, and by turns we led the way, no one of the three speaking, but hastening on, intent upon our errand, until about the midnight hour or a little beyond it, when Osseo, who was then in advance, stopped and pointed with his forefinger. I saw far in the forest a faint gleam, no more than that of a firefly, but steady, and to the eye of a frontiersman significant.

"What do you think it is, Osseo?" I asked.

He shook his head.

"Looks like a camp fire," he replied, "but can't say. Maybe not, maybe so. Suppose we see?"

His suggestion was quite appropriate, as no true forester ever passes by anything unexplained, not even a trifle, not to mention such an important matter as a light in the night.

We pushed our way carefully among the trees, and there was good need of caution, as I have seldom seen a more dense growth of forest and underbrush. The soil beneath our feet was as black as tar, and everything seemed to have grown upon it spontaneously. Twigs and boughs were so thick that, despite the fall of the leaves, we could scarce see the sky overhead. Coming thus through a screen almost impervious, the light did not grow rapidly, but remained steady, and we were soon confirmed in our belief that it was a camp fire.

"Some great fool," repeated Osseo. "He lies down to sleep by the warm fire, and when he wakes he may find his scalp swinging at the belt of the Miami or Wyandot."

Yet it seemed incredible to me that any one should go to sleep alone, even beside his own bed of coals, in a country infested by hostile Indians and not twenty miles from the scene of St. Clair's great defeat. I had no doubt, however, that Osseo was right.

We continued our approach, Winchester making his way with great difficulty through the bushes and briers, but doing very well for one of his limited experience. As we came near, a most appetizing odour arose; it told of frying venison and beaver tail.

"The man does not sleep," said Osseo.

His remark was superfluous. The stranger or strangers, whoever he or they might be, evidently were engaged in cooking supper, late though the hour was. In truth, it must be a man or men with the most childlike faith in the innocence of the wilderness. Osseo was a little in advance, and lying down he crept closer, while we crouched in the brushwood, awaiting his report, but he stopped when he had gone a few yards, and signalled to us. We approached, and then we heard distinctly a low, humming sound. It came from the vicinity of the fire, and I recognised it as the voice of somebody who sang softly to himself.

"It is one man!" said Osseo. "Behold!"

I rose to my knees and looked over the tops of the bushes, getting a view of the camp fire and the man who sat beside it, or rather moved about it. As well as I could see, he was young, with blonde hair, blue eyes, and a fair face. His dress was a strange mixture of the American frontier style and Old World fashion, being composed of tanned deerskin except the coat, which was a sort of tunic of black velvet trimmed with silver lace, and the hat, which was a splendid three-cornered affair, also adorned with silver lace.

He carried a pistol and knife in his belt, and his rifle lay on the ground at least ten feet from him, which on the frontier is a most rash and foolish distance. But the stranger seemed to have never a care. The song that he hummed was gay and careless in tone, as if dealing with love and war, and he bestowed not a single look upon the Indian-haunted wilderness about him. All his attention was reserved for the late supper which he alternately cooked and ate, cutting most appetizing strips from a haunch of venison and grilling them over the coals on the end of a sharp stick. Near him lay a small leather case bound with silver, which evidently contained baggage.

Winchester snuffed the odour of the venison.

"It makes me hungry," he said.

But the stranger's appetite was nearly satisfied when we arrived, and in a few moments he ceased his culinary operations and threw away the sharp stick. Then he lifted a blanket from the ground and spread it over a fallen log, turning the next moment to the little silver-bound case, which he unlocked with a key. He lifted from this a very much smaller case, and after relocking the first opened the second.

"What under the sun is he about?" whispered Winchester.

The stranger took from the little case three or four hollow and polished pieces of wood, mounted with silver, and fitted them together. Then he sat on the blanket-covered log and put his mouth to one of the little holes in the tube.

"He is about to make music," whispered Osseo. "Lo! the strange white man is in the keeping of Manito. He is mad."

"Listen!" said Winchester.

The man began to play the flute—not like a mere amateur, not like one who blows his breath into a piece of hollow wood that he may hear himself make a noise, but like one who played because the soul of music was in him; in truth, like a master. His own face proved it, because, serving as a mirror for the mind beneath, it showed that his thoughts wandered away with the music to whatever land of fancy the latter led. It was a mellow note, at times low and pathetic, then wild and high, and I too, like the player, wandered with it; I saw my boyhood, the great days in the early years of the war with my brave comrades, felt the fire of battle, endured my disgrace a second time, and beheld Rose Carew's face again. I looked at Osseo; his eyes glistened. It was instinctive in this noble man to love music, and I wondered where he was roving on the note of the flute. But I did not dream of asking him.

The player ceased, took his flute apart again, and returned it to the box.

"Lo! he is mad and in the keeping of Manito," repeated Osseo. "He walks the forest as safe as the papoose in its father's wigwam."

He spoke of the fact, so well known, that the Indians consider all insane people in the special keeping of the Great Spirit, and therefore never harm them, no matter what their race. But the man turned toward us a clear-cut, thoughtful face, and I saw well enough that he was not mad, at least according to white standards—perhaps all whites are mad according to red standards. The features were of one not over thirty, and seemed French to me, much like those of the gallant young men of high birth who came over to help us in the last days of the Revolutionary contest.

"Let us speak to him, Osseo," I said.

Rising, we walked into the little glade in which the stranger had pitched his tent—I say tent metaphorically, as besides his arms he had only a blanket and the little leather case and its contents. He showed no surprise at our approach, receiving us with a politeness which was neither slight nor overdone, but just what it should be.

"Will you share my fire?" he said. "I have no seat to offer save this log, which is at a convenient distance, but not so soft as a chair. Sit there and let me fry you some venison. It is of the best quality, I assure you. *Sapristi*! I should know. I have never eaten better from the king's own forest."

We would travel fast, but we knew that food was necessary to those who would arrive in time, and we sat silently upon the log, awaiting the service of this strange man, who upon his own part proceeded with much deliberation.

"Are you aware," I asked, when I had eaten a slice of the venison, "that your life is in the utmost danger?"

"I did not know it," he replied calmly. "Not from you three, at least. You have accepted my hospitality, you have broken bread with me, you have eaten of my salt, and it would be a wicked deed now to turn a hostile face toward me."

He looked at the three of us closely and then smiled.

"No," he said, "I do not fear you."

"I did not mean that there was danger from us," I continued. "All this region is infested by Indians of the most warlike and ferocious nature, and you are now not more than a half day's journey from the villages of the Miamis, the most powerful of the tribes."

"I am not an American," he replied, "and the savages are not at war with my nation nor me."

"But you are a white man, and the savages do not make nice distinctions. They might shoot you first and make the inquiry as to your nationality afterward."

"I take the chances. Would this life be pleasant and interesting unless chance played so great a part in it? I surmise not."

"At all events, you can not be as indifferent as you pretend," I persisted.

"And at all events," he replied quickly, "the precision of your language and your manner indicate that you are not the mere hunter you seem."

It was obvious that I could not get at him by such manner of questioning, and so I told him of St. Clair's defeat and the slaughter, and then of our errand. His eyes kindled into interest as I proceeded with the narrative, and he made many comments in a quick, sharp way.

"It was a trap," he said, when I concluded, "and a raw army following a blind general walked into it. We French have our faults, but we would never do that. We are the best woodsmen, we know the Indian, we can make ourselves his friends, we learn his ways; we find the land first and we give it a name, but what does it profit us? The blind Saxon in the end takes it from us."

He was sad momentarily, and stared into the coals, but then his face brightened, and he said quite cheerily:

"Now you have told me who you are, and it is fitting that I should tell you of myself. The courtesy of the wilderness demands it. I am Hector de Chamillard, baron of France. I do not mention the title as a boast, but as an explanation, and the name Hector has no significance in my case. My barony was wasted, not by me, but before my time, until there is naught left save for the money lender and the tax gatherer. The wars are over for the moment, and since the birth of Hector de Chamillard does not allow him to work, he brings himself to the New World in the vague hope of finding a good fairy, and, moreover, to see the splendid regions which France has owned and lost—it would take him a long time and the circuit of the globe to see them all; so I am at present, and contrary to your supposition, a mere wanderer."

"But great events have been happening in that France of yours," I said. "Rumours of them are coming even here to us in the American woods. A cool head and a bold mind might make a high place there for themselves."

"I have heard them, too," he replied, the momentary sadness returning to his face, "and that is the best reason of all why I can not return to France now. By birth I am with the nobility, by sympathy with the peasantry. My position is very difficult: my birth does not allow me to associate with men of my own sympathies, and my sympathies do not allow me to associate with men of my own birth; so I remain in the forest until I can see a path clear before me. Truly it is a great forest, and man may admire."

He looked up at the dark woods which encircled us like a wall.

"And you will not go back to France?" I asked.

"I do not say that," he replied. "I do not scorn civilization; far from it. Paris has many delights, and it is still the capital of the world. I could take my pleasures there if circumstances were fitting; meanwhile I take them here. I hunt and explore, and man so far has not disturbed me; the forest is my dining-room, and my good rifle the gargon who serves me with a bill of fare that pleases me. I wander where I will, and see mountains, great rivers, and great lakes; my life is not bare, and it will please me in my old age to remember these things."

Clearly the man was a philosopher, and I could appreciate his resignation, having in mind my own case.

"I have been in Paris, too," said Winchester, who had not spoken hitherto, "and I know its contrast with this forest. But you are right when you say that each has its pleasures."

De Chamillard looked inquiringly at Winchester.

"You are an Englishman, I take it," he said, "and you and I have been enemies for a thousand years. Let us be friends for the moment. Your hand, Mr. Winchester."

Winchester extended his hand frankly, and the Frenchman shook it with heartiness. We four stood there a moment—the Indian, the American, the Englishman, and the Frenchman—but in perfect accord. Then I gave the Frenchman a parting salute, as we did not have time to tarry, but he put his rifle on one shoulder and his portmanteau on the other and said:

"Messieurs, I travel with you."

"Ours," I said, "is an errand full of danger, in which you would be involved."

"I have heard your story; there is a beautiful lady who must be rescued, and since I have been a knight errant of no use, I should now become a knight errant of some use. I shall help you."

It was said with an air of decision and finality that showed him a man of courage and will, and likely to prove a strong addition to our party. Moreover, a sudden idea concerning him occurred to me, so I said:

"Come with us and be sure that you do not lose your flute."

"Part with my best friend? On the faith of a De Chamillard I swear not! But why do you value my flute?"

"Because you play it so beautifully."

He took off his cocked hat and made me a sweeping bow.

"I thank you for your compliment, which I know was intended as an evasion of my question," he said. "And now lead on; I follow."

Thus, and without further discourse, we adopted him into our party, resuming our journey through the woods.

Winchester and De Chamillard dropped a little in the rear presently, and talked in low tones.

"Of what do they speak?" I asked Osseo.

Dark as the night was, I distinctly saw a twinkle in the eyes of the chief.

"The Frenchman and the Englishman," he said, "conduct a great war between themselves. They go back many, many moons, and they tell of mighty battles in which the children of Onontio[8] and the children of Corlear[9] fought against each other, and lo! as one tells it the children of Onontio have always won, and as the other tells it the children of Corlear have always won. Manito alone knows which is right; he has not given to Osseo the wisdom to judge between them."

"You think them both mad, Osseo?" I asked.

He shook his head sorrowfully.

"It is the will of Manito," he replied, "that it shall take many kinds of men to make his world, and who is Osseo, to question his wisdom?"

But I knew full well that Osseo's conviction of their madness did not injure them in his good opinion. It was part of his lofty nature to consider it a quality with which they had been endowed specially by God, and hence entitled to all respect and consideration; I say again that perhaps there was something in his claim of red superiority over the white race.

---

[8] The French Governor General of Canada

[9] The English Governor of the old Province of New York

CHAPTER 11 A Magic Flute

We lay down in the forest at sunrise and slept soundly, all but one man, who was relieved in turn by the others, and we did not approach the Miami village until late in the afternoon. This, comprising several hundred lodges and log-cabins, defended by a triple palisade, was pitched upon the banks and hills of the Wabash River, and around it were small fields, in which crops of maize and melons had been gathered before the frosts, but which stood bare now, forbidding our further approach, especially as various mangy curs, wonderfully keen of sight and scent, like all the Indian dogs, wandered about the open spaces.

We knew by the calm appearance of the village that the victorious warriors had not arrived yet, though they must be very near.

The sun was still an hour above the earth when we heard a high-pitched cry at our right—not a war-whoop, but a swelling shout of triumph, the signal that the warriors were approaching. It was answered from the village, and then the old men, the squaws, and the children, who had been left behind, came forth to meet the victors, silent at first while the warriors were shouting their own Indian whoop, and imitating, too, the howl of the wolf and the panther, and the growl of the bear. Then these non-combatants answered with a great cry of triumph, after which the squaws began to sing and dance their queer dance, which consists more in jumping up and down to the rhythm of a monotonous chant than anything else. But the song increased in volume when they saw what a magnificent spoil the victors were bringing, enough to stock the village more years than any of them would live.

When the warriors ceased the answering halloos, they marched in silence and with dignity between the applauding lines of squaws.

They crossed the fields and reached the outer palisade, where they fired their rifles in the air as the fine finish of the celebration. Then they went to the lodges with their spoil, while the old squaws sang the death song of those who had fallen, and the young women cooked venison and buffalo meat for the returned.

The singing and wailing of the squaws ceased after awhile, and the sun dropped low in the west. Osseo looked inquiringly at me.

"Has Lee a plan?" he asked.

"I have, Osseo," I replied.

He asked no more, but stood waiting until in my own good time I should make it known.

I turned to De Chamillard.

"Will you play the flute again for us?" I asked.

He stared at me in surprise.

"You seem to have my flute upon your mind, Monsieur Lee," he said. "Did I ever think that my poor music was to win such applause in these vast and lonely woods?"

"Will you play the flute for us again?" I repeated, "and play it not only like a musician, but also like the brave man that you are?"

He laughed.

"It shall not be said of Hector de Chamillard that he resisted such a flattering appeal as that," he replied.

"Then give us your arms, take only your flute in your hand, and as you play it walk into that village like some pilgrim of old, seeking alms."

"Monsieur Lee," he replied, "I give you this credit: when you ask for a favour you make it a large one; you are not a small man in any particular."

His tone was complimentary rather than accusing, but I hastened to explain.

"If you approach the village unarmed and playing your flute, the Indians will consider you insane," I said. "Nothing else that you might do could shake them in this belief. Even Osseo, who has seen more of the white men than most Indians have, thought you mad when we approached your camp fire in the forest, and he thinks so yet—do you not, Osseo?"

Osseo nodded his head gravely.

"On my honour," exclaimed De Chamillard, "I have never before been accused of madness."

"It is not a discredit," I continued, "and just now it may be of great service to us. Go among these Indians; you may enter wherever you wish, for, as one mad, you are, so they think, a special favourite of Manito, which is Indian for the Great Spirit, otherwise God. Find where Miss Carew is kept—we are sure that she is there; tell her to be of good heart, that her friends are by and will rescue her. To-morrow afternoon come back into the forest as near this point as you can. When you hear the cry of the whip-poor-will, walk toward the sound as quietly and secretly as possible. You will find us there, and then you may tell us all you have seen and heard."

"Which means that I am to act like the woman in the Bible and spy out the land?"

"Even so."

"Then I accept the proposal. If any man had told me yesterday that I would do such a thing, 'Liar' would have been the first word on my lips, and I would have defended the epithet; but to-day I do it. The De Chamillards were never practical people, which perhaps is the reason why I am here, a beggar, embarking upon such a venture. But it is well to risk one's life even for the lady love of a new friend."

I know that I flushed a little, because he laughed and looked at me with a twinkling eye.

"There is one promise I make you, Monsieur Lee," he said, "and I make it on the oath of a De Chamillard."

"What is that?"

"All our family love beauty, and women have been one of our weaknesses, but I pledge you my word that I will not seek to make love to the lady."

"I have no claim upon her," I said.

He laughed again.

"Perhaps not," he said, "but you wish to have. No, I go only in behalf of my friend, not in my own."

I could not help smiling at him, his fine-drawn point of honour, and his rising gaiety as he embarked upon this strange venture. I saw clearly that the errand appealed to a romantic and daring spirit. Chance had put in our hands the best man to carry it through.

He gave us his arms, took the flute in his hands, and entered the field that lay between us and the village.

"He is really mad," said Winchester.

But I knew that in his English heart of hearts he thought all Frenchmen mad.

When De Chamillard had gone a few yards into the open he put the flute to his lips and began to play a chansonette, some pretty French tune, which I dare say had been heard in the halls of the Great and the Little Trianon, with small thought by any one that it would be repeated here in these wilds. He changed in a moment to an air of love and longing that moved us with its pathos.

He walked steadily on toward the village, and I knew that he was seen now by the warriors. One raised his rifle as if to take aim, but quickly dropped it, for when this warrior looked again he saw that the strange white man was in the keeping of Manito.

De Chamillard's ancestors were Crusaders, I am sure, sent by the spirit of adventure as well as the love of Church to the Holy Land, as even from our covert we saw that he bore himself in the most jaunty manner; and I am equally certain, too, that his soul was in what he now did. The warriors, the women, and the children were coming forth in a great swarm, gazing at him with the most intense curiosity, and making no sound. Their opinion, as one knowing the Indian nature and the Indian manner could tell, was formed already. The Frenchman was to them a man blasted by a stroke of Manito's lightning, and therefore under his protection. They made no further movement, but waited in front of the village as he advanced.

De Chamillard presently took the flute from his lips, and to our surprise began to sing with much expression in a clear, strong voice, evidently a voice that had been trained by good masters. This was his song:

> En mon coeur n'est point escrite
>
> La rose ni autre fleur,
>
> C'est toi belle Marguerite
>
> Par qui j'ai cette couleur.

I had heard the song before; I knew that its name was The Young Captive, and the fitness of it moved me. I thought not then of De Chamillard, but of Rose Carew. He sang other verses, and then changed suddenly to a new song, an air with a hop and a skip and a jump and a merry note, and these were its words:

> J'ai toujours, Bacchus
>
> Célébré ton jus
>
> N'en perdon pas la coutume;
>
> Seconde moi,
>
> Que peut, sans toi
>
> Ma plume.

> Coule à long traits
>
> Dans mon épais
>
> Volume
>
> Viens, mon cher patron
>
> Sois mon Apollon
>
> Viens, mon cher ami! Que j' t' humer!

When he ceased the song he danced one or two steps, just the suggestion of a dance, and then, putting the flute to his lips, began to play again. I have always thought that De Chamillard, were it not for his birth, might have been an actor. In truth, he had the gifts. To fill such a rôle as the one he was playing now he did not have to act; he lived it; he was in very essence and being a child of God, as the Indians term it. He continued his steady progress until the crowd of savages closed behind him, and we saw him no more, although the notes of the flute still came to us faintly.

"I told you that he was really mad," said Winchester. "He did not have to play the part."

Even Osseo smiled. Then we withdrew farther into the forest, not caring to risk the notice of some stray warrior. Having nothing now to do but wait, we sought sleep again, wrapping ourselves in our blankets, with the exception of one who watched. A wise frontiersman always rests and sleeps when there is opportunity, knowing that it may not come again soon. We had a sufficient supply of jerked venison with us, and when we were hungry we ate. Thus the night and most of the next day passed, and when the sun dropped low Osseo imitated the cry of the whip-poor-will so perfectly that even I, with the experience of years in the woods, could not have told the difference.

"He will never come," said the incredulous Winchester. "The Indians have burned him at the stake long before this."

"The Indians have not burned him at the stake, and he will come," was my rejoinder.

Osseo repeated his cry, all the time intently watching the forest in every direction, since others than the one wished might answer the whip-poor-will call. He put his ear to the earth presently, and when he rose again he said:

"The Man-who-blows-the-hollow-stick comes, and he is alone."

Osseo once more gave the cry of the whip-poor-will, and then, waiting a little longer, we saw at a great distance the figure of De Chamillard advancing among the tree trunks. But we did not remain where we were until he could reach us; instead, we moved farther and farther to the right, continually drawing him after us with repetitions of the whip-poor-will cry. We adopted this course in order to be sure that no Indians were following the Frenchman, and at last, when we were convinced, we stopped. He came to us presently, flushed with exertion.

"I had begun to think that whip-poor-will was the most evasive bird that ever uttered his lonesome note," he said. "*Ma foi*! but I have had a walk."

"Have you seen her?" I cried.

"I have," he said, "and on my honour, Monsieur Lee, it was only my promise to you that kept me from trying to make love to her, and I may say to you this very moment that I am sorry I gave the promise, although I think it would never have got further than an attempt."

"What of her—the girl?"

"She is well, and she hopes again, since she has heard that her friends are near, seeking her rescue. But I will begin where the story does, and tell you the whole of it. When I left you, playing the flute and marching toward the village of the savages, I, the madman, the man who is in the keeping of God—as our Indian friend frankly puts it, and as our English friend secretly believes—began to feel the grandeur of my task, and my bosom swelled with inspiration—it is our French way sometimes; and I played the flute with a new mastery and sang French lyrics as I had never sung them before. The savages met me, and what you told me, Monsieur Lee, was even so; they deemed me perfectly mad, and I confirmed them in the belief, playing my flute at intervals and marching wherever my changeful mind might incline me, sometimes into the lodges of the warriors, where I helped myself once to a piece of most succulent venison, and none said me nay—just as if I was the Lord's anointed, Louis of France, honouring one of his peasants by taking what he fancied from the contents of his cottage. It is a pleasant emotion, to feel that you may do as you choose and pay no price, and I continued in my lordly career.

"Two white men present—renegades, I suppose—seemed to suspect me, but they dared not molest me, as the chiefs sternly forbade any interference with my career. Moreover, my music pleased the savages, and I wandered about the village, looking with all my eyes and listening with all my ears—I know a little of the Miami dialect—learning presently that the captive lady was kept near the centre of the village in the largest hut until such time as the chief, Hoyoquim, her captor, could carry her to his own village. Meantime they were treating her with proper respect; and deeming it best not to proceed too rapidly, I lay down in the most comfortable wigwam that I could find and slept the night.

"I wandered about in the village a little while this morning, playing my flute at times, and at last undertook to enter the hut where the lady is imprisoned. The warrior on watch made no resistance, no more daring to lay a hand on me than if he were in truth a French peasant, and I the Lord's anointed. There I found the maiden in great grief, and near unto despair, but her spirits rose wonderfully when I told her that her friends were near, particularly when I mentioned you. Truly she has a courage! 'Is Mr. Lee out there in the woods?' she asked, and you alone she called by name. 'He is,' I answered; 'and he will not go away without you.' 'Nor will he,' added she, very low and under her breath, although I heard her. She was much excited at first, but after that she was quite calm, and seemed to contemplate the future with more confidence than I can. When I came away I asked if she had any message to send, and she said only, 'Tell Mr. Lee that I have the utmost faith in him,' and so I relate it, although it seems to me that she might also have faith in messieurs the red gentleman, the English gentleman, and the French gentleman."

I thanked De Chamillard briefly for his achievement, feeling that he, like Winchester, would not care to listen to many words of gratitude, and then Winchester spoke.

"It is now my turn to go among the savages, Lee," he said. "I am of a nation that is not at war with them, and they will not harm me. Moreover, I am a fur-trader, and I know the chief, Hoyoquim, who is not without certain chivalrous instincts. It may be that he will take ransom for Miss Carew, and I can offer it."

I pondered awhile over his suggestion, and then I decided to improve upon it. I had feared at first that Winchester's presence with our army might involve him too in the Indian hatred, but since he was without apprehension on the point, it was not for me to imagine dangers for him, when the fate of Rose Carew perhaps depended upon his help.

"See Hoyoquim or Little Turtle, if you are able," I said, "and tell either that I wish to come with you and buy back Miss Carew. I know the Indian ways, and perhaps I can attract them with an offer. If they say that I may come in safety it will be even so, for they are men of honour."

He departed at once upon his mission, and returned about midnight.

"The head chief, Little Turtle, is absent," he said, "but the Wyandot, Hoyoquim, who captured Miss Carew, is in the village. He says that you can come with me under the white flag, so to speak, and talk about the girl. If you and he do not agree, you may return to the forest in peace."

This was sufficient, and we prepared at once to enter the village, while Osseo and De Chamillard remained in the woods to await our return.

"If you do not return I shall go for you," the Frenchman said. "*Nom du chien*, how could I desert so interesting a friend?"

It was just at sunrise that we approached the village, and the barking of many mangy curs warned the Indians of our approach. One of those horrible, weazened old squaws who are always on watch about the outskirts of an Indian encampment came forward to meet us, and she was followed presently by others. We held up our hands to show that we were peaceful, and I said in Miami:

"We come with a message to the great chief Hoyoquim."

Then they conducted us to Hoyoquim, who received us beside the council fire, having made ready for our approach with all the formality practised by the Indians upon such occasions, and we, knowing that it was wisdom, paid heed to his ways.

CHAPTER 12 A Bargain Made

The firelight flickered and fell upon the face of the chief. He sat unmoved, his bronze features expressing a gravity that became one of his port and place, and naught else. I thought him a splendid type of savage man, massive and strong, the complete master of himself.

The coals smouldered and died down a little, making but a tiny point of fire in the forest, which stretched away in endless miles. The lodges of the Indian village were still dusky behind us, in the shadows of the trees, but the east was rosy with the rising sun.

Winchester and I, knowing the customs of this race, were silent too, gazing into the coals rather than at the face of the chief, and affecting indifference. Hoyoquim presently took his tomahawk from his belt and held it thoughtfully by the handle between his thumb and fore finger. It was a curious and beautiful weapon, the blade small and highly polished, and the head scooped out like a pipe. The handle was of white horn, hollow, and carved in fantastic designs. Winchester's eyes met mine for a moment, and then passed on. But I understood his look. He believed that the chief would consent to our request.

Black Eagle, as Hoyoquim was called by most of our people, took a small piece of tobacco from the deerskin pouch at his belt, put it in the hollow head of the tomahawk, and placed on top of it one of the red coals. He drew two or three whiffs of smoke through the slender horn handle, then passed the pipe of peace to me, and it seemed especially fit that on this occasion the same pipe should have been the moment before the weapon of war. I, too, took the stem in my mouth, and having drawn the smoke, handed it in turn to Winchester, who, his duty performed, returned it to the chief.

Black Eagle let the fire and tobacco drop out of his tomahawk, and thrust the weapon back into his belt. Then he said to me:

"You are a man."

"It is my belief," I replied with a little pride. I trusted that I had borne myself well in my ten years' life in the wilderness, and the thought was not unpleasant.

"You are a man," he continued with the utmost gravity, "and so am I. Who should know this better than Hoyoquim and Lee?"

We sat face to face, old enemies who had sought each other's life more than once. I was completely in his power, but I had put myself there by my own choice, and I never doubted that he would keep faith. The group of warriors ten yards away were silent and solemn, apparently gazing with the deepest interest at vacancy, but I knew that no movement of ours escaped them. Around us curved the mighty forest, a wilderness that I liked and of which I had yet a certain fear at times, despite ten years of use and habit. Its depths and its immensity now and then oppressed me.

I was anxious to be at the business in hand, but I knew better than to hurry. I glanced again at Winchester. He was as grave as the chief, the early sunshine falling across his ruddy cheeks, his blue eyes calm and untroubled. I thanked him once more in my heart for his service to me in the affair, and swore silently that some day he should have repayment.

"Is the captive, the girl whom he took in Kentucky, unharmed in the lodge of Black Eagle?" I asked at last, and unconsciously I bent forward to hear his answer. I saw the pink in Winchester's cheeks deepen, and his gaze rested directly upon the chief. But there was no expression upon the carven bronze of Black Eagle's face.

"The captive is as she was when she was taken in the far land of Kain-tuck-ee," he replied.

I breathed silent thanks. I remembered even then the pale face and agony of that mother in Kentucky, to whose entreaties I had said that I would bring back her daughter, should it be within my power.

"I would buy her from you for her own people," I said.

"What does Lee offer?" asked the chief, after another long silence.

"One hundred coins like this, to be paid into the hands of the friend of us both, the English trader," I replied.

I held up a golden guinea fresh from the mint of King George III. The sun glittered across it, and I saw a faint reflection of the gleam in the chiefs eyes—the savages had begun to learn the value of gold; where does it not go?—but he shook his head.

I was surprised, and, let me confess it, a trifle bewildered, too. One hundred guineas on the frontier, where money was so scarce, was a great ransom, and I had not expected a refusal. But I kept my countenance.

"Does Black Eagle choose well," I asked, after another long silence. "One hundred golden coins like this I hold between my fingers will buy many muskets and much powder and ball at the British post."

"The muskets of the English are good," he replied, "but the rifles of the Long Knives are better."

My glance turned to my own favourite rifle lying in the hollow of my arm, a piece with a long, slender barrel of blue steel and a carved stock, a rifle at once light, beautiful, and unerring. I knew that there was pride in my eye as I looked upon the weapon which had served its master so often and so well. Then I held it up that the gaze of the chief might fall directly upon it.

"If you will give me the girl," I said, "you shall have thirty rifles of a pattern like mine. How good this is you and your warriors should know."

It was a desperate throw to make such an offer, being held as treason among us to furnish rifles to the savages on any pretext; but I knew not what else to do, and at the moment I saw once more the face of that mother in far Kentucky. I felt that the deed would find forgiveness.

The eyes of the chief glistened for the first time as he looked at the rifle and heard my words, but it was a brief emotion. I beheld the next instant only the bronze of his face and the inscrutable black of his eyes.

"Hoyoquim would like the rifles," he replied, "but he will like the white girl better."

I glanced at Winchester and I saw his face fall. It was clear to me that he now regarded the case as hopeless. But I would not give up.

"Why does the chief wish to keep the white captive," I asked, though well I knew.

"She shall be a light in the lodge of Hoyoquim," he replied.

"Hoyoquim has wives of his own nation; why does he seek one of another race?"

"The white prisoner is fairer than the red maidens," he replied.

I saw Winchester shudder. He had told me more than once of a girl waiting for him in England, and I fancied that his imagination now put her in the place of the Kentucky captive. Well might he shudder, and well may you, who learn at what a price this land of ours was won.

I paused again and for a longer time than ever. I knew naught to say nor which way to turn. And yet that pale face in Kentucky forbade me to go with empty hands. It was Black Eagle himself who ended the silence.

"Lee is a hunter and a warrior," he said, "a man worthy to be the enemy of a great chief. Were he Hoyoquim he would do as Hoyoquim will do. The white captive would shine like the sun in the lodge of the mightiest chief. She is beyond price. He shall see for himself."

He rose and waved his hand to the group of warriors, two of whom approached. The chief spoke to them in the Wyandot tongue, and they walked toward a lodge of large size that I had noticed near the centre of the village. When they returned they brought Rose Carew with them.

I see now the light that leaped into her eyes when, raising them from the ground, she beheld Winchester and me. A great wave of delight and surprise flowed over her face, and I too felt joy because I was there to behold it. Perhaps she had never expected to look upon a white face again.

"You have come to save me?" she exclaimed, and her tone was imploring.

"We shall save you, Miss Carew, do not fear," I replied, deeply moved by the appeal in her voice. (I asked God to forgive me for the lie. Even as I spoke there was faint hope—in truth, none at all—in my heart that we might rescue her, but how else could I answer the question in that young face?) But I saw her raise her head and look proud defiance at the savages.

She stood there, the beams of the brilliant morning sun falling full upon her figure, her hair flowing in loose waves down her back, her dress torn by the bushes and brambles of her long journey. I felt, gazing upon her, that Black Eagle had told the truth when he said she was beyond price, and as I caught the look then in his eyes I could have killed him, his guest though I was. But I said to him in even tones, speaking his own language:

"The words of Hoyoquim are the words of wisdom; the maid is in truth beyond price—beyond any price that was ever before paid for a captive. But I will give for her one hundred rifles, such a reward as no chief, however great, has yet received."

"You behold her," replied the chief, "and you know if you were Hoyoquim you would, like Hoyoquim, refuse all ransom."

I shook my head, but at the bottom of my heart I was sure that he spoke the truth. Man is wild and evil where the law runs not, and the mercy of Black Eagle was but the mercy of his kind.

"What does he say?" asked Miss Carew, looking at me with the infinite trust that I deserved so ill.

"It is about the ransom," I replied, again saying the thing that was not, without scruple. "He asks a high price."

"Tell him," she said, "that my family is rich. They will pay him what he asks, however great it may be."

I met Winchester's gaze once more, and my eyes fell before his. He, too, was awaiting the answer to the girl's question.

"I shall neglect nothing, Miss Carew," I said, bowing to her with deep respect.

"And you will take me to my home?"

"I will take you to your home," I continued, repeating the words mechanically.'

I would have avoided her look then, but I could not, and again my soul grew sick. And yet her gaze held me, it was so full of faith, of an absolute faith in me, of an unspoken belief that I would do what I was promising to do, when I had no power to keep even the smallest of my pledges. Black Eagle understood all that we said. English was not a strange tongue to him, but his face was still unspeaking bronze. The girl turned with simple dignity to Winchester.

"And I have you, too, to thank for my rescue," she said.

"Yes," I interrupted. "Mr. Winchester opened the way that I might come here for you."

She told him her gratitude in fit words, but he did not reply, bending down his face, which suddenly had gone pale. The chief spoke again to the attendant warriors, motioning at the same time to the girl to go with them. She made no resistance, but she addressed me once more before returning to the lodge.

"In good truth I might have guessed that it was such a man who would come for me," she said.

I had some pride in my wilderness skill and the reputation that I, in the beginning a man of another kind, had won among the wild borderers, but now it was like the turning of a knife in a fresh wound.

"You will not fail me," she said, the smile of faith overspreading her face.

"I will not fail you," I forced myself to reply, cursing John Lee for the weak liar that I knew he was. Then she was gone, and I was glad that my eyes no more beheld her.

"She does not doubt your promise," said Winchester. I knew that he did not mean to taunt me, the words being involuntary, but they added to the bitterness of my mood. There was even a moment when I felt regret ever to have come upon such a mission.

Black Eagle did not stir, and the silence among us was very long. It was again the chief who at last broke it.

"Lee is troubled or his face does not tell truly the words of his heart," he said, although, with a delicate politeness which perhaps I did not appreciate, he never looked toward me.

"It is true, Black Eagle," I replied. "I have promised the maid that I will take her back to her people, and I can not do it. If a great chief were to make a pledge and find himself unable to keep it, would not his heart be heavy?"

He nodded assent, and then for the first time let his eyes fall upon me. I thought I saw pity there, and I flushed with a slight feeling of shame that a savage should so regard me.

"You have seen the maid," he said presently, "and you know that neither gold nor rifles are fit to buy her. But there is yet another way, with a price so high that few have ever paid it. I have known none who did so, but it is said that in the ancient and greater days of our race men have been found who were willing."

Curiosity flamed up in my mind, and I tried to divine his meaning, but the bronze repose of his face was unbroken and I could read nothing there. Winchester, too, leaned forward with a sudden increase of interest.

"Speak on, Hoyoquim," I said, adopting his sententious manner. "We listen."

"The chief would refuse all the offers that the hunter could make, except one," said he.

"And that?"

"Yourself."

"Myself!" I cried in amazement.

The cold eyes of the chief glittered.

"Will you become my prisoner in place of the girl?" he said. "Will you give yourself, my great enemy, for her? You have told her that you will send her back to Kain-tuck-ee. A true warrior never lies. How can you keep your promise? Think what it is for Hoyoquim to give up the one who would become the light of his lodge, the captive taken in honourable battle. There is none save Lee for whom he would give her."

Now, I am like other men. I appreciate a decent bit of flattery, but I make the small demand that it be spoken at the right time; moreover, Hoyoquim's proposition was so sudden that I scarce knew how to take it.

"And after the exchange is made?" I asked, speaking upon the spur of the moment.

"Lee shall have a death worthy of a brave man and a great warrior," replied the chief impressively. "There is no torture which he shall not show himself able to endure. When the fire is rising around him and the women of our tribe thrust blazing splinters into his flesh, he shall laugh at them, and calmly sing his death song. When the men taunt him and tell him that he will never see his home again, he shall smile upon them, and over his ashes the Black Eagle and his warriors will say, 'He was a great white chief in death as well as in life, the bravest foe that we have ever known.'"

The look upon my face must have been most rueful. Had Hoyoquim been a white man I should have called his speech irony, but I understood the Indian character, and I knew that he meant to pay me the highest compliment that could enter his mind. I glanced again at Winchester, and I caught a strange expression in his eye. He seemed to say, "Would you—would you dare?" and then the thought came to me—Would I, could I?

I believe it was the questioning look of Winchester that troubled me: it seemed a sort of challenge; without it I should never have permitted such an idea. I reread in an instant the tale of my life as I had lived it so far. I was alone; no father, no mother, no sister, no brother to mourn me—none at all, in truth, save some good comrades of the hunt or the forest battle, and they would quickly find another to take my place. And then, too, that old story would be buried forever. Yet this life was pleasant in spite of-all. I was not thirty, and I felt the blood flushing in a full tide through my veins. I knew the secrets of the wilderness which curved around us, and I could find zest there for thirty, forty, or more years yet.

"It is impossible that you should do this thing," said Winchester. "But what a fate for the girl!"

He was thinking, I knew, of that other girl in England.

"And why impossible?" I demanded sharply, rising to my feet. I saw then Rose Carew's face, and another like hers, but older, in distant Kentucky.

He did not answer, but there came back into his eyes the questioning look which was to me a challenge, though far from his intent that it should be such. I hesitated no longer, but turned to the chief.

"Does this forbid escape?" I asked.

"It does not," he replied. "The same chance that was open to the girl is open to you. If it be the will of Manito that you escape, you shall escape."

"I am your prisoner, Black Eagle," I said.

He looked at me gravely for full two minutes, and there was in his eye a momentary gleam that I did not understand. Was it admiration, or pity, or regret? Then he said:

"Lee is a man."

I turned to Winchester.

"Will you do this thing for me?" I asked. "Will you take the girl to Kentucky, holding her as you would the one you have left in England?"

"As God is my witness!" he replied, and he gave my hand the strong English grasp.

"Don't tell her anything about it," I continued. "Say to her that I have gone on a long expedition into the land of the Shawnees, and that you have taken my place. Tell her the ransom was money."

"I will say to her all that you ask," he answered, repeating the grasp, and I knew that he would keep his word, if man could.

"I am at your service, chief," I said to the impassive Black Eagle.

He bowed and led the way to a small hut built of logs. Thus was the bargain made.

CHAPTER 13 White Face, Black Heart

Winchester left me at the door of the hut, with one last hand clasp, and I troubled myself no more about that part of the bargain. It was never in my mind that Hoyoquim would not keep faith, and the girl could have no more trusted guardian in her flight than the Englishman.

The floor of my prison was the bare earth, on which was spread a buffalo-robe, the sole article that the place contained. I sat upon it in the Indian fashion, and looked up at Black Eagle and the two Wyandot warriors who had come with me there, awaiting their wish. I felt the pangs of hunger, not having eaten for some hours, and I mentioned it to the chief. He sent one of the warriors at once, saying that the white man was his guest and brother, and the choicest afforded by the village should be at my service, or words to that effect, my mind at the moment not dwelling on trifles.

Two Miami maidens—light brown, slender, and graceful—brought me cakes made of the beaten maize, strips of venison, and a slice of buffalo tongue, a delicacy that I had appreciated these many years. They must have been the daughters of a chief, as their moccasins and leggings and deerskin tunics were brilliant with many-coloured beads, and small feathers of red, blue, and yellow glittered in their hair. Whether they felt pity for me I know not, as I could see no expression upon the face of either, yet they were most gentle in their ways.

I ate with hearty appetite. Even in the face of dissolution in its most hideous form my body demanded its due, such was the healthy life I had led. I do not think that the strong man ever appreciates fully the approach of death; his physical senses do not permit the idea. Perhaps this feeling led me into the rash bargain.

I admit, however, that some of my hope was lost when Hoyoquim told me that I must be bound, and again in the telling of this unpleasant fact he sugared it with a compliment. The white hunter had the cunning of the wolf and the strength of the bear; if a hand or a foot were left free even for the width of the narrow hut he would slip from the Indians, though a hundred warriors guarded him. As I have said before, I like compliments; but now whenever Hoyoquim began to pay me one I felt a chill; I knew that it was but the preliminary to another reduction in my chances of life.

Two warriors bound me tightly with thongs of green deerskin, and then Hoyoquim informed me that he would leave me to myself that I might commune with the Great Spirit, as it was the custom of all warriors to make their peace with

Manito before going to the happy hunting-grounds. He might have spared me that last allusion, so I thought, but the suggestion of a taunt was far from the chiefs mind.

They went away, and when I was alone in the hut, chained upon the bosom of Mother Earth, I missed his grim politeness. My courage declined still further. I could not account for this sudden blotting out of hope; but when a man who has hunted all the way from the head waters of the Ohio to those of the Mississippi and then back again finds himself limited to an orbit of six inches, he understands that his life has undergone a mighty change.

It was only a hut of the Indian fashion in which I lay, strong enough to hold a prisoner, but with wide chinks between the logs, through which the winds of heaven blew as they wished. They brought upon their breath the odour of summer flowers and tales of the great, free world outside, through which I had roamed in thoughtless content. Ah, how I wished to be there again! I did not want to die, and it was a bitter thought to me then that perhaps when my old comrades heard of it some of them would say, "He was a fool for doing it, and he deserved his death." If we have to leave life we wish to leave it gracefully and with honour.

I lay there a long time. The varied sounds of the village came through the chinks to my ear and the winds still blew, bringing with them that note which now had become taunting. I heard after a while a light step, and looking up, beheld a white man.

There are among us of the West certain creatures with a white skin and the shape of men who have the soul of neither the red nor the white; in truth, I know not whether they have a soul at all; perhaps they are possessed of a devil which drives them to the commission of all manner of crimes surpassing those of either race with which they have so often come into conflict. Their names are spoken among us with horror, and their deaths are matter for public rejoicing. These are the renegades, men of white birth belonging to the superior breed who have taken abode with the savages, fighting against their own kind, and practising every foul snare and treasonable stratagem.

It was the worst of them, all—Moses Blackstaffe—who was now before me, a man who had achieved great power among the Northwestern tribes, because his cunning intellect brought to them many a triumph and much spoil.

He was of most hateful presence, short, broad-faced, almost as dark as an Indian, with stringy black locks, cruel eyes set close together, and sensuous lips.

He folded his arms across his breast and gazed at me awhile without speech. We were not strangers. Twice had I looked upon his face in forest ambush, and thrice at the British fort. Twice had I taken from his hands prisoners—once a girl destined for his lodge, as Rose Carew was destined for the wigwam of Black Eagle. I knew that he remembered it now as he gazed at me lying there helpless, and even had he been prone to forgetfulness I should have reminded him. One can not live so long in the Indian fashion without acquiring a touch of the Indian manner.

"I salute you, Mr. Blackstaffe," I said. "I did not expect to meet the worst villain outside of hell, but it gives me opportunity for pleasant conversation. Do you remember that fight on the Muskingum when you fled from me? But I knew before then that you were a coward. Do you remember that time two years ago when I took from you the girl whom you had chosen as your share of the spoil? She is happy now with the white people, her own people; I saw her last summer, and she asked me if the dog Blackstaffe still lived. I told her yes, but that he would yet meet the death of the dog he was!"

For answer he spat full in my face, and I saw the red flushing under the brown of his cheeks. I continued to look at him with the scorn that was burning in me.

"You speak big words for a man in your position," he said.

"I am here in this hut, bound to this spot of earth, by my own free will and choice. If I die, it is a death that I could have avoided, and there will never be a day when such a thing can be said of you, Blackstaffe. That you know!"

I felt for the first time a thrill of exultation. I believed myself so superior to him that in comparison I seemed a very good man. I trust that the emotion was human.

He flushed again under his brown skin, but in a moment resumed his self-command and said dryly:

"No, I have more sense."

I did not reply, and closed my eyes, as if I were weary and would be rid of his presence.

"If it is any pleasure to you to know your prospects," he continued, "I tell you that you are to run the gantlet, and then you will be burned at the stake."

I gave him no answer, and presently he went away, without further ado, and as his shadow became less in the hut I rejoiced greatly thereat, hating the sight of his evil face and the sound of his cruel words.

The chief unbound me about noon and the Indian maids again brought me food. I stretched my muscles, and felt the blood still flowing full and warm in my veins. When I had finished my farewell repast the girls withdrew, and I was left again to lonely thought. The night came presently, and with it a chill that reached my marrow. Hope blazes up in the sunshine, but sinks in the shadow. My chance of escape seemed to dwindle. I was now in the hands of a most cunning foe, and as my life suddenly shortened, the living of it seemed the sweeter. Yet mine in truth had been a most wretched career, now about to end obscurely in the wilderness, and the manner of its ending stirred me to anger. I should be repaid, I thought, for some things that I had suffered, and it was a hope always in my heart until this moment, when it died with other hopes.

But I did not permit such sad thoughts to go far, attuning my mind to a better frame, and seeking sleep with such good result that when I awoke again the morning sun was creeping under the mat that hung over the door.

CHAPTER 14 An Unexpected Offer

The mat was lifted after awhile, and Little Turtle himself, the head chief of the allied tribes, a man of strong countenance, stood before me. Now I knew that it was he and not Hoyoquim with whom I would have to deal.

Mechecunnaqua was dressed with great splendour, his tunic, leggings, moccasins, and head-dress being of the finest Indian make, vivid with many-coloured beads and small feathers of brilliant hue. But his chief garment was a great robe which he wrapped about his person, much as a general infolds himself and his dignity in a military cloak. It was not a blanket such as most Indian chiefs of this region wore, but a robe made of the skin of a young buffalo bull, like the kind affected by the chiefs of the plains Indians, with the soft, silky hair left on and turned outward, the inside decorated beautifully with porcupine quills in such fashion that the setting of the quills depicted the most famous battles and single combats in the life of Mechecunnaqua. It was a splendid garment, but Mechecunnaqua was a splendid man of the Indian type, and he had won most worthily the right to wear it. He took presently from the recesses of his clothing a tiny medicine bag, made of brilliantly dyed beaver-skin such as warriors of the Western tribes carry, passed it before his face two or three times, and then returned it to its concealment.

"What is your wish, Mechecunnaqua?" I asked.

"To talk to you of many things," he replied.

"Proceed."

"Lee is a great warrior," he said, "and his name fills our ears. I, Mechecunnaqua, know that fame does not lie. The war-cry of Lee is as terrible as Annemeekee."[10]

Now, I had no war-cry at all, but it was merely his way of paying me a compliment, and it would have been poor courtesy to refuse it. So I said, adopting his tone:

---

[10] Thunder.

"Proceed. In the presence of Mechecunnaqua, Lee is but Pahpukkeena[11] staring at Gheezis.[12]"

"Lee, though our enemy, did not come to take our country or slay our warriors," he continued. "When the moon hangs over the forest and the wind breathes from the south the Indian hunter, too, seeks his mate. I know not all the ways of men nor the will of Manito, but I suspect that the heart of the white hunter is like that of the red. He, too, would seek the face that he loves, and when he goes upon such an errand labours and dangers become a little thing. Even so has Lee come into the lodges of the Miamis because a white girl's face has led him on. Now the heart of Mechecunnaqua turns toward Lee. It is the will of Manito. Listen, the white girl is not yet gone from our village, but at the noon hour she starts, if Lee does not say the words that are sweet in my ear."

"Proceed, o Mechecunnaqua!"

"You are a prisoner, and nothing can save you from the stake but the words that please me, and which you alone can speak. You love the white maid. Become a Miami, and she is yours. Even more, you shall be a chief among the Miamis second only to Mechecunnaqua. I, Mechecunnaqua, say it. Forget the ways of the white man. Remember the Long Knives only to fight against them. The woods from the mountains to the great Father of Waters and beyond shall be yours. If the white maid does not please you long, then you shall have your choice among the red. You shall be adopted into the tribe as my son, and when I grow gray and my eyes fail and Manito calls me away, then you shall be head chief in my place."

The chief paused a moment, but before I could speak resumed the thread of his discourse:

"Lee knows both the ways of the white man and the red," he said, "and his wisdom will aid us in driving the Long Knives back over the mountains. Then our hunting-grounds shall remain such forever. The Western tribes—the Miamis, the Shawnees, the Wyandots, the Ottawas, the Pottawatomies, the Sacs, the Foxes, and all the others most warlike—shall form a league like that of the Iroquois in the East, but more numerous and of much greater power, of which Lee shall be some day the chief, even as the Yengees,[13] call it in their language, the king. And we shall have, too, the help of the Yengees. We have an old and very wise man, Kahgagee.[14] Many moons have whitened his head; he fought long ago in the wars between

---

[11] The grasshopper

[12] The sun

[13] English.

[14] The Raven

Onontio[15] and Corlear;[16] now he does not wield Dayanoaqua[17] or Osquesont,[18] but his heart still throbs at the beat of the war drum, and he would send his children, the warriors, to battle. Just before Behmagat[19] began to dry in the chill autumn winds he went in Cheemaun[20] to Canada to talk with the big white chief in the red coat,[21] and Keewaydin[22] has not yet brought him back again; but when he comes he will bring news that the Yengees will help us against the Long Knives."

I doubted the accuracy of this statement, not his belief in it, but it was not for me to say him nay at that moment.

"Your offer is that of a noble spirit, Mechecunnaqua," I said, "and in its way is greatly beyond my desert, yet I must cling to my own kind. But I tell you truly, Mecheeunnaqua, and to your face, I could wish that God had made us brethren in race."

"Even so could I," he replied, "but my heart is sad because Lee will not listen to my words, and a wind of Peboan[23] blows between us. And yet it would have been heavier still had I not spoken. Farewell, Lee."

"Farewell, Mechecunnaqua."

He lifted the mat that hung over the door of the hut and went out, his footfalls making no sound. I was left a prey to mingled feelings. My own race had cast me off. Then why should I not take the great reward that he offered and join his? I thank God that I never looked at this question with serious intent, but merely as a vague and curious thing that passed before my mind.

I had once more a fine opportunity, lasting two or three hours, to commune with my own unpleasant thoughts, and at the end of that time the mat was raised

---

[15] The French Governor General of Canada

[16] The British Governor of the Province of New York

[17] The scalping knife.

[18] The tomahawk

[19] The grape-vine

[20] A birch-bark canoe

[21] The British Governor General of Canada

[22] The home wind

[23] Winter

again, and a figure entered. It was that of Rose Carew. I motioned her to the wolfskin. I shall not tell how glad I was to see her, but I affected an easy and careless air.

"It is little that I may offer you, Miss Carew," I said, "but I do the best I can. This castle of mine lacks furniture."

It was poor gallantry, but I scarce knew what to say, and she did not reply, looking for the moment beyond me and over my head As if she had some purpose in mind. I was surprised, too, to find that she had not gone, and I said so.

"The Wyandot chief is a man of his word, and Little Turtle, who now supersedes him here, would not break any promise that Hoyoquim had made. Why have not you and the Englishman started for the South?" I asked.

"There is no breaking of faith," she replied, "and we linger at my request. Why are you held here a prisoner, Mr. Lee?"

She was looking at me with strange eyes, and I felt a sudden fear, but I answered:

"It is an old matter, Miss Carew—a quarrel between Hoyoquim and myself, but it amounts to little. I am a sort of hostage, and I shall be released in a week or two."

"And when you are released you will come back to Kentucky?" she asked.

"Oh, yes," I replied, but I knew then that she did not believe me.

"The chief, Little Turtle, let me see you," she said. "It was a favour that I asked, and he was willing to grant it, as you behold. I know, Mr. Lee, that you are in truth held as a hostage, but not as one who is to be released. I know the real reason why you are here. Do you think that I can accept such a sacrifice? Do you think that I could have any peace hereafter if I did? I am not willing to buy my life at the price of another's!"

She stood up before me straight and tall, her cheeks flushing a deep red with nervous excitement, and her eyes full of fire.

"It is too late," I said, "to make any change. What has been done has been done, and perhaps you are mistaken."

"I am not mistaken."

"Then if one should grant that you are right, which I do not, what purpose could you serve by refusing the offer? You would but destroy yourself and help nobody else. You must go. You have a father and mother waiting for you. Have they no claims upon you? I saw that mother and her face of misery, and I promised to send you back. And what am I? There is nobody of my blood to grieve for me. If I don't die here I might fall the next day in battle with some wild beast or wilder man. It is but the risk that we of the forest take."

"But I can not have you die for me," she exclaimed.

"I shall not die for anybody," I said, and I laughed with a simulation of indifference. "Even if the Indians do not release me I shall be rescued. A friend of mine, the most skilful woodsman in the world, is out there in the forest. He comes and goes when he pleases, he is an Indian himself; he will reach me here in the night, and we shall go away together."

She put her face in her hands and was silent for awhile. I too was silent, watching her. I felt a deep pity for her, torn as she was by conflicting emotions. She raised her face presently and it was pale now, but there was a strange fire in her eyes.

"The chief, Little Turtle, has spoken to me," she said, "and he has told me perhaps more than you know. Did he not make you some kind of an offer?"

"I do not recall any," I said, although I did full well.

"Perhaps he forgot it when he spoke to you," she said, "but he mentioned it to me, and it may be that there is a way for you to save your life."

Her gaze now met mine directly, and that strange fire was still in her eyes. I felt a sudden quiver in the blood and a thought shot through my head like lightning. But that inward voice said, "Who are you and what are you, John Lee, to dream of such a thing?" The hope that had flamed up so suddenly died.

"I can not think of any way but the one way," I said, "and that is for my trusty comrade to come for me."

"I did not mean that," she said. "Is there no other?"

"None."

Her cheeks became red again, but the fire did not go from her eyes. Nor did she take her gaze from me.

"Think, and think well, if there is not another way," she said.

I had admired her from the first—her beauty, her strength, her mind, and all her womanly qualities—and now I admired her more than ever. Truly, she was worth winning by any man, and it was well that I was able to send her back to her own race. Then that persistent thought came to me again. Life could be pleasant. But I crushed it once more, and said for the second time:

"No, I can not think of any other way."

Her face became white again.

"Who are you and what are you?" she asked, "and why should you do this thing for me?"

"I am but a wilderness hunter," I replied, "and there are many others like me. Death—although I do not care to die for many years—does not seem terrible to us, as it is always by our side, and we grow familiar with it. What I do is from choice, and because it is the first chance that I have had in a long time to be of real service to any one. You would not deny me the pleasure of such a feeling, would you?"

I laughed lightly, pretending to indifference, but I saw a mist appear in her eyes.

"But think," she said, "to die here in this vast wilderness at the hands of savages!"

"It is not to happen," I said; "and even if it should happen, remember it is but the fate which in any event is sure to overtake me some day."

"And you will stay? Nothing can change your mind?"

"Nothing. I shall stay until Osseo comes for me, which I do not think will be long, and then he and I shall go together into the wilderness again, and you shall return to Civilization unharmed. Winchester will take you safely. I know it. Believe in him."

"I will go," she said. Then, stooping suddenly, her face aflame, she kissed me on the forehead and rushed from the lodge.

I will not deny that I felt regrets when she was gone, but I was marked with one deep scar, and I did not wish another. My own conscience gave me approval, however great was the weakness of the flesh, and it was very weak.

It seemed that Little Turtle now had no wish to treat me ill before my time, and shortly he gave me food in abundance, in wooden or earthenware bowls, and consisting of dried buffalo meat, fresh venison, corn cakes, a sort of pudding made of roots and succulent to the taste, and wild plums. It was all very good, and I can not say that its character as a farewell feast given before sending me into the Supreme Presence interfered with my enjoyment of it, so I ate with slowness and dignity.

As I sat there I thought of Rose Carew returning to Kentucky. I was sending her back to Jasper. I had not thought of that when I made the sacrifice, but I was glad, nevertheless, that I had helped her to escape. Yet I could not keep from my mind the picture of her as Jasper's wife and Jasper and her father again planning great schemes for their advancement in the West. St. Clair had been beaten and the Northwest was not yet to be divided, but Mr. Carew's fertile mind would form fresh plans. He and Jasper and Knowlton would speedily be plotting something else, and perhaps it would not be so innocent as the acquisition of new land. The wish to know added to my wish to live.

At times they left the door of my prison open, and I could see much that passed in the village. Warriors had been coming continually, bringing some fresh trophy, or if too late to have a part in the battle and pursuit, to share in the triumphal songs and dances.

One of these parties arrived as I was looking forth, and the squaws welcomed the warriors with the chant of triumph. I was about to turn my face away, finding no joy in the spectacle of Indians coming with the scalps of my own people, when I noticed that the song was for a prisoner and not a scalp; and then, when I looked again, I saw that the prisoner was my cousin Jasper, wounded in the shoulder, his clothes torn and his face pallid.

The hurt did not seem to be serious, but his situation was, and the lack of colour in his face showed clearly that he knew it. I had much cause to dislike Jasper, but at this moment I felt only pity for him, knowing what would be the fate of a white man taken by the savages. I wondered, too, that they had spared him so long, as he must have been captured while near Fort Jefferson, and that was two days' journey away.

They hurried him by me, and he passed so near that I could have touched him with my hand. Then they carried him on to one of the wigwams, in which he was imprisoned. His ambitions, I thought, were to end like mine, and as badly. Rose Carew was to be for neither of us.

The afternoon and night passed without event and another day of my captivity came—a day that found me wondering at the delay of my fate. The door of my hut, closed at night, was opened again in the morning to admit the fresh air, which, however, was not wholly a blessing, as it brought with it stronger recollections of the freedom that was lost.

A strange and faint but musical note entered the lodge.

It was the sound of a flute, scarce higher than that of a gentle wind, but I could not mistake it. I smiled in momentary amusement. De Chamillard the "madman!" Then I silently begged the forgiveness of the gallant Frenchman. Until that moment I had completely forgotten his existence.

The voice of the flute playing a plaintive old French air grew louder, and I smiled again. Now that I had no use for him and his flute, I regarded his continued appearance in the rôle of a madman as a childish act; once was well enough, twice was folly. Then I knew that I had wronged him. De Chamillard might be eccentric, but he was not a fool; perhaps it was curiosity that brought him back to the Miami village. His music did not cease, but steadily growing louder, changed from the pathetic to the gay, and at last De Chamillard played his cheerful air directly before the door of my prison. I could see him as he stood there, facing the warrior on guard. He played the tune to the end, waved the man aside, and entered. He stared at me a moment, put the flute to his mouth again, played another short tune, and then said:

"Do you think that I am really insane, my dear Lee? I merely do this to maintain the character which chance gave to me. The warrior outside has that opinion, and he did not dare to resist my entrance here, lest his Manito should strike him down with a bolt of lightning. I came to tell you, Monsieur Lee, that Monsieur Winchester and the girl have gone southward, but your friends who are left, and particularly the red gentleman who calls himself the son of the evening star, are alert, and.are determined that your captivity shall not be of long duration."

"I am grateful to you, De Chamillard," I replied. "I have played double and quits with death before, and I do not give up hope now, especially while you and Winchester and Osseo are free to help me."

"I thank you for your confidence in me, *nom du chien*, I do," he said with much dignity, "but I am only an amateur in this wilderness life, and I think you shall owe me merely for good wishes and not much for material help."

Then he took his flute and cheerful countenance from the wigwam, and presently I heard the notes of music in the village—dying soon, however—and I imagined from the circumstances that De Chamillard was wandering into the forest once more.

Again the mat before the door of my prison was lifted, and now the amazing spectacle that greeted my eyes was my cousin Jasper walking with the renegades, Blackstaffe and the still more famous Simon Girty, much of the colour returned to his face, and his manner suggestive of liberty and relief from fear.

"The Long Knife whom we took near the fort," said Little Turtle, who visited me again, "has had a message from Manito, and it tells him to join the red men, as Girty and Blackstaffe have done, and fight against the white men who have come to take from us the country which is ours. He is adopted into the tribe of the Miamis, and presently he shall go upon the war path with us."

And so my good cousin had become a renegade to save himself from the torture! Perhaps, too, there was something in the man that would reconcile him to such a life. All the pity I had felt for him the day before went away, and in its place came contempt. It should be known that on the border we always hated the renegades more than the Indians. In a bitter spirit but in silence I wished Jasper in his change of life the luck that he deserved.

Thus the time passed.

CHAPTER 15 A "Madman's" Idea

The silence and loneliness of my prison were soon broken by the sound of De Chamillard's flute, and observing that its note was of an unusual, even excessively gay, character, I was compelled again to smile to myself. The Frenchman undoubtedly had a happy temperament, and that is not a possession to be despised. I heard his music alternating with song for nearly an hour, as if he were entertaining the savages, and then when the twilight had begun to come he appeared at my door, and, as before, pushing aside the sentinel in such manner that one would have thought the world his private property, he entered, letting the mat drop behind him until it covered all the door.

"Quick, Monsieur Lee!" he said, "bind me and take my clothes!"

As he spoke he cut my thongs.

"What do you mean?" I asked in surprise.

"After all," he replied gayly, "you do not have every clever idea. It is I who have one now and then. Do you not see? I am mad, wisely mad. It was your suggestion at first, and now I complete the plan. I am mad and the savages will not harm me, no matter what I do or what is done to me. Quickly bind me, take my flute, put on my clothes, pull your hair about your face as mine is, and go forth to freedom! *nom du chien*, do not delay! The night is coming and your features will be hidden. I shall rejoin you and the others when the savages release me."

"I will do it," I cried, struck by his idea, "but before God I swear, De Chamillard, that if the Indians hold you, I shall return and yield myself in your place! Little Turtle, the head chief, is in a way my friend, and he will see that justice is done."

"I have no fear, Monsieur Lee. But hasten! Opportunity, like a lady, is coy, and once refused, will not come again."

He had divested himself of his outer clothing already, and as we proceeded with our talk he blew an occasional note on the flute in order to maintain the illusion to the warrior at the door. The task was done in two or three minutes. De Chamillard, his arms bound behind him with the cords that he had taken from mine, lay placidly on the wolfskin, and I, flute in hand, paused a moment, unable to express to this gallant gentleman the deep gratitude that I felt. He saw my lips move, and he guessed what I would say, or at least its meaning.

"Let it wait! I understand," he said. "Can you blow a few notes on that flute?"

I nodded. I had learned a little of this art, too, from the French officers with whom I served in our Revolution, although I did not have, like De Chamillard, a real talent for the music. But I stepped boldly out of the hut, thankful now that a forest life had compelled close observation of the minutest details about me as I was able to imitate De Chamillard's walk and even his gestures. I blew a few stray notes from the flute and wandered off toward the centre of the village, the warrior on guard scarce giving me a second glance as I passed, so sure was he that I was the madman.

Our most reckless moments usually occur when we have passed half a danger triumphantly, and now one of those impulses from which I had suffered sometimes in my earlier youth seized me. I felt for the moment a sense of recklessness, and I invited attention rather than shunned it, so confident was I that my rôle as a madman would serve better than my disguise as an Indian, and carry me out of the village and into safety.

I blew a wicked tune or two upon the flute—I call them wicked because they deserve no other name—and danced a few steps in imitation of De Chamillard's French gavottes.

These maiden efforts were received with admiring glances, chiefly from the squaws and papooses, whose experience of music and the dance, as practised by the civilized nations, was not great. It was easy to see that De Chamillard in his two or three visits to the village had become a character of high privilege, and I was not willing that his reputation should suffer at my hands; therefore I put as much heart as I could into the notes of the flute and the quickstep. My curving course brought me soon into the presence of the three renegades, whom I met walking among the wigwams and conversing with deep earnestness. It was natural that these men, like ill-omened fowls, should cling together. The fall of the dusk was now so great that they could not distinguish my features even had suspicion incited them to a close look, and when I, stopping in front of them, blew a few notes on the flute, Blackstaffe said:

"That madman again. If it were not for the foolish superstition of the Indians I'd have him burned at the stake."

"Wherein you show that you are not a statesman, Blackstaffe," commented Girty reprovingly, "and also wherein you are likely to limit your power among the tribes. Now, I have no objection myself to seeing a man burned at the stake, but it is not worth while to go to so much trouble without a purpose. Besides, you ought not even to ridicule the popular beliefs of the Indians; that is a thing concerning which a people is always most sensitive. Float with the stream, Blackstaffe, or you'll be sure to strike a snag and sink."

I knew that Girty was right, and I understood why he had risen to such power among the savages, but I did not linger over his words, the reckless impulse that had taken possession of me bearing me on. I seized Blackstaffe's hand in mine and gazed at the lines in the palm with all the intentness of a sorceress.

"The white Indian," I said, in as wild a tone as I could assume, "is a man of great passions and quick temper. Manito so made him and he can not help it. Once he lived far to the East and another white man crossed him in some darling wish; but he slew that man, and when the friends of him who had fallen came to hang him he fled to the forest and the red man for refuge."

"Damnation!" cried Blackstaffe, snatching his hand away. I knew a little of the wretch's history, and the story that I told was the truth, not mere guess-work. Girty laughed with malicious enjoyment.

"Let him go on," he said. "He has made a chance hit at your past, Blackstaffe; now let us see what he will say about your future."

This emboldened me still further, and I seized Blackstaffe's hand again.

"Your future is doubtful. *Ma foi*, but it is," I said. "You have another darling wish, and more than one opposes you in it. You are a brave man—*un brav homme*! but they fight you with treachery. I see death, whether yours or theirs I can not tell. But if you fall it will be the fall of a very brave man—*un tres brav homme*."

"What is that you say?" he cried angrily. "I have enemies, treacherous enemies? Who are they?"

He looked suspiciously at Girty and Jasper.

I shook my head.

"That I know not," I replied. "The God of the white man and the Manito of the red man both hide it from me."

"At least you have an equal chance, Blackstaffe," said Girty, laughing again. "He tells you that some one is to fall, but he does not say whether it is to be you or an enemy. Therefore the question is still open."

"But the man guesses too well," said Blackstaffe, whom my truthful narration of his beginnings in the greater wickedness seemed to have impressed deeply. "Perhaps the insane can see into the future sometimes."

"Now, that doesn't look unreasonable," said Girty thoughtfully. "They say that Nature always gives compensations, and as she has made the mind of this man weaker than those of other men, perhaps she has given to him something that she denies to us. Still, it has never been proved and I doubt it.—Now, Mr. Madman, what fate do you assign to me?"

"You," I replied, "shall live to see the power of your friends destroyed and your own fate none shall know."

This was by intent an ambiguous answer, and yet it was a true prediction, a guess that chance carried to its mark. But Girty did not dream of its truth, merely seeing the doubtful nature of my reply, and he said again, laughing as if I and all my prophecies were a jest:

"You are a cautious witch doctor, my friend, and I don't blame you; in your business I should think that a madman would fare better than the sane.—Ah, Mechecunnaqua, we merely jest with the mad Frenchman who has come among us."

"It is not well to jest at those whom Manito has in his special care," said Little Turtle gravely. He had approached unnoticed while we were talking.

"I used the wrong word when I said jest," added Girty, correcting himself hastily. "The madman was telling what the future had in store for us, and we listened to him with interest."

"I know not whether the mad can tell what our lives shall be next year or the year after," said Little Turtle, "but wherever the mad may be, and in whatever guise they come, they are the beloved children of Manito, and the red man would not lay hands upon them."

I started in surprise and apprehension at his significant tone. The eyes of Mechecunnaqua could reach to the bottom of a well: had they pierced my disguise? He stood there, calm without emotion, the bronze of his face as expressionless as that metal itself. I laughed, whistled a bar or two of some backwoods tune, and then, putting the flute to my lips, lounged toward the outskirts of the village. None followed me, but I needed no inward monitor now to tell me I should hurry. Yet I could not hasten toward the forest in a straight line like an arrow from the bow lest I arouse suspicion in the minds of these ever-suspicious children of the wilderness, and I lingered to blow an occasional note on the flute or to stare vacantly about me. It was thus that I was passing the last fringe of wigwams, when a warrior who brushed past me said in my ear:

"When Lee reaches the forest let him go straight toward the point where the sun last showed itself before going behind the earth. When he has gone about ten miles he will come to a little lake. Let him wait there."

I started at the sound of the name Lee, but in a moment I was reassured, knowing the voice to be that of Osseo. I turned to speak to him, but he was gone in the darkness, disappearing as silently and completely as if he had been but a shadow himself.

I entered a melon field, and there I paused to look back at the village now almost in darkness, as the only light of an Indian town at night is the moon, if that be shining; otherwise none. My venture into the place had been a success, and I felt that I had kept my promise to the sick woman in Kentucky.

No one disturbed me; even the prowling curs passed me by without notice, and thus I entered the forest. Following Osseo's directions, I arrived at the tiny lake, just a bowl of water set in a rim of hills, and soon Osseo came to me there, bringing with, him also arms for my use.

"The English trader and the girl have gone southward on a course that I chose for them, and we may overtake them before to-morrow's sunset," he said.

"Then come on, Osseo," I said, flushed with triumph, and not willing to delay a moment.

He did not say me nay, and we started with great speed upon the indicated path.

CHAPTER 16 Autumn's Last Glory

Our way led through the wilderness, where oak and beech and hickory grew in dense clusters, the space below their boughs now filled with twining thickets, through which we forced our way, now open like the aisles of a park, where we trod a carpet of turf with naught to hold us back. Modest little flowers of pink or purple, blooming late, peeped above the grass or snuggled between the roots of the trees. We leaped the brooks of running water, and when we came to a creek too deep for wading or jumping we swam it with swift strokes, holding our rifles and ammunition in one hand above our heads. Once we disturbed a deer with mighty antlers who crashed through the thickets, and at the crossing of the creek the beaver dived from their new house in the stream into the deep waters.

It was the mighty wilderness as the first white man found it, a country of great forests and little prairies, with the fiercest foe that our race ever encountered lurking in its depths.

There is no finer region on the globe, and I knew that it was destined in the next century to be the seat of many cities and a great population, but I felt a regret that the forest and its true inmates should ever go. I think it will be a dreary world when all of it is known and measured by the land surveyors, and there is no place left where man may hunt the wild deer and perhaps be hunted by wilder man.

These were but fleeting impressions, the vague thoughts of a moment, and we never ceased our race to the south. Osseo was beside me, stride for stride, the earth giving back no sound as his moccasins touched it, the leaves and bushes silent too as he passed through them. How he did it was his secret, and sometimes I used to think that the forest contained no mystery for him. He read all its signs and understood all its tongues.

We came in the afternoon to a little glade, in the centre of which lay some charred pieces of wood. Here was where the Englishman and the girl had camped the night before, and we stopped but a moment, following swiftly upon the traces of their footsteps.

The sun was now dropping down in the west, and touching the edge of the forest with a glow of red gold. Presently we saw a thin dark line like a thread appear against the horizon, and Osseo's white, even teeth showed in a smile.

"See, the trader signals to all the wilderness that he is here," said he. "Verily, the children of the cities are as babes when they come into the woods, and the white learns wisdom but slowly from his teacher, the red man."

We reached in fifteen minutes the little glade in which Winchester had made the camp. I must give him the credit of good selection, as he had chosen a spot in the lee of a hill, sheltered, moreover, by the trunk and roots of a large and half-fallen beech tree. Here he had scraped up a heap of leaves, evidently intended for the girl's resting-place in the night, and now he was bent over the fire, cooking some venison, his honest red face glowing with the heat. The girl sat on a log near by, resting from the long journey. Yet she seemed cheerful, and her face was not so pale as it was when I beheld her in captivity.

"Listen! she is talking of Lee," whispered Osseo, putting his hand on my arm.

"You said to me that Mr. Lee would escape, that his Indian comrade would rescue him; how do you know this?" she asked.

Winchester's red face grew redder.

"No one can be sure of the future," he said, "but this I think will come true."

I knew that Winchester did not expect it to come true.

She said nothing, but looked sadly into the coals, and I felt a strange pleasure to see melancholy in her eyes.

"Come, let's join them," I said to Osseo.

We walked silently into the glade, and they did not see us until we were very near. Then both sprang to their feet, the girl with a cry of fright, the face of Osseo the Indian first meeting her eyes, and Winchester with an exclamation of surprise and confusion because he had not seen our approach sooner. Miss Carew turned her wide bright eyes upon me, and a deep flush swept over her face. I could read her thoughts as clearly as if she had told them herself. She remembered first what she had said back there in my prison lodge, but the flush gave way in a moment to a look of glad surprise. She held out both her hands, and as I took them I felt a supreme content.

She said but little, but I knew that her joy was great, not because I was John Lee, but because she could never have been happy knowing that another had suffered to save her. Then I introduced Osseo as my best and most skilful friend, and she gave him, too, both her hands while he looked his admiration.

My attention was arrested a moment later by a splutter of indignation from Winchester. Osseo was kicking apart the sticks of his fire and trampling upon the coals. Nor did he stop until the last of them ceased to smoke.

"It is necessary," I said to Winchester.

"Why so?" asked Miss Carew.

"The forest is haunted," I replied.

"I know," she said, and she shuddered. Truly she knew.

"I beg your pardon for forgetting," said Winchester to me a little later, "but I thought that we had come far enough to escape pursuit."

"So we have, I think," I replied, "but in the wilderness one can never omit caution."

Ours was a most cheerful party despite our lack of a camp fire and the knowledge that danger still hung on our skirts. We made for Miss Carew a bed of leaves and soft boughs under the sheltering foliage of the largest tree, and then we induced her to wrap herself in the blanket that Winchester carried and go to sleep there. It required but little persuasion, as she was weary, and, moreover, she was fast learning the discipline of the wilderness. In a short time we heard her regular breathing, and we knew that she slept. As for ourselves, we watched by turns, and I stood guard near the morning hour. I was restless, but my nervousness came from neither fear nor sorrow. A strange satisfaction took hold of me, and when I looked at the sleeping form of the girl I felt that I had done a good deed. None of us can afford to despise the memory of such a thing.

We rose at daylight, and, having eaten a little dried venison, resumed our flight, curving in a wide semicircle toward the northwest, as we knew better than to travel straight toward Fort Jefferson, with the chance of being caught on the way by war parties, which were certainly between us and the fort. We preferred a long road around to the short and dangerous path.

We adopted under the guidance of Osseo many cunning devices to hide the traces of our flight from a pursuing enemy, such as wading for long distances on the pebbly bottoms of brooks; stepping now and then from one fallen tree to another, which often in the great Northwestern woods are spread thickly thus for miles, and again walking where the fallen leaves lay in dense showers of russet brown. So we travelled, and we neither saw danger before us nor heard the sound of it behind us. Swiftly my fear of a recapture in which the girl might be included passed. We were three men with her, all strong and alert, and at least two of us adept in forest lore. Fortune, in truth, would be a most fickle jade if she did not serve us now.

It seemed that Fortune, instead of being fickle, had become most kind. The wilderness, its treacheries stilled, lay at peace, and over it hung the glory of Indian summer's last days. But little snow had fallen where we trod, and the forest was yet red and yellow and brown, and every colour grew deeper in the clear gold of the late sunshine. We walked on the brown carpet of leaves, and the air that blew in our faces was tonic in its freshness.

I watched Miss Carew curiously, and I saw the influence of the wilderness peace fall upon her. She was a child of the East caught suddenly in forest dangers, and yet she showed all the border courage and endurance. Rescued from the worst of fates, her spirits rebounded, and she became the gayest of forest maids. She deemed all danger past now that her eyes saw none. The colours of the woods were too intense, the world was too beautiful for foes to be lurking there, and she was the brightest of creatures, talking of many things, asking us of our own lives, and now and then humming to herself little songs, the familiar notes of which after all these years gave me a deep and painful thrill. She was a constant wonder to us; her variable moods, though never a bad one among them, her deep interest in all things around her, and her good fellowship, kept us watching to see what phase of character she would show next. Once she said to me:

"This wilderness is beautiful now, but I have known that it can become terrible." She looked around at the glowing forest, but at that moment its vivid hues did not appeal to her. Instead, I saw her shudder.

"Why should one choose to live in it?" she asked. "I can understand why white men as wild as the Indians, men who know nothing of civilized life, should come here and roam the woods far away from the things that we value most, and exposed every moment of their lives to the danger of a cruel death. But you? You are different."

She was looking straight at me, and there was the old inquiry, even curiosity in her gaze. I was startled a little, but replied:

"And how am I different, Miss Carew?"

"Your speech, your manner, are those of an educated man; they are habits that you can not discard. You have not passed all your life here. Does shooting wild animals and fighting savages gratify your whole ambition?"

A glow appeared on her face as she asked me these questions, and her look became eager. She had touched again that old chord in my nature, and I was surprised to find how it vibrated. The ancient memories came back, fresh and strong. But I would not allow them place. I closed my mind again to that part of my life, and lied to her, deliberately lied, with that earnest young face before me.

"In truth, Miss Carew," I said, "you give me credit for what I never had, and you make me more than I am. I am but a plain hunter, not without some skill in the trade, I hope, nor wholly lacking in knowledge of the white man's and red man's tricks. I know that I can never equal Osseo there in forest lore, because he was born to it, but I am willing to match myself against anybody of my race that I know."

She sighed gently, why I was not sure, and I continued:

"And you wrong the wilderness, too, Miss Carew. It has its delights, attractions that can not be found elsewhere. Think of its freedom. I may roam my own master from the Alleghanies to the Pacific, a matter of three thousand miles, and in all that space there is not a foot of land fenced and shut off by the white man from his kind, nor is there any day's march in it in which my rifle will not find me all the food I need. There are wolves on the way, it is true, but they are not wolves in sheep's clothing."

"It may be well enough for men," she said, "but not for women."

I would not dispute with her upon that point; in truth, I agreed with her fully, and she herself at that very moment was an example; yet she seemed in a few moments to forget what she had said, as if it were a mere fleeting emotion, and again she became the forest sprite.

It pleased her for awhile to consider herself a queen, us three her subjects, and the forest her kingdom, which latter was so contrary to the truth that her fancy gave me a curious pleasure. Yet we were most willing subjects, obeying all her little commands with a zest and quickness that drew high approval from her Majesty. Once she plucked a little purple wild flower in late bloom, and asked me to wear it in my cap. I had thought my time for such youthful folly long past, but I put it in the cap and wore it all that day, though Osseo said to me when none other could hear:

"Beware, Lee! A little maid may blind the eyes of a great chief."

His words sank deep in my mind. Now the joy that I found in her presence was uneasy because I knew that it must soon cease. I was troubled, too, by a sense of wrong, because I was not what I seemed to her. Yet she did not notice it, making me the mark for the shafts of her wit and fancy, and then repaying me by her constant intimation that I was the chief cause of her rescue, and the one to whom her debt was greatest.

She could not understand our caution when we refused to build a fire at night. She said she wanted to see the light of the flames shining through the great forest, and hear the crackle of the wood as the blaze ate into its fibre. It would have been a most cheerful sight, as she said, but neither Osseo nor I would have dreamed of such an act; and even Winchester, with his limited experience of the wilderness, merely shook his head now and smiled when she spoke of it. But we made excuses, saying the first thing that came into our minds, and thus we went on, the great forest dropping behind us, mile on mile.

It is an old story that the taste of forbidden fruit is pleasant, and after many years of loss the society of a woman, one's equal, who can talk of the things one values most, has an intoxicating effect. Despite Osseo's warning, I lingered near her, and surely as leader of our little party I had good excuse. I did not know until then how I longed to hear over and over of that old life of mine and those who had been a part of it, and she, though all unaware, was the link between. Once, I think it was about the third day of our flight, she said:

"Ours is a strange country. Truly, extremes meet in it. What a contrast between these great and silent woods and a town like Philadelphia, crowded with human beings!"

"You speak truly," I said. "'Tis in reality a great town back there. I wish that I could see it now."

"Then you have seen it before?" she exclaimed, "and you are not the mere hunter that you pretend to be. I knew it—I knew it from the first."

And unless I was much mistaken I saw an eager light in her eyes, a wish that I should confirm what she said. I was confused for a moment, but then I recovered my poise and shook my head. "It is as I told you before," I replied. "I know naught of the great towns. These woods are my home."

She laughed and looked at me with a provoking smile.

"Then yours must be a most peculiar mind," she said, "since you cultivate a speech and accent that men acquire only on paved streets. I predict that you shall soon he again in New York or Philadelphia, and that you will not find the ways of either strange."

Her smile became most winning. I knew that the Mother Eve in her was finding delight as thus she touched upon what she thought a mystery, and I fell into her humour.

"Your prediction can not come true," I said. "Do you know, Miss Carew, that all the prophets have been men?"

"Why?" she asked.

"Because the Superior Wisdom knows whom to trust."

"Now, I am sure that you have not lived all your life in the woods," she cried, "or you could not talk that way."

I did not answer her, contenting myself with silence, and she did not return to the subject. She perceived now that I would avoid it, and it was not in her nature to hurt or embarrass any one through mere idle talk. There was a fine delicacy in all her words, whether she chose to banter us or to pretend that she, too, was of the woods. She drew easily from Winchester his secret of the girl in England, and showed an interest not by any means assumed, that won his heart completely, and established a frank friendship between them. But it was not such a friendship of which any lover of hers back in Kentucky could be jealous. A third and invisible person, a blonde girl five thousand miles away, was the tie between them.

"Lee," he said to me one night, "she could be dangerous if she wished."

"But a good woman never wishes," I replied.

He looked at me critically, and then smiled.

"I do not know much about women, but I know better than that," he said.

The glory of the lingering autumn grew as we advanced. The wilderness seemed to have acquired a strange new splendour. Always that fine haze softening and deepening every colour hung like a misty veil in the air. The trees were brilliant masses of red and yellow and brown foliage, and when the leaves, shaken by the wind, fell to the ground, they fell softly and without complaint.

The game was plentiful and wondrous tame. Troops of deer were grazing in the glades, and scarce raised their heads unless we passed too near. The fish leaped up in the brooks and the silver bubbles marked where they sank again. Thus the peace of the wilderness infolded us, and each night the red sun sank in a blaze behind the black forest, to come up again in the same splendour the next morning, with the bars of red and gold piling above each other like terraces in the sky.

When a few days had passed, Miss Carew would fall into brief periods of depression, as if she were troubled by her thoughts or memories, but she would soon cast them off and become cheerful again. I wondered that they did not last longer, not understanding how she was able to bear herself so bravely, but I said nothing, knowing that she would not wish to hear such words.

She spoke sometimes of St. Clair's great defeat, and of all that it would cost us, but said that another American army would be sent against the tribes, and sooner or later we should surely win.

At last I told her that in a few days we should be at Fort Jefferson. She was silent, and a minute later I saw her turn white. I threw my arm around her and held her just in time. She had fainted. Osseo stopped and turned. Nothing—not even a long-drawn breath—seemed to escape his notice.

"There is a brook near, I hear its trickle," he said. "Take her there. The water will bring her back to the earth."

I lifted her in my arms. How slender and weak she felt! I wondered again how the women who helped us to conquer our Western world could ever be paid back for their sufferings. In very truth, they were forced to tread the wilderness road. Osseo led us to the brook, a silver thread winding through green moss under the shade of mighty beech trees. The cool drops on her face revived her, and for a moment she did not recall where she was. When memory came back she was ashamed, the pink flushing into her cheeks while her tone became appealing.

"I promise, Mr. Lee, that I shall not faint again," she said. "It was weak and unworthy, but—but I could not help it."

I assured her that no woman in the world could have endured more or have been braver than she had been, and Osseo came to her relief handsomely. She was fully recovered in a few moments, and then we went on.

CHAPTER 17 A House of Glass

My fool's paradise lasted long. We pressed on, finding the forest as peaceful and friendly as a gentleman's park in the Old World. Rabbits leaped up from their coverts, once or twice a deer ran across our path, but of human beings there was no sign save ourselves, and we rejoiced because in the wilderness one expects enemies—he merely hopes for friends.

The joy of escape was still upon Miss Carew, her passing weakness swiftly ceasing. Lightness of heart now remained with her; she was going back to civilization, and the dangers of the forest would no longer be hers.

I suppose that all of us have our moments of supreme weakness. I was a hardened man near to thirty; in my youth, in the gay days, when I was twenty, I had known beautiful women, and—well, I was near to loving more than one of them; but now, with such a past as mine, I should have known better. But she led me on, not that she meant to do it or knew that it was so, but it was the revulsion in her mind, the lightness of heart coming after escape from so many and such great dangers, because as we two walked together in the forest, Osseo and Winchester coming on behind, she talked of many things, and I heard her low laugh more than once; she told me again of her life in Philadelphia, where she called the names of men and women whom I too had known in those thoughtless days of my youth. Thus did I find a link between us, though saying nothing of it to her. She knew well that old life of civilization, that larger world than this of the wilderness; and a hope to see it and taste it again, a longing which I had persuaded myself was dead, thrilled me. And with it came the old bitterness, stronger than ever because she was by my side. Were it not for that ancient stain I could walk with her, so I thought, as her equal, and measure myself in this gentler competition against any man who chose to enter, and I doubted not that they would be many.

I paid little heed to the forest then. My eyes were upon the rosy face beside me, noting the delicate curve of her chin and the wonderful deep blue of her eyes. Her hair was in two long braids, after the Indian fashion, and they hung far down her back, two tawny cables that glinted in the sun, pure gold, slightly tinted with a faint reddish gleam. This may seem a strange time to speak of or even note such matters, but mine was a peculiar situation, and this girl who walked beside me, trusting herself to me with such faith, stood not for herself alone, which would have been sufficient, but also for that old dead past which now in a foolish moment I almost persuaded myself might live again.

We walked as fast as we thought we ought to tax her strength in view of the journey that yet lay before us. The days were beautiful, more like late Indian summer than early winter, and the air was crisp and fresh. The wilderness was in a frolicsome mood, and presented a smiling face. Rose Carew had forgotten its treachery.

"How long will it take us to reach Fort Jefferson?" she asked.

"We should arrive there in two days."

"And then?"

"And then?" I repeated, not knowing her meaning.

"And then," she said, "what is to be done?"

"You," I replied, "will go back to your relatives in Kentucky. I shall return to the wilderness with Osseo."

"I think it likely," she said, "that I shall go at once from Kentucky to Philadelphia; after such an experience as this my father would consider me safer there. And why not come to Philadelphia too? You say that you know only the wilderness; then it is time that you knew the cities also. It is worth the visit."

"Do you ask me to come?" I said.

"Yes," she replied, looking straight into my eyes. "I wish to see you there."

The tempter spoke loudly to me then. I knew that I loved this girl, and I was sure that she did not hate me. Perhaps I might rebuild my ruined fortunes, and my soul was full of longing.

"It may be that I shall come," I said.

She did not reply, but for a moment there was a deeper colour in her face, and a sudden thought made me tremble with happiness. I have said that she did not hate me; that I knew, and I began to believe that, disgraced man as I was, I might hope for more.

We stopped one day by the side of a brook, and saw only peace around us. The forest was still friendly and protecting. But a little anxiety began to creep into my mind. Miss Carew noticed the cloud on my face, and quickly asked me its cause; I sought to dismiss it as nothing.

"You will come to Philadelphia; remember that you have promised," she said, misinterpreting the subject that I had upon my mind.

We resumed our flight as soon as we had taken a little rest, travelling nearly all of a beautiful starlit night, no enemy disturbing us, and nothing occurring to indicate that a hostile hand was near. When it was within an hour or two of daylight we told Miss Carew to rest. Osseo spread his blanket upon the ground for her, and Winchester had another with which he proposed to cover her while she slept. But she would not accept our suggestion. "No," she said, "I can go on, and I will not have you risk yourselves further by delaying here on my account."

But I knew that she should stop, and I told her to do as we said. Her lip quivered a little, and she looked at me reproachfully, but she yielded with surprising meekness. Exhaustion has a way of playing us queer tricks, and five minutes after the blanket was spread over her she was asleep, only a pale wisp of her face showing above the covering.

Osseo left us for awhile, and presently returned with fruit of the wild paw-paw; but as Miss Carew was still sleeping, and we did not wish to wake her, we waited. All of us needed rest, and while the girl slept the men reclined against tree trunks, gathering fresh strength and watching the forest. None of us spoke, because of the sleeper.

We were so much nearer safety, and by as much did my spirits fall. I was no longer alone with her; I was not bewitched by the sound of her voice, and my fool's dream was over. I was what I was before I met her—John Lee, the condemned traitor—and while I might dream such a fool's dream once, it could not be done twice. It would be as well for her to be tied to a stone and dropped in a river as tied to me—the difference would not be great. And I was a fool, too, for thinking that she could ever consent to such an alliance when she learned what I was, as she speedily would do.

She woke with a pretty start of surprise to see the sun so high in the sky, and began to make excuses, pleasant for us to hear, but most unnecessary.

"Miss Carew," said Winchester, with a smile, "you sleep well for one who does not want to sleep at all."

She retorted in like fashion, and while Osseo produced his paw-paws and some dried venison from his pouch she shot the shafts of her wit and fancy at both Winchester and me. Her gay spirits evidently were on the increase, and she rallied me on my glum face.

"What has occurred since I slept that you have grown so sombre, Mr. Lee?" she asked. "One would think that you are about to become a missionary among the Indians instead of a scout and hunter who fights them. But, in truth, has anything wrong happened to you?"

She looked at me with such clear eyes of sympathy that my spirits fell to greater depths than ever, but I responded that my countenance was a deception, a law unto itself, and that often I was most joyous when it seemed most gloomy.

After our brief breakfast we resumed the flight toward Fort Jefferson, which we reached on the following day without interruption, and behind the walls of which we at last placed Miss Carew in safety.

We found the fort filled with soldiers, other troops having come and officers of high rank present, among the latter Captain Hardy, who had shown me sympathy before St. Clair's defeat. Nor was he less friendly now.

"Tis a great deed that you have done, Mr. Lee," he said, "this saving of Miss Carew."

"Others have done as much as I," I replied. "Besides Osseo there were Winchester, the Englishman, and a wild Frenchman named De Chamillard, whose fate I do not know."

"You were the leader," he said, "and by this deed you have made new and powerful friends."

"It may be so," I replied, "but I shall not use them. I return to the forest when this task is concluded."

He put his hand upon my shoulder and his manner was most friendly. It was like the touch of a brother.

"I think that you do wrong, Lee," he said. "Finish this campaign with us and go back to the East. There are few things so bad that they can not be cured. No one can overlook your work here on the border; friends may do much; you may return to your original position, and you may marry."

I saw plainly by his eyes what he meant, but I shook my head.

"Do not tempt me, Hardy," I said. "I have already been tempted enough, God knows!"

And then in a weak and unmanly moment I put my face in my hands and groaned. He said no more, but he sounded my praises in the fort, as many things proved to me, among them the deference shown me by the soldiers and young lieutenants as I passed.

About midnight after our arrival the sentinels were aroused by a strange, clear note from the forest. I too heard it, and I went to the palisades, where I found that Osseo had preceded me. Captain Hardy was on watch, and turning to me he asked:

"What is that odd sound, Mr. Lee?"

It rose upon the still air, clear and melodious, and I knew it at once.

"What is it?" repeated Captain Hardy.

"That," I replied, "is the mad Frenchman of whom I told you. Won't you kindly warn your sentinels not to shoot at him?"

"He is not so mad as he seems," replied the captain, "since he is wise enough to play his flute when he approaches the fort at night and save himself from a bullet."

I made no mistake when I said it was De Chamillard, as he emerged presently from the woods, playing another flute, and approached the palisade. When Captain Hardy admitted him he saw me, and cried out with joy.

"*Ma foi*, but you are a welcome vision, Mr. Lee!" he said. "Did you bring the beautiful lady with you?"

I replied in the affirmative.

"Thanks to your help, M. De Chamillard," I said. "You have risked your life nobly in her service."

"'Tis a small matter to risk one's life for such a lady," he said. "The debt is mine."

Then he informed me that the Indians found him bound in my place a few hours after my flight. There was a great uproar, but no one thought of blaming the man who was in Manito's special keeping. He was released, and again he wandered as he chose, and his choice took him in a few days to Fort Jefferson, his desire to know of us urging him on. He was truly rejoiced over our escape, the sincerity of his manner permitting no doubt of it, and avowed his intent to pay his humble respects to the beautiful lady, as he insisted upon calling her, at the first opportunity, a purpose which I could not criticise.

I was near the palisade early the next morning, and Rose Carew came to me there. I saw at once by her face that she knew. Some one—and there are always such—had taken the trouble already to tell her. Here, in her presence, stubbornness and that sense of defiance came to my aid, as they had come when I faced others.

"They have told you of me; you know now what I am," I said.

"I did not hear until a few minutes ago the charge against you," she replied.

I looked at her, and I saw in her eyes the glow of confidence in me. I knew then that I was to her the man who had rescued her from the savages and who had guided her safely through the woods. To a pure mind like hers it did not seem possible that such a man could have done a great wrong. My heart sank, but it was no time for evasion or subterfuge.

"You have heard of the charge soon enough," I said.

"But I do not believe it."

She was refreshed by her sleep, and the colour had come back to her cheeks. Her clothing, torn by the bushes and briers, had been repaired by the loans of other women in the fort.

I met her questioning look with firmness, but I knew that I cared greatly for this girl's opinion.

"I am waiting for you to deny this odious charge, Mr. Lee," she said.

"I have not said that I was innocent."

The old warlike passion rose stronger than ever in me—not against her, but against the situation in which I found myself. Let her believe it if she wished to do so! Strengthened by this feeling, I beheld without flinching the incredulous look in her eyes change to surprise, then to brief aversion, then to momentary bewilderment, and back to disbelief—all these variations as swift as the shifting colours of water under sunlight. 'Tis pleasant to feel that you have one's faith, but 'tis bitter to shock that faith. So I said, with some hesitation:

"Miss Carew, I was tried and convicted of the crime with which you have heard me charged."

"Then you were guilty?"

I was silent, and the momentary look of aversion returned to her face.

"Why don't you deny it?" she cried. "I would not have believed it had everybody in the world save yourself told me that it was true—and after all that you have done! And throughout our flight you had the look and manner of a true man! And you were concealing the truth even then! Why did you bear yourself so? Why did you seem to be the most honest and unselfish of men? Was it merely a part that you played to deceive others?"

I had offered myself a sacrifice in her place, and for the moment, under the influence of other emotions, she seemed to forget it. But she was white; she could not have the simple creed of that gentleman in red, Osseo, who took me for what I was, not for what I may have been years before. After all, might not there be something in his contention that his was the superior race, simpler perhaps, but also more majestic? So I met her eyes again—so firmly that hers, not mine, fell. Then she suddenly extended to me her hand, which I did not take, because I felt anger in my soul.

"Mr. Lee," she said, "will you not take my hand?"

"Why?"

"Because I wish to beg your pardon. What right have I to inquire into your past? I can not believe you guilty. I do not think that the man who risked his life again and again to save a stranger could have committed so base a crime."

"And if I had committed it you would despise me. You would let the past outweigh the present. You have just credited me with a good deed: then a bad one done long ago is to have more effect after so many years than a good one done now?"

"I am not different from other people," she said, half in bewilderment, half in appeal.

I had Osseo in mind, and I did not answer her.

"Mr. Lee," she said, "let us be friends. If you did this I know that you have since undone it a hundredfold. I spoke foolishly just now, but it was under impulse. It is not for me to be the judge of any man, and I can only say in apology that I cared for your honour. I did not wish to hear any one speak against you. 'Tis but human, I think, to wish well to those who have done us a great service."

I took her hand then, but I saw that her manner was not quite the same. She was now making an effort to like me. Yet I was re-enforced by pride, which can bear great burdens.

She went away without saying more, but presently she came back to me, and her manner was winning. "Your breakfast is ready, Mr. Lee," she said.

A bright spot of colour appeared in either cheek, and then faded. Her manner was embarrassed, and I surveyed her for a moment trying to discern her meaning. She flushed again, but, as before, the colour was fleeting.

"I know it is waiting," I said, "and a place is left for me over there."

I pointed to a group of scouts and hunters who were enjoying the morning venison and coffee.

"I have prepared your breakfast myself, Mr. Lee," she said, "and I hope that you will not refuse it. I wanted to give you something better than the common camp fire."

So I went with her and found that she had made ready with her own hands the best food that could be obtained, and, moreover, she insisted upon serving it herself. I was grateful, but there yet seemed to be something lacking in her manner. She was singularly silent as she attended to the duties of this office, and suddenly it occurred to me that she was doing penance. She did not like me now; she could not forget what she had heard, but she was seeking to show the gratitude that she believed she ought to feel. So a resolution was formed in my mind—that is, it formed itself; I always felt that my will had but little to do with it. It was, I suppose, another ebullition of warlike temper.

I began to find fault with the breakfast; I remarked that the venison was not well cooked, at least not so in the opinion of a hunter of experience; the coffee had a suspicious muddiness and weakness; In fact, I was so captious and fault-finding that perhaps I should now be ashamed of myself. She flushed and pouted after her quick fashion at my first complaints, and then flaming red spots remained in either cheek. But she endured it awhile in silence.

Then I shifted my comments to the hollowness of human protestations. I asked if one really had friends; was there ever a time when they did not cast one away at the slightest excuse? She said nothing, and I returned to my criticisms upon her breakfast, although it was really of the best.

"Mr. Lee," she said at last, "I told you in the forest that you could not have always been a hunter and wanderer through this Western wilderness, as you seemed to have in your speech and manner a reminder of the cultivated East."

"Well?"

"I am convinced now that I was mistaken."

"But you have just been told that I was a Revolutiomary soldier."

"It was some other Lee."

She would say nothing more after this, but I did not change my manner, still feeling belligerent, and resolved not to wish sympathy and friendship unless they were spontaneous. Her own attitude became somewhat hostile, but she forced herself to finish what she had undertaken.

"Miss Carew," I said carelessly, when the breakfast was over, "I thank you, and I tell you now that in a day or two we start south. I shall not leave you until I give you back to your parents."

But she did not show aversion to me again. She seemed rather now to seek my presence, and I did not avoid it. Whether it was the feeling of penance that still urged her I did not know, and I began to feel ease while with her.

De Chamillard heard of my conviction, but, like Winchester, he scorned it.

"If I do not know whether a friend of mine is innocent or guilty," he said, "it is certainly my part to believe him innocent, or I am no friend. It is pleasanter to me, Monsieur Lee, to consider you innocent, and I swear I will not listen to anything else!"

CHAPTER 18 The Terror

It was my plan to return at once to the forest with Osseo, thinking my use past, but on second thought I lingered yet a few days at the fort. Such confusion and discord reigned in our councils, and there were so many rumours of an Indian advance in numbers far greater than at St. Clair's defeat, that deep alarm reigned. Officers and men began to fear for our safety even behind log walls; and although I knew that the army of the savages had scattered for the present, it was a vain effort to tell them so. I was not believed. Moreover, the remnants of our force were indulging in fierce recriminations; the militia called the regulars fools, the regulars called the militia cowards, and the hunters agreed that both were right. Not having fought well against the enemy, we now fought well among ourselves.

It was at this juncture that Captain Hardy delivered to me a message.

"The militia are going home," he said, "and they go whether General St. Clair wills it or not. They say that they have had enough, and I can not find it in my heart to blame them. All the women who survive will accompany them, including Miss Carew, and I ask you and your Indian comrades to go with them too. They need such men, for the danger from the savages will not be past until they cross the Ohio, and perhaps not then. Miss Carew wants you, as she has more confidence in you than in anybody else, and I make it a personal matter also."

I could not refuse such, a request. Moreover, having gone so far, I was not willing to leave Miss Carew while she was yet in danger. I had given my promise to bring her back safely to Kentucky, and the task was unfinished.

So we started the next day, our party consisting of the militia, the women, and some of the scouts and hunters, including old Joe Grimes and Winchester. Few affectionate regrets were exchanged by the regulars and militia as they parted. The hunters and scouts said little, but that little burned.

"I hate a fool more than a coward, and a coward more than a fool," said Joe Grimes to me. "These soldiers are mighty small potatoes, and mighty few in a hill. Look how they've been beat. I tell you a short horse is soon curried."

"But it was a surprise, Joe," I said. "Both regulars and militia did well under the circumstances. The blame was with the leaders. Think how Braddock's army was cut to pieces in the same way by the savages at Fort Duquesne! The Hessians scarce made any resistance when we dropped on them that cold morning at Princeton, and they are fine soldiers, too."

"What's the use of good fighting when your general leads you straight into a hornets' nest?" he repeated stubbornly. "The hornets sting you, but you can't catch 'em. Now, I never put my hand out farther than I can draw it back. To the Old Nick, I say, with all soldiers! They're sticks of wood with coloured clothes on. Kentucky had better cut loose and paddle her own canoe. If she don't, she'll sink where she stands. The Spaniard or the Frenchman would be a better friend than the Gov'ment back there in the East. You're barking up the wrong tree when you praise it to me."

Old Joe but spoke a feeling too prevalent in Kentucky, based upon the impotence of the Federal Government to protect its people from the savages and its weak dealings with them, a belief that had come to an alarming pass a little before in the Spanish intrigue; but I refused to listen to him, though seeing well that the great rout of St. Clair would stir it anew. Again I thought of Mr. Carew. He was just the man to take advantage of such a moment and turn it somehow to his own profit. One great plan of his had failed. He would be ready with another.

We travelled fast; in truth, we fled to the southward through the wintry forest and across the frozen streams. It was a lone and desolate wilderness now, without sign of human being save ourselves. Nowhere did the scouts behold the Indian token, and I was sure that our path lay clear before us.

"The tribes rest," said Osseo. "Their hunger for scalps is great, but now their stomachs have been filled. We flee in peace."

But our troubles nevertheless were great. Winter came upon us in full swing. On the second day of the march the sky turned a dirty gray, and the clouds trooped by in unbroken battalions. The wind blew out of the northwest, raw and chill. Daring the risk of the savages, we built, lest we freeze to death, a great fire in the forest, throwing upon it heaps of the fallen timber with which the wilderness was littered until the blaze rose higher than our heads and the popping of the dry wood was like volleys of pistol shots. I have learned that nothing can confer gaiety like a red and blazing fire on a cold night, and despite the horrors of the past, we began to grow cheerful. The women spread their hands before the flames, and I watched Rose Carew as she stood there, luminous in the glow, the red coming back to her cheeks, and all the spring and elasticity of youth and strength returning to her figure. I had, after all, much to be grateful for. I had saved her, and I was taking her back to her parents in Kentucky. Then I turned away with a sigh, not knowing why I was unhappy when I should be happy.

The clouds opened toward morning, and snow fell to the depth of several inches. When the women awoke and came from their blankets they saw a white wilderness. Earth and forest alike were covered, and the risen sun shining in all its glory was reflected back in rays of yellow and silver. The trees stood up, great cones of white, and the breaking of the branches under the weight of snow as we moved on through the wilderness made a steady crackle around us, like the fire of skirmishers. The skies were blue and clear once more, and the air was crisp and cold. It was a world in all its white beauty and splendour, and we pressed on with as much speed as Nature would allow, often in silence, save for the tread of our footsteps, the cracking of the branches, and the sighing fall of snow into snow. The brooks were frozen in their beds, and we passed them, scarce knowing they were there. By night our camp fire blazed through the forest, telling to all who would look where we lay, but no enemy came to our beacon light. The wilderness that curved around was yet lone and bare, and when we rested before the blazing logs we slept in peace, save those who watched.

The gaiety of our company increased, and the rebound of spirits was greatest in the women. I wish to give them full credit for all the courage that they had and showed. But there were some of us still gloomy. We were looking ahead, and saw the storm that would be let loose on the border by our great defeat. The savages would hang upon Kentucky like a cloud of hornets, and I beheld already the empty cabins and heard the mourning for the slaughtered. Moreover, I knew well what was passing in the mind of old Joe Grimes, and also in the minds of many other Kentuckians.

"What's the good of a gov'ment that can't protect yon?" he said on the fifth day of our march. "All these men from the East are tarred with the same stick, and when it comes to helping the West they stand back like a bound boy at a husking."

"Give the Government another chance, Joe," I said.

"It's had too many already," he replied passionately, "an' you, John Lee, have the least cause of all men to defend it. When I've got a gun that's no good I throw it away an' get a better one; I don't stand blinking like a toad in a thunderstorm; an' that's what men ought to do with a gov'ment. I tell you we've brought our pigs to a poor market."

"But you don't believe in any sort of government, Joe."

"No, I don't," he replied with increasing stubbornness. "Abolish 'em all, I say, and let every fellow fend for himself: Then you won't waste your breath singing tunes that nobody will listen to."

In which opinion Joe Grimes was not alone among frontiersmen.

Winchester chanced to come near him at this moment, and old Joe turned upon him furiously.

"It's you English that's doin' it!" he cried. "You keep the Northwestern posts, breakin' the treaty, an' you arm the savages an' turn 'em loose upon us. You are as black as they are!"

"I don't know the full facts about this question," replied Winchester with dignity; and then, with a slight humorous smile, "the English Cabinet did not consult me about it, and so I decline to be responsible."

"You know, Joe," I said, "that Mr. Winchester is our friend, and there are some among us who owe him much."

"That's so," he said with a revulsion of feeling.—"Shake hands, Mr. Winchester; I eat my words if they don't strike you right."

But I saw him a little later in deep conversation with some of the Kentucky militiamen, and I judged by their actions that they would not care to have their talk overheard by those in whom they did not have the utmost confidence.

Some rumour of the discontent reached the ears of Rose Carew, because she came to me that evening as I eat by the camp fire and asked:

"Mr. Lee, what do you think will be said in Kentucky when the tale of this slaughter shall have spread throughout the settlements?"

"Many things that will not be pleasing in the ears of the President and his Cabinet."

"I do not doubt it, but they are making a great mistake."

She sat on a log near me, and remained silent for a long time. Many thoughts were in her mind, and I believed myself able to read them. Her face was luminous in the fire, and it expressed her emotions as they passed. Her heart wept over the scourged and scarred border, and she feared, too, the black brows of the men who marched with us.

"Don't blame them too much," I said. "They have suffered and expect to suffer more. It's a fit of passion that will not last."

She looked up in surprise.

"You have guessed what I was thinking," she said. "But I did not believe you would be so quick to say the feeling would pass. You have no cause to love this confederation."

"Is love always logical?" I asked.

She did not answer me just then, but leaned her face upon her hands, where it was full in the red glow, and presently I saw a fire in her eyes which was not that shining from the red coals.

"No, it is not logical," she said at length, "not even the love of country; but is it any the worse because of that? I love my country with a love that I do not wish to measure, and for which I do not try to account. Sometimes I think that women are better patriots than men, because we do not seek to reason about it. The fact is enough. If I were a man nothing could shake this love in me; even if I had done my country a great wrong or had been falsely convicted of such wrong, I would turn a cold ear to the disappointment and discontent of my countrymen. If guilty myself once, I would prove that I could never be so again; or, if suffering from the greatest injustice, I would show that the fact could not incite me to wrong."

"Miss Carew," I said, "the advice that you give me is good, and is meant well, nor do I wish to be impolite, but I did not need it."

Her cheeks flamed into deeper red.

"I should ask your pardon, Mr. Lee," she said. "What right have I, for whom you have done so much and who has done so little for you, to offer you advice? Yet I will not ask it, because I think that my motive was right."

Then she rose and walked toward the women's quarters.

We were now approaching the Ohio, and all that we had foreseen came to pass. There was a thin fringe of settlements along the northern shore of the river, scattered cabins, lone families seeking a new home in the wilderness under the very edge of the scalping knife, as others had done a few years before in Kentucky. Full of hope, they had seen the army of St. Clair go northward, and they waited to hear that the Indian power was destroyed. Now they saw a wretched remnant of that army returning, and terror spread to the farthest cabin. There was no longer any protection for them. Women and children alike would be given to the tomahawk. On any night they might find the savages at the door, and that would be the end—and, in truth, their fears were realized too often. Torch and the tomahawk soon raged along the border, and the smoke of the burning cabins told what St. Clair had cost us. The tale ran to the uttermost limit. There was naught that a man could rely on now save his own arm and eye. The Government could do nothing, or rather it made the bad worse; and now, after its great defeat, it was about to desert us. It was not a wonder that terror reigned; that the women in the lone cabins saw the edge of the tomahawk in every flash of sunlight, and heard the tread of the savage in every fall of snow from the overweighted bough.

Some of the families joined us as we marched southward, but most remained ready with a silent stubbornness to face whatever fate might come. It was the character of our borderers. When the wave of people had once rolled forward it never rolled back. The tomahawk, the scalping knife, the burning cabins, and the torture were alike unheeded. Now they had come to hold the land, and here they would stay.

"Why don't they flee, Mr. Lee? Why don't they cross the Ohio into Kentucky, where the white power grows strong?" asked Miss Carew of me as we passed a cabin whose inmates, though knowing the danger and appreciating our warning, refused to go.

"For the same reason that those who came to Kentucky would not turn back," I answered, "and what that is I know not. Perhaps it is the love of a new land that grips our race so and makes it scorn death and torture. Look at Kentucky! It is watered with the blood of the white man, but a new commonwealth is rising there as surely as we live, and it was won in the way that these people will win the Northwest."

I have heard that it takes an old country with many historic associations to inspire the love of its people, but the saying, I know, is not true. Already the men in Kentucky, not one of whom was born upon its soil, loved it with a passion not surpassed by the devotion of any Frenchman or Englishman to his native land.

As we advanced the terror grew. We found in many cases that the tale of the slaughter had preceded us, and it did not suffer in quantity or quality as it passed from cabin to cabin in the great woods. The fugitives, though still the exception, gradually gathered in our train, and they were a pitiful sight to see, mostly women and little children fleeing from the mercy of the red man, which in all but rare instances is no mercy at all.

It was now that I saw Rose Carew in her noblest character. She had passed through enough to break the spirit of most women, but in the presence of those poor fugitives she was all strength and elasticity. She tended them and she encouraged them. She said that another army would come and better generals would lead it; the savages would be crushed and the border made safe; the President himself would see to it, and there was no occasion for despair. She would not listen to any of the talk against the President and the Government; and once, when she heard old Joe Grimes upon his favourite topic, she denounced him so fiercely that he shrank back in affright, and then with a true backwoodsman's gallantry would not say a word to her in his own defence.

Her bearing toward me changed. She treated me now as a comrade—as one with whom she had shared dangers and with whom she had triumphed over them, but to my great relief she said nothing of gratitude. She seemed to know that I did not wish it, but often she would call upon me to help her in her errands about the camp as if we were brothers in arms, and I acquired an ease in her presence which I had not known before.

Thus our march continued in the white world of winter, through snow-covered forests, over frozen streams, and across little prairies, until we reached the Ohio, which was running deep in its wide channel, and covered with floating ice, a formidable barrier to all but the most skilful. But the scouts brought a half-dozen canoes from coverts in the brush and rushes, and after many trips the last of us were taken over in safety. Osseo stopped here to await my return from the homes of the white men.

Now we entered Kentucky, and the terror spread there too. The savages would come again, and all the old tale of atrocity and suffering lasting so many years would be repeated. There was hardly a home in this new land which had not lost some member under the tomahawk, and they expected to see its flash again. The cry of alarm was heard in every home, and mingled with it was another and angrier cry—a cry of rage against the Government beyond the mountains because it had allowed such a scourge to be let loose upon them. It swelled into thunder, but I listened little to it then, hastening on with Miss Carew to Danville, where I expected to find her parents. I heard that Mr. Carew had organized an expedition of his own to secure her rescue, but I surmised that he was now on his way back to Danville, or was there, having heard of her safety. And I was sure, too, that his crafty ally, would be with him.

CHAPTER 19 A Whisper of Intrigue

Winchester left us to go to Lexington, where one of his agents lived, and a day later we were in Danville. I was among friends again. They inquired little in Kentucky about a man's past. All were too new themselves for that, and the force of circumstances had made the best fighter the best citizen. I was valued, and once again I saw that I was among friends who thought of to-day and not yesterday.

We found that Mr. Carew had gone to meet us, but following another road by mistake, had passed us by. The mother, that invalid with the noble and gentle face, took Miss Carew in her arms, and I turned away from a scene which affected me powerfully. There was no reward now for which I would have traded the memory of the sacrifice in the wilderness, and of all the words that Mrs. Carew said to me, those that pleased me most were these: "I knew that you would bring her back to me, Mr. Lee; when you gave your promise I never doubted."

Mr. Carew came on the afternoon of the same day, full of gratitude, pouring out his thanks to me, calling me his daughter's saviour, and a hero of whom the West should be proud. It seemed to me that on the whole he was effusive, and by the rush of quantity wished to end the supply as soon as possible. I was aware that he must know now who I was, and wishing to relieve him, I withdrew into the free air. He urged me with but faint heart to stay and share the hospitality of his home, but his daughter said nothing.

While the atmosphere into which I stepped when I left the house of Mr. Carew was free, it was also surcharged, and I was soon to discover it. Kentucky had received already the permisison of the Union to become a State, and its political capital was this town of Danville, a sprightly village with some fine houses built of bricks brought in wagons across the Alleghanies, and inhabitants who had received the best culture that the East could afford side by side with the wilderness rovers. It was a strange mingling, and yet the diverse elements were fusing already.

The surcharging of the atmosphere was of the same tone and texture that I had noticed in crossing the Ohio, but there was a great increase here. They were not mutterings, they were open and violent curses that I heard: "Have we been deserted by the Union?" "Does the Government merely send us imbeciles to lead us to slaughter?"

Now I saw the beginnings of the Kentucky character as it is developing to-day, that openness and frankness of dealing, the tendency to give all or nothing, those fiery bursts of passion when enraged—the whole making a nature generous but uncalculating. I am of the opinion that this character was formed by the long years of Indian fighting on the soil of Kentucky, which certainly merited its name of the Dark and Bloody Ground,

Much to my surprise, I saw in Danville old Joe Grimes, an inveterate woodsman, a man who was seldom willing to come where the smoke of a half-dozen chimneys troubled his view.

"Why, Joe," I exclaimed, "what do you in a town?"

"May I not come here if I want to, as well as you?" he replied defiantly.

"I know it," I said, "but I tell you, Joe Grimes, that you did not come without a good reason."

He looked at me suddenly, and I saw that it was not now his intent to evade my question any longer.

"I'm troubled, John," he said. "I think there's too much gov'ment in this country. I thought maybe I might help cure it. I want to go the whole hog or none. I'm going to make a spoon or spoil a horn, and I think, too, that you might help us, John Lee, considerin' that you haven't much to be thankful to the Gov'ment for."

"Joe Grimes," I said, giving him back his steady look, "I think it is impossible for you to be a villain, but I am not sure that you can't be a fool."

His face was tanned to the colour of leather. Nevertheless the red came flushing through.

"I won't quarrel with you, John Lee," he said, "because I've fought beside you too often."

"I know it, and for that reason I dare to speak to you as I have done."

"You can't fight battles with popguns, and you can't win wars with armies that don't know how to fight. Besides, I don't believe in govment nohow," he repeated, as he left me and entered the little inn which received visitors in Danville—not an inn really, but a private house, whose owner consented to take travellers for money. It was one of the few places in Kentucky where a man paid for his food and lodging.

It was a varied company gathered there, and it surprised me by its size. The cause must be powerful, I thought, that drew so many into so small a place. There were hunters in buckskin hunting shirts and leggings and 'coonskin caps; two or three lawyers in black garb, among them the thin-faced Knowlton; and two men in fine small-clothes and powdered wigs. One of the latter was the heavy man Curry, his face now sullen and resolute.

A great fire was burning in the fireplace, which extended almost across the end of the room, and the apartment looked most cheerful, for it was bitter cold outside, and those who entered came with red ears and noses. Joe Grimes sat in the chimney-seat calmly smoking a pipe. Occasionally he tapped with a meditative forefinger the pods of red pepper that hung beside him.

Knowlton had been talking, but he ceased when I entered.

"Speak on, Master Knowlton," said Grimes. "It's John Lee; I guess you know him; a true man, if there's one in the West; a man who has less cause even than we have to love the Gov'ment."

The lawyer gave me a knowing leer—I hated him for it—and resumed the thread of his discourse. I took my seat without comment.

"The weakness of the Government has been exposed," said Knowlton, his sharp eyes watching every one of his auditors, "and with the greatest force by this horrible defeat of St. Clair. Would any Kentuckian, would any man of sense, have led an army into such a snare? Didn't the Kentuckians say that St. Clair was an imbecile, and doesn't all the world know now that they were right?"

He paused for his words to sink deep, and all gave approving signs, none with more emphasis than Curry and his companion, who was a younger man and weak of brow and chin.

"What can the Government do for us?" resumed Knowlton. "Nothing. What have we to do with the East anyway? We are cut off from it by great mountains. Our outlet is down the current of the Mississippi, and there the French and Spanish lie. It is with them that our great dealings in the future must be."

"Do you mean to say that we should cut the tie connecting us with the East, and treat with the Frenchman and the Spaniard? That was tried a year or two ago, and the people would not have it," said the young man with the weak face.

"Softly, softly, Master Harvey," replied Knowlton in gentle tones. "Don't put in my mouth words that have not come from it. I have not advised, I have not even suggested, that we treat with the Spaniards and the French. I but stated the facts in regard to the weakness of the Government and its small value to us. Perhaps if those who were concerned in the Spanish intrigue had waited until the present they would find the times riper."

"That is not a surmise; it is the truth," said Curry, with an emphatic snap of his strong jaws.

"Undoubtedly, Master Curry," said Knowlton in his smooth tones, and then putting his pipe in his mouth he began to smoke. I saw well that his words went far, and I knew to what end they tended. I judged that Curry was his strongest ally, and I still deemed it fit to keep silence. I saw through the open window the expanse of hill and meadow, beautiful even in its winter garb, and I thought it too fine a land and won too hardly to be lost. And I thought, too, as I looked at Knowlton and Curry, that when I sat in the lodge of Little Turtle, deadly foe to us though he was, I was in the presence of a nobler man than they.

Knowlton renewed the conversation presently, and kept it upon the same note. By artful device and insinuation, he dwelt upon the sufferings of Kentucky, her great services in winning the Northwest from the British, and the small reward that she had received; her desertion by the Government, he called it. Should this new State beyond the mountains tie herself to a lifeless Union, which would hang but a dead weight upon her?

This was plain talk, although no purpose was mentioned, but it was a land where a man might say what he chose, being held to account for his deeds, not his words, and I yet kept my peace, being willing to listen since they were willing for me to hear. The door opened presently, and a new figure entered.

It was Mr. Carew who joined the group around the fire, and the familiar manner in which they received him persuaded me that he was not a stranger to such conversation as had been going on. It was most disagreeable news to me, though not wholly a surprise, that such projects, vague though they might be, should flit through the head of Rose Carew's father. Yet I had read his character in his face, ambitious and of the world, to the last degree.

A seat of honour near the fire was given to him and a glass of one of those noble mixed brews, for which this State is achieving fame, was brought. When he drank he looked inquiringly at me, but I said nothing and gave him back no answering glance. Nevertheless, he seemed satisfied.

"What news do you discuss, Master Knowlton?" he asked.

"There is but one topic now present in every man's mind," returned Knowlton, in the rhetorical strain that he had adopted; "it is the future of this fair land which we have so recently won with our blood"—I was willing to wager that no drop of his had ever been shed for such a purpose—"and we dread what the future will bring."

"We have good cause for such dread," rejoined Mr. Carew.

Here Curry broke in with abrupt utterances. He was a downright fellow given to impulsive speech, as any one could see, and he said that the men who had treated with Spain were not far wrong. Kentucky, in truth, had nothing to gain from the confederation of States; there she would be a subordinate member, serving merely as a bulwark against the Western tribes, giving all and receiving nothing; her place was in a Western empire, of which she should be the head and her first citizens the leaders.

The others were silent, willing that this headstrong man should do all such direct talking, but I saw the eyes of Knowlton and Mr. Carew light up, and I knew that both were dreaming of a great place in this Western empire. Old Joe Grimes was uneasy. Speech so plain had an unpleasant sound in his ears. It was the precious and inalienable privilege of our borderers to speak bitterly of our Government and our people, but they liked it little when the same words were used by others. Now I understood the feelings of Joe Grimes much better than he did himself: slow anger against Knowlton was rising in his mind.

I left the room presently, Mr. Carew following me. When we were outside he approached me in most friendly fashion, and hooked his arm in mine. Despite the fact that he was Rose Carew's father I felt aversion, but I did not withdraw my arm.

"You heard what that hot-head Curry was saying, did you not, Mr. Lee?" he asked.

"Ay, I heard it," I replied, "and I paid heed to it."

"It was rash talk; and yet, when one considers, it might seem much less foolish to think such a thing than to say it."

"It would be treason," I said.

"I do not know," he continued; "Kentucky has done much for the Union, but the Union has done nothing for her. I should think, Mr. Lee, that Curry's idea would appeal especially to you. A great wrong has been inflicted on you by our Government."

"How do you know that?" I asked.

"It must be so," he replied after some hesitation. "And it would be a fine opportunity for you too. You are loved on the border for the deeds that you have done. Your words are of weight and influence with the people. In this new land, if it were cut off from the old, you could rise to high position should you wish it."

"I do not wish it," I said.

"That's strange," he replied. "Most young men have ambition, and few would refuse a prize that is ready to be placed in their hands."

"It is treason."

"Treason is a harsh word, but it is sometimes used carelessly. If a portion of a country is abandoned by the remainder, it is scarce treason in that portion to take care of itself as best it can."

"I will not share any plan to sever Kentucky from the Union or to plot with the French or Spanish," I said, resolved that such talk had gone far enough.

He dropped my arm and faced me with a look of amazement. Then he laughed lightly. I discovered now that he was an adept at intrigue.

"My dear Lee," he cried, "I think he is a bold man who should propose such a plan, and yet one likes to speculate now and then concerning the notions of others. Even now I am seeking to put myself in the place of that hot-head Curry, and imagine the feelings prompting him to such foolish talk."

"Yet one may have too strong an imagination, or he may let it go too far," I said.

"Quite true," he rejoined, "and I advise you, Mr. Lee, not to let yours trifle with you."

Then, as if to apologize for the sharpness of his remark, he began quickly to talk of my services to his daughter, and again was so profuse in his thanks that I would have escaped from him had he not held me by the arm. I much preferred Miss Carew's own manner of scarce alluding to her rescue, but I listened perforce to her father's. I did not believe him to be wholly bad; merely somewhat blinded to other things when his own interests were concerned.

We passed a man, a stranger to me—it was but my second visit to Danville—a tall, thin man with a pale face and the look of a student, to whom Mr. Carew gave a contemptuous nod. As the stranger glanced twice at us, I was moved to ask Mr. Carew who he was.

"It's only Underwood," he replied.

"Only Underwood? Why do you say 'only'?"

"Well, Underwood hasn't a very good name in one respect. You know that personal bravery is a quality greatly needed in this region, and, to put it mildly, Underwood is possessed of a somewhat excessive caution. He is a sort of schoolteacher and law student. I believe that he hopes to be a great lawyer."

I looked back at the retreating form of Underwood, and I felt first aversion and then pity. The border despises a coward most of all men, but I had been through the Revolutionary War, and I knew that one might be a coward because of Nature's decree.

"Perhaps it is not his fault," I said. "It may be that he is so because God made him so."

"True," replied Mr. Carew, "but men do not have time to make such inquiries. They take people as they are."

He left me presently, and I found in talk with others that the complaints against the Government were increasing. Many men had come to Danville, and discontent was the note of all, a note aggravated by reports of atrocities now coming from the border. The red terror was spreading, despite midwinter. Daring bands of savages had crossed the Ohio, and the tomahawk was busy.

Although it had been my intent not to linger, and Osseo was waiting for me, I concluded, in view of what I had heard, to stay yet a little longer in Danville.

CHAPTER 20 A Man of Fear

On the morning of my third day in Danville I met Jasper Lee, smart and dapper, and clad once more in American costume. I did not seek to conceal my surprise at his appearance, but he was complete master of himself, greeting me with an appearance of great warmth—it was in the presence of others—and hastening to explain how he had come back to his own race. I was fain to confess to myself that his statements were ingenious and plausible, because he told half the truth, and thus had a solid basis upon which to proceed with his lies.

"You know, cousin," he said, "that I was forced to adopt the costume of those hideous red wretches, and pretend that I had become one of them. But only a day or two after your own escape I managed to slip from their village, and after countless hardships reached the Ohio. Ah, it is like a terrible dream, those days in the Indian village!"

Jasper could have made his fortune as a play actor, and there was none present, save myself, who doubted the sincerity of his words. Perhaps many in like circumstances would have done the same, and how could one situated as I prove that his motives had been bad?

And I was in doubt whether I should speak, even were my words to carry conviction. So I kept silence, not seeking to restrain Jasper from pluming and disporting himself as he would. Nor was he at all neglectful in this particular, making himself with his fine tale much of a hero in Danville, and soon establishing a more intimate friendship than ever with Mr. Carew. He was restored too into a sort of place with Rose Carew, persuading her that he had been an injured man—in fact, somewhat of a martyr. I saw readily the drift of his design, which, in truth, was not new, and I was bound to own that all the chances were in his favour. Even one less worthy than Mr. Carew might well favour Jasper's suit for the hand of his daughter.

Three days after Jasper arrived Captain Hardy came, and his mission was to call for volunteers to serve in the regular army on the border. His appearance was at a most inopportune moment, the passions of the Kentuckians being inflamed and the mind of every man full of anger against the generals who had led the army into such a snare. He asked for those who would serve to meet him on an appointed day in the public square; but instead there came a mob which began first to jeer and then pelt him with snow-balls, although I noticed the "coward" Underwood seeking to restrain them. Poor Captain Hardy knew not what to do.

He put his hand upon the hilt of his sword, and evidently his first thought was to draw it and lay about him with the flat of the blade; but he saw that such an act would not serve. These were people who would retort blows with death.

The jeers increased in number, and a lump of snow hardened in water knocked the captain's cocked hat from his head. It was then that a woman interfered, and it was fortunate that it was so, as I know not whether a man could have commanded like respect. The crowd was about to rush upon the captain, and perhaps he would have received much rougher treatment than a mere snowballing, but Rose Carew burst through the ring and upbraided them for such conduct.

"This is the act of cowards," she said. "If you must do violence, why not go forth and fight the savages?"

The point of her remarks reached them, and they saw, too, the humour of what she said. Moreover, our Kentuckians are an impulsive race, and if there is one quality more strongly developed than another in them it is deference to womanhood. Captain Hardy, defended by Rose Carew, was as safe as if he sat undisturbed in his own home.

"I think you are upon a poor business," she continued, "and there are some among you who have set themselves to another task still poorer. I know of it, I have heard of it, and I tell you to take care lest you do yourselves a mischief."

She paused and looked around, her face glowing, and her look was so accusing that the gaze of none in that crowd could stand before it. I made no movement then, because I was occupied with admiration of her quick and generous action. To me a beautiful woman is more beautiful than ever when she is moved by noble anger.

"This man to whom you would do harm," she continued, "is far braver than any among you. He was in that battle on the Wabash, and he risked his life many times. I was there and I know. Which of you has done as much?"

They gave no answer and began to scatter in the town, though not neglecting to applaud her as they went. Such was their impulse.

Captain Hardy took off his hat, which he had replaced, and which was somewhat indented by its contact with hardened snow. Nevertheless, its damaged condition did not affect his politeness.

"It is pleasant at any time to be saved, Miss Carew," he said, "but when one has so fair a rescuer one knows not what to say."

"Then say nothing," she replied, and she laughed —I think it came as a relief to her tense feelings. Then she turned to me.

"Why did you not stop them, Mr. Lee?" she asked.

I reddened. I could not deny that I had been somewhat slack in moving to Captain Hardy's relief.

"You did not give me the opportunity," I said. "You were so much readier than I."

She accepted my apology, but whether satisfied with it or not I did not know. Then we walked on with Captain Hardy, and he told us that the Government must have volunteers to protect the border, since the President could send no more troops at present. I gave him some hint of the state of public opinion in Kentucky, a hint that perhaps he did not need after his recent experience, and in a few minutes he left us, as his time was pressing. I, too, had begun to excuse myself, but Miss Carew asked me to go with her to her father's house, and I could not refuse.

"Why have you not come there since our return?" she asked.

"I did not know that I would be welcome," I replied. "My cousin Jasper is here now, and he is able to do all the honours of the Lee family."

"Your cousin Jasper is himself, not you," she said, "and I tell you, Mr. Lee, that you are cherishing a false pride. No man is more honoured here than you. Why should you keep yourself from the public view? You might become a great figure in this new land."

"I do not wish it," I said, and I was sincere then.

Her face was grave and sad, the flush of strenuous action having passed.

"You wrong yourself," she continued. "Kentucky occupies a position of much danger, and it needs men of tenacity and steady conduct. Your voice might do much good here."

"It would not be listened to."

"You do not know that. Your help is needed in Kentucky as much as it was back there in the wilderness with St. Clair. Do you think that I am blind and deaf because I am a woman? I know the feeling that has arisen here, and how artful men are fomenting it for their own selfish ends. I think they are the worst of traitors to take advantage of such a time when we are under misfortune, and the minds of men turn naturally to new things."

She spoke the condemnation of her own father, and because she used such words I was persuaded that she did not know of his complicity.

"You will not have a part in any such affair," she said to me.

"Did you think that I would share it?" I asked.

She replied in the negative, and I saw that she was sincere. Then she began to talk freely, and it was a relief to her to make this confidence. I repeat that women are better patriots than men, because their patriotism is never tinctured with calculation; it is always sentimental and of the heart, like their love for husband or child. Because they had suffered much in behalf of the country, and had received no reward, the Kentuckians, she thought, ought to stand all the more firmly in its defence. Were she a man she would help Captain Hardy in his mission to the utmost of her ability. I should mention here that even as a woman she was of great aid to him, perhaps greater than if she had been a man. While she spoke thus I resolved to keep her ignorant of her father's duplicity and complicity if I could. I believed that he talked one way to her, and another to Knowlton and Curry and their like.

The night following this conversation was cold and dark, and wearying of the little inn at which I stayed, perforce, for lack of a better place, I strolled outside for the sake of the brisk air so necessary now to me, a man of the wilderness. I looked at the forms of the buildings rising obscurely, and the dozen lights or so, twinkling here and there; then I looked at the dim figure of old Joe Grimes hastening past. I knew his slouch in an instant despite the darkness, and I hailed him.

"Why such a hurry, Joe, at this time of the night?" I asked.

"Ask no questions an' you'll get no lies," he replied, and was for passing on; but I seized him by the arm, and as I was the stronger man he was compelled to stop. Joe Grimes was always a poor dissembler, and I knew by the tone of his response that mischief was afoot.

"Joe," I said, "you are about to do something of which you are ashamed."

He flushed guiltily and then grew angry, endeavouring to snatch himself loose, although I held to his arm.

"What's my business to do is yours to let alone," he said. "You've been a good comrade of mine, John Lee, but I've lived in the wilderness a long time, and I don't mean to begin asking you now if I may go out in the dark by myself."

But I knew him thoroughly, and therefore I could afford to talk to him as I did.

"Joe," I said, "you've never needed to ask me before, but you do now. I told you the other day that you could not be a villain, but you can be a fool, and you are proving it."

He pulled loose from me with an oath and hurried away. That he was troubled by a guilty conscience I felt sure, or he would not have been so impatient about it, and I was moved to follow him; an impulse that I obeyed, and I felt right in doing so. He walked toward a small wooden building in the outskirts of the town, which I recognised as the home of Underwood's little school. It was unlighted, but when old Joe knocked on the door he was admitted, and I formed at once the conclusion that the conspirators were meeting there. I was alarmed. I had not really believed that the matter would go so far, and the fact that Rose Carew's father, led on by some fantastic dream, was among these men did not lessen my trouble. I was amazed, too, that the schoolmaster should be one of them. I did not think him so bold.

I lingered there long, trying to decide what I ought to do, or rather what I would do. It was my duty to denounce these men and to put a stop by what means I could to their treasonable plottings. And yet I hesitated; they would retort upon me with that old conviction of mine; they would say that there is nothing like the zeal of the converted, and that I was trying to win credit by accusing others of what I had done. And there, too, was Rose Carew's father.

I was aroused from my doubts by a light step, and I beheld the schoolmaster, Underwood himself, approaching. My impulse when I saw him was one of distinct aversion. I remembered the epithet that had been applied to him—the basest of all names upon the border, "coward"—and now to find him a conspirator also, sneaking through the darkness, was too much for my feelings.

"You are late for your wicked work, Mr. Coward," I said to myself, "and 'tis no wonder; cowards usually are."

I expected him to glide past me like a shadow, sure that a schoolmaster's eyes would not note me in that darkness; instead, he turned and came straight to me.

"Have you seen any one go into that house, Mr. Lee?" he asked, pointing toward the school building.

"Yes, Mr. Underwood," I replied; "all your fellow-plotters are there; they wait for you only; you should hasten."

"I do not understand you," he said.

I laughed. I felt in a bitter humour, and this man rubbed me the wrong way.

"I ask you to come with me, Mr. Lee," he said with sudden vigour. "I wish you to be a witness of what is about to occur."

He put his hand upon my arm, and his fingers felt like iron. The man's manner changed, and his eager face, which was close to mine, showed strength. There was mastery, too, in his eyes, and I yielded to his request without a word.

We approached the house, and he knocked upon the door. It was opened but a few inches, and some one was about to ask the name of him who came, but Underwood pushed past him, and I followed.

It was an odd place in which to hold such a meeting, but perhaps the best that could be found in Danville, as it was untenanted at night. It was a single room with wooden benches for the pupils, and a split-bottomed chair, beside which stood a little table, for the teacher. The room was lighted by one window, the clapboard shutter of which was now closed, keeping any ray of the dim candle that burned on the table from reaching the outside. In the room were Mr. Carew, Jasper, Knowlton, Curry, Harvey, old Joe Grimes, and a half-dozen others. Faint as the light was, I saw a look of apprehension upon all their faces, when we entered, but it disappeared gradually.

"I see that you have reconsidered, Lee," said Mr. Carew in familiar tones. "You do well."

It was my intent to answer him, but I lacked opportunity because the schoolmaster spoke with such quickness.

"You do not do well, Mr. Carew," he said. "You do ill to turn such a place as this into a nest for conspirators."

"Be quiet, Underwood," said Curry fiercely, with a snap of his aggressive jaws. "You are but a teacher in this house, and you do not own it."

Curry was a man of influence and wealth in the community, and Underwood was in a measure dependent upon him for his place. But the schoolmaster was not daunted. He might be a physical but certainly he was not a moral coward, and at that moment I admired him.

His long thin finger swayed a little as he spoke, but his eyes, which had appeared dull to me before, were burning.

"I know the purpose for which you have come here," he said, and his eyes roved from one to the other of the conspirators, "and if these proceedings are not stopped at once I shall denounce you. There is law in Kentucky for such things as this, and there are plenty of men who will enforce it. None of you is so high that he may not be brought down."

As he said these last words he shook his finger in the face of Curry, who sprang to his feet with an oath, his face as red as blood, ready to strike at the accuser had not Mr. Carew pulled him down.

"Underwood is excited," said Mr. Carew, easily and smoothly. "Too much reading of books has given him a vain imagination. We are here to discuss measures for the protection of the border as becomes good citizens, and the schoolmaster's fancy attributes to us some strange purpose of which perhaps no one ever dreamed."

"That, Mr. Carew," said Underwood, "is a clumsy falsehood."

But Mr. Carew yet kept his temper. Nature had fitted him to be an intriguer.

"Will you kindly give me the name of your tipple, Underwood?" he said, "because when I wish to see things which are not of this earth I shall have merely to taste it."

But Underwood was not abashed. He spoke again vehemently, and I was surprised at his eloquence. Nor was its effect lost.

"You can not deceive me, Mr. Carew," he said. "You do not even persuade yourself that you have done so. I know well what has brought you here, and if you do not put an immediate end to such proceedings I swear that I will arouse Kentucky against you!"

It was then that Jasper spoke. He had been sitting at his ease, his expression slightly satirical.

"I am glad, Mr. Underwood," he said, "that in your great task of casting out devils you have brought with you my good cousin, John Lee. It is said in the wise book that he who is without sin should cast the first stone, and so, what more fitting than that John Lee should accuse this worthy company of gentlemen?"

I was about to speak, but again the schoolmaster was too quick for me.

"I know John Lee's history," he said, "and I know too that he is loved by the people of this land whom he has served well. He shall tell with me to-morrow what he has seen and what he knows. And I warn you, Jasper Lee, that the people of Kentucky will pay much more heed to his words than they will to yours."

Jasper shrank a little, but in a moment or two recovered his coolness.

"Shall we proceed with our discussion, Mr. Carew, when our unbidden guests withdraw?" he asked.

I noticed that the young man Harvey was moving uneasily, and his weak mouth was trembling. I judged that his spirit inclined him to leave them, but Curry suddenly clapped a heavy hand upon his shoulder, and he collapsed as if the touch of that hand had bent him to the will of the older man.

"Come, Mr. Underwood," I said, putting my hand upon the arm of the schoolmaster, "you have delivered your message here, and none could have done the task with more spirit and directness. Let us go."

He walked to the door with me, but he turned there and said, with much solemnity, to the assembly in the room:

"You have had your warning. Heed it!" Then we went out together, and we heard them closing and barring the door behind us.

CHAPTER 21 Plain Talk

The night was not dark, a clear moon sailing in silver skies, and a skim of snow covering the earth. The wind too was softened, having shifted to the southwest, and the air felt pleasant. So the schoolmaster and I strolled on together, and for a little while were silent. I was attracted to him at that moment despite his reputation for physical cowardice. In truth he had shown none in the presence of the conspirators, and he had been so bold there and had cut so directly to the marrow of the matter that I could find it in my heart to forgive him for a defect, the cause of which was nature.

I glanced once at his face, pale usually, but lighted now by an inward fire, and I asked:

"What made you go there to-night and speak to those men as you did, Mr. Underwood?"

"It is because I love my country, and would see no part of it wanting in its duty," he replied. "This talk of a Western empire is but a dream, as vague and unsubstantial as any that ever passed in Hamlet's mind. The people do not want it, nor in truth do those men themselves in the house back yonder. They are filled with anger against the East, because of the great disaster that has befallen us and the criminal folly of St. Clair; so they say words to-day which they do not mean to-morrow. Even among those conspirators there are but two, perhaps three, who are really dangerous—Mr. Carew, because he has seen the Old World and dreams of the honours and station which the republic of the New can not give; and Curry, who is one of those foolish men, so headstrong that they can see only what they desire at the moment. The third, the doubtful character, is your cousin Jasper, whom I can not fathom."

"How did you know of this plan?" I asked.

"Know of it?" he said, and he laughed for the first time. "They have scarce sought to conceal it. We are breeding here, Mr. Lee, a race hasty and hot, but true of heart. It is not a race that will ever go masked. What it intends to do it will announce to all the world; and if the intent is bad, frequently it will not do it."

I saw that he was moved by strong emotion, and I was glad to hear him talk. Why he had chosen to say these things to me I did not know, but I believed it to be the accident of the moment—he was a recluse, even under a ban, as it were—and he wished to speak his feelings to some one. I had known the desire myself, and I had known, too, what an effort it was to crush it.

He laid much of his soul bare to me, and then I found that he, too, dreamed dreams. He would see the republic spread across all this Western country, and the fertile lands become the home of a great race.

"As for their wars with the savages," he said, "they are terrible for the moment, but they will pass; the Indians are like a cork that the wave of the whites picks up and carries on. I feel sorrow for them—at times—but what else can happen?"

I had listened to the dream of another man, not long ago—the dream of the great Miami chief, Mechecunnaqua, and his mind then seemed to me to be like Underwood's now; but it was not possible that both dreams should come true—the one destroyed the other.

His had been a silent tongue. I knew by the way his words flowed now when the check was once removed. His pale face was illumined more and more by the vividness of his thoughts. Kentucky, he said, which was about to become a State, should feel an increase of honour, because of her great sufferings. It would be said of her hereafter that she was the mother of the West; it had been her duty as the first outpost beyond the mountains to fight for all that vast empire, and so far she had not failed; now, when the Government in the East was weak, it behooved the people in Kentucky to prove themselves strong, and, as much as they could, redress the balance.

He found in me a willing listener. I could not contradict anything that he said, nor, in truth, did I seek to do so; it was my wish rather that we had among us more such as he. But when he ceased I made one request of him.

"Will you not, as far as you may, keep Mr. Carew's complicity hidden from his daughter?" I asked.

He looked intently at me, and I felt my face redden through the tan. But there was a rare smile in his eyes when he gave my hand a hearty clasp and said:

"It is right that you should make this request, John Lee; and Miss Carew, whose truth is enough to redeem her father's falsity, shall be protected, if it lies within my power."

I thanked him, but he had not come to the end.

"I have more to say," he continued, "and do not censure me if I use plain speech, because it is of your interest that I am thinking. You love Rose Carew. Nay, man, do not flush and grow angry; it is nothing of which one need be ashamed. Why not stay here and win her, and become a great man in this new State? It lies within your power."

"Which?" I asked, "to win Miss Carew or to rise to a place of importance?"

"Both," he replied, and his eyes would not turn aside from the gaze of mine.

"She could only feel aversion for me," I said, "and even were it not so, how can I ask her to unite her pure life with that of a man whose history is like mine?

My place is there," and I pointed toward the northwest, where the great wilderness lay.

"The past is the past; it is not the present," he said.

"No, but the present is based upon it, and grows out of it."

He said nothing more upon the subject, and presently we parted. I awoke early the next morning, wondering what course Underwood would take, and in some fear, too, on Rose Carew's account. But freshly returned to her people from captivity, it seemed hard to me that she should now hear her father called a traitor.

CHAPTER 22 A Messenger from the North

The morning was quiet and Danville seemed peaceful. I met Jasper, and he nodded as if nothing had occurred to disturb the placid course of events. Yet this quiet was of short duration, although its end came in a way that I did not expect.

A messenger, riding hard, arrived in Danville shortly before the noon hour, and he had news that made women and many a man, too, shudder. The tribes, flushed by their great success, and scorning midwinter, had crossed the Ohio in force, and already the torch and tomahawk were busy in Kentucky. The band numbered many hundreds of warriors, the messenger said, and Hoyoquim again led. They had burst in a flood of fire upon the undefended settlements, and along a line of many miles the bodies of women and children lay amid smoking ruins.

The messenger was but one of those who rode throughout the land for help, and it was a message that in the last fifteen years or more, or since the first house was built at Boonesborough, had been borne often through the settlements, and here, after the first shock, it was received with the usual stoicism of the border. To fight the savages, to be on guard against a treacherous and cruel foe, seemed to our people an eternal condition, and they did not complain. Nor was there any delay in the answer to the cry for help. A few minutes after the messenger came I met old Joe Grimes. His excitement was visible, his eyes flaming with it, and he clapped one hand heavily upon my shoulder, pointing with the other toward the north.

"They are calling for us there, John!" he cried. "We must make haste! They need us! It's the people of the West now who must do the work; they've got to save Kentucky and the Northwest for the republic!"

I looked him squarely in the eyes, but he did not see the humour of his words.

"And if you are to save the West for the republic what is to become of the great conspiracy in which you are such a master figure, Joe?" I asked. "Surely you have not forgotten your Western empire?"

"That Spanish business?" he said. "Oh, I've changed my mind. I'll never put my arm out farther than I can draw it back; besides, I haven't time."

Then he was off in a moment seeking for volunteers to go against the tribes. It was the note of the war trumpet ringing in his ears that had changed his mind overnight. He was willing to conspire as long as his anger lasted, but he was not willing that others should do the same, and now at the cry for help he hurried to the defence of his chosen land. Curry and Harvey showed the same spirit, and it was obvious that the Indian alarm had blown away many noxious vapours, serving at least one good purpose. The little town was soon full of men coming with rifle and ammunition pouch, and ready to march northward against the foe. There would be no lack of zeal.

I went in the afternoon to see Rose Carew, having formed a project, the execution of which I had at heart. She received me in a manner most grateful to me, as it indicated that my coming was not unpleasant, and I felt at ease in her presence. She too had heard of the message brought across the Ohio, and her woman's heart thrilled with sympathy for those exposed to the tomahawk, a feeling all the greater because she herself had been under the edge of that weapon, and knew its terrors. And she showed a spirit like unto that of Underwood. Kentucky must go to the relief, and go at once. Naught else could be thought of at such a time. When the East was loaded down with its own troubles the West must show how it could defend not only itself, but the interests of the republic to which it belonged. She took it for granted that I should go, not only willing, but eager to accept such an opportunity, and it was then that I approached my subject.

"In truth I shall go," I said. "I had no thought of anything else; and I should be glad if I were in a command with your father, Mr. Carew. He is sure to distinguish himself."

She gave me a look of surprise.

"I did not know that he was going," she said. "Perhaps he is—is old for such an arduous campaign,"

I saw clearly that she did not wish Mr. Carew to join the expedition, but I was resolved that he should; it seemed to me a loophole for escape from many dangers, and so I ridiculed the idea of his being too old, as, in truth, I had a right to do, since he was not past fifty, and in the height of health and vigour. I told, without direct reference to him, what an obligation lay upon every man to go for the defence of the border; even the thought of that poor invalid wife did not deter me, and I saw conviction growing upon her face. As I have said before, I think that women are the truest patriots of all, and if one woman sends her son or husband to war another may well send her father.

"You will see that he comes back to us again, will you not, Mr. Lee?" she said, as I was about to leave. "You have done us one service, and I do not hesitate to ask for another."

"Mr. Carew is able to care for himself," I replied, "but if he should need help he shall have all that I can give."

The glow of gratitude appeared in her eyes, but she said only:

"I shall look first for his coming, Mr. Lee, and then for yours."

When I went from her presence I felt much joy, mingled with much pain. The old disgrace was now all the more bitter to bear because, had it not been, I believed that the way I longed most to tread might be open for me. I was a fool, I told myself, to be thinking of the curve of a girl's eyebrow, and I turned at once to sterner matters.

In the short time left to me I assiduously spread the report that Mr. Carew was eager to go against the savages, as he had great interests in Kentucky, and on that account felt the weight of his obligation to assist in the defence. So when they came to him and gave compliments to his zeal he was somewhat taken aback; but seeing no way of escape with honour, made the best of it, and pretended to the zeal that he did not feel. There was in him something of Jasper's shifty character, though the grain of it was better. Jasper himself had made a hasty journey to Lexington, and he slipped through our sieve.

The expedition drawn from many parts of Kentucky started in three days, so rapid were our preparations, but it was none too soon, as the entire border lay under the tomahawk, and the tale of slaughter did not cease to come.

Ours was a little army in which every man commanded himself. We had colonels and captains selected by ourselves whom we could turn into privates when we chose, and who could give advice which might or might not be taken. In truth, we represented the sort of government in which Joe Grimes believed—every man for himself, and "devil take the hindmost." All were brave and strong, sons of the forest, who knew the Indian trail when they saw it, and were confident of their own powers.

As we advanced rapidly northward our numbers increased, and it was a picturesque little force variously clad and well armed. These men, with their fiery spirit and eager desire to close with the foe, presented a striking contrast to the drooping army of St. Clair which had perished in the great woods.

The zeal and rage of the borderers increased as we approached the Ohio. The full tale of slaughter had not been told. The tomahawk was flashing along a line of two hundred miles, and the savages were showing no mercy. We talked of these things, and the desire for revenge burned in every bosom. Hoyoquim's army, in great force, it was said, was besieging Winston's Station, near the Ohio, and increasing our speed again, we hastened to its relief. When within one day's march of the Station, Osseo joined us, coming into camp at daybreak, and taking his place without a word beside me at the camp fire. Nor did I speak for a half hour, merely helping him to food and waiting until in his own good time he should choose to talk. Then he looked around at our motley little army and said:

"In the camp of the General-who-never-walks the fire burned too low; here it burns too high."

I sighed. I could not help it. I had seen already the fault of which Osseo spoke, but I was reluctant to mention it. Sanguine of success and eager to show the regular troops how superior the borderers were in the conduct of Indian war, they thought only of finding the foe. Osseo said no more, and while we sat in silence another approached us, and to my surprise it wag Underwood.

"How happens it that you are here, Mr. Underwood?" I asked, and then I would have given much had I not spoken the question, as his face flushed a little, and plainly he knew the cause of my surprise. But he answered:

"My errand is the same as yours, Mr. Lee. I come to fight the savages."

His face, the flush departing now, seemed paler to me than ever, but the spirit I saw that night when he denounced the conspirators burned in his eyes.

"I am not much of a forester," he said, "and I know little of Indian war, but it is not a time when any of us should shun the conflict."

I welcomed him at our fireside, and Osseo gave his approval. I felt an increasing liking for this man. It seemed to me a fine thing that he should so far overcome his physical impulses that he could force himself to come upon such service. I not only liked him, I admired him. His delay in joining us, I learned, was due to an effort to raise additional volunteers.

Our halt was brief, and as we approached Winston Station a messenger informed us that the heroic band of defenders from the cover of their wooden walls had repulsed every attack of the savage army, which was now retiring, in fear of our advance. Then our men shouted their joy, and their fiery zeal swelled higher and higher. They would follow the horde of Hoyoquim and destroy it. Now, they said, the difference between soldiers and borderers was plain to every one; even the savages were aware of it, and while they would never retire in the face of the regulars they knew too much to await the attack of the true foresters.

"Across the Ohio and after them!" was the universal shout, and all were eager to strike a blow which should balance the defeat of St. Clair. Curry sprang upon a log and made a speech full of heat. The man in truth had a rude eloquence, and it was sufficient for his hearers. We pressed forward at once upon the trail of the savage army, crossing the Ohio, and after passing a low range of hills we entered a beautiful prairie country.

The air turned warm; the light snow melted and, despite lingering winter, the grass and foliage showed here and there.

CHAPTER 23 At the Ford

The next day was one of those strange days that we have sometimes in the Western lands between the great colds. The grass bent in little waves like the ripples on a river, and the brown tint of leaf and stem was almost lost in the golden flush of the sun. The wind that came over the brow of a hill fanned our faces like a perfumed breath, and all around us was a flood of colour, the gold of the sunbeams softened by the snowy white clouds through which they came.

I turned my face to the wind and inhaled its breath. It filled my lungs, and heart and brain alike expanded. I felt again the joy of the wilderness. I could understand the philosophy of the old Greeks who believed in fauns and satyrs, and that in the morning of time we roamed the scented woods, happy and harmless.

Our course now took us toward a river which flowed into the Ohio, and presently we saw in the distance the faint line of its stream. The condition of the trail showed that we were advancing faster than the Indian army, and we increased our speed again.

The river grew broader, and its silver shaded into deeper blue. A haze of hills beyond it became purple, and the line of a distant forest cut the sky like a sabre's edge.

We halted presently, and I looked around at my comrades, who had gathered in a great group, on foot and on horseback, two hundred strong men, faces darkened and seamed by sun, wind, and rain, figures spare but nervous and powerful, some clad in homespun, others in tanned deerskin trimmed with long fringe and little coloured beads which flashed in red and blue and yellow as the sunbeams fell upon them. All carried the Western rifle, conspicuous with its quaintly carved stock and long, slender barrel of blue steel. Looking upon them, I was proud of my comrades, though I did not forget Osseo's warning of "too much fire."

The leaders now talked together a little, and I preached caution.

"Caution!" cried Curry; "while we are lingering here the savages are escaping."

His words, not mine, were grateful in the ears of the men. So I stepped aside.

"Do you think we'll overtake them this side of the river?" asked Joe Grimes of me.

I looked at the long stretch of forest and the blue band of the stream, and saw nothing but peace and stillness, save where our men gathered. The outline of purple hills beyond the river showed no change. But through the deep grass led the trail of many footsteps which were not a puzzle to me, for as my eyes turned away from the forests and the water, I bent over and examined the traces with a trained eye. Then I shook my head and Underwood signified his agreement.

"I believe they will make their stand at the river," he said. "That is the best place for them."

I thought him right, and even old Joe in his confidence seemed to have lost his habitual caution. He and the others feared only that the warriors would not wait for us, that the rapidity of their flight would leave us behind, no matter how strenuously we pursued, and they were consumed with impatience at the delay. Some had talked of caution, of the superior numbers of the warriors, and the danger of ambush, but the great majority laughed at the conservatives, and did not hesitate to call them unpleasant names.

"There are a thousand of the warriors, and we are but two hundred," said Underwood as we stood there. "We ought to wait for re-enforcements."

Old Joe flamed out at him and boldly called him a coward. I felt pity for the man, and told Grimes that he should be ashamed of himself, but I was unheeded. Underwood did not resent the affront, merely turning away.

The council ended and our leaders rode toward the river, thus giving the sign that we should continue the pursuit. A fierce shout of approval arose, and then we poured forward in a picturesque stream, the sun flashing over the rifle barrels and the brown, eager faces, the beads on leggings and moccasins shimmering in many colours.

The river, first seen a silver thread in the morning, was now a dark-blue sheet of water, and very near; yet I looked little at it, keeping my eyes on the line of the woods which filed past on either side of us. I searched them continually for the glimpse of a brown form or the steel of a rifle barrel glinting as some stray sunbeam struck upon it. The traces that we were following led straight toward the river, yet it seemed natural in me to watch everywhere for an ambush. The lightest sounds came to my ears, and I felt a familiarity with all the phases of the wilderness. This was home.

But the woods were silent and unoccupied. My eyes could find nothing there. The peace was the same that had hung over the land in the morning. A redbird glowing in his deepest scarlet sat on a bough just over my head, and did not move as we passed.

We reached the river and stopped upon its bank, staring at the line of bare hills on the farther shore, the hills that had shone deep blue in the distance and then purple. We were astonished for the moment, and our little army, breathing deeply, expressed its opinions with freedom.

We could not see a human being on the other side. The Indian force which the men had expected with such confidence to find waiting for us there was gone.

Even then it might be far on its way toward the deeper wilderness, and many hearts beat with fierce anger at its escape.

Again I eagerly searched the line of silent hills, but saw nothing. The blue bluffs and the white stone gleamed in the sun, and there was the river, flowing in blue where the channel was deep, but rippling in silver bubbles and white foam over the shallows. The peace of the world was still about us, and the little white clouds sailed calmly on in turquoise heavens.

"If necessary we should follow them even to the lakes," said Joe Grimes to me.

"But it will not be necessary," I replied. "Look!"

Two Indians had appeared on one of the hills beyond the river. They were Shawnee warriors in all the glory and hideousness of their war-paint, each carrying a rifle in his hand. They came a little nearer, and sitting on a rock looked intently at us. There was something particularly insulting in their stare, their air of unconcern, even disdain, and the angry blood flew to my head.

"Scouts or skirmishers," said Grimes.

"Yes," I replied, "and they are daring us to cross and attack them."

"We'll be cowards if we don't," he said.

"Joe," I said, "remember one of your own favourite sayings—'Never bite off more'n you can chew.'"

He gave an angry snort, but did not answer me. Then he raised his rifle, but it was too far for a shot. Others too had made threatening motions with their weapons, but the warriors either knew that they were safe or scorned them. One ran his fingers carelessly through his long scalp-lock, and then leaned back against the rock as if he would go to sleep.

Our leaders drew together again, and there was much talk. But I foresaw the result of it. There was the long, easy slope worn by the crossing of buffalo herds, and a dash into the fordable river would soon put us on the other side.

The talk continued. Underwood, unabashed by the name of coward, which had been applied more than once to him, pushed into the circle and advised them not to attempt the passage of the river in the face of the Indian army. Some voices were raised in his support, mine among them, but the others turned upon him and rebuffed him so hardly that he withdrew and stood at a little distance, leaning upon his gun. Even those who shared his opinions would not be his friends because everybody knew that he was a coward. I watched his face, but if he felt shame he did not show it. I could not understand him; a man might be a coward, but I had never before heard of one who did not try to hide the fact. Once Underwood's eyes met mine, but they seemed to take no note of my look, and passed on toward the river and the two warriors who sat on the hill, combing their scalp-locks with their fingers.

The younger men were nearest the river, and they moved about in their impatience, swearing now and then under their breath, the metal of the guns clicking against metal. The scent of the great woods that had followed me all the morning came to me still. The same little white clouds sailed peacefully past the sun and left the huge coppery ball to shoot its rays upon us.

I looked at the debating leaders, and then turned my gaze back to the hill. I saw the Indians sitting upon the rocks and then I did not see them. I rubbed my eyes to remove the film which had dimmed my vision, for I could not believe that they had gone, thinking it only an illusion. The rubbing did not bring the warriors back. I saw the bare, blue hill, its outlines cutting the sky as sharply as ever, the stone outcropping seeming to smoulder in the sun, but it was lone and desolate, as if men had never been there.

"See, they have fled!" shouted old Joe; "the band is afraid of us!"

Again the cry that we follow at once was raised. I saw Underwood's lips move as if he were about to utter another protest, and I wondered at the man's hardihood and lack of shame. But he crushed the impulse, and closing his lips tightly, remained leaning upon his rifle's muzzle and intently regarding the leaders.

Most of our band had closed around those who were to decide our course, urging their older comrades to delay no longer and lead them forward in the pursuit, if they were really brave men. It was a circle of hot, red faces, angry eyes, and swaying forms. Suddenly one of the officers on horseback, a large man with the reddest face of all—Curry himself—pushed his horse out of the circle and rode toward the ford. He paused near the brink, wheeled his horse about until he faced us, and cried in a voice that was a mixture of swagger, courage, and scorn:

"All who are not cowards follow me!"

Then he wheeled again and galloped into the river.

His taunt was the touch of fire to dry grass, and we poured after him, a tumultuous horde, horse and foot alike eager to be first at the crossing, leaders now as wild as the men with enthusiasm. I was in the front, but I did not forget to look again at Underwood and see whether he would go or stay. He kept pace with the rear ranks, and then I lost him as I dashed into the stream. These were my comrades, and I could not leave them.

The water rose to my waist, and for the moment I was blinded by the foam and spray kicked up by so many men and horses. A clamour of shouting and splashing water rose around me, but I cleared my eyes, and holding up my gun and powder to keep them dry, pushed for the farther shore, stumbling over the boulders and the uneven bottom.

The river was neither deep nor wide here, and its waters were churned up now by many feet, and men and horses blocked the way. A horse fell with a great splash, and he and his rider struggled up again, everybody giving way and deepening the confusion. I looked at the blue hills, and I was alive with apprehension. It was here that we expected the Indian army to make its stand, disputing with us the passage of the river, and if the warriors were to give us a fight at all it seemed to me that this was the best place for it. I expected them each moment to appear on the summits and pour a deadly fire upon us as we struggled in the river, but the hills remained as bare as ever, shining in the sun, and there were no sounds save those that we made.

Our wet and wild little army, thinking nothing of the cold, pulled itself out of the water and stood upon dry land, triumphant, the obstacle that we feared most overcome, our foes still fleeing the sight of our faces.

The sun was rapidly drying our clothes, though wet or dry it was a matter to which the men gave little thought, as we climbed the hills and stood upon their summits, seeing only the wilderness before us. But the scouts soon found the trail of the warriors, leading on straight ahead, and we followed. I confess that I too shared somewhat in the enthusiasm of the moment.

The ground remained rough, and we proceeded along the crest of a ridge that ran back at an angle from the river. The confused talk ceased now, and we heard only the footsteps and heavy breathing of men and horses, upon whom the long pursuit was beginning to tell. As we left the river the open nature of the country ceased, thickets of bushes and clumps of trees appearing, while farther on curved the wilderness.

I watched the dark line of the forest, sure that it now hid the fleeing warriors.

The ridge broadened a little, and seemed to extend to the distant woods in which we believed the Indian army to have sought refuge, offering us an easy path of pursuit along its crest. Full of zeal and spirit, the borderers forgot now the weariness which had begun to creep over them, and pressed on with rising ardour. I was in the front rank, keeping pace with the horsemen, and I watched the forest as it rose like a wall from the earth, ending in a sharp black line against the blue sky. A tremulous haze like that of Indian summer hung over it, and it seemed to form so secure a covert that I wondered if we should ever be able to find our enemy in its depths.

Osseo was by my side, saying nothing, though I knew well his thoughts. We had sunk into silence now, our course decided, and no breath to spare for talking. The ridge flattened out somewhat, and I noticed that it was cut on either side by a great gully, filled with a dense growth of bushes.

We halted here a moment to examine the trail, which seemed to veer about as if the warriors had become uncertain in their flight, and I glanced toward the ravine on my right and its thickets of bushes. My eyes lingered there a moment, and were passing on when they were caught by something and turned back. It was a metallic gleam, a flash quick but bright, like the sparkle of a firefly in the dark, that drew me, and I looked for it again.

That passing gleam of steel was not more sudden than my comprehension of it, of its awful nature, of the catastrophe. I knew that it was a flash of sunlight falling across the polished barrel of a rifle. I knew that a thousand sharpshooters lay concealed in the bushes of those two ravines, and we—rash fools!—had marched directly between, making of ourselves a target as full and fair as the most ferocious warrior could covet. What right had we now to taunt St. Clair?

Involuntarily I seized the arm of Osseo in so fierce a grasp that he turned upon me in surprise. This movement of my hand, this succession of vehement emotions, passed in a second, and I opened my mouth to shout the warning, but it was never uttered.

The cry was checked at my lips by a burst of fire on either side of us, like the two long, flaming edges of a sword. The red blaze seemed to reach from either ravine to our faces, and inclosed us in a rim of death. The crack of hundreds of rifles uniting made a roar as of cannon, columns of smoke arose, and the odour of burned gunpowder snuffed out the perfume of the wilderness.

The flame of the rifles fired so close flashed in our faces. The cry of death mingled with the cry of pain. Our little band reeled under the leaden sleet and dripped blood. Horses and men dropped together and the screams of wounded animals added to the confused and terrible uproar.

I was used to Indian warfare, but this was so quick that for the moment I was dazed. It scarce seemed real.

A man beside me suddenly asked what we ought to do. I was about to reply, but before I could speak a word he fell dead at my feet, struck between the eyes by a rifle ball.

A wounded horse, shrieking in pain, plunged past me, and fell among the bushes from which the red sharpshooters were pouring their fire.

The paralysis of the terrible surprise was still upon us, the fire which scorched us from all sides still drove us toward a common centre, the huddle of man and horses becoming every moment denser and more confused. Some of us were firing at random into the encircling rim of smoke. Men would pitch out of the mass and fall headlong to the ground where they lay; most of our leaders were killed already, many of those who still stood were bleeding from wounds, and all the time our ears were filled with the fierce, triumphant peal of the war-whoop.

They pressed closer and closer upon us, five times as numerous, with all the advantage of a surprise and the first volleys, using every bush and tree and stone as shelter, until sometimes we saw only the curling smoke and the dim outlines of the undergrowth.

I looked at our blood-stained group, the brilliant deerskin tunics dyed now with many a red stream, and still saw upon many faces that dim look of surprised horror, of vague dismay, borderers though they were. All the grass was torn up by our tramplings, and upon either side of us the bank of smoke had become a solid mass, through which the steady fire of the rifles blazed in hundreds of red streaks.

A warrior dashed out of the smoke, and bending over a fallen man, drew his knife to scalp him. One of our band raised his rifle and shot the savage. That seemed to arouse our army from its apathy of despair, and with a universal impulse we turned our faces toward the river, which we had crossed so gaily a few minutes before. The thought in every mind then—and they were brave men—was flight. Those who have never been surprised by the appearance of death when least expected—death in its most terrible form—may boast of their courage, not otherwise. Ours were the best men of the border, and yet for a little while the panic was the same as that of St. Clair's day.

The warriors, when they saw the attempt of their victims to break from the trap, began to shout more fiercely than ever, and increased the vigour of their fire. The clouds of smoke grew thicker and blacker, the volleys flashed faster, and the bullets, when they did not strike flesh and bone, whistled incessantly in our ears. The men choked with the smoke and were blinded by it; they stumbled over bushes and their comrades, and had no means of knowing which way they were going, save that instinct was carrying them toward the river, now become somehow in their imagination a line of safety. Yet through all the horrible tumult, the smoke, the blaze and rattle of the firing, the groans of the wounded and the death cries, the force of old teaching and habits prevailed; the borderers mechanically loaded their rifles, and as fast as the bullets were rammed home fired into the encircling walls of smoke.

Our band, though confused, was still a compact mass, held together by the enemy, who was pressing so fiercely upon us from all sides, but the terror of death and the love of life were urging us on. We wanted to get away from those rifles that were stinging us, from that enemy hidden in his veil of smoke who found us a perfect target, while we could only see figures appearing and reappearing with the quickness of shadows on a screen.

The mass of slowly moving white men in the centre of this ring of death suddenly heaved up and broke from a walk into a run toward the river. The warriors had not closed in entirely on what had been the rear of our army, and there the line of flitting phantoms was weakest. We drove at the place where the smoke was thinnest, leaving behind us our dead, firing the loaded rifles, clubbing at savage heads with the unloaded, shouting in rage, resembling nothing so much as a buffalo with weakening strength and torn flanks surrounded by a herd of fierce and famished wolves.

The fever rose into my eyes and brain. I became a savage myself. The barrel of my rifle, hot with the frequent discharges, burned my hand; once when I touched my face it felt as hot as the rifle barrel. The blood in my eyes and the drifting smoke enlarged and distorted everything, and the faces of my comrades became as wild and savage as my own. Everything had over it the tinge of bloody redness. The skies were no longer blue, though the blue was still there. This, however, was but the rage of battle. Otherwise I retained my presence of mind, and remained a part of the circle of my comrades, the compact though bruised body that was driving at the thin point of the Indian line, firing and shouting as it came.

We struck the line of smoke and savage faces and dashed through it, a feeling of triumph flushing us for a moment as we passed. But the horde poured after us, now counting out our fallen, outnumbering us seven or eight to one, hanging in a swarm on both our flanks, pressing upon us from the rear, never giving us a moment's rest, and keeping our wounds bleeding.

"To the river! To the river!" our men shouted incessantly, as if that river had suddenly become an impregnable fortress, destined to receive us and give us shelter.

The same instinct was in possession of all, and toward the river we went, the merciless fire of our enemies scorching our flanks and rear, the warriors still whooping and yelling their triumph. Yet the borderers already began to recover from their confusion. Retreat was necessary, but the fight was not done. I saw better now—the smoke was broken into pillars and columns, the rifle flashes were scattered more widely, but around us there was always the same reek of blood and sweat. Some comrade would press against me, shoulder to shoulder, straining like myself, and then he would go down, to become a victim of the tomahawk. Those who fell did not rise again.

We were a huge bank of fire and smoke moving over the ground, ourselves the front of it, the Indians the rear and sides, and always the bank was rent by many flashes and shouts and cries, and it left a trail of the dead that it spat out; yet there was some order among us, and it was not our men alone who fell. The savages, too, were beginning to pay a price.

Still the bank of fire and smoke rolled on, giving forth a volume of harsh and confused sound, and increasing its speed as the blue streak of the river began to shine before it. The gleam of the water was like a magnet to many; they believed that beyond it lay safety, but, however they struggled on, the streak broadened too slowly.

Osseo was beside me, fighting as he had fought in St. Clair's defeat. Despite the confusion, I was now able to watch the attack, and when a warrior dashed out of the smoke to scalp one of our wounded who had begun to lag a little from weakness, I raised my rifle and shot the savage through the head.

"Well done!" said a voice near me, and looking through the film of smoke I beheld Underwood, whom they had called a coward. It struck me even then that I saw no fear upon his face.

The fight and the flight seemed to me to grow in ferocity as we approached the river. The great cloud increased in density and hung closer to the earth, the firing of the rifles made an unbroken crash, and the yelling of the savages was as steady and fierce as the howling of a pack of wolves. They spread farther along our flanks, and tried to overlap us and pass in front of us before we reached the ford, but we drove them back for a moment; then, with these wolves again hanging to us, we reached the river, and into the water we rushed, pursuers and pursued, white men and Indians together, still fighting, some of us now hand to hand, knives against tomahawks, the gun muzzle pressed upon the target, the silver of the river's current already flowing in red streaks.

That terrible cloud of fire and smoke which had followed us so far was not turned back by the stream, but still hovered over and inclosed us, and the core of it was now a fighting jumble of white men and red. The water was dashed into bubbles and foam by whistling bullets and striking arms. Men stumbled on the rough bottom, and falling, disappeared. Some came up again and others did not. A floating body struck against me and passed on. The stream from bank to bank was full of red and white men, in whom only the animal was left, shooting, stabbing, and striking, and filling the air with shouts, yells, and groans. More savages lined the bank and fired at every white face they saw. The river now seemed to roar and splash around us and encourage us with an evil song to kill. The ferocity of the battle in the water excelled anything that we had seen on the land this day, and I began to believe that with all these Indians clinging to us and hacking at us we could never reach the farther shore.

Nothing oppressed me so much as that horrible river. I hated its hiss and gurgle, and my heart revolted at the sight of the bloody bubbles that floated past me. When I fell once and came up with my mouth full of water I spat it out as if it were so much poison.

As we rocked and reeled about in the stream we struggled always to burst from the grasp of the savages, to throw them off, and to escape to the shore. There was no order, no plan in our fighting, and we were without a leader, until at last I heard one voice raised above the uproar—a voice that had the tone of a commander. Wiping the smoke and spray from my eyes, I saw Underwood, up to his waist in the river, but calm.

"Comrades, men!" he shouted in a voice that everybody heard, "stand together! We must beat them back now, or none of us will be saved! Won't you help?"

His voice resounded above all the tumult of the battle, and his face was that of a man without fear. He inspired the defence anew, he brought back the courage that was natural to our little army, though partly beaten out of it by the sudden ambuscade and overwhelming attack. He dashed here and there, encouraging one, directing the efforts of another, and all of us found ourselves obeying him, as if he were our natural and chosen leader, which he now was, become such by supreme fitness. Though the bullets sang their venomous little song around him, he paid no heed to them, but continued to encourage us with voice and hand, to fight with us sometimes, and always to direct the combat. I knew then that his was the wisest and bravest mind among all these men, and for a moment I was overwhelmed with shame that I had ever called him a coward or thought of him as such.

The violence of the fight in the water deepened. The Indians, despite their superiority in numbers, had not been able to pass us, and the panic that had assailed the men began to give way to a kind of fierce exultation.

Underwood was unremitting in his exertions, and presently we found ourselves formed into a line of battle—a rough line, it is true, but one that presented a defensive front to the enemy, bristling with rifles, and more dangerous to them than the wild *mêlée* of single-handed fighting in the river.

The warriors, savage as they were for our lives, shrank a moment from this little band, dripping with blood and water, wholly desperate, conscious that the time to make the last stand, if a single one was to escape, had come, and animated with the courage that the wounded beast has when he sets his back against a rock and faces his enemy. But that moment quickly passed, and then, more lustful than ever for our blood, they rushed upon us, each uttering the war-whoop. We had reloaded our rifles, and under the command of Underwood awaited the shock, half of us delivering a volley at only a few yards into their faces, the other half following it up with an equally deadly fire as they reeled back under the first blow. Then we charged them, smashing with clubs and stabbing with knives, and so great was the impetus of our slender force, borne on by the last courage which is the most desperate, that their line bent before ours and was driven back toward the shore. Numbers and their daring, of which they had a full share, were of no avail; we were a band of wild men, and elated with the triumph of the moment we forgot death, the desire to escape, and everything else save the wish to end the lives of the yelling savages in front of us. And always Underwood led the men on, calm, watchful, unwounded.

Fighting thus, we drove them back across the river and up the hills, and so heavy was the blow we gave that the whole numerous band shrank from us, and their fire sank just as the effort and impulse which bore us on had begun to die. But the precious time to get our wounded and ourselves out of their grasp and across the river was gained. The men rushed about, still under the guidance of Underwood, and reached the farther shore as the howling pack recovered their courage and came swarming after us. But we stood upon the bank and received them as they plunged into the water with so fierce and deadly a fire that they recoiled again, and we exulted in our triumph.

CHAPTER 24 Back to the South

The river, which in our retreat had threatened to be our destruction, was now, repassed, our bulwark. It sometimes happens that men who have lived hitherto peaceful lives, suddenly and under the pressure of necessity develop military talent. And the pale, reserved schoolmaster, whom all called a coward, now furnished such an instance. He shouted to us to hold the ford, and he was obeyed. The spirit and courage of the borderers rose again. They were not like the raw soldiers; they might bend to the sudden blow, but they would not break, and though rash leadership and their own hot blood had led them into disaster, they sought now for revenge.

I thought it well to imitate the example of Underwood, and I too cried to the men to attack, and helped in forming our forces for the defence. Curry had been mortally wounded in the river, but managed to reach the shore, where he died presently, paying for his folly with his life. Harvey, he of the weak chin, who had been drawn into the plot by the stronger man, Curry, was wounded too, but his hurt was slight, and he was fighting with valour, all his treason gone from him in such strenuous moments like a skim of snow melting before a hot sun. I looked, too, for Mr. Carew, and I saw him lying wounded at the very edge of the stream, unable to come farther, and in his position a fair target for the Indian rifles on the other shore.

I did not in the first moment feel pity for the man. His death would be a great grief to his daughter, but it might save her from keener sorrows, and I turned my eyes from the sight of the wounded man lying there, his feet in the water. Then I felt shame and remorse because such a thought had entered my mind, and springing forward I dragged him to the cover of the rocks.

"I thank you, Lee; my debt to you grows great," he said, and there was genuine gratitude in his tone.

I had no time to answer him, as the savages, rushing forward with a fierce yell of triumph, were beginning their attempt to force the ford, though they came now to meet a foe full of courage. Our men, sheltering their bodies behind rocks and hillocks., received them with so true and deadly a fire that they fell back to the shelter of the farther bank, leaving many dead to float off with the stream. Twice and thrice they returned to the assault, but they could not force the passage, being hurled back each time with increasing loss, and then the war-cry of the borderers arose, in its turn triumphant.

All day we held that bloody ford, and at nightfall the savage army, tired of so vain and costly an effort, resumed its march to the northward, while we, taking our wounded with us, turned to the south, sad because we had rushed into an ambush, but with the saving memory that at the last we had regained our courage and driven back our foes. We had been hot with folly, but our valour had saved us.

I heard as we marched little criticism of the mistakes of others. Our own were too fresh in our minds, but the common danger now bound the men together in a brotherhood that could not be broken. Old Joe Grimes for the first time in his life was subdued, and talked to me in the most temperate manner.

"We bit off more'n we could chaw," he said. "You can scorch a cat once, but it's mighty hard to git him too close to the fire twice."

"You must help to defend the border now, Joe," I said.

"I'm not thinking of anything else," he replied.

And I believe that his words were true. Harvey, too, spoke to me a little later. His left arm was in a sling, caused by a flesh wound, but his downcast look was not due to his hurt.

"Mr. Lee," he said, "I have been indulging in a dream as foolish as it was wicked, and it took a man whom I once despised, Underwood the schoolmaster, to awaken me from it."

"But you waken in time," I said.

"Will you say nothing of what you saw and heard in Danville back there, that night?" he asked.

"You do not need my promise," I answered; "the occasion will never arise."

His face grew clearer, and presently I saw him talking in the most cheerful manner to others. In truth, he was but a boy, and Curry had drawn him into the mischief. Mr. Carew, on his part, was silent and moody, a frame of mind for which his wound gave him good excuse, and I kept away from him. Underwood by unanimous consent remained in command, though he was kind enough often to ask the advice of Osseo, myself, and others, and he conducted us safely across the Ohio into Kentucky, where the little army divided, all returning to their homes or duties elsewhere. Osseo again was to wait for me at the Ohio, and I continued the journey with Underwood and Mr. Carew to Danville. It was my first impulse to stop at the Ohio, but I wished to see Mr. Carew safe again with his wife and daughter, and I did not deny to myself that the sight of Rose Carew once more would be pleasant to my eyes. Not in all the years since its beginning had my disgrace borne so heavily upon me as it did now. Were I only free to seek her, I said over and over again to myself, I might pick up the challenging glove of any one, even that of Jasper himself, with all his worldly wealth and smooth ways. I renewed the events of our life together, the long flight through the forest, the idyllic days, and the revelation. I could remember each incident, and the order in which it came, and her look and smile when she spoke.

Mr. Carew remained silent and gloomy. His wound, though still painful, did not prevent him from travelling on horseback, and I was glad now that he had been struck in the battle, since to any who might hereafter taunt him with projected treason he could point to the honourable scars received in his country's cause. But Underwood was my friend, and we talked freely. There was a certain change in him. The man had found himself. He was now conscious of his own powers, and yet scarce knowing whence the knowledge came. I saw in him a force which had not appeared until that night in Danville, when it was disclosed by the presence of supreme emotion. I was drawn to him, too, by the faith that he showed in me.

"You must remain with us now, Lee," he repeated. "'Tis not a matter to be dismissed lightly, and I beg you to think long upon it before you refuse. You were one of those who did not fall into a panic back there at the ford. The debt that Kentucky owes you has grown. Here you have the respect and love of everybody. Stay with us and become one of our great men. We need your like."

He did not know then that he himself was to win such a place—member of Congress and then Governor of his State, a national figure of importance—but I dimly foresaw it even at that moment. I confess that he tempted me strongly. I could go back to the old community and show the honours given to me by the new, but stronger than that was the vision of a woman's oval face, with fair hair rising above pure eyes.

"Don't ask me, Underwood," I replied; "I feel that I ought not to stay."

He said no more, but often I caught his eyes dwelling upon me with a wistful look, and I was troubled much, for the flesh was weak.

I felt that our defeat—defeat it was despite the final repulse of the savages—was not in one respect a bad thing for the Western people, as they could now look with more leniency upon the mistakes of their Eastern brethren, and the community of disaster would bind them together. The news of the fight at the ford was received with calm, showing another phase of their character. It was their own who had made the mistake and suffered, and they would not complain; rather, it would encourage them to new efforts in defence of the border, and they would make expiation; they would hold the Western marches until the new relief expedition which the Government was now said to be preparing could come. The people strengthened themselves again for the great task that lay before them, and in the face of defeat that must be repaired the last phase of Spanish or French conspiracy disappeared like a dead leaf before a wind.

Our advance southward was slow, owing to Mr. Carew's wound, and suddenly spring, which often in that latitude makes unkept promises, began to breathe upon us with south winds. Tender blades of grass sprang up amid the dead stems of last year, and a faint tint of green appeared on the foliage. I looked at the beautiful land rolling so gently over hill and valley, the brooks of clear water, and the noble forests of oak and hickory and beech; and Underwood, following my eye, swept his hand in a wide curve.

"This is too fine a country for our race to lose," he said, "and I know, too, of none better for the making of a man's career."

His eyes met mine directly now, and his look was most meaning, but I shook my head. He sighed slightly, and was silent.

Joe Grimes and others had gone on before, and we found our fame ready for us. The skill, courage, and quickness of Underwood were praised by all, and he had ample repayment for the measure of contempt which once was given to him. I too, it is said, had borne a part second only to his, and my denials seemed only to increase the emphasis of the statements. Mr. Carew was applauded as a hero who had received a desperate wound in a successful endeavour to cover the retreat of his comrades, and soon he brightened visibly, for he loved praise. His confidence returned, and he speedily became his old complacent self, ready of speech and courteous of manner. Jasper met us at Lexington, and his joy at the sight of Mr. Carew, alive and wrapped in glory, was quite wonderful to see. He wished that he could boast of such honourable scars; it had been a painful thing for him to stay behind, but necessity was the step-mother of choice, and he was the sufferer, yet the knowledge of Mr. Carew's achievements almost repaid him. It was all hollow to me, but Mr. Carew's delight was manifest, and soon the attention of Underwood and myself was not required by him, as he found ample pleasure in the society and flattery of Jasper.

I went with them to Danville, where I saw Mr. Carew restored to his daughter and wife, as Rose Carew had been restored to her father and mother. She said but little to me then, but asked me not to go to the Ohio before seeing her again, and I promised.

CHAPTER 25 For Honour's Sake

Sprinq was in the air when Rose Carew and I walked together on the border of the little town that was to be the capital of the new State. There had been a brief period of peace among us, a rest before beginning anew the struggle in the Northwest. Not a breath of the Spanish conspiracy came to our ears. It seemed to be dead.

Mr. Carew was recovering from his wound, and his most faithful attendant next to his daughter was Jasper, who knew now all his moods, and, without fail, anticipated them.

I had been thinking of Osseo, and how he was waiting at the Ohio, but after my promise I could not go until Rose Carew sent for me, and now I had come. She seemed to me somewhat changed in these later days. I missed the humour and varying moods that marked her in our first flight through the wilderness. She was graver and paler, and yet she had passed through much to make her so.

I had heard for some days the voice of the wilderness calling in tones that would not be denied, but now as I walked with Rose Carew in this new and beautiful land just given to the uses of man, I heard another voice calling too. I was not by nature the wilderness hunter; the forest had its glory, but so had the homes of men. I was not one to scorn honours, and I loved to gaze upon the beautiful face of a woman.

The sunshine was like gold in the clear air, and the houses glittered under its rays. Slender columns of smoke rose and seemed afar like silver spires. All around us stretched the noble country. I felt the influence of such a scene, and I saw that she too was touched by it. Her lips were parted a little, and the red in her cheeks deepened.

"Yes, it is beautiful," she said, divining my thoughts.

"Almost too beautiful for one to leave," I answered.

"One need not leave it," she said.

We were silent for a while, and then she continued, somewhat as if speaking to herself:

"Pride is a fine thing to have, and often it may serve to keep one's honour clean, and again it may make its possessor stubborn, and blind his eyes to the right. I knew a man once to whom a great wrong had been done, and his heart was filled with bitterness toward those who had done him the wrong. He left his home and came to this new land. Soon he became known on the whole border for his valour in defence of the defenceless, and all loved him. When there was any great service of danger and daring to be done they sent for him, and he never refused. A girl was taken from her people and carried into the far Northwest by the savages, and this man followed to rescue her. When naught else could avail, and the Indian chief made the suggestion to him, he gave himself for her. He was rescued, but when he made that sacrifice he did not know that he would be."

"It is a fable," I said. "The man is a border boaster. He merely claimed to have made such a sacrifice in order that he might rise in the favour of the rescued girl."

"It is not a fable," she said. "He made no boast of it, but tried to keep it a secret. She learned of it from another. She did not at first know of the great injustice that had been done to this man, and when she heard the story of the charge against him, and which he did not deny to her, she felt aversion toward him. She could not help it, because she believed then that the charge was true."

She faced me now, her eyes gazing into mine, and I felt that she was like one who had come to a confession and was resolved to make it. I would have stopped her, but I could not.

"But she continued to watch him," she resumed, "and when she saw his deeds and the sacrifices he made for others she felt that whatever he may have done, it was in a moment of rash and heedless youth, and his was now a great nature, all the nobler because of what he had suffered."

"It was her generous heart that made her think so," I said. "Men often wear false faces, and because of his fancied service she saw him not as he was, but as she wished him to be."

"Not so," she said, "She saw him better than he saw himself. She would have him take all the rewards which other men covet, and which might be his if he would seek them. Perhaps no wish would be denied him. But his pride stands in the way, and there he wrongs himself and others."

I had no answer then to make her. The note of the wilderness was silent at that moment, and I heard only the voice of my own kind calling to me. It was, in truth, a most beautiful land in which to live and be happy. I looked at the oak groves and the rolling hills in the tender green of young spring, and then at the tall girl with the luminous eyes, and I thought that never before had the homes of white men seemed so fair.

"You do not know how many friends you have here," she said presently, "and I now owe you two great debts of gratitude—one for myself and one for my father. Oh, I have heard how you rescued him at the ford, and I have heard how you and Mr. Underwood saved our little army from destruction and turned the day."

"My friends are overkind," I said. "It was Underwood who did it all. My part was no more than that of any other."

"Those who were with you do not say so. Kentucky is filled with your praises. None sings them louder than Mr. Underwood, who is sure to receive great honour from the State. Why should you refuse the same reward?"

Then she painted a picture which was in truth most beautiful, though I knew it, too, to be most dangerous. It was the same story that Underwood had told me, and the colours were the same, but there was something else in her voice of which he could know nothing, and it was that which I dreaded most. I asked myself how any woman could ever hold in her heart the man who does not keep his honour clean. The thought decided me, and I was about to tell her that I should depart the next day for Osseo at the Ohio, but she, seeming to divine the nature of what I would say, exclaimed:

"No, do not give me your answer now; I shall have more to say presently."

Then she changed, and the change was so sudden that it took my breath, while I admired. She became again the piquant, elusive girl whom I had known in the forest, with all her variable moods and merry humour, speaking of one topic, and then flitting to another like a butterfly on the wing. I felt my blood leap under the influence of her gaiety, but I soon noticed that she talked most of the East, of old places and people whom I knew, touching here and there upon the things that were vital to me and which I loved most, arousing in me such a longing to see it all again, and to see it when she saw it, that I was forced to put myself in bands of iron.

Then she stopped suddenly.

"Now I must go back to my father," she said, "and I wish to see you again to-morrow, Mr. Lee, if you will come. But first I have another promise to exact of you. Go to the inn to-night. Some one who wishes very much to see you will be there. No, don't ask me who it is, but go."

Of course I gave such an easy promise; and that night, shortly after sunset, I sat in a little room at the inn with a thick-set, large-faced, stern-lipped man, of whom I had heard often, but whom I now met for the first time. It was Isaac Shelby, one of the heroes of King's Mountain, a valiant patriot and defender of the border, who by almost unanimous consent was now about to become the first Governor of Kentucky.

"We are well met, Mr. Lee," he said. "I have long heard of you, and I have heard good only. But now to business, understanding, of course, that what we say is in the confidence always existing between gentlemen."

I bowed. In truth, he was wasting but little time upon preliminaries, though his welcome to me was warm, and all the more grateful coming from such a man. He fixed his eyes upon me, seeming to mark every expression of mine as he spoke.

"You are a man of note in this region, Mr. Lee," he said. "You have a long claim upon its gratitude, and your fame is extending. Your rescue of Miss Carew was a most gallant affair, and your services in that last fight across the Ohio were great. Don't look embarrassed, man; I but speak the truth. And there is something else to your credit. I know of your visit to the school-house that night with Underwood, when you two faced the Spanish conspirators, and I know every one of them, too."

I felt a sudden fear for Mr. Carew, and the fear was because of his daughter. He was a stern man who sat before me, and soon great power would be in his hands.

"I knew that such an affair was breeding here," he continued, "and you need not think that it could ever have succeeded; doubtless you do not; I had some part in defeating the schemes of that wretch Wilkinson and his associates, and I could crush this, were it not dead already, with a single pressure of my thumb, for, as you know, I am about to become the first Governor of this State, which I mention merely as fact, and not through vain boasting."

"But these men are all repentant," I said.

"Those who have a chance to be so with one or two exceptions," he said. "The two lawyers are too much frightened ever to raise their heads in such an affair again, and Curry, who under certain circumstances might have been the most dangerous of them all, has died for his country's sake. Now there is Mr. Carew."

He did not take his eyes off me, and unless I deceived myself I saw a faint twinkle in them.

"But Mr. Carew is safe," he continued, "only he will have to be careful how he walks, despite the great credit he has received for that wound in the recent battle. When Kentucky calls upon him for service he will have to respond."

He spoke with emphasis, and his lips shut tightly together. I saw that Mr. Carew was in truth in a trap, and I could appreciate the grim humour of it all the more because it put him in a safe place.

"His daughter need not fear for her father," he said, and again I saw that faint twinkle in his eye—a twinkle that set me to guessing.

"And there, too, is your cousin Jasper," he continued. "I wish I could find some proof against him, but he has been too cunning. We should only weaken ourselves by proceeding against him. He is a bad fellow, Mr. Lee, for all his cousinship."

I was silent.

"And now for yourself," he continued. "You were one of those who denounced this affair. There you did us a service again, and we would reward you. I am not unaware of your past. Your pardon for mentioning it, but it was a necessity. Stay with us and you shall have one of the greatest offices in the gift of the Governor. You are a swordsman and a rifle shot, and if any one speak ill of you, warn him that he does so at his peril. Here in this land you are within a hedge of friends."

I was moved to the depths and I felt myself trembling. I would have remained then, when this offer so fair was made to me, but I was afraid of a woman's face. With her constantly before me I could not be true to myself, and I said again under my breath that the duty rested now more heavily upon me than upon most men to keep my honour clean.

"Then you will not stay?" he said, when I had given my answer.

"No," I replied.

"Not even if others should ask you?"

"Others have asked me, and I have given them the same answer, I do not think that I should stay."

"It seems a pity," he said. "We shall have troublous times here, and God knows that this community needs strong men."

"I shall have other work to do yonder on the border."

"Ay, that you shall, and I know that you will do it well. My good wishes attend you, Mr. Lee."

He gave my hand a strong clasp, and I left him, to find Osseo waiting for me at my lodgings. The chief had grown impatient, and he came now from the Ohio to find me. He asked me no question, but merely waited there in silent inquiry.

"We shall go to-morrow, Osseo," I said.

The next day in hunter's garb and with my rifle on my shoulder I bade Miss Carew good-bye. She looked at me steadily, and her eyes were full of reproach.

"What does this departure mean, Mr. Lee?" she asked.

"I return to the place in which I belong—the forest," I replied.

"And your promise to me back there across the Ohio that you would come to Philadelphia?" she asked.

"There are some promises which it is more honest to break than to keep," I replied. "What right have I to go to the East? What reply could I make to those who should ask me why I came?"

"But I asked you to come," she said. "Do not go back to the wilderness. Stay and live the larger life for which you are fit. Prove to all your enemies what you can be."

I shook my head.

"It is too late," I said.

"It is not too late!" she exclaimed, and her tone thrilled me in every fibre. "Won't you come? What does something that happened long ago matter now? Of what importance is it now whether you were innocent or guilty then?"

"Does it matter to you?"

"No."

Her eyes told me that she spoke the truth, though the crimson in her cheeks was deeper. She did not know now how much I was compelled to cast aside. The forest was calling to me in a yet louder tone of duty.

"Good-bye," I said.

"Will you go back to the wilderness?"

"Yes, I have no choice."

She turned and ran into the house, leaving me standing there like one dazed, and I felt to the centre of my heart that I should never see her again.

A friendly hand was put upon my shoulder, and the voice of Osseo, as low and sweet as that of a woman, said in my ear:

"The forest is calling to us, my brother."

"Ay, Osseo, I hear it; let us go."

We started at once, and soon were deep in the great Northwestern wilderness.

CHAPTER 26 Two Years Later

"You will find him in the fort on the hill yonder," said the man. "He has been there for the last hour talking with his officers."

Time had passed, and I was now in the village called Cincinnati, a little place in its fifth or sixth year, built of log huts and shanties according to the border fashion of making its beginnings. But it was a picturesque village set between high hills, and with the wide and deep Ohio flowing at its feet.

Before me was Fort Washington, its square logs rising to a height of two stories and glistening with whitewash, the mouths of cannon appearing at its bastions, while to the eastward stretched a well-filled garden and the houses of the officers, all forming an odd combination of war and peace.

I walked up the hill, full of my resolve, and came to the fort, where I was stopped by a sentinel, rifle in hand. I gave him my name and business, and when he reported them to those inside I was conducted to a large apartment, but ill lighted by a single window. A half-dozen officers were sitting about, and evidently they had been debating subjects of importance, as maps and papers lay upon a table. He whom I sought was on the far side of the table, a short, thick, rosy-faced man, dressed in a splendid Continental uniform, each garment arranged with such care that its wearer could have been called dandyish, and might have been depreciated by strangers had not the dignity of his manner and penetrating gaze forbidden it. A three-cornered hat with a great rosette upon the side lay at his elbow.

I distinctly saw a sneer upon the faces of several of the officers as I entered and was announced, and the most pronounced of all was that which disfigured the countenance of my cousin Jasper. But I treated such insolence with the coldness and scorn it deserved, and kept my eyes fixed upon him to whom I came. He rose to his feet at the mention of my name, gazed fixedly at me a moment or two, with an expression of surprise changing rapidly—yes, I could not mistake it— to one of pleasure. Then he came forward with a quick, nervous step, and holding out both his hands, cried:

"It is the same John Lee who was by my side that night on the rocks at Stony Point!"

I took the two hands that he offered me, and he must have felt mine tremble as they clasped his own. He knew all the old story, and yet he never hesitated.

"Good old Jack Lee! Brave Jack Lee! Where have you been all these years?" he cried. "They told me in the East that you were dead, that you had been killed somewhere in the woods by the Indians. Out upon such a lie; 'twas past believing! 'twas impossible! What, the warm-blooded youth whom I used to know, the lad who never feared death, slain, obscurely, by breech-clouted savages! 'Twas a lie I believed then, and I know it now! And you have come here now, Jack Lee, to help me in this pass!"

I was looking into the honest and steadfast eyes of Mad Anthony Wayne—what a pity many others were not affected with his particular kind of madness!—and I knew that I stood, as I had hoped, in the presence of a man my friend once, my friend yet—and always. He gave me ample and immediate proof.

"Gentlemen," he said to the others, and there was a touch of warning in his tone, "John Lee, of the Continental army, one of its most gallant and meritorious officers; one who never flinched in a desperate cause—I who was his comrade ought to know—and who, as some of you perhaps remember, was most unjustly accused and condemned of an infamous crime, but whose innocence all the world shall yet know—gentlemen, Mr. Lee!"

Then he presented them to me one by one, some bowing slightly and coldly, others with more warmth; and last of all was Major Carew—he was a major now—smiling and self-collected as of old.

"We are no strangers," he said as he took my hand. "I owe him much, and, moreover, we are comrades of the field."

I saw that he had no fear of me, expecting me to spare him if he would spare me. He was safe from words of mine, but my chief reason was not the one that he had in mind.

"None, general, can be more glad than I to meet Mr. Lee. This is the man who saved my daughter from the worst fate that may befall a woman," he continued.

"'Twas like honest Jack, brave Jack," said General Wayne. "He ever had a weakness for the fair sex, and while willing enough to lay down his life for his country, he was more than willing to lay it down for woman, beautiful woman."

I was sorry that the general's warmth of commendation carried him quite so far, but 'twould have been a shame to complain. Major Carew merely smiled.

"General Wayne gives you a character concerning the ladies which youth does not despise, and which in my own time I was anxious to have," he said.

I was not thinking then of his words, but of Rose Carew. Where was she? In Kentucky or in the East? Married, doubtless! What else could I expect? Still I asked no question about her. General Wayne poured wine; he seemed to be in an excellent humour; we had been loyal friends once, though he was the superior in age and rank, and, thank God, were yet, as I could see; and, lifting his glass of wine, he said again, with that note of warning in his voice:

"Gentlemen, drink with me to the health of honest Jack Lee; to the lost who is found; to John Lee, late captain of the Continental army, and now captain in Wayne's army of the West."

All drank more or less, and I stared at him in amazement. He put his hand upon my arm as in the old days, and said, in the gentle and winning way that he knew so well how to assume:

"Jack, dear old Jack, will you not oblige me in this little matter? I have power here to give you the commission, and you know how badly I need men like you. This is to be a most arduous campaign. We are to fight a hidden foe, and you, they tell me, know more about the wilderness and its ways than any other man living. Underwood, your new member of Congress, vouches for it too. Now, good old Jack, don't say me nay."

It was he who was doing the pleading; it was I who was to grant the favour—it was Mad Anthony's way. There was water somewhere at the back of my eyes, but I let it come no further, holding it meet that I should bear myself as a man without emotion. I saw at that moment the deepening sneer on Jasper's face, but it did not have power to touch me; I knew far worse things of the smooth and silky villain than he thought of me, and I took now a firm resolution, the precise opposite of another I had taken that time when a woman's voice and eyes spoke to me. The friendly touch of an old comrade's hand and the welcoming sound of his voice aroused a hope that I might reconquer that former world which I had believed dead for me. The others began to say their adieux, Major Carew giving me his hand again ere he went, and then I was alone with Mad Anthony. He pushed me into a seat and bent upon me a look of grave reproach.

"Jack, it was wrong of thee," he said, theeing and thouing me after the fashion that he sometimes adopted with me in the earlier time, learned perhaps from his Pennsylvania Quaker brethren. "Thou shouldst have outfaced 'em all. It was a lie, and your friends knew it. There was Buxton, of the Jersey Horse, who fought a duel in behalf of thee, running his man neatly through the shoulder. I should have fought one myself had my rank permitted it. I repeat, Jack, it was wrong of thee—wrong to thyself and to thy friends."

"Nay, general," I said. "What else was left to me? The evidence was against me, and the verdict of the court. I was lucky in not being hanged—or perhaps unlucky. I say again there was naught else for me to do but to hide myself and my honour."

"Ever the same stubborn fool!" he said with vehemence. "But we knew that you were innocent, Jack, and by all the gods that are in the mythology—Greek, Roman, Egyptian, and every other kind—it shall yet be proved!"

I shook my head.

"Nay, general," I said; "I expect to keep the stain, faded a little, perhaps, by time."

"And I maintain that you shall not!" he said, smiting the table with his fist. "I would have you to know, sir, that I am commander here, and when I say a thing shall be done it will be done."

I was about to speak, but he turned upon me with a sudden change of tone.

"Nay, Jack, don't tell me anything," he said. "I heard but vaguely about the trial, but I sha'n't believe you guilty, even if you swear that you were. As your friend, not as your commander, I now entreat you not to say another word upon that subject, but to come to the reception to my officers and myself to-morrow night at the residence of Mr. Converse, and to come, too, in your uniform as captain. Montrose, my aide, will furnish you with the uniform."

Not pausing for an answer, he knocked upon the door of an adjoining room, and Montrose, an honest-faced man of six- or eight-and-twenty, came forth. General Wayne introduced me as one of his new captains, and whether Lieutenant Montrose knew my history or not, he gave me a hand grasp that was warm and sincere.

"Now, Captain Lee, I leave you for the present in the care of Lieutenant Montrose," said General Wayne. "Don't forget that I expect you to-morrow night at the house of Mr. Converse."

I could do nothing but continue with Montrose, while General Wayne closed the door upon us. In my soul I was deeply thankful to Mad Anthony, but knowing no way to express my thanks to him, I determined to attempt none. Had he not taken such advantage of me I should have refused to go to the house of this man Converse, but I suddenly asked myself, "Why should I not go?" The kindness of General Wayne seemed to open new ways for me; I would go! The glimpse of friendly faces had set the old world to calling in a louder voice than ever, and I was in a mood to heed its note.

An errand took me from the town into the forest an hour or two later, and I did not return until the next day, but I was in time for the reception to be given to the officers of the army by Mr. Converse, hastening at once to my new friend, Lieutenant Montrose, who was ready with the uniform, a spare one of his own that sat upon me well. It had been years since I arranged a toilet with such care, but I felt now with great force the need of making a good, even fastidious, appearance; and when I contemplated the result in a small handglass I felt a reasonable degree of satisfaction. It is true that I was almost as brown as an Indian, but, after all, tan is not unbecoming, and while I had been reckoning myself old I realized with sudden force and delight that I was young. A small but tempting voice whispered in my ear, "You are young enough yet, John Lee, to win back honour and happiness," and I felt come over me a sudden glow like the memory of a lost joy that may be brought back again. All young soldiers are dandies, and I had been such in my time, but I saw that my forest life had not injured me; instead, it had given somewhat more flexibility, as the youthful military officer is likely to be a stiff figure.

When the inspection was finished I clapped upon my head a gorgeous cocked hat, and buckled by my side a fine sword that General Wayne himself sent me, and thus accoutred I felt ready for the social fray, howsoever fierce it might be, at the house of Mr. Converse, although I fancied that its nature could not be very grave in this little backwoods town. Still, it was a great step for me, inasmuch as I had not taken part in any such affair, not even of the humblest kind, for years, although once extremely fond of them, and I felt my heart beating like that of a youth about to make his first venture upon the floor of a drawing-room.

"Let us go together," said Montrose, linking his arm in mine in most friendly fashion. I was soon sure that General Wayne had been talking to him about me, and his naturally good heart accounted for the rest of his geniality.

He hung a lantern upon his other arm, as Cincinnati was too early in its infancy and too far in the wilderness to be provided with any lighting at night save that of the moon, which is of a most inconstant nature. 'Twas thus that we approached the home of Mr. Converse, a place of some pretensions and considerable size, built of logs and oak boards, and showing many corners and angles. However rude a house so constructed may seem to some, it is truth that such primitive abodes in the West often shelter people of breeding and quality. Many families of the finest education and manners are among those who went over the Alleghanies, risking the perils of the wilderness and Indian wars, to find homes on the lands of the West, which are richer than those of the East. Hence I knew that, despite appearances, I should be in no mean company. In truth, as we approached we saw several carriages in front of the house, which stood on the crest of one of the lower hills, while boys bearing torches like the link boys in the East were running about, and lights were glittering in every window. We beheld already, even before entrance, a scene of pleasing bustle and gaiety, and again I felt my youth, for, as I have said before, I liked these things, and still like them. The background of wooded hills, yellow, winding river, and wilderness added the picturesque touch that was needed, and I began to feel most glad that I had come. Montrose saw my face, and he said:

"You are right, Lee. As an officer of General Wayne 'tis your duty to be present, and 'tis well when duty and pleasure go together."

CHAPTER 27 Old Faces in New Guise

We reached the house, entered, and our names being announced, we found in truth a brilliant company present, glittering with many of the gayest fashions of the East, golden epaulets, and laces and shawls of India, and gold and silver shoe-buckles, and other such adornments, to which my eyes had been a stranger for years. Moreover, the wooden walls of the house contained much mahogany furniture dragged painfully over the mountains from New York or Pennsylvania.

I noted my reception with curiosity and a prepared stoicism. It was of a mixed nature, some showing warmth and others holding aloof, but none dared to offer insult, since General Wayne, who was the first to-greet me, had so evidently constituted himself my champion, while Major Carew came forward to salute me with even greater warmth. Jasper himself did not risk more than a sneer. He had regained his position in the army through powerful influences, and now, ranking as a major, had come West again with Wayne. I wondered why he ventured a second time upon such dangerous ground; but here he was, in a most resplendent uniform, and beyond a doubt confident of his position and himself. My gaze lingered on him for a moment only, passing on to an honest, square, and ruddy face—in truth, the face of Winchester, whom I had thought in England. We gave each other that silent hand clasp which speaks so much, and then he said:

"I concluded to make one more trip in the fur trade, and I have brought Mrs. Winchester with me. She is in the next room, and you shall see her presently."

There was a small matter of wine to be discussed by the gentlemen, and then Winchester, hooking his arm in mine, said he would take me into the adjoining apartment and present me to the ladies.

So many lights glittered in the drawing-room that at first they quite dazzled me, having been unaccustomed so long to anything of the kind. But I heard the words of Winchester as he presented me to his wife, and then, my eyes clearing, I saw her. She was a young Englishwoman of the familiar type, quite as ruddy as Winchester himself, very blonde and handsome, and watching with delighted curiosity the incidents so strange to her that she beheld in the American backwoods.

"Mr. Winchester has told me ten thousand things of you," she said in the deep, low voice which is among the finest possessions of Englishwomen. "I wonder if they are true?"

"I should like first to know what they are before I vouch for them," I replied.

She laughed, and said:

"I will tell you of them another time, but now I wish to present you to some one else."

I looked up and it was Rose Carew—but not the Rose Carew that I had known in the forest. Then she was a simple Western maid fleeing with me through the wilderness and seeking to save life and honour; now she was the woman of quality in splendid raiment, and bearing herself as one to whom tribute was due. I seemed to be further from her than I had felt on that day when I believed I could win her and had put the chance aside. I was for a few moments without the power of speech, and there was a mist before my eyes. I had thought that I should never see her again, and now I saw her, but she stood there, a stranger.

"Am I forgotten, Mr. Lee," she said calmly, "and will you not take the hand that I offer you?"

I recovered my presence of mind and took her hand. Then my old facility of speech came back—'twas said when I was a youth that I knew what sounded sweet in a lady's ear—and I made her the handsomest compliments that my tongue could fashion.

"You have become a soldier now, Mr. Lee," she said, "and all soldiers are alike; it is a large part of their business to make pretty speeches to ladies."

I disclaimed any intent of flattery, and she continued in this vein for some time, reminding me more and more of the world that I had left behind in the East. She scarce alluded to those tense days when we fled together from the savages, and I began to feel that she had changed in more particulars than one; she had grown more splendid and beautiful, but she was thinking little now of us in the West. It was a painful impression, although I knew that I had no right to feel pain. A sudden chill came over me; the sense of comradeship which had existed between us seemed to be gone forever; certainly I had no right to claim its restoration. I was sorry for a moment or two that I had entered the Converse house, and then the feeling of stubbornness which is often such a bulwark came to my relief. I had resolved to hold my head erect before all men; I would do so before all women too.

I could not monopolize her attention, and soon I yielded my place to another, she letting me go without show of either joy or reluctance, but saying that we should be sure to see each other again before the evening reached its end. I came to the conclusion—and it gave me a pang—that she would rather forget our acquaintance, and it was wholly in reason that she could wish to forget that last interview.

If Miss Carew's welcome was cool, not so was that of others. I had friends, warm friends, present, who knew that I needed championship, and they came quickly to my relief. General Wayne gave me his especial help, and spoke more than once of my services to the border in such terms that modesty compelled me to enter a disclaimer. Winchester and his wife, too, repeated my praises, and there also was young Harvey, now serving in Wayne's army. I saw that Mrs. Winchester was already a prime favourite in this little frontier settlement, and her influence was great; she was likely to prove the most efficient of all my champions. Major Carew, also, had not abated one whit from his warm and friendly manner—in truth, as in our earlier acquaintance, I wished that he would be a trifle less effusive—and with the aid of such allies I felt that I should have sufficient courage and resources to maintain my position. Then, despite Rose Carew, I began to feel a warm glow about the heart. There was much present to appeal to me. I was with people who came from the world to which I had belonged, and all the old chords in my nature were touched; mingled with this and stronger than before was the returned knowledge that I was yet a young man, and the reconquest of the world that I wished seemed not impossible. Perhaps my faculties for such lighter affairs as these were strengthened and refreshed by their long disuse, but I felt that I was bearing myself well and that I did not suffer in the passages of words. Once Winchester whispered in my ear, "Keep on as you have begun, Lee."

But to whomsoever I was talking or whatsoever I was doing I kept a side look on Rose Carew. The fancy that she was not the same girl whom I had known in the forest returned to me with increased force: then she was in every respect simple and unpretending; now she practised all the arts of the finished coquette; she seemed to crave attention—of a certainty she had it; apparently she wished all the men at her feet, and they were there; and despite myself she drew me toward her with as much strength as the simple forest maid had ever done—yes, more.

Jasper approached her presently. I thought that she would turn from him with repulsion, knowing as she must know what he was; but her brightest smile had been saved for him, and soon I heard their voices laughing together at some quip or jest of his. I turned my eyes away with a feeling of anger and a great sinking of the heart. If such deeds as his were to achieve the greater reward, one might well lose faith, not only in the justice of man but in that of the Supreme Power. Yet it was unreasonable of me to find fault with her for believing Jasper's tale about his presence among the savages, since it was a most plausible one, and evidently had deceived the American officers.

I found that my reputation as an expert in forest lore and combat had reached nearly all the people present, and soon I was called upon to tell about the savages whom Wayne was going to fight for the sake of protecting the border and cleansing away the disgrace of St. Clair's defeat. I was surrounded by a group and I was compelled to describe with some detail the ways of the Indian, and the dangers that white troops going against him were bound to incur.

"What cruel beings they are!" said a lady.

"It is true," I said, "but they are savages, and such are the ways of savages. There are some men among them far more guilty than the Indians."

"Who are they?"

"The renegades, white men who have turned Indian," I replied—I had introduced this subject purposely, because Jasper was near, and could hear—"white men who have joined the vices of their own race to those of the red man, and who scorn the virtues of either. The blackest souls in the world are among them—Girty, Blackstaffe, and others not so well known."

I let my eyes fall upon Jasper, but he met my gaze firmly. In truth, I must say that the man was a perfect actor. He laughed lightly, and then said:

"I can vouch for the accuracy of Captain Lee's statements. When I was captured by the Miamis just after St. Clair's defeat I was compelled to pretend that I would join them in order to save myself from being burned at the stake, and then I saw Girty and Blackstaffe—and horrible scoundrels they were—ugh! the memory of it is like poison to me yet!"

He gave a shudder of repulsion, and the ladies murmured their sympathy. 'Twas most effective, and yet I was not sorry to have reminded him of the episode, as I wished him to bear in mind that while he was armed against me I also was armed against him. In a few minutes he was playing Miss Carew's most devoted cavalier, and search as I would for signs of dislike on her part, I could find none; to all his jests and small talk she listened with close attention, and when he made a point her smile and laugh were forthcoming as a matter of course, and at the sight my heart again became most heavy. She was forbidden to me, but I could bear it better to know that she was in the arms of any other man than Jasper. When I saved her from Hoyoquim I did not save her from a worse fate. My opportunity to talk with her came again soon, and it was but to receive a rebuke.

"Why did you speak with such point of renegades in the presence of your cousin?" she asked.

"You know before the telling, Miss Carew," I said, resolved not to be evasive. "Surely you can not have forgotten how he walked in the Indian village with Girty and Blackstaffe."

"No, I have not forgot," she replied; "but how can I know that he was in truth and reality a renegade? You only say so, and you seem not to like him."

It was bitter to me to hear her words, because I saw now that Jasper had made her believe me to be the villain and himself the martyr, and I do not know what reply I should have made, but there was a murmur and buzz just then near the door, and my chosen comrade and loyal friend Osseo entered, looking the chief and magnificent warrior that he was.

Osseo, though he played the Sphinx on most occasions, was quite subject to human emotions, and he always had a keen eye for the approval of the ladies which I hold to be not unbecoming in him. Therefore he had some very splendid toilets, and I had never seen him looking finer than he was that night. There was not in the whole assembly a man of more dignity and presence—not Mr. Converse, not Major Carew, nor General Wayne himself.

The colour affected by Osseo that evening was dark blue. Such was the tint of his head-dress and of the little eagle's feather symbolizing the chief rising from the centre of it. The short blanket which hung in folds from his shoulders was of blue, and of the richest texture. His deerskin leggings and moccasins were of light blue adorned with a multitude of little beads and porcupine quills, most of which were dyed a darker shade of the same colour. Around his waist and inclosing his tunic was a broad belt of similar hue, beautifully worked and containing his tomahawk and hunting knife, both with polished horn handles. When I add to this that Osseo was six feet three inches high, with massive shoulders, and a waist as slender as a woman's, you can easily conceive what a figure he made.

There were little cries, half of terror and half of admiration, from the ladies when the splendid Indian entered, and some of the men who knew him went forward to greet him. But Miss Carew was the first to meet the warrior, and I noticed how much warmer his reception was than mine. In truth, she took his hand in both of hers, and told of her pleasure to see him again.

"You gave me my life, Osseo," she said, "and I can never reward you."

Then she proceeded to make a great commotion over the chief, although 'tis not for me to say that he did not deserve it, in which pleasant work she was assisted by most of the other ladies. They hovered around him like a covey of partridges, and the ingenuous red man, with a taste for which I give him credit, made no effort to disguise his pleasure—these Indian chiefs, like white men, know well when they are being made heroes of, and, like white men, they enjoy it. I begrudged Osseo his place for a moment or two, and then I was ashamed of myself for such unworthy thoughts. Truly I should wish my best friend success equal to his desert.

Yet Osseo a little later was the cause of some embarrassment, which fortunately was witnessed by but two or three; 'twas when Miss Carew had joined Winchester and his wife and I was approaching, drawn, I suppose, like the moth to the flame. Then Osseo gave Miss Carew and me a benignant smile, and asked of me, with a significant look at the lady:

"When does Lee take the White Rose to his wigwam?"

Winchester and his wife looked embarrassed, while Miss Carew turned scarlet from neck to brow. I thought it best to take his question as a jest and I replied:

"The White Rose, Osseo, has never yet signified her willingness to go to my wigwam."

"Why is Lee so foolish as to ask her?" said Osseo with great earnestness. "Let him take her first, and then if he choose ask her when she can make no answer but yes. Lee is a great warrior, and she will soon be happy in his wigwam."

I was quite confounded. The savages are usually very plain and blunt in the matter of speech, which has its advantages at times and at other times is most awkward; but I replied:

"'Tis not our way, Osseo, and the customs which the white man has practised so long he can not change."

He shrugged his shoulders as if still believing that the red way was the best, and Miss Carew soon gave me her shoulder, letting me see most plainly that the incident was not to my service. Presently she was with Jasper again, and I withdrew into a little room set aside for the men. There chance placed me next to Major Carew, and it was my impression that his large ambition and worldly views were unchanged. His wife, she whose piteous face had sent me upon the arduous quest, was dead a year and a half, and having come back to Kentucky again to look after his lands, he had found it incumbent upon him as one of its beneficiaries to join in Wayne's expedition for the relief of the border, at least in its preliminary stages.

He was a man of position, wealth, and reputation, and certainly he would expect his daughter to make a match with one of similar importance. He was yet under fifty, with a youthful, ruddy face.

Major Carew seemed to feel his daughter's indifferent bearing toward me. The weight of obligation rested upon him and he sought to make amends, speaking for himself with such warmth that my own sense of discomfort increased. I wished to be exactly like other men, and not one whom it was necessary to address in an apologetic way, as if he desired to like me and did like me despite the effort that it cost him. He said much of the Western country, its beauty and fertility, and the rapid growth that would attend it when the Indians should be conquered.

Jasper entered the room while we were talking, and turned his back upon me, which I thought decidedly preferable to his face, but he soon wheeled about and showed me a countenance expanding with triumph. He was firmly convinced, so I felt, that he was making good progress with Miss Carew, and was quite willing to let me see his satisfaction because of it. Jasper in the worldly sense was certainly a good match for her, as Major Carew could not fail to know. But I was silent, not wishing to reply to him in any form or fashion, and I realized that, despite the favour of General Wayne and others, I should have difficulty in maintaining my position in the army. Now that the first step had been taken, this made me all the more determined to go on to the end of the road upon which I had started.

I walked with Mr. and Mrs. Winchester to the two-story log house which they occupied for the present, and each of the two men carried a pistol in his pocket, as the wilderness still converged so close about Cincinnati that a prowling Indian might seek in the darkness to take a scalp and then dash to the woods with it.

I seemed quiet and sad to them as they accused me of being in a gloomy state and rallied me upon it, but I made some trivial reply and disclaimed any such feeling. Then they spoke of Miss Carew, her beauty and her grace.

"It is reported that she will marry Major Jasper Lee," said Mrs. Winchester, "and she seems to have a mind for him; but I do not trust the man. The heart in him is not right, or his eyes lie. Yet she will marry him, unless some other bold wooer defeats him."

But I inveighed against women, saying that with a few exceptions, such as Mrs. Winchester, they were of a heartless nature, and overfond of conquest.

CHAPTER 28 The Prize of Skill

It was not the intent of General Wayne, having conferred honour upon me, to let me live a life of leisure. He had been selected by the President for one of the most onerous tasks ever allotted to man—the conquest of savages inhabiting an unbroken wilderness half as large as Europe and the protection of a border a thousand miles long. He was to do this with three thousand raw troops, reenforced by a few hardy frontiersmen, while the fierce savages, flushed with their great triumph over St. Clair, roamed the forest at will, as elusive as phantoms, but incessantly striking here and there when least expected, and keeping the entire border one line of flame and blood. Such was the work that now lay before Mad Anthony, and I was soon to know that the iron soul of this man, the most daring and sanguine general of the Revolution, sometimes despaired, though it was only for a moment, and none but the officers nearest him knew it.

The Government was weak and its means were small, but it did the best it could, sending troops which, as in the case of St. Clair, were poor, while the Kentucky militia rallied nobly to the common cause. Major Carew had brought a detachment from Kentucky, which he was incessantly drilling, while I was set to work with some of the raw recruits from the East, Osseo standing by, and regarding me with a mixture of amazement and amusement.

It was the third or fourth day after my arrival, and I had my men upon the little parade ground teaching them the sort of open-order tactics we expected to use in our forest campaign, a more flexible discipline than that of armies intended to act against a white enemy in the open country, and despite the perversity of my exceedingly independent troops, I found a very keen pleasure in the task. I had done this often ten or twelve years before, whipping awkward York and Jersey countrymen into shape for combat, and the old work brought back to me the light feelings of former days. I have noticed that there is nothing so effective as a familiar occupation to restore the average frame of mind. Thus I was engrossed in my task, shouting orders at my men, and telling them not to do the things they were doing, when I noticed that Osseo had the company of other spectators. They were Miss Carew, Mr. and Mr. Winchester, Jasper, and a young officer named Lawless, who was much with Jasper and whom I did not like.

I left the men presently and joined the spectators, Miss Carew receiving me with the same unconcerned manner that had marked her before. We talked somewhat of the coming campaign and its prospects, and young Lawless at length commented upon the fact that I was now a drill master.

"I should think of you, Captain Lee," he said, "in any other rôle than that of a teacher."

It was a pointed and gross insult, when my history is considered, and I had no doubt then, as I have none now, that Jasper suggested to him this line of conduct. I had expected, situated as I was, to encounter sneering remarks, and I merely replied, though with intentional point:

"There are many of us, Mr. Lawless, who need teachers."

He said nothing, restrained perhaps by the presence of the ladies, and I was of a mind to let the matter pass, but presently, when he found an opportunity to speak to me in their absence, he said:

"I should resent your insulting remark were you or could you be on an equality with me, but all here know what you are and have been."

I saw that he was merely a snapping little puppy, set on by the larger dog behind him, Jasper, and I was able to reply quite calmly:

"Then, Mr. Lawless, you should charge that fancied inequality to your good fortune, for if we were to fight I should most certainly kill you. I give you this warning in order that you may not force a quarrel upon me. You can ask Major Lee there if I was not known as the best swordsman in the Continental army, and every frontiersman in Cincinnati will tell you that I am at least as good a shot as there is in the West. I say these things to you not as a boast, but as simple facts, lest you risk your life rashly."

He turned pale and his under lip whitened. I fancied that he was beginning to find the baiting of the bear not the delicate sport of his hopes. But Jasper hastened to his relief.

"Come away, Lawless," he said. "I doubt whether you could insult Captain Lee."

"He could not," I said with emphasis, "nor could you."

They turned their backs upon me and swaggered off together; but as I have alluded to the baiting of the bear, I foresaw that more sport of the kind would be attempted, and I was of a mind that those who tried it should suffer. Of a certainty I should not turn the other cheek; I fancy that the authority of the Bible was intended for particular cases, and not for general practice.

As we were leaving the parade ground, the drill being finished, Miss Carew came over to me and said:

"You will, of course, fight that man who insulted you?"

I was surprised at the question, likewise at her emphasis, but I replied that such was not my intent.

"How can you maintain yourself in General Wayne's army if you do not resent such attacks?" she asked.

"Do you really wish me to retain my position in it?"

"You saved me from the savages, and I would be ungrateful if I did not desire your advancement."

I think that "gratitude" and "grateful" become at times the most hateful of words; they can stand sponsor for so many things which one would like to credit to another cause; so I could answer only with a shrug of the shoulders, and at this moment Winchester and his lady joined us.

I heard the next day that young Lawless was assailing my reputation with great assiduity, but having no wish to pose as a duellist or to foment broils at a time when union was necessary, I let the matter run for the time being; and I noticed that the officers were soon divided into two camps concerning me—one which gave me the cold shoulder, and the other which received me as a welcome addition. Old Joe Grimes came at this time from one of his scouting expeditions, and the pugnacious borderer, true to his instincts, seemed to think that I had lowered myself greatly by becoming a soldier.

"I thought you were too good for that, Lee," he said. "Soldiers don't know anything; and to think of you putting on a uniform! It's like a chief in a petticoat."

He shook his head more in sadness than reproach, and would not be pacified; yet he was forced to admit that General Wayne showed some evidence of common sense, and was undertaking his business in a more promising manner than any other general who had come to the West.

Miss Carew was still in the town, and so far as I could learn had no intention of returning soon to Kentucky. It was now said that she purposed to go with Major Carew to our advanced post, Fort Greeneville, far to the north, and noticing the extent of her influence over her father, I was convinced that she could get his permission if, in truth, she wished to go; nor was General Wayne himself, though no longer a young man—which, however, is no bar—at all impervious to the smiles of fair young womanhood, and I felt sure that she could obtain his consent too.

I was certain now that Rose Carew had become what would have been called in the Old World lady of quality; at this little frontier village she reigned a belle, and though there were present many young army officers who knew the best that the society of the East offered, she could call any of them to her feet when she chose. It was evident too that she enjoyed admiration; I do not undertake to say that such a feeling is not natural in a young girl, but it may be carried a trifle far, I think.

Although we were very busy with drill and preparations, there was time for amateur gaieties, and I managed to procure for myself a new uniform, attired in which I sometimes hung upon the outskirts of the festivities and held short converse twice or thrice with Miss Carew. Upon such an occasion I told her that it was my intent to go once more to my old haunts in the East when the present campaign was finished. She gave me an odd look, and then said in a tone that was quite without expression:

"You told me once that you would never go back."

"I have changed my mind," I said.

"It is always one's privilege to do so."

"I shall come to see you there," I said boldly.

But she did not answer.

We had target shooting the next day on the hills back of the river, this being a most necessary practice for the recruits from the East, and General Wayne as an incentive had offered some prizes for which all might compete. 'Twas natural, too, in such a small place, that the civilians should come forth to see, and among them were Miss Carew and Mrs. Winchester. Two or three rude benches had been fitted up for these spectators, and the rest of us stood about watching the shooting. Jasper was present, and constituted himself the shadow of Miss Carew, making comment upon the marksmen, not all of which was flattering. I kept aloof, although Winchester and his lady were most friendly and would have me come and talk with them, but I had small fancy for Jasper's company.

The chief prize was a tiny silver bugle, and of course the ordinary soldiers had no chance whatever to win it in competition with the frontiersmen, although two or three of them entered. Nevertheless, the test excited much interest, and I learned presently that Jasper would make a trial. It was Winchester who informed me, and he added:

"He is sure to win it. Major Lee is a fine shot, and he is anxious to distinguish himself in the presence of the ladies. I don't know that I like him, and I would beat him if I could. He means to give the prize to Miss Carew."

His last statement contained suggestion, but I did not accept it, and presently they began to shoot at the targets. As Winchester had foreseen, Jasper soon proved himself superior to the others, but the competition was still open. A test of this kind is always sure to arouse my interest, and I joined the group about the marksmen.

"Why do you not enter, Captain Lee?" asked Mrs. Winchester. "Mr. Winchester has told me marvellous tales of your skill with the rifle."

"The skill was his once, but he lost it," said Miss Carew.

I looked steadily at her. I was surprised that she should speak such words, and also that she should speak at all. But I would prove them false, and take from Jasper the pleasure of presenting her the prize, and from her the pleasure of receiving it at his hand. An orderly quickly brought me my rifle, which even as an officer I had not abandoned.

"Then you really have the courage to try?" said Miss Carew as I took the firelock from the man.

"Miss Carew," I replied in a low voice, for her tone had cut me, "you should be the last to ask me such a question."

She reddened and for a moment her lip quivered. Then the look of cold pride which she now wore habitually returned, and she said:

"You need not remind me of the past, Captain Lee. I do not speak of it now because I am not able to express to you the greatness of my debt."

Then she began to talk to Jasper, who had just made a splendid shot, drilling out the centre of a sixpence at forty yards.

"Don't let him beat you," whispered Winchester. "The man loves to triumph over anybody, and most of all over you."

I nodded to him and asked them to move the target back a considerable distance, which being done, I also drilled the centre of a sixpence. Osseo, in the brilliant garb which he always wore in the village, was near me, and he uttered his satisfaction at my shot.

"Lee shoots straight while pretty squaw looks on," he said.

"Well, Osseo," I replied, "would not you do your best under the circumstances?"

His eyes twinkled, but he said nothing.

Jasper equalled my shot, and so did old Joe Grimes, whereupon the target was moved back yet farther, and Grimes failed, but both Jasper and I hit it fair and true.

"Your cousin is also a great marksman," said Miss Carew to me.

"You wish him to win the prize?" I said.

"I wish it to go to the one who deserves it," she replied.

I may not boast, but the shooting that had been done was really child's play to me, inasmuch as I had a natural gift for marksmanship, and it had been trained by a lifetime of practice. So I asked one of the soldiers to take a sixpence and toss it in the air at a convenient distance. Jasper frowned at this; and young Lawless, who was near him, said in a low voice something about me, all the words of which I did not catch, but it was of the purport that a man with my history ought not to be allowed in the contest. I saw well that I should have to punish Lawless for insolence, and I made a silent note of the matter.

"Proceed," I said.

The soldier tossed the sixpence in the air, and I sent a bullet through its centre before it touched the ground. The frontiersmen and the soldiers gave me much applause, and so did Mr. and Mrs. Winchester. Miss Carew made no demonstration. "She thinks that Jasper is beaten," I said to myself, "and she does not like me any better because it is I who is about to defeat him."

Jasper made some demur about the test, claiming that it was most unusual, but the officer in charge would not listen to his grumbling. So the sixpence was tossed up a second time; Jasper fired, missed, and the prize was mine.

"You have won," said Jasper, turning away and shrugging his shoulders, as if that which I had won was not worth the winning.

They gave me the prize, and I, knowing well that it was the custom upon such occasions for the winner to present it to a lady, did not hesitate, as I had made up my mind beforehand. I took the silver trifle and, placing it in the hand of Miss Carew, said:

"Will you accept this from me? Even had my opponent won, I think that it would have come to you."

"Is that why you offer it to me now?" she asked.

There was, in truth, a question in her voice as well as in her words, and I replied:

"No, I offer it to you because it is mine to offer, and because it is you whom I wish to have it."

She took the trifle, but with only a word of thanks, and then all of us left the parade ground, the sport being over. I believed that my gift had embarrassed Miss Carew, and I was sure that Jasper, Lawless, and two or three others would insist that I, a man with a black page in his history, should not have had such an opportunity. For that reason I rejoiced at my action.

Winchester escorted the ladies, and as I walked toward my quarters Lawless brushed by me and again made supercilious remarks, half under his breath, which he could claim were or were not meant for me, as he chose. But I did not intend to allow him such latitude, and I seized him by the arm.

He demanded in most indignant tones that I unhand him, but I retained my grasp.

"Mr. Lawless, you have purposely and with malice made yourself offensive to me on two or three occasions," I said, "and I warn you that its repetition will be dangerous to you. I told you the other day what I could do with weapons. You saw just now my ability with the rifle. Look at that squirrel in the tree across the ravine."

He looked in spite of himself, and drawing my pistol from my belt, I fired. The squirrel dropped from the tree, dead.

"Now come into the room of Captain Hardy," I continued, "and I will show you what I can do with the sword."

As my hand was still upon his arm, there was nothing for him to do but to comply, and Captain Hardy at my request produced two swords.

"Here's your weapon," I said, thrusting the hilt of one into his hand while I took the other. "Now touch me if you can; I promise not to hurt you."

He gave me a look of rage, and thrust at me with the sword, but I caught it upon the blade of my own, and with a twist of the wrist drew it from his grasp. It fell ringing upon the floor.

"Do you wish to try again?" I asked.

He was furious, and, snatching up the weapon, ran at me. But the sword was drawn from his hand a second time, and was thrown against the wall. He made a third attempt, and the result was the same.

"I hope you are now convinced," I said, "that if you seek a quarrel with me your life is mine to do with as I choose. Do not seek that quarrel, and let us be friends."

He shook my hand, though with small grace, and hurried off to his quarters.

CHAPTER 29 A Feathered Message

I slept in a small log-hut on the fringe of the village, the rooms in the fort being limited, and Osseo now and then shared my quarters, but oftener passed the night in the woods upon some mysterious errand, coming into Cincinnati or leaving it as he chose. I knew that if he received proper treatment, his dignity being considered at all times, he would prove of great value to the commander, and General Wayne showed good understanding in the matter. Osseo visited him more than once at his quarters, and they were long in secret consultation.

"The Black Snake[24] is a great chief," he said to me after one of these conferences. "He will not ride into the forest on the shoulders of his men."

One morning, about an hour before daylight, I was awakened by a light sound at the door, as of something striking against it. I was alone, and one trained to forest life is suspicious of every noise; so I sprang to my feet, and seizing my rifle, rushed out. No one was there, and the sound was not repeated, but when I glanced at the door I saw by the wan light an Indian arrow buried deep in the wood, the feathered head still quivering with the force of the impact. It had been discharged from a bow, bent by a man of great power. That I knew at the first glance, and I cast about me for some point at which the bowman had been hidden. Then I remembered a clump of bushes inside our lines and at a considerable distance from my cabin, but not so far that a man of unusual strength might not reach it with an arrow. Moreover, an Indian of great daring could creep at night into the clump of bushes and then escape unobserved, save by the most watchful sentry.

It would have been the impulse of a man without experience of wilderness life to rush for the clump of bushes that he might catch or at least pursue the bowman; but I knew that the savage, ere the arrow left the bow, had glided back into the impenetrable forest, and I knew, too, that the missile was not sent in search of a human target; it was a sign, a signal, a message of some kind from somebody, and to me.

I looked thoughtfully at the arrow and the little black feathers still faintly quivering in the head of the shaft. Then I bent down and examined these feathers more closely. They were small and black, a jetty hue, but they were from the wing

---

[24] The Indian name at that time for Wayne; they called him after his victory "The Storm," or "The Tornado.

of the eagle. Now I knew. It was the arrow of Hoyoquim, the Black Eagle, the Wyandot chief, the man who had held Rose Carew in his power, and who beyond a doubt was seeking to hold her there again. He had been in the clump of bushes, and I knew it as well as if I had seen him when his mighty brown arm drew the bow.

My heart sank with a sudden dread for Rose Carew. She was a wilful woman, and she was going with us to Fort Greeneville, our most advanced and dangerous post, far into the Indian country, where naught save strong arms and strong hearts could protect her. She might fall again into the hands of Hoyoquim, and then there would be none, neither Osseo nor I nor any other, to save her. I had a bad quarter of an hour, after which I took my resolution. I would put the case to Rose Carew in such manner that she must change her purpose and stay behind.

I made haste to find her while still hot with my plan, and I had not far to seek. She was sitting alone upon the portico in front of Mr. Converse's house. All our early builders of pretentious homes in the West followed the Greek styles of architecture, and were fond of columns and pillars, of wood most often, but painted white to resemble marble. As I saw her sitting there among the white pillars, and herself in white, she seemed to me more than ever out of place in the Indian-haunted wilderness, a flower whose home was in the peaceful and cultivated garden, and not in the wild woods. It was impossible for me to change again this sophisticated woman into the shy maid who fled with me through the forest. And yet I was not willing to lose either.

I had expected to be received with coldness, and the warmth of her manner, while a surprise, pleased me more than I am willing to confess. She gave me both her hands—an impulse I thought it, due perhaps to a sudden memory of the days we had spent together in the forest, for as I saw her now she was a woman of variable moods.

"You are in your uniform, your true uniform, Captain Lee." she said. "I told you long ago that you should return to your place in the world, but you would not believe me then."

"You were right and I was wrong," I said, "and while I rejected your advice at the time, I am wise enough to accept it now. I mean to win back my old position. When this campaign is finished I shall return to the East."

I spoke with decision, meaning that she should understand me clearly, but she was silent, nor could I draw from her looks either approval or disapproval of my words.

"'Tis, however, a matter of small importance compared with another of which I shall speak to you," I said, "and if I have ever served you in any wise I pray that the memory of it will make you give some heed now to what I say."

"Tell it to me," she replied, neither by word nor tone making any promise.

"I hear that you intend to go with the soldiers to Fort Greeneville. I ask you not to do so."

She bent upon me a look of inquiry—a look that was without surprise, as if she had half divined my question before the utterance of it.

"Do not go," I repeated. "Fort Greeneville is far in the Indian country. None can ever tell what will happen when opposed to such a numerous and active foe as the northwestern savages. Remember the fate of St. Clair's army, and your own narrow escape. You know that the Indian chief, Hoyoquim, will seek to recapture you. There is no place in this column for a woman."

"But other women are going with it?"

"Not such as you."

"Their lives are as precious to them as mine is to me. Besides, my father is going. Should I not watch over him and tend his hurts if he is wounded? Is it the custom of our border women to shrink from danger? I shall go to Fort Greeneville with the army."

"Even if I beg you not to do so by the memory of your former dangers?"

"I shall go in any event," she replied firmly. "It is now for me to make a request of you, Captain Lee. Do not seek to persuade me against my will. My reasons for going, perhaps, are good."

"I can not accede to the request," I said.

"And I can not accede to yours; so I am not more obstinate than you," she said.

Then I told her of Hoyoquim's arrow, its obvious intent as a threat, and the extent of the danger to be dreaded from the chief's wily and tenacious character. But I could not shake her in her purpose, and I could not alarm her either with the threat of dangers to be incurred, or with reminders of those past. "I shall go," she would say, and she seemed to me to show a resolution most singular when time and circumstance are considered.

"Would you have me to be less brave than other women, who you say are of a lower grade than I?" she asked,

She smiled upon me for the first time since the conversation took this course, and then, shifting the subject, she became again the girl of the wilderness, my wood nymph, simple, unaffected, speaking of the dangers that we had shared, and from which I had saved her. It was but a brief glimpse of this Rose Carew that she gave me; then she was the woman of the drawing-room once more, talking wittily and brilliantly of social life in New York and Philadelphia, and speaking with the ease and familiarity of one who was in the heart of it. I felt her power; she had been able in former days to call up with vividness that larger world to me, but now she made the reality itself pass before my eyes. I was seized with an inextinguishable longing to become a part of it again, and take my ancient place there, and I knew even then that it was she, however unconsciously, who was most potent in drawing me on. And she did so all the more because hers was now an elusive character to me. I seemed to meet her here and there, and my mind touched hers, but it was only for a moment; then she was gone, and I was left in the air.

"My father and Major Lee are coming," she said presently.

"Then I shall go," I said.

But she bade me stay, and I passively waited, while her father and my cousin Jasper walked side by side along the footpath that led up the hill to the house.

Major Carew greeted me again with warmth, a warmth that seemed to me slightly in excess of reality, and Jasper nodded coolly, as was his wont.

"What do you think your cousin has been asking me?" said Miss Carew to Jasper.

"Nothing that he should not, I hope," replied Jasper stiffly. I fancy that he did not like her use of the word "cousin" when speaking of me, though he used it at times himself, and perhaps I had as little reason as he to be pleased with it, though far from resenting such a use by her.

"That I do not go with the column to Fort Greeneville," she said, supplying her own answer.

"Miss Carew rejects my advice, but I am sure that I am right," I interrupted, and I related again the incident of Hoyoquim and the arrow, Jasper and Major Carew listening intently. I glanced at Jasper as I came near to the end of my story, and I saw his lips turn quite white. I knew full well that he saw the shadow of Hoyoquim across his path.

"I think that Captain Lee judges correctly," he said when my tale was finished. "You should not go to Fort Greeneville, Miss Carew, as beyond a doubt you would be in great danger there. It is not even sure that you are free from it here. And, moreover"—his air growing gallant—"if you stay here I may be able to watch over you."

She looked at him in surprise, not seeming to take his meaning. But I could have sworn that I was reading the processes of Jasper's cunning mind.

"It may be that I shall stay at Cincinnati when the army advances," he said quite coolly. "This is a sort of base for us, and it is likely that I shall be put in command of it by General Wayne. I should prefer to go on and meet the savages, but in war one must obey."

His manner seemed quite real, and, I was sure, deceived all but myself. But he changed the drift of the talk quickly, leading it upon lighter matters, and addressing himself more particularly to Miss Carew. Jasper, as I had often noticed, was not without a certain, charm for women. He possessed a power that seemed to draw them despite themselves, and now I observed with pain that Rose

Carew hearkened closely to him, his conversation being of that light nature pleasing to a woman. I saw, too, that Major Carew looked upon Jasper with approval, particularly when Jasper was speaking to his daughter, and I recalled with a sudden sinking of the heart that there were no reasons why he should not; to any one who did not know him so well as I he might in very truth seem most desirable. My own position was of the lowest when compared with his, but when one has been battered about much by Fortune he sometimes reaches a point where fresh blows, instead of shattering, merely harden, and my resolution grew stronger as I matched myself anew with Jasper in the contest apparently so unequal. Jasper and I left the house at the same time, and when we were yet within hearing of Major Carew and his daughter he tapped me on the shoulder with an appearance of great friendliness and said:

"Let us walk together, John; there are some matters which I wish to discuss with you."

I signified assent, and side by side we strolled down the path. Almost any one beholding the two men proceeding in such manner might have taken them for the best of comrades.

We passed on until our figures were lost to the observers at the house, if there were any, and I waited for Jasper to lead the way to the topics upon which he desired to speak with me. We were upon a slope of the hills which inclose Cincinnati, and a beautiful spectacle was spread out at our feet—the clustering houses of the little town almost hidden in the foliage, the broad and curving flood of the yellow Ohio, and beyond it the dark green mass of Kentucky, hidden in its deep woods, with the silver thread of the Lacking winding through.

"John," said Jasper at length, "I think it well that we should know each what the other means."

"The knowledge is already attained," I replied. "I do not believe that either is mistaken about it."

"Whatever your crimes may have been," he said with some appearance of passion, "I have never taken you for a fool before. But now what else can you be? You, a convicted traitor, a broken man, an exile in the woods, to pretend to the hand of Rose Carew! Withdraw from such an absurd position and I shall help you all I can to regain your old name. You know this border warfare, and your services here may be an offset. I am not without influence in the East, and a good word for you there can go far."

Long and silent meditation in the woods may give one the power to read the hearts of men, and I believed that his thoughts then were not unknown to me.

"If I am so low and my rivalry is so preposterous," I replied, "why, then, do you fear it?"

He winced a bit, as if I had made a hit, and then he replied:

"You have some claim on Miss Carew's gratitude, and that, as you well know, is a strong influence upon the mind of a girl."

I felt the hot blood coursing through my veins, but I was able to restrain my temper, responding, I think, with a fair degree of coolness:

"Cousin Jasper, you and I often look at the same thing in a different way, and for that reason perhaps you are unable to understand that it is impossible for me to remind Miss Carew of such a thing as gratitude."

"Your folly is greater than I can understand," he said, affecting not to notice the point, "and I give you fair warning that if you presume to oppose me in my dearest wish I shall fight you with all the weapons at my command. Having an inclination to spare your feelings, I have said very little concerning you here. But I shall not be so considerate now. I make no bones about it. I shall let everybody know what you are. As you yourself are aware, you are not fit for the society of gentlemen."

"Gentlemen of your kind—certainly not!" I replied.

We walked on together, and the chance observer might still have thought that we were the best of friends, as he kept his temper admirably, and I was careful never to raise my voice above its usual pitch. But he uttered further threats, and on the whole I was glad to hear them, preferring this open declaration of war to a false politeness. When we parted I was aware that I was likely soon to encounter unpleasant incidents, but I was quite resolved to give him blow for blow, and my mind glowed with the strength of its hostile purpose.

CHAPTER 30 Hot Heads and Cool

These was no immediate military duty for me to perform, and I went to the little cabin which I occupied with Osseo, and staying there awhile, turned over in my mind the events of the day. The chief was gone in the forest upon some errand of his own, probably one of those scouting expeditions that he loved, and I was alone.

I had spoken to Jasper in hot blood when I made my boast that I would fight him to the end; but now, when I sat in silence and the heat was gone from my veins, I felt a sense of despair. Could I surmount such obstacles, and if I could, should I? Was I not right that day in Danville when I turned from the welcoming light in Rose Carew's eyes? I wondered if I had become a worse man than I was then. But the absence of that welcoming light now, her very elusiveness, as I have said before, drew me on. It is an old tale that we want most that which we can not have, and crushing down all compunctions, I resolved to follow the course that I had chosen. Nevertheless, my deep depression continued, and although I would not have had it so if I could, I felt that it were better had I never seen her; then I might have continued my way in the woods, content with a life which, however different from the old, was not without its allurements. "Ah, Osseo," I said, "you are the truest and most unselfish type that I have met. You alone have been faithful to me in the face of everything!"

I did not hear a step in the cabin, but felt a heavy hand upon my back, and a cheerful voice cried in my ear:

"John Lee giving himself over to a fit of the blue devils! I never saw you, lad, at such a business before. What ails you?"

It was Winchester, and I was most glad to see him. I could never look upon this Englishman's honest, ruddy, and open face and not feel that I had another friend as trusty and stanch as Osseo himself. Although he could not but be familiar with the tale about me, he asked me for no syllable of defence, and never showed by either word or deed that he was so much as conscious of it.

Then he sat down and told me the gossip of the little town. The advance to Fort Greeneville would take place very soon, and it was now known to all that Miss Carew would go with the column, and for the matter of that Mrs. Winchester also would accompany us, as he expected to take her with him through the Indian country on his way to a British post near Lake Erie. He had no fear of the savages, the British being on excellent terms with them.

He talked so gaily and brightly, retailing the news of this little frontier town, that all my cares fled away like a mist before a fresh wind, and then, when he saw that I entered into his spirit of lightness, his own face took on a shade of gravity.

"I think I should warn you, Lee," he said, "that your road is likely to grow a trifle rougher, and that, too, pretty soon."

I divined at once that my good cousin was at work. Well, he did not delay with the task that he had set himself, and on the whole I was not sorry. When one is expecting a hard fight he does not like to linger.

"I heard that fellow Lawless say something about you as I came up here," continued Winchester.

"And naturally you inferred, as I should have done in your place, that it was prompted by my cousin, Major Jasper Lee," I said.

He was silent, not wishing to deny it.

"I have been fighting in one war or another since I was sixteen years old," I said, "and I have no impulse to shirk it now."

"Nor would I if I were you; the sooner an inevitable trouble is brought to an issue the better." And then, with a sudden apparent change of the subject, "there is to be a gathering of officers to-night at the quarters of Captain Romney—General Wayne allows a little relaxation now and then, wisely, I think—and almost all the men whom you know will be there; some who are civilians, too, myself included. Romney told me to ask you in his name to come. You'll do it, won't you?"

I saw that he wished me to accept; I saw, too, that he expected my situation there to be made unpleasant, but would have me go despite it. This confirmed me in my determination, and I replied promptly in the affirmative.

"Then wait here, and I'll come by about dusk for you," he said.

I thanked him with a look for his friendly act, and in the afternoon when I went upon the parade ground to drill my little troop I felt a certain exultation at the sense of coming conflict.

When the time arrived I made a most rigorous toilet. In my early and callow years I may have been somewhat of a dandy, which I take to be a harmless vanity, it being better to err upon that side than rush to the other extreme, and to-night I felt a return of the old fastidiousness. I brushed my uniform, not a bad one in itself, with utmost care, and I tied a very full and flowing neck ribbon in a fancy knot at my throat. Then I saw that the sword at my belt made a correct angle with my body, and I was just putting on my buckskin gloves when Winchester entered.

"On my soul, Lee," he cried, "you snuff out a civilian like myself as if I were a cheap tallow dip! May I indeed have the honour of going with you, or shall I remain here overpowered?"

"Shall I do?" I said, standing before him.

"Admirably. Faith, John, you are quite resplendent," he replied, and hooking his arm in mine, after the fashion of our time, he led the way to Captain Romney's quarters.

A friend of the worthy captain, an immigrant to Cincinnati, had built a large double house on one of the hills, and in the owner's absence our prospective host had been permitted to take it as his camp, a privilege to be valued, as General Wayne himself did not have a better place in which to live.

Lights were flashing from the windows of the house, and as we approached we heard the clatter of joyous voices, some of which were raised already to an unusual pitch. I should say here that our border armies always brought with them the virtues and vices of the East. We were then, as the nature of our lives made us, often a fiery and violent race. Officers were quick to resent real or fancied insults, and the finger flew quickly to haft or trigger. The duello, practised in all the polite world, travelled with the army into this immeasurable wilderness. General Wayne himself, with all his sternness, could not prevent it, and I remember that upon this very campaign two young officers scarce in their twenties quarrelled over a trifle, and fought with such fury that both were slain. Nor was this a solitary example. So I knew that if any trouble were to arise at the gathering I should be expected to make good my point of view with sword or pistol. I was not loath, and my hand unconsciously slipped to the handle of the weapon that hung by my side. The "feel" of it was good.

Captain Romney gave us welcome, my reception not differing from Winchester's, and I judged that the captain was willing to accept me as one of his brother officers without either coldness or undue warmth, with which I was content.

The two rooms of the cabin were filled with men, and Romney had made a brave and not altogether unsuccessful effort to reproduce Eastern splendour, or what seemed splendour in comparison with the border. He had decorated the place rather handsomely with furs and skins, spreading the larger out as rugs, and there were wine and cards for all who chose to drink or play, and if I knew my own time and race, most would choose both. Soldiers ever take their customs with them.

I saw Jasper in a corner laughing and talking in the most expansive manner, and near him his satellite Lawless, his face already flushed with wine. Not far away was Captain Hardy, and scattered about were nearly all the younger officers of our army. It was just such a scene as I had witnessed more than once in the days of the Revolution after the French came over to join us. But here the wilderness setting gave a different effect.

When time and place are suitable, one quickly resumes old habits which circumstance has compelled him to drop, and soon I was playing bezique at a table as carelessly as if it were not a dozen years since I had sat at the game. We played in one room and we talked in another. I was never a gambler by nature, merely hazarding a few shillings and pence for the sake of social feeling; and presently, when my wagers left me as I was at the beginning, I quit the table and went into the room where conversation was going forward. The older officers had gathered there, and were telling stories of their experiences, to which I was soon asked to contribute. There was an ancient tale of an escape of mine from the savages well known along the border, and growing unduly, perhaps, as it passed from one to another, which I was called upon to relate. Just as I finished the story a great burst of laughter came from the next room, where everybody was visible to us, the wide door between standing open.

We naturally looked up to see the cause of this laughter, which was followed by perfect silence, interrupted in a moment or two by the high-pitched voice of Lawless, whose face had grown redder under the influence of the cards and more liquor. The expression of his eyes indicated his arrival at the degree of intoxication which breeds utter recklessness, but the attention given him proved that what he was saying was not without interest.

"Believe me, gentlemen, it is most preposterous, but it is true," he said. "I swear it, and if my oath be not sufficient I can produce witnesses. Such presumption I never heard of before, but it only proves how shameless the fellow is. He was drummed out of the old Continental army for treason—cold-blooded treason. I have seen a copy of the records myself. How he escaped the rope I don't know, but they let him come out here in the woods to live with the bears and the Indians. Now, this fellow, as he enters the settlements, happens to clap eyes on one of our maidens from the East, a girl beautiful, rich, and among the best born. Instead of keeping his proper distance and admiring her from it as any dog might, he immediately pays court to her and sticks to her like an army to a besieged city— 'pon honour I'm telling you the facts—and I think the fellow ought to be driven back into the woods with the lash across his bare back, 'pon honour I do."

Lawless was a fool; moreover, he was drunk, and he was prompted by a far more cunning man, or he never would have made this speech.

There was a dead silence, and everybody began to look at me, for of course my story was known to all, and Lawless's meaning was too plain. It was broken a moment later by the clear voice of Jasper, asking:

"Are you quite sure of all that you say, Lawless? Have you yourself witnessed it, or is it a story that has been told to you by others?"

"My own eyes have given me the proof and yours have done the same for you," said the reckless youngster.

Again the ominous silence of expectation ensued, and now there was not a pair of eyes in the room, unless Lawless's be excepted, not bent on me. I saw that I could not linger in my reply, as the identity of Lawless's "villain" was too obvious; it was well for me to begin at once, but I felt a deep regret that Rose Carew should be mentioned, as there could be no doubt about the identity of the girl whom Lawless meant any more than there could be about mine.

I rose to my feet—I was glad that so many were looking on—and I walked to the table beside which Lawless sat. I do not boast when I say that I was quite cool, because I had prepared myself for such scenes.

"Mr. Lawless," I said, "you are a fool when you are sober, and you are a greater one when you are drunk, which you are now. You have attempted to insult me—not for the first time, be it said—and I have tried to avoid it, but I suppose that I shall have to kill you as a warning to those who are pushing you on."

I looked at Jasper here, and his face did not change; but I saw his fingers twitch.

"I did not call your name, Captain Lee," said Lawless, "but since the cap is such a fine fit for you, on your head it must sit. But I will not fight you. I have not yet sunk so low that I can cross swords with a condemned traitor."

"Perhaps then the Long Knife whose mouth is full of vain words will fight me" said a voice over my shoulder.

There was a start of surprise from everybody. Osseo had entered so quietly, and the attention of all was so thoroughly concentrated upon Lawless and me, that his presence was not noted until he spoke.

"The Long Knife is not a great man among his own people," resumed Osseo. "He is but that"—and he snapped his fingers—"and Osseo is a chief; he has looked upon danger as the Long Knife looks upon the face of a fair girl, and the ways of the white man are not his ways, but he will fight the Boy-of-big-words as he chooses, because he loves Lee, by whose side he has fought many good fights, with whom he has shared his last venison, and whom he knows to be such a man that the Boy-of-big-words can never be his equal, though he live more years than the oldest chief in all the woods."

Osseo spoke with the sententiousness of the Indian, standing perfectly erect, his tall form towering over all and his coal-black eyes passing defiantly around the circle. I saw that the chiefs words had made a deep impression. The Indian does not practise the duel in our set and formal fashion, and such an offer, coming in such a way, surprised the officers and pleased the more reckless.

"A duel with swords or pistols between an Indian chief and a lieutenant! 'twill be worth seeing," I heard one mutter.

But Captain Romney interfered, and I did not know until afterward that Winchester had been talking to him while Osseo was speaking.

"Yours is a noble offer, chief," he said, "and does credit to your friendship; but if there is to be a duel, Lieutenant Lawless must meet Captain Lee."

"But consider what Captain Lee is!" exclaimed Jasper, seeing the plan to disgrace me suddenly go wrong. "How can Lawless meet him?"

"I am the host here," said Captain Romney with dignity, "and I have already consulted with those who know the code. Lieutenant Lawless must meet Captain Lee, if the latter wishes it. All of us know of the charge against Captain Lee—a charge that unhappily ended in conviction; and yet there are many who still do not believe him guilty—I among the number, I am proud to say. Neither does our commander-in-chief. At any rate, Captain Lee is one of General Wayne's most trusted officers; as such no one can insult him and refuse him satisfaction."

A murmur of approval arose from more than half of those present, and I was deeply grateful to them. It seemed that wanton fate, the sport of which I had been so long, was determined now to make some amends.

"Do you insist that Lieutenant Lawless meet you?" asked Captain Romney of me.

"I do," I replied.

Lawless was silent. I think that the effect of his liquor was wearing off, and he turned ashy pale. He gave Jasper a furious glance, and then turned whiter than ever. He knew perfectly well that he was no match for me with any weapon, and either he must avoid the meeting with all the implication of cowardice or leave his life in my hands.

"General Wayne forbids duelling, but it is not my affair," resumed Captain Romney. "I have nothing more to do with it."

Then he turned away to a game of cards, and we knew very well that while he would make no preparations for the duel he would likewise be no tale-bearer.

"I fancy that the nicely prepared scheme of somebody has come to grief," said Winchester to me a little later. He, too, so I saw, had divined Jasper's plan, and I surmised that he was not without a hand in the spoiling of it.

While I had friends I also had enemies, and the company seemed to divide over me, making me an issue, a circumstance which I found very unpleasant, but which for the present I could not avoid. Lawless was playing cards noisily in the next room, and laughing frequently with an air of the most reckless gaiety. But his mask was transparent; his nerves were upset, and he plainly saw death before him. However, I had no intention of sparing his feelings; he had insulted me too grievously to be let off lightly; moreover, he was the willing tool in a plot, and I deemed it right that he should suffer such mental agonies. Jasper spoke only when he was compelled to do so, but he could not refrain from biting his lip, and I enjoyed his anxiety.

I stayed an hour or more after the quarrel, and then, when I felt that I could leave without forfeiting my self-respect, I said my adieux and departed. I sat at the window of our little cabin, it now being after midnight. Osseo, who came in later, also sat down near the window. By the clear moonlight I saw that he was smiling to himself, and I waited patiently until he should condescend to explain.

"White man great fool," he said presently. "He drinks much fire-water before he goes to fight his enemy; Indian fight his enemy, take his scalp, and then drink fire-water."

"So Lawless drank more after I left, did he?" I asked.

"Much! much!" said Osseo with great emphasis, and he raised his hand to his lips five or six times. "But white man again big fool; if young Indian wishes to prove he is brave, he does not attack the greatest warrior he can find. No, Manito has given him too much wisdom; he fights another young brave and passes the chiefs by until he is a great warrior himself. White man be as wise as Indian some day, and get what you call civilization."

He smiled at me in a quite superior way.

"I am sorry that I can't fight Boy-of-big-words," he resumed. "His scalp look well hanging here. Will not Lee give me the chance?"

He fingered his belt meditatively, as if Lawless's long auburn locks were already swinging there. But I knew that it was only a jest, as Osseo had long since given up the practice of scalping.

The news that a duel was to be fought caused a stir in the settlement the next morning. Everybody seemed to know it, except the commander-in-chief and his higher officers. I believed that the affair was likely to hurt me greatly in General Wayne's esteem, and would appear almost as a breach of faith, but I had no choice save to meet Lawless; stern methods were now needed.

I kept as closely to my cabin as possible that morning in order to avoid trouble, and shortly before noon, when I was alone, Osseo having gone to the camp, there came a light knock on the door. I called, "Enter!" and Rose Carew stepped over the threshold.

She gave me no time for surprise or inquiry, but exclaimed at once:

"You are to fight a duel, Captain Lee?"

I noticed that her face was flushed and her eyes glittering, showing excitement. But I bowed in answer to her question.

"You fight with Lieutenant Lawless?"

Again I bowed.

"I ask you not to fight this duel. You have done much for me; will you not do this also?"

I was surprised at her deep interest, her evident apprehension, and I sought a reason for it. Could it be that she cared for that red-haired chucklehead? He seemed a poor choice for such a woman, and yet I knew that the most brilliant women often choose the most ridiculous men with whom to fall in love. I looked straight into her eyes, but she did not notice my gaze, standing there, nervous and eager, awaiting my answer. Then it was true, she did care for Lawless. I had felt the most profound contempt for him, but now I honoured him with my hate.

"I can not make you the promise you wish, Miss Carew," I said, shaking my head. "My position here would be untenable if I did not meet Lieutenant Lawless."

"That is true," she said with sudden comprehension, and then she looked down and wrinkled her eyebrows as if in thought. When she looked up again her expression had changed entirely, as only a woman's can in so brief a time. She gave me a most intoxicating smile, and I, though knowing well that she was smoothing the way to ask something else, and though calling her under my breath the boldest of little deceivers, smiled back. I was angry at her while I smiled.

"Now you are yourself, the brave hunter who saved me, the best-natured man in the world," she said with a little laugh.

"But I am not good-tempered at all," I protested. "On the contrary, I am morose and obstinate."

"Oh, no, you are not; you may give yourself a bad name, but others refuse to accept it. You can not hide behind such a false reputation in order to refuse me what I ask."

She smiled upon me again, and so bewilderingly that I felt myself without the heart to refuse her. I was a fool, although knowing it.

"If you fight with Lieutenant Lawless you will not kill him. Will you not make me such a promise?" she asked.

Now, it had never been my intent to slay Lawless, but when she asked me that question I felt a sudden desire to run my sword through him. A woman must be blind indeed, or excessively brilliant, to love such a man. But I would make her show her feelings more plainly.

"You wish very much that I should spare him?" I said.

"I do indeed."

"Then his life is most dear to you?"

Her eyes met mine firmly.

"Do you think you have the right to ask me such a question, Captain Lee?" she said.

I was somewhat confused, but I replied:

"Ah, well, it seemed to me that you should not have a monopoly of asking."

She laughed.

"Your point is fairly made," she said, "but you will promise, will you not, Captain Lee, to let Lieutenant Lawless escape with his life?"

"It has never been my intent to take his life," I replied, not willing for her to think that I had yielded to her intercession alone.

"Then you do give me the promise!" she cried, ignoring my meaning, and she looked so joyful that my heart smote me for the feeling of hatred that I bore toward Lawless. I was about to say more, but she hurried from the house.

I watched her light figure descending the hill, and then I reflected seriously on our conversation. My blood was cool now, and I became convinced that she could not really care for Lawless in the way I had feared. It must be Jasper, wishing to save his tool, who had sent her. He was the man, and my belief did not improve my feeling toward him.

CHAPTER 31 A Red Actor

A young officer named Myers came to me in the afternoon, saying that he was Lawless's second, and would arrange the terms of the duel with any one whom I chose. I had expected Jasper to act for Lawless, but second thought showed me that he would avoid it. So I named as my second Winchester, who accepted at once. I offered to fight Lawless with swords, since every one knew my vast superiority over him with the rifle or pistol, and I saw the look of relief on Myers's face when I named the weapons, although Lawless himself had felt my swordsmanship. I left the rest of the matter in the hands of Winchester, promising to abide by all his decisions, and after a conference they told me that we could not meet for two or three days, as all of us would not be off duty at the same time until then. So the matter of the date was left open for the present, and, to tell the truth, it was almost driven out of my mind by a piece of news that Osseo brought me an hour later. Our Government was engaged, after St. Clair's defeat, in several futile and, I think, rather shameful efforts to treat with the savages; but then the Government was light in resources and heavy in responsibilities, and there was some excuse. Now an answer to one of our missions was coming, and Hoyoquim was the chief bearer of it, so Osseo said.

I felt a thrill at the idea of looking into the eyes of my old enemy in such a manner, and I was stirred, too, by Osseo's report that Mechecunnaqua was no longer the head chief of the allied tribes. He had been shorn of much power by his enemies. This was good news for General Wayne's expedition, as Little Turtle was a great general, by far the ablest among the savages, but I felt a sense of personal regret, too, at his deposition, as I had received nothing but kindness from him.

The embassy from the savages, composed of five men holding the rank of chief, arrived that afternoon. There is no human being more dignified than the Indian when he comes under the flag of truce on a mission to his enemy, and Hoyoquim and his comrades of a certainty bore themselves as if the world and its whole fruitage were theirs. All the tribes were mightily puffed up over their victory at the Wabash, perhaps not unjustly, and the efforts of our Government to treat with them but seemed to increase this swollen pride, an inevitable result which a President and Congress many hundreds of miles from the border could not see. I was curious to know what reception Jasper would give to Hoyoquim, and I noticed that he kept to his quarters with singular pertinacity. I chanced to be near him when he first heard of Hoyoquim's coming, and his lips became like ashes. That was the only sign; he held his countenance otherwise, and doubtless it was noticed by none else, yet afterward he invented excuses, some of them very feeble, to remain in his tent.

I was present with General Wayne when he received the delegates with all the formality and courtesy due upon such occasions. Hoyoquim and his comrades were arrayed in the extreme of Indian splendour, gay headdresses, red or blue blankets, hunting shirts, leggings and moccasins of bright-coloured buckskin, adorned with many-coloured beads, and their bearing was both haughty and condescending. It was evident to those who knew the ways of the savage that they came not to treat with an equal, but to announce their terms to an inferior. It made my blood hot to see them assume such an air, although I knew that we had given them good excuse for it. Hoyoquim was the spokesman of his party, and after he and General Wayne had smoked the pipe of peace and exchanged the usual compliments he turned to me, extending his hand.

"It is my brother Lee," he said. "I offer him my hand in the white man's fashion."

"And I take it as it is meant, Black Eagle," I replied. "You are a fair and open foe, which I can not say of some white enemies whom I have."

His eyes flashed an inquiry, but I gave no explanation. I half suspected that he guessed the man whom I meant most of all. When I was escorting him a little later to a tent set aside for him he saw Rose Carew. It was only a sudden glimpse. She was walking some distance away with Mrs. Winchester, but not all the bronze of his skin and gaudy paint could hide the gleam of savage delight and anticipation that swept over his face. I knew Hoyoquim's intent and his ruthless tenacity, and with a momentary faintness at the heart I recognised the danger of Rose Carew, which she herself would not see. But Hoyoquim uttered no word until we reached the tent. Then, when he and I were alone, he said:

"Lee, the white maid who was once my prisoner is again with the army of the Long Knives. 'Tis Manito who brings her back that she may sit in the lodge of Hoyoquim and call him her warrior."

"Not so, Hoyoquim," I replied. "You are cunning and swift and strong, but it is not the will of God that she shall ever sit in your lodge."

He gazed at me without resentment.

"You love the white maid," he said, "and so does the other Long Knife whose name, too, is Lee, the false dog whom we shall yet burn at the stake, but I will take her."

He spoke with the most absolute confidence, and I shuddered at the possible fate of Rose Carew. There was nothing that I could do, save to watch over her with redoubled vigilance, and trust to Osseo for the rest.

General Wayne entertained the delegates on the evening of the second day at his quarters, seeking perhaps to impress them with a view of white civilization and its power. All the chief officers in their best dress attended, and the ladies came too, drawn partly by curiosity and partly because any kind of diversion was rare in a frontier town. There was a dinner, some dancing, and a little playing by the ladies upon the harpsichord and spinet to the accompaniment of their voices. Jasper was present—I had seen to that myself, with a little suggestion to the general that, as Jasper had been among the Indians, he might be able to assist with advice; I am not unwilling to confess to some malicious pleasure in the suggestion. I also managed it in such manner that Hoyoquim and Jasper met suddenly and almost face to face, and this time Jasper was so little master of himself that he became deathly pale, and for a moment or two was in a nervous tremble. But Hoyoquim was content with a veiled threat.

"Your skin is white again," he said to Jasper, "and it is well, for now I know you best."

Rose Carew's manner at the sight of the chief was wholly different. She seemed to have no fear of him—or is there a quality in woman which prevents her from dreading any man whom she knows to admire her?

"He is in truth a striking type of the savage race," she said to me, I chancing to be near her at that moment.

"Ay, of a race that has brought much woe to the white women of this country," I replied. There was wrath then in my heart against Hoyoquim, and a little, too, for her, because she would not see how greatly she ought to fear him, and instead wasted upon him words of admiration, though I think, in truth, that she spoke in all innocence.

Osseo too came presently, and he had not been less sparing of adornment than Hoyoquim. My Indian comrade had the vanity of dress and that love of colour which is an instinct with the primitive races. To-night he glittered in reds and blues, and the beads upon his garments flashed in a dozen tints under the flare of the candles. He was, as I have often said before, a magnificent specimen of his race in physical development as well as mental endowments, and he and Hoyoquim made a striking pair. But they could be coupled in name only, as I was conscious at once of a deep animosity between the two. They exchanged only a single glance, but it was so full of hate that I was startled. I wondered at the cause of their enmity, but I was not sorry for it, as such an ardent foe might thwart any attempt by Hoyoquim.

When Rose Carew played the harpsichord and all of us gave our applause, I saw again that look of complacent triumph on the face of Hoyoquim, and I longed to have him before my rifle in the forest.

The formal courtesy with which the chiefs had been received reigned throughout the evening. General Wayne and his staff, acting upon the advice that had been given them, never abated a jot from their dignity, nor did the savages. They drank wine which was presented to them with great gravity, not smacking their lips nor giving any other expression of content. But I thought a little later that I saw Hoyoquim's eyes sparkling, and I believed that, despite his will, the wine had crept into his blood—savages yield much more readily than we to the influence of liquors. Osseo, with superior judgment, touched no wine, and even the youngest and handsomest of the women—my comrade was never insensible to beauty—could not induce him to do so. "White man's medicine red man's poison," he said briefly to Rose Carew, though with no intent of impoliteness. I repeat that Osseo had a keen eye for beauty, and he proved it by devoting himself with all a red dandy's gallantry to Miss Carew. When next he had a chance to speak to me unheard by others, he said with that faint, almost invisible smile of his:

"Lee should not get jealous and blame me. I can not help it. The white maiden is a sun, and she dazzles me."

"It is not I whom you have to fear, Mr. Son-of-the-evening-star," I replied, meeting him in the proper spirit, "but the Wyandot chief and the Long Knife whose name is the same as mine."

"Let them meet me in the wilderness," he said with a sudden flash in the eye, and now I knew that he was not indulging in easy trifling. "I pray Manito that the day may come quickly."

Thus proceeded this singular entertainment, in which the most primitive and the most advanced of our country met on an equal footing, and I saw more than once the mounting fire in Hoyoquim's eyes. I believed that his surroundings and the wine together were having some influence upon the Wyandot chief, and I watched him with eager curiosity. Presently one of the ladies hovering about him—he seemed to have for them the fascination of the snake for the bird—asked him to illustrate some custom of his race, following the lead of the whites who had sung or played. Hoyoquim was not loath, and while his eyes sparkled he replied:

"It shall be as you wish; our ways are not your ways, and Manito alone knows which are better."

But it was obvious enough from Hoyoquim's tone which he considered better. He spoke to his comrades, the centre of the room was left clear, and while they chanted in low, monotonous tones he danced the scalp dance, throwing the blue cloak from his shoulders and drawing from his girdle the tomahawk, through the horn handle of which he and I had once smoked the temporary pipe of peace. The subordinate chiefs never took their eyes from the face of Hoyoquim, bending upon him a look most intense and vivid, while he in torn, with the same concentration of vision, followed imaginary foes.

The scalp dance varies according to the tribe, and sometimes acording to the taste of the dancer. Hoyoquim gave to his all the tricks and adornments of his savage fancy, expressing ferocity, anticipation, triumph, and every other warlike emotion of his savage nature. His shoulders and arms were bare, and all the great, brown muscles stood out upon them as he bent and gyrated. It was no secret to me that Hoyoquim was not seeking to conceal his primitive ferocity. In the disguise of the dance, and with the maddening chant of his comrades in his ears, he let it all come forth. I knew full well, as he nourished the tomahawk, that he was looking forward to the day when he could swing it in deadly earnest over the same heads—this was but the foretaste—and Osseo, standing like a statue against the wall, knew it too.

The lady whose suggestion had been the cause of the dance repented soon of her too fertile mind, and shrank back with a cry of fright when Hoyoquim swung the tomahawk before her face. The others only laughed, liking the jest, as they called it, and applauded Hoyoquim.

The chant of the Indians ceased presently, and Hoyoquim, stopping his dance, stood erect and motionless, and began to speak, also in the monotonous tone that the Indians like.

"Listen, my white brethren," he said, "and you shall hear a story of a great chief and a white man. The chief lived far in the wilderness, and Manito loved him, for he made him straight and strong and great in war and the chase. The chief took in battle a white maiden who was as fair as the rose, and whom he coveted for his lodge. His comrades took a white officer, a Long Knife like yourselves, and the Indians carried the white maiden and then the Long Knife to their village."

Hoyoquim's blazing eyes were fixed upon the face of Jasper, who was white to the brow. Osseo moved not, but both he and I knew well the tale that Hoyoquim would tell. The chief spoke with all the expressive gesture and mimicry of the Indian, his face now and then becoming so ferocious that the women shrank back afraid. But Rose Carew followed him with strained eyes and a dawning comprehension.

"The captured Long Knife," said Hoyoquim, "loved his life and he feared the torture post. He did not wish to die like a brave warrior amid the flames, laughing at his enemies; the forest and the sky were sweet to him, and he prayed to his gods not to take him away. They heard his prayer, and told him to be no longer a Long Knife, but to become a red warrior, and he heeded. He was adopted into the tribes, and he became a brother of the chief. He put on the blanket and wore the scalp lock, and there was a tomahawk at his girdle. But his heart was false. It was blacker than the black mud of the swamp, and as foul."

Hoyoquim paused again, and swept the circle with fiery eyes. Jasper tried to shrink back, but there was Winchester just behind him, and the muscular form of the Englishman would not yield.

"The great chief," resumed Hoyoquim, "would take to his lodge the white maiden whom he had captured, the prize of his skill and courage, but there were other chiefs who hated him, and they said that he must wait. The Long Knife looked upon her and he coveted her too, but another Long Knife, whose skin, like his heart, is always white, that both his friends and his enemies may ever know what he is, came and gave himself for her that she might return to her own people; and the Long Knife with the black heart, breaking his oaths before Manito, slipped from the red men and went back to the whites, telling them many lies."

Hoyoquim paused for the third time, and then, as if he were a medicine man who could learn the secrets of the future from Manito, began to prophesy.

"But the great chief only waits," he said in his chanting voice, "for Manito has given to the red warriors both the patient heart and the strong arm. He sees from afar the white maiden who was stolen from him, and he watches her. She is yet his, and he will claim her again, taking her to his lodge, from which none can rescue her; and he watches, too, the Long Knife of the black heart, whom he hates for his broken oaths, and for whom he sharpens his tomahawk every day. When the time comes he will drive his tomahawk through the traitor's skull, thus!"

He sprang forward, swept the tomahawk in a glittering circle over Jasper's head, and then whirled it aloft. All the women shrieked, and Jasper stood as if paralyzed, powerless to move. But Hoyoquim, with a low laugh, let the tomahawk fall, unstained, to his side, saying, "A great chief will deal as is fitting with both his loves and his hates," Then he stepped from the circle, and throwing his gaudy blanket again over his shoulders, resumed his phlegmatic calm. When I looked at Jasper a few moments later his face was covered with great beads of sweat, while Rose Carew was shrinking back as if frightened.

"'Twas a fine bit of acting, Black Eagle," said General Wayne, "though perhaps savouring somewhat too much of the real to soothe the nerves of the ladies, but we thank you."

Whether he knew the meaning of Hoyoquim's words I could not tell from his manner, but the reception ended presently, and we went home.

CHAPTER 32 The Demand of the Tribes

It was not in reason that Hoyoquim's most real acting should not create talk, but no opportunity was permitted me to hear it the next morning, as at rise of sun there came a message for me to attend at once at General Wayne's quarters. Again was I sensible of the great kindness with which he treated me, and the manner in which he upheld with his power an outcast like myself. He received me in his usual sincere manner.

"I have sent for you, Jack," he said, "because you know the ways of the savages, who are on the whole strange stuff to me. It was the wish of the Government that I first seek to treat with them before trying the edge of the sword. But I lack faith in the softer measures. It seems to me, Jack, that the bearing of these Indians since they have come among us is that of masters toward slaves, and it goes sorely against the grain of me to dance to the crack of a blanketed savage's whip. What thinkest thou of it, Jack?"

"General Wayne," I replied, "when the Niagara shall have drawn all the water from the Great Lakes, then will it be wise to be humble to the Indian."

"'Tis my way of thinking, Jack, but the President is a man of peace, and the arm of the Government is not long—but it may grow, Jack—and we must even try what soft words will do, though 'tis wise at the same time to have the sword unsheathed. The Black Eagle and his comrades will be here with their demands within two hours, and I wish you to keep at my elbow, Jack, and advise me what they mean. They deal so much, in the sun and the moon and the stars and metaphors and allegories that they quite befog my brain, and I would know what they say."

I laughed a little at the general's vexation, although I knew that it came from good cause, and promised to be at hand for reference. In truth, I felt pleased at his trust, and would have been the most ungrateful of dogs not to have served him to the utmost. Major Carew, my friend Captain Hardy, and several others arrived presently, and at the appointed time the delegates from the allied tribes, in all their brave raiment, stalked into the general's quarters. Then the usual interchange of courtesies and formalities followed. Both sides smoked the pipe of peace, talked for awhile of matters far from that in hand, and then through devious courses approached the true one. Hoyoquim's bearing was haughty in the extreme, and it was apparent to one like myself, who knew the Indian nature, that the demands of the tribes would not be light.

General Wayne, as I saw very well, was thoroughly angry, but though he had the reputation—often a true one—of being a hot-blooded man, he held a fine rein over his temper on this occasion, and deflected not a hair's breadth from the formal politeness with which he had received the delegates.

"And now," he said at last to the chiefs, "I wish to tell to you the words of our Great Father in Philadelphia. His heart is full of grief because of the wars between the white man and his red brother. He hears of the brave men who have fallen on either side and the captives taken, but he would put an end to it all, and have the two nations smoke a pipe of peace that will last forever."

"It shall be as the Great Father in Philadelphia wishes," said Hoyoquim gravely, "if he will listen to the words of wisdom, and give to the tribes of the red men that which is theirs. What these are I, Hoyoquim, called in your language the Black Eagle, have been chosen by my brethren to tell."

"What are these demands?" asked General Wayne. "Let the Black Eagle whose words are wisdom tell them and the white men will listen."

"In the beginning," replied Hoyoquim, "the red man owned all the land. The woods and the waters and what were in them were his. Then the white man came, and he was poor and sick, and he begged for a little land, only enough for him to build a cabin on, and the red man gave it to him. Then the white man grew strong, and more came with swords and rifles and great guns on wheels, and then they took all the land from the red man and drove him over the mountains. Now they cross the mountains and seek to take more land, that they may cut down the forests and drive away the game. But the Indians, who before fought among themselves, now fight together against the white man, and he can not stand before them. They have destroyed the army of the General-who-never-walks as they will destroy that of the Black Snake if he comes."

"Your demands, Black Eagle?" said General Wayne patiently.

"My brethren of the allied tribes," continued Hoyoquim in the same haughty tone, "have had a great talk, and they have chosen that I and those who come with me should tell to you their message. They bid you and all the white men to go back beyond the mountains, give up all the land of Kain-tuck-ee, and all the land on this side of the Ohio, the tribes to keep all the captives that they have taken in battle; when this is done there will be peace between your nation and mine."

I saw General Wayne's eyes flash at this preposterous demand, but again he was master of himself, and replied in even tones:

"You have given to me the message of the chiefs, Black Eagle, and now do you take mine to them. Tell them that the Great Father in Philadelphia is patient and loves his red children. But when madness like a fever creeps into their veins he must punish them. You have chosen to dig up the war hatchet, and he says that it is well. He has sent me with many soldiers to punish you, and I shall come and burn down your villages and slay your warriors, and the tribes will become as weak as a starving wolf!"

"The General-who-never-walks came with many soldiers," replied Hoyoquim, "and where are they? Their women and children will never see them again. Their bones lie rotting in the woods, and their scalps hang in the Indian wigwams."

"It is true," replied General Wayne, "but I come with men who know the Indian ways, men who never sleep, men who see the Indian trail in the forest, though he pass as lightly as the deer, and even as you served the army of General St. Clair so we shall serve you."

"Be it so," replied Hoyoquim, and his whole manner expressed nothing but defiance. "Let the white general come, and, however soon, it will not be too soon for the Indian. You have chosen war, and our hearts are glad."

He plucked the tomahawk from his belt, and with a mighty stroke buried it deep in the wood of the wall. Then his four brethren did likewise.

I knew the Indians' ways, and taking from General Wayne's hand the pipe of peace that he had been smoking, smashed it in pieces on the floor. The general took his cue at once.

"It is war," he said, "and thus have we destroyed the pipe of peace. Go home to the old chiefs and tell them that I shall come with an army!"

Hoyoquim and his comrades said no more, but, drawing their tomahawks from the wall, strode haughtily from the room. An hour later they were again in the forest on the way to their villages in the north.

As I left the general's quarters I met old Joe Grimes.

"What have they been saying in there, John?" he asked.

"Not many words, but they had meaning, Joe," I replied.

"The chiefs are mighty stuck up," he said. "I don't have no use for an Indian any time, barrin' Osseo and one or two others, an' I can't abide 'em at all now. If I had my way I'd fight 'em to the end. What did they ask?"

"That we give up Kentucky and all the Northwestern Territory, leave to them all the captives that they have taken from us, and go back east of the mountains."

Old Joe's face became as red as the rush of blood could make it, and he uttered a series of rapid and unintelligible oaths.

"And the general—what did he say?" he exclaimed at last.

"Of course we agreed," I replied. "Next week we begin our march to the eastward; all the settlers go with us."

Then the volcano burst. Old Joe despised soldiers; he believed them of little use, and now he consigned them to more warm places than are contained in all the theologies that I ever heard of. But in the midst of a fiery outbreak he saw my face.

"John Lee," he said indignantly, "you've been stuffin' mush in my ears."

"Of course I have, Joe," I replied. "What do you take General Wayne for? Don't you know that he's the kind of man who makes peace at the edge of the sword? He's sent those chiefs back to the tribes with a message that he's coming at the head of an army, and they'll have to fight"

Then old Joe did a dance of delight, and swore that General Wayne was one of the few soldiers who knew anything about fighting Indians, and he, Joe Grimes, would prove it anywhere and to anybody. There was neither sentiment nor poetry in Joe's nature, and, like so many other of the rugged borderers, he believed that the best way to settle the Indian question was to kill all the Indians, and truly, whenever a new tale of their atrocities came in, it seemed that he was right.

An hour later I was in General Wayne's quarters again, called to him by a new message. He had dismissed his staff, and though he smiled, it was sourly. It was apparent enough that the blood was hot in his veins. When I entered he burst out, though not against me.

"By my soul, Jack!" he cried, "I have never before had such a struggle against myself. I, a man of hot temper, called upon to hold my tongue in the face of such insolence! Why, I could have seized that red savage, Black Eagle or Hoyoquim, by the throat! He tried to dictate as if I were in the dust with his foot on my neck."

"He is a cunning Indian," I said, "and a dangerous foe, but not so able as Little Turtle, who beat St. Clair."

"Whatever he and his comrades are," he said emphatically, "we march against 'em as soon as possible, and I pray to God that we beat 'em. Jack, do you know that I tremble sometimes at the responsibility. In the war with the British we were fighting a civilized foe, and if we failed we did not expect to see our women outraged and our children brained as we do here. They beat Harmar and St. Clair, and if they beat us too, God knows what will happen, for I fear much that the Government can do no more. You don't know, Jack, how glad I am to have with me a comrade like you who understands this wilderness, and whom I can trust. It is enough to make an iron man weep when these tales of outrage come in, and if we are beaten again I hope, Jack, that I shall not be spared to tell it; and I love life, too."

"General," I said, "you must beware of an ambush. That is the thing which the soldier who goes against the savages should never forget. They can not stand before us in the open, but when they fight the white man in the forest they will beat him unless he has learned their ways."

"Just what the President himself said, and as he was present at Braddock's great slaughter he ought to know."

Then he began to tell me his plans, and to ask about the country and where I thought the savages would meet him. These were points on which I could in truth be of service to him, and I drew some rude maps for his use; but above all I repeated my cautions as to the nature of Indian attacks. When you know the savage and his rules of warfare, which are wholly different from ours, you are much better fitted to advance against him. At the end of a half hour I said:

"General, you have done much for me, now will you add to my gratitude by granting one little request?"

"What is it?"

"Forbid Miss Carew to go with the army to Fort Greeneville."

He looked at me in some surprise and then asked why.

"You heard the story of Hoyoquim," I replied, "and you know well that it was Miss Carew whom he meant."

"And I know, too, that the man whom he called a traitor was your cousin Jasper. I would that I had the proof; then I could at least send him back to the East; now I must keep him, though he shall have no responsibility—you know well, Jack, that a general can not always choose his own officers, and his influence was too much for me. But Miss Carew has my promise to go to Fort Greeneville, and I can not withdraw it. She is very anxious to go—perhaps she has reasons which seem good to her—a woman's reasons are not always a man's reasons, you know. Don't ask me to break my word, Jack; I can not do it."

I knew the uselessness of pursuing the quest further in that quarter, but when I left General Wayne I went straight in search of Rose Carew, and was fortunate enough to find her alone as before.

"I trust, Miss Carew," I said, without preliminaries, "that you listened well to the tale Hoyoquim told last night."

"I did, and it was an interesting story," she said defiantly.

"You know that the white girl of whom he spoke was you, and the white man whom he called a traitor Jasper Lee?"

"And if so, what then?" with increasing defiance.

"You heard his threats and how direct they were; you know what a dangerous savage he is, and what your fate will be if you fall into his hands. I beg you again not to go with the army. If you do not think of yourself, think of others who would rather die than hear of you in the power of the savage chief."

"Who, for instance?" Her eyes were sparkling, and she gazed at me with an intentness that made my own eyes waver. But I did not flinch in spirit and I answered her proudly, for I was not ashamed of the love I bore her:

"Myself!"

A deep blush suffused her countenance, but whether of anger I could not tell with my half-averted gaze. But when she replied it seemed to me that there waa some softness in her speech.

"I must go," she said; "I think that I shall be safe with General Wayne's army—he is not a St. Clair—and, moreover, I wish to be with my father when he is about to incur great danger. There are, too, other reasons——"

Here she hesitated, and my jealous heart, so ready to make Lawless her choice, now shifted to Jasper. She wished to watch over him and to save him from the particular wrath of the savages. Feminine influence even in the strictest of camps might be great.

"A woman must have her way even though she pay for it," I said, the anger that rose in my veins making me forget my manners.

But she did not fling back at me as I expected.

"I owe you a great debt, Captain Lee," she said, "and I would pay it if I could, but do not speak harshly to me now. I pray that you do not. I must go to Fort Greeneville. I have reasons that you yourself would call the best in the world if you knew them, but I can not tell them to you."

I was ever discovering some new phase of her character, beholding some mood or passing fancy of which I had not dreamed—perhaps that was why she attracted me so much—and now she chose suddenly to appear as the most bewitching of supplicants, and to me. There was the suspicion of a pout in the curve of her lips, as if she feared that I would speak harshly to her, when God knows that I was not in a position to deal roughly with anybody, least of all with Rose Carew.

"We are good friends, are we not?" she said, joining her hands, still in a beseeching attitude, but a smile illumining her face like the rosy dawn driving away the night; "we are even partners in a way, as we fled through the wilderness together, and it is not an unhappy memory. You won't refuse me my request, will you? You promised, you know, to spare Lieutenant Lawless, and you will do this, too, won't you?"

A soft heart is the curse of man, and woman, knowing it, wheedles him; and man, knowing that she is wheedling him, lets her. I plead no immunity. I claim to be no exception, and I said no further word against that which seemed to be her heart's desire, though my anger toward Jasper grew.

CHAPTER 33 A Great Trust

The general pushed the preparations for our march, and there were a few days so crowded with the details of work that my duel with Lawless was perforce compelled to linger. I met the lieutenant two or three times in the interval, and I speak truth when I say that I pitied him. The heat of wine was gone from his head, and he saw the affair that he had forced upon me in all its cruel reality. My skill with firearms—and I mention it here not to boast, but to explain the case—was known to all the frontier posts; indeed, I had given an exhibition of it in Cincinnati, as you know; and a half-dozen of the old Revolutionary officers now with Wayne's army were spinning marvellous tales of the way I used to handle the sword in the old days. They would say, as I heard from Winchester, that I might have lost a little of my skill through lack of practice, but it could not make much difference, and then some one would take the report to Lawless.

How much the youth suffered in those days it is impossible for me to estimate, but I think that he never forgot it. Jasper, who had drawn him into the trouble, gave no sign, confining himself to his military duties, and abandoning for the time his plan to make me trouble. In truth, Hoyoquim had given him much to think about, and I heard that he was making further efforts to escape the march into the wilderness, but without success.

The duel was arranged at last, and late of a bright afternoon we met in a fine open space on the Kentucky shore near the confluence of the Licking and the Ohio, swords being the weapons. Winchester was my second, and Myers acted for Lawless. Lawless was quite pale, but on the whole his bearing was creditable to him—I was sure that he had prepared himself for death. There were four or five spectators, including Jasper and Captain Hardy, and they stood in a group, talking in low voices and waiting for us to begin. I was somewhat apart, and Jasper, approaching me, said in a tone that could not be heard by the others:

"John, if you kill this boy it will be murder."

"Quite true," I replied, "but it is you, not I, who will be the murderer."

He was silent, and I added:

"I know well, Jasper, that he was egged on to this by you. It was part of your plan to make the camp so hot for me that I must leave it, but I propose to show that those who do not respect me shall at least fear to pick a quarrel with me."

He turned on his heel and joined the group of spectators. Winchester produced the swords, a fine pair of weapons, with edges like razors, and he ran his fingers along the shining blades in a manner most appreciative.

"You shall not be able to say that you lacked the use of a good weapon for your maiden duel, lieutenant," he said to Lawless with a smile.

The boy's lips quivered, but he did not answer. In truth, the world about him, if he chose to look at it, seemed fair. The surface of the two rivers shone in alternate play of silver and gold as the sunlight fell upon the water. Hills and valleys were clothed in forest green, and the air was balmy. One would not wish to leave it all.

The seconds handed us our swords, and we stood on guard. Now, in my youth I had learned the use of the weapon from three masters—an Englishman, a Frenchman, and a Prussian—to which was joined a natural aptitude; so I knew the tricks of all the schools, and I waited, looking straight into Lawless's eyes. He lifted his sword and thrust at me, but I caught his blade on mine, gave a quick and powerful turn of my wrist, and his weapon fell on the turf a dozen feet away. He became paler than ever, and his lips quivered again. But the boy was brave. He stood erect and motionless and said:

"It is my chief regret to die at the hand of a traitor."

"Lieutenant Lawless," I said, "when you are older you will learn manners as well as knowledge of the sword. Until then good-day."

I bowed to him, replaced my sword in its scabbard, and hooking my arm in my friend's said:

"Come, Winchester, we will cross to the other side of the Ohio; my work awaits me there."

We bowed politely to all the officers, and proceeded toward the river. As we approached our skiff I heard the sound of hasty footsteps behind me, and turning, beheld the flushed face of Lawless.

"Captain Lee," he cried, "I hope you don't think I'm ungrateful. I value my life, and I take it from you with thanks. Besides, you are a braver man morally than I am, and what they say about you must be a lie! Will you shake my hand?"

Our hands met in a hearty grip. We have been the best of friends to this day.

The affair never came to the ears of General Wayne, or if it did he said naught upon the matter. It grieved me much to go against his orders on the subject of duelling, in particular since I owed him such a great debt, but I felt the necessity of making an example. Those who are of doubtful character must speak with great emphasis if they would be believed. I may add also that a slanderer grows cautions in the presence of a sharp sword, and I noticed after the duel that the air about me had become perceptibly more pleasant. Winchester said that the number of my defenders showed a sudden increase.

On the morning following the duel I met Rose Carew.

"I have fought with Lieutenant Lawless," I said.

"You spared him?" she asked.

"He called me a traitor on the duelling ground in the presence of all the others," I replied.

"Did you kill him?" she exclaimed, and there was a sudden flash in her eyes.

"I promised you that I would not do so," I replied.

"And of course you kept your word, because you are a man of honour," she said. But the expression had gone from her face, and she seemed cold and indifferent.

"I kept it," I replied, "and Lieutenant Lawless has since withdrawn his words. We are friends now."

"It was well of him," she said.

We departed four days later for Fort Greeneville, about fifteen hundred strong, carrying with us several cannon, much baggage, many camp followers, and about twenty ladies, mostly officers' wives, though there were two or three exceptions, like Rose Carew, who seemed to have forgotten the danger, and who was full of interest in the wilderness.

We had scarce left out of sight the log houses of Cincinnati before we saw on every side of us the Indian sign.

"The warriors expect to make another great slaughter," said Osseo, "and they will wait until we are far in the woods."

"But 'tis not the General-who-never-walks who commands us now," I said.

"No," replied Osseo, casting an approving eye upon the well-drilled troops, "and it is not the same army that follows. Manito does not will that the same thing shall be done twice in the same way."

But the Indian portent was invisible to the majority of the soldiers; they saw only the deep-green foliage, now in all the royal flush of early summer, and the birds of brilliant hue that chattered and sang around them; they admired the brooks of clear water sparkling over the pebbles, and the gigantic oaks and hickories that grew so thickly in the forest. It was a beautiful land—a land of temperate climate and deep, rich soil, for which opposing races might well fight. The wilderness showed only its peaceful and beautiful side to them, and the new explorers could scarce believe that dangers lay hidden in it.

"It is so interesting and yet so strange," said Mrs. Winchester to me, "and how unlike England!"

"They have been building houses and making roads there for two thousand years, and they haven't begun here," I replied.

"And do you really tell me that there are hostile Indians all around us?" she asked, a look of incredulity on her blonde countenance.

"I told you so, and I repeat it," I replied. "There hovers about us continually a foe more dangerous, so far as forest fighting is concerned, than any other in the world."

"How do you know this?"

"The leaves tell it, the turf tells it, and the birds sing it."

"The birds sing it? You are becoming poetical, Mr. Lee."

"Not at all; I am speaking most commonplace prose when I say that the birds sing it; they usually sing it about nightfall, and it is not the song of a bird at all, but the imitation of it—Indian signalling to Indian."

"Then the voice of the wilderness is not always a voice to be trusted?"

"It is full of treachery."

"I can scarce believe it; it looks so beautiful!"

I could see the beauty as well as she, but I saw, too, what a lure it was. This same beauty had drawn many thousands of the ignorant to torture and death. The wilderness is only for those who know it.

Old Joe Grimes beheld but the other side. The beauty and the peace were nothing to him. Old Joe may have had the spirit of the picturesque and the romantic concealed somewhere in his soul, but "concealed" was certainly the word.

"'Tis well that our general has some brains in his head," he said, "though where on earth a soldier got 'em I don't know. The forest is full of savages, John, an' they are countin' our scalps already."

"Let 'em count," I said, "if they find any pleasure in it; but I tell you, Joe Grimes, Mad Anthony Wayne knows the work that he has to do."

But Joe shook his head doubtfully and would not be consoled.

Nevertheless, we reached Fort Recovery, built on St. Clair's battlefield, a good log stronghold, without incident save the loss of three or four stragglers, the fate of whom was concealed from the ladies. The latter rejoiced greatly over the safe journey, and maintained that we had exaggerated the dangers. But I was glad to notice how thick and solid were the walls of Fort Recovery, and I was quite able to endure the taunts they levelled at me as a prophet of disaster proved false.

"Where are your savages?" said Mrs. Winchester to me. "Still hidden in the woods?"

"Still hidden in the woods," I replied, "and none the less dangerous because of it."

Rose Carew was not so incredulous. She needed no proof now that the wilderness was full of snares, yet she seemed to fear none.

The stay of the main column at Fort Recovery was but brief. Two nights after our arrival General Wayne called me to his cabin, where I found him alone and thoughtful.

"Sit down, Jack," he said, "I have much to tell you, lad, and a great trust to confide to you, too."

I would have given my thanks for this new proof of faith, but he would not listen. "Tush, Jack! do not bore me with such words," he said; "I select you for the work that I am going to name because you are the most fit. My purpose is wholly selfish. I can not afford to fail in this campaign, and, as you know, the fate of every general is in the hands of his subordinates; therefore it behooves me to choose the best."

I was silent, while he waited, deep in reflection.

"You know that I must concentrate my men toward the Maumee," he resumed presently, "in order that we may strike there at the heart of the Indian power. Therefore I advance day after to-morrow with the main part of the army now here. But Fort Recovery is one of our most important way stations, and it must be held by an adequate garrison. You are soldier enough to know that a garrison needs a commander"—here he smiled—"and you are to be that commander. I promise you that you shall be released in time for the final campaign, but you are to be in charge at Fort Recovery until I send for you."

I was a hardened man, but tears rose in my eyes at this new and great proof of confidence, while at the same time I felt a sense of awkwardness.

"General," I said, "there will be officers here who are my seniors. They would rebel against this even under ordinary circumstances, but consider what I am."

"I have considered everything," he replied shortly, "and I don't make any request; I give an order. If you do not obey it I shall have you locked up in your own guardhouse. Now go back to your quarters and begin to think about what you will have to do. I fancy that yours will be no easy task, but if you do not perform it, then I, as well as you, shall suffer from the disgrace, and I imagine that John Lee does not wish that."

In addition to his verbal dismissal he turned his back upon me and began to read some documents. Then I went to my quarters, overwhelmed and embarrassed, but feeling, too, a secret pride. Presently confidence also began to rise. I would show my critics, whatsoever they might be, that I knew how to command.

The knowledge that the commander-in-chief would advance again was general at the fort the next day, and when I met Rose Carew just inside the stockade wall she spoke to me about it.

"All the women are to be left here, so I hear," she said.

I answered in the affirmative.

"Why?"

"The general thinks they would be in the way," I replied, quite plainly. "It is certain they would be of no use in fighting the Indians."

"You have the merit of brusqueness sometimes, Mr. Lee," she said.

"'Tis often a merit," I replied.

"It depends upon the man," she said. "But do you know who is to be commander here in the absence of General Wayne?"

I fancy that she knew even when she asked, although I did not think so then.

"Yes," I replied, "the general has selected a man in whom he has the most implicit confidence."

"It is a difficult post."

"That is true, because in addition to the soldiers there are at least a dozen women whom this man will have to reduce to obedience."

"And do you know this paragon?"

"I do. It is myself, John Lee, the man who stands before you."

She looked thoughtful.

"It is a long time since you have been a soldier—that is, a regular soldier," she said. "Don't you think the responsibilities are very heavy?"

I flushed at this expressed doubt of my ability.

"At any rate," I replied, "I shall see that my orders are obeyed."

"By all?"

"By all—men and women alike," and I looked straight into her eyes.

Her gaze fell, and the red in her cheeks deepened. I fancy that she was not often spoken to as I spoke to her then. Yet sternness with a woman is not always misplaced.

"You shall find me obedient," she said, as she walked toward the women's quarters, but before disappearing she turned and added, "if you are a reasonable commander."

I ascertained before the close of the day that Major Carew and Jasper would remain at the fort under my command, an embarrassing fact in its way, but not without a grim satisfaction for me. I resolved that both should obey me. But for the present, in order to avoid any awkward situation, I remained rather closely at my quarters. There, shortly after sundown, Major Carew came, and I knew at once what he would be about.

"I hear, Captain Lee, that you are to command here in the general's absence," he said.

"The report is correct."

"It is a great honour."

"Quite true, but no greater for me, I trust, than for anybody else."

I spoke coolly, determined that he should make his meaning plain. The only respect that I felt for him was due to the fact that he was Rose Carew's father—a circumstance that she could not help. He flushed a little, and spoke evasively. He did not mean to refer to anything unpleasant, he said—anything that ought to be forgotten—but there was already much comment among the officers who had to remain; there might be trouble, and perhaps if I were to speak to General Wayne he might change his mind. But I cut him short.

"General Wayne chose me for this place because I have had much experience in Indian warfare," I said with intentional brusqueness, "and to tell you the exact truth, I think that he has made a good choice. Let those officers who are murmuring be assured that I shall find means to enforce my authority. I shall have the power of life and death here."

He flushed again, this time a deeper red than before, and then hastened to make apologies; he disliked extremely to be the bearer of disagreeable messages, he said, but he was older than the others, and he thought that perhaps he might relieve an awkward situation,

"There is no awkward situation at all," I replied. "I shall be commander here and I will be obeyed."

Then he went out, and I was sure that his coming had been instigated by the crafty Jasper. I began now to take a joy in the situation. These fine gentlemen from the East should know that here in the woods I was their master.

Following Major Carew came a more welcome visitor. It was Osseo. He sat for a long time in silence, seemingly buried in meditation after his fashion. Then he said:

"Lee is to be the great chief here. My heart is glad. The Black Snake knows a wise warrior. He is a warrior himself."

"It is your partiality, Osseo," I replied. "We have long been good comrades, and therefore you credit me with more virtues than I possess."

"Not so," replied Osseo, the twinkle coming into his eyes. "Does Lee take Osseo for a white man who says one thing with his lips and has another in his heart? No, Osseo is a red man, and his tongue is not crooked; if he thought Lee was a fool he would call him a fool; since he is not a fool, but a wise man, Osseo calls him a wise man."

Thus he dismissed the subject in the most airy manner, and I knew that he was not speaking wholly in jest, although Osseo loved to tease me about the weak points of my race, and point out the many particulars in which, according to his view, the red man was our superior.

But the joy of old Joe Grimes was undisguised.

"I'm tarnation glad that no soldier is left to be big chief here," he said with his customary contempt of all organized authority.

"But I'm a soldier."

"You're not soldier enough to hurt," he replied, which did not sound like a compliment, although he meant it for one.

General Wayne left the next day, and I came into my command.

CHAPTER 34 The Defence of a Fort

I increased the guard of Fort Recovery as soon as General Wayne and his force disappeared in the forest, my fears of attack, which surpassed those of the Commander-in-chief, inciting me to the utmost vigilance. He did not know the secret motives impelling Hoyoquim, whose power among the allied tribes was now greatly increased, and the renegade Blackstaffe would be driven on by the same impulse. I also sent forth Osseo, Joe Grimes, and other trusty scouts to beat up the woods for Indian signs.

I was just beyond the palisade, giving instructions to the last of the scouts, when Rose Carew came through the gate. I thought it well to show her at once that I was a commander who commanded.

"No one is allowed outside the palisade without a pass from me," I said.

"Well, what of it?" she replied, giving me a look that I could not call anything but saucy.

"It means," I said, "that you must go inside at once."

"And if I decline to go?"

"Then I shall take you."

"You would not dare."

She remained where she was, looking defiance.

I advanced and put my hand upon her arm. I wish to say, too, that it was my firm intention to pick her up and carry her into the fort, although I doubt whether she expected it, as she flushed red, and shrinking away from me ran through the gate. I followed her and I said reproachfully:

"Miss Carew, my position is difficult enough; don't make it more so."

"Forgive me," she replied, her face still red, and turning, she walked away.

I proceeded with the men as if I had been in command for years, thinking then that this was the best way, and I am convinced now that I was right. I summoned Major Carew and placed him in charge of the guard for the rest of the day. He received my orders without a word, and, although he was Rose Carew's father, I took a pleasure in speaking to him sternly. Lawless I made my chief aide, and he accepted the place with such frank pleasure that I could count upon him beyond a doubt. But there were great grumblings among the other officers; I saw that, however they may have felt toward me personally, they did not relish being placed under the command of a man with my history. I soon beheld an instance of it. I had assigned a lieutenant named Worthington to the duty of assorting some ammunition, and when I passed by in order to inspect the work I found him lolling in his tent. I asked him the reason, and he responded with a supercilious curl of the lip that he did not think hurry was needed.

"Are you in the habit of deciding upon the necessity of orders after you receive them?" I asked, controlling my temper.

"I did not do so when I had them from previous commanding officers," he replied, still sneering.

"Then you will not do so now," I said.

Whereupon I sentenced him to three days' solitary confinement in our little guard-house upon a diet of bread and water, and I saw in person that the sentence was begun. The effect of this speedy action was most-enlivening, and the officers went about their duties with great briskness. As for the privates, there was no discontent among them even from the first, and I felt now that I had affairs well in hand.

Shortly after the arrest of Worthington I met Jasper.

"I congratulate you upon your advancement, cousin," he said with sleek politeness. "Times change and you ride high."

"It is true," I replied, "that I am on horseback, and I may keep the saddle while others who used to ride will have to walk."

He started a little, a movement that did not escape my eye.

"I do not quite take your meaning, cousin," he said, "but I for one certainly have never had any wish to keep you down."

"And perhaps none to help me up."

"You do me great injustice."

I had no wish to bandy words with him, in particular when it was his affectation to be polite, and I merely added:

"Since General Wayne has seen fit to leave me in command here, I shall be glad if all will co-operate with me."

"It shall give me great pleasure to obey any order that you may issue," he said, in tones that were almost mincing. I preferred that he should be openly hostile, but I walked away without replying.

Thus three or four days passed without incident, but at noon of the fourth day Osseo returned from the forest. He had discarded much of his attire, and he was now the warrior pure and simple.

"What song have the birds of the forest sung in your ear, Osseo?" I asked.

"They have sung many times," he replied, "but their song is always the same. They tell Osseo that the hostile braves come as thick as the leaves before the whirlwind, and Hoyoquim and the white renegade, Blackstaffe, lead them on. They have heard that the Black Snake is gone, and they wish to take the fort and gather many scalps. Hoyoquim and Blackstaffe hope, too, to capture again the white maiden who was stolen from them."

"Which they shall never do!" I said with emphasis.

"Manito alone can tell," replied Osseo solemnly.

His news was of the deepest importance, but I could do nothing now save to wait the attack. In the afternoon Joe Grimes returned with the same report. At twilight, heavy with cares, I walked by the palisade, and Rose Carew again joined me.

"You are thoughtful, Captain Lee," she said.

"I have need to be," I replied, glancing at the forest.

"What do you expect there?"

"You know this ground?"

"I do," she replied, blanching a little. "It is here that the great slaughter of our army occurred."

"Then what do you think can come from that forest?" I asked.

"The savages."

"Ay, we are threatened with an Indian attack; it is more than a threat—it is a certainty, and your devoted admirer, Black Eagle, and the renegade, Blackstaffe, lead them on."

I was angry at her for coming to Fort Recovery, or I would not have spoken thus. Her face blanched again, and she turned upon me an appealing look.

"You do not mean to say that it is I who will be the cause of this attack?" she asked.

"Oh, no," I replied; "you are merely an incident"—yet I believed in my soul that she was the cause—"and do not fear, Miss Carew; behind these log walls we shall beat them off, no matter how great their numbers. Now go into your cabin, if you would oblige me. An arrow might fly over that palisade and strike you down."

"And might not one strike you too?"

"Ay, but I would be a poor soldier if I did not take the risk. Now, I ask you to go."

She went as obediently as a little child.

Several more days passed, and there was no attack; in truth, so far as the soldiers and the officers from the East could see, there was no indication that a single Indian was within a thousand miles of us, and I began to hear murmurs at the excessive watchfulness which rested somewhat heavily upon the more slothful. I was sure that Jasper was instigating these complaints, but I took no notice and did not relax our caution. I was confirmed in my apprehensions by Osseo's repeated warnings.

A few days later a pack train reached us, and, discharging its load of supplies, prepared to return. Its commander, over whom I had no control, insisted upon camping outside the palisade, claiming that he and his men and animals would be crowded too much inside; and despite my repeated requests, even entreaties, he had his way. I gave him up for lost, knowing well that the savages would not let so tempting a bait escape them. I resolved to remain awake that night, and when I saw Rose Carew passing between the women's cabins I beckoned to her. She came, though reluctantly, and hanging back like a child that had been scolded.

"You see those lights?" I said, pointing through a crack in the palisade toward the camp fires of the pack train.

She nodded assent.

"Know, then," I said, "that General St. Clair is not the only fool who has come into the wilderness. There are others, though perhaps not on so large a scale. The commander of those men out there is one."

I spoke with some bitterness, and she looked surprised.

"Why, they are in no danger," she exclaimed. "Many of the officers say that there is not an Indian within a hundred miles of us."

"That only proves what I said about the abundance of fools."

"Then you feel sure that the savages are near?"

"There can be no doubt of it. I have not been able to go forth and see for myself, but Osseo tells me so, and I would sooner trust his pair of eyes than all the others in the Northwest."

"Shall we beat them off?"

"I do not doubt it," I again assured her, "and you shall go back in safety to the East to wed the man of your choice. I begin to understand now why you have come again into this dangerous country. Your anxiety for him would not let you stay behind."

I spoke plainly, but it was because I felt that I had certain rights over her, almost paternal in their nature—I had saved her from the savages. But I was surprised to see how deeply her face flushed, and her figure wavered like that of a frightened deer about to flee.

"I do not understand you," she said. "Do you mean to assert that I came to watch over any one besides Major Carew?"

"Ay," I replied. "My cousin Jasper is a lucky man. Fortune has seemed always to fight for him, and never more ably than now."

The red did not depart from her cheeks and brow, but otherwise she recovered her self-possession, and changed the subject abruptly, at which I did not wonder, as a girl naturally does not like to discuss with an outsider her coming marriage. She pointed toward the forest, which inclosed the fort with a black and circular wall.

"I have ceased to wonder at your fondness for the wilderness," she said. "There is a spell in that forest even for me, one who has felt its dangers—an uncanny spell, I grant you, but it is upon me. I feel a desire to search its depths, although I know that danger is there."

"It draws the woodman as the sea draws the sailor," I said. "I think that the chief charm lies in its majesty and silence—I don't use silence in its strict sense, because neither the sea nor the forest is ever wholly silent."

She made no reply, but stood gazing at the impenetrable wilderness. She had moods in which she was grave, even solemn, and I liked to look at her then, when her beauty took an aspect, severe like that of a vestal virgin. It endured but a few moments. Then she said with a little laugh:

"I am rude, but this wilderness took my thoughts far away."

"Since you have condescended to come back to Fort Recovery," I replied in the same tone, "I have a command to repeat to you, and it is that to-morrow during the battle you stay in one of the cabins under shelter."

My tone was grave now.

"I know that we shall have one," I replied. "You see the provocation to it," and I pointed again through the crack in the palisades at the twinkling camp fires of the pack train.

A phantom rose out of the ground beside us, and resolved itself into the shape of a man, tall, erect, and but half clothed. It was Osseo.

"What song do the birds sing to-night, Osseo?" I asked, wishing to speak in a light tone in the presence of a lady. But there was no lightness in his reply.

"The warriors come," he replied, "as many as when they slew the army of the General-who-never-walks, and more. Before the sun marks the noon hour tomorrow the scalps of those will hang at the belts of the warriors! Manito has made them mad that they may go laughing to death!"

He stretched out his long arm and pointed toward the supply train.

"I know it, Osseo," I said, "but I can do nothing. I have even begged them to come inside the fort."

But I made another effort. I went forth to the packers, repeated Osseo's news and again asked them to come in. They laughed at me, and two or three went so far as to hint that I was a coward. But I refused to take offence, repeated the attempt with similar failure, and then, returning to the fort, placed nearly half my force on guard, making ceaseless rounds in person to see that nothing was neglected. It was not my intent to take any sleep that night; in truth, I could not have slept had I wished it, and the hours passed with terrible slowness. The forest made no sign, the fresh foliage there sighing gently in the wind, and naught else stirring. But I knew that this stillness was ominous; the savage loves a sudden onslaught, and when the ignorant least expects him he comes. The night passed, and the first light of day as narrow as a sword-blade showed under the edge of the horizon. Then the war-whoop, issuing at once from thousands of throats, burst from the forest, and the warriors in swarms poured forward among the trees.

I was watching by the palisade, and I saw their first onset, as they swept like a flood upon the camp of the pack train. I beheld a multitude of flitting brown forms, the flash of upraised tomahawks, and the puff-puff of white smoke from the rifles. The war-whoop, which had swelled at first in one mighty yell, now fell and then rose again, becoming shriller, but continually piercing the drum of the ear as if with the thrust of a knife.

My men fired from the palisade, and here and there one of the flitting brown forms fell, but the wood still poured forth its savage horde. The men in the camp beheld upon them the death of which they had been warned, and at which they had laughed. They grasped their rifles, and at the same moment the stroke of the tomahawk fell. The camp was destroyed as if by one of our Western tornadoes; most of the packers were killed before they could fight, and the rest, driven on by terror, fled to the fort, where we scarce had time to admit them before the horde was upon us too. The attack was so sudden, though expected by many, and the result so sweeping, that the effect of it was unreal. Our eyes seemed to deceive us, but our reason told us it was true.

No man fattens upon his food faster than the red savage, and swinging aloft the bleeding scalps and filling all the forest with their triumphant whoops, the horde rushed upon Fort Recovery, eager for the prize which they had no doubt of winning. Had I been without responsibilities I should have sought the figure of Hoyoquim, sure that he was somewhere in the van, in order that I might send toward him an unerring bullet. I bore the chief no special animosity, but with him fallen the spirit must go out of the attack. The duties of command, however, lay heavy upon me, and I ran from point to point of the wall, urging the men to keep their coolness and to fire with certain aim.

The rattle of our rifles ran in a ring around the palisade, the men standing in the face of all this yelling and frightful swarm with a firmness that was beyond praise, and a storm of bullets broke full upon the brown mass that was launched against us. I expected that the savages would fall back, knowing their dislike of the open assault; but motives of unusual power urged them, and shouting their war-cries and firing their rifles, they rushed to the very foot of the palisade, some hewing at the wood with their tomahawks, and others, drunk with blood-lust, seeking to climb up and spring among us.

I thanked God in that moment for a long experience of Indian warfare, and, knowing that any case of faintheartedness on our side would give to the savages their opening, I watched every point, and always, despite our scanty numbers, I sent relief to any part where the soldiers seemed to yield. Old Joe Grimes rushed past me once, his face black with powder smoke, and a real joy shining in his eyes.

"Didn't I tell you men'll fight better without any commander?" he cried. "See how they stand! A fool of a soldier would 'a had us all beat afore this."

Which I thought rather hard upon me, but I had no time to argue the matter with Joe.

Three of the savages cleared the wooden wall and sprang among us, but they were shot dead before they touched the ground. Yet others took their places and made the same attempt. Never before had I seen such tenacity in assault by the Indians, and now I began to hear the powerful voice of Hoyoquim driving them on, though I sought in vain for the sight of his figure. He was hidden from me by the palisade.

The wall was lowest on the western side, and suddenly it was crested with the forms of the savages. The defenders recoiled for a moment at the sight, and I sprang forward to lead them anew. Two or three of the Indians fired at me, and at the same time I heard a cry from a point inside the wall. A bullet whistled by me, but with involuntary motion I turned at the sound of the cry, which had in it a familiar note. I saw Jasper, a smoking rifle in his hand, and Rose Carew standing before him, her hand upon the same rifle. That picture was impressed upon my brain in the flash of a moment; what caused it and what followed it I knew not, as the savages on the wall demanded all my attention. We drove them back with our rifles, and when I turned again Rose Carew and Jasper were no longer there.

I had no time to ask questions then, as our little fort was a vortex of flame and smoke. We were scarce two hundred within the walls, and more than two thousand outside were seeking to reach us, panting with a desire for another revel of slaughter. We kept close to the palisade, and their bullets, passing over our heads, fell on the ground. I could hear the steady patter-patter behind us like the beat of heavy rain. However fast they fired, they never ceased to utter their war-whoop, a cry so appalling to the inexperienced, and which more than once has routed white men with its suggestion of torture and death. But my soldiers were stanch and true, and the savages fell fast before their rifles.

A long time they pressed the assault, and at last they gathered themselves for a rush fiercer than any that had gone before. It too was beaten back at the wooden wall, and the war-whoop ceased so suddenly that the silence was astonishing. The Indian army melted away as if the hand of a magician had waved it into space, and when I looked again I saw only the bodies of the fallen lying here and there in the open, and beyond them the woods silent and dark as ever. Nowhere was there a sign of a living human being.

"They have fled!" exclaimed Lawless, my aide, who had stayed close beside me throughout the assault.

"But not far," I replied; "they are lying there in the woods ready to shoot the first of us who venture beyond the palisade."

"One would think that the earth had swallowed 'em up," he muttered to himself. And in truth it seemed so. We saw only the forest fresh in its spring foliage, and heard only the wind blowing through the leaves and boughs. But I knew well that the crafty savages were still near, despairing of the open assault, but hoping to win by trick.

I began the round of the palisade, and I came to the little bastion where Jasper had commanded a small detachment.

"Well, we have beaten 'em off for the time, cousin," he said.

"Ay," I replied, "but it seems to me, Cousin Jasper, that at the most critical period of the assault one of your bullets flew wide of the true mark."

He retained his presence of mind wonderfully.

"You saw that, did you?" he said. "I fired at an Indian inside the palisade, thinking that he was an enemy, when it was Osseo. It was a natural mistake at such a moment of excitement. Fortunately, Miss Carew knocked up my gun in time."

It was a glib and plausible answer, as Osseo in truth was near me when the shot was fired, and I was in doubt. So I passed on to note what damage had been done, and strengthen the garrison as best I could. We had escaped most marvellously well. But a single man of ours had been killed, and the little garrison, triumphant and sanguine, was eager for the savages to attack anew. I felt a great swell of joy. We had beaten off the largest army of Indians ever yet gathered in the West, and I believed that all other attacks upon us would fail in the same way. And in thinking upon it I could not forget my own personal advantage. Few would dare to reproach me with the past in the face of this. Again I was deeply thankful to General Wayne.

I ordered food and drink to be served to the soldiers, and then I entered the women's quarters. I found Mrs. Winchester and Rose Carew together. The young Englishwoman was very pale, but her quiet manner showed that her courage had not failed.

"What awful sounds!" she said. "The shrieking of those savages was more frightful than their bullets."

"We have driven them off," I said, "and I do not think that they will make such another assault, though we may be besieged for some time yet."

To Rose Carew I said:

"You promised me that you would remain in the cabin during the fighting."

She showed again that I could never anticipate her mood, for her reply and manner were as meek as those of a nun.

"It is true," she replied. "I gave you the promise, and I broke it. But I have no excuse to plead."

Her look was not only meek but appealing, and I could say naught else. Had I known more of the incident which I had but half witnessed I felt that I could have spoken further, but as it was I left the cabin and returned to the defence, a duty that I could not neglect for any personal matter.

The savages, finding that none of us came forth to be shot down from ambush, soon gave proof of their continued presence by opening a scattered fire. Their best marksmen crept from cover to cover, trying to pick off all who incautiously showed their heads over the palisade, but succeeded in wounding only two or three of our men, for which we took a tenfold revenge.

"We broke their hearts when they tried to rush us," said Joe Grimes in great glee. "Mr. Red Man has made a big mistake."

"Yes," I said, "the storming of forts is not to his taste. He will never get inside this palisade."

An hour or two later we saw a white rag fluttering among the trees, and I ordered my men to hold their fire, that the flag of truce might be brought forward. Its bearer proved to be the renegade Blackstaffe. Then I called Osseo and Joe Grimes.

"I am going to talk to Blackstaffe," I said. "If any one of the savages fires at me, kill the renegade instantly."

They made no reply, but the careful manner in which they handled their rifles showed that in case of trickery Blackstaffe was a doomed man. I raised my head above the palisade and asked the renegade what he wished.

"It is you, Mr. Lee, and you are in command; I know that it must be so, or this garrison would not have made such a clever defence."

You can catch a goose by sprinkling salt on its tail, but I was not to be taken in with such compliments.

"Bring forward the chief, Hoyoquim, the Black Eagle," I said, "and let him vouch for the fact that I shall not be fired upon while we talk. Otherwise I shall order my men to begin shooting again."

He looked injured.

"You are unfair," he said; "you see that I trust you, but you do not trust me."

"We understand each other perfectly," I replied. "You know that I am to be trusted, and I know that you are not. You know, too, that I know both of these facts."

He did not argue the matter, but disappeared in the forest, returning presently with Hoyoquim. The chief was in all the glory and hideousness of his war-paint, and in truth was a ferocious and impressive figure.

I felt some one tugging at my arm, and turning, I saw that it was old Joe Grimes.

"Let me fire at him," he said. "Just one little bullet, and it will save the border at least a thousand lives."

"Don't think of such a thing, Joe," I replied severely. "It would be the basest treachery. He comes under the flag of truce."

"It's right to kill a snake whenever you find him, then you get rid of p'ison. Jest one shot, John, and Osseo at the same time can pick off that d—d renegade, Blackstaffe."

His voice became pleading.

"Nonsense, Joe!" I replied. "It can not be thought of. Be silent."

"Do you guarantee that I shall not be fired upon while we are talking?" I shouted to Hoyoquim.

"I promise you that it shall not be," he replied. "May Manito strike me with his lightning if I lie!"

I was satisfied, and I told Blackstaffe, who evidently was chosen spokesman, to go on.

"You have made a good defence," he began in the smooth tone that he had adopted from the first, "but you must see that final success is impossible. The warriors of all the allied tribes, the bravest and the best, are here. They outnumber you ten to one. They are the same men that destroyed St. Clair and his soldiers. A thousand skulls bleaching in the forest tell you what the Indians can do. We ask you to surrender and to trust to our mercy."

I laughed.

"Your mercy?" I replied. "I know what that is—outrage for the women, the stake for the men!"

"There you make a mistake," he replied. "I admit that the Indians are not particularly soft-hearted, but I am a white man, and I shall use all my influence with them. I do not boast when I say that I have much. As it is, we shall certainly take you, and you know what the Indian is when he is inflamed by battle. I could do nothing then."

"I have no more to say to you except to come and take us if you can," I replied, and with that I ended my colloquy. The renegade and Hoyoquim quickly retreated to the woods, and I came down from the palisade. There was another hour of silence, and unconsciously I found myself strolling back toward the quarters of the women. Moreover, I had been revolving a project in my mind, and I asked Rose Carew what I should do with Jasper while the siege lasted.

"It is necessary for some one to be here in charge of this part of the fort," she said. "Let it be Major Lee."

Now I understood her, and I was sorry that I had asked the question, although more than half expecting her answer; in truth, it was my desire to oblige her that had prompted me to ask it. I now knew that she wished to keep Jasper out of danger. So, with a sense of self-martyrdom, I sent him to the post that she sought for him.

The savages by and by began a desultory attack, again pursuing their favourite methods, firing from the cover of grass, stumps, and logs, and exposing themselves but little. They did no damage to us save the infliction of one or two slight wounds, and old Joe Grimes laughed with derisive glee.

"I could live on things like this," he said. "I haven't had such fun in ten years."

"Perhaps Blackstaffe would like to rush us again," I said, sharing to some extent in his grim satisfaction.

"Not he," replied old Joe. "He ain't goin' to hire a dog and bark himself. He'll let the Black Eagle do all the rushin' an' keep his own dirty skin in safety."

This crackling fire lasted throughout the afternoon. The bullets often flew over the palisade and fell in the inclosure with a light pit-pat like the drop of hailstones, but we seldom replied, preferring to keep our ammunition and to watch vigilantly for another rush. Major Carew came to me in the course of his duty, and began to pay me extravagant compliments on the success of our defence.

"We should have been lost without you," he said; "and second to you only has been your cousin, Major Lee. He risked his life a half-dozen times in repelling the assault."

I looked fixedly at him, and his eyes fell. He was not so bold and determined as Jasper, and in truth I did not consider him a villain at all, despite his inchoate treason; merely smooth and self-seeking, and desirous of a brilliant match, in a worldly sense, for his daughter, and yet for the moment I despised him. So feeling, I turned my back upon him without a word and went to another part of the palisade. I could have reminded him of what he and Knowlton had said one night in my presence in Danville, but I thought it an ungenerous revenge. Knowlton was back there now, as quiet as a lamb, though carefully praising the Government at times.

The afternoon waned and night came. I feared the darkness, knowing well that it was most suited to the wiles and strategems of the savage, but an hour or two later Osseo, who had slipped from the fort, returned and said to me: "Let Lee rest easy; there will not be another attack." He added nothing to this brief statement, but I doubted not the correctness of his words. Then in truth the savages must have had their faces burned finely if, despite the eagerness of Hoyoquim and Blackstaffe, they refused to continue the siege.

The night deepened and darkened, and then glimmering lights appeared here and there at the edge of the forest. It was the savages bearing torches and seeking their dead. We might have picked off some of them from the palisade, but I forbade my men to fire. Old Joe Grimes considered it a waste of mercy, and swore furiously at what he called my foolishness, but obeyed the order nevertheless.

I was standing beside the palisade watching the twinkling lights through a crack and wondering what were the thoughts of these savages, who considered us interlopers, when I heard beside me the light step that I had learned to know so well. Rose Carew, in virtue of her experience among the savages, had become in some sort a privileged character, and now that the battle was over, I could not blame her for coming forth from the cabin. I moved a little to one side and let her look between the two stakes of the palisade.

"What are they doing?" she asked.

"Carrying away their dead."

"Then the attack is over?"

"I think so. Savage races do not like the open assault. It requires the training of white men to carry through such attempts. They have failed where they expected another great triumph."

"I can imagine their feelings," she said. "We know what ours would be if we held this country and saw some one coming to take it."

Now, I have a certain sympathy for the savage, but my knowledge of him does not permit it to go very far. There are too many of our own people who wish to charge all the faults of our wars with him upon the white man, but that is only the sentimental view. I know the red man's noble qualities, but I can not forget his great faults either, and the history of his relations with us is filled with his atrocities. But I did not reply, merely continuing to watch the removal of the dead.

The last light died by and by, and the last Indian figure vanished. But I stood there yet, watching the black forest and the girl beside me. Then from those sombre depths came a strange wild note, but clear and sweet. It rose, filled the air, and did not die.

Rose Carew looked at me, and I saw a smile pass over her face.

"It is he," she said. "It can be none else."

I nodded. The note following a plaintive air swelled higher and higher, and approached the fort. Numerous heads now appeared upon the palisade, and I did not restrain them, knowing well that the Indians were gone. I called to Winchester, and he came.

"You, too, should be here to greet him," I said.

"I am glad to have the chance," he replied.

The figure of a man playing the flute presently emerged from the forest, and then the features of De Chamillard came into view. I ordered the gate thrown open, and, still playing his flute, he walked through the palisade. But when he saw Rose Carew and me he let the instrument fall from his lips, and made one of the finest bows that I had ever seen.

"It is indeed Miss Carew?" he cried, "or—or Mrs. —Mrs.—you shake your head—then it is Miss Carew still! Truly it was a good angel that prompted me to leave the red man and come back to the white man. And it is the great hunter, too! And behold, here is his companion, the red chief, who poetically styles himself the Son of the Evening Star; and yonder, too, is the brave Briton, M. de Winchester! On my soul, 'tis quite a family reunion."

Thus he chattered in the gayest manner, and I could not tell whether he was in jest or earnest. Yet I doubted not that he was most glad to see us; and as for himself, I could note but little change in his appearance since last we parted in these woods. I cast a look at the forest and he followed it.

"Do not disturb yourself about the savages, mon cher Lee," he said. "They are gone far from here now. You know how they can speed like ghosts through the wilderness. Your hospitality was too great, and they would flee from a repetition of it. That is why I am here. I do not like such rapid flights, and I concluded to come and stay with you awhile, a matter of the utmost ease to me, as I am still playing my rôle of one stricken by Manito—a great advantage, M. Lee, I assure you, as I am the only man, perhaps, in all this vast northwestern wilderness who has perfect freedom. It was a happy thought of yours that suggested the part to me, and again I thank you."

I could not tell for the second time whether he was in jest or in earnest, but leaving the palisade, I walked toward the cabins. Osseo, who would not have moved for a king, was in our path, but he stepped quickly aside for De Chamiilard, bestowing upon him a look that was half pity, half reverence. None, not even De Chamiilard himself, could ever persuade Osseo that the Frenchman was not in truth stricken by the lightning of Manito, and therefore in his special keeping.

I was entitled now to a little rest, and I determined to take it while I played host to De Chamillard. I introduced him to Mrs. Winchester, to whom he paid the same deference that he had shown to Rose Carew, murmuring that while their countries might quarrel and go to war, no Frenchman could ever forget the beauty and grace of the English ladies. Then over a little wine he told me the tale of his wanderings.

"I have been all this while with the savages," he said, "taking no part in their wars or their cruelties, but roaming as I wish, even to the head of the Great Lakes and past the Father of Waters. The character which I took upon me and of which I could not now rid myself if I would, protects me everywhere. I have seen mighty rivers and mightier lakes, and great forests and savage men, and I have seen life. And now, dear Lee, if you can, tell me of that France which has perhaps forgotten one of the humblest of her sons, but which I can not forget though I go deeper and deeper into the woods, where no word of the dear land can follow me."

I told him of all the strange and terrible things that were happening there, or at least the story of them as it came to us in the woods, and I saw all the lightness of his manner disappear for the while. He was silent a long time, but at last he said:

"Poor France! I suppose that I ought to be there, but how can I go when my conscience will let me fight for neither party?"

I too was silent, contemplating this exile of old Versailles, seemingly so bizarre here in our wilderness, and yet taking his place in it with such ease. And I knew also that while he was of the old order his heart was more with the new than the old.

The next day all traces of sadness were gone from his manner, and he dropped too the rôle which he had so long played among the savages. Instead he was the courtier, giving the greater part of his devotion to Mrs. Winchester and Miss Carew, but neglecting none other of the ladies.

"Had I known that they were here, my dear Lee," he said to me with the utmost sincerity, "I should have come sooner. The only flaw that I find in the wilderness is the absence of the feminine gender, as one knows it in the capitals of the world. Primitive man is well enough, but may the gods save me from primitive woman! Civilization is necessary on woman's account."

He was an established favourite with men and women alike in less than twenty-four hours, and I also found that his report concerning the savages was correct in every detail. They retreated northward so fast that our scouts could scarce keep pace with them, and not long afterward I read with abounding delight General Wayne's letter of congratulation to me.

"It is the most brilliant success that we have won in the West for a long time, dear Jack," he wrote. "In truth it is the only one, and God knows that it came at the right time! I have described it in full in the report that I have just forwarded to the President, and do not be afraid that I have not done you full justice."

Did ever man have a better friend than I had in him?

CHAPTER 35 A Full Confession

"I tell thee, Jack, thy debt of gratitude to me is not half as heavy as mine to thee. That victory of thine at Fort Recovery has maintained my credit and put heart in the soldiers as nothing else could. Let me hear no more of this nonsense. I use thee because thou art the best tool that my hand can find."

It was General Wayne who was speaking, and we sat alone in the little log room at Fort Deposit, another post that we had built in the Northwestern wilderness, and yet farther than Fort Greeneville toward the heart of the Indian country. All our army save small garrisons was united there, and we were preparing for the great stroke. And with us, too, was Rose Carew. After the battle at Fort Recovery she might have had to return to Cincinnati perforce, but the way was closed by the savages, and of necessity she came on with us to Fort Deposit. Now we knew that the Indian power was assembling in our front, and we expected a speedy trial of the issue.

General Wayne turned his attention to a piece of paper, across which lines ran in zigzags, with here and there the picture of some wild animal. It was a map made by Osseo, each wild animal representing Indian warriors of a particular tribe, and I have seen many a map drawn by European experts that was not half so good.

"Your red friend gives me the disposition of their forces," he said, dropping his thee and thou, "and I think we can meet them, Jack, trick for trick. We may rely on Osseo, may we not?"

"As surely as on the rising and the setting of the sun," I replied with emphasis.

He smiled.

"I know that you are right," he said. "But, Jack, I wish to talk of the future—that is, your future. There is a matter, Jack, near your heart, of which I want to speak, and you will excuse the freedom of an old comrade in mentioning it, because it is now as a comrade and not as your general that I do speak. You were a fine blade in the old days, Jack, and you had a glib tongue with the ladies. Nor have your years in the woods been unkind to you. I have seen the eyes that you make at Miss Carew. What! blushing? a reprobate like you! But, Jack, you love her—I know it; don't fib to me about it."

"It is true, general," I replied; "I do love Miss Carew, but the best that a man like myself can do is to conceal it, or at least try."

"It is because you are such a fool, Jack, that I have wished to speak to you of this matter. And it is because of it, too, that I shall send you back to the East. She will be there before you—her father has had enough of the wilderness—and I tell you, Jack, you must go in and win, if for no other reason than to upset that cursed cousin of yours. The fellow has power, and he has tried to weaken me in my command here. I tell you, Jack, you must beat him in love as you have beat him in this war!"

He was the fiery, enthusiastic Mad Anthony Wayne of the Revolution who was now talking, and I caught from him the spirit of hope. "Never mind the past," he would say, "follow the girl, Jack; follow her, I tell you."

It seemed a singular chance that another friend of mine should speak to me upon the same subject the next morning. This was Mrs. Winchester. The Winchesters were still with us, though they were to pass to the British post on the Miami the following day.

"Your cousin expects to wed Miss Carew," she said, "when this war is over and they shall have returned to the East."

"Has he her promise?" I could not refrain from asking.

"That is a question that you had best ask her."

"He might say that he had it, but I would not believe him," I continued.

"You do not love your cousin," she said, looking at me curiously.

"As much as he loves me," I replied.

Then she began to tell me of Major Carew and his ambition for his daughter; he was fond of place and power, perhaps excessively so, and he would have his daughter to wed to advantage. Although not saying it in so many words, Mrs. Winchester indicated plainly that Jasper was the choice of Major Carew, and well he might be, since he was one of the richest men in our country. All my own property, escheated after my conviction for treason—I had been treated like the loyalist exiles—had been obtained by Jasper, and at small cost to himself, as I learned. He was now swollen with mine as well as his own, and my heart burned with a fierce rage that he should steal this girl too. Nothing now should keep me back. I, too, would go to the East, and if I could not obtain her for myself I might at least keep her from his arms. I was so much lost in these emotions that I did not notice until presently that Mrs. Winchester was watching me with the greatest keenness and curiosity. But she turned her eyes quickly away when they met mine.

"You are resolved to go back to your old home, are you not?" she asked.

"Yes," I replied with emphasis.

"You should tell Miss Carew so," she said.

That was an odd remark for Mrs. Winchester to make, but I did not notice its nature at the time, my mind being so full of Rose Carew and Jasper. Yet it chimed well with my wishes. I would see Miss Carew, and I would tell her the kind of man

Jasper was!—No, I could not do that—it would not be the act of a gentleman—but I must talk to her before this battle. I was glad of any excuse now to seek her presence. In the narrow space inclosed by the palisade of Fort Deposit such an opportunity was not long lacking. When we walked together on the little parade ground I told her that we should march without further delay against the Indian power, and the chiefs would not avoid a battle; either their strength would be broken, or they would regain all the Western country.

"But I have decided," I said, "that in any event I shall return to the East," and then I added, with an effort at lightness, "you see that you can not escape me; you shall see me there."

Her face was turned from me then, and I noticed only the gravity of her reply: "You are right to come."

"Others who know my history might not say so," I replied.

"But all the world will know of your great services here," she said. "How many people on this Western border have you saved from torture and death and worse than death?"

She turned her eyes upon me then. They were luminous and moist with the suspicion of tears. She felt pity for me, I knew. One does not always want pity, but I was moved by it.

"If there is any credit due me," I said, "I wish to have it. I am not such an affected fool as to deny it. And I should like to have my good name back again. Do you think, Miss Carew, that all these years in the wilderness among savage red men, and almost as savage white men, have hardened me to the shame or made me forget it? I persuaded myself once that it had, and I believed it—almost believed it—until you came. You called me back, not that you meant to do it, or that I meant you should. But all the old rebellion and fierce desire for revenge upon the world that had condemned me rose up again. Do you think I could ever forget that time? Remember that I was only a boy, and the world seemed bright and good. I had name and station, I had won honours in the war, I had comrades of my own age, and I was trusted by great men far older than myself. Think, then, of what I was called upon to endure—this sudden blow! Could you have wondered if I had become the worst of criminals in very truth?"

She turned her eyes upon me then, and they were still luminous and soft with the mist of tears. But she did not speak. My heart was hot within me. I had held down my grief and rage so long that now, at the first lifting of restraint, they burst forth in a flood.

"Do you suppose that I have forgotten it, any detail of it?" I repeated fiercely. "Do you not know what it is to feel that you are despised by all men, that you must always have their contempt? Do you not think that all of it, as hideous as ever, came back to me when I saw you and saw how far away you were? Do you not think I felt as deeply as if I were still the convicted boy, every word of my cousin Jasper, when we met again and he taunted me with that old memory?"

"But you were not guilty," she said gently.

"No, I was not," I replied, and it was the first time since my conviction that my pride had ever let me deny it; "but what of that? The evidence said I was, and the court could not do otherwise than it did. The world, the world that was mine, is convinced that I am guilty, and I might as well be."

"Now it is not your better self, John Lee, that is speaking," she suddenly interrupted me. "If you are not guilty you are not, and the opinion of all the men in the world can not make you so. I would go back to the East, I would assert my innocence, and I would prove it; even yet I would do so."

Her eyes were shining, but there were no tears in them now; instead, they sparkled with brilliant fire. It was this that bewildered me for the moment and drew me on.

"I will go back," I said. "I have finally resolved on that, but whether I shall prove my innocence I know not. It is not alone the hope of regaining my old position that induces me to go; it is less potent than something else." And now I lost my head fully. "When a man knows that he is condemned, and a woman speaks the only word of sympathy that he has heard in ten years, what can you expect of him? Would he not fall in love with her, even if she were not the best and most beautiful woman that he had ever seen? And when a chance came to him to help her would he not do it, and would not that help itself make him love her the more? You know well of whom I am talking, Rose, dearest Rose! I can call you so because I love you and I can not help it, nor would I help it if I could."

She tried to say something, but I would not hear her. The words came up from my heart like a flood all the more powerful because held back so long.

"I know that it is folly—nay, more, presumption—in me," I continued, "but I will say what I feel. You do not understand what a luxury it is to speak one's real mind after being denied it for many years. I know that I am a miserable object to utter words of love to a good woman, but I say them because I love you!"

"Oh, hush! hush!" she murmured. "Do not talk so!"

"You will be offered love by better men," I said, "but none will offer you a better love than mine, and I am glad to avow now what I feel."

I spoke the truth. It was a joy to me to say to her that I loved her. What I had sworn to myself to keep secret I now told her with all the fire and passion of a boy in his first love, and I was proud of it. She turned her head away and said nothing. What feeling looked from her eyes I knew not, but I could not check the torrent of my speech. At last I repeated:

"If I am spared by the battle I shall return to the East, and you shall see me there."

Then I turned, and not looking back, hurried into the fort. She murmured some words, but I could not stay to listen. I could not bear to hear her reproach me for my folly.

It was folly, I repeated in my cooler moments, yet I was not sorry for it; instead, I felt mental exaltation.

CHAPTER 36 The Fallen Timbers

The August sun swung clear of the earth and threw a flood of light over the army as it advanced through the deep woods. We had started from Fort Deposit at daybreak, leaving there our heavy baggage, the women, and a small garrison, and at last we were marching to meet the gathered power of the Indian tribes. The fate of the Northwest hung upon the event, yet around us was only the silence of the wilderness, the murmur of the wind through the deep foliage, and the singing of the birds. Even the soldiers, who usually, in the face of death, see the lighter side of things, refrained from jest or other comment and walked solemnly on to meet the elusive and terrible foe, against whom another army had marched only to slaughter.

I felt a thrill alike of pride and apprehension as I looked upon those around me. I knew how the iron hand of their general had moulded them into shape until they were fit to meet the savage tribes, and I knew, too, that it would be a mortal blow to him if he failed. Yet the fate and hopes of one man were but little compared with the desolation that torch and tomahawk would spread along the border behind us if we were beaten. Surely if men ever had a spur to valour it was we.

The sun, a ball of red and gold, crept up the arch of the sky. The army, still silent in speech, gave forth the usual murmur of arms and the tread of men and horses. The sunbeams glanced along the leaves of the trees, not yet burned brown by the summer sun, and shot in long arrows of light over the surface of the Little Miami. But the woods were yet silent. They gave forth no sign of the enemy. We knew that the allied power of the Northwestern tribes lay near us, but the waving of no scalp lock, the glint of no tomahawk, met our eyes. That foe whom we were going to meet was as wary, as elusive, and as terrible as ever. The silence was oppressive, ominous, and I longed to hear the defiant war-whoop.

General Wayne signalled to me. His face was anxious, and he made no effort to disguise it.

"Are you sure that they are before us, Jack?" he asked.

"Osseo says so, and the chief is never mistaken. Moreover, old Joe Grimes and a dozen other scouts bear witness to the truth of his words."

"I did not doubt them, Jack, but I like not this silence. I hate a hidden foe. 'Twas not this way in the war with the English, as you know, Jack. Then it was hammer and tongs, give and take, and the best man to win, with no ill feeling afterward. But here it is an enemy whom you can not find, and you know not what to expect when you do find him."

But Mad Anthony Wayne would not allow impatience to defeat caution. Forward we went, hugging the Little Miami on our right, that we might not be flanked there, the scouts swarming on our left and in our front. Near me was Lawless, now my devoted friend, and farther on was Jasper. His face was turned from me, but I knew that his lips were as white as chalk, and that he saw the figure of Hoyoquim in every glade. The footsteps of the army were softened by the deep turf. The wind rose a little and sang a song through the leaves of the trees. But there was no hostile sound. Our eyes saw and our ears heard only the peace that we had learned never to trust.

On we went, still hugging the river as a swordsman hugs a wall, and the wilderness deepened. The trees were denser and the grass grew higher. Before us rose a dark mass of fallen forest thrown down by a tornado, and looking toward it I suddenly saw a spot of faint pink appear against its background and then darken into flame. The crack of the rifle shot, sharp and distinct, came to our ears, and it was followed by another and others. A sputtering fire came too from the high, grass on our right, and then the scouts bounded into view. But we needed no word from them; we knew now that the Indian army lay in the grass and the fallen timber. And we were ready. There was fierce exultation in that thought.

General Wayne was near me when the Indian attack began. He turned and brought down a heavy hand upon my shoulder:

"We are face to face with 'em at last, and it is not a surprise; I thank God for that, Jack!"

I think that he spoke unconsciously, and because the long and great tension of his mind found relief in the sudden opening of the battle.

The fire of the Indians rose to a steady crackle, with the defiant war-whoop swelling at intervals above it. Yet the warriors still lay hidden. Not one of their brown faces could we see, and our soldiers already were falling. But the army remained steady. I noticed it with joy. The long and diligent training had paid. Always the men had been told to do that most difficult of things—to remain firm in the face of hidden death; and now they obeyed. The bullets flying from the fallen trees and the long grass whistled among us, and the soldiers here and there continued to fall; but on the army went, steady and resolute, into the deepening fire.

I kept close to General Wayne, and I marked the unconscious workings of the mind of this man, who was prone to speak as he thought.

"Good lads! good lads!" he said in a rapid under-tone, like the patter of a subdued fire of musketry. "They don't flinch! Look how they go against a death that they can not see, but which they know is there! Ha! this is worthy of Stony Point! No, on my soul 'tis better!"

He stopped suddenly and called me. The fire on our left was growing extremely heavy—as heavy as any that I witnessed at St. Clair's defeat, and it was spreading, too, around our flank. They were seeking to repeat their old plan of surrounding us, pressing our army into a huddle, and then shooting us down from covert. But the general's eye was quick to see.

"We must have none of that, Jack," he cried. "Bid the left flank advance with the bayonet and we'll rouse up these fellows."

I delivered his order and galloped back to the general, and then we faced the fallen timber. Innumerable spouts of flame came from the tree trunks and upthrust boughs, and through the smoke now we could see the brown and naked forms of the warriors as they leaped from one covert to another. From the left came the boom of the cannon and the crash of our own rifle fire preparing the way for the bayonet charge. Then it died suddenly, and I knew that the men were advancing with the cold steel which no savage who was ever born can face. At the same moment the general gave the word to us in the centre. Up went the bayonets in a flash of light, and our line swept down on the fallen trees.

My horse was killed by a bullet, but I sprang clear of him, drew my sword, and rushed on in the charge. The fire in our faces seemed to redouble, and the flash of the exploding powder became one great, blinding blaze; but on we went into it and through it, and then we leaped among the fallen trees.

The bayonet was raised and the savages fled from its cold touch. We roused them out of the brush like a swarm of partridges, and they could not stand before us. Then they learned that they had not come against an ambushed rabble like St. Clair's force, but a trained army led by the best men in the West. Again I felt the thrill of exultation as the line of bayonets flashed in the brushwood, and the naked warriors, leaping from their coverts, ran in terror. On our left we saw the same gleam, and we knew that it came from the bayonets of our comrades who were driving the enemy before them with a speed not less than ours.

The savages ceased to utter the defiant war-whoop. On all sides they fled, a frightened swarm, pursued by the avenging bayonets and stricken down by the rifle fire, the forms of their dead scattered all through the brushwood and high grass.

A tall figure rose out of the smoke beside me and a voice shouted in my ear:

"Who's blinkin' like a frog in a thunderstorm now, John?"

It was old Joe Grimes, his face one great blaze of triumph.

"You're right," I replied. "They can't stand the flash of the bayonet in their eyes."

"Bayonet, hell!" he cried. "It ain't the bayonet that's doin' 'em! It's this!" and he tapped the barrel of his rifle as he spoke. The next moment he was gone in the timber, hot upon the trail of the beaten savages. But I knew that he would never allow any of the credit of the victory to the regular soldiers, or to that weapon despised by all frontiersmen, the bayonet.

We passed on through all the grass and fallen timber, driving the savages so fast that our run never dropped to a walk, and winning the victory so soon that only our vanguard was unable to get into the battle, the rear ranks panting and rushing through the hot sun only to find the work done when they arrived.

I came near General Wayne again in the pursuit.

"It was quick—eh, Jack!" he cried, his face not concealing his triumph.

"Ay, quick," I replied, "and thorough too."

"After 'em, lads!" he cried. "Don't give 'em time to turn on us!"

It was a difficult matter to pursue the savages. They melted before us like ghosts in the dark, but we knew as we pressed on that they would have no chance to rally and cut us down with a fire from ambush. I was hot with the pursuit, and having a better trained and keener eye than the soldiers for such work, I marked the tall form of a warrior fleeing through the woods, and kept it in sight.

The chase led me directly from my comrades and into the deeper forest. The scattering fire behind me became feeble, but I noticed little else in my eagerness to overtake or bring down the warrior. I judged from his size and the splendour of his garb that he must be a chief at least, and my zeal increased. I strove to reload my rifle as I ran, but he led me in such a rapid chase that I could not do it, and giving up the attempt, I loosened the pistol in my belt.

I was scarce twenty yards away when the warrior suddenly stopped, and turning about, stood stock still, gazing at me. Then I recognised the lofty features and haughty gaze of Little Turtle, the great chief of the Miamis.

He struck his hand upon his breast and said in a tone of mingled dignity and sadness:

"Fire, my brother! Mechecunnaqua, this day, has seen his people beaten and their power destroyed forever. The land was once the land of the red man, but it is now the land of the white man. The will of Manito is done. Since Mechecunnaqua is to die, he is glad that he is to die by the hand of a brave enemy—an enemy whom he has loved."

I lowered my pistol. I remembered that night in the Miami village when he looked upon his escaping prisoner and then looked away.

"You did not command the Indian army to-day, Mechecunnaqua?" I said.

"No," he replied. "I was but the chief of my own tribe."

"Wherein God was kind to us," I said.

He bowed to my compliment, but I saw the flash of his eye, and I knew that he believed it true.

"Be our friend, o Mechecunnaqua," I said, and I turned away.

I left him standing there alone in the forest, a defeated and fallen king, a prey to I knew not what gloomy thoughts, but never have I had cause to regret lowering my weapon. He was the leader in making the great treaty of peace the next year, and now the mighty chief, Little Turtle, who more than once led the allied tribes to victory, lives among us, our long-time and faithful friend.

CHAPTER 37 The Only Way

I returned toward the battlefield, thoughtful and sobered. I had seen the other side of the victory. But before I reached the fallen timbers Osseo rose up in my path.

"Manito has been kind to Lee to-day," he said. "Manito loves him."

"How so, Osseo?" I asked in some surprise.

"He has moved Lee's enemy from his path. Lo the Long Knife, whose name is the same as Lee's, was taken to-day in the battle by the Wyandot chief, Hoyoquim, and the white Indian Blackstaffe, and they have carried him away to work their will upon him."

I was struck with horror. Those who have followed this narrative know that I had no cause to love Jasper, but I shuddered when I thought of the hideous tortures that Hoyoquim and Blackstaffe would inflict upon him for his desertion. And after this came another thought: perhaps Rose Carew loved him! Could I bear to see her grief when she heard of his doom? When this second thought came to me I hesitated no longer.

"Come, Osseo," I said, "lead the way; we must bring my cousin back again."

"Lee is a strange man," he responded. "The Indian rejoices at the torture of his worst enemy, but the white man would rescue him. Manito has made us different, and it is not for Osseo to ask why. Come!"

He led the way through the forest, and I knew that we were upon the trail of Hoyoquim and his captive. I was to some extent a free lance and I was troubled by no qualms of conscience as I left the battlefield and the army behind me and sped on in pursuit of the Wyandot band. The trail lay broad and plain before us, but its state showed that the warriors were travelling fast. If we would rescue Jasper it must be done quickly. Yet we were sure that Hoyoquim did not anticipate pursuit, and this aided us, as, fearing no ambush, we travelled at great speed.

It was a brilliant day, the August sun pouring a flood of light upon the world. The forest stood out against the perfect blue of the sky like carved tracery. But the old silence, save for the murmur of the wind and the song of the birds, had returned to it. One could believe that the battle of the morning and destruction of the Indian power was a dream.

"The captive lagged here and they prodded him with their knives," said Osseo, not looking up. "Then he hastened."

I did not wonder that Jasper hurried before the knife points, and it was but a foretaste, too, of what awaited him.

The footsteps followed the bank of the river through woods and grass and across tributary creeks, and Osseo, watching with keen eyes, said that the warriors had not stopped once. Evidently they had some purpose in such a rapid and sustained night, since the danger of ordinary pursuit had long since passed.

"Why do they hurry so fast and far?" I said to Osseo.

"Lee knows," he replied, without raising his head from the footsteps.

He spoke the truth. I knew even when I asked.

Noon came, and then the afternoon began to wane, but the sky was still a brilliant blue, save where little clouds made spots of fleecy white upon its azure surface. The murmur of the wind did not cease, and by the river's brink wild flowers of red and purple and white nodded to its breath.

"The footsteps shorten," said Osseo. "The warriors do not hurry so much." Then he added, a few moments later: "Now they stop and talk with each other. The prisoner stands in the centre; and see, he falls to his knees!"

Poor Jasper! I knew why he was upon his knees, and I knew too how vain was his sacrifice of the white man's pride.

"Come, Osseo," I said, "let us hasten on."

"It is not far now," he replied. "Hoyoquim is sure at last that he is beyond pursuit, and he will soon begin the work for which he has come."

We followed more cautiously and slowly for about a half hour, and then Osseo, without a word of warning, sank suddenly to his knees. I imitated him at once, knowing that he did nothing without good reason, and then he pointed silently with his finger to the far side of the river.

The savages had crossed and already had begun their horrible task.

Jasper was bound to a tree with green withes, not so tightly that he could not move, but fast enough to cut off all hope of escape. The warriors and Blackstaffe were gathering dead wood for the torture and heaping it about his feet, while Hoyoquim stood before him and taunted him after the Indian fashion.

We crept forward among the thick bushes and high grass until we were separated from them only by the river. I can not forget the look of terror and despair on Jasper's face. Had the withes fallen of their own accord to the ground I do not believe that he could have made an effort to escape.

"Had they only waited until the morrow for this we might have saved him," I whispered to Osseo.

"'Tis too late," he replied. "Manito has spoken his will."

Hoyoquim turned presently, and then I saw his face also. It was the incarnation of savage and malignant triumph. To him Jasper was a traitor for whom the worst torture was too good, and he would spare him nothing; God had not delivered him into his hand that he might show him mercy. Hoyoquim was always an Indian of Indians and a Wyandot of Wyandots.

The warriors proceeded slowly and with care. It was a delight that they loved to linger over. One stopped now and then to join Hoyoquim in the task of taunting Jasper, but in a moment or two would return to his work of collecting dry wood and heaping it around the prisoner's feet.

Jasper never moved or uttered a word. The look of horror and despair in his eyes seemed to be fixed there. It affected me strangely. He was my enemy. That I knew. But he was my cousin too. We were of the same blood and the same name. I had seen other men in like position, but none stirred me in such a manner. How could I hide the story of this from Rose Carew? I longed for him to struggle against his thongs, to cry out, to reply to the jeers of the chief, to do or to say anything, rather than stand there, motionless and senseless, with that fixed look of horror upon his face. I shivered despite myself, but in a moment the face of Jasper drew me back. No matter what his faults, he was receiving his punishment and more.

We crept to the very edge of the bushes and trees that lined the brink, drawn by the hideous fascination of this scene. Higher grew the heap of wood around Jasper's feet, reaching now to his knees, but he noticed not, still staring with terrified eyes straight into the air and seeing nothing. The renegade Blackstaffe presently joined Hoyoquim, and he too began to taunt Jasper, laughing with atrocious mirth at the face of the victim.

We could hear the taunts, but beyond this single blur there was nothing to disturb the peace and beauty of a summer day. Bubbles in delicate tints of purple and pink and blue floated for a moment on the silent sheet of the river, then broke and were gone. The gentle current made a murmur like a sigh that matched the note of the wind through the forest. In the open the long grass rippled like the surface of a lake swept by the mildest of southern breezes, and little birds in brilliant plumage sang, unscared, almost at our feet.

Hoyoquim spoke to one of the warriors, who presently came with a piece of dry wood burning at the end. The chief took it from his hand and waved it before the face of Jasper, who noticed it not, merely staring with that horror-stricken gaze into the blue of the skies.

Hoyoquim bent down and applied the torch to the heap of wood built around Jasper. The dry boughs ignited readily and little blazes began to rise.

The savages stood in a semicircle before the victim, their faces expressing triumphant anticipation.

I looked into the eyes of Osseo. His gaze met mine, and he understood.

"There is no other way," he said.

The warriors came a little closer to their victim, but the next moment there was the sharp crack of a rifle, a puff of white smoke, and a vacant look came over Jasper's face. Then his head fell forward on his breast, and he passed forever from the power of his captors.

CHAPTER 38 The Meeting of the Chiefs

Osseo and I, after the shot, leaped from the bushes and ran southward, knowing well that Hoyoquim and his warriors would follow hot upon us. Yet we could not use our utmost speed at first, as it was needful for one of us to reload his rifle. But when this was done we ran faster. We heard nothing after the shot save one long, fierce war-whoop, and then came the silence of tenacious Indian pursuit.

We expected no easy escape. The cunning chief and the renegade would guess from some clew who we were, and every motive would urge them to our capture. Yet our blood thrilled with other emotions than those of fear. It was a test of skill and endurance, but if overtaken that was not the end; we should be as hard to hold as a wounded panther. Then my mind went back again to that ghastly face beside the river. I looked at Osseo, and, as before, he knew of what I was thinking.

"It was the will of Manito that it should be done," he said.

We paused a moment at the top of a little hill, and, glancing back, I saw the long grass moving at the edge of the forest. I knew that the warriors, having crossed the river at once, were there, and were following us at great speed.

"We may have to fight, Osseo," I said.

"It may be so," he replied, "and I ask Lee that he leave the chief, Hoyoquim, to me."

I was surprised at Osseo's tone, and when I looked at him I saw that his eyes were flashing. He seemed to be moved by a deep emotion that broke through the Indian calm. There must be some feud between him and Hoyoquim, as I had guessed before, and I spoke at once.

"I shall not stand between you, Osseo," I said.

We resumed our flight, plunging once more into the deep forest, running with long, easy strides.

"Let us go now in a curve, like the bending of a bow," said Osseo presently.

"Why so?" I asked.

"The Wyandots will see it and think then to cut us off," he replied, "and the warriors will divide. One party will follow the curve of the bow and the others will follow the string. Then if we be overtaken it will be by fewer warriors, and, if we must fight, Manito alone knows whether the Wyandots or Osseo and his friend are to be the victors."

I turned as he wished without another word, and we went on in silence for many minutes. Then I noticed that Osseo's speed was slackening, and I was surprised. He was as if made of steel, and never had I known him to show fatigue in so short a time; but, looking at him carefully, I saw no sign of weariness.

"Why do you check your speed, Osseo?" I asked.

"Why should we hurry and waste our breath?" he replied. "Are we fawns, that we flee thus from the hunter?"

I saw again that flash in his eye, and I knew what was passing in the soul of Osseo.

"How many are following us now?" I asked.

He dropped down suddenly and put his ear to the earth.

"But four," he replied, springing up.

"Think you that the chief, Hoyoquim, is among them?"

"As sure as the sun shines."

"Then we shall lead them farther away from their comrades."

We made a deeper curve of the bow, turning far to the westward, and went on for almost an hour. Then Osseo, looking at me with that old faint, humorous twinkle in his eye, said:

"I grow as weak as a sick woman, and I can run no farther."

There was not a drop of sweat on him, and he was as strong as steel.

"I must rest, or I die," he said, his eyes yet twinkling.

"Then, Osseo," I said, "it is better to rest than to die."

He sat down on a fallen log, and I sat down beside him, each holding his rifle across his knees.

"Lee," said Osseo, "it seems to me that some one comes for us."

"Osseo speaks the truth," I replied.

The bushes parted suddenly, and our pursuers leaped into view—Hoyoquim, the renegade, and two warriors. They uttered the triumphant war-whoop at sight of us, and fired just as our fingers pressed our own triggers.

Their bullets, discharged with hasty aim, missed the mark, but not so ours; our hands were steady from the rest, and we had marked the target true. The two warriors fell dead.

Then Osseo, casting down his empty rifle, drew his tomahawk. Hoyoquim did the same, and the two rushed into the glade. Each threw his tomahawk and each lightly sprang aside, the weapon whizzing by. Then, drawing their knives, they closed in a fierce combat.

I had lost my pistol somehow in the battle, and I was reloading my rifle with all the speed that I could command. The renegade was doing likewise, but my weapon was levelled again and my finger on the trigger just as he withdrew the ramrod.

"Don't raise your rifle!" I cried. "This is no fight of ours!"

He let the weapon drop to his side, and stared at the two chiefs twined now in deadly strife, their black eyes flashing with hate, the great muscles standing upon their brown arms, and their breath short and spasmodic with their tremendous efforts. Yet neither uttered a cry, and neither sought with his eyes the help of the friend who stood near. I could have sent a bullet more than once into the body of the Wyandot chief, but I had given my word to my comrade, and there was no excuse for me to break it.

So evenly matched were they that they scarce shifted from the spot upon which they stood. Each grasped the other by the wrist, and neither could strike with his knife or tear the hand away. Watching them, I was unable to say that either had the advantage by the breadth of a hair.

How long a time passed I know not, but when I will it I can yet see those two fierce faces so close to each other and so full of hate. Nature had made them a splendid pair, equal in height and breadth and weight, and now she had brought them together to see which was the finer work of hers.

They began presently to move a little in their struggle, feet crushing upon the earth, and arms swaying slightly. I heard their loud, spasmodic breathing. Presently the form of Hoyoquim bent back a little, and Osseo bent over him. It was the end. Osseo with a sudden supreme effort tore his wrist loose from the hand of Hoyoquim, his knife flashed aloft, and the next instant it was buried in the breast of the Wyandot chieftain.

Hoyoquim reeled away, but Osseo stood where he was, motionless, his face without expression. The Wyandot plucked the knife from his breast with all his failing strength and hurled it at his enemy. Still holding himself erect, he gave us one look of defiance from drooping and bloodshot eyes, then uttered a long and thrilling war-whoop, which died away in a quaver as he fell dead at our feet.

I heard the snap of a gunlock, and wheeling about, saw the rifle of the renegade levelled at Osseo. I fired instantly and without raising my weapon to my shoulder, but the bullet sped true. The renegade fell on his face without a cry, and the earth was one black scoundrel the less.

Osseo looked down at the face of the dead Wyandot chief.

"He was a great warrior and a brave man," he said.

When he had spoken this simple tribute to his enemy we resumed our flight.

CHAPTER 39 The Outcast's Return

The coach-and-six swung rapidly forward in the beautiful sunshine, and I looked about at the peaceful country, the neat farm-houses, the stone fences, and the cultivated fields. The wilderness is fine in a way of its own, and the inhabited country in another, also its own. It is not for me to preach the beauty of one to the exclusion of the other, particularly when I see both.

Yet it took my eyes a long time to grow used to the sight of houses and fences and men working in the fields. I was coming home after nearly fifteen years in the wilderness, and habit was still strong upon me. It was hard for me to believe that no danger lurked in the wood ahead; and our driver, as he swung his great whip and cracked it over his horses with a sound like a rifle shot, seemed to me to approach it with criminal carelessness. I felt instinctively for my rifle, but the weapon was not there, and I laughed softly to myself.

"Yonder is Philadelphia!" exclaimed Winchester.

We were on top of the coach, and rising to my full height, at the imminent risk of being pitched into the road on my head, I gazed at the tips of Philadelphia's church spires shining in the late afternoon sun. Yes, it was our great town, the old town in which so much of my boyhood had been spent, and of which I had so many memories.

I did not wish to speak, and Winchester, understanding, was silent. Fate had decreed to me a life full of striking contrasts so far, but none greater than this. We had come at once from the wilderness by the way of old Fort Duquesne, where we took the coach for Philadelphia, and now we were at the heart of our civilization. It was like a sudden trip from a different world.

But I was not to enter Philadelphia at once. Another and greater duty awaited me. The driver, obedient to my request, stopped at a point where a small road led off from the main line of travel.

"I leave thee here, Jerry," I said to the driver—he was Jerry Goddard, a veteran of the Pennsylvania line, and I had known him at once, though he did not know me—"and here's one of Mr. Hamilton's new dollars for thee, Jerry, to drink to the memory of the old days."

He took the money and stared at me. Then he shook his head. He could not remember—I had not told him my name. He blew his horn, and the coach swung forward at a lively rate, driver and horses alike eager for their supper in Philadelphia. I saw him looking back at me from the top of the next rise, but I had not moved from the roadside, and he was compelled to go on, his curiosity ungratified.

Then I turned into the narrow road and walked toward a grove of trees which looked black and impenetrable at the distance. Yes, it was I, John Lee, I said to myself as doubts arose; John Lee in a sober suit of gray, though his hat was cocked and there were silver buckles on his shoes; John Lee, of Philadelphia, not the wild hunter who carried his life, night and day, on the touch of his trigger—that seemed now to be another man.

The wood thinned out as I approached. Then the slate roof of the house and the red of the brick walls appeared through the trees. A western window blazed like fire in the light of the setting sun. It was at once a joy and a pain to see that nothing was changed. Well, Jasper had been a good tenant, and he was past blame now.

There was a field on my right, and a man who had been at work in it was riding his horse home, the harness rattling about him. I wondered if he knew me, and half feared, half wished, that he would call my name. But he did not turn his face, and rode on, unnoticing.

The road, well kept I observed, led straight to the gates of the little park in which the manor-house stood. All about me was neat and thrifty, and I said to myself again that Jasper had been a good tenant. I stopped a moment at the park gate of iron with the brass filigree work at the top which my grandfather had brought from England, and of which he was so proud. The same old griffins stared at me from the tops of the stone posts beside the gate, and I found myself staring back at them as I used to do when I was a child. Then, passing my hand inside the gate, I pressed the spring that opened it and entered the park, walking along the shell avenue between the great elms. They looked smaller to me than when I last saw them, yet in truth they were larger; fifteen years makes a difference in perspective. The catalpa trees in front of the house were in fresh and full bloom, great masses of white that almost hid the building.

The park, though showing the same care and neatness that marked the fields, was deserted. All seemed to be prepared for human life, but human life itself was lacking. A dog came at last from behind one of the outbuildings and looked at me. Then, without opening his mouth, he trotted back to his covert. "I am not of sufficient importance to be barked at now," I said, with a sort of self-pity.

Ours was a fine mansion—nay, it has been called a great one—of red brick, three stories in the centre with a two-story wing on either side and a handsome portico, the pillars, wreathed with vines, framing the main entrance in the centre. Some of the leaves from the roses blooming on the vines had fallen on the floor of the portico, but there was naught else to see. Here was still the same fresh cleanliness and the same lack of human presence.

I lifted the heavy brass double knocker, and then, taking second thought with myself, I pushed the door; it opened easily, and I entered the house in which I was born. Here, too, there was no change. The great hall, wainscotted with polished mahogany, and the mahogany balustrade of the grand staircase, looked neither blacker nor older than when I left. This balustrade, carved by hand to represent baskets of fruit and flowers, was another object of my grandfather's pride, and there just above the floor was the little notch which I had cut to show my youthful prowess, and for which I received a just punishment.

I pushed open a door on the right-hand side of the hall and entered a room that had been my father's, a large, light apartment. It was precisely as it had been in his day, each piece of furniture in the old position, and there on the wall hung the famous portrait of my grandfather, Geoffrey Lee, painted in London by Sir Godfrey Kneller, a heavy but handsome man in a velvet coat, ornamented with silver lace and buttons, the face clear and strong and surmounted by the large, flowing wig of the period—a fine, courtly man, whose firm character showed in every feature. It was he who built Stoneham, our house, and created the estate; and here was I, the last of the race, upon which I had brought disgrace, staring into his eyes. But he did not reproach me nor did he commend.

The face of my father, painted by a lesser artist, was not so strong, but more benignant; and there, too, was my mother, a slender woman with mild blue eyes.

I sat by the table in the centre of the room, how long I know not, in that strange silence, until I heard a step behind me as light as that of a cat; and then old Godfrey, faithful old Godfrey Landale, was beside me. He seized my hand, and the tears that ran down his withered cheek fell upon it.

"It is you, Master John! It is you at last!" he said. "I have been waiting for you!"

"Through all these years, Godfrey?"

"Through all these years."

"And through all the disgrace, Godfrey?"

"It was a lie, Master John. I never believed it."

"No, Godfrey," I said, "you did not believe it, and you would not have believed it had I been guilty, which I was not."

Then we both fell silent, for our memories were heavy upon us. He had always been an old man to me, but seen now by the older eyes which diminish effects, his age did not sit more heavily upon him than fifteen years before.

"There have been no changes here, Godfrey," I said at last.

"The other one made them," he said, "but when I heard of his death I put everything back as it was."

I knew that he was speaking of Jasper, but Godfrey would never recall him by name. He always spoke of him as the "other one."

He brought me my supper there presently, and insisted upon serving it with his own hands, watching me with jealous care. He asked me no questions. Whether he knew aught of the fifteen years I could not say, but he seemed to have no curiosity.

"Do you wish to see any of the others, Master John?" he said presently.

"Is Sam still here?" I asked.

Sam was the black coachman. He left the room and returned soon with Sam, a gigantic man who cried like a baby at sight of me, and yet stared at me curiously, as if he were not quite sure that I was I. Then I told them both to say nothing of my presence until I bade them. I was not yet sure of my position. The estate was mine; though escheated from me once, it had come back to me as Jasper's heir, and surely they could not take it from me again, after my work in the West, which General Wayne had been kind enough to call good. But Winchester was to come on the morrow and tell me the news. I wondered what effect the arrival of the traitor, John Lee, would have upon Philadelphia. Perhaps this great town of fifty thousand people, occupied with many things, had long since forgotten him! It was likely.

After Godfrey and Sam went out I took from my pocket an envelope of pale blue, sealed with red wax, and stamped with the arms of the Carews. It was inscribed to John Lee, Esq., and the letter inside, written in a small, clear hand, was but a line or two; it said:

I beg to remind you of your promise that we should see you in Philadelphia, and to tell you that we hold you to it.

Y's,

Rose Carew.

To Captain John Lee,

at Cincinnati, on the Ohio. It had reached me at Cincinnati, and if I had felt any weakening of my resolve this would have roused my courage. I had not seen Miss Carew immediately upon my return to Wayne's army, and I had sent Winchester to tell her of Jasper's death, which I said had occurred under the tomahawk of the savages; in truth, I saw her only once before her return to the East, and I did not have the heart to speak to her of Jasper. Major Carew, however, had talked of him with deep regret, and mourned him as one of the best of men.

I went to sleep that night in my own bedroom, in the high brass bed upon which I climbed by means of a little ladder, drawing the curtains around me, and about the middle of the night I awoke with a strange, oppressive feeling as if I were suffering from a nightmare. I sprang from the bed, sure in my semi-somnolent condition that enemies were upon me. I grasped at a weapon, and then remembered with a foolish little laugh that none was there. I opened the window, letting the free, fresh air flow in, and again I laughed at myself. I, a son of the wilderness, who slept under the trees, had not been in a curtained bed in fifteen years. I would not tell Godfrey of this. I must accustom myself gradually to bedrooms.

I slept the remainder of the night in front of the window, and Winchester came to see me early the next day.

"This Philadelphia of yours," he said, "is a fine and bustling town. I saw the President himself out driving, and the streets are full of macaronis. There's life here."

"I mean to see a little of it," I said.

The desire to see this old town with which my early years were united was so strong, now that I was near, that I would have risked everything to go there. Then, too, Rose Carew had asked me to come. But she could scarce do less for a broken man to whom she owed so much. It struck me for the first time what a trifle her letter was. She might have said more to one who had saved her from the savages.

But I let Winchester see nothing of these thoughts. He was manifestly in high spirits, and I sympathized with him. His wife was with the Carews on High Street, and both anticipated a period of gaiety in Philadelphia. He brought letters from General Wayne and other influential men in the West, and despite some coldness which then existed among us toward the English people—due rather to trouble over the Northwestern posts than to memories of the Revolutionary War—there could be no doubt of his kind reception. I felt for a little while a strange sort of jealousy of Winchester. He, a foreigner, could enjoy himself in my native town, while I was debarred, and debarred unjustly. I had looked in the mirror again that morning and found myself yet young, without a wrinkle or a gray hair, and I felt that I could have sported it with the gayest macaroni of them all. But the feeling of envy disappeared in a few moments. One could not hold it in the presence of Winchester.

"Have they heard of my arrival in Philadelphia?" I asked, "or am I wholly forgotten?"

Now, I wished him to reply that I was not forgotten. I preferred persecution to oblivion.

"You are not forgotten," he replied, "and your arrival is known. I heard it mentioned by two or three persons, but only casually, and not in a way that had meaning."

He was to return to the city in the afternoon, and would see me again on the morrow. Meanwhile I would remain at Stoneham.

"Bring me a newspaper," I said to him as he departed, and he nodded.

I was hungry for the sight of the Gazette or the Advertiser, merely to see familiar names, and the old routine of news, or perhaps there would be something about myself, showing how the town was likely to take me.

But when Winchester came the next day he was taciturn and evasive. I asked him for the newspaper, but he shrugged his shoulders and said that he had forgotten it. "At any rate, there is nothing in those little sheets but advertisements of sales, notices of arrivals at the port, and other uninteresting trifles," he said. I saw him a half hour later talking in a low voice to Godfrey, and when he noticed me he seemed confused and troubled. I inferred at once that my affairs were going badly, and I determined that he should not burn his fingers to help me.

"Winchester," I said, "it was wrong for me to come here. My presence in Philadelphia will not be taken well."

He pursed his lips and replied slowly, and, as I saw, with caution:

"'Tis past human wisdom, Lee, to tell about such matters, but having come, I would even go through with the business. 'Tis not in your nature, I think, to retreat now."

No, it was not my intent to withdraw, but I felt a great sinking of the spirits, of which, however, I did not tell Winchester.

CHAPTER 40 The Visit to the City

I remained at Stoneham four days, a hermit, or rather a prisoner, in my own house. Winchester visited me once more, but intimated that I should not leave until he came for me. Godfrey and the remainder of the men on the place seemed worried, and I caught them more than once whispering to each other, a conference that always broke up in a confused manner at my approach. But I was too proud to ask what troubles were before me or let them know of the sinking of the heart which I now felt so often.

Winchester returned on the evening of the fourth day.

"I think it best for you to come into town with me to-morrow, Lee," he said. "The news of your being here is spreading, and 'tis the cause of some talk. I would face it at once. And if I were you, Lee, I would put on my bravest apparel—your captain's uniform, you know—and choose your best horse, and we will ride together to the Carews. Mrs. Winchester is anxious to see you; she says that you have been secluding yourself too long."

Winchester seemed to me to take a just view of the affair. It was poor and discreditable tactics to be so bold at a distance and then to flinch in the face of the enemy. Hence I arrayed myself in my captain's uniform, shaved with extreme care, and selected the finest horse in the stable, a very presentable bay, having throughout the assistance of Godfrey and Sam. I knew, that whatever might befall, these two faithful souls, would remain loyal to me.

But I did not use the horse which I selected, as a handsome coach, with gilt panels and drawn by four horses, rattled up to the gates of Stoneham.

"It's mine," said Winchester, "or rather I hired it; 'twas the best that money could find in Philadelphia, and, I think on the whole I have done well. Honour me by getting in, will you, Lee?"

I sprang in, and there was Mrs. Winchester, very blonde and very beautiful, in silk of lilac and rose, with her hair drawn up monstrously high on her head in the fashion known as the "Queen's Nightcap."

"Since you would not come to see your friends, Captain Lee," she said, "your friends have come for you."

She was a good woman, and I was grateful to her for upholding me thus, feeling in truth somewhat ashamed that I did not have fit words in which to thank her.

Winchester entered the coach after me, the liveried driver cracked his whip, and we whirled away toward Philadelphia. Winchester, although it was a brilliant sunny morning, closed the coach door, and when I remarked upon it, said that we should at least go to the Carews unobserved. He seemed to me to be right, and I sighed that I should have to enter Philadelphia, in a way, concealed.

But I knew by passing glimpses through the glass that we had turned into the Germantown road, and would thus enter the city. This recalled to me the battle there, in which I, a mere slip of a boy, had borne my part, and when I aroused myself from these memories we were entering Philadelphia itself. Then I could not be restrained from looking through the glass door at the familiar houses, the streets, the church spires, and all the old sights known so well. But the streets seemed very silent for the great town that I had known and the greater town that they said it had become.

"Why, Philadelphia is as dull and sober as a New England village on Sunday," I said to Winchester.

"The active part of the town has shifted since your time," he replied. "Scarce any business is done in this quarter now."

Our carriage now approached the heart of the city, and suddenly I heard a great shout ahead of us.

"'Tis the soldiers," said Winchester, "and the people are cheering at the sight of the arms and the gay clothes. By my faith, Lee, despite all the Yankee talk about the dignity and rights of freeborn citizens, your populace is as frivolous and fond of the spectacular as any that we have in England."

"And behold Captain Lee himself, who for so many years has practised the stoicism of the Indian, showing as much vain curiosity as any of them!" exclaimed Mrs. Winchester, leaning forward and putting her shoulders between me and the glass door.

"As I can not see through a lady in any sense," I said, "I yield," and I leaned back in my seat.

The shouting increased, and 'twas a great tumult made by many thousand voices. Then I heard the crash, not of one band, but of two or three or more, and so much sound, falling upon ears long accustomed to the silence of the wilderness, was doubled or tripled in effect.

"'Tis a great celebration evidently," I said to Winchester.

"Ay," he replied; "I think it is the anniversary of one of your battles with us. There's to be a review of a great number of your old troops by the President. I've told our driver to take us by, and perhaps we may see a little of the spectacle."

We went on, and the shouting continued to grow, and as the coach began to proceed but slowly, I judged that we were now well into the crowd. Then we stopped suddenly, and Winchester said:

"Let's get out, Lee."

He threw open the door, and without giving me time to ask the reason of his strange action, plucked me by the arm. I was out of the coach in a moment, blinded by the dazzling sunlight, and deafened by the roar of ten thousand voices in my ears.

But I distinguished the cries:

"It is he! it is he! Lee! Lee!"

All the blood rushed to my head. I had not expected such fierce and prompt resentment as this.

"Forgive me, Winchester, for bringing you and your wife among such wolves as these!" I cried, and I tried to draw my sword that I might drive back the leaders of the mob.

But he seized my arm and, laughing in my face, cried out:

"Save your sword for another day, Lee!"

Then he released me, and the shouting of the crowd ceased, a deep murmur taking its place. I looked around me and saw that I was in front of Independence Hall. The street was crowded with people as far as my eyes reached, but in a moment they separated, forming a narrow lane between. My arms were suddenly seized by two men, and even in that moment of confusion and excitement I knew them. They were the colonel and lieutenant-colonel of my old regiment in the full uniform of the Pennsylvania line.

Then the shouting was renewed, with double strength, so it seemed to me, and all the bands played at once. The officers walked forward, and I, as one dazed, walked with them, without resistance. We passed through the crowd, and then between lines of soldiers, and I began to see around me many faces that I knew—good comrades of the camp and field. The shouting and the music never ceased, and my eyes were blurred with tears, but I was conscious in a few moments that I stood in the presence of a very tall man in the Continental uniform, our immortal leader himself, and beyond him I saw Hamilton and Knox and Lear, and then a tall girl whose eyes were dewy. The shouting and the music stopped, and the President said:

"John Lee, you were accused and convicted of an infamous crime once, and now after fifteen years we find that you were not guilty. Yet with dishonour falsely resting upon you, you have served your country and served it well. 'Tis never too late to undo a wrong. Therefore the Congress of the republic presents you with this sword in place of the one that was broken before you, and also with this resolution of thanks, and with other perhaps more solid rewards of which you shall hear later. And may I shake your hand, John Lee?"

They thrust forward a great, gold-hilted sword and a roll of rustling parchment, and the President grasped my hand in both of his.

Then the thunder of the crowd and the crash of the bands began again, and I was glad of it, because I could not speak.

The President took my arm and led the way to his carriage, a great cream-coloured coach drawn by cream-coloured horses with white manes, and helped me in with his own hand. Then Mr. Hamilton and Mr. Knox, and Mr. Lear, the President's chief secretary, followed us there, and I became conscious that we were moving.

"Where are we going? What is to be done?" I said.

"We are going where we are welcome, and we shall do what is pleasant," replied the President, gravely taking a pinch of snuff.

The shouting continued and followed us, and when the coach stopped a great crowd was still around it. But it made way for us, and we approached a red-brick house with three stone steps leading up to the front door.

"Mr. Morris's place," I cried. I had played in the woods before it many a time.

"Ay, it's Mr. Morris's," replied, the President, "but I live there now."

It was true. This was now the home of the President of the United States, and I entered it arm in arm with its tenant, the others following behind and the crowd yet lingering about. They showed me the finest guest chamber, and left me alone, though Winchester presently joined me there. He sat down near a window and laughed with deep content.

"Well, Lee," he said, "was your reception sufficiently hostile to please you?"

Then I laughed too. I was compelled to do so, as a relief to my feelings.

"Winchester," I said, "how did this happen?"

"Ask your President," he replied. "He seems to be the master of ceremonies, and I am willing to swear that none could manage them better. But keep yourself composed, Lee. There is to be a great state dinner, with your distinguished self as the guest of honour, and while you are waiting you might look at this newspaper, which I would not give you the other day."

He tossed me a copy of the Gazette, and then I read the story how John Lee had been accused and convicted, and now was proved innocent. For the sake of the dead man who was of my own blood I will not dwell on the wretched tale. It was Jasper who was the traitor, who had plotted with the enemy, and who, when he was in danger of detection, had placed his incriminating letters among my belongings, where they were found. He was Lieutenant J. Lee and so was I; with cunning prevision he had used in the correspondence only the initial J., and he had spoken of himself, too, in such a manner that it seemed to be I and not he who was meant. In the face of such evidence my denials amounted to nothing. I wonder if Jasper ever felt remorse? Then the newspaper told that Congress had voted me a sword, a resolution of thanks, the restoration of Stoneham, and a great tract of land in the Northwestern Territory which I had fought with such valour and skill—I quote the Gazette—to save for the republic.

"There is more to the tale than the newspaper tells," said Winchester, "but you are likely to hear of that later."

We were summoned after a while to the best drawing-room of the President's wife, a large chamber with a great crystal chandelier hanging in the centre of the ceiling, beneath which she stood, a little lady with hair drawn, like Mrs. Winchester's, high upon her head, in order to give her the effect of greater height. She remembered me well, she said, a brown-haired boy, noted for his recklessness and excessive trust in human nature, and spoke as if there had been nothing unusual in my life since then.

We went presently into the dining-room, where the state dinner was served, the President of course presiding, a magnificent figure in black velvet knee-breeches and coat, and pearl satin waistcoat set off with fine linen and lace and glittering buckles. I saw around me the foreign ministers, the members of the Cabinet, Mr. and Mrs. Winchester, Underwood, now member of Congress from Kentucky, my old colonel and lieutenant-colonel, a French gentleman of distinguished appearance whom I afterward learned to be the Due de Liancourt—I have just read in a French journal his account of "eette affaire extraordinaire," as he termed this event; and beyond him two familiar faces—one that of De Chamillard, and the other, to my deep surprise, Osseo; yes, it was the Son of the Evening Star, his magnificent embroidered blue blanket drawn in graceful folds over his shoulders, and the humorous light twinkling in his eyes as they met mine, the son of the woods himself not one whit abashed by the mahogany and china and silver and brilliant uniforms, but calm, perfectly poised, and never looking more thoroughly the chief than at that moment.

"And in all your glory can you not find one word for me?"

It was Rose Carew, who had slipped quietly into the seat beside me.

"'Tis not my fault that I am sitting in this chair," she said. "The President's wife made me come here. 'Twas your duty to bring me out, but they forgot to tell you somehow, and behold, I am come."

She looked up at me with eyes brightly smiling, and I felt a great rush of happiness. There had been two Rose Carews before, the girl whom I had rescued in the woods and the proud woman of fashion, but now they were the same; my wood nymph and the most beautiful woman in Philadelphia were one.

I have never had a distinct recollection of that dinner, because even then my impressions were only of light, colour, many bright faces, and a great joy. And yet it was ceremonious in all its aspects. It was superintended by the famous Uncle Harkless himself, a dainty macaroni in black small-clothes, blue silk stockings, and huge blue cloth coat with velvet collar and great metal buttons shining like silver. But too many great surprises had burst upon me at once to leave me in a calm mind; and when at last they toasted me, standing, as one whom his country could never repay, but would try, the President himself pronouncing the words, I could stammer but a little in reply.

I met Osseo later, and he saluted me with much gravity.

"Well, Osseo," I said with some pride, "I am at last proved to be an innocent man."

"It is so," he replied; "but Lee is no better in the sight of Manito now than he was before."

Such was the faith of this Indian. When he liked one, the opinion of the world concerning that man was nothing to him.

"I have come to see the great city where men tread upon each other," he continued. "The Tornado asked me to come, and I have brought with me the mad Frenchman, who is not less mad here than he is in the forest."

I stood alone with the President at last, an opportunity for which I had been waiting long, and I poured out my thanks.

"It is you and the Congress who have done this," I said.

He laughed.

"You deceive yourself easily, Captain Lee," he said. "I believed your case closed, and even had I thought otherwise I have had no opportunity in all these years to review it. Nor do Congresses occupy themselves with the old wrongs of an individual. You must look elsewhere, Captain Lee."

"I am at a loss," I said, and truly I was.

"There is no one," he replied, "who would do so much for a man but a woman. There is no one in the first instance who would have the faith in his innocence but a woman, and there is no one who, having it, would come here from the West, toil two years to prove that innocence, searching among mouldy old documents, sending to England to procure from my Lord Cornwallis himself the proof that it was Jasper Lee and not John Lee who was the criminal, and then, even before her case was complete, going back into the wilderness to follow this man and save his life from the treachery of another. She must have had a powerful motive to do so much, and I think that on the whole he will be repaid for all that he has suffered. Go into the garden and you will find some one who can tell you about it."

CHAPTER 41 Paid in Full

There was behind the presidential house a walled garden, bright with summer fruit and flowers, and I stepped into it, my heart filled with thankfulness for all the great repayment that was being made to me, and yet I was oppressed too by a sense of diffidence. She seemed for the moment further away from me than ever, too good for any man of whom I had ever heard.

I saw her there on a stone seat beneath a great rosebush that curved over her head, and from which petals of pink or white fell one by one upon her or at her feet. And her face was alternately the colour of the petals.

I stood for a little while gazing at her, and the feeling of my own unworthiness grew upon me. I remembered now that in all our troubles and dangers it was she who never uttered a word of despair; it was she who bade me hope that I might yet win back my name, and at last it was she and none other to whom I owed the success of my effort. In those old days in the wilderness I had believed that she was in my debt, but now she had repaid me and more, and I felt the need of humility.

"Are you so soon tired of all your honours?" she asked.

"No, I am not tired," I replied. "It would be false to say that I do not enjoy them, but a magnet even greater has drawn me away."

She did not speak, but bent her head a little lower. The roses still fell at her feet, and the colour in her cheeks yet matched them.

"A man was condemned once by the world and condemned unjustly," I said. "Then he fled into the wilderness and grew hard and bitter. He thought that the old wrong done him would never be undone. He began to believe that the wild men were better than those whom he left behind. He even felt a certain pride in his condemnation, false though it was, because he was strong enough to bear it. But a woman came into the wilderness, and she showed him, but not by words, how wrong were his pride and stubbornness. He loved her, and, though she was above him and far from him, he told her so, not because he believed that his love would be returned, but because he was proud to love her, and proud, too, to avow it."

She was yet silent, and now did not look at me.

"He was glad to serve her," I continued, "and he felt much secret joy to have done so. He was glad to have her under obligation to him, and when she went back to the city and he to the woods he still rejoiced, because he thought her in his debt, and that he would keep her there. But he did not know her full nobility. While he was nourishing such a foolish pride she was toiling and planning for him, and now his debt to her is so great that he can never pay it."

"You estimate her too highly," she said at last.

"I do not. It is you, and you alone, to whom I owe this reparation," I said.

"I knew from the first that you were innocent, and it would have been poor repayment for all that you saved me from had I not proved you so," she relied. Then she continued, "I suppose now that your good name is restored, you will go back to the West."

"I do not know," I replied. "There is yet something lacking, and if I do not win it I shall. But it may be that there is another way."

A sudden deep colour suffused her face, and she looked down.

"I search my heart," I said, "to find if there is not another way, but I know that the answer is only in yours. I told you once, back there in the forest, Rose, that I loved you, but I told you then without hope. I tell you again that I love you, and shall love you always. It is only this that keeps me waiting. I do not want now to go back to the West."

"It may be that there is another way," she said, flushing rosily, and dropping her eyes.

"Can it be," I cried, seizing her hands, "that you love me enough to keep me here?"

The red was still in her cheeks as she whispered:

"You have found the other way."

THE END.

Made in the USA
Coppell, TX
09 July 2024